DATING DRACULA

DATING MONSTERS BOOK ONE

PROLOGUE

All right, boys and girls, listen up, cuz I'm only going to say this once.

When someone says your plan is downright stupid, perk up those ears and start taking notes. Otherwise, you might end up like me, cornered in a filthy alleyway, staring down the business end of a pair of fangs.

Let me back up a moment. Don't worry, this won't take long. Fang-face here will just have to wait the few seconds it'll take me to fill you in. After all, I want you not only to mourn my death, but learn from it as well. Maybe this lesson will save your ass one day.

Where should I start? Not the beginning—that's boring. No one wants to know my life story. So, let's fast-forward twenty-four years to tonight. The night I die.

First, an important note: It's been a week since the vampire community came out of their bloody coffins, so to speak. Which means everything is still so fresh. Humanity has no idea how to cope. Well, most of humanity. The small percentage of remaining Goths are walking around rubbing everyone's faces in the knowledge, like they've always been part of the cool kids' club.

As if.

And the second: I'm a professional vlogger. Or *was*, anyway. Maybe that doesn't mean much to anyone, but I swear it's relevant to *all* of this. See, I thought it'd be a fantastic idea to use my vlog as a media source for all things "vampiric." To learn all I could about these elusive blood drinkers and post it on my vlog for the entire world to see. Use their popularity to bolster my fame. I mean, what do we truly know about vampires? We've all read the books and watched the movies, but those were fantasy. And this is reality. As a social media influencer, it's my responsibility to shed a little light on the truth, right?

Unfortunately, during my search, I attracted the attention of a very unfriendly vampire—the kind who stars in horror films. I honestly hadn't expected to run into such an animal. Naïve, I know. Clearly, vampires aren't the friendly beasts the media portrays. My ex-boyfriend warned me this would happen, but I never believed someone would actually turn me into a Happy Meal.

Nothing but a comedy of errors led me to this dreadful moment.

Maybe you should look away now, because I highly doubt my death will be a pretty one.

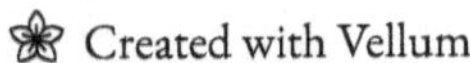 Created with Vellum

CHAPTER
ONE

"This is so stupid. Remind me again why I always go along with your plans?"

I huffed and rolled my eyes. I loved Lucy. She was the best friend a girl could ask for. But damn, sometimes she was a real stick in the mud, always cautioning me to smarten up and think things through. Well, where was the fun in that? Last thing I wanted was to tiptoe through life. Live fast and free, I always said. Gotta grab life by the horns. Yadda, yadda, yadda.

"We'll be fine, I promise. Let's go! It'll be fun." I gripped Lucy's hand and dragged her to the front of the ridiculously long line.

Still, she dug in her heels. "You do know they don't allow cellphones in the club, right?"

She was referring to Fallen—New Orleans's hottest new vamp club. Of course, since vampires had only recently come out of their coffin-closets, who knew which club would make it to the very top of the five-star list. For now, this was the *one*.

In the week since I'd learned about this club, I'd researched the hell out of it, and came across some very interesting, albeit mildly disturbing, information. If my sources were trustworthy, this club had been around for a while, disguised as a Goth club. But true horror lay in the underbelly of this beast. A "blood farm," as the dark web called it.

Apparently, all the big-named bloodsuckers frequented this establishment. And why? Because the owner/manager supposedly supplied the club not only with the newest synthetic blood products but also, as rumor had it, the *real* stuff too. The *good* stuff. As in, bottles of fresh human blood drained directly from the tap. Further digging revealed that someone had also sent an anonymous tip to the police, but the club had managed to clean up before the authorities had arrived. Imagine my surprise when I stumbled across that juicy nugget of gossip. The perfect story just *waiting* to be revealed.

"Earth to Anna," Lucy said, tapping the back of my head. "Did you hear me?"

I gave a casual nod. "I did. And I do know about their no cellphone rule. It'll be fine."

"Fine?" Lucy laughed. "Girl, I haven't seen you go five seconds without your phone since you bought your very first one. You expect me to believe you're okay with this? Ms. Modern Vlogger? Ms. Can't Go Two Seconds Without Retweeting Someone?"

I snorted a laugh. "Oh, shut up."

Sadly, she wasn't wrong. Far from it, in fact. But I'd planned for this. The club definitely didn't allow any form of cellular devices, but since I absolutely *needed* my phone tonight, I'd taken some precautions. My very dreams hinged on the success of my plan.

It'd been a week since vampires had made their startling debut, announcing their so-called "peaceful" presence to the world. A moment that would surely go down in the history books. In that time, there'd been mass confusion, a little hysteria, definitely some full-blown panic, and a whole lotta online chatter. While most people were still confused, wondering if this was some kind of prank, others—like myself—remained skeptical. Literary vampires had been around since long before the modern era, though the current stories seemed to focus on dramatic teenage romance. Some "lucky" girl who caught the eye of a big, bad—but actually good—vampire.

Pfft. I highly doubted such a thing existed.

There was no way a species that fed off human blood could be qualified as "peaceful." In one night, these creatures had restructured the entire food chain, knocking humans down a peg. Sure, they'd tied in the release of their synthetic blood line with their show-stopping announcement, but I wasn't fooled.

And that was the whole purpose behind Lucy's and my presence here tonight.

I wasn't a professional journalist—I lacked the credentials—but I still possessed a hungry appetite for uncovering the truth. And luckily, we lived in a digital age where any mook with decent equipment could build a story and slap it up on their website.

Enter, *moi*.

Despite my best efforts, the world had yet to discover me. But after tonight.... Imaginary stars shone in my eyes. After tonight, I would be famous. Celebritized. Viral. If the rumors were true, I would be the one to crack this story wide open. Just imagine, an exposé on vampiric blood slavery on *my* vlog. Everyone would know I'd scooped it. Not the police. Not the real journalists. Me. An eager twenty-four-year-old armed with a cellphone.

I shivered with excitement—nothing would stop me tonight.

Clutching Lucy's hand, I dragged her into the line, butting in front of three women wearing more makeup than a burlesque performer and racy outfits that blatantly exposed their throats. In the last week, I'd seen so many articles about women like this—desperate for a nibble, flagrantly flashing their jugulars with the hope of catching a vampire's attention. It didn't surprise me. Too many vampire romances out there, glorifying sexy love bites and eternal life. I couldn't imagine ever letting anyone—man or beast—sink their teeth into my throat. Didn't these people realize how many germs the mouth contains? *Yeesh* and *shudder*. No thanks.

"Hey!" the woman closest to me shouted. She grabbed my arm,

her dangerously sharp nails catching my skin. Make no mistake, these cougars were on the *prowl* tonight. "Back of the line, bitch!"

I ignored her shrill voice and instead stared up at the bouncer. I instantly knew he was a vampire, and my breath caught in my throat. Wow. I'd never seen one up close before. He was, in a word, impressive. I'd expected muscles—bouncers were always ripped. But this guy went beyond muscular to downright bulging with veins.

His keen gaze caught mine, and he watched with a raised brow as I grabbed a crisp hundo and slipped it into his pocket. After a slight hesitation, he gave an almost indecipherable nod and pointed to our purses. "Gotta check those. No electronics allowed inside."

Damn, his voice was *deep*. The sort of deep that awoke something in the lady bits area. But now wasn't the right moment to let his voice distract me. He needed to check our purses, and I most definitely had a cellphone in there. If found, they would ban us from the club. I couldn't let that happen. We had to get inside. So, earlier today, I'd sewn a small pocket into the liner, hidden from sight—or rather, human sight. Then, just in case, I'd dumped silver shavings I'd purchased online into my purse and covered it up with a Styrofoam container chock-full of garlic bread.

I had absolutely no idea if this would work. I was working under the assumption that the myths were true. Supposedly, silver weakened a vamp's senses, and they were apparently all allergic to garlic. Personally, I loved garlic. But I could see how someone with an enhanced sense of smell might not appreciate it.

I only hoped these two things combined convinced him not to look too closely.

The bouncer leaned in to inspect our bags. I popped mine open and shoved it toward his face. With a choking gasp, he staggered backward, clutching his nose. Even in the dark of night, I saw his lip curl upward as he wafted the air near his face.

"Oh!" I feigned horror. "I'm so sorry! My friend and I grabbed some pizza along the way. A girl's gotta eat before drinking, you know. It came with free garlic bread. I wasn't thinking when I put them in my purse. Just let me throw it out, then you can take another look."

The offended vamp garbled something I didn't understand, then pointed at the doors and waved us inside. If I wasn't mistaken, the poor guy looked to be tearing up. I was tempted to lean closer and study his face, fangs and all. But seeing as how my dream had just been delivered to me on a silver platter, I choked back my curiosity and hurried inside.

Darkness and deafening noise instantly consumed us. The emphatic beat of what sounded like horrible techno music echoed off the walls and thumped beneath our feet.

I grasped Lucy's hand and dragged her farther inside. A dimly lit staircase greeted us, leading us down to a sunken dance floor. Once we braved the first step, the entire place suddenly lit up with colorful strobe lights, as though the club had simply been waiting for us.

I grinned and squeezed Lucy's hand. This was what I lived for. The excitement of a new story, the energy of chasing a lead, and the thrill of experiencing a new adventure. My mama always called me an adrenaline junkie with a penchant for gossip, which made me laugh, considering it described me to a T.

At the bottom of the stairs, mystical fog swirled around our feet. I snickered—trust vampires to be stuck in the past. Techno music and fog machines. Could they be any more '90s?

"It's loud!" Lucy shouted over the incessant noise.

I was used to clubbing and the expected deafness that tended to last for days afterward. Lucy often tagged along, seeing as I never gave her a choice, but she always remarked on the noise. I suspected she preferred dark and dank bars. Quiet, lonely, withdrawn—all the words I often used to describe her. How the hell we'd ended up friends, I had no idea.

I turned my attention toward the surrounding crowd and clapped my hands with delight. Now, *this* was a club. Everywhere I looked, I saw someone writhing and grinding against another person, their hips gyrating shamelessly. It reminded me of the movie *Dirty Dancing* when Baby first stumbled across the *real* dancers. The brazen touches, the heated embraces... hell, someone was actually necking off to the side of the room. And at closer inspection, fingering. Yup, that's right. Some random guy stood pressed up against a woman, her skirt hiked up to her hips, his fingers boldly going where I assumed every man had gone before.

"Well, that looks fun," I shouted, nudging Lucy's shoulder and gesturing toward the scandalous couple.

If I had to guess, the no cellphone rule likely encouraged such dirty behavior. Easy to be naughty if there weren't any repercussions to fear.

"Oh. My. God!" Lucy cried out. If the woman owned pearls, no doubt she would have been clutching them right now.

I grinned and shook my head.

Mr. Shameless ground against the woman, then slid his knee between her legs and pushed her panties down. With her ass and other goodies bared to the entire club, he continued to ravish her without a care in the world. And she seemed quite content in the moment.

Vampires, man. Guess they really did see things differently than us mundane humans.

It was difficult to tear my gaze away from the couple. They were like a freaking car crash. You kept looking back to see if things got worse, and every time I snuck a peek, they most definitely were. I had a feeling if we didn't stop watching now, we'd catch the full act in a matter of minutes.

Every fiber of my vlogger-being wanted to whip out my phone and film this. It'd definitely get me some hits. Everyone loved a good sex scandal. But that wasn't what we were here for, and I couldn't risk exposing my cell for something so mediocre. No, we were here to investigate illegal bloodletting. I couldn't allow something like this to distract me, not when there was a real story to unearth.

We had to dance if we wanted to blend in with the crowd. Any nearby vamps had to believe we were here for the same reason as Mr. and Mrs. Shameless over there. If they got even the slightest whiff of my true intentions, they'd shut me down faster than a restaurant infested with rats.

I led Lucy out onto the floor. With a teasing grin, I buried my hands in my hair and started dancing, swaying seductively to the beat. Lucy mimicked me, though her movements were stilted. Her attention seemed elsewhere, like she was imagining a million other places she could be right now.

Some sidekick she was turning out to be.

"Hey!" I tugged her hand and placed it on my hip. Touching didn't bother me. We'd seen each other in our birthday suits more times than I could count. "Loosen up!"

She grimaced, her gaze still roaming the club.

I shook my head and chuckled under my breath. Typical Lucy. Here we were, in New Orleans, for crying out loud, getting our groove on in the hottest vampire establishment, and she still couldn't relax and have a little fun. Most of our friends back home called her Mother Hen. Always pecking at us, nagging us to take our vitamins and wear sunscreen, because vitamin deficiencies and melanoma were two very serious problems. I loved her to death, but sometimes I wanted to shake the sensibility right out of her.

With an impish grin, I cupped her hips and drew her close, hoping to evoke some sort of reaction. Instead, she leaned forward and pressed her lips to my ear. To any common observer, I knew it looked sexual. Like she was taking a little taste of Anna. The guy beside us laughed and gave us two massive thumbs up.

Men.

"Vampire," Lucy said, distracting me from Douche McDoucheson. "Up above. Your six o'clock."

Excitement stirred my blood. I quickly spun and pressed my back flat against her chest, my hands now gripping her thighs and my booty shimmying against her abdomen. McDoucheson cheered and lifted his beer in our direction. I ignored him, like most men, and let my gaze stray across the upper floor. Sure enough, a single vampire prowled above.

Pardon the expression, but *holy shit*. This vampire looked *nothing* like our bouncer outside. Our bouncer had looked friendly. Muscled, yes, but in a way that suggested he worked out. Nothing dangerous had stuck out to me.

But this guy? He had a giant invisible sign above his head with a flashing arrow that read *Vampire*. Everything about this one screamed *predatory*. The vamp was tall, broad, muscular, everything my lady bits generally wanted in a man, but I didn't like the way his hungry gaze raked over the crowd. In search of his next meal, maybe? One would assume Fallen's patrons knew what they were getting into by frequenting this type of club, but I had to wonder if they'd come for the thrill or to be a snack.

Legally, a vampire had to get permission before feeding on a human. It was the quickest I'd ever seen a law pass. So quick that I, and many others, had our doubts. Maybe the government had known a little something-something in advance. Maybe they'd taken the time to pass this law before announcing to the world that vampires existed.

My wannabe-journalist brain didn't believe a law could be passed in under a week. Government never agreed on anything. Seemed unlikely they'd agree on a law insisting on consent when cases involving rape were still being thrown out of court.

"Anna," Lucy hissed in my ear.

I whirled around to face her.

With a pinched expression, she pushed her hands through her hair and quietly gestured over her shoulder. My gaze followed, and sure enough, another vampire was serving drinks behind the bar. His movements were downright fluid, and damn if I wasn't jealous. My ballet instructor had tried for years to impart that particular lesson on me. It'd never stuck. I was as graceful as a drunken gazelle wearing six-inch heels and a purple tutu.

I scanned the crowd in search of more. Now that I'd seen the two of them, I knew what to look for. Impossibly pale faces, smooth complexions, thick luxurious hair, devastatingly seductive smiles. As though their exclusive club only accepted the incredibly beautiful.

Well, that left me out. Lucy could make the cut—the woman's skin was pale and flawless and her eyes as vivid as emeralds. Me? I was a mess. Tousled dirty-blonde hair tossed up into a sloppy bun and boring hazel eyes that never caught a man's attention. Not with Lucy standing right next to me. I didn't care though, or so I'd convinced myself a long time ago. Lucy was gorgeous, and she knew it, but thankfully, she wasn't the sort to rub it in other people's faces. And I appreciated that about her. She possessed a modesty and kindness that many lacked.

Focusing back on the task, I danced around Lucy in a tight circle and scoped out the rest of the club. Four doors that I could count. Emergency exit, two bathrooms, and then an obscured door toward the back of the dance floor guarded by a single vampire. A storage room, maybe? But why guard a storage room? Unless that's where they kept all the blood. I could definitely see a need for a guard then, to ensure no one made off with their supply.

I studied the rest of the club. My attention landed on the bartender, and I watched as he served order after order. I'd never seen someone mix drinks so quickly before. And his martinis looked downright delicious. But now wasn't the time to get distracted by yummy gin and vermouth.

Interestingly, though, he never seemed to serve blood. Every customer at his counter had been human so far.

So then where did the vamps get their drinks?

Or were *we* the drinks?

No. My intel had specifically mentioned illegal bloodletting. That had to mean a back room somewhere. My gaze drifted back to the guarded room. Maybe it wasn't for storage after all. Really, there was only one way to find out.

"In about two minutes, I want you to create a distraction," I shouted to Lucy.

Her sweaty brow creased. "What?"

"A distraction. You know, a ruckus. Big enough to attract *everyone's* attention." I slyly gestured to the lone guard near the back of the dance floor. I needed him to abandon his post so I could sneak in.

She closed her eyes and muttered something to herself, something I couldn't catch with the music droning in my ear. But I imagined it was something similar to "why am I friends with you?"

"Two minutes," I reminded her, holding up two fingers.

"What do you suggest?"

I shrugged. Then, with a naughty smile, I danced my way toward the women's bathroom, all the while silently talking myself up. Oh yeah, tonight was gonna be *the* night. I was about to crack this story wide open. I was gonna show the world that vampires were far from the docile little pets they wanted us to believe they were. That their friendly neighborhood PR couldn't save them. One video was all it would take. If something unsavory was happening in that room, I was gonna be all over it like white on rice. They had fangs, for cripes' sake. Fangs meant to sink into our fragile little throats and drain us dry. I mean, humanity could barely tolerate mosquitoes sucking at our veins. How the hell were we planning on cohabitating with vampires?

I paused in front of the women's room door and peered back into the crowd. By my Mississippi counts, Lucy had thirty more to go. Hoping not to attract any unwanted attention, I bent down and fiddled with my shoes. Men didn't understand heels. They simply enjoyed the look of them in the bedroom. I could play with them for minutes, and no one would be the wiser.

At twenty Mississippis, I heard it. A scream. A shout. The crowd roaring with excitement. Then, suddenly, the music cut off with a grating screech. I watched as everyone turned toward the center of the dance floor, where my bestie stood eye-to-eye against Douche McDoucheson. Even from back here, I could hear her screaming a series of unflattering names that would have deeply offended his mama.

When she reached "self-righteous motherfucker," the vamp guarding the sketchy door broke protocol and wove through the crowd to sort out this new problem. I, however, skedaddled my pert ass toward the newly abandoned door and gripped the doorknob. It turned without resistance, startling me. Who left a guarded door unlocked?

Whatever. Not my problem.

I snuck into the room, then skidded to a stop, my jaw slack.

This was *not* a storage room. Nor a kitchen. Nor a frickin' back office.

No—this was a damn whorehouse. I honestly couldn't think of a better term.

Naked women everywhere. Writhing. Moaning. And on top of the naked women were naked men. Naked *vampire* men.

A blood orgy?

I needed a second to adjust. Except, I didn't have a second. *This* was my bloody story. The club wasn't providing bottles full of fresh human blood. No. They were providing their vampire clientele with *victims*.

Holy guacamole.

No wonder I hadn't spotted a single vamp buying a drink out on the dance floor. Why buy when you could get fresh from the tap back here, holed up in a room that looked like the decorator had taken notes from Hannibal Lector, their greedy mouths latched onto the women?

And the sounds.

My God, the sounds.

I'd seen porn, and this didn't compare. The sucking, the lapping, the moaning, the groaning, the thrusting... I couldn't decide if I needed to throw up or slip someone a twenty. How the hell had they kept this so quiet? And no wonder they'd stationed a guard. Gracious! Imagine if an unknowing customer stumbled across this.

Someone like me!

I rifled through my purse and freed my phone from its fancy hidden pocket, then activated the camera. I had *just* hit record, and hadn't even looked at the screen yet, when one of the closest vamps positioned himself between a pair of long legs. An unconscious woman lay beneath him, her head turned to the side, brandishing a fresh bite wound.

Oh hell no!

I refused to stand here and let *that* happen. Dead or alive, rape was rape. But before I could so much as move, he thrust into her.

Indignation rose hard and fast within me. I aimed my camera at him and opened my mouth, about to scream something—*anything*—when an ice-cold hand clapped over my mouth.

How quickly my rage turned to fear. Before I could so much as react, another arm snaked across my waist and dragged me back against a hard chest. His arms were like vices, too strong for me to struggle against.

He wrenched me backward, and my Jimmy Choos caught against the tiles, falling off my feet. The second my bare feet hit the floor, instinct flooded me. I would *not* become one of these women! I would not become some pin cushion for them to sink their fangs into while they sank something *else* in down below.

I dropped my phone, then screamed and kicked, slapped and bit, twisted and struggled. But no one so much as batted an eyelash in my direction. Hell, no one even bothered to look up, so consumed with their conquests to notice a woman in distress. Doubtful they even cared. And my attacker? All he did was laugh, the vile prick.

He dragged me down a dark hallway, and I heard him kick open another door. Fresh, cold air assaulted me, cooling my fear a few degrees. Maybe it was just the bouncer from out front, kicking me out for breaking the rules. Or maybe the guard had returned to find me inside and was ridding the club of a little problem—namely *me*. Honestly, I didn't care which, so long as they didn't hurt me.

My abductor spun me around and shoved me backward. I staggered from the force and toppled into a metal fence.

Gasping for breath, I clutched the fence and finally glanced up.

A vampire stood in front of me. And it was neither the bouncer nor the guard. And from the looks of the dumpster next to me, he hadn't dragged me out into the street. No, he'd dragged me out the back, into a freaking alleyway.

This wasn't good. Vampires weren't legally allowed to feed on the unwilling, but hey, when did laws ever stop someone from doing what they wanted? And watching this predator pace in front of me didn't fill me with any reassurances.

The vamp lifted his head, his eyes closed, and inhaled. "I love that smell."

His voice. Oh God. He sounded like Death.

"Do you know what fear smells like?" he continued, enjoying his little monologue.

I didn't bother answering. Instead, I searched for something I could use as a weapon. But apparently Fallen liked to keep their alleyway squeaky clean. The *one* time I wouldn't have minded being thrown into a garbage pile.

Without waiting for my answer, my attacker darted forward. Ivory fangs flashed in the pale streetlight, his face terrifyingly monstrous. He slapped the fence by my head, then lifted his other hand and gripped my throat.

Fear snaked down my spine as a million thoughts raced through my mind.

Can't breathe!

Can't scream!

Lucy!

Help!

"You smell like peaches," the vamp rasped, his rank breath brushing against my throat.

Mouth gaping like a fish out of water, I beat him with closed fists, kicked him with bare feet, clawed at his face and arms, *anything* to get this monster *off* me.

Instead, he leaned forward and nuzzled my cheek. He gave another painful squeeze, then released the hold on my throat. I reared back, coughing, choking, gasping. But before I could so much as catch my breath, he struck. Like a viper, his fangs plunged deep into my neck.

I screamed, the hoarse sound likely to be the last thing I ever heard.

Because I was going to die here.

Strange how fast the darkness came. And when it completely consumed me, my last thought was *I should have listened to Lucy.*

CHAPTER
TWO

Reckless—that was the word Lucy always used to describe me. And every time, I grinned and nodded. I couldn't help it. I liked that word. It suited me perfectly.

For instance, in fifth grade, one of my classmates had dared me to hang upside down from the monkey bars for the entire recess. If I fell, I had to cough up my lunch money. If I won, I got hers. Maybe that didn't seem like a crazy bet, but for a bunch of ten-year-olds, it'd seemed insane. When I won, because of course I did, I used my classmate's money to buy lunch for the homeless man down the street. Lucy and I hadn't been friends at this point. In fact, we'd classified each other as archnemeses. She'd hated me, and I'd hated her. Elementary drama and whatnot. But she'd heard the story from everyone in the school. I was the *wildcat* who'd hung upside down for fifteen minutes without losing my breakfast.

In eleventh grade, I'd punched my soon-to-be ex-boyfriend in the face when he'd spread the rumor that I was a minx in the sheets. Wasn't long before the *truth* had spread around the school. Dude had been too scared to touch me, let alone steal home base.

In twelfth grade, I'd egged *and* toilet-papered our hometown's mayor's house. Now, before anyone starts judging me, I feel like it's important to note that the mayor was—and still is—my father. And like the upstanding citizen he is, he'd just cheated on my mom and kicked us out, so I'd been feeling a little vengeful. And how had my so-called wonderful father responded? He'd called the cops and had me picked up for littering and vandalism. Thankfully, no charges were ever laid, but as a punishment, I'd had to clean up the mess, thereby forcing me to spend time with my father's new she-bat of a mistress who'd moved in soon after my father had kicked us out. I'd returned the favor by giving the bitch's overpriced Agent Provocateur lingerie a spin in the washer and dryer—and *not* on delicate mode. Her horrified screams had kept me grinning for a year.

My point to all this was that sometimes I don't think things through. I occasionally react rashly. Like, *maybe* it hadn't been such a great idea to storm a vampire club in the middle of the night. And *maybe* it hadn't been such a great idea to film an illegal blood orgy instead of getting the hell out of Dodge and calling the police. My quest for fame had gotten me into trouble more than once, but this time, things had gone a little too far.

Unfortunately, I was now paying the piper. Because, believe me, there was no romance in dying. True death wasn't anything like in the movies. No weepy music as I sucked in my last breath, no final peaceful sigh as my eyes closed, no one gracefully sobbing as they begged me to wake up. Instead, there was a hell of a lot of screaming, some horrible slurping sound echoing in my ear, and the indecency of being discarded in the alleyway like I was nothing more than a piece of garbage.

And the worst part? The absolute catastrophe on top of my horrendously shitty night? I somehow could see all this happening. I'd heard of out-of-body and near-death experiences, but I never believed they were real. It didn't seem possible that your soul or essence or whatever could take a little vacation from your body.

Well, now I knew it was possible.

I stood there and watched as that asshole drained me of almost every last drop of blood, slavering over me like a starved dog drooling over a Big Mac. And when he was done, he wiped his hands on his pants like I was filthy or something and casually strolled back into the club, not a hair out of place. I glared at him the entire time, committing every detail of his face, down to that stupid hairy mole on his chin, to my memory. I wanted to memorize the murderous bastard, because I had every intention of haunting his stupid ass for the rest of my incorporeal existence.

I'd seen *Ghost*. I knew what was happening here. Knew I'd be trapped here until I solved my murder. That was how these things worked, right? Ghosts were the definition of unfinished business, and oh baby, was my business now unfinished. I just needed to find someone nearby who could speak to the dead. This was a club full of vampires, for shit's sake. If they existed, and I, a ghost, existed, then surely there *had* to be a psychic somewhere who could talk to me.

Right?

Except, weirdly enough, things were growing a little... hazy. Was that normal? It felt like a fog had settled over me, like it was trying to erase me from this world.

I rubbed my eyes and turned back to my body, crumpled and broken against the cold cement. Strangely enough, I could feel my connection to it weakening. I wasn't *fully* dead yet, but I could feel the inevitable moment closing in on me. Like a phone counting down the minutes until it died. I estimated I had about four percent left on my life's battery.

Coldness crept into my center. I clutched my chest and staggered toward my body. This was bad. Like, *really* bad. Why punt my soul from my body just to watch this happen? That had to rate pretty high on the torture scale. *Here, kid. Just stand here and watch yourself die, knowing you can't do a single thing about it. Sound good?* No! It absolutely did not!

The closer I got to my body, the more everything faded. The edges were dark-gray now, and it continued to creep inward, robbing my world of all the color. I couldn't see much beyond my body, and even that had begun to blur.

Two percent remained, which I assumed equated to a few minutes.

I kneeled next to my body and reached for my hand, only for my fingers to pass right through. I wanted to scream and curse, but when my lips parted, no sound emerged. Stupid deathly rules.

I was so focused on my situation that I barely noticed when the back door suddenly slammed open. But I definitely noticed when a shadow fell over me. I gasped and shot to my feet to find a stranger hovering over my body.

For the first time, a sliver of hope pushed back the darkness. I knew it was too late for anyone to actually help me, considering I was ninety-nine percent dead now. But at least now, I wouldn't die alone. And for some reason, that comforted me.

I squinted through the foggy haze to find a man crouching next to me. Everything about him was dark, from his hair to his shoes. So dark that I wondered if he was Death himself. I'd always pictured the Grim Reaper cloaked in black with a face so skeletal it scared people to death. Maybe this was him? I couldn't see the man's face, hidden from sight as it was, but everything else fit.

In one fluid movement, he scooped me into his arms and rose. I looked so small, so broken, pressed against his chest.

Less than one percent remained now. I was hanging on by a thread. Barely.

If this guy meant to help, it was too late. No one could survive such extreme blood loss—even I knew that.

At half a percent, the man moved. I couldn't see what he was doing, but if I strained really hard, I could catch a hint of his face. He stood utterly still, but I'd never forget his eyes. So dark, so piercing, like black coal burning in the darkness. And for one brief moment, I let myself believe he was staring through the veil *at me*.

He shifted his weight, then pressed something against my mouth, something I couldn't make out. But the instant we connected, I *felt* it.

A strange electrical current zipping through my body. It almost felt like a horse had kicked me in the chest. I gasped and wrapped my arms around myself.

Another zap. Stronger this time. And with it came a little clarity. Like there was a light at the end of the tunnel, barreling right toward me.

When the third jolt came, I was ready. Excited, even. With every little kick, I felt stronger, alive, and pissed as hell. I had no idea what was happening, and I didn't care. All that mattered was my countdown had begun to reverse and my battery meter climbed upward. Like he'd plugged me into the wall. Half a percent became three; three became ten; ten became thirty; thirty became fifty.

At seventy-five percent, my soul slammed back into my body and my eyes flew open. I sucked in a sputtering gasp and choked. Something warm and bitter filled my mouth. It tasted like pennies and ambrosia mixed into one strange cocktail. I coughed as the liquid trickled down my chin. But none of that mattered when I caught sight of the man holding me. The man with eyes as dark as night.

He stared down at me, his mouth curved upward. I caught sight of his *sharp* pearly whites, but for some reason, they didn't scare me.

"Ah, there you are," he said in a voice as smooth as silk.

Mm, I'd always loved a man with an accent, and his was to die for. I tried to think of a witty response, something biting and hilarious to break the tension. It wasn't every night a girl woke up in the arms of a beautiful man who'd saved her life, after all. But my savior chose that moment to unleash his hypnotic gaze on me once more. Damn, it was mesmerizing. I couldn't tear my eyes away. They seemed to swirl like dark, warm chocolate syrup. So delicious. So manly. So beautiful.

"Thank you," he said with a wide smile.

Shit. Had I said that out loud?

"Shh." He repositioned me in his arms. "You're safe now, Anna. Sleep."

He didn't need to tell me twice.

A SHARP JAB in my ass startled me awake.

I sucked in a startled breath and froze. Oh fuck. Was that... a dick? Was there a *dick* poking me in the *ass*? That was impossible, right? Except, it felt distinctly similar. The hardened tip, the long ridge— holy shit, that *was* a dick! There were so many things wrong with this scenario, the most important of which was that I had no idea whose dick it was! I couldn't recall *anything* from last night after Lucy and I infiltrated Fallen.

Wait, wait, *wait*. Fallen was a vamp club.

Oh. Oh no.

Did I get drunk and fuck a fanger? No. No! Surely, Lucy would never let me go home with a vamp.

Unless... what if we'd been enthralled? Enraptured? Hypnotized? Whatever they frickin' called it. I'd heard vamps could do that. Tamper with our minds, make us believe things, make us think we were attracted to them—their own personal form of Ecstasy and Rohypnol.

Oh, this had all the potential for an epic disaster of catastrophic proportions.

Okay. The most important thing at this moment was not to freak out and certainly not to move until I figured everything out. I couldn't afford to wake the beast attached to the wanker still knock-knock-knocking at my backdoor.

Think, Anna. Think!

If a vamp had hypnotized me, I wouldn't be aware of it. And I certainly wouldn't be in the right frame of mind to question what had happened. So, by that twisted logic, it seemed safe to assume I hadn't been mind-raped.

Was there a second option? A possible drunken fling with some junkie human obsessed with vamps? I didn't *feel* hungover. And I knew without a doubt I hadn't taken even the slightest sip of alcohol last night. I never did when working, because I liked a clear mind.

Regardless, I needed to get the eff out of here and find Lucy. Vamoose my poor violated ass out the front door and never look back. Thankfully, the hard member digging into my backside hadn't so much as twitched, meaning my bed partner was still snoozing away. It also meant I needed to be careful. Quiet. Sneaky. But first, I had to crawl out of this bed without waking anyone, which might be a little difficult, considering it was absolutely pitch-black in here. I was surrounded by so much darkness that I couldn't see an inch in front of my face. Whoever lived here owned some killer sun-blocking curtains, which would make escaping super difficult.

I only hoped to hell I never gave him my phone number.

I reached out a hand, searching for the edge of the bed, but cursed when my fingers slammed into a wall.

Uh... okay. That was unexpected. And more than a little nerve-wracking.

I flattened my palm against the wall and followed it upward. But when my palm found a corner and took a sharp forty-five degree turn inward, I sucked in a panicked breath.

What the *hell*?

Fuck this. I didn't care anymore if I woke someone, so I flipped onto my other side and felt around. That thing jabbing me in the ass? My damn shoes. The stupid heels I'd worn to the club last night. But that didn't make sense. I remembered them falling off my feet at some point. So how were they here?

On the upside, at least I wasn't in bed with some stranger.

I reached out, hoping to find the other edge of the bed, but instead, found more wall. A wall that climbed upward and took another forty-five degree turn inward.

I started shivering and gasping for breath.

There was only one thing that explained the walls surrounding me. But it couldn't be happening. I wasn't trapped inside a....

Cripes, I couldn't even finish that thought.

What the hell happened last night? Had a serial killer kidnapped me? Locked me in a box and left?

I inhaled through my nose and froze at the unmistakable scent of pine and satin.

Now fully panicking, I patted the material beneath me and the plush pillow under my head.

Holy effing hell.

Either someone had placed bedding inside this box, or I was locked in a *coffin*.

Yup, I screamed. And when my breath ran out, I screamed some more. This was everyone's worst nightmare come true. Had someone buried me alive? Or was this some sort of horrible joke? Like a hazing? And if so, who the hell would play such a cruel prank?

It didn't take long for me to realize that screaming was likely using up all my air. Eyes wide, even in the darkness, I clapped a trembling hand over my mouth. This was bad. So very, very bad. And I had no idea what to do. No one ever taught a class on how to escape a coffin. Tied to a chair, I could handle. Self-defense, sure! I could kick a guy in the balls better than any woman. But this was *beyond* anything I'd ever imagined possible.

Someone had *buried* me. In a coffin.

Okay. Calm down. Think your way out of this.

I waved a hand near my face just to feel the air move, to convince myself I hadn't used it all up screaming. Scenario: what if I'd died last night? Was that why I couldn't remember anything? No, that didn't make sense. Dead people didn't come back to life.

Or rather, not *all* dead people.

Vampires sure as shit came back to life.

Except, I didn't feel like a vampire. I felt like *me*.

And where the hell was Lucy? My blood ran cold just thinking about her also being buried somewhere out there, screaming my name, worrying about me as I was her.

No. I had to get out of here. If not for me, then for her. I couldn't let my best friend die out there all alone.

Coffins were made of wood, evidenced by the smell. That meant they were breakable. It might hurt like hell, but I could handle that. I tightened my hand into a fist and pulled it back next to my head. There wasn't enough room for a solid punch, and there wasn't enough room to pull my knees up for a decent kick either. Who the hell designed these things? And why were they so small? A girl needed some leg room to kick her way free, right?

Breathe, I told myself. *You can do this. You've taken self-defense classes. You know how to throw a punch. It's gonna hurt, but hey, a broken hand is better than suffocating to death.*

Nodding to myself, I struck, then gasped when my fist punched right through the top of the coffin. *Whoa.* Wood splinters rained down on me, but I didn't stop to contemplate what that meant. My hand was *outside* the coffin, and that was all that mattered. I pulled it back, then peered through the jagged hole. I'd expected dirt, mud, cement, but instead, I found only air.

So I hadn't been buried then. Relief loosened my muscles. Things were looking up. I could handle this now. Just knowing I wasn't entombed six feet under soothed my frayed nerves.

Palms flat against the lid, I gave it a hard shove. It slid off without resistance. Huh. Maybe I should have tried that first before going all Chuck Norris on the coffin's ass. Meh. I felt surprisingly little guilt. Whoever had pulled this shitty little prank could pay for repairs, because I sure as hell didn't find this amusing.

I gripped the edges of the coffin and launched myself over the edge, landing silently on my toes. I cocked my head and stared at my feet, surprised by my sudden cat-like nimbleness. That sort of move usually landed me on my ass, listening to people laugh as they uploaded the embarrassing video online.

I shook my head and turned away from the coffin. I needed to focus on location. Where was I? At first glance, I appeared to be standing in the middle of what looked like an attic—albeit a reinforced one. I groaned and shuddered. Nothing like waking up in a creepily enclosed room, complete with a coffin to freak a girl out.

So then whose attic was this, and why was I here?

"Anna!"

I whirled toward the familiar voice, a grin spreading across my face at the sight of Lucy barreling toward me. Thank heavens she was fine! At least now I knew she wasn't trapped in a coffin somewhere too. But why was she here? She never would have arranged this little stunt, considering she didn't possess a single funny bone in her body. These sorts of pranks weren't her style. Lucy lacked *all* imagination for such things.

She screeched to a stop in front of me, her cheeks streaked with tears.

Whoa, what the hell? Had someone hurt her? If so, I felt a sudden need to punch that specific person for hurting my Lucy.

"Are you all right?" I demanded, then froze when something sharp scraped across my tongue. I instinctively reached for my mouth but paused when Lucy started rambling.

"Me? Are you insane?" She wiped her snotty nose against her arm. "I should be asking you that question! Asks *me* if *I'm* all right...."

Huh? A deep frown pinched my eyebrows. I felt fine, considering my recent circumstances. Yet, she still seemed quite upset by something.

She took a deep breath, then ran her hands over her hair and exhaled. "Okay. Are you okay?"

"I'm fine. Why wouldn't I be? Oh, because I just woke up in a fucking *coffin*?"

She paled. Like visibly paled. I'd never seen someone do that before. All the blood just suddenly drained from her face. It was mesmerizing. I stared at her cheeks, fascinated by the tiny veins and arteries beneath her skin.

Lucy took a giant step back and glanced behind her. "He... he said it was necessary."

"Who said?"

"Now, don't get mad."

"Girl, I'm already spitting. Out with it already."

Lucy swallowed. My gaze dropped to that little hollow in her throat, and I watched the seductive movement. I'd never noticed how beautiful her neck was before. So lean and graceful. And warm. Wow. She looked *very* warm. We'd never been more than friends, but I suddenly felt a strange desire for her.

I wanted to bury my face in her throat. It looked so inviting. So delicious. So—

"Lucy, step back," a male voice commanded, one that sparked a hazy memory, almost like a dream.

Dazed, I tore my gaze from her newly flushed neck and flicked a quick glance at the shadow hovering near the doorway. I barely paid him any mind, my focus all for Lucy. She was all that mattered right now. Eyes half-lidded, I stumbled forward and mindlessly reached for her. Distantly, I heard myself mumble something incomprehensible, with absolutely no idea what I was trying to say. I just knew I needed her. I needed something *from* her.

She turned away from me and glanced over her shoulder. "What?"

"Step back. Now," the shadow ordered.

Lucy bolted out of reach, and instantly, full-blown anger erupted within me. It took control of my body, rising hard and fast like a volcano. I'd never felt this monstrous presence before. It seemed to invade every inch of me until all that remained was a senseless creature with one thing on its mind.

To feed.

My lips peeled back, and with a savage snarl, I lunged forward, my clawed fingers swiping at my best friend's throat.

The shadow man swept into my path, but I ignored him completely. I saw his arm rushing toward me. I meant to duck beneath it, but instead, he turned his hand and grazed his wrist against my mouth. He must have nicked himself against something sharp. I knew it the second his skin split. It was like my senses kicked into overdrive. I *smelled* the blood before I saw the wound—I'd never noticed how mouth-wateringly delicious blood smelled before. Never craved something the way I craved *this* right now. It was like Lucy didn't exist anymore. The only thing that mattered was his blood.

I snatched his arm and yanked it to my mouth.

With a soft sigh, my lips closed around his wrist, and I sucked. The instant his blood coated my tongue, I sank into mindless bliss. I barely registered the feel of his fingers stroking my hair or the sound of Lucy sobbing in the corner. The only thing I knew was this incessant hunger and endless thirst.

Guess I really had died.

CHAPTER
THREE

WITH EVERY GULP OF BLOOD, I felt my sanity returning. But with it came this annoying yammering sound, and it took a few more swallows for me to realize it was coming from Lucy. My eyes were closed, but I could smell her. She stood—more like hovered—nearby, fretting over every damn little thing.

"Should she still be drinking?"

OMG, yes.

"Hasn't she had enough yet?"

Not nearly.

"Why is this taking so long?"

Because I'm thirsty!

"Shouldn't you be doing something?"

He is! Calm your tits!

This man's—whose name I *still* didn't know— blood was so sweet, so fulfilling. Every mouthful made me want more. A part of me never wanted to let go, but there was a smaller part of me, the lingering human part, that screamed wordlessly in my head.

I was drinking *blood*, for crying out loud. From a stranger, no less.

What had my life become?

My senses slammed back into place, and I reared back from the bleeding arm with a choking gasp. My stomach instantly roiled, so I clapped a hand over my mouth and spun away without so much as a thank you. Just like that, the blood turned sour in my gut. I couldn't believe this. I just drank someone's blood. Their blood. Their blood! No matter how many times I repeated it, my brain refused to comprehend.

Yesterday, I was a normal girl. Lucy and I had left our hometown and driven to New Orleans with a single goal in mind: getting into Fallen and busting open the truth. We'd rolled the windows down as we drove, singing into the wind as we sped toward the city. We'd left all our problems back home—including my freshly minted ex-boyfriend of one week—with the grandiose expectation that I'd be famous upon return.

Oh, I was going to be famous all right. Or maybe infamous was the better word.

The first resident of Perish, Louisiana, to be turned into a vampire.

A *vampire*.

My mama had always told me my busybody nose would get me into trouble one day. I absolutely hated the idea of returning home to prove her prediction true.

"Anna?" Lucy whispered.

"Stay back." My voice shook with strained effort. I could still smell her. Hell, I still craved her. If she so much as took another step, I might lose control again. And I refused to let that happen. She was my best friend—no way in hell I'd be responsible for her death.

Of course, she didn't listen. Lucy never did. She did what she wanted, when she wanted.

Her footsteps practically echoed in my ears, but it was nothing compared to the sound of her thunderous heartbeat. Saliva pooled in my mouth, and it took every ounce of restraint I possessed not to seize her by the throat and drain her dry.

"Anna?"

"I said stay back!" I shouted, whirling around to face her.

The pungent stench of fear splashed me in the face. Eyes wide, I cupped my cheeks and staggered backward. That damn monster had risen inside me again. Was that the vampire within? Would it always be this hungry?

"I—I'm sorry." I shook my head over and over, hoping it would help clear my thoughts. I reminded myself again and again that I didn't *actually* want to eat Lucy. I didn't want to eat *anyone.* Unfortunately, though, it seemed like I no longer had a say in that matter.

This was too much.

I needed to focus on something else—*anything* else.

So, instead, I turned toward the man who'd just fed me his blood. The second our gazes clashed, my jaw dropped. I recognized him! He was the shadow from the alleyway. The man who'd saved me. Even now, his eyes burned, enthralled, in a way I'd never seen before.

"You," I whispered.

He matched my stare with a faint smile. "Me."

"You two know each other?" Lucy asked. "From before all this, I mean?"

I shook my head. I seemed to be doing that a lot tonight. "No, I don't *know* him. But he saved my life."

"Um, I think he failed," Lucy snapped, her frustration painting her cheeks with a lovely splash of color. "Epically."

"No, he saved me," I whispered as memories assaulted me. This was the man from the alley. The one who'd jump-started my heart and saved me at the very last second by apparently turning me into a vampire. The evidence was undeniable at this point.

"Can someone *please* tell me what the hell is going on here?" Lucy demanded, her voice shrill. "And start at the damn beginning please, because I have no fucking clue what happened."

I winced at the sound of Lucy cussing. I'd only heard her swear maybe once or twice in our life. She'd always been the nice one. Not me. I cussed as much as possible.

"Start at the point where you insisted I cause a distraction," she said.

Right. The distraction. The club. The vampires. The orgy. It was strange—I remembered it all, but it felt like the memories were from another life. All hazy and dim, like my brain was already struggling to forget the traumatic event. Self-preservation, perhaps?

"Well?" Lucy insisted when I didn't immediately respond.

"Give me a sec. It's hard being dead."

"Undead," my savior corrected.

"Same diff." I rubbed my eyes and groaned. "Okay. So, I had you cause a distraction to draw away a vamp guarding the back door. When I snuck in, I found a blood orgy. I got a little video, but before I could leave, someone grabbed me."

"A vampire?" Lucy asked.

I pinned her with a droll look that clearly said *duh*. "He dragged me outside and... killed me."

"Almost killed you," the stranger said.

I caught his gaze again and felt my nerves settle. There was something odd about him. Something calming but equally mysterious. I didn't even know his name, but I owed him so much. Without him, I'd be flat on my back in a morgue right now with a lovely tag dangling from my toe.

Even more interesting, I felt a strange fluttering in my chest when I looked at him. It wasn't my heart, because sadly, that little gem was long dead. I hadn't noticed it at first, but now that I knew I'd crossed into the undead, I realized my body was *quiet*. As a living, breathing human, I'd never paid attention to my heart unless it did something funky like skip a beat. But now, my entire body felt hollow. Nothing beat beneath my breast, no blood flowed through my veins. I was walking and talking like it was any other day, but my body seemed to be firmly dead.

I cleared my throat and refocused my attention. "You knew my name."

My savior quirked a thick, dark brow.

"After you changed me. You said my name and told me to sleep. How did you know who I was?"

His expression shuttered. I watched, mesmerized, as his mouth flattened into a grim line and his eyes narrowed, as though he didn't want to answer my question. "Does it matter?"

"Definitely. Especially to me."

"And me," Lucy chimed in.

My savior sighed, his broad shoulders rising and falling with the dramatic movement, considering we didn't *need* to breathe other than to smell things. I pulled my gaze from his face and inspected the rest of him. He'd draped himself in black clothing, right down to his shoes. The dark shade contrasted against his pale skin but blended with his ear-length, wavy, midnight hair and obsidian eyes. Monochromatic or not, I had to admit, he made it look good, like an avenging dark angel.

"You wouldn't believe me if I told you."

Laughter burst past my lips. "That evasion might have worked yesterday, but not so much today."

The stranger stepped toward me and extended his hand, as though inviting me to touch him. And for some unknown reason, I wanted to. No doubt about it. I reached out and brushed my fingers across his palm. The instant we connected, warmth bloomed within my chest. For a brief moment, I wondered if my heart had restarted. But then the moment passed, and I realized it was nothing more than a wave of attraction for a man I didn't know.

Interesting.

His fingers closed around mine, and he pulled me toward him, murmuring quietly, "I heard your name in my head."

I peered up at him with a small frown. Had he just admitted to being able to read minds? Because that was impossible—said the newborn she-vamp. Was there even a word for us? Besides monster?

"You what?" Lucy asked, saving me the embarrassment of asking him to repeat himself.

He brushed his fingers along my knuckles, then released my hand and stepped back. "I heard her name. It was whispered to me."

"Like you can read minds?"

"No, I don't have that ability." I wanted to dig deeper into this whole hearing my name in his head thing. Because that didn't seem natural. But he pressed onward. "When I realized Anna was in trouble, I stepped in."

"And turned her into a vampire!" Lucy accused.

"Her options were that or death. Perhaps you would have preferred a deceased best friend? Someone to bury six feet under?"

Lucy's mouth snapped shut.

I choked back a laugh, knowing she wouldn't appreciate it. I understood her concerns, but really, she couldn't complain about his methods. I'd been there. If he hadn't turned me, I would have died. That other vamp had done quite the thorough job. He hadn't drunk every last drop, but he hadn't left me enough to survive the ordeal either.

And speaking of which... "Do you know the other vampire? The one who killed me?"

"Almost killed you," my savior intonated. "And no, unfortunately not."

"Super handy," I mumbled. "So, what are the rules here? Do I file a complaint somewhere? Or even better, get to hunt the bastard down and kill him for killing me?"

"If that's your desire."

I blinked. "Which one?"

His mouth curled into a small grin, leading me to believe he'd been referring to the latter.

"Okay. Good. I want to kill him back." I could already imagine it. The second I got my hands on that asshole, I was going to break every bone in his body and shove something super long up his dickhole. No one killed me and got away with it.

"What? Are you insane?" Lucy screeched. She rushed forward, grabbed my hands, then gasped and stared down at them. "Holy crap, you're ice-cold."

"No, I'm not. You're just boiling hot." I drew my hands back and wiped them down my shirt. "Geez. Do you have a fever or something?"

"Human temperatures run around ninety-eight degrees," my savior commented. "Vampires run much cooler than that. It's noticeably different."

"Fun," I muttered.

"Just more information to store away for later." Lucy hugged her arms around her waist and shook her head. "Look, I know you want to kick your murderer's butt and all that, but don't you think that's maybe a little dangerous? And reckless? He *killed* you last time, remember?"

"Almost killed me," I said at the same time as my savior. We shared a private grin, then I turned back to Lucy. "I think I'll be a little more equipped this time."

Lucy's face hardened. "What about your family?"

I froze. "What about them?"

"Don't you think they might deserve to hear what happened? To see you? To grieve you? If you go off guns a-blazing, and *he* kills *you*, you'll be really dead this time. Like *dead*-dead."

"So, you'd rather I just let this go?"

"Yes!" She threw her arms up into the air. "Anna, you got off lucky this time! Okay, something bad happened, and yes, your life has been irreparably changed, but you're *alive*, sort of. Walking and talking. Maybe you drink blood now, but that's better than a tombstone! If you go after him, I'll be the one returning home with the news that you're truly dead."

"Oh, don't be so dramatic. I'm only half-dead."

"Undead," my savior clarified.

"Yeah—that." I waved a hand. "So, why does it matter when I tell them? Don't you think someone should track this guy down? What if I'm not the only one he's killed?"

"So what? Aren't there vampire police who can handle this?"

"I have no idea. I just woke up, remember?"

"We have a protocol for these situations," my savior commented. "Someone who will open an investigation on your behalf."

"There!" Lucy cried out. "See! Someone else can handle this."

"Maybe I don't want someone else to handle this," I growled, remembering how vulnerable I'd felt in that alleyway, how broken. That vamp had stolen everything from me. He'd sunk his teeth in my throat and drained me—and he'd *enjoyed* it. I didn't want some vampified cop dealing with this. I wanted to be the one who ripped out my murderer's throat. How many victims got that chance in life?

Lucy scoffed and shook her head. "This is so stupid. You're risking your life, *again*. You dragged me to that club. Then left me without any idea as to what you were doing. When you didn't come back, I had no idea how to find you! Do you know what that felt like? They kicked me out when I started making a scene. I luckily found this guy holding you in the alley"—she stopped and released a slow exhale—"and you're doing it again. Your half-cocked ideas got you killed once, and now they're going to get you permanently dead."

"Lucy—"

"I'm not staying," she blurted out.

Betrayal stabbed me in the chest. "What?"

She met my gaze with tears brimming in her eyes. "You think I want to stay here and watch you hunt down some vamp in the name of justice? Sorry, vengeance. What if he wins the fight? What then?"

"Lucy." I walked toward her but froze when she waved her hands in the air and spun around, giving me her back.

The scent of her anger was rich, like a sweet perfume filling the air. But beneath it, I caught the scent of something more primal, bitter. Grief, I realized. Strange that I could smell emotions now.

I caught the sound of her soft sobs. They were almost deafening now with my sensitive hearing.

I wasn't sure how to process all this. Lucy and I had been best friends since high school, after we'd finally buried our frenemy hatchets. We were Lucy and Anna, sisters from different misters. Our parents had often remarked how we were always attached at the hip.

She'd never said no to me before, and certainly had never abandoned me in a moment of need. Then again, my shenanigans had never gotten me killed before, and I'd never tried to hurt her before.

Seemed my death had put a small damper on our relationship.

"I'm sorry," she whispered with her back still to me. "I just.... You died, Anna. You're *dead*."

"Undead," my savior clarified for like the third time.

"It's still dead!" Lucy snapped.

Even I glared at him. Now wasn't the time for his little comments.

"I—I don't know how to handle all this. Do I grieve for you? Or celebrate the fact that you're still walking around? You're a vampire, Anna. For frick's sake, do you know what that means? You drink blood, you sleep in a coffin... you aren't *you* anymore. How am I supposed to handle this?"

My dead heart shattered. "You're supposed to accept me as I am," I said, struggling to keep my voice steady. "We're sisters. Always. Forever."

"Except always and forever means two very different things to us now," she said.

I forced myself to swallow. From the sounds of it, Lucy was breaking up with me. Which almost made me laugh. She was my longest relationship ever. And she wanted to walk away from it? All because of an accident I had no control over?

I ran a hand down my face and turned toward my savior. Someone whose name I *really* needed to learn. I couldn't keep referring to him as my savior or I was going to develop some major hero worship issues.

"Anna, I'm sorry," Lucy repeated. "But I think I need some time to process all this."

I nodded, all the while keeping my gaze trained on my savior. He was the only thing keeping me calm right now. The thought that I might lose my best friend over all this was too much. I couldn't show her how much this hurt, because if I did, I might never recover. Lucy had stormed into a vamp club at my side, but apparently, she drew the line at death.

And honestly? I didn't blame her. This time, tears really did spring to my eyes, but I blinked them back before they spilled. If I started crying, I had a feeling I'd never stop.

"I'm going to head back to the hotel," she said. "I've been staying there the past few nights." Wait, what? Past few *nights*? But before I could question that little tidbit, she continued speaking. "Do you want me to call your parents for you? Explain what happened?"

"No," I rasped. That wasn't her responsibility. If anyone was going to tell them about my transformation, it would be me.

"I'll text you," she mumbled, but her voice was already fading. She was leaving.

Text me. Ugh. Why not just tell me you hope we can still be friends?

I hated this. What happened to best friends forever? I'd like to think that if this had happened to her, I'd still be standing by her side. Lucy was my world. Nothing could have convinced me to leave her.

"I'm sorry" was her final comment before I heard the door shut.

I took a few minutes to absorb everything. Thankfully, my savior let me brood in silence. I appreciated that. I wasn't in the mood to hear platitudes right now.

Once I was sure I had schooled my expression, I turned toward him and nodded. It was embarrassing to have someone witness a break-up, but there wasn't anything I could do about that now.

I needed a distraction. I didn't want to think about Lucy right now. I'd reserve that for later, when I was alone and could process everything myself. Instead, I stared up at him, once again stricken speechless when our gazes met. Why did I find him so enthralling? So fascinating? It felt like I could stare at him for hours.

Clearing my throat, I rubbed the bridge of my nose and asked, "Well, do you have a name?"

His brows shot upward, and an amused smile claimed his lips, exposing the tips of his fangs. Intrigued, I reached for my own, poking them with my fingertip. They must have been what scraped my tongue earlier. Seemed they were a permanent fixture too. I'd have to remember that when talking and laughing. Vampires might be public knowledge now, but as seen by Lucy, humans weren't one hundred percent ready to accept them yet.

"Forgive me," he said, his voice deliciously rumbly. "I'm so accustomed to being recognized wherever I go that I often forget to introduce myself."

So, he was like vampire royalty or something?

Fangs still peeking out from behind his lips, he gave an old-fashioned bow, one he executed flawlessly, then peered at me through long, dark lashes. I shit you not, the boy almost breathed life back into me. He was just that gorgeous.

"My name is Vlad." He took my hand and lifted it to his lips before brushing a gentle kiss across my knuckles. "But most know me as Dracula."

I wish I could say I absorbed that information with grace and poise. But that would have been a lie. Instead, I burst out laughing, and said, "No shit!"

FOUR

Did he just say Dracula?

Like... *the* Dracula? *I vant to suck your blood,* Dracula?

My shoulders shook with gentle laughter, but the more I thought about it, the more hysterical this seemed. Dracula! The big guy himself. I was hardly a fan of bloodsuckers, but even I had to admit, I was starstruck. This guy was positively the most famous man in the world. Hell, maybe even more famous than the British monarchy. Everyone knew Queen Elizabeth, sure, but Dracula had stuffed dolls, movies, TV shows, books.... He even had Halloween costumes based after him!

I snorted with laughter—a very unappealing habit, I admit—then laughed harder when I caught sight of his wide-eyed expression. My first night diving into the world of vampires, and I meet the Count himself. What were the chances?

As for dear ole Drac, he seemed a little put out by my reaction. If I'd thought his expression dark before, it was nothing compared to now. Rage flashed across his noble countenance, and his nose crinkled like a pissed-off lion. At the sight of his whetted fangs, my laughter morphed into a choking cough, and I covered my mouth with the back of my hand.

"I'm sorry, I'm sorry," I sputtered. I waved my hand in front of my face, then reached toward him. Unsurprisingly, he stepped out of reach. "It's just... wow. I mean, Dracula."

"I prefer Vlad," he growled. And damn, the man could growl. Ever heard a human attempt that before? It always made me laugh. We—or *they*—weren't designed to truly growl anymore. But the sound rumbling deep in Dracula's throat made all my little hairs stand on end. Seemed wise to remember not to piss him off.

Before I could attempt another apology, Dracula—sorry, *Vlad*—grabbed my hand and pulled me out of the room. He didn't grip me hard, but he pulled with enough force to keep me skittering after him. Clearly, he wasn't impressed with me right now, and I couldn't blame him. I wouldn't appreciate someone laughing at my expense either. I needed to try apologizing again. You know, when my sides weren't hurting from laughing so hard.

He led me down a flight of winding stairs, then guided me through a series of rooms. He refused to let me peruse, so I studied each room fleetingly, catching sight of things like four-poster beds, ornate bathtubs—yes, there was more than one—marble flooring, and oh yeah, regal statues of him everywhere. Pretty much everything one would expect to find in Dracula's estate.

As we hurried down another flight of stairs, I caught whiffs of humans, and my mouth began to water. Despite the fact that I'd just fed on him, my stomach twisted with hunger. Thankfully, Dracula tightened his grip on my hand and tugged me along, away from the delicious humans. Before I could thank him, he took a hard right-hand turn into a sitting room.

And holy crap on a cracker, what a sitting room it was. It had to be bigger than my entire apartment. I stepped forward, noting that he held onto my hand as long as possible before finally releasing it.

"Fuck me," I whispered.

Like, holy shit, maybe even twice as big as my apartment. The ceiling was at least two-stories high, and in the middle hung a glimmering chandelier. Whistling softly, I spun in a slow circle and studied the rest of the room. Beautiful paintings and elegant sconces graced the warm-toned walls, and across from me was a wall-to-wall fireplace gently flickering with small flames. I stepped closer, only to hear the charred wood popping away. Which meant someone had to attend this freaking fire *all night long*.

Must be good to be rich.

I returned to Dracula, then grimaced when I caught sight of a truly horrendous pair of couches behind him. Fainting couches, I believe they were called. I'd seen them in movies before—usually historicals—all velvet material and wooden framing. Ugh, I *hated* velvet. Even though it suited the slightly Victorian décor, it screamed *uncomfortable*. Clearly, this room wasn't meant for relaxing. I felt drab in comparison, my naked feet leaving a slight dirt trail thanks to the frightening events that had led me here.

Guess no one had bothered to clean me up before slapping me in a coffin.

A quick glance down revealed my unkempt condition. My outfit was in tatters, my feet bare and filthy, and blood crusted my hair. I must have looked quite the fright. Thankfully, Dracula—ugh, *Vlad*. Man, I really needed to get into that habit—didn't seem overly concerned about my current state compared to his pristine room.

Which had me wondering... "Live here long?"

He followed my gaze and took in the surroundings as though trying to see the room from my perspective. "A few years now. I bought this place from a dear friend who wished to leave New Orleans. He'd grown tired of all the tourists."

"And would this dear friend be, oh, I don't know, the King of England or something?"

Vlad's gaze strayed from the chandelier to the plush fur carpet beneath our feet. "Another vampire, actually. He'd lived here for a few centuries and decided it was time to move. Grew tired of the famous life, I suppose."

"He was famous before vampires came out to the public?"

Vlad nodded. "He's a central character in a popular book series. People wanted to see his house, even if they didn't believe he was a real vampire. He left a few things behind after he moved, and I found I liked them enough to leave them."

My brows darted upward. Just who were we talking about here? Another famous vampire? I only knew of a couple, and Vlad was the main one.

Vlad waved a dismissive hand, clearly not the sort to name-drop, much to my annoyance. I was itching with curiosity, but I forced myself not to pry. Seeing as how there weren't *that* many famous vampires, I figured I could take an educated guess as to who he meant. And if I was right, that would explain the wolf fur draped across the back of an antique dining chair sitting across the room and the picture of a fancy violin hanging on the wall, assuming those didn't belong to Vlad.

"Well then." Vlad crossed the room and took a seat on one of those dreadful couches. "I imagine you must have some questions."

He removed his jacket and flung it over the back of the fainting couch, then gestured for me to sit next to him. I grimaced at the sight of all that velvet. In all my life, I'd never liked the feel of it. It made me itchy just thinking about touching it. I didn't find it soft like everyone else. It was like touching Styrofoam. Whenever I *did* touch it, I felt this strange catch in the back of my throat, almost like it was suffocating me. Velvet and I certainly were not friends, and I felt no desire to bridge that gap.

Instead, I skirted around the couch and perched my big ole butt on what I assumed, and damn well *hoped*, was a stool.

Vlad gave an amused smirk but ignored my preferred seating and instead indicated that I should speak.

Right. Questions. I had so many I didn't know where to begin. My whole life had imploded. Where would I even start? Maybe with the simplest things? Then go from there? See where the conversation led us?

"So..." I tapped my fingers against my knee. "I guess I'm a vampire, huh?"

The corner of Vlad's mouth tipped upward. "Indeed."

"And just to be clear, you're the one who turned me?"

He inclined his head.

"And that makes you my... master?" I cringed when I said that word. I was a woman of the twenty-first century, I didn't dig the whole *master* vibe.

To Vlad's credit, he seemed equally horrified by the notion. "Not even remotely."

Thank goodness for that. Yuck.

"What does it make you then? Is there a title for someone who turns another into a vampire?"

"A sire," he said, settling into the couch. He rested an ankle against his thigh and laid a hand on his knee.

Sire. That sounded fancy. While the last thing I wanted to do was fangirl in front of Vlad, I had to admit, I found this part fascinating. Not the dying bit, of course, but the being turned by him. Imagine what this could do for me and for my vlog. Bloody freaking Dracula. Vlad the Impaler, for cripes' sake. If I could interview *him*, the man himself, imagine how my popularity would skyrocket. People all over the world would tune into my vlog because of my personal connection to the most famous vampire in history. Hell, the most infamous tyrant, if you considered his human life.

"I'm not him," Vlad suddenly said, interrupting my inner monologue.

I blinked. "Not who?"

"Vlad Tepes."

"I thought you said you couldn't read minds," I accused.

"I can't. But your expression is quite transparent. Not to mention, I have quite a bit of experience in this area. When I tell people my name, they tend to jump to this first conclusion."

"Okay, but you did say you're Vlad."

"My birth name is Vlad Vasek," he said, his other arm now

stretching along the back of the couch. He looked the picture of comfort and ease. Every bit of me was dying to video him during this line of questioning, but considering I'd just woken in a coffin, I had no idea where my phone was.

"I'm far from the man you're thinking of," Vlad continued. "Tepes was a cruel, vindictive monster. Unfortunately, Vlad was a common name at my time of birth. It might interest you to know I'm older than Tepes, by about a decade or so. It's difficult to keep track of the years when you're as old as I am, but I remember someone telling me a decade once."

I stared dumbfoundedly. "But you called yourself Dracula."

"Indeed. There are those among your kind who associate Dracula with Tepes. And why not? The man was as bloodthirsty as they come. They would be wrong, however. Dear Mr. Stoker wasn't writing about Vlad Tepes. That's an assumption made by scholars, fanatics, even family members."

"Stoker was writing about *you*?"

Vlad nodded. "He was an insightful man and saw through my guise in minutes. He lived at a time when humans believed in the supernatural. Most feared ghosts and goblins, and they certainly feared the undead. In fact, where I'm from, graves were often reopened after five or so years and the corpses checked for vampirism. Things like simply not following proper burial procedure could result in the rising of a vampire. Humans lived in fear of a great many things back then. The concept of staking a vampire came about from the belief that staking a body to the ground would pin the monster to their grave, leaving them unable to rise.

"Stoker sought me out to learn about such creatures. To this day, I'm not sure when he figured out I was a vampire, but he soon offered me a sip of his blood. I was younger then, foolish even, and I took him up on that offer. To him, I was the confirmation of all his pursuits.

"However, while visiting my country, he came to learn of another man. One truly long-dead but equally intriguing. Vlad Tepes fascinated him. I cautioned him against writing his book, warning him that others of my kind might not appreciate the release of our secrets. But Stoker's imagination would not be silenced, and I found him too engaging to kill. Thus, Dracula's legend was born."

Huh. That put a small damper on my buzz, but not entirely. "So, you're not Tepes."

"No."

While slightly disappointed, I was also relieved. I couldn't imagine being tied to such a tyrant for the rest of my existence. "And Tepes is not Dracula."

Vlad shook his head. "People made their assumptions, but we vampires know the truth. Especially considering quite a few of us were born before Tepes and knew the man himself. Cruel, yes. Vampire, no."

I bit my lip and considered my next question. Finally, after a moment's hesitation, I decided to go for it. What was the worst thing he could say? "Would you be willing to let me interview you?"

The sight of his widening eyes brought a shy smile to my lips. Had my question surprised him?

"Interview me about what?"

"Just you. The truth behind Dracula. Let the world meet the real you and not the fictional character in the books and movies."

"And how, might I ask, would you interview me?"

This time, I was the one to wave the dismissive hand. "I have a vlog."

His blank stare wasn't encouraging.

"Um. Like a movie, except I'm filming you and asking questions for the public to view."

Understanding dawned on Vlad's face. "I'm afraid that won't be possible for two reasons."

I tried not to show my disappointment. This was exactly the sort of thing my vlog needed. A human—well, vampire—interest piece with someone famous. I knew a journalist would push for a yes, but somehow, I also knew Vlad wasn't the sort to concede.

"The first is that every vampire in the country has been given a hush order," Vlad continued. "The queen felt it was time to announce our existence to the world, but under no circumstances are any random vampires to give interviews without her express consent."

I'd learned of the vampire queen a week ago when she'd signed a peace treaty with our president, but it still sorta blew my mind. "But you aren't a random vampire."

"I am to her," he said. "While I might possess notoriety, I am not part of the queen's inner circle and have no power beyond my own."

"I wouldn't think something like that would stop you."

He offered another fangy grin. "Tell me, Anna. What do you know about vampires?"

I shrugged. In my last week, I'd done some research, as journalists were wont to do, but the information always seemed to contradict itself. Some sites claimed they—*we*—could only subsist off human blood, while others claimed animals would do in a pinch. No one ever seemed to know the right answer.

No human, that was.

"I know vampires drink blood, as seen by our little interlude upstairs."

He nodded.

"One would assume sunlight is a problem, considering the coffin."

"Very insightful. Direct sunlight will reduce us to ash. Some vampires can tolerate dusk and dawn depending on their age. I've also heard of vampires who could remain awake during the day when under duress. But for the most part, the sun renders us completely useless, and our coffins provide us protection while in that state. Typically, vampires are traditional creatures. Coffins used to be the only thing that could provide us with enough cover both from the sun and humans. Some took a more direct approach and dug little nests in the earth while others hide in the walls. But those of us who preferred something more..."

"Comfortable?"

He nodded. "That'll suffice. Those of us who preferred something more comfortable relied on coffins. We hide them in our attics or secret rooms barred from within."

I nodded. Of those choices, the coffin definitely seemed preferable. "So if sunlight is a problem, I would assume that fire is too."

A twinkle sparkled in his eye. If I wasn't mistaken, he seemed almost proud of me. His newly born minion. And didn't that warm the cockles of my dead heart.

"And since decapitation seems to work for just about everything, I assume it can also kill us."

"Very good."

"What about stakes?"

A shadow darkened his face. "Regretfully, quite effective at killing us."

"All right. Did I miss anything?"

"A great deal, actually. I assume you've heard of our queen and her council?"

"Beyond the press release from a week ago, no."

Vlad nodded. "Very well. Regarding your previous statement, that you wouldn't think someone of my caliber would be bothered by the queen's decree, I need you to understand something. We aren't governed like humans. The queen is our law. And her laws are absolute. You cannot successfully imprison a vampire—even permanently trapping us in coffins is difficult. Therefore, when one breaks the law, death is often the immediate punishment. We're immortal. We can always make new vampires. But our queen refuses to allow wayward vampires to run amok in this world. So when I tell you she's issued a hush order, know that disobeying merits strict punishment."

I forced myself to swallow. "Okay, so she's a tyrannical queen."

"No." Vlad sighed and repositioned himself on the couch. "Genevieve isn't cruel or unforgiving, but she must remain stout and stand by her laws. Otherwise, the vampire world would descend into anarchy, and the humans will pay the ultimate price. It's our responsibility as loyal subjects to obey her laws, and it's her responsibility as our queen to maintain control of our people."

A spark of anger flickered within. Listening to him, Vlad made it sound so idealistic, so perfect. But I'd already seen the darker side of vampirism, and I wasn't yet a week old. "If your queen is so strong and vampires fear her, then how the hell did I stumble across a blood orgy? I know for a fact that the human government worked with your queen to pass a law stating no vampires may take blood from unwilling victims, and yet look what I found."

A shadow whisked over Vlad's face. He lowered his arms from the couch and braced his elbows against his knees. "I was hoping not to have this discussion with you yet. Not until you'd had more time to adjust. But perhaps it's best I tell you now. Those women weren't unwilling."

I sucked in a sharp breath. "What?"

"The scene you stumbled across was sanctioned. It's not ideal, I'll admit, nor is it good PR, considering we've only been made general knowledge within the last week, but each attendee there signed a consent form. Those types of parties have been around for centuries."

My mouth gaped as I struggled to find the words. This was insane. Surely those people wouldn't have signed away their rights like that. The things I'd seen in that back room. Most of the—what? Customers? Patrons?—hadn't been aware enough to know what was happening. It honestly seemed no different than taking advantage of a drunk person.

"How...?" I shook my head in an attempt to clear my thoughts. "How do you know they all signed consent forms? Have you seen the documentation?"

"I know it's in your nature to distrust—"

"Of course I'm distrustful!" I shouted. "You're sitting here telling me about this mysterious tyrannical queen that holds complete power over every vampire subject beneath her, who *allows* these blood orgies to take place because the humans consented. Well, hello? Do you not see me sitting in front of you? I absolutely did *not* consent to this. That vampire, whoever the hell he is, literally dragged me out of the club, threw me up against the fence, and drained me dry before discarding me next to a fucking dumpster like I was trash. And you expect me to trust you? To believe you when you just say those people consented? I saw those humans with my own eyes. I saw the delirium, the lack of inhibition, the complete and utter lack of awareness of anything going on in that room."

Tears welled in my eyes, and I bit my lip to silence my shouting. Vlad didn't deserve my anger. He was just the messenger. But this whole situation was becoming incredibly distressing and not at all how I expected my weekend in New Orleans to turn out.

"Anna." Vlad cupped my hands. The instant we connected, I felt a sense of calm wash over me. Something about him soothed me, as though he could reach inside and ease my nerves. "As a general rule, humans crave a vampire's bite. It can be erotic, sensual, and heighten the pleasure one feels while engaged in intercourse."

My cheeks burned. Hearing Vlad utter things like "erotic" and "sensual" gave me some naughty visuals. Ones I didn't find particularly welcoming right now.

"Fallen has been hosting those blood parties for a very long time, so I assure you, those who joined in were vetted. Most, I imagine, already belonged to other vampires."

"Wait, what the hell does that mean, belong?"

"There's so much you don't know yet. So much I have to teach you."

"Well, we're in it now, so you may as well continue."

He squeezed my hand and nodded. "Vampires tend to employ humans, keep them on 'staff' as part of their harem. Many of us dislike hunting. It's exhausting to constantly be on the prowl. So, it became common practice to keep a few humans in our homes to feed from. These people are always made aware of their circumstances and sign an NDA agreement on threat of death should they break them. Usually these people are in need of help. Homeless, drug addicts, et cetera. We meet their needs while they feed ours."

"So you extort them," I accused.

Vlad held my gaze without a flicker of remorse. "Yes, we extort them. But it's a symbiotic relationship that's worked for millennia. These people prefer their lives with us as opposed to living like a junkie on the streets. I've heard of these little blood parties, and more often than not, they're attended by those particular humans. Those employed by a vampire. Believe me when I tell you, no innocents were harmed."

No, no innocents were harmed. None whatsoever.

Except me.

My breath caught in my throat, and tears pricked at my eyes. Suddenly, this wasn't fun anymore. I no longer cared who Vlad was or about his past. Now, I wish he'd just left me to die. Surely that would be an easier pill to swallow than these truth bombs he kept lobbing at me. At least then, I wouldn't be a walking, talking monster from beyond the grave who'd apparently died for *nothing*.

I pulled my hands from his and scrubbed my cheeks before my tears fell.

Later, I'd cry. In the safety of my own hotel or whatever. Not here. Not in front of Vlad. He might have turned me, but that didn't mean he got to see me at my most vulnerable.

I pressed the heels of my hands against my eyes and released a slow breath. "And your second reason?"

"Pardon?"

"At the beginning of this conversation, you said you couldn't give me an interview for two reasons."

"Ah, right. The second reason." He injected a little humor in his voice. "Well, have you ever seen any vampire movies? Or read any novels about us?"

"Of course."

"Good. If you were to name off let's say five things most commonly understood about vampires, what would they be?"

Great. A trivia game. Just what I wanted right now. "I don't know." I waved a hand in the air. "Aversion to sunlight, sleep in coffins, death by stake, allergic to garlic..."

He raised a brow. "And the last?"

I wracked my brain, then focused specifically on the latest book I'd read as part of my research. My eyes slowly widened, and I met Vlad's gaze. "No reflections."

He inclined his head.

But why would that matter for an interview? Unless... I made a small disbelieving sound. "You expect me to believe that we don't have reflections? Even in videos?"

"They're all reflections."

I blinked. "So mirrors, cameras?"

"Water, windows. All of it. Our clothes are visible, but not *us*."

"Our clothes?" I repeated, flabbergasted. I suppose in a way it made sense. Our clothes weren't magical. We bought them in stores, for cripes' sake. I sat there, completely silent and entirely flummoxed. I had no idea what to make of all this. It was so much information in such a short amount of time. Almost like he'd given me a lecture in Vamp 101.

"It's a lot," Vlad said, as though he actually could read my mind. "Why don't you get some rest and digest everything you've just learned."

"Um." I hesitated at the sound of my voice, breathless and weak. "Yeah, maybe a good idea. You didn't happen to find my things at Fallen, did you? Phone, purse, all that stuff?"

Vlad nodded.

Relief flooded me. At least that would save me some money. "Then if you'll just tell me where they are, I'll head to my hotel."

"Ah. About that."

All my hopes suddenly deflated. His tone was very telling, even if he hadn't spoken the words. Seemed I wasn't the only one with a bit of transparency issues. "I'm not allowed to leave, am I?"

"Not yet."

I gave a slow nod. "I'm too tired to argue about that."

Emotion flickered in Vlad's eyes, but I couldn't read it. I didn't know him well enough yet. A part of me guessed it was pity, and that only enraged me further. I didn't need his pity.

"Your friend Lucy placed your things in one of the spare rooms one level up. It's your room to use as you see fit for as long as you need. I've asked my servants to steer clear of your space for now until you've had a few days to adjust. In the meantime, sunrise is in"—he peered at a massive grandfather clock across the room—"approximately seven hours or so. Might I suggest you take the time to unwind, perhaps clean yourself up, and check your emails. From what I understand, you'll have one in particular awaiting you from the queen."

"What?"

"Well, it'll say it's from the queen, but rest assured, it isn't actually from her. One of her inner circle members is responsible for registering new vampires and providing them with all the material needed to make this adjustment. As your sire, it was my responsibility to register you as a newborn vampire upon turning you. Your friend Lucy assisted by providing your contact information. The queen is very determined right now to make a good first impression with all new vampires. I'm afraid I have no idea what they've sent you, but I do know you've been sent something. Lucy confirmed the arrival of the email the night I changed you."

If I wasn't already overwhelmed, this might have done me in. To think I'd been registered and my personal information handed over to the queen's flunkies without so much as a request for permission just chapped me the wrong way. But bitching about it would accomplish nothing. The damage was already done.

"Thank you," I forced out. "If you don't mind, I'd like to just...."

Vlad rose from the couch in a fluid motion that rendered me speechless. "Of course."

I rose from my stool and approached the winding staircase. Before taking the first step, I glanced over my shoulder to find Vlad standing in the sitting room, his dark gaze trained on me.

"Find me before sunrise," he said. "I'll escort you to your coffin."

Because that sounded like a barrel of laughs.

I quickly climbed the stairs and found the room he'd mentioned. It was quite simple, actually. I'd recognized the scent of my purse, interestingly enough, and found it sitting on the bed when I entered. Not in the mood to peruse my surroundings, I crossed the room and snatched my phone from the bedspread. It seemed Lucy had even plugged it in for me. Maybe there was still some hope for our friendship.

I activated the cellphone screen. My finger hovered over the camera app, the last thing I'd been using before that asshole had killed me. Part of me didn't want to look, too afraid of what I'd see in my last moments. But after a while, curiosity got the better of me, and I entered my gallery. The video was the last item in the folder, and with a trembling hand, I quickly tapped it, then hit play.

Except, it was nothing like I remembered. I could see the woman closest to me moaning and panting, her eyes half-lidded like she was high. But Vlad was right. Not a single vampire was visible in the video, except for their clothes. The air sort of distorted around them, like watching a bad television feed. A few seconds later, the video jerked, and fear crept up my spine as I watched myself being dragged through the club, Jimmy Choos abandoned on the tile.

Terror grabbed hold of me, and I soon found myself on my knees gasping for unneeded air. Seemed the video of my murder had inspired a panic attack. At the sound of my screams rising from my phone, I scrambled for it and shut it off. Then I dragged myself to the bed and let it all out. One ragged cry after another.

Everything that had happened to me was all for nothing.

I'd *died* for *nothing*.

Those words kept echoing in my head until I finally threw myself onto the pillows and gave into the tears.

CHAPTER
FIVE

Tears were the bane of every man's existence, regardless of age.

A few seconds after I broke down, I heard a gentle tap on the door. I hadn't welcomed Vlad into my room, but I felt the bed dip as he sat beside me. He offered a few words of encouragement, murmured a few helpless platitudes, but I still asked him to leave. It wasn't that I didn't appreciate him saving my life, but I firmly believed sobbing was a private affair. I'd never been one to share in the misery, so once the tears started, I just wanted to be left alone. And Vlad was so eager, he practically blurred from sight as he made his escape.

I didn't blame him.

No one wanted to be trapped with a hysterical person.

Truth be told, Lucy was the only person I wanted to see right now. In all our years together, this was the first time one of us had bailed on the other. I wanted nothing more than to reach out to her, to convince myself that she was still my best friend, that I hadn't done anything too damaging. But I knew I needed to give her space.

Death was difficult. While I hadn't *truly* died, I was now an official member of the undead country club. And Lucy wasn't. Were the roles reversed, I could only imagine how I would feel. And regardless of my current undead status, this had to be causing her some grief and loneliness.

Had she stuck around, though, she would have seen I was struggling with this as well. This change would not be easy for me. I had to come to grips with this new reality and learn who the hell I was now. Because, damn it, my life had taken a complete one-eighty.

Once my tears dried, I slowly sat up and wiped my cheeks. A flash of red caught my eye, and I stared down at my palms, flabbergasted. I looked like Lady Macbeth, my hands utterly stained in blood.

I cried out, darted to my feet, and bolted into the nearest bathroom. Careful not to stain the sink, I ran the hot water until it steamed up the mirror. Only then did I plunge my hands into the basin and scrub, all while muttering, "Out, damned spot."

Even though they didn't take long to clean, I still felt the blood on my skin. It was all in my head, and I knew that, but it didn't change anything. Exasperated, I grabbed a nearby cloth, rinsed it, then scrubbed my cheeks until my skin felt raw. The thin material was covered in blood, even after I washed it out. I stared down at the tinged water and sighed. I needed to relearn everything about life and what it meant to become a vampire. I'd always loved surprises, but this was one thing I felt I needed to be prepared for. Maybe that would help me adjust to my situation a little better.

Finally clean, I dragged my soggy ass back into my bedroom and plopped down on the wooden bench resting against the bed's footboard. I fetched my phone from the floor and, once again, unlocked the screen.

The first thing I noticed this time was the date. April fifteenth. Good lord. Lucy and I had infiltrated the club three nights ago. She'd mentioned that earlier, that it'd taken a few nights for me to wake, but I hadn't been able to give it much thought yet. Or anything for that matter. Had I really slept in that coffin for that long? Was that how long it took someone to become a vampire? Ugh. I really needed to learn what else to expect.

I pulled down my notifications bar and grimaced at the sight of them all. Texts and missed calls from my parents, a few texts from my ex-boyfriend checking to make sure I was still alive—oh, the irony—some Facebook notifications, and sure enough, an email from "The Queen of Vampires."

The email was quite sparse. They welcomed me to their lifestyle—like I'd had a fricking choice—issued me a username and temporary password for their website, and included a few links to what looked like an online forum.

Curious, I clicked one of those links first. It took me to their website and prompted me to sign in using the name and password provided in the email. Once logged in, I pulled up their forum and began to investigate.

When I first started researching vampires after their big announcement, I'd noticed Google only consisted of personal websites and a bunch of Wikipedia pages based on vampire *myths* and *fiction*. At the time, I'd found it all entertaining. Now, I wanted the real info. The nitty gritty.

This site was far more professional than the blogs. Clean cut, easy to read, with a look about it that screamed *government*. Everything was categorized into a beautifully organized Q&A, followed closely by what looked like personal accounts.

I settled in for some quality learning time.

HELP. I've been changed into a vampire. What do I do?

Well, first off—let us offer both our congratulations and our condolences. We understand this choice is a personal one. If you've willingly been changed, we suggest turning to your sire for any assistance you may require in adjusting. By Queen Genevieve's law, your sire is required to mentor you for three months after your awakening. If, unfortunately, you were not turned willingly, please contact the council as soon as possible. You will require a great deal of support, and we have people who can help. Click <u>here</u> to be taken to our contact page with a list of applicable emails, phone numbers, and addresses.

. . .

I PAUSED at the sight of those emails and numbers before finally jotting a few down. Maybe there was *something* they could do to assist me with this change, other than handing me a website and sending me on my way.

I glanced at the next question.

WHAT CHANGES SHOULD I expect once I've been changed?

Vampires are extraordinary creatures. Over the first week, your body will undergo extreme changes. Anticipate an immediate awkward stage as your body learns to adjust to its new abilities. The initial change takes three nights, during which you'll remain unconscious. Upon waking, you'll begin to experience heightened senses, strength, and most importantly, hunger. While becoming a vampire is a majestic transformation, it, of course, does not come without challenges. And a newborn's hunger is unlike anything you'll ever experience. The queen recommends that you sequester yourself from all loved ones for the first week as a means of protecting them and yourself while you adjust. Fear not, though. This hunger will eventually pass. And soon you'll become a normal, functioning vampire.

For more information, click here.

I IGNORED the link for now and instead contemplated what I'd just read. Maybe it was for the best that Lucy had left. I'd never forgive myself if I hurt her. Or anyone else, for that matter.

After promising myself that I'd text her once I was finished, I finally clicked the link and groaned when I saw the stupid headline.

YOUR VAMPIRIC BODY AND YOU!
This is one of the most common discussions, so we felt it best to

dedicate an entire page to this topic. The vampiric body is nothing like a human's. Our breed is stronger, faster, and deadlier. And whereas humans weaken as they age, vampires grow stronger. Take heart in knowing that you'll never be as weak and useless as you're feeling right now.

I SKIMMED THE ENTIRE PAGE, noting interesting little tidbits like how newborn vampires could immediately lift upwards of five hundred pounds. Further research concluded that since our bodies were able to take more damage and heal faster, we were less encumbered by things like strained muscles.

I couldn't help but think about Vlad. If newborns were already that strong, and vampires only grew stronger with age, what did that mean for someone who'd lived for more than half a millennium?

The rest of the article continued in the same vein, mentioning how vampires can count the craters on the moon and hear approximately ten miles away. I hadn't been given the chance to experience any of that yet, but I also hadn't left the house. Unluckily for me, our fangs were *not* retractable, and it was our responsibility to try and hide them while speaking—to avoid scaring the normies. Guess that meant I'd have to learn how to speak without chomping on my lips and tongue. And even worse, yes, we cried blood tears now. Repulsive. I made an immediate mental note to stop crying entirely. Some women were attractive when they cried, but I had a feeling female vampires weren't among them.

The next question gave me a hard pause.

CAN VAMPIRES PRODUCE CHILDREN?
No.

. . .

THAT WAS IT? No further discussion on the topic? I hunted around on the page but found nothing. So, I opened a new Google tab and searched this specific question. The answer wasn't encouraging. According to one of those horrid blog sites, even though vampires were classified as the undead, the fact remained that the body *did* die. As such, all natural bodily functions cease, such as a female's reproductive system. The dead couldn't give birth to the living.

My chin wobbled as I read the words, but I banished the traitorous tears that threatened to spill. I was twenty-four years old—I'd never really given thought to children. However, I absolutely hated that the decision had been stolen from me. There were upsides, though. No more monthly cycle, which, yay! And no more using the bathroom. Another plus. Still, the sting of that particular loss lingered.

I moved on before any dark thoughts took root.

Is it true that vampires are immortal?

Yes and no. All vampires are long-lived, but you're only as immortal as you allow yourself to be. Therefore, we recommend living your everlasting life in such a way that doesn't result in someone cutting off your head.

GOOD UNDEAD LIFE ADVICE, there.

So, really, what they were trying to say was I'd spend the rest of my "long-lived" life lonely and barren, provided I didn't attract the attention of an axe-wielding lunatic.

This was fun, and yes, that was sarcasm.

CAN VAMPIRES LOVE?

Vampires are creatures of heightened and intense emotions. When we find our mate, it's chaotic, messy, and yes, eternal. Unfortunately, few ever find their true soulmate, but when they do, it's an unbreakable bond.

OH BOY, did this question stop me in my tracks. There were so many thoughts racing through my head. I'd often heard it said that vampires were soulless. That when they died, their souls passed on, but their bodies remained, reanimated by magic and a consciousness that lacked morals. If this was the case, wouldn't that mean us soulless monsters were incapable of love?

We were entering an existential philosophical debate here, and I had no one to argue with.

The most important question being: Did we or didn't we possess a soul? The debate hinged entirely on that answer. I wasn't a religious person—far from it, in fact. I was, in a word, an atheist. There was simply too much bad shit out there in the world for me to be able to believe in an all-powerful deity. And if our destinies were actually preordained, then the "Big G" up there truly hated us all.

But that didn't mean I didn't believe in souls. The thought that I might have lost mine twisted my insides. Without my essence, my being... what did that make me?

Ugh, all this research was giving me a headache.

I rubbed my temples, then froze when my phone buzzed, and a notification flashed across the top of my screen. I sucked in a sharp breath at the sight of Lucy's name and nearly dropped my phone in the mad dash to tap the bubble.

L: *Did you see that your hair and nails will stop growing? That every night they'll revert back to whatever you looked like when you were changed? Good thing we got a manicure before coming here.*

What? No, I hadn't read that part. And grateful for the distraction, I flicked a glance at my hands. Relief rounded my tense shoulders. Thankfully, I'd opted for a classic manicure with rounded tips and a clear polish before hitting the road. No need to ever work on these bad boys again. My feet, on the other hand, were a whole other battle. Rough heels and ugly nails. Guess I now got to spend eternity suffering through endless pedicures. Ugh. I hated when other people touched my feet.

Who was I kidding?

My feet were strictly a no-touchy zone for me. Ah well. Someone had invented socks for a reason, right?

I glanced back at my phone to see the three little dots on the screen. I hadn't yet responded to Lucy, but she was typing another message. I couldn't begin to describe how happy that made me. She'd left, but I clearly hadn't lost my best friend.

L: *Apparently all vampires are born with a special gift. Did you see that?*

A: *No, I haven't. Sounds rad, though. What kinda gift?*

L: *Dunno. Maybe that's how your dude knew where to find you.*

A: *Did he ever introduce himself to you?*

L: *LOL. No. I never asked.*

Three nights and she never asked his name? Guess they hadn't spent much time together. And while I was thinking about that....

A: *What did you do while I was out of it?*

L: *Fretted, mostly. Sat in our hotel and stared at the walls. Read up on vampirism. You know, normal stuff.*

Nothing about that was normal.

A: *Did you tell anyone about what happened?*

L: *Yeah, right. I didn't even know what to say. Mostly, I just worried.*

Remorse swelled within me.

A: *I'm so sorry, Luce. I can't imagine what this must feel like for you.*

A few moments passed in which she didn't respond. Maybe she wasn't ready to talk about her emotions yet. Lucy was like that. I hated sharing emotions in general, but Lucy clammed up when something was too much for her. Like this.

The three dots popped up, and I waited anxiously, so grateful my best friend was still willing to talk to me.

L: *So, what's his name, then?*

A: *Vlad.*

L: LOL. *Of course it is.*

A: *What's that supposed to mean?*

L: *Aren't all vampires named Vlad, or Lestat, or Dracula, or something? Wannabe bloodsuckers, right?*

I bit back a laugh. She'd nailed two out of three already.

A: *He's the real Vlad. Also known as Dracula.*

The message quickly turned to *read*, but Lucy didn't immediately respond. My mouth twitched with amusement. I could only imagine how she was taking that little bit of information.

L: *You shittin' me?*

I snorted at her message.

A: *Nope. The legend is based on him. Insane, right?*

She left me on *read* again. I decided to change the topic.

A: *Have you left town yet?*

She didn't immediately respond. I sat perched on the edge of the bench, nibbling on my thumbnail. Finally, when the three dots popped up, I sighed.

L: *No.*

Relief bloomed through my chest. The site recommended a week's separation. I could handle that if it meant seeing her again.

A: *Are you going to stay?*

Another long pause. Clearly Lucy hadn't decided on anything yet and was making this up as she went. I knew my best friend better than anyone. I was no stranger to her thought process.

L: *Do you promise not to go after the vamp who attacked you?*

I considered her question and understood the implication. If I pursued my bloodlust for this vamp, she'd leave, and I'd likely lose my best friend. No matter what happened, nothing was worth that. So I gritted my teeth and answered.

A: *Yes.*

L: *Then yes, I'll stay.*

I fist-pumped the air. Everything was so strange right now. And there was so much to digest. But with Lucy at my side, I felt like I could do anything. She was my rock and always had been.

A: *Thank you. Love you, Luce.*

L: *Yeah, yeah, just don't think about ever taking another bite out of me, got it?*

A: *Yes, ma'am.*

L: *That's better.*

A: *The sites say we shouldn't see each other for a week. What are you going to do in the meantime?*

L: *I thought I'd go back to the vamp club, see what I can learn about your... well, that guy.*

That guy, meaning the vamp who'd killed me. Adoration swelled within me. This girl was my life. And even though I'd been sorta murdered at that club, she was still willing to go back, if it meant helping me. I must have done something great in a past life to end up with a friend like her.

But no way in hell was I going to let her tackle that place without me. Or ever. It was too dangerous. And I loved Lucy way too much to let her risk her life like that, regardless of her reasons.

A: *No, absolutely not.*

L: *Girl, just cuz you're a badass vamp now, doesn't mean you get to tell me what to do.*

A: *Lucy, I'm serious. It's too dangerous. Promise me you won't. At least wait until Vlad and I can go with you. For backup.*

Yet another long pause. Finally, after a few minutes of me fretting over whether I was about to break quarantine to ensure her ass stayed put, she responded.

L: *Fine. I'll just go do some sightseeing during daylight hours then. You know, when all you little vamps are a-snooze in your coffins. Don't worry about me. Just focus on you. You're going to need to master your control before we go home. You can't be munching on townies.*

A: *Aww, why not? Bet Christopher tastes delicious.*

And wouldn't my ex-boyfriend just *love* me snacking on him.

L: *Har, har.*

Christopher had been my first *real* boyfriend. I couldn't use the word serious, because it definitely hadn't progressed to that, but our "relationship" had lasted longer than all the others I'd dated. Christopher and I had broken up a week ago, when he'd learned about my plan to come here in search of a vampire to interview. He'd warned me I was going to end up dead, and I'd broken up with him. Guess life really did have a way of punching you in the face. Still, if ever there was anyone who deserved a good necking, it was him.

L: *Go relax. Get comfy being in your own body again. I'll message you tomorrow night once the sun goes down.*

A: *Can do, girlfriend. Gab at ya later.*

Lucy sent a massive thumbs up, thereby ending the conversation. I took the time to scroll a few social media sites and reacquaint myself with the people from my hometown. Perish's population hovered near the seven-hundred mark, meaning everyone knew everyone. Seeing their faces and reading their mundane posts helped ground me and remind myself there was a big ole world out there continuing on as though nothing had happened. It helped, seeing how normal their lives were.

Yes, I was a vampire. But with luck, most people never needed to know. Of course, seeing as how I was now undead, luck had never really been on my side.

CHAPTER

SIX

It seemed safe to assume, based on the cellphone laying smack dab in the middle of my face, that I'd fallen asleep while scrolling the feeds. Weirdly, I didn't recall drifting off. I remembered chuckling at something my former high school principal had posted in one of our town's local groups, then instant darkness. Not even a droopy eye to hint I'd been hovering on the edge of sleep. I could only assume it was because of the change. The Q&A I'd read had mentioned something about it taking a week for your body to completely adjust. Maybe it needed more sleep during the transition. Had to take a lot of work to reanimate a dead body.

I plucked the phone from my face and stretched out my jaw. Then I lit up the screen and peered at the time through slitted, light-sensitive eyes. If the clock could be trusted—which, let's face it, I always trusted my phone—it was three in the morning. Or "witching hour," as my mother had taken to calling it. Two weeks ago, she'd never believed in the paranormal. But after the press release, she'd begun to take stock in everything. And witching hour had quickly become a time of night she now feared. Apparently, it had something to do with witches, demons, and ghosts being at their most powerful or some nonsense. All I felt was groggy. So guess there was no truth to that myth. She'd be so pleased to hear that.

And since the thought of telling my mom I'd been vampified filled me with abject terror, I chose to change my mental direction to something a tad less nerve-wracking—like personal hygiene. Because *blech*, I stunk. I guess three nights of marinating in my coffin hadn't done me any favors. Not to mention nearly dying. I had to imagine a body experienced some intense levels of stress when going through this sort of thing, meaning sweaty B.O. And since I was currently rooming with another vampire, taking a shower seemed a wise idea.

Yawning, I waddled my drowsy ass into the closest bathroom. Though I was hardly an expert, I figured I had a few more hours until sunrise. Of course, even that raised more questions. It felt like every few minutes I thought of a dozen more.

What would happen? Would I "die?" Did I need to sleep in that damn coffin again? Would I immediately wake at sunset? Or did I need to set some sort of vampy alarm to wake me?

And if I did have to sleep in that coffin, why? There had to be other options. Surely these people weren't content with literally crawling into their death beds every night. I shuddered at the thought. Maybe other vampires were okay with that, but not me. I definitely needed to make some changes. Sunlight was a problem, but that was fine. I could work around that.

I didn't bother turning on the bathroom light, thanks to my newly improved vision. Everything was crisp and clear. Who needed light anyway, right? *Hello darkness, my old friend....*

The first thing I noticed was the mirror. There it sat above the sink, brazen as sunlight, as though taunting me to stare into it.

Nope. I wasn't ready for that.

It was one thing to *know* I didn't have a reflection. It was entirely different to experience it. And somehow, I just knew that would be the thing to send me over the edge tonight. So, avoid the vanity.

The next thing I noticed was the massive amount of products stuffed onto the shelves next to me. Enough to stock an entire beauty salon. My gaze leapt from item to item, and I bit back a laugh. Had Vlad done this? Or had a servant done his bidding? Considering the four-poster beds and massive tubs that could fit a small house party, it seemed safe to assume he'd ordered someone to do it for him. I hadn't spotted any servants yet, but I sure could smell them. In fact, I could pick out their individual soap and shampoo brands. Thankfully, Vlad's blood still filled my tummy, so I wasn't feeling especially hungry right now.

I grinned when my gaze snagged an item of interest. My mouth felt grimy, seeing as how I hadn't brushed my teeth in three nights. It seemed my thoughtful host had anticipated my needs and provided me a toothbrush. Or at least what I assumed was a toothbrush. I grabbed it and held it up for inspection, laughing at the sight of it. Guess there was a special brand for vamps, one specifically designed for cleaning our fangs. It had this weird triple-sided head that formed a triangle. After a small experimentation—and yes, a Google search—I learned that I was supposed to insert my fang through the center. Once positioned, I pushed the button and listened to the electric hum as it cleaned and polished my dangerously sharp canines. Afterward, there was a button on the side that once pressed, opened the triangle up into a flat brush for the rest of my teeth.

Handy.

Now with squeaky clean teeth, I rinsed it off, then snapped a photo of it and fired it off to Lucy with the caption "Fangtastic." After a few moments, in which I considered the other products, Lucy sent back a laughing emoji. Hey, we had to laugh about it. Otherwise, we'd cry, and I'd already established a no-crying rule. I couldn't break it on my first night.

Unable to resist, I picked up a tube of lipstick and chuckled when I spotted the name Eternal Blood. The mascara brand was Everlast. And the eyeliner? Yup. Undead Black. My laughter echoed through the bathroom. An entire line of makeup designed for the everyday vamp-girl. Including Bite Me perfume. I couldn't even make this shit up. But someone had. And likely made millions off the product. Man, it sure hadn't taken the marketing companies long to dip their toes into the supernatural pool, considering how recently the queen had made the announcement. Made me question so many things. Like, had some companies known in advance? Had they been prepared, waiting to jump on the opportunity the second the treaty was announced? It also made me wonder if they'd manufactured anything for the men. Something like Immortal Cologne for the undead man in your life.

I'd always been fascinated by makeup but sadly had never mastered it. I always ended up looking like a circus clown who'd gotten into a bar fight. The few videos I'd watched had intimidated the hell out of me. Contouring, highlighting, shadowing, and oh lord, the blending. So much blending. I wasn't a painter. I barely even knew what those things meant! Kudos to those who'd figured it out, though.

And hey, guess it didn't really matter anymore, considering the whole no reflection thing. Seemed like an impossible task to master the art of something I'd never be able to see again, right? Besides, if I hadn't learned how to perfect my makeup in the last ten years or so, I really didn't think the next hundred were going to make a difference. With luck, maybe a bar-fighting clown would be the look then. I just needed to wait for my moment to shine.

After snapping a final picture of the undead makeup line for Lucy, I ran the water and hopped into the shower. I instantly ducked under the hot spray and let loose a groan worthy of the bestest orgasms. The water felt amazing as it pummeled the top of my head and trickled down my body. I didn't realize how badly I needed this. I'd always heard water was a symbol of renewal and rebirth, and right now, I was eager for those things. But the best part was it washed that murderous bastard off me. With my new senses, I could still catch whiffs of him, enough so that I knew I'd recognize him if we ever crossed paths again.

I lathered up and washed the blood from my hair, then moved on to the rest of me. I scrubbed, scrubbed, scrubbed until I shone, then leaned back against the shower wall and closed my eyes. There was something about the calming sound of water that soothed my nerves. I had a feeling I could stay in the shower all night and not run out of hot water, but that seemed rude. Vlad was letting me stay here. I didn't need to take advantage of the amenities.

Once dried off, I brushed my hair flat. I generally tied or braided it back to keep it off my face and shoulders, but the thought of exposing my neck bothered me. A vampire thing, maybe? Or residual trauma from the attack? I couldn't say.

I stared at the products on the counter, then decided on a whim to apply a little of the Bite Me perfume to my wrists and throat. I wasn't *trying* to catch Vlad's attention or anything—not that I would have minded it if I *did*. No, I was just curious about the smell, or so I told myself.

But when I lifted my wrist to my nose and sniffed, I winced. The bottle claimed the perfume possessed floral notes mixed with a hint of an aphrodisiac. All I smelled was sterile alcohol. *Blech*. I turned the sink taps, wet a cloth, then scrubbed it off as best as I could. The overwhelming stench didn't give me hope for the rest of the products. Maybe Vlad thought this was what vampire women wanted. Or maybe his servants had bought it all, and he hadn't the foggiest idea about any of it. Either way, I wouldn't be wearing any of this stuff.

I returned to my bedroom to find a set of pajamas laid across the bed. Someone had found some spare clothes for me, it seemed, and slipped them into my room while I was showering. I pulled on the sweats and oversized hoodie and took comfort from the soft material. Nothing like wrapping yourself up in fleece and cotton to make the world feel right again.

Once dressed, I set out to hunt down the Count. Sunrise was approaching. I could feel it in my bones. And he'd asked me to find him beforehand. It didn't take long to find him. I knocked on a pair of giant oak doors and waited for his acknowledgement. When it came, I pushed one open and strode inside.

The moment I entered, I was struck by the staggering amount of wood in the room. Seemed our man here enjoyed himself some mahogany bookshelves alongside cherry wood floors and furniture. From roof to floor, wood, wood, and more wood.

"Geez, you suicidal?" I asked.

Vlad sat in a cushy-looking computer chair. He spun around at the sound of my voice, his brow lifted in question.

I gestured all around us. "One would think a vampire wouldn't want to be surrounded by this much wood."

"One would assume I'd be safe in my own home," he retorted.

"You know what they say about assuming."

He rolled his eyes, effectively communicating that he did indeed know that saying, and he remained unconcerned. "I only welcome those I trust into my home."

"And me?" I asked.

A whisper of a smile crossed his face. "If I didn't, I wouldn't have turned you, wouldn't you agree?"

"But how could you even begin to believe you can trust me? We don't know each other. You appeared out of nowhere to save my life. And speaking of... why were you even at the club?" My eyes widened. "Were you taking part in the orgy?"

Vlad's eyes grew comically wide. After a moment's bluster, he shook his head. "I assure you, I have no need for blood orgies." He cocked his head. "Are you always this inquisitive?"

"Oh, definitely," I said, laughing. By habit, my teeth scored my bottom lip. I winced when my fangs punctured the flesh, then moaned when a drop of blood coated my tongue.

Vlad's eyes flashed—with desire or anger, I couldn't tell—but he half-rose from his chair before he seemed to realize he'd even moved. With great effort, he appeared to restrain himself. He closed his eyes and drew in a deep breath, his fingers digging deep into the armrests.

Eyes still closed, he tilted his head toward me and began to speak, his words a tad clipped, as though he found this entire conversation tedious. "Let's begin with the club. I was there waiting."

"For a meal?"

"No" was all he said.

When he didn't offer any more information, my mouth opened with the intention of digging deeper, but the grim slash of his lips told me this topic was off-limits.

He swallowed, and my gaze dipped to his throat, mesmerized by the motion. It was no surprise that Vlad checked off everything I liked in a guy. Tall, dark, handsome, strong, severe, smart—I stopped myself from listing more adjectives and instead forced my gaze back up to his. Heat flared within his dark eyes, like embers flickering against coal. Maybe I was just hungry? Or *maybe* I was hungry for something more primal.

Vlad blinked, snuffing out the flames. "I knew when I saw you...."

"Knew what?"

He shook his head. "I'm explaining this wrong."

"Technically, you aren't explaining anything."

Vlad sighed and narrowed his eyes on me. "If you'd let me finish."

I bit back a chuckle and pantomimed zipping my lips shut. What could I say? I loved to needle him. He was needle-worthy. Few guys were worth poking.

"I was nearby when I spotted you in the crowd. You were talking to your friend, and your voice cut through the deafening din, so soft, so sweet."

Not words people usually used to describe me, but I'd take them as a win for now.

"I admit I followed you for a bit. Watched as you and Lucy moved through the club. I lost track of you for but a few moments."

And I could see from his deep frown that this flustered him.

"I followed your scent, curious about you. When I discovered you'd entered the back room, I knew you were in trouble. Then I found you in that alleyway. Broken, bleeding, dying."

"So, you just turned me? Without even asking?"

"Who would I have asked?" Bitter laughter slipped past his lips. "Who was there but me? Had I left you, you would have died."

No doubt. I remembered the countdown looming in my head.

"Would you have preferred that?"

Truthfully, I wasn't sure. So, I refrained from answering that question. "*Why* change me then?" I demanded. "Seeing me in the crowd was reason enough to turn me?"

"Yes." He caught my gaze again, his features smooth with compassion. "And no."

This time, I frowned. "What does that even mean?"

"I wouldn't wish this existence on my worst enemy."

Um, okay. Then what did that make me?

"But you're the furthest thing from my worst enemy. And the thought of losing you before I even had a chance to know you... I couldn't bear that."

Remember that little headache from earlier? It came screaming back with a vengeance. Nothing this man said made any sense. And I was getting tired again. Too tired to keep digging. I would have bet my last dollar that my newfound exhaustion was all vamp-related. But that didn't make it any easier.

I rubbed my brow and released a small sigh.

Vlad was on his feet and swept across the room, all majestically. "Are you in pain?"

"Only the literal kind."

His fingertips touched my cheek, and I had to resist the urge to lean into him. Cripes, everything was just so confusing.

"What hurts?"

"My head," I mumbled.

Without a word, his fingers brushed my cheek and settled on my temples. He rubbed them in small circles with just the right amount of pressure. I moaned and closed my eyes, sinking into bliss. The man knew how to give good head—massages, that was.

"It's part of the transition," he told me. "It takes about a week for our bodies to fully adjust."

"I know. I read the website."

"What website?"

If it weren't for my headache, I might have laughed. Of course

Vlad knew nothing about a website. He was as ancient as they came. And from what I'd read in books, ancient ones always abhorred modern technology.

"The queen's lackey sent a link in the email you told me about," I replied. "Stuff about the changes our bodies go through, recommendations to listen to our sires, since it's their responsibility to guide us for three months post-change. And since you're my sire, I guess that means I have to listen to you."

"Heaven forbid. Sunrise is less than fifteen minutes away. We should get you settled."

I groaned. "Do I have to go back into the coffin?"

Vlad cupped my cheeks, and I opened my eyes, meeting his gaze. I saw the truth in his face, and my hopes plummeted. I *hated* that stupid coffin. As if it wasn't bad enough to wake up in it post-death, I had to look forward to it for the rest of my life.

Hmm. Or did I?

I mean, was there an unwritten law stating vampires must retire to their coffins every night? Some vampy nonsense about pine boxes and cramped living conditions?

Gently nibbling on the inside of my lip, I considered those questions. Maybe there was another solution now. "Now that you guys are public knowledge, why not just black out your windows?"

"Black them out how? With black paint? That's not exactly attractive aesthetically."

I nodded. "What about mesh liner? Or blackout curtains?"

Vlad considered me while lowering his hands. "You haven't experienced sunlight yet. Believe me when I tell you it's no laughing matter. We can't risk our lives for simple comforts."

"Then what's the point of living?" I mumbled. "Look, there has to be something better than a coffin."

"It upsets you," he stated.

"Duh. No one wants to be trapped in a coffin."

His gaze turned distant. "I've done it for so long I barely give it a thought now."

"Well, wouldn't you like to sleep somewhere more comfortable? Like a giant California king bed?"

A chuckle rumbled in his chest. "I'm not sure I've ever slept on one."

"Trust me, it's worth risking being burned alive."

That chuckle turned into full laughter. "I'll take your word for it."

"What about an attic suite without windows? Could have a bed, a dresser, whatever. Something more comfortable."

"Building code states that all bedrooms must have windows for emergency access."

"Okay." I considered our options. Maybe I could try sleeping in the earth? Buried under a mound of soil. But that sounded horrible. I'd never been claustrophobic before. Guess I was now.

Vlad's thoughts were clearly elsewhere. After a few moments, he nodded. "I'll make some inquiries and see what can be done. There might be some new options now that we needn't hide our existence anymore."

Hope blossomed like a flower in my chest. "Really?"

"Give me a few nights to discuss our options with contractors. I have some ideas, but I don't know if they're possible. There are building codes we must abide by, unfortunately."

"You would do that for me?"

He studied me silently. I could tell there was something he wished to tell me, could practically see the words hovering on the tip of his tongue, but instead, he merely nodded and strode toward his office door. "Let's get you settled. There's not much time left before sunrise. We can discuss this at length once I have some answers."

Together, we went upstairs, and I started to sink into depression. I really didn't want to sleep up here tonight, but I wouldn't push it any further. He'd already heard my complaints and promised to do something about them. I couldn't ask for more.

We entered the attic, and I spotted a second coffin sitting next to mine—now complete with a brand new lid. Curiosity piqued, I stole a glance at him to find him very studiously staring at the coffins.

"Do you always sleep in this room?" I asked.

"Yes" was all he said as he approached my coffin and eased the lid back. My shoes sat inside, tucked up amongst the silk lining. I'd completely forgotten about them and was dismayed to find the heel had snapped off one. My poor Jimmy Choos. It'd taken me *months* to pay them off, but a girl *has* to have a pair of Choos. Now I needed to save up to buy another. I could pay to have them repaired, but they'd always be tainted in my head now.

I removed them from the liner and set them on the floor. Didn't need them poking me in the bum again.

With one hand holding the lid, Vlad offered me his other to help me inside. I climbed in, then stretched out on my back, my breath already hitching.

"My people know not to disturb us during daylight hours unless it's an absolute emergency."

"Thank you," I whispered, relief loosening my shoulders. The thought of being caged in the darkness again would have given me palpitations if my heart could beat.

"I'll be right next to you all day," he said, his voice soothing those lingering anxieties. "I wake an hour before sunset. You won't be able to yet, but just know I'll be here when you wake."

"Okay. Good morning?" I prompted, unsure of the proper terminology, since technically the sun was rising.

"Sleep well, Anna," Vlad murmured as he sealed me in.

Before I could respond, he'd vanished. I heard the soft sounds of his own lid being moved, then nothing but silence. I had a moment to wonder if I could crawl into his coffin with him, when the sun suddenly rose and knocked me out.

CHAPTER

SEVEN

I NEVER WAS A MORNING PERSON. Usually it was ten a.m. before I hauled my ass out of bed in search of waffles and coffee. And my damn coffee mug needed to be empty before I was willing to so much as converse with another human being. Lucy had always teased me about this, told me I was pissier than a mama grizzly bear. She'd even made me a special mug for Christmas one year that read "Cranky Bitch Medicine."

But, thanks to my new *condition*, I didn't need to worry about any of that anymore. The instant sunset hit, my eyes popped open without a hint of lingering grogginess. One moment, I was dead, the next awake again. Almost like someone had flicked on my power switch, and now I was raring to go.

I palmed the coffin lid to the side, hopped out with all the elegance and grace I'd lacked as a human, and glanced at Vlad's coffin. It sat open and empty, the silk pillows fluffed and pristine. Guess he really did wake an hour before sunset, earlier than the rest of us plebs.

A quick glance down revealed pristine pajamas. Normally when I woke, I looked like I'd been mauled in my sleep. Rat's nest for hair, half-rumpled pj's, sheets tangled between my legs, drool stains on my pillow—though I'd never admit to that one aloud. But not anymore it seemed. My pj's looked like I'd just ironed them. Not a wrinkle to be found. Guess we didn't move around much during daylight.

I didn't want to think about that. Just the thought that I might actually be dead during the day gave me a ragin' case of the heebie-jeebies. I needed to adjust, and I knew I would with time, but that night wasn't tonight. Probably not even tomorrow.

One upside, though. I didn't feel an immediate need for a shower as I had when human. My hair was smooth and unknotted, no gunk in my eyes, no yawning or lingering grouchiness, and—after blowing a quick puff of air into my hands—no morning breath either.

Now *that* was a miracle.

I had a huge hate-on for halitosis. My number two rule—which came after removing your shoes in my house—was no making out until teeth were brushed. The human mouth was disgusting. I didn't think it was too much to ask that my boyfriend handle that situation before handling mine.

"Good evening, madam," a monotonous voice said.

My head snapped up, and I spotted a rather old man standing next to the attic entry, dressed in—I kid you not—a penguin suit with a white towel draped over his forearm. I bit back a chuckle as I inspected him. He *had* to be Vlad's personal butler with that appearance.

"The Count awaits your presence downstairs," he said, gazing down his hawkish nose at me.

"He does, does he? Well, the Count can wait until I'm ready to be seen."

"That would be unwise," the old man said, his British accent emphasizing his words. "My instructions are to bring you to him immediately."

I shook my head. "I'd like to change my outfit first, if that's all right with your lordliness."

"Your attire can be addressed after your meeting. Master Dracula wishes to bid you a good evening and ensure you're fed a quality meal before seeing to the rest of your night."

A quality meal? Like what? Raw steak and potatoes drenched in blood with a Bloody Mary on the side? I snickered against the back of my hand and nodded. But when I took a step toward Mr. Butler, he gave a distinguished gasp and stepped backward.

"Please, madam. I will leave first. You haven't fed, and I don't wish to upset your delicate appetite."

Delicate appetite? What the hell did that even mean? Besides, I wasn't even hungry. "It's fine, Beauregard."

"My name is Harold, madam."

"Honestly, I prefer Beauregard."

"Yes, I imagine you would."

Was that sarcasm? Seeing as how I was fluent in that language, I was definitely picking up what he was putting down. If I had to guess, I'd wager Mr. Beauregard didn't like me.

With a dismissive wave, I took a few more steps toward him.

Beauregard's eyes went comically wide, but it wasn't until he started to protest that a mouth-wateringly delicious scent smacked me in the face like a wet towel. Holy guacamole, it was wonderful. Perfectly sweet with a hint of spice. Saliva pooled in my mouth, and my eyes fluttered shut. It wasn't until I outstretched a hand that I realized the delectable aroma came from Beauregard.

"Should I leave?" he asked in a soft voice.

It took every ounce of strength I possessed, but I managed to hold my breath and nod. Maybe if I didn't breathe, I wouldn't be tempted, because him leaving was the last thing I wanted. No, I wanted to sink my fangs into him and suck him dry until nothing remained but a withered, empty shell.

Distantly, I listened to the sound of his retreat. Only when he was two levels below me and well out of range did I exhale. His scent rode the air and could lead me to him if I wished, like a giant bright arrow lighting up the way. I had to fight the urge to chase him down. Surely, Vlad wouldn't appreciate me chomping on his butler's neck.

No. Beauregard was a human. I didn't eat humans.

Yet.

Hopefully never.

I just wished they didn't have to smell so good. It was like every food fantasy I'd ever had rolled into one delectable package. Beauregard had reminded me of chocolate ice-cream sundaes topped with Bailey's. My former favorite Sunday afternoon snack.

I needed to focus on something else—*anything* else. So, I took the stairs two at a time and hurried to Vlad's office, where I was sure I'd find him. I knocked, then slipped inside without waiting for a response. It had to be safer in here, under Vlad's watchful eye.

Vlad glanced up from his desk and gave me a slight nod. He held a phone to his ear but from the sounds of it was on hold. For some reason, that made me laugh. A house full of employed humans hired for exactly this purpose, but he was the one on hold.

"I'll just...." I pointed at his surrounding library.

Books, books, and more books, all in alphabetical order. Not a single trinket donned the shelves, as though he felt they were unwelcome amongst his library.

I casually perused his selection. His tastes differed from mine. Unsurprising, really. The man was from an entirely different era than me. He'd already died before authors like Voltaire, Austen, and Shakespeare wrote their works.

I preferred more contemporary fiction, with a taste for fantasy when the mood struck. I'd never been one to enjoy the classics. But to each their own.

"Very well," I heard Vlad say as I rounded one row of bookshelves and started down another. "Yes, that'll suffice. We'll see you then. Thank you."

At the sound of his call disconnecting, I circled back around the stacks. The nosy journalist in me wanted to pepper him with questions. What was he planning? When he said "we," did he mean me and him? Or did he mean the royal we? But the manners my mother had instilled within me as a young child flared up, and I bit my tongue.

"Apologies." Vlad tipped his head. "How are you feeling tonight?"

"I'm okay, I think. Not as tired as last night. Less frazzled."

Vlad nodded. "Good. Are you hungry?"

My mind instantly went to donuts and coffee. Ugh, I would kill for a glazed anything right now. Even just a nibble. Something to soothe the sugar-addicted beast within me. "Can we eat human food?"

"Ah. No. Our systems can't handle it."

A polite way of saying *now that you're dead, only the lifeblood of the living will keep you alive.* Cute. I tried not to let the disappointment bring me down, but damn it, I *lived* for crullers. What a cruel existence—to live forever without ever again relishing a donut or pastry. It had to be illegal.

"So, just blood?"

He gave a single nod.

"Great. An eternal liquid diet."

His mouth twitched with the hint of a smile. "I assure you, it's not so bad. The different flavors make it quite appetizing. And our hunger is not so easily sated. Believe me when I tell you, you won't ever grow tired of blood."

Ugh. I think that was the most unappetizing thing he could have said.

"Does it have to be human?"

Sympathy softened his face. "I know of some who subsist off animals. But believe me when I tell you, that type of diet will weaken you. I admit I don't know the science behind it, but human blood is the best nourishment for us."

"What about other vampires?" My stomach warmed with the thought of last night, suckling at Vlad's wrist. The honeyed taste of his blood lingered in my memory.

Some sort of emotion flashed deep in Vlad's eyes, but it was gone before I could figure it out. For a moment, I wondered if it was rage—if my question had angered him. But then I wondered if it was lust. Was the idea of me drinking his blood again as erotic for him as it was for me?

And if so, what did that mean?

Vlad cleared his throat. "There are *some* vampires out there who feed off one another."

"And...?"

He sighed and rubbed the bridge of his nose. "It's usually reserved for lovers. They share blood in the heat of the moment."

Heat of the...? Ahh.

"Sharing blood can be thrilling for both parties. To give yourself wholly to someone you care about deeply. However, many choose not to partake in such a way. The older the vampire, the more powerful their blood—and unfortunately, the more addicting. Drinking from an ancient, for example, is harmful to younger vampires."

"I don't understand." None of this was explained in the forums I read last night, so I was a bit lost here.

Vlad sat in his desk chair with a pinched expression. "Vampires require blood to survive. We subsist off humans because their blood contains no magic or power beyond simply providing life. But vampiric blood contains an essence humans lack. Younger vampires who drink from older vampires tend to experience exponential growth of their own power. But often, their minds and bodies aren't prepared for such a thing."

"So, what happens to the younger vampire then?"

"They succumb to madness, unable to handle the power. We vampires develop our powers naturally over the course of centuries. Over the years, I've grown into two abilities. But when a younger vampire drinks from an older one, the process is accelerated. And their young bodies can't handle the transition."

"Then what about last night?"

"It was an emergency," Vlad said. "A few small feedings won't harm you. But we do need to tread carefully. I am over five hundred years old. And you are...." He gave a small shrug.

"Two nights old," I answered, if we didn't count the three nights I'd spent marinating in my coffin.

"The age-gap is dangerous."

"So no more feeding off you. Got it."

Vlad's jaw tightened, and for a brief second, I wondered if he actually wanted me to feed from him. He'd mentioned sharing blood was addicting. Perhaps he wasn't as immune as he thought.

Which got me wondering... "What about those who are in a relationship and share blood while—" This time, I cleared my throat. I was a grown-ass adult, but for some reason, I couldn't say the word "fucking" in front of Vlad. And "making love" seemed far worse.

"Yes, well, there's always an exception, and those in a relationship make that choice for themselves. Sadly, we've seen situations arise where the younger partner needs to be contained, or even killed, due to sharing too much blood. Those are sad days."

My breath rushed past my lips. "You kill them?"

"We have no choice, Anna. We cannot allow rabid vampires to run rampant through the streets. And those who've lost their minds to bloodlust can't be reasoned with. Imprisoning them would be a life worse than death, since their minds never heal. Death is a blessing in that case."

Okay. *Definitely* no more drinking from Vlad. No matter how badly I wanted to wrap my mouth around him. It was strange how that disappointed me. I hadn't known Vlad long. Yes, he'd saved my life, but really, I didn't know anything else about him, other than his approximate age. And yet, I felt this loss keenly. A weight pressed on my chest, almost like I wanted to cry. I remembered how sweet his blood had tasted, how it'd brought me back from the brink twice now. Once the night of my death, then last night. Was this the addiction he'd mentioned? Why vampires began to crave one another?

It had to be in my head. He'd said a few small feedings wouldn't harm me. Probably boiled down to me just wanting something I couldn't have. Typical Anna Perish behavior—and yes, before anyone asks, my family name is the same as my hometown name. Thank my great-great-and-so-on-grandfather who'd founded the town.

Anywho, growing up, my parents had constantly used reverse psychology on me, because anything they said I couldn't have, I wanted. Seemed Vlad's blood was no exception.

I shoved those thoughts to the back of my mind. Focusing on them would only deepen the craving. "Okay, then what's on the menu tonight?"

"I had Harold fetch you some bagged blood. It's human. However, not fresh from the source. You may not like it, but you can't leave the house for the rest of the week, so I'm afraid this will have to suffice."

I grimaced. Bagged blood did not sound appetizing whatsoever. "What about another vampire my age?"

This time, rage flashed across Vlad's face. "Absolutely not."

I blinked. "Why not? If the age discrepancy is the only issue, and I'm not allowed around humans for the rest of the week, wouldn't it make sense—"

"No, Anna," he snapped, his words edged with a growl.

I startled at the severity of his tone.

After a few tense moments, he drew in a deep breath and rose from his chair. "I apologize. I didn't mean to...." He sighed and raked a hand through his hair. "My emotions are a bit charged right now. Let me call for Harold. And we'll get you fed."

His emotions were charged? Why? Yet again, I bit my tongue to keep from asking him the question. My inner journalist was getting frustrated with me. She wanted *all* the answers, and I kept holding back. Afraid of his responses, perhaps?

Vlad strode toward the door, then pressed an intercom button and summoned Harold.

The minutes passed in silence, with Vlad's back to me, as though he couldn't stand to face me right now. Clearly, something had upset him. And even though I was dying for answers, I knew better than to push.

Finally, Harold appeared, as calm and composed as he was in the attic. He held a bag of blood in one hand and an empty wine glass in the other. I grimaced at the sight. Maybe a black cup would have been better for my first time, to hide the dark-red color.

Vlad took the supplies from him, then beckoned me closer. He still seemed so distracted, even as he opened the bag and poured it into the glass. Something was clearly bothering him.

Harold eyed me as I approached, but I ignored him. The scent of blood had reached my nose, and right now, it was the only thing I could focus on. Much like in the attic, it didn't smell disgusting at all.

Vlad offered me the glass. I held the stem between my fingers and gave it a swirl, like I'd seen wine aficionados do. The blood was too thick to swish, but it gave a small slosh, freshening the scent. I felt the monster within rise at the sight. Hunger grew within me until it was all I could think about. I wanted blood, *needed* it. And I didn't care how I got it. Even if it meant slurping it out of a glass.

I lifted it to my mouth, took my first sip, and instantly winced.

Bitter. Rancid. To the point where my stomach lurched.

I gave the liquid in the glass another sniff and realized *this* blood wasn't the one giving off the marvelous smell. This smelled like plastic and copper pennies.

No, the delectable fragrance came from in front of me.

I lifted my gaze over the rim of the glass and eyed Harold.

This was the closest I'd come to a human since Vlad saved Lucy from me last night. His scent was like coming home to the sweet smell of fresh cinnamon buns. My eyes fluttered shut, and I drew in another deep breath.

Without warning, the monster within took hold.

Before I realized it, I dropped the glass to the ground and lunged.

Chaos erupted within the room. Shattering glass and a man screaming, but none of it mattered. My fingers locked around Harold's arms, and I rode his body down to the ground.

Distantly, I heard Vlad order me to stop, but his words were a muffled haze, lost to my bloodlust.

I descended without a thought and struck like a snake.

My fangs pierced Harold's throat, and blood gushed into my mouth.

Mm. Heaven.

Nothing like fresh blood direct from the tap to appease a hungry vamp tummy.

EIGHT

I'D BARELY TAKEN a few sips of blood when a pair of cold, strong hands clamped around my arms and hauled me backward. I felt Harold's flesh give, tearing beneath my fangs, and another splash of blood coated my tongue. An animalistic growl tore free of my throat as I mindlessly dashed after my meal. All I saw was red, and all I could taste was blood.

I needed more.

Something struck my shoulder, and I flew backward, colliding with the nearest bookshelf. Pain ricocheted through my head as I slumped to the ground. I blinked and shook my head, clearing away the haze.

The scent of blood still rode the air, teasing and taunting me, but with distance came a bit of clarity. My vision returned to normal, and I stared across the room. Vlad leaned over Harold, hand clamped to the human's throat, but his furious gaze blazed at me.

"Oh shit," I whispered, my hands rising to my blood-smeared mouth. What had I done? I'd injured poor Harold. Possibly killed him? I'd felt my fangs rip through his throat. "Is he okay? Vlad? Is he okay?"

"There's a first aid kit in the bathroom, under the sink. Get it. Now."

I didn't even think to argue. I scrambled to my feet, clapped a hand over my mouth and nose, and tore through the room like a dervish. The stairs whirred by in a blur, and I barely acknowledged grabbing the first aid kit before I returned to Vlad's office and dropped to my knees at Harold's side.

"Hold your breath," Vlad warned, though his voice was calmer now. "It'll keep you from scenting his blood."

I nodded.

"Open the kit. I need a needle and sutures. You'll see a small bottle of alcohol, pour it over the needle."

I did exactly as he commanded.

"I'll need both hands to close these wounds, so I'm going to remove my hand now. Harold, I need you to hold still. This will be painful. I apologize for that, old friend."

Instantly, Vlad removed his hand from the wound.

Harold's neck pulsed, and a fresh stream of blood began pouring out. I continued to hold my breath, knowing that scent was my worst enemy right now. The sight of it, though, was almost enough to undo me.

No. *No.* I had to have better control than this. I couldn't walk around ravaging every human I saw.

Vlad barely paid me any mind as he snatched the newly sterilized supplies from my hands and set to work. By the way he moved, I could tell he'd done this before. Made sense. He'd been around quite a long time. I was sure he'd picked up little bits of information and knowledge that most of us didn't have.

It didn't take long to sew Harold up, thanks to Vlad's quickened speed. Soon, Harold's neck was stitched and wrapped in gauze, the edges taped to the top and bottom of his throat.

"There," Vlad whispered, sitting back on his haunches. "You'll be all right."

I still didn't dare to breathe. Not with so much spilled blood.

"Anna, go wash up. Then wait for me in your room while I handle all this."

I nodded. I didn't dare meet Harold's gaze. I wasn't brave enough to face the accusation within. I shouldn't have attacked him, but I couldn't speak to apologize. Not without releasing my breath and sucking in a new one. It'd have to wait.

"Go," Vlad snapped.

I shot to my feet and retreated down the hallway and back up the stairs toward my room. I snatched up yesterday's clothes from beside my bed and ducked into the bathroom. With the lights still out, I gripped the sink and *finally* released my breath. My chest burned with relief, but I hadn't felt the need to breathe once while down there. Guess air was only needed for talking and using our senses.

I don't know why, but that hit me hard. Another nail in the coffin, pun intended.

I was dead. And now, I'd almost killed a man. His blood still stained my hands and pajamas.

Fighting back tears—because I swore I wouldn't cry ever again—I stripped, then lifted my head and stared into the mirror, only to be met with *nothing*. No reflection. Not a hint of the person I was or had been. Nothing but empty glass, as though the mirror was taunting me.

This was what I'd become. A monster with no reflection who fed off humans.

Those damn tears were welling in my eyes, but I refused to succumb.

Instead, I snapped the shower curtain back, turned on the water, then stepped under the spray. In the shower, I could pretend like everything was all right. I wasn't a vampire. I was just a normal woman. I gave myself ten minutes to wallow, then washed up and stepped out.

This was my situation now. Crying about it wouldn't change

anything. And sobbing over Harold wouldn't change the past. I needed to learn from this and improve.

There was a reason the queen recommended a week of isolation.

I patted myself dry before tackling my wet hair—a new challenge considering I couldn't see myself in the mirror to line up my part—then brushed my teeth. I *needed* to get Harold's taste out of my mouth. I scrubbed my fangs until my bristles came away tinged with pink.

Only then did I dress and venture back into my room.

Vlad stood near the window, his hands clasped behind his back. "I should apologize again."

I startled. *Him?* Apologize?

"I wasn't thinking. I shouldn't have had you walk to me to receive your meal. I should have brought it to you. I was distracted and let you get too close to Harold. This was my fault."

"What?" I whispered. "Vlad, no. You didn't do anything—I screwed up. I attacked him. I—"

"*You* are barely out of your grave." He turned from the window to face me. "You don't understand how alluring humans can be. I do. It's my job as your sire to teach you and to protect those within my care. Including the humans."

I considered his words. "Of course I accept your apology, but I'm sorry too. I'm going to work on this. I need to be able to be around humans. I can't hide away for the next hundred years. So I'm willing to do whatever it takes. Even if it means drinking that dreadful bagged blood."

A whisper of a smile crossed Vlad's face. "Perhaps that wasn't the best way to start."

"I'm open to other options," I gently teased, remembering the rancid taste of that crap compared to a fresh human. "How is Harold?"

"He'll live. Thankfully. I've given him and my staff the rest of the week off. I feel it might be safer for the time being."

I hated that such precautions were needed, but I'd rather that than me inadvertently killing someone. That was something I couldn't live with.

Vlad walked toward me. With every step, my breath hitched. The man was so beautiful up close. I'd never seen anyone's eyes so dark—like obsidian gems.

After a moment's pause, he lifted a hand and tucked a wet rope of hair behind my ear. "I've never done anything like this before." When I lifted a questioning brow, he clarified. "You're the first person I've ever sired."

"Really?"

"Yes, well, don't let it go to your head."

I laughed, grateful when my shoulders started to relax. "Well, we can learn together."

Vlad nodded. "I've reached out to a few friends I trust. They'll educate me on how we should proceed. In the meantime, here." He pushed his sleeve back and offered me his wrist.

My mouth pooled at the sight of it, and my eyes widened. "But I thought—"

"One more feeding won't hurt you. You must feed, and I can't have you snacking on my employees."

A shiver rolled down my spine. Oh, I wanted this. Wanted *him* in my mouth. My chest quickened as I sucked in one breath after another. "Are you sure about this?"

"Yes."

I forgot about my fangs and bit my bottom lip. I winced when they punctured the soft flesh. Blood welled over, and Vlad's eyes flashed at the sight. I knew desire when I saw it. That was one emotion I'd always been able to easily read. Would it hurt to give him a little of my blood? From what I'd learned in his office, it didn't seem like my blood would do anything for him, other than provide a thrill.

His eyes were locked on my lips, so without warning, I eased up on my tiptoes and pressed my mouth to his.

Vlad hissed and jerked back, his expression wild. "What are you do—"

"Shh." I slid my hands over his shoulders and offered him a second taste. That the proposition included my mouth was a bonus.

"You shouldn't be so giving of your blood," he scolded. "You don't know—"

"Just shut up and enjoy the moment."

Apparently, I didn't need to tell him a third time. I watched his throat move as he swallowed in anticipation, then his hands found mine and he wrenched me against him. His mouth crashed against mine with a hungry growl, his tongue sweeping across my bleeding lip. Vlad groaned and tilted his head, deepening the angle as he fed from my mouth.

The instant our tongues touched, I gasped. Desire uncurled in my belly, like a cat waking from a nap, and spread through my body. I wound my arms around his neck and plunged my fingers into his hair. So soft and thick. It made me wonder about the rest of him. What would I find hidden away beneath his clothes, and when would I get the chance to find out? I wanted to unwrap him like a Christmas present, taking my time to appreciate the gift within.

Vlad's fingers dug into my hips, and he lost himself to my mouth, ravishing me with a single kiss. I quickly learned how talented a five-hundred-year-old man was—because *damn*. I felt his touch everywhere, even though his hands hadn't moved.

The man undoubtedly had skills, proven when he artfully pierced my tongue without my notice, taking from me what I'd soon be taking from him. I had to admit, I preferred his method to mine. The wrist seemed hardly as provocative now that I'd experienced this way of taking blood.

Vlad's fangs scraped my bottom lip as he slowly drew back. We both panted for breath, his cheeks flushed with my blood. I immediately touched a hand to my tingling mouth, too stunned and aroused to speak. I'd never experienced anything like that, and I was far from a nun. I'd had my share of boyfriends—all former now. But Vlad wasn't a boy. My exes paled in comparison to him.

"I—I...." I had absolutely no idea what to say. I sucked in a slow breath and shivered. "Damn."

Vlad clenched his jaw tight, as though afraid to speak. Instead, he held my gaze and offered me his wrist. Veins ran beneath his flesh, pulsing with excitement. My mouth watered at the sight. If our kiss was any indication, I was in far more danger than developing a minor blood addiction. That alone should have been reason enough to pull back, thank him, and find another blood bag to choke down. But I couldn't seem to walk away. I *wanted* to taste him again.

I shot him a questioning glance, and when he nodded, I cradled his arm in my hands and lifted it to my mouth. Damn, I wanted this so bad.

Correction. I wanted *him* so bad.

Crazy, right? I'd known the man for two nights! Well, three if you counted the night he turned me. Maybe this attraction was a vampire thing? A sire-apprentice connection? The forums last night had mentioned heightened emotions and raging hormones while our bodies adjusted. Was that all this was? Did my emotions include desire? Did I care?

These were all questions for another time.

I bowed over his wrist, then slowly bit, sinking my fangs into his flesh. His hissed breath made my own catch. But it was the taste of his honeyed blood that had my eyes fluttering shut. I needed to focus on the feeding and not the throbbing between my legs. So he was an attractive man. That didn't mean I needed to jump him. But my brain took off with the imagery and started wondering what sex between us would look like.

It took every ounce of self-restraint I possessed not to jump Vlad right then and there.

Cripes, I needed to get a hold of myself.

It didn't help that his fingers were running through my damp hair, pushing it off my neck. The darkest part of my fantasies imagined him biting the soft part of my throat while I fed from his wrist.

Oh man, this was bad.

I couldn't be attracted to my sire, right?

My five-hundred-year-old sire named Dracula.

Because that would be insane.

And yet, when I pulled back from his wrist and lifted my head, my dead heart stuttered at the sight of him watching me, his gaze practically searing.

Seemed I wasn't the only one in this predicament.

CHAPTER
NINE

Reality came crashing down, and I jerked back. I'd just kissed Dracula. Vlad. The Count. Whatever. The man had more names than I did panties at the moment. Which, speaking of, I needed to phone Lucy and ask her to go shopping, since we'd only packed weekend bags.

But that was a different, easily solvable problem. Nothing like this. Kissing Dracula had to rate stupider than busting into a vampire club to expose illegal bloodletting, which turned out not to be illegal. Impulsive, remember?

This right here was proof. Two nights under this man's roof, and I was making out with him and swapping blood like we were lovers. Gah! I shouldn't have thought that. I didn't need the word "lovers" in my head right now. Not with him standing so close, eyes still blazing, and certainly not with my lady bits still waving their pom-poms and cheering me on.

Kissing Dracula was stupid, right?

Maybe?

Who the hell even knew anymore? "I, uh, should go."

Vlad inched toward me. "Go where? This is your room."

Right. My room. Because I'd just showered after *attacking* Harold. And here I was, getting my freak on with the Count himself. If he could just stop watching me like I was the cherry on top of a very delicious strawberry sundae, that would be greatly appreciated. I couldn't think with him standing there, all smoldering eyes and swollen lips.

The invitation was clear, as were his desires. I wasn't one of those women who was blind to the opposite sex. If I so much as gave the word, Vlad and I would tumble into that tiny bed next to us.

And damn, I was tempted.

On the one hand, I was a grown-ass woman, allowed to kiss whoever the hell she wanted. But on the other, this man was five hundred years older than me—which, *ick*—and a vampire. All right, maybe that last one was unfair, considering I was also a vampire. But if he'd never been turned, he would be rotting away in a grave right now. Then again, so would I. Not a very sexy thought. Why focus on the what ifs, though? He *had* been turned, and instead of a rotting corpse, he was a downright gorgeous beast of a man who I wanted to dry hump like a randy mutt. Decisions, decisions....

"Okay, then you need to go," I told him. "I, uh, need to be alone. Is that okay? I need to think. And I can't do that with you here."

Vlad inclined his head and blinked, the heat fizzling from his gaze. "Very well."

"Thank you."

"Of course. I'll be in my office, should you need anything."

A shiver rolled through my body. I could think of one thing I needed, but my last impulsive decision had gotten me killed. I really needed to start thinking things through. And since I wasn't allowed to go to a bar and get wasted—probably wouldn't even work anyway— there was only one other thing I could think to do and that was call Lucy.

Vlad took my hand and kissed my knuckles before exiting my room.

I slumped against the wall and blew out a relieved breath. Man, he knew how to wind me up. And he hadn't even done anything. Just walked into my room. Was that all it took now to get my engine revving?

Plucking my phone from my back pocket, I ignored all the missed notifications from my family and dialed Lucy's number. Texting wouldn't do for this situation. I needed to hear her voice when she told me this was a stupid idea.

She answered on the third ring. "How are you?"

The sound of her voice brought a smile to my well-kissed mouth.

"Slaughtered half of New Orleans yet?" she asked, not waiting for my answer.

That smile slipped. "Har, har. Considering I'm not allowed to leave the house, I think New Orleans is safe."

"For now."

Her words stung. Until I remembered that I'd just assaulted Harold. And then made out with his employer. Geez! What was becoming a vampire doing to me? How could I go from savaging a poor man's neck to ravaging my sire's mouth all within an hour?

Clearly, I was losing my damn mind. And I blamed the hot piece of ass I'd just booted from my room.

"I...." My words died. I, what? Nearly killed a man? Lucy wouldn't take that very well. Should I tell her I kissed Vlad? A fanger? Cripes, her mind might implode with that one. Which was the lesser of the two evils?

How much was I even willing to say? Vlad's office was only one level down, meaning he could hear everything we said. Did I care, though? A gentleman wouldn't pry, and based on my experiences with him, I had to believe he would refrain from listening in. Maybe it was a part of vampire etiquette? Thou shalt not eavesdrop? And if he did, well, that was his problem, not mine.

"Anna? What's wrong? Are you all right? Did he hurt you?" She fired off her questions like ping pong balls.

"No, nothing like that. I just.... Lucy, I did something."

She drew in a sharp breath, then released it. "Okay. It's okay. We'll get you through it. Do you know who it was? Do they have family?"

My brows knotted. "Huh?"

"Honestly, it's okay," Lucy repeated. "Just tell me what happened. I was expecting this. So I'm prepared."

Prepared for what, exactly? For me kissing Vlad? What could have possibly given her that impression in the two minutes she'd seen us together? The one and only conversation I'd had with him in her presence had mostly involved Lucy and me fighting. Vlad had barely been involved.

I opened my mouth, about to confide in her the whole story, when that damn light bulb went off in my head again. Lucy's sympathetic voice, telling me she'd expected this. She hadn't been referring to me kissing Vlad.

No.

She thought I'd killed someone.

I wanted to be mad. Hurt even that she would suspect such a thing. But honestly, who was I to cast stones? I'd almost murdered Harold. Me. A newly bloodsucking fiend from beyond the grave. Eating humans sort of came with the territory. Was it really so surprising that she'd prepared herself for the worst-case scenario?

Maybe instead, I should be grateful that she was still willing to be my friend and listen to my confession—had I actually murdered someone.

"It's nothing like that, Lucy. Although, I did accidentally bite Vlad's butler. I lost control."

"But he's alive?"

"Yes. Vlad assures me Beauregard will be fine. Vlad also gave his staff the rest of the week off so there won't be anyone else for me to hurt."

"Oh, okay. I mean, great! Really. That's great."

I frowned. She sounded unsure. Like she was trying to convince herself more than me.

"Well, if you didn't kill someone, then what did you do? Or were you just referring to this Beauregard guy?"

Oh boy. Here we go. I couldn't put my finger on why I was so nervous. So Vlad and I kissed. Big deal, right? Besides, Lucy's disappointment was second nature to me. She constantly waggled her finger at me about this and that—her impulsive and irresponsible friend.

"Okay, so, here's the thing." I pinched my brow and mustered up the courage. *Just spit it out, girl.* I cupped my hand around the phone and quietly hissed, "I kissed Vlad."

Silence.

And then came more silence.

With my newly heightened senses, I could hear her mouth opening and closing even though no sound came out. Her small inhalations. Hell, I could practically hear the gears spinning in her head.

"I'm sorry. I thought I heard you say—"

"You did. I kissed Vlad," I whispered.

"Okaaay." Nervous laughter bubbled across the connection. "I gotta say, Anna, I really don't know how to react to that."

Better than her immediately scolding me.

"Did he force you to kiss him?"

"Cripes, Lucy! No, he didn't force me!"

"Well! I don't know!" Her voice rose. "I hardly know the man. All I know is he changed you into a vampire. That doesn't exactly give me a good feeling about him. For all I know, he's the kind of guy who extorts sexual favors! And if he is, you tell him I don't care who he is, I'll march down there, stake in hand, and stab him in his vampy ass."

I snorted back a laugh. "Oh wow, Lucy. There are so many things wrong with that statement. First, you can't stab a vampire in the ass with a stake. Well, that's not true. You *could*, but I think you'll only piss him off. Second, Vlad really isn't the type to force himself on anyone. I don't think he has that problem."

"Oh shit, girl. Are you falling for him?"

"What?" I sputtered. "No!"

"Good! You better not! Because we're going home, remember? To Perish. To your folks and my family. Besides, you *cannot* fall in love with the first vampire you meet. That's so cliché!"

"No one is falling in love, Lucy. You don't need to fall in love with someone to suck face with them."

"Ew, Anna! Suck face? Really?"

A teasing grin tugged at my lips. Knew she'd appreciate that one. "Well, there was some sucking. Some biting. Some bloodletting."

"Oh, gross!" Lucy feigned gagging. "That's disgusting. I don't want to know about your nasty vamp ways. It has to be impolite to discuss your new plasma-enriched diet."

"I'm sorry. My what now?"

"Well, it sounds better than drinking blood, doesn't it?"

"Whatever helps you sleep at night," I said, laughing.

"Okay, can we get back to the issue at hand here?"

"I don't know, can we?"

"Girlfriend, I can think of half a dozen reasons why getting involved with the man who turned you is a bad thing."

"Sire," I told her as I sat on the small chest pressed up against my bed. I stared out the window, my gaze immediately leaping to the stars.

Holy shit.

I'd always loved astronomy as a human. To stare up at the stars and name the constellations, watch the planets rise and set, count shooting stars. I'd even gone to a planetarium once and saw Saturn through a telescope. Absolutely breathtaking seeing the planets in all their splendor.

But none of that compared to now. The stars were so much crisper. Hell, I could count the craters on the freaking moon. Utterly incredible.

"Anna?" Lucy's voice called through the line.

I blinked and tore my gaze away from the twinkling sky. I found it comforting to know the night would never be empty again. I could see for miles now, even through the thick veil of darkness.

"Sorry, got a bit distracted there."

"You okay?"

"Yes. I'm just starting to comprehend the changes my body is going through. Like, I can see things I've never seen before. Lucy, I can hear people talking a few miles away."

"That sounds... uncomfortable."

"Anyway. You were saying?"

"Yeah, I said that it doesn't seem wise to get emotionally involved with your sire."

"Okay. Reasons?" I needed to hear them.

"Well, he's older than you."

"So were your last two boyfriends."

She scoffed. "By like three years, Anna. I highly doubt that qualifies."

Fair point. "What else?"

"He's a more experienced vampire than you."

"Isn't that a good thing?" One would assume that would help me become the best vampire I could be.

"Maybe. Okay. Um, he's Dracula?"

"And? Are you saying I can't be with someone because he's famous?"

"No, of course not." She sighed. "I don't know. This just feels weird to me. And unwise."

I bit my lip, careful this time not to puncture the flesh. For some reason, I suspected he'd be able to smell my blood all the way downstairs, and the last thing I needed was another make-out fest with the man in question.

"There's something else you should know," I told her.

"Uh oh, I don't like the sound of that."

"Earlier, Vlad told me it's dangerous for a newborn vamp like me to take blood from an older vamp like him. Apparently, there's a bit of a power transfer when taking blood from an ancient vamp or whatever."

"I'm gonna need you to explain that a bit more."

I sighed. I really didn't feel like recapping all this, but I couldn't keep this a secret from Lucy. It was a part of my life now, and secrets were like cancerous tumors. "Younger vampires have been known to go mad if they ingest too much blood from an older, more powerful vampire."

"All right, and how old is Mr. Dracula?"

"He's over five hundred years old," I admitted. "And he has two of those special ability thingies."

"Anna," Lucy whispered. "I don't like the sound of that."

I nodded. I wanted to reassure her that everything was fine. But I already felt the pull from his blood.

"You drank from him last night," she continued. "Before I left."

"And the night before, seeing as how he changed me."

"Right." She exhaled. "Okay, so maybe—"

"And, um, tonight too," I said, interrupting her.

"Anna!"

"I know. It was after I hurt Beauregard. I needed to feed. He said a few feedings wouldn't hurt me, but that we needed to be careful."

"Careful? Why? What happens if a vampire loses their mind?"

"I think you already know the answer to that."

Lucy groaned. "I hate this, Anna. So much. I hate it! You're dead."

"Undead," I repeated softly.

"Don't start that up again. Or I will literally come to Vlad's place just to slap you."

My lips twitched.

"My point is there's so much we don't know about this world. I know you read up on it a little last night, about what becoming a vampire means. But that doesn't tell us anything about the actual vampire world. Do you realize we don't know anything about this queen of theirs? Only that she signed a treaty with our president? But what about everything else? Are there laws you have to follow? Are you indebted to Vlad? Are you trapped with him forever now? Do you have to do as he says for the rest of your eternal life? Or obey the queen without question? We know *nothing*. Can you even go home to Perish?"

All fangtastic questions, ones I didn't have answers to.

"They have you isolating for a week. Then what? Do they just toss you out into the wild to sink or swim? Will they teach you how to feed? What about employment? Can you still work? You can't *not* work. How will you survive? You still need housing and whatnot. Just because you don't need to buy food anymore doesn't mean you don't need other necessities."

"Lucy—"

"And what about your family? How are they going to react? Is there any sort of program in place to help them adjust and accept that their daughter is, in fact, undead?"

"Lucy—"

"Or your friends for that matter! Or do you just vanish into the good night and start your new vampy life over without us. Because I can't lose you, girl. I just experienced how that felt, and I'm really not eager to go through that again. But what if it isn't safe for you to return to human society? What if that's forbidden? There's so much we just don't know!"

"Lucy!"

She sucked in a shivering breath. Even through the phone, I could hear the sounds of her impending panic attack.

"Okay, take a breath, hun."

"I really hate this, Anna." Her voice grew thick with tears.

Guilt sucker-punched me. I hated that I couldn't be there to help her through this. "I know. Just take a deep breath for me, okay? And when you're ready, let it out." At the sound of her exhalation, I nodded. "Good. A few more times. In and out. Just keep doing that while I talk."

She didn't respond.

"I want you to listen to me when I tell you I'm not going

anywhere. Ever again. Literally. I'm immortal now, which means you're stuck with me until you're wrinkled and gray with dementia, crowing about your best friend the vampire. All your questions are valid, and we're going to find the answers to them, I promise. But believe me when I tell you, no queen or otherwise will ever keep me from you. Take another breath."

She did as I commanded.

"Do you feel better?"

"No," she croaked.

"I love you. You know that, right?"

"Yes."

"Good. That's all that matters right now. We'll figure everything else out together. After tonight, there's only five more nights until we can see each other again. We'll both feel better after that."

"Sure."

"Hey, we got this. We're two strong, kick-ass women. Dead or alive, it doesn't matter. Nothing's gonna tear us apart."

"Okay, INXS," she teased, sounding a bit like her old self.

A bark of laughter slipped past my lips. "It's getting late. Why don't you go take a bath or something, stop worrying, then get some sleep? If you're up for it, feel free to go shopping tomorrow. We both could use some clothes."

"Yeah, I thought about that. I'll hit the stores tomorrow. You should call your mom, though. I told mine we were staying a few more days. But yours should hear it from you."

I nodded, even though she couldn't see it. I didn't love the idea of reaching out to my family. Not yet. My family wasn't exactly a happy one to begin with. Their divorce burst our happy little bubble. But I couldn't ignore them either. My mom was expecting us home earlier today, so our absence would be noted. Especially considering Sunday nights were her version of family night. The one night a week my brother and I were forced to go to her place for a fancy dinner and games.

"Yeah. I have a few missed calls from my mom already. Dad

probably hasn't realized that I'm not even home right now. You know how oblivious he is when it comes to his *real* family. I didn't answer their calls. I'm not ready."

"You'll need to make something up. Lie to them about why you're unavailable during the day. Until you're willing to tell them the truth, that is."

Just another problem to handle. I knew my parents. They were both going to lose their shit. Lucy was already panicking, but my mother would slip into full-on hysteria. It certainly didn't help that my dad was the mayor of our town, or that both my parents were churchgoing people, even though they were divorced. Honestly, I wasn't sure if they'd even see me as their daughter anymore, and I wasn't eager to find out.

"I'll call them both," I said, glancing at the clock. A little before ten. Mom would be in bed, but she'd still answer her phone. She generally stayed up until eleven or so. Dad was a bit of a night owl, considering he had his business and the town to contend with. But I wasn't ready to face either of them yet, so I amended my statement with a "Tomorrow."

"Anna."

"I'll call them tomorrow, Lucy. I promise. I'm just not ready yet."

"Okay," her voice softened. "You know, I never got to say how sorry I am this happened to you."

"What?"

"Last night, I was really worked up and frightened. I hadn't seen you in three nights. I thought you were dead. My thoughts had gone to a very dark place. But I want you to know, I'm so sorry. I never should have agreed to go to that club with you. If I hadn't...."

"I would have gone alone," I admitted to her. "This is so not your fault."

"I know, but—"

"No buts. No what ifs. This is absolutely, unequivocally not your fault. The blame rests on me. I got myself into this situation, but I can handle it. It might just take a little time."

"Still," Lucy continued, "I want you to know that what I said last night, about me leaving, I didn't mean it. You know you're my bestie. I'm not going anywhere."

Relief eased my shoulders. "Good, because I'd hate to have to bite your ass."

"Oh, there won't be any biting. I... I need to be upfront about this. What happened to you is about the worst thing I can imagine. I don't want to become a vampire. Ever. Okay? If something happens to me, and I'm dying, let me die."

"Lucy."

"No, Anna. I know you can handle this, because you're so strong. I'm not. I couldn't handle having to feed off people or living forever while all my loved ones passed on. I'm not religious, but I—I can't become that."

I tried not to let her words hurt me, but they truly felt like a knife in the gut. Not that I'd even considered turning Lucy. But to think of her dying while I lived on... that was true pain.

"Anna?"

"I hear you," I told her. "And I understand."

She blew out a relieved breath. "Good. Thank you. Try to have a good night. Don't maul anyone else, 'kay?"

"'Kay."

"Night, girl."

"Night." I disconnected the call, then lowered my phone into my lap and stared out the window, letting the emptiness creep in.

CHAPTER

TEN

I spent the next couple nights thinking about my past, present, and future. Truthfully, I had nothing else to do except avoid any further inevitable hanky-panky. At least not yet. But OMG, was I borrred. Wasn't being a vampire supposed to be exciting or some shit? Becoming a creature of the night *sounded* majestic and mysterious. Stalking my prey through the shadows, thirsting for their blood, living a life ripe with tragedy, caught in an eternal struggle between light and darkness.

Guess those ideas were rooted in fiction.

The truth was far more mundane.

Four nights had passed since I'd first woken—two since I'd played tonsil hockey with Vlad. For those two nights, I'd done little more than aimlessly wander his mansion, looking for something—anything —that might entertain me, all while avoiding what I assumed was an inevitable conversation. Vlad kept eyeing me *that* way, as though he wanted to discuss our kiss, but I sure as hell wasn't ready for that. Nor was I ready to talk to my parents yet. I was avoiding that phone call like herpes.

On the upside, thanks to Lucy, I had new clothes. She'd dropped them off the night after our phone call, giving me enough to last until we returned home. It'd sucked donkey balls not being allowed to see or talk to her, but I'd obeyed Vlad's instructions for Lucy's sake.

I'd also mastered drinking blood from a bag. Believe me when I say it was absolutely disgusting. Nothing like chasing down your drink with the smell of burned microplastics. Vlad promised he'd teach me how to feed off humans after my week's isolation. He kept pushing me to start considering who I'd welcome into my harem. I couldn't think of a single soul who would willingly donate blood to me nightly. That wasn't something I'd ever thought about before.

I spent my time combing through the many, *many* websites about vampirism to suss out fact from fiction. My readings had resulted in a lot of peculiar tests. Ones that I think were driving Vlad to the brink of frustration. I had to admit, he was really patient with me, considering the stunts I'd pulled.

The night before last, he'd feigned a heart attack when I dropped from the ceiling to the floor beside him. Fact: Vampires could defy gravity by scaling walls and perching upside down on rafters like a bat. Guess I hadn't mastered enough stealth yet to sneak up on him. But he'd been a good sport about me messing up his papers.

Before "bed" this morning, I'd forced him to race me once around his house, just to see how fast we could run. He'd consented to the challenge, deciding it was best for me to learn these things before releasing me back into the wild. Unfortunately for my competitive soul, Vlad whooped me hard. Before I'd cleared half the distance, he'd done a full lap and was coming around for a second one. My own Captain America. Swoon.

Tonight, he'd found me in the kitchen, only to learn I'd cracked open every single jar of pickles, salsa, olives, you name it, just to test my strength. All because I *could*. No more grunting and cursing while struggling to open some obscure jar of food. Not that I'd need to open any jar ever again. But hey, I could totally open things for his human staff now. Huge win in my books.

His baffled expression had me doubled over with laughter.

Lock me up for a week and weird shit happens. I didn't know what else to tell him.

After that, he'd agreed to simply answer my questions instead of me destroying his house in the name of science. Which led us here, to his sitting room. Vlad eased onto his stupid fainting couch and faced me with a knowing smirk. I returned to my stool, but this time I had a notepad resting on my lap and a pen in hand, my mind buzzing with everything I'd recently read.

"Flying," I said, jumping right in.

"Fact."

My head snapped up. "Seriously?"

"Well, semi-fact? It's a power some vampires have developed."

Ah. Okay, so not fact for everyone. "Accelerated healing?"

"To save you the hassle of stabbing yourself to test that theory, that one is fact. I wouldn't wish to see you waste the blood."

I grinned. Less than a week together and he already knew me so well. I probably wouldn't stab myself, but there would have been some experiments. "Shapeshifting."

"Fact. But again, only as a power some vampires develop."

If I had a choice, that was the power I wanted. I would love nothing more than to romp through town as a stray dog. See the world through their eyes. "Running water."

"Fiction." He rolled his eyes. "I assure you, water running has never affected me in the slightest."

"Holy water, then?"

"Fact. It's a very unpleasant experience. I don't recommend it."

I nodded, then quickly jotted an X through it. "Crosses."

"Fact."

I raised a brow. "Care to elaborate?"

"There's not much more to say. Religious artifacts as a whole repel us. Being in the presence of a cross is as unpleasant to me as the first rays of sunrise."

"All religious artifacts?"

He considered that. "I've never had anyone throw a Star of David at me, but I'd imagine it would have the same effect, being religious and all."

"I'm an atheist," I told him. "I don't believe in religion or God at all."

He lifted a brow, as though that surprised him. Not sure why. Many people were atheists now. "I would imagine the artifacts would affect you similarly, but I can't say for sure. I've never tested the theory."

And I highly doubted he had a cross sitting around. So I moved on. "Entering a house without permission."

Vlad nodded. "Sadly, fact. We must be invited to enter a home."

Huh. Definitely needed to store that away for future information. "Silver."

"Has no effect on us. That's specifically a werewolf issue."

My jaw dropped. "Holy crap on a cracker! There are *werewolves*?"

"Fact." He rested his ankle on his knee. "I do not suggest seeking them out, though. Terribly ornery things. More bite than bark, and they have a distinct hatred for all things vampire."

"So *Underworld* was accurate then."

He lifted his hands, palms open, as though to say he didn't understand.

"It's a movie." I waved off his unspoken question. "Okay, hypnotism."

"Fiction. I can't think of a single vampire who has the power of compulsion."

Boooo. That would have been another cool power. Walk around flashing my eyes at everyone and telling them to do the chicken dance in the middle of the street until sunrise. Ah well, *c'est la vie*.

"Tell me about these so-called powers we develop."

Vlad chuckled. "I feel like I'm being interviewed."

He was, in a way. I gestured for him to speak. I was dying to know about this.

"As the centuries pass, you will begin to develop very specific abilities such as reading minds, telekinesis, flight, et cetera. There's no way to know which you will possess until it happens. As you already know, I, myself, have developed two."

"Is that normal?"

"For one of my age, yes. You must remember, even the queen is younger than I." Another person I had so many questions about. But I needed to pace myself. If I asked him every single question I had, we'd be here 'til the end of time.

"How many vampires are there your age?"

"A few. Some older still."

"Care to tell me about your abilities?"

He shrugged, then drummed his fingers against the sole of his fine Italian leather loafers. A girl could spot a good shoe a mile away, regardless of who wore them. "One of my abilities is the power to shapeshift."

I leaned forward on my stool, excitement lighting me up. "Really? That's the one I want! What can you turn into?"

"A bat and a wolf."

Oh man. I tried not to fangirl. But seriously, how *awesome* was that? "And the second?"

He seemed to grow uneasy with this one. His fingers continued to drum against his shoe, but the rhythm quickened. A case of nerves? But why would he be nervous about this last one?

"Let's move on."

I blinked. Just like that? What could it be? Something bad? But what kind of powers were considered bad? I wanted to press the conversation so badly. In the grand scheme, though, his second power had little relevance to our discussion. Not when there were so many other things I could ask.

I considered Lucy's many questions from last night. Now was as good a time as any to get the answers. She'd definitely appreciate them. "What can you tell me about vampire society?"

"Vampire society," Vlad said, chuckling as though this phrase amused him. "What do you wish to know?"

"Well, there's the queen and her council. But what about below that? Is there a full monarchy? Does she have complete control over us all?"

Vlad shifted position on the couch. He dropped his foot to the floor and leaned forward, his expression amused. "Perhaps someone should write up a manual for new vampires. Especially for curious ones like you."

"Give me the answers, and I might do just that," I teased, then gasped when a new idea struck. "Or do a vlog on it!"

"You'll have to explain this vlog thing to me at some point."

Aww, I was touched he cared enough to ask. "Not a modern-day technology kind of guy, huh?"

"I like a quiet life, contrary to popular belief."

"Oh yes, fame and fortune can become so taxing." I laughed. "But seriously, how cool would it be if I created a vlog for all new vampires? A web series!" My mind started spinning. "Oh wow. This could be a really great idea. 'Welcome to The Undead Channel.'" I squealed and quickly began scribbling down notes. "I could provide them with *all* this information. This could be huge. It could be the hit I've been looking for to expand my reach."

"I don't know what any of that means, but I see a flaw in your logic."

My head lifted of its own accord, and I caught Vlad's gaze. "Huh?"

"You seem to have forgotten we have no reflection."

Crushing defeat crashed down on my shoulders. Shit. How had I not thought about that? I mean, there was so much going on, so much to acclimate to that things were guaranteed to be missed. But my lack of reflection was kind of a big one. Especially for someone who was seeking fame from her vlog.

"So I can't be recorded," I whispered. My mind flashed back to the video I'd taken of the vampires at Fallen. The playback had shown their clothes, but nothing else. Nothing recognizable. No faces to commit to memory. Fuck! How had I not connected the dots?

I pressed a hand to my lips and drew a deep breath. This ruined everything. And in so many ways. How the hell could I even continue my own personal vlog if I couldn't video myself? Everything I'd worked so hard to achieve was going up in flames right before my eyes.

"Anna?"

I blinked and gave Vlad a dead-eyed stare.

"Are you all right?"

"It's all ruined," I whispered.

"What is?"

"Me. Everything I've worked so hard for. Everything I've sacrificed. If I can't be seen on camera, all my hopes and dreams are over."

"I fail to see how this is that detrimental."

"You would," I whispered. "You don't even know what a vlog is."

"True, but—"

"I'm, uh, gonna go for a walk," I said, interrupting him. "Get a little fresh air."

"Are you sure you wouldn't like some company?"

"Oh, I'm sure." Deathly sure. I wanted a little peace and quiet to absorb this realization.

Man, becoming a vampire fucking sucked. Pun absolutely intended.

I CIRCLED Vlad's grounds a few times, stopping now and then to really absorb the changes in my body. Anything to distract myself from the knowledge that I'd never achieve my dreams.

The things I could hear now—birds chirping in the surrounding marshes, cars backfiring miles away, the buzz of New Orleans, even though Vlad's estate sat a good ten minutes outside the city.

I could even hear people nearby, chatting in their houses. Each residence sat on a good-sized portion of land, five or so acres. Vlad's seemed larger than the rest. I wasn't a professional surveyor, but it seemed like twenty or thirty acres to me. All surrounded by marshy wetlands and, from the sounds of it, many, *many* alligators. I *so* wasn't okay with that. Sharks and alligators were my two biggest fears. And one of those had no problem coming onto land. Where *I* lived. How inconvenient was that?

Thankfully, I could easily kill them if they strayed too close. Small consolation.

The sound of nearby bullfrogs and boars had me chomping at the bit to try out animal blood. They had to be better than tearing out a human throat, right? Vlad had promised to teach me how to safely feed, but I wasn't convinced I was ready, or ever would be.

What if I lost myself in the moment? Or started bathing in the blood of innocents? All right, maybe I'd read too many vampire novels recently, but those novels existed for a reason, right? Animal blood would weaken me, according to Vlad. Maybe that wasn't such a bad thing. Maybe it would keep me in check so I didn't hurt anyone else.

My mind flashed to the memory of Harold, sprawled on the ground, his face pale while blood gushed from his throat. I never wanted to experience that again. Perhaps animal blood was the answer. Considering how much I hated gators, I wouldn't mind putting a dent in their population.

I started toward the sound of the nearest beast, eager to test this theory, when I caught movement out of the corner of my eye. I glanced in that direction and scanned the perimeter. Hmm. Nothing. A figment of my imagination then? Probably just a random animal. Stray dog or something.

Back to the nearby gator... I braved another step when something streaked by me, as quick as lightning. My hand flew to my chest, and I sucked in a startled breath. Something was out here. Something moving across Vlad's property. And fast. Faster than both animal and human.

I inhaled and tasted the air, searching for a particular scent. But only magnolia and pine tickled my nose. My senses were still evolving, so I didn't quite know how to use them yet, how to fine-tune them into something useful.

Another flash of movement, so fast I barely saw it. Fear strangled me, my breath quickening as I scanned my surroundings.

"*Anna*," a voice came, like a whisper carried on the breeze.

I choked on my breath, my hand still clutching at my shirt. I didn't respond—I knew better than that. Thanks to the plethora of horror films I'd watched as a teenager, I knew never to run upstairs, and never call back to a strange voice. The safest course of action was to get inside and tell Vlad what I saw.

"*An-naaa*," that damn whispered voice came again, dragging my name out.

Something brushed the back of my neck, like fingers combing through my hair. I cried out and whirled around, slapping at empty air. Nothing. I stood alone in the middle of Vlad's back yard. Whoever it was, they were gone as quickly as they came.

A vampire then? Their movements were so quick. But they knew my name. And the only vampire I knew was Vlad.

Was this all in my mind?

Was I imagining things?

No. I'd felt those fingers on the back of my neck, heard its voice in the darkness.

"So beautiful. So delicious. So very mine," it whispered.

Something brushed against my side an instant before cold fingers touched my cheek.

And me?

I fucking *screamed*.

CHAPTER

ELEVEN

VLAD MATERIALIZED beside me with a gust of wind. I knew he couldn't fly in human form—that wasn't one of his powers—so he must have raced toward me the instant he heard my scream.

He stood in front of me with a pinched face. "What is it? What's wrong?" His hands cupped my cheeks, and he frowned. "You're shaking."

I gave a frantic nod. "There's someone out here." He opened his mouth, but I cut him off before he could jokingly tell me it was me. My mother used to do that when I told her I had something in my eye. She'd tease me and say, "Yeah, your finger." But I wasn't in the mood to be teased. "And I mean other than you and me."

Vlad held my gaze and cocked his head. For a moment, I thought he meant to contradict my statement, but then I realized he was *listening*. I could only imagine what his ears might pick up that mine had missed. I waited silently, my nerves jumping with anticipation. But the sight of his frown didn't instill me with confidence.

"Are you sure?" he finally asked.

"Of course I'm sure! I'm not insane. Something touched me. Called my name—"

"It called your name?" His face hardened.

"The voice said I belonged to him, called me delicious. Vlad...." I clutched his forearms, my fingers digging into his flesh.

"Him," Vlad repeated. "It was male?"

"I—I think so? The voice whispered, but yeah, yeah, I definitely got the feeling it was male." I forced myself to release Vlad, then took one giant step back. I needed space to think, to sort through everything. "I was standing right here, just listening to the sounds of nature. Considering trying to feed off an alligator—"

"What?"

I waved a hand. "Not important. Then out of nowhere, I started to see movement. Quick. Like a vampire."

Vlad's face turned thunderous. "A vampire?"

"I don't know, maybe? He was fast. Like you. When I screamed, you were here within seconds. This thing could move like that. Then he started whispering my name."

"Get inside."

"What? But—"

"Get inside, Anna. Go to my office and wait for me."

Oh, I didn't like the sound of this at all. First of all, I didn't want to be alone. Second of all, what if that thing, person, whatever, followed me into the house? That big, creepy mansion that I now realized was completely empty except for me and Vlad, since he'd given his staff the week off.

I gulped and glanced at his house. The lights were on, but literally no one was home. And the goose bumps running up my arms told me I *really* didn't like this idea.

When I didn't immediately move, Vlad's face softened, and he smoothed his hands down my arms, soothing the pebbled flesh. "Everything will be all right. Remember, no one can enter my house without permission. You'll be safe there."

Finally, I relented and hurried back to Vlad's house. I wasn't as quick as him, but that didn't surprise me. Once inside, I slammed the door behind me and shivered. Even the little hairs on the back of my neck stood up. I had to remind myself again that no one could enter without permission, but that didn't ease my fears. These new vampiric laws meant very little to me right now.

I bolted into Vlad's office, then took a seat in his chair and drew my knees to my chin. Now that I was inside, and safe and warm, I started to wonder if maybe I *had* imagined it all. Maybe the darkness had frightened me. Maybe it was a side effect of the change. My body was still evolving. Could have been my ears playing a trick on me.

I scoffed at myself. I'd felt those damn fingers on my cheek and neck. I hadn't imagined *that*. I needed to trust my instincts, and right now, they were screaming at me.

The minutes passed with only the sound of the flames in Vlad's fireplace crackling away. I turned in his chair to peer out the window, but I didn't see anything questionable. Nothing but the night growing long.

Eventually, a shadowed figure stepped out of the darkness, jacket fluttering in the breeze as he strode toward the house. My heart leapt at the sight, then settled when I realized it was only Vlad. He strolled across the land, stopping now and then to listen to his surroundings. Hopefully, he'd found something. That would put my mind at ease.

I listened as he made his way inside, his footsteps growing louder as he approached his office. He wasn't moving with liquid vamp speed, so maybe everything was fine.

But if it was, did that mean I *was* going insane?

Vlad eased into his office and shook his head. "I'm afraid I didn't find anything."

My hopes plummeted. What did that mean exactly?

"That doesn't mean there wasn't anything to find," he said. "If it was another vampire, he likely ran off when you screamed. It's one thing to face a newborn like you, but an entirely different situation when faced with someone like me."

"Someone has an ego," I mumbled.

Vlad's mouth twitched. "Ego has nothing to do with it. It's simply a fact. There are very few vampires out there who would willingly face me."

"Why? Are you some badass vamp with a penchant for murder?"

He held up his hands as though to say *well?*

All right. Fair enough. He was older than half a millennium. I suppose if it came down to it, I wouldn't want to provoke the infamous legend either.

"Vlad." I sighed and dropped my head back against the top of his chair. "He knew me. He knew my name. I swear, I didn't imagine that."

"I believe you. It's a strange process, becoming a vampire. But I've never known anyone to suffer hallucinations while transitioning."

I briefly closed my eyes. Vlad believed me. That shouldn't comfort me, but it did. Like his words validated everything. I needed to trust in my own instincts and not rely on his. But there was something powerful in being believed.

"Who do you think it was?" I asked. "Who all knows about me?"

"You were registered upon your undeath," Vlad told me. He crossed the room and perched against his desk, his hands gripping the edge. "The queen insists on this procedure. She feels it's the best way to keep tabs on her kingdom."

"Kingdom." I laughed under my breath. Apparently, becoming a vampire was the equivalent to time traveling. Never thought, as an American, that I'd fall under a queen's reign.

"Upon registration, your name is added to a database that she and her council arranged a decade or so ago. That database is accessible by every vampire in the world."

I squinted at Vlad. "Are you serious? What about privacy?"

"No such thing exists. We cannot have wild, rebellious vampires on the loose."

"Yeah, you mentioned that."

"And it's as true now as it was then. As one of the queen's subjects, it's my duty to abide by her laws. As it's now your responsibility."

Yeah, yeah, yeah, typical monarchy loyalty rubbish. "Except that means any vampire out there can access my name. What else does the registration include?"

"Location of death and sire."

"Perfect." I groaned and squeezed my eyes shut. "So, all it took was your name. You're one of the most infamous vampires out there. Everyone likely knows where you live. In other words, this vampire could be anyone."

"I don't believe that to be the case," Vlad said after a small pause.

"Hmm?" I opened my eyes and stared at him, enjoying the sight of him leaning so elegantly against his desk.

"You said he called you delicious?"

I shuddered. "Yeah."

"Anna."

My brows rose. "Vlad?"

"Only one other vampire has tasted you."

And just like that, my blood froze. "What?"

"I don't mean to frighten you, but we mustn't blind ourselves to a possible truth."

"You think...."

Vlad placed a comforting hand on my shoulder. "I've been waiting for a specific guest to arrive, one I made plans to meet with a few nights ago, if you recall. He should be arriving sometime tonight."

I remembered that phone call. The one before I attacked Harold. In all the commotion, I'd completely forgotten about it. "Who?"

Vlad rose from his desk and strode to his fireplace, holding his hands out toward the flames. "Queen Genevieve holds complete control over the vampire population. Her reign isn't the same as what you're accustomed to. Your kings and queens are more like figureheads. But Genevieve is absolute in her rule. She believes her laws should be unequivocally obeyed. To ensure that, she has placed what you would call sheriffs throughout different parts of the world. We call them reeves. These men and women are imbued with her trust. She allows them to police their territories as they see fit, so long as they follow the letter of her law. Our reeve is a vampire by the name of John Johnson."

I blinked, a tiny smile playing at my lips. "I'm sorry. I thought you just said—"

"I did. John Johnson is his name."

I tried not to laugh. I wasn't eight years old anymore. But who the heck named their child John Johnson? Poor guy.

"John and I spoke a few nights ago. I asked him to pay us a visit, hoping you could pass along any information regarding the vampire who attacked you."

Right. "Then what?"

"Then we leave the rest in John's hands. It's up to him how he progresses."

"What if he decides that hunting this vampire down isn't worth it?"

Vlad glanced over his shoulder and grimaced. "There's a chance of that. But Queen Genevieve wouldn't appreciate a murderous vampire running amok in New Orleans. Not while she's trying to secure a peace treaty with your human president. I have faith John won't ignore this."

"Do you really think it was the same vampire?" I whispered, my mind circling back to the current issue. "The one who attacked me at Fallen?"

"I can't say. I didn't see anyone out there. But the words you heard, calling you delicious and claiming you belong to him, make me wonder."

"I belong to no one," I snapped. "Least of all some murderous bastard."

"No one would question otherwise," Vlad assured me. He stepped away from the fire and crouched in front of me. When he took my hands, I relished in the heat from his palms. "Nor would I allow this vampire, or any other, to harm you."

"Because you're my sire?" I whispered.

Vlad hesitated, then after a moment offered me a small smile. "Of course."

       🦇

AFTER VLAD'S and my particularly disturbing conversation, I returned to my bedroom. I texted a bit with Lucy, then retreated into a book I'd stolen from Vlad's office, needing something to distract myself from tonight's events. The thought of that vampire hunting me down gave me more than chills. My entire stomach had become a nest for imaginary bats, all dive bombing my nerves. And the more thought I gave *that* night, the more I started to remember. Like the feel of my attacker's cold breath on my skin before he struck, and the feel of him feeding at my neck, lapping at my blood like a thirsty puppy.

So lost to my thoughts, I hardly remembered anything I'd read. As much as I wanted to turn off my brain, it seemed impossible. These memories haunted me and probably would for the rest of my life. I only hoped with time I could start looking at them objectively. But tonight wasn't that night, sadly.

A soft knock broke through my thoughts. I blinked and lifted my gaze only to find Vlad standing in my doorway. Seemed he'd changed his clothes in our time apart, and now he wore a tightly fitted Henley —black, of course—and dark slacks. Why wasn't I surprised? Twenty bucks said his entire wardrobe consisted of black clothing. He had a reputation to uphold, after all.

"Reeve Johnson is here and would like to speak with you," Vlad said.

I swallowed, then nodded and put down the book. I had to remind myself that this John was here to help. Hopefully. I'd done nothing wrong. Well, except infiltrate Fallen and bust in on a blood orgy, but I'd been human then. Surely vampire sheriffs couldn't hold me responsible for things done while human?

Knowing *my* luck, though, that was exactly what would happen.

I rose from the bed and approached Vlad. He offered a hand, one I immediately took. The feel of his fingers joining mine settled the bat cave. Vlad wouldn't knowingly endanger me. As my sire, he was duty bound to protect me. But I knew his dedication went deeper than that.

"John is a kind but resolute man," Vlad said as we headed downstairs. "He will hear what you have to say and decide on an appropriate course of action afterward."

Instead of entering his office, Vlad led me into the kitchen. I hadn't seen this room yet, and my eyes widened at the size and design of the room. Based on the rest of the house, I'd expected something Victorian in appearance, and mildly gaudy. Instead, the kitchen possessed a more modern feel. Gleaming stainless-steel appliances, a light-colored marble floor, even pale-toned walls. Eggshell, probably. The only splash of color came from the tiled backsplash behind the sink and stove—deep red, because of course it was.

A man sat on a nearby stool, his elbows and forearms braced atop the island's marble counter. A mug sat in front of him, steam curling up from inside.

I frowned, wondering what the heck was in there. "I thought we couldn't tolerate human food?"

Vlad's gaze followed mine, and a small smirk tugged at the corner of his mouth. "That's not coffee. John prefers his blood steaming-hot."

My stomach soured. Did he microwave it? I could barely tolerate microwaved food as a human—I doubt that'd change as a vampire.

"Evening," Vlad said, nodding once to John.

The man lifted his mug and held my gaze as he took a long sip. I fought to control my gag reflex. Bagged blood and I weren't pals. And the thought of super-heating it made me want to throw up. I couldn't wait for this week to be over. Vlad would teach me to hunt, and I would begin building my harem. And that sounded a hell of a lot more appetizing than overly processed blood.

"It's better when you spice it," this John fellow said in a slightly southern accent. His deep voice raised the hairs on my arms. He sounded like someone who'd smoked a pack of cigarettes a day before dying. "A bit of cinnamon does the trick for me."

My eyebrow jumped. "Cinnamon? But how...?"

"He mixes it into his blood. So his system doesn't reject it."

Interesting. Made me wonder what sorts of flavors I could add to mine. Anything had to be better than the plastic taste.

"So, you're Vlad's new gig."

"Gig?"

"My newborn, or apprentice, if you prefer," Vlad replied.

Oh, I *definitely* preferred apprentice. Newborn made it seem too familial, and considering our recent kiss, I really didn't want to picture Vlad as anything remotely father figure-ish.

"Well, let me have a look at you, darlin'," John rasped.

Vlad released my hand and gestured me forward. I stepped into the middle of the room and watched as John rose from his stool and circled me. "Hmm. She's pretty enough. Young, though. How old did you say she was?"

"I didn't," Vlad responded, his tone dry. "And since *she* is standing right there, perhaps you should simply ask her yourself."

I bit back a smile. Five points to Vlad for treating me like a person instead of a possession. "I'm twenty-four."

"Quite young."

"My age has nothing to do with this," I retorted.

"Wrong." John circled around and came to a stop in front of me. His gaze narrowed as he took all of me in. "Blonde hair. Brown eyes."

"Hazel," I corrected.

He lifted a brow.

"My driver's license has it listed as hazel."

"Brown will suffice," he replied. "Slim. Almost no curves whatsoever."

"More than enough for me, thank you. And absolutely none for you." I fought back the urge to grab my chest and show him exactly what curves I possessed. Two minutes in this John Johnson's presence and I already didn't like the guy. What was the point of this little assessment?

His mouth quirked. "Fiery. That mouth, though. Did you say somethin' to piss someone off, lil' darlin'?"

I was about to flip him off when Vlad stepped forward and rested a hand on my shoulder. "Are you intentionally trying to provoke us?"

Us. This time, I did grin.

"No. And I apologize if I am." John dipped his head respectfully. "My intention here is to build a profile. Blonde, dark-eyed female, young, slim. Murdered outside Fallen, you said?"

I shuddered at the word. After days of convincing myself I was undead, *murdered* seemed so final.

"In the back alley," Vlad commented. "I found her discarded alongside the garbage bins."

"Then the vamp in question didn't mean for her to survive."

"I think not," Vlad said. "If I hadn't found her when I did, she would have truly died."

"Hmm." John stood back and assessed me once more. "Well, let's have it then."

I shot him a startled glance. Have what?

"Your story, darlin'." John waved a hand at me. "I'll take your statement, and we'll go from there."

It took me a few seconds to decide where to begin. I wasn't sure how much to reveal. Would I be punished for snooping around the club? I couldn't avoid it, though. This so-called reeve needed to know where I was when abducted.

So, I started at the very beginning. It didn't take long to regale him with my story. But I left Lucy out. I didn't need anyone else knowing about her involvement, just in case. Once I reached the back-alley part, John held up a hand.

"Tell me about him."

"Who?"

"The vamp. You said you got a good look at him. Describe him to me."

I closed my eyes and recalled his memory. I grimaced the instant he filled my mind. That was a face I never wanted to see again. "Four or five inches taller than me," I said, remembering how he towered over me. "He wasn't thin, but he wasn't big either. Medium-sized. He had dark hair, blue eyes, angular face. And he had a mole on his chin. I remember that very distinctly. It was quite large and located here." I tapped the side of my chin.

John's gaze leapt to Vlad's. The two didn't speak, but I sensed the tension rising between them.

"What's wrong? Do you know this vamp?"

John carded a hand through his hair and returned to the island where his mug of blood awaited. "His name is Petrik Kamen."

I shot Vlad a curious look, only to find his expression completely shuttered. As though he feared giving something away.

"You know him too?"

A single nod.

Their reactions weren't very encouraging. "Okay, and why do you both look like the shit just hit the fan?"

John sighed and took a sip, then met my gaze. "He's the queen's sire."

CHAPTER
TWELVE

My attention bounced between the two men. Clearly, this Petrik was a big deal. I couldn't believe he'd sired the queen. If he had the queen's ear, why was he at Fallen? And why attack me?

Vlad's and John's expressions told me everything I needed to know. Petrik was bad news. Like, *whoops, I'm pregnant* bad news.

John cupped his mug and lifted it to his lips, breathing in the aroma. His gaze lifted to mine over the rim. "Hate to tell you this, darlin', but you've attracted the attention of the oldest vampire I've ever met."

My lungs squeezed out my breath. Older than Vlad? Crap on a cracker, that *was* bad news.

I turned to Vlad and cringed at his sympathetic expression. "You too?"

He sighed, then nodded. "Petrik dates back to William the Conqueror. He was one of William's many soldiers."

My jaw gaped. Growing up, I'd hated history class, but William the Conqueror was a well-known name across the entire world. If I remembered correctly, he'd conquered England sometime in the eleventh century, making Petrik nearly a thousand years old.

"Holy shit," I wheezed.

I reached for the nearest stool, my hand trembling as I pulled it close. I needed to sit. My damn legs had turned to jelly.

"That is, of course, if Petrik is indeed the one you saw," Vlad said. "We mustn't jump to conclusions until we know for sure. There are many vampires out there with moles on their faces."

My eyes fluttered shut, and I thought back to *that* moment, the one where my murderer had clutched my throat and leered over me. I remembered staring into his face, drinking in every last detail.

"He, uh... had a small scar," I said, my voice frail. "Right above his upper lip. I remember because the streetlights emphasized it." I traced the location, above my lip leading up to my nose. "Jagged. Like he'd taken a piece of glass to his face."

John's shoulders sagged, and he cursed under his breath. "Yeah, that's Petrik. No doubt about it."

Panic bubbled beneath the surface like molten lava just ready to explode. "Okay, okay. This is bad. Really bad."

Panic gripped my insides and twisted. I leaned against the island and dropped my head into my palms, cursing myself out over and over. I never should have left Perish. I never should have gone to Fallen. My ex-boyfriend had warned me this would happen. He'd straight up told me I'd die if I followed through with my plan. And I'd responded by dumping him. Thankfully, I didn't regret that part. He'd pissed me off by trying to forbid me from coming to New Orleans. No thank you. But he'd been right—for fuck's sake. Like that wasn't ironic enough, now I had a thousand-year-old vampire possibly hunting me.

"Vlad," I croaked into my palms. "Tell him about tonight." Because I sure as hell couldn't.

"Anna was exploring my grounds when she was graced by another vampire's presence. I believe it was Petrik. He seems to have staked a claim on her. Called her his and told her she was delicious."

"Delicious," John repeated.

I groaned and dropped my head onto the counter. This was

ridiculous. What happened to my happy-go-lucky life? Blood, death, vampires, I didn't want any of it. What was the saying? It was all fun and games until someone lost an eye? Well, I hadn't lost an eye, but I think my lost life definitely fit the bill.

"Sounds like he wants another taste of her blood," John said.

"Thank you, Captain Obvious," I muttered. I lifted my head with a glare. "I'd like to state for the record that I do not consent to this Petrik so much as touching me. I'd also like it stated that if he comes near me again, I'm gonna do whatever the hell I can to murder *his* stupid ass."

John's lips twitched. "She's a cute one."

I growled under my breath, my lip curling up to reveal my fangs.

"Oh, just adorable," John said, laughing. "Darlin', let me drop a few what you kids call 'truth bombs.' You don't stand a friggin' chance against Petrik. Hell, I don't stand a chance against him. And I'd bet every last dollar of my wealthy estate against dear ole Drac here too. Petrik has five hundred years on him, and seven on me. You wouldn't be able to harm a hair on his head, lil' one."

I ground my back teeth together. "I'm not useless. Stake, beheading, fire, sunlight. There's more than one way to skin an undead cat, and believe me, I'm looking to do some skinning."

John chuckled. "I see why you changed her."

"No, you don't" was all Vlad said.

I blinked at Vlad but chose not to inquire further, not with present company.

John cast me another curious glance. "You look like one solid gust of wind would knock you down, darlin'. Petrik was a soldier. He's been fighting in wars since before you were a twinkle in your great-times-twenty-grandma's eye."

"I've taken self-defense classes," I muttered.

John burst out laughing. "Against vampires?"

"Well, no. But how hard can it be to drive a wooden stake into a vampire's heart, for crying out loud?"

"All right. Stand up, kitten."

"Do *not* call me kitten."

"Darlin', whatever. Up, up, let's go."

I slapped my hands on the counter and rose. This guy wanted a fight? Good, because I was hankering to do a little damage right now too. He made me feel weak and useless. Like I was some fragile little woman who needed the strong manly men to protect me.

"Anna, might I suggest refraining from this little demonstration?" Vlad implored.

I ignored him and held up my hands like I'd been taught in self-defense.

John snickered, then without warning blew past me and snagged me by the throat, his other arm like a vice across my shoulders. "See, darlin'? If you can't handle me, a mere three-hundred-year-old, how are you gonna handle someone of Petrik's pedigree?"

I caught Vlad's gaze, then winked. John might have bested me, but his position was sloppy. He thought he had me beat. His frame was loose and his grip relaxed. So, instead of wrenching away from him, I pushed backward until our bodies were flush, further loosening his arm at my shoulders. Then I spun around, wincing when his nails caught the flesh at my throat.

Now face-to-face, I had a second to catch John's surprised expression before I snapped my knee up and landed a solid blow to his boys below the belt.

John instantly howled and dropped. Once he finished rolling back and forth, mewling about his "damn balls," I kneeled next to him and pushed a lock of hair off his sweaty forehead.

"I may not be some ancient vampire, but I'm not useless either. Women have been dealing with this sort of abuse since the beginning of time. We have our tricks. Believe me when I tell you that Petrik will rue the day he attacked me."

"For the love of all that's tender, woman..." John rolled to the side, then rose to his knees, his hands still cupping his bits. "Back off and give me a moment to breathe."

"You're a vampire. You don't need to breathe," I quipped.

He chuckled, then slowly pushed to his feet, still rubbing his afflicted area. "I wish I could say I like you, but my balls might disagree. And I'm rather attached to them. Tell you what, darlin', I'll put in a grievance report to the queen, tellin' her all about her precious sire and what he's been up to. Whether she hears me out or agrees to let me handle this situation my way is hard to tell." He coughed into his hand, then repositioned himself below the equator. "In the meantime, Drac, might I suggest calling in a few friends. The more vamps surrounding your precious cargo here, the less inclined Petrik might be to take another bite."

"Noted," Vlad agreed.

"And that's it?" I frowned at John. "You submit a grievance? This guy almost murdered me. Or did, depending on your point of view. Who's to say how many other women he's killed?"

"I'll be lookin' into that. Missin' women aren't exactly a rare thing down here. Sadly, the human authorities have a lot of trouble in that regard. All the surroundin' gators, if you catch my drift."

I shuddered, pretty sure he was implying that these abducted women were killed then fed to the local wildlife. I knew I hated alligators for a reason.

"I'll see if I can rummage up a pattern and hopefully track our boy down."

"I thought all vampires were registered?"

"Sure, but that doesn't mean much for an ancient like Petrik. And it ain't like we put trackin' devices in everyone. If he doesn't wanna be found, there ain't much we can do about it."

Sarcastic laughter rushed past my lips. "Are you kidding me?"

"Now isn't the time for this discussion," Vlad said, finally speaking up. "The sun approaches. I need to get Anna into her coffin before retiring myself. John, if you feel you can't make it home in time, I keep a few spare coffins in the small mausoleum out back. It secures from the inside."

"Mighty grateful. I'll definitely take you up on that offer. This conversation took longer than I'd anticipated." He grimaced and tugged at the inseam of his pants again.

"Very well. Tomorrow, I'll summon those loyal to me, but I expect to hear from you regarding the grievance immediately."

"You got it, Drac."

Vlad rolled his eyes, then held his hand out to me. I instinctively took it, only afterward noticing how John's attention zeroed in on our embrace. Still, I didn't pull away, even as Vlad led me out of the kitchen and up to the attic. Vlad's touch soothed me, and right now, I needed as much comfort as possible.

Once next to our coffins, he released my hand and sighed. "There's something I wish to discuss before we retire for the day. You asked me about my second gift."

I nodded, sparing the inside of my coffin a dreaded glance.

"In light of all this new information, Petrik's identity and whatnot, I feel I should tell you what it is."

Curiosity lit within me, and I gave Vlad my full attention.

"Do you remember how I told you I heard your name in my head?"

"Of course." That wasn't something a girl forgot.

"I have the gift of foresight," he finally said. "Visions of the future, if you will."

"What?"

He inclined his head. "That night at Fallen, I *knew* I was looking for you, because I'd seen you in my dreams many years ago. In my dream, someone whispered your name to me. I knew then that we were fated to meet that night. But my gift is flawed, as it's still developing. I hardly ever receive all the pieces of the puzzle. I never saw Petrik or what would happen. Nor have I seen what's yet to come."

"Okay." I couldn't wrap my head around this. We were *fated* to meet that night? Did that mean I was also fated to become a vampire?

Shit, I didn't believe in fate! I'd always believed a girl made her own path, her own choices.

"I'm telling you this, because I need you to understand me when I tell you I will *not* let Petrik lay another finger on you." Vlad cupped my cheek, then leaned in and brushed a chaste kiss against my mouth. "We are fated to mean so much more to each other than this. I know you're conflicted about what you may or may not be feeling for me, but remember that I've had more time to prepare. I first saw you in my dreams fifty years ago."

My breath rushed past my lips, and I stared at him, dumbfounded.

"I've been waiting for you for half a century. And now that I've found you, I refuse to let anything ruin what we have the chance of becoming."

With a small smile, Vlad took my hand and assisted me into my coffin.

I slipped in without complaint, my mind whirling with everything he'd just told me.

Fifty years, fated to meet... I just... couldn't comprehend this at all.

My thoughts were deafening as he slid the coffin into place. But not so deafening that I didn't catch his soft "sleep well" before he climbed into his own coffin.

Thankfully, the sun rose, silencing my thoughts for the rest of the day.

CHAPTER

THIRTEEN

I HAD SO many questions when I woke the next night. Almost like my stupid brain had refused to switch off even though my body sure as hell had. My thoughts kept going 'round and 'round, to the point where it felt as though I hadn't rested at all. My first night with Vlad, I'd asked him how he'd known where to find me. Yes, he'd been elusive, but he'd eventually mentioned hearing my name in his head. At the time, I'd assumed he meant he could read minds. He'd corrected me, but he hadn't been too forthcoming with the details afterward.

But foresight as his second gift? What did that even mean? I couldn't wrap my head around any of it, especially the whole waiting for my arrival for the last fifty years.

I absolutely did not believe in God, religion, or predestination. The thought that two people were fated to cross paths, that the world aligned specifically to bring them together, was too mind-boggling for me. Hell, it downright terrified me. I'd always believed I marched to the beat of my own drum, cut my own path through life, and that my choices—and consequences—were my own to bear. Now, here came Vlad with evidence to the contrary. How could he have possibly seen me in his dreams twenty-five-ish years before I was even born? And who was on the *other* end controlling our destinies? Who had woven the threads of our lives together?

Mythology had always intrigued me, so I knew all about the Greek Fates, the Norse Nornir, even the Egyptian god, Shai, but I'd never considered that any of those entities may have actually existed at some point. Or perhaps still did. Cripes, it was like someone had set a bomb off in my life, destroying everything I ever thought I knew, then leaving me to pick up the shattered pieces.

Okay. Time for a deep—albeit unnecessary—breath.

Here were the facts.

Número Uno: I was a vampire. Check.

Número Dos: *Señor* Vlad was my sire.

Número Tres: We were connected.

Those were three facts I could live with. So long as no one went around talking about fate and destiny, I could handle that.

Ugh, this was far too much to consider at seven-thirty in the evening. I hadn't even had a sip of blood yet and was already contemplating philosophy, which, side note, was a perfect example of hell. My brain wasn't awake enough to handle this kind of heavy thinking. And I certainly couldn't hide in my coffin all night, as much as I wanted to.

I stretched the kinks out of my body, then pushed my coffin lid back and climbed out with less fanfare than the last few nights. Even though I was *dead* during the day, I was exhausted.

I still yearned for a bed too. Something I could stretch out on and snuggle up to some pillows. But with everything hanging over us, it was doubtful that would happen anytime soon. We had a baby vampire to train—me, I was the baby vamp—and a villainous monster with tight connections to the queen to track down.

Boy, all that sounded about as fun as a trip to the gynecologist.

Damn, I really wished I could go back in time and slap myself upside the head before entering Fallen. Give myself a solid kick in the ass and point me home, tell myself to smarten up. All this in search of fame and fortune, and where had it landed me? Dead and completely unremarkable. I couldn't even host my vlog anymore, thanks to the whole no reflection thing.

Sighing, I smoothed a hand down my pajamas, then beat a quick path to my bathroom one floor down. Though I was hankering for a nice sip of AB+, I also felt the desperate need for a shower. Was I avoiding Vlad? You betcha. I so wasn't ready to face—or discuss—the truth bombs he'd set off in my life early this morning. Nor was I ready to contemplate what it all meant.

Could this whole "fated to meet" thing explain why I was so attracted to him? Was there some sort of deity out there getting her jollies by pairing me with Vlad? If so, I bet she was getting one hell of a laugh out of all this. Shit, I *hoped* she was. Someone ought to be laughing somewhere.

I reached for the shower taps, about to turn them, when I heard movement downstairs. Unfamiliar voices greeting Vlad like old friends. All right, so I might have perked an ear and eavesdropped a little. But it didn't take long for me to realize the voices belonged to his allies. The ones he'd mentioned calling on tonight. And since he woke a good hour or so before me, it sounded as though he'd already summoned them. They must have lived nearby, to be here so soon. Probably in New Orleans.

I wouldn't learn anything more though until I showered and dressed. So, instead of asking myself unanswerable questions, I turned on the taps, then ducked under the spray and quickly scrubbed. If showering was an Olympic sport, I would have won gold. Once finished, I climbed out, only to scream at the sight of an unfamiliar woman sitting on my toilet.

"Sweet baby Zeus!" I shrieked, clutching my towel to my chest. "Who the fuck are you?"

The dark-haired beauty slowly raised a brow. "You really are a baby, aren't you?"

Holy shit—her voice was like liquid butter. "Excuse you, I'm twenty-four."

Her lips parted, and I caught sight of her shiny fangs before musical laughter rose from her throat. "I mean a baby vampire, you naïve little dolt."

Holy guacamole, I could listen to her talk all day. Her voice was pleasantly pitched—a bit lower than most women—but it flowed with the cadence of a professional singer.

But then I blinked. Had she just called me a dolt? Wasn't that something kids called each other in grade school? And did that mean we were about to get in some sort of hair-pulling fight? I hoped not. I liked my hair right where it was, attached to my skull.

"You let the water dull your senses," she said before slowly standing and rising to her full height, a good few inches taller than me. Whoa, I wasn't used to looking up at other women.

Damn, this woman was absolutely breathtaking. Her golden-brown skin shone like the sun on Mediterranean sand, and her dark eyes sparkled with humor. She looked like an Egyptian goddess, even while dressed in a modern loose cable-knit sweater, black tights, and thigh-high boots.

"Who are you?" I demanded.

A small smirk tugged on her pale rose-petal lips, so perfectly painted that I had to wonder how she'd done it without a mirror. "My name is Camilla."

I waited for her to offer a little more information—like maybe a last name and why she was here—then sighed when she gave me nothing else.

"And why are you in my bathroom, Camilla?" I asked politely.

"To meet you, of course. To introduce myself to the woman who finally stole Vlad's attention."

Oh shit. I didn't like the sound of that. Was Camilla some past lover of his? Did she intend to stake her claim on him or something? Because I *so* wasn't interested in getting into a pissing match with a former lover.

"Calm down," she said, her lilting voice rising in a chuckle. "I'm not here to fight."

Phew. That was a relief. "Then do you mind if I get dressed?"

She lifted a delicately stenciled brow, her dark gaze assessing me. "If you wish, though I'd prefer you didn't if you're offering me a choice."

I bobbed my head, then froze. What?

Her suggestive smile and wink raised even more questions. "Um, okay. I'm going to get dressed then. My room is—"

"I know which room is yours, little vamp."

"Right. Then I'm just gonna...." I clutched my towel tightly and practically bolted out of the bathroom into mine.

I grabbed the first things I could find, then paused. Vlad had invited his allies here to help protect me. Logic dictated Camilla was one of those allies. And based on her appearance, I couldn't just throw on sweats and a T-shirt. If I'd learned *anything* from all the vampire fiction out there, it was that they took their appearances seriously. Vlad himself never dressed down, though that might have more to do with his personality. But even Camilla looked like a living goddess. Perhaps it was time to give my wardrobe the same consideration. Unfortunately, I didn't have much to play with. Lucy had bought enough to last me the rest of the week, but nothing fancy. She knew my style. I was a jeans-for-life type girl.

Thankfully, she did understand my penchant for shoes. So, I slipped on a pair of ripped skinny jeans paired with knock-off Gucci heels—because who could afford the real thing?—and a black sleeveless shirt, topped with a leather jacket. Fuck, I loved my bestie. She always seemed to know exactly what I needed.

Afterward, I towel-dried my hair—le gasp, I know—and considered a style. My usual one was a low messy bun. But I had a feeling these vamps wouldn't appreciate the look. Not to mention, walking around with my neck exposed felt like a giant *come bite me* sign. Especially with Petrik out there. Instead, I grabbed some mousse, finger-tousled my locks, then scrunched them up as best I could. Whether that gave me the beach waves I was going for, I had no idea. And I really didn't feel comfortable asking Camilla for her opinion.

So, regardless of my final appearance, I was going to own it. Walk out there in my knockoffs and strut my stuff, like I belonged here with the rest of them.

But before I could reach for my door, it opened, and in Camilla strode.

Her eyes widened a fraction before a tiny smile played across her lips. If I had to guess, I'd impressed her, at least. Hard to say, considering I didn't know her.

"It's Anna, right?" she asked.

I nodded.

She circled me like a shark, the sound of her leather boots soft against the floor.

"Does Vlad know you're up here?" I asked.

Her laughter sent a shiver up my spine. "Sweetie, he's a vampire. Of course he knows I'm up here."

Right. Just like how I'd heard them arrive, he would have heard her come upstairs. I attempted a different tactic. "Is there something you want from me?"

"Not yet," she mused. "I just wanted to meet you. It isn't every day someone catches the eye of the infamous Dracula. In fact, you're the first he's ever paid a lick of attention to, other than his darling Mina."

My heart sank like a stone. "Mina?"

"Mm. His precious wife."

And just like that, everything within me shattered into a million pieces. "His wife," I rasped. He'd never mentioned a wife. But I'd never asked. And why did this bother me so much? Yes, we'd kissed. Once. It didn't mean anything, right? And maybe he'd dreamed about me fifty years ago, but that didn't *mean* anything either.

Yet, I burned. With anger, with hurt, with heartbreak.

"Oh, sweetie." Camilla gave a twinkling laugh. "Mina was his *human* wife, before he was turned. She died years before he did."

I frowned. "Then why mention her?"

"To see how you reacted." She shrugged, then flounced over to my bed and flopped against the pillows. "Oh, I always loved Vlad's guest beds. That man definitely knows comfort."

"I... don't understand. What game are you playing?"

"Game?" A wicked smile spread her lips, and she patted the bed next to her. "Sweetie, if you want to play a game, I'm all for it."

"What? No. Why mention his dead wife? Why test my reaction? What do you want from me?"

Her face sobered, the vampire within peeking out. "Vlad is one of my dearest friends. I've known him for more than three centuries. When he called me this evening, I was stunned to learn that he'd sired a new vampire. A young woman. One who has apparently caught the eye of dear Petrik."

I winced. *Dear* Petrik? There was nothing dear about that monster. My hand instinctively rose to my neck.

"I have agreed to help protect you," Camilla continued, once again studying my reaction. "But I want to know what you two mean to each other before I involve myself. Petrik is the queen's sire, as I'm sure you know."

I gave a jerky nod.

"Then you should know any harm done to him will come back on us twice-fold. The queen is not so forgiving when it comes to the people she loves. And she loves Petrik dearly."

"Well, maybe she should have kept an eye on her *beloved* then, considering the dude is walking around murdering innocent women."

Camilla's brow shot upward. "You're hardly innocent in all this."

Oh no, she did *not* just go there. Maybe there would be a catfight after all. Twenty bucks said all that beautiful hair of hers were extensions. I could easily rip those out. "Excuse me?"

"My sweet summer child, ignorance is not an attractive trait. Vlad has already told us your intentions at Fallen. To expose the blood orgies."

"Yeah, so? How does that make it okay for someone to murder me?"

"You're far from dead."

"Not this again. Look, Petrik intended to kill me. It was just luck that Vlad came across me."

"Luck. Yes, I suppose you would consider it that."

I blinked. "What?"

Instead of answering, Camilla rose from my bed and crossed my room. When she reached the door, she paused and crooked her head toward the hallway. "Well?"

This time, I raised my brow. "Well what?"

"Your audience awaits. Come tell us your woeful story about the nosy reporter who dug too deep and now has to live with the consequences."

My gaze narrowed. "You know, I don't think I like you."

Her mouth grew into a fangy smile. "A shame."

Shaking my head, I trailed after Camilla, my gaze unabashedly dropping to her swaying hips as she prowled through Vlad's hallways. Damn, the woman could move. She reminded me of a lioness stalking her prey, while I looked like... well, remember? The drunk gazelle? I loved wearing heels. Loved the shape they lent my legs, *loved* the sound of them clicking against the floor, but I was horrid at walking in them. Lucy always teased me about it, how I looked like Bambi on stilts. With luck, tonight, I'd manage something halfway between a sashay and faceplanting.

Once we reached the stairs, snippets of conversation began trickling in. I immediately recognized the deep timbre of Vlad's voice and had to stave off a shiver.

"My, you *do* have it bad," Camilla teased, glancing back at me.

"What?"

She tapped her nose and threw me a salacious wink. "Our sense of smell is our strongest ally. It doesn't develop immediately, but soon, you'll be able to pick up on anything. Including"—she waggled her brows at me—"people's emotions and desires."

My cheeks flamed. Sweet mother of all things bloody, was she trying to suggest that she could smell how I felt for Vlad? That wasn't possible, right? Surely desire didn't have a scent?

But the sight of her waggling brows told me otherwise.

"Oh my God," I lamented.

Camilla immediately shrank back, and her lip curled up—a monstrous caricature of her previous playful face. "Don't utter that name in my presence."

"What name?"

Her jaw tightened. "*That* name. I won't repeat it. You know what you said."

"Oh, you mean G—uh, the big G upstairs?"

"Have you no manners?" she snapped. "What is Vlad teaching you?" She sighed and came to a stop on the stairs, her hands perched on her narrow hips. "Listen closely, little vampire. *That* name is not spoken among us. It's an offense to our existence."

I frowned. "Okay."

"Maybe you new millennial vampires"—she rolled her eyes— "don't see a problem uttering that name, but those of us who have been around for more than a few nights take great offense to it. If you don't want some older vampire taking yet another chunk out of you, I suggest you refrain from speaking it again."

This time, I rolled my eyes. "I get it, thank you. Let's move on."

She scoffed. "Newborns, I tell you. Absolutely no couth or gratefulness for the life they're given. You're not the first new vampire I've met this week, and I must say, so far, I'm not impressed."

"Yeah, yeah, you're the big bad. You used to walk to school uphill both ways in the snow. I get it."

"I beg your pardon?"

The stark confusion in her expression made me laugh. "It's a saying. Something our grandparents used to say to us when we were children and whining about something they never had the pleasure of experiencing. They'd tell us we didn't have it hard, that we didn't know what hard even meant, because when they were our age, blah, blah, blah."

Camilla huffed under her breath. "Ungrateful wretch."

"Undead fossil," I retorted.

"Undead what?" Anger morphed her features into something almost ugly.

"Fossil. Dinosaur? Ugh, it isn't funny if you make me explain it."

Camilla gaped at me. "I can't believe I'm having this conversation. You're like a five-year-old."

"I'm rubber, you're glue," I needled. I wish I could say I regretted the comment, but I didn't. She was just too fun to piss off. And clearly my comments were lost on her.

"Just... get in his office," she muttered. Camilla smoothed down her hair, as though I'd frazzled her to the point of giving her split ends —my new goal in life—then continued down the rest of the stairs.

I chuckled and followed her into Vlad's office, where from the sounds of it, other vampires awaited.

Oh boy.

CHAPTER

FOURTEEN

My phone buzzed the second I stepped into Vlad's office. It had to be Lucy. Even though both my parents were likely still awake, it was beyond what either of them considered an acceptable hour for phone calls. They were the sort who believed any interruptions an hour past dinner was rude. But as much as I wanted to take Lucy's call—and tell her all about my new "friend" Camilla—I knew now wasn't the right moment. Not while four strange vampires were staring me down like I was nothing more than an insect meant to be squashed.

"Anna." Vlad strode toward me and extended his hand.

I instinctively took it, clinging to the one ally I had in this room. Camilla had sought me out upstairs, eager to meet Vlad's new apprentice, but I had a feeling she wasn't quite as interested in being besties now. Nor did any of the others look at all welcoming. Good first impressions and all that.

"I see you've already met Camilla," Vlad said, gesturing to the goddess on his left.

She stood closest to the door, her hand on the knob as though she meant to bail on us. The smile she wore reminded me of all the teachers in my life who had sent me to the principal's office. That

148

eager, knowing grin that told me I was about to get my ass chewed out by Mr. Penuckle.

"This here is Eli," Vlad continued, drawing my attention to the man standing closest to Camilla. He reminded me of a young Idris Elba, with his dark, flawless skin, broad shoulders, and tapered waist.

Eli's eyes narrowed on me, and if I wasn't mistaken, there was a flare of annoyance in them, as though he'd already decided to blame me for this entire mess. *Welcome to the club, kid.*

"You didn't tell us how young she is," Eli muttered, his lip curling up over his fangs.

Oh yeah, we were going to be great friends—*not*.

Vlad tensed but ignored Eli's comment, then politely gestured to the vampire standing at his right. "Breccan O'Connor."

I bit back a smile at his clearly Irish name. Breccan seemed more at ease in my presence, even going so far as to crack a grin at me. The tension eased from my shoulders, and I grinned back. There was something so likable about him. Maybe it was his warm brown eyes or his mussed sandy blond hair that gave me the impression of a careless teenager. Whatever it was, his friendliness put me at ease. Of course, sharks could grin too, so I knew not to take his kindness as reassurance that he wouldn't kill me.

"The infamous Anna," he commented in a brogue thicker than his eyebrows.

"And this is Rebecca." Vlad gestured to the fourth vampire.

Rebecca stood alone across Vlad's office, perusing his bookshelves, much like I had a few nights ago. Except, she seemed rather impressed by his collection. With her back to me, I couldn't make out more than the long curtain of shiny black hair that fell to her waist. When she finally turned, I gaped at the sight of her beautifully sculpted face. If I thought Camilla gorgeous, she was nothing compared to Aphrodite here. Geez, didn't Vlad know any ugly vampires? Or was that a statistical impossibility? Were all vampires drop-dead gorgeous? Emphasis on dead.

"Evening," she said, her soft voice somehow carrying across the entire room.

I offered a smile, hoping it was enough. I really didn't know what more to say. I'd never been the sort to envy another woman's appearance. Self-assurance wasn't something I lacked. I was attractive, sure. But compared to Camilla, Rebecca, and even Lucy, I looked like someone's awkward little sister. And for the first time ever, I felt it, a tiny prick of jealousy.

"Anna, I've already filled them in on our little problem—"

"Her," Eli interrupted. "*Her* problem, Vlad. None of this has anything to do with you."

Vlad growled, a terrifying deep sound that raised the hairs on the back of my neck. He took a step toward Eli, then stopped and drew a deep breath. "I am her sire."

"Yes, well, we all know that doesn't always work out. You could walk away from her right now. There's no need to endanger yourself like this. Petrik will eviscerate the lot of us if we go against him. And if by some miracle we survive and Petrik doesn't, the queen will pike us so that everyone else can see what happens to bad little vampires who betray her."

"We aren't betraying Genevieve," Camilla chimed in, surprising me. I honestly hadn't expected her to side with me. "We're handling her rogue sire who has been stirring the pot for some time now. Are we to be blamed for solving a problem the queen should have handled long ago?"

"Of course you would see things that way," Eli snapped. "Your loyalty only runs as deep as your cunt."

I gasped, but before I could even think of a response, Camilla shot across the room, snatched Eli by this throat, then heaved him through the air. He sailed clear across Vlad's office and slammed into one of the bookcases before crumpling to the ground.

Vlad stood next to me, anger radiating down his body. He stared at Eli with a terrifyingly murderous expression, hands fisted at his sides and fangs peeking out from beneath his upper lip. Seemed Camilla wasn't the only one angered by Eli's rude outburst.

"If you don't wish to involve yourself, then see yourself out," Vlad uttered, his voice as dark as the surrounding night. "But if you choose to stay, you will conduct yourself appropriately. If I hear one more disparaging remark from you, I'll feed you your guts before piking you myself."

Eli picked himself up from the floor and dusted off his jacket before nodding curtly at Camilla. "I apologize."

She sneered and turned away—not that I blamed her. Why did men always go after a woman's sexuality in order to shame them? As though it was the only way they knew how to control a woman? In my opinion, he was lucky Camilla had merely tossed him around a little. I might have gone for something a little more permanent, like turning him into a eunuch.

My phone buzzed again, disrupting the uncomfortable silence rooted in the room. I grimaced, then reached into my pocket to silence it once more. Lucy would just have to wait until this meeting concluded.

Vlad turned to face the other three vampires, purposely giving Eli his back. Perhaps Vlad was comfortable with this display of dominance, but I sure as hell wasn't. So I positioned myself to keep an eye on the temperamental vamp.

"All I ask is that you remain in my mansion for the next few weeks until I can resolve this matter with Petrik. I will provide you all a harem to feed from. Reeve John is petitioning the queen as we speak. He's also submitting a formal grievance on Anna's behalf, explaining the details surrounding her attempted murder. I'm not asking anyone to hunt Petrik down. That matter will remain between me and the queen. I'm merely asking you to help me keep Anna safe until the queen has contained her sire."

"Of course," Rebecca said, her icy-blue gaze cutting to me. "We all understand the protective nature between a sire and apprentice. I'll remain to assist, regardless of how long it takes."

"As will I," Camilla chirped, flashing me a wink.

"I'm here for ya, mate. I'm sure we'll have a whale of a time with Anna here. I wouldn't abandon ya in your time of need."

Vlad nodded at the three of them, then turned to Eli. "And you?"

Eli cut me a scathing glare, as though I'd personally offended him, when I had yet to speak. I think it had to be a new record for me. Must have hated my face or something.

"Fine," he muttered. "But under protest."

"Coward," Camilla scoffed.

Clearly, there was no love lost between these two, and I made a mental note to steer clear of them during their time here. I really didn't feel like cleaning up body parts for the next few nights.

I cleared my throat, then winced when all five vampires turned to face me. Phew, this was almost as bad as speaking publicly in front of my classmates.

"I, uh, also want to thank you." My gaze bounced between them all. "You guys don't know me, so this means a great deal to me—"

"We're not doing this for you," Eli grumbled.

I blinked at him. "Got it—you're the dickhead of the group."

"Watch it," he snarled.

"I just call it as I see it." I shrugged. "If you don't want to be known as a dickhead, don't be a dickhead."

Camilla chuckled under her breath. "Told you I'd like her."

Vlad's hand came to rest on the small of my back, a movement the other four seemed to instantly take notice of. Heat rushed through my body, responding to his touch. I arched into him, and my eyes fluttered shut when a strangely erotic scent teased my nose. I'd never smelled anything like it before. Heady, hot, and intoxicating. And I wanted more.

My words ran dry, and instead, I inhaled, savoring the potent aroma.

"What is that...?" I stumbled over my question.

Vlad cleared his throat. "Let's return to business, shall we?"

I shook my head, hoping to clear away my muddled thoughts.

There was something entirely too distracting about this scent. It reminded me of chocolate-covered strawberries, and champagne.

"Anna?" I distantly heard Vlad's voice calling to me. His hands cupped my cheeks, and he caught my gaze. "Anna."

It took me a few moments to snap out of the trance. When I did, I came to only to find the room silent again except for the incessant ringing in my back pocket.

"Perhaps you should answer that," Vlad suggested.

Answer what? Thankfully, the scent was gone now, and I still had no idea where it'd come from. I gazed up at Vlad, wondering if it might have come from him. He'd been the only one standing near me, and it'd happened when he'd touched me.

"Anna." Vlad's voice came out sharper this time.

I gave my head another small shake. "Sorry. Distracted, I think? What happened?"

"We'll discuss it later." He gestured to my backside. "I think it might be best to answer that. It won't stop ringing."

Right. My phone. That was the chirping I kept hearing.

"It's just Lucy," I said. "She can wait 'til we're done."

"You're sure?"

I nodded. "We were discussing the plan?"

"Were we?" Vlad asked, his mouth quirking.

"Well, that was my intention before I was interrupted." I shot Eli a scowl. "I meant to ask if you had a plan other than sitting here waiting for Petrik to show up."

Vlad nodded, then addressed the entire room. "Reeve John has agreed to investigate Anna's case. However, I feel we'd be remiss if we didn't take some matters into our own hands."

"Like?" Camilla asked.

"Due to the extreme nature of these circumstances, I believe we should accelerate Anna's training. I intend to teach her how to feed starting tonight."

"What?" I gasped. "What about the rules? The weeklong isolation and all that?"

"Your circumstances differ from most newborn vampires." Vlad gave me a reassuring smile but was careful not to touch me again. "If something *does* happen, and we're separated or worse, I need to know you can take care of yourself. Learning to feed is the most important lesson I can impart upon you. Hopefully, you will never need to use it."

I bit my bottom lip, careful not to puncture it with my fangs.

"Camilla, I called on you because I would like for you to teach Anna to fight. She may need to know how to defend herself in the coming days."

Camilla's grin broadened. "Gladly."

Wait, fight? This was spiraling out of control so fast.

"Rebecca, Eli, Breccan, you three will be responsible for keeping an eye on the grounds. Petrik knows Anna is here. We could move her, but he's proven able to track her. I think instead we should focus on security."

Rebecca and Breccan bowed their heads, but Eli stood by like a sullen child.

My wide gaze darted between the five of them. "This is your plan?"

"Do you have a better one?" Vlad asked.

"Weapons? Police? I don't know, werewolves even?"

Vlad laughed under his breath. "I assure you, such extremes won't be necessary. More than likely, John will convince the queen to undertake Petrik's punishment. And he'll be out of our hair without another glimpse of him."

Hmm. Why didn't I believe that?

Before I could probe any deeper into Vlad's plan, my damn phone went off *again*. This time, I sighed and dug it out of my back pocket. The second I lit up the screen, a flutter of *something* passed through my chest.

I had eight missed calls—three from Lucy, five from my parents, all spanning from a few hours before I woke until now. Then there were a dozen text messages from Lucy and my brother—which was beyond disconcerting, considering my brother and I never texted—and tons of notifications on social media, along with quite a few Google alerts.

Something was wrong.

But before I could read any of the texts or listen to the many voicemails, my phone lit up again. *Mom* flashed across my screen with a silent urgency even I could feel. I shot Vlad a startled glance and noted the concern in his eyes.

With a deep breath, I answered the call, only to be met with the sound of my mother's panicked voice.

CHAPTER

FIFTEEN

"Anna?" My mother's sharp voice rang across the line. "Anna, answer me!"

"Mom?"

Her relieved sigh carried like the wind through my phone. "Thank God. Oh my God. Thank God."

I didn't wince, but the five other vampires in the room did, as though my mother's prayers were like hot pokers under their skin. I don't know why the word *God* didn't bother me. Maybe because I didn't believe in him? My parents did, though. Absolutely. They still went to Church twice a week and prayed with all their friends. My father called himself a God-fearing man. They'd always hated how I rejected all religion and turned my back on their precious Lord. More than once, they'd told me I was going to hell—huh. Guess they were right. Welp, no point belaboring on that.

"Are you alright?" my mother demanded, her tone rising with every word.

I cradled the phone against my ear and stalked across Vlad's office in search of a little privacy. "I'm fine, Mom. What's wrong? Are *you* okay?"

"No, I am *not* okay. Anna Marie Perish, tell me you aren't dead!"

I froze, my breath forming a lump in my throat. "Of course I'm not dead. I'm talking to you, aren't I? What a silly question."

"Don't play dumb with me, young lady!"

"Mom, come on. I'm not a teenager—"

"Well, you damn well—sorry—darn well act like one."

Whoa, my mom never cursed. "Um. Okay? What is it I'm supposed to have done this time?"

She released another aggravated breath. Before she could respond, another incoming call chirped in my ear. I quickly glanced at the screen and noted Lucy's name once more. Frowning, I returned the phone to my ear, not that I necessarily needed it.

"I saw... pictures," my mother hissed. "Of you in that godforsaken club."

Oh. Shit. My hand shot to my mouth. "I can explain."

"Really?" Hysterical laughter rang through the phone. "You can explain why you and Lucy went to a monster bar? How you ended up *dead*?"

Did Lucy rat me out? Was that why she was calling? What the hell was going on? "Mom, I'm not dead. Listen to me."

"You're one of them!" she shrieked, her hysterics ramping up another notch. "Aren't you? I saw the pictures, Anna! Of you being turned!"

I winced. My chest grew cold, as though it'd frozen into a block of ice. "What pictures?"

"What pictures? You expect me to believe you haven't seen them? They're all over the internet! Your brother and I were in *church* when this was brought to our attention. The entire town is talking about it. Anna! What have you done?"

Fuck. Fuck. Fuck!

"I haven't seen any photos, Mom." I cradled my head and closed my eyes. This was bad. Like *nuclear war* bad. So much for maintaining a little anonymity.

"Tell me it isn't true! *Tell me* you're not some... some... *vampire*."
Utter revulsion dripped from her words.

My mouth opened, but nothing came out. What could I even say?
I refused to lie about this, because when I returned home, she'd see the
truth for herself. But I hadn't imagined my "coming out" like this.

"Anna," my mother moaned. "Tell me this isn't true."

I swallowed and forced out the words I never wanted to say. "It's
true."

The scream that tore across the line deafened me. I cringed away
from my cell, my ears ringing from the assault. But before I could
reassure her that I was fine, my mother succumbed to deep nerve-
wracking sobs.

Tears pricked my own eyes but I quickly blinked them away. No, I
wouldn't cry about this. And I couldn't let my mother's hysterics drag
me down.

A heavy hand came down on my shoulder, and I glanced up to
find Vlad standing behind me, his eyes warm with sympathy. "We'll be
outside. Give you some privacy."

I nodded, then mouthed "Thank you." I had a feeling this call was
going to take some time.

Vlad and the others left, leaving me alone with my emotional
mother. Listening to her heart-wrenching cries was difficult, but I let
her sob in peace, knowing she'd calm down once she was finished. In
the meantime, I sat in front of Vlad's fireplace and warmed my now
frozen body.

This wasn't how I'd imagined this playing out. I'd planned on
waiting a few months if possible, until things between the vampire
and human communities settled, until people were more forgiving
and welcoming of us fangers. Then I'd intended to take my parents to
dinner—separately, of course—and explain everything there. By then,
they'd see I hadn't changed, because I would have been there in person
with them for a few months. They would have accepted the change
more gracefully. Not devolved into a hysteric mess.

"Anna!" my mother wailed.

"I'm here, Mom."

"Come home. Right now."

The ice in my chest fractured. Honestly, I'd feared her rejecting me entirely. Telling me to never step foot in Perish again. Telling me I wasn't welcome there anymore.

"I can't right now, but I'll be home soon."

"Why?" she demanded. "I want you here, now. I want to see my daughter."

My eyes fluttered shut. She wasn't going to like my answer, but in for a penny, in for a pound, right? Might as well tell her everything and let her adjust all at once. "Because it isn't safe for me to leave right now."

"Safe?" she shrieked. "Why isn't it safe? What's going on?"

"Where's Caleb?" I asked.

"Your brother didn't want to be here for this conversation."

Another nod. Of course he didn't. Because Caleb avoided anything that made him unhappy. Ignorance was bliss in his perfect little world. My brother was the type who'd gone to college on a football scholarship. He'd never made it into the NFL, but he'd come close enough to be considered a star in our little town. People had compared the two of us our whole lives. Troublesome Anna and perfect little Caleb. Well, now they had something else to gossip about.

My mother blew her nose, then sniffled. "Tell me what happened."

"Are you sure, Mom? This isn't pleasant conversation."

She whimpered. "I—I need to know. I need to know what happened to you."

Sighing, I crossed my legs and rested my elbows on my knees. How much should I tell her? I couldn't imagine the truth would help matters. But if someone out there had scooped the story, I knew better than to lie. The truth might be painful, but lying was worse.

So, I told her everything. From infiltrating Fallen to Petrik's attack to Vlad saving me. When I mentioned he was Dracula, my mother just about fainted.

"I can't handle this, Anna," she whispered into the phone. "You're dead. My daughter is dead."

"I'm not dead, Mom. I'm right here. You're talking to me."

"You're one of *them*, though."

"This doesn't need to be an *us* versus *them* situation."

"Anna, you're a fucking vampire!" my mother screamed.

I winced. I could recall on one hand the number the times I'd heard my mother swear and so far, she'd cursed twice in this conversation. She was a southern belle, through and through, unlike her daughter. A church-going, debutante ball, dress-wearing, tea-drinking southern belle. Guess the apple really did fall far from the tree.

"This isn't how I wanted you to find out," I said. "I was going to tell you myself."

"Just another thing you screwed up," she snapped.

Oh. I felt that one.

"I—I'm sorry," she mumbled. "I didn't mean that."

Yes, she did. My mother had always considered me a fuck-up. Because I hadn't followed in her footsteps. I'd chosen my own path—and look where it'd landed me.

"Mom, I should go. I'm needed elsewhere."

"Elsewhere? Where the heck could you possibly need to be right now?"

I didn't mention that Vlad wanted to teach me how to feed. That wouldn't soothe her already broken psyche. Nor did I mention that Petrik was still hunting me. That was vampire business and none of hers.

"I'll call you in a few nights, okay?"

"Anna, don't you dare hang up on me—"

I hung up and dropped my cell into my lap. Even now, my phone was blowing up. Notifications from every social media site, along with countless text messages pouring in.

I'd officially been outed as Perish's first vampire.

Lucky me.

◂▸

AFTER SCOURING ALL the posts about me, I texted Lucy that I'd call her later, then turned off my phone. I hadn't bothered reaching out to my father or brother. It seemed pointless now. My mom could pass along what I'd told her. In the meantime, I needed to stay off the web.

I'd always longed for fame, but not like this.

I held my cell in my hand and attempted to digest everything I'd just read. Apparently, a tabloid reporter had spotted me and Vlad in the alleyway and had snapped a few quick pictures. She'd caught herself a big-time story—a vampire changing a human. Even though Vlad wasn't visible in the photo—other than his clothes, and let me tell you how *odd* that looked—I was. I looked dead in it, arms dangling at my sides and blood gushing from my neck. With Vlad unable to be photographed, no one knew his identity, but mine hadn't been hard to find, thanks to my online presence. And that was all it'd taken to spark this piece into something larger.

The reporter had gone to my hometown and interviewed my friends and my damn ex-boyfriend. She'd dug up everything she could on me, including how Lucy and I had left for New Orleans in search of illegal bloodletting. My weasel of an ex had gone on and on in the article about how he warned me not to go, how I left determined to get myself killed.

Then it'd circled back to Lucy. She'd been "unavailable for comment," but this same damn reporter had photographed Lucy coming and going from "Dracula's mansion," leading them to believe that I had indeed been turned. There was even a "Where is she now?" article, speculating that I was hiding in Vlad's estate, mourning the loss of my human life.

Kaboom. Instant infamy.

I couldn't focus on this right now, though. Not with Petrik still in play. After the dust settled, I'd worry about the photos and the articles. Maybe with luck, the story will have petered out by then. Some new celebrity story to steal the attention from me.

"Anna?" Vlad rapped his knuckles against his office door. "Is everything all right?"

I honestly couldn't say. It was all so fresh still, and I felt a little numb. Fame was my life's dream. For everyone to know my name. And now, I just wanted to curl up and die. Again.

"Everything's fine," I finally said. "Just a small hiccup. Apparently, someone took a photo of us outside Fallen."

Vlad stepped into his office and closed the door behind him. "I fail to see why that's so upsetting."

"You would. They can't see you. All they see are your damn clothes, for crying out loud. Me? They can see everything. Just what I wanted, for the whole world to witness my death. The stupid reporter posted these photos everywhere. And now everyone knows I'm a vampire."

"Ah." Vlad crossed the room and came to a stop in front of me. He slipped his arms around my waist and drew me into his chest. I went willingly, hungry for some comfort right now.

"Will this get us in trouble?" I whispered, my head resting against the swell of his chest.

"From whom?"

"The queen? Seeing a photo like that, with me being turned into a vampire when she's in the middle of peace talks with the president... isn't this bad?"

Vlad didn't answer immediately, so I tipped my head back and stared up at him. A flicker of something darted behind his eyes. Concern, maybe?

"John would have already notified her about Petrik and the developing situation. She may not like how public this has apparently become, but I can't see why she would punish us."

"Um, she can punish us?"

"It's within her rights as the queen." He smoothed my hair back from my face. "But don't fret over things that aren't in our control. We must focus on the issue at hand, yes?"

I groaned. "I had a quiet life before this—and I hated it. Now, I would give anything to have it back."

"I admit, I'm not as well versed in the internet as you, but I imagine it'll pass. As all things eventually do."

I nodded.

"In the meantime, we need to focus our attention on other matters."

"Like apparently teaching me to feed."

Vlad gave me a small smile. "And teaching you how to be a vampire."

"And then what?"

"Hmm?"

I flicked my tongue against one of my fangs, a stark reminder of my future and all it entailed. "I just... what happens to me after you're done teaching me how to be a vampire? After I'm self-sufficient. After I establish my harem. Am I expected to leave?"

Vlad frowned down at me. "Leave to go where?"

"Anywhere. Do I go home? Do I strike out on my own, away from you? And what about you? Do you move on to greener pastures? Move on to someone else?"

Vlad's expression cleared the second I uttered those two final words. "Ah, I see."

"What? What do you see?"

"Allow me to ease your worries."

Without another word, he leaned down and claimed my mouth. I sucked in a surprised breath, then moaned when he took advantage of my parted lips to deepen the kiss. His hands pressed into my lower back, holding me in place—not that I minded. I melted into him, eager to taste all he had to offer.

I'd had a few days to think about our first kiss, whether or not I regretted it. And I knew now, without a doubt, I most certainly did not. Vlad was unlike anyone I'd ever met before. His touch made me burn, made me ache, made me *want*. It was like he awoke something within me I'd never experienced before. This *need* for someone else, like he completed me in a way none of my previous boyfriends had. Almost as though we were made for each other.

That thought terrified me.

He'd dreamed of me fifty years ago. He'd saved me, then literally changed me by turning me into a vampire. But with him, everything felt right. Like nothing in the world could touch us. With him, I felt invincible.

I nipped at Vlad's mouth, then groaned when my fangs pierced the plump part of his lip. The taste of his blood blinded and inflamed me. I slipped my arms around his neck, then sighed contentedly when he cupped my ass. One small hop, and I was in his arms, my core pressed against his stomach. I didn't even care that there were four other vampires in the house with extremely sensitive hearing. I wanted Vlad. Right now.

He broke from the kiss and pressed his forehead against mine. "Careful. You haven't fed tonight. And you shouldn't feed from me again."

Shouldn't. Not couldn't.

I licked my lips, my eyes drifting to his throat. I cupped his neck and ran my thumb along the vein. That strange scent from before returned, so warm and inviting yet delicate. Desire, I realized. That was what I scented earlier when Vlad touched me in front of the others. Whether it was his or mine, I had no idea, but I knew the smell now. And I reveled in it.

"Shh," Vlad whispered. "It's difficult to separate passion from hunger at first."

"I know the difference," I told him. "When you touch me, I come alive."

Vlad's throat bobbed as he forced himself to swallow. "That's just your bloodlust talking."

"No, it's a different part of my body talking," I teased. "The one pressed against you right now. And it's *starving*."

The shadows lifted from Vlad's face when he chuckled. "You're incorrigible."

"I know." I stole another kiss, swiping my tongue across his. Yup, I could do this forever. The feel of him pressed against me was addicting. And all I could think about was pinning him to his bookcases and ravishing him.

"We can't," Vlad rasped, pulling back from my kiss. "Not right now. Not with the others in hearing distance."

"Aren't all vampires always in hearing range?" I teased, nipping at his jaw.

Vlad's fingers gripped my ass, as though he was struggling to maintain control. I loved it.

"Anna, stop. I can't believe I'm saying that right now." He groaned and shook his head. "There are things we need to do tonight."

"Yup—each other."

He gave a breathy laugh. "What am I going to do with you?"

"With me? Or to me?" I waggled my brows.

With a sorrowful sigh, he lowered me to my feet and stepped back. "Our first time will not be in my office while my allies are in listening distance."

"Aww. Party pooper."

He blinked at me, then chuckled and strode toward the door. "Come. Let's get you dressed and teach you about vampire dining etiquette."

"Don't think I'm not onto you," I called after him. "You still haven't answered any of my questions."

He turned and lifted a brow. "Haven't I?"

Hmm. Pretty sure he'd avoided answering them. But that was okay. Just meant I could pester him some more. And if that resulted in more schmexy times, I was game.

CHAPTER
SIXTEEN

The "Big Easy" was anything but. The sights and smells—*especially* the smells—were nearly enough to undo me the instant we stepped foot in the city. I'd visited New Orleans many times throughout my life, particularly during Mardi Gras, and I'd always noticed how badly the city stunk. But it was so much worse now as a vampire. There was an acrid mixture of body odor combined with stale food and the bitter tang of what I assumed was sex and alcohol that made my nose crinkle.

Live music poured out of every building and off each street corner, and the hum of the city lights nearly gave me a headache. It was all incredibly overwhelming. And so very intriguing at the same time. Things I hadn't seen as a human were now overtly visible. Like the fine craftsmanship of the buildings and the beauty of the entire city.

Crescent City was alive and pulsing with humanity, but Vlad and I stood in the shadows, like creepy little stalkers. After my recent debut on the internet, the last thing I wanted was for someone to spot me.

"The most important thing to remember when feeding is not to drain the human completely," Vlad said. "Unless you intend to turn them, of course. But I would counsel against such a decision until you've aged a few centuries."

His hand brushed against mine, and I glanced down in time to watch as our fingers joined together. Vlad followed my gaze and offered his own little smile at the sight. Nothing like a midnight rendezvous in the middle of New Orleans to get a girl's blood pumping. Considering we were getting a meal, I decided to call this a date.

"A vampire's bite can be sensual when done correctly. Humans tend to think they've engaged in a little foreplay. They remember more the 'necking' part and less the 'biting' part. So take care to leave them with good memories."

"How often do you need to feed?"

"Once a night, but I haven't dined out in a long, long time."

"What?" I stared up at him. "Why not?"

"I have no need. My harem feeds me."

"Then why bother teaching me this? Why can't I just use a harem?"

Vlad sighed. "Not all vampires can afford to keep one. It's expensive to house and feed humans. If you cannot own a harem, you'll need to know how and where to properly feed. I refuse to unleash an uneducated vampire on society."

Right. And since I was a former twenty-four-year-old human with very little money to my name, it seemed unlikely that I would possess a harem any time soon. Why hadn't I gone to college for something a tad more lucrative, like medicine or law? Nope. I had to shoot for the stars, aim for fame, and all that nonsense. Well, where did that leave me? Penniless and undead. Score one for me.

"Okay. So, what's the game plan here?"

"Come."

Vlad's hand tightened around mine, and the next thing I knew, we were jogging through the streets. The feel of the residual heat from the day and the nighttime breeze against my face made me smile. After five days of isolation, I'd been about ready to climb the walls... more than I already had.

Vlad led me through the French Quarter, past Marie Laveau's House of Voodoo, to a quaint little shop. I'd heard of Boutique Du Vampyre before, but I'd never visited it, seeing as I wasn't one for the touristy gimmicks.

"What are we doing here?" I asked as he pulled me inside.

He led me through the store, pausing only to catch the eye of the storekeeper, then guided me to the back. We approached a velvet-framed door where Vlad lifted his hand and gave a rhythmic knock. Without delay, the door swung open, and the strong scent of incense and blood wafted out.

I gasped, overcome by the delicious notes floating through the air.

"Hold your breath if needed," Vlad counseled. "You'll adjust in time. But the scent of blood to a newborn can be a bit much."

I fought the urge to plug my nose, then followed him inside.

The door slammed shut behind us, but Vlad didn't seem to care. Instead, he slipped the doorman a crisp fifty-dollar bill, then approached a booth near the back. Once seated, a human server approached and untied a silk ribbon fixed to the wall. A curtain slipped free and closed us off in our own private nook.

"What is this place?" I whispered.

"The Vampire Lounge. It's a private club owned by the Voodoo Queen."

My jaw gaped. "The Voodoo Queen? You mean Marie Laveau?"

"Shh." Vlad patted my thigh. "It's an unwritten rule that we don't speak of her. She hasn't been seen or heard from in decades, so we allow her some privacy."

"Decades? But she died over a hundred years ago."

Vlad gave me a look, the kind that suggested I was being naïve.

"Her people opened this lounge a few years ago, but it's always been a well-kept secret. I imagine business will spike now, thanks to the treaty. Here, we can order our meal. All the humans are consenting, which makes it far easier for us, since we now can no longer drink without permission."

"Wait, *this* is what you meant when you said you wanted to teach me to feed?"

Vlad lifted a brow. "What did you expect?"

"I don't know, some wild frat party where we feed off drunken humans—"

"Illegal."

"Okay, catching some would-be murderer and exacting some vengeance—"

"Illegal."

I blew out a breath. "Okay... um, luring in some young stud and—"

"Illegal, Anna. All of that is illegal now. The classic vampire ways are now dead, thanks to Genevieve. She's brought us into the twenty-first century so we can feed openly."

"Geez, talk about taking all the fun out of being a vampire."

"You think it would be fun to murder people?"

"No!" I scoffed. "Who said anything about murder? Whatever, just show me how this all works."

Right on time, the curtain fluttered open and our server appeared. "Good evening. My name is Rainn, and I'll be your server tonight." She lifted her head, then gave a dramatic gasp. "Oh! Dracula. Wow. It's an honor, sir."

I stifled a stunned laugh. Of course Vlad would be recognized. No wonder the man chose to feed off a harem.

Rainn's gaze swung to me, and she blinked. "And holy shit—sorry, I didn't mean to curse—but you're Anna! Anna Perish!"

If I'd thought myself stunned before, it was nothing compared to now. "Um...."

"I saw your photos online! Everyone's been wondering where you are. But you're here! And you're a vampire! By the blood, you *have* to tell me what it was like. Being turned, I mean. I am like your *biggest* fan. Ah! To think, you're here. You're really here! Oh my G—sorry, no, I won't say that. I'm just so excited! I didn't think it was possible. Did Dracula turn you? Was he the one in the photo turning you? My G—" She slapped a hand over her mouth, her wide, unblinking eyes boring into mine.

Holy. Shit.

Was this what it was like to be famous?

"Um...." That was all I could think to say. This was all so new to me, and completely unwelcome. Yes, I wanted fame. But I'd wanted it on my terms. Not accidentally. Not because someone had taken a few photos of me on the worst night of my life. I mean, sure, I could turn lemons into lemonade, but I really wasn't ready for that kind of sickening positivity yet.

"AB+ please," Vlad commented, his tone lacking all warmth.

"Right. I'm so sorry. This is only my second night on the job, and I wasn't expecting to meet you two, like ever. Man, you are a beautiful couple. Has anyone told you that before? Did you two know each other before Anna became a vampire?" She gasped loudly, her hand clutching at her tattooed neck. "Oh wow, are you two in love? So you turned her? To spend eternity together?"

Vlad and I were deathly silent. When it was clear she had no intentions of leaving, Vlad slowly exhaled and answered. "I assure you, I would never turn someone I loved in the middle of a dark alleyway unless there were no other options. I was providing Ms. Perish a service. Otherwise, she would have succumbed to her injuries."

Rainn practically melted on the spot. "You saved her life? How romantic."

Wow, she and I were on completely different wavelengths here. I appreciated what Vlad had done for me, absolutely. But romantic? No. Not even a little.

"Our order?" Vlad implored.

"Right. Gosh, I'm so sorry. AB+ for the Count, and for you, Anna?" Yet another gasp. Rainn needed to calm down before she started hiccupping. "Or would that make you the Countess now?"

Before I could correct her, Vlad held up his hand, and said, "O+ should be fine."

Rainn practically curtsied before fleeing our secluded booth.

I exhaled and slumped against the seat. "That was...."

"You'll get used to it," Vlad said. "Yet another reason why I keep a harem."

"How did she even know who you are? I get me. My picture's been slapped all over the web, including the damn vamp gossip sites. But you?"

"There are a few portraits of me here." Vlad waved his hand dismissively. "I let Marie talk me into sitting for a series about a hundred years ago. I'd forgotten what I'd looked like, so I'd agreed to them."

Oh wow. I needed to see those before we left.

We were barely alone for a minute before the curtain fluttered open and Rainn returned. Two humans stood on either side of her, their expressions equally as gobsmacked.

"Wait, what is this?"

Vlad gestured to the open seats next to us. "Have a seat."

"Oh my gosh." One of the women sat next to me, giggling with wide eyes. "You're her. Aren't you? When Rainn told me, I couldn't believe it."

"What's going on?" I shot Vlad a dark look. Was this some sort of creepy fan club?

"Our meals." He gestured to the woman who sat next to him. Hers was more of a silent wonderment, but I could see the stars in her eyes as she gazed up at Vlad.

"Enjoy," Rainn murmured, apparently trying to regain a little professionalism. She stepped out of the booth and fixed the curtain to ensure we had our privacy, then vanished.

Vlad's companion extended her arm, wrist facing up. I watched as he gently cradled her arm and brought it to his mouth. His eyes flicked to mine, then his mouth parted and he slowly bit down.

My breath caught at the scent of fresh blood welling over her skin, but something south of the border practically quivered with excitement at the sight of Vlad's mouth closing around the girl's wrist. His eyes closed, and he sank into the feeding. Sensual, he'd said. Yeah, I definitely could see that.

"Ready?" my meal asked.

I turned to her, my nerves fluttering anxiously. "I've never done this before."

"I know. I'll walk you through it."

"Do you feed a lot of vampires?"

A sweet smile brightened her face. "I'm here every week. We're not allowed to come too often. I consider it an honor to be your first meal."

Vlad had actually been given that honor. And I would cherish those memories for the rest of time. Especially the aftereffects. I just hoped I didn't respond to every meal like that. I liked to think there was something special between me and Vlad.

"What's your name?"

"Maybelle," she answered.

"Is that your real name?"

She winked. "No."

"Fair enough." I wouldn't want to give a bunch of strange vampires my real name either. "Well, Maybelle. Shall we give this the ole college try?"

She offered me her arm the same way Vlad's companion had. So I mimicked his movements. I cupped her forearm and lifted it to my mouth. Her scent practically smacked me in the face. So mouthwatering. My eyes fluttered shut, and I nearly lost myself. But then I remembered Harold. How horrible I'd felt after attacking him. I couldn't allow that to happen again, no matter how intoxicating her scent.

"Take your time," Maybelle cautioned. "Let your fangs do all the work. You don't need to bite hard."

I licked my lips, then pressed her wrist to my teeth and exerted the slightest amount of pressure. She was right, my fangs did all the work, sliding into her flesh with hardly any resistance. Her blood instantly flooded my mouth, and I bit back a groan, not wanting to frighten her. I needed to maintain complete control of the situation here. I would make Vlad and myself proud by not becoming a savage beast.

Maybelle sighed contentedly and leaned into me. Guess I'd done something right.

I drank deeply, reveling in the warmth that spread through my body. Maybelle's blood differed from Vlad's. Delicious, but hardly as exhilarating. There was something about his that excited me, whereas Maybelle's simply nourished me.

"Anna." Vlad's voice called to me through my feeding haze. "That's enough."

For a moment, I almost ignored him. The hunger within wasn't sated yet, but after a moment's hesitation, I regained my senses and gently pulled away from Maybelle's bleeding wrist.

My eyes fluttered open to find my companion leaning against the booth with a satisfied grin.

"You did really well," she breathed, almost as though she'd enjoyed my bite a little *too much*.

I shot Vlad an anxious glance, but he seemed unperturbed. In fact, his companion had practically melted into her seat, her eyes closed while she hummed to herself. Rainn magically appeared and led our meals away as though she'd been watching.

"Very good, Anna," Vlad said. "How do you feel?"

I released a shivering breath, then catalogued my emotions. My hunger was abated, but there was a different craving rising beneath the surface, one that I was fairly sure only Vlad could satiate.

That same sweet scent from his office rose between us, and Vlad's eyes widened. He chuckled and cupped my cheek, rubbing his thumb along my lower lip. I nearly pounced on him right there.

"Feeding can be sensual for both parties. You'll learn to separate it in the coming days."

"She didn't taste like you," I whispered.

"No human ever will."

I dampened my lips with my tongue, then caught Vlad's finger with my teeth, careful not to split his skin. I wouldn't be able to handle that right now. So many thoughts ran through my mind, all more deafening than the last. I'd bitten Vlad's wrist more than once, and now Maybelle's. But how did it feel to feed from the neck?

"What does it feel like?" I finally braved asking. "To be bitten by someone who cares for you? I mean, you sort of tasted me when we first kissed..." Blood warmed my cheeks. "But I've only really been bitten by...." I couldn't say his name. I didn't want to ruin this moment by even thinking about him, but I couldn't stop myself.

A shudder swept through Vlad's body. He leaned forward and rested his forehead against mine. "Would you like to experience it?"

Heat flushed my entire body, and I shuddered. I hadn't realized it was something I wanted until right now.

"Mm. I'll take that as a yes."

I wanted Vlad's teeth in my throat, if only to erase the memory of Petrik's. I wanted to experience what Maybelle just went through. What Vlad had experienced when I'd bitten him. I wanted to experience it all.

"My neck," I said.

Vlad drew back and met my gaze. "Are you sure?"

I gave another jerky nod.

"I know that's where Petrik bit you. I'd understand if you aren't ready to share such an intimate thing with me so soon after his attack."

"I trust you," I whispered. I *yearned* for this, more than I'd ever yearned for anything before.

"Anna—"

"Vlad, please. I want this. You. Everything."

His eyes fluttered shut, but I caught the sight of a soft smile. "And I you."

He shifted his weight and leaned into me, pressing his mouth against my neck. I shivered against him, my hands sliding up his thighs. Maybe this wasn't the right place for this, but the curtain was drawn, secluding us from sight. His mansion had four other vampires present. But here, it felt like it was just the two of us.

"Anna... I—" Vlad's teeth found their mark, interrupting whatever he'd meant to say.

The slight pressure made me squirm, but the instant his fangs slipped into my flesh, my entire world imploded.

CHAPTER
SEVENTEEN

I CERTAINLY WASN'T AS calm and collected as Maybelle—far from it. The second Vlad's teeth made their mark, I had to forcibly restrain myself from molesting the poor man. *Poor man*—yeah, right. I'm sure he wouldn't have minded a little molestation. But since his fangs were deeply imbedded in my neck, it seemed wiser to hold still. The reality was a bit more sexual though. Little moans escaped my throat, and I practically squirmed in my seat.

Vlad's hands seemed to have a mind of their own. One cupped my hip, locking me in place, and the other threaded in my hair, holding my head still. His lips were soft and warm against my skin, but his bite was erotic—the stark opposite of Petrik's. Vlad's intention was to pleasure, and boy, was he a master. Seconds into the bite, heat had already begun spiraling through my core and spreading through my limbs. Far faster than my vibrating boyfriend back home.

A girl could get used to this sort of thing. If I wasn't mistaken, he was seconds away from causing a massive eruption in my lady bits without even touching them.

"Vlad," I moaned.

His teeth slowly came free from my throat, and he leaned back, running his tongue over his lips. His skin was just as flushed as mine. Apparently, it'd been just as good for him.

I watched him visibly swallow and shivered. How did he make that look erotic?

"I think we should leave," he murmured.

My head jerked. Oh yeah. We needed to leave. Now. Stat. Pronto. Because someone—namely Vlad—had awakened the horny little beast within me, and it was desperate for more.

Vlad cleared his throat and blinked. "You need more blood first."

"I do?"

"I just fed from you."

"Can I feed from you?"

He shook his head. "I'd fear the ramifications right now if you did."

Yeah, me too. If I had my mouth on him, I had a feeling The Vampire Lounge would be catching more of a show than they'd bargained for.

Vlad stuck his hand outside the curtain, which seemed to summon Rainn. She appeared a few seconds later, her grin telling me she'd seen more than I would have liked. Curtain or not, guess we hadn't been entirely discreet.

"More blood?" Rainn asked me.

"Can it come from Maybelle again?"

Rainn nodded. "She has a few more feeds in her tonight. I'll grab her."

"You liked her?" Vlad asked when Rainn left.

"She helped calm me, and right now, I think that's what I need."

Vlad gave a very knowing and manly chuckle.

It didn't take long for Rainn to return with Maybelle. She slid into our booth and, with a soft smile, offered her other arm. "Glad to be of service."

So formal. It was quicker this time, and certainly easier. I knew how to hold her arm, how to bite, and when to pull back. Maybelle left for a second time, her hand cupped over her wrist. But she was still standing, alive, and happy. That was all that mattered.

Vlad dropped a few bills on the table, then grabbed my hand and started to guide me out of the Lounge. I hurried behind him, my body pressed against his, chuckling under my breath. Guess I wasn't the only eager one. I just hoped we made it home before either of us lost our patience. Twenty bucks said it would be me who caved and jumped him first.

Distracted by the feel of Vlad's back against my chest, I didn't realize his hand had tightened into a bruising grip until he shoved me completely behind him, shielding me with his body.

"What—"

"Petrik," Vlad growled. "What the hell are you doing here?"

Ice ran through my veins. Petrik was here? Right now? I released Vlad's hand in case he needed it and gripped the waist of his pants, holding on for dear life. I pressed my forehead against his back and closed my eyes.

This wasn't happening.

This wasn't happening!

"Vlad," Petrik drawled in a faint English accent. "How wonderful to see you here, old friend."

"We're hardly friends," Vlad spat.

"Such animosity. To what do I owe the honor?"

Vlad sucked a breath in through his teeth but didn't respond.

"I smell our mutual friend. I would know that scent anywhere. You needn't hide her."

Tension zipped through Vlad's body, and I hugged him even tighter. Terror coursed through my freshly fed veins. A part of me knew I wouldn't be able to handle seeing Petrik, or even speaking to him. The memories of that night returned in full force, blinding me to everything else. It was like I could feel the cold fence against my back and his fingers gripping my throat, choking me. I gasped and buried my head against Vlad's back. I hated feeling this weak and cowardly. But Petrik downright terrified me.

"Stay away from her," Vlad growled. "John and I have already petitioned the queen for your punishment."

Petrik scoffed under his breath. "Such a waste of bureaucratic time. You and I both know the queen will do nothing of the sort. If you feel I've slighted you, then let's handle this now."

My gaze caught sight of Vlad's hands tightening into fists at his side. "What exactly do you think a duel would accomplish?"

"For you, absolutely nothing. For me, it'll remove the one thing currently standing in my way."

Vlad, I realized. Petrik was referring to him.

"Ask yourself this, Count. Is she worth your life?"

"A thousand times."

I froze, Vlad's response startling me. I knew he cared for me, but enough to die for me?

"Your affections for the girl run deeper than a sire's," Petrik mused. "How adorable. You've convinced yourself you love her."

My fingers tightened on the edge of his pants.

"Leave," Vlad snapped. "And if I catch you sniffing around my house again—"

"You'll what?" Petrik laughed, and the sound lifted every last one of my hairs. "Let me remind you, boy. You're nothing but a name. You may be famous, but fame means nothing. I'm five hundred years older than you and can destroy you in the blink of an eye. So don't push me. Give me what I want, and you'll live to see another night."

The thought of Vlad facing Petrik made me sick to my stomach. All that fresh blood was about to come rising up. I couldn't let him do this for me. I needed to be able to stand on my own two feet. Be the vampire Vlad wanted me to be. I'd told John I could handle Petrik, but here I was, cowering behind Vlad like some child.

I drew a deep breath, ignoring my trembling bottom lip, and stepped out from behind him.

Petrik's cold gaze instantly latched onto me, and his cruel mouth curled into a malicious smile. "There she is. Tired of hiding behind your sire, are we?"

Emboldened by the fact that we stood in a public place, I braved a step forward and jabbed a shaking finger into his chest. Petrik's eyes widened with amusement.

"Leave me the hell alone," I growled, though it sounded more like a meek puppy than a vicious wolf. "If you ever come near me again, I'll consider it a threat. And I don't give two shits about the laws or your precious queen. My face will be the last thing you see."

Petrik's mouth split into a wide grin, exposing his fangs. "How adorable—Ms. Perish, is it? I never did catch your name."

My hand curled into a fist. "Keep pushing me, you misogynistic asshole."

"Anna," Vlad warned.

"No. I'm not going to stand here and listen to his threats, and I certainly won't let him terrorize me. I may not be a thousand years old, but I will *not* let you threaten me or those I care about. Maybe it's you who should be watching *your* back, Petrik. Because fire burns us all. And while you're a fucking mummy from ancient times, I'm not. I have people who would *love* to set your ass on fire during the day."

"Anna!" Vlad snapped.

Petrik's face darkened, and his frosty gaze narrowed on me. "Oh, Ms. Perish, I think you're going to be a fun little toy to break."

I swallowed but managed to maintain my bravado. "Try it, old man. Let's see who dies first."

"That's enough!" Vlad grabbed my hand and yanked me away from the developing scene.

"I'll be seeing you again soon, Ms. Perish," Petrik called behind me.

Vlad cursed under his breath and rushed me out the front door, muttering something about me being a foolish newborn. Guess he hadn't appreciated my little show.

No one had spoken in a good ten minutes. I was pretty sure no one had moved either. Supernaturally freaky. Not a single eyelash batted, or even a twitchy finger. All five vampires simply sat in Vlad's office, staring at... well, me. And it was fucking unnerving. I wanted to clap my hands in their faces, slap their cheeks, anything to get them moving again. But they sat as still as statues.

"Okay, fine." I tossed my hands in the air. "Maybe I was reckless. But that guy absolutely terrifies me."

"Another fine reason to keep your mouth shut," Vlad suggested.

My brows shot upward. "Excuse me?"

Vlad sighed and dropped his head into his open palms. "I apologize. I didn't mean it that way. I just wish you hadn't spoken to Petrik."

"Why? What's the big deal?"

"The big deal?" Camilla rose from her seat and stalked toward me. "You really don't understand the first thing about vampires, do you?"

"Considering I've been one for like five minutes, no, I can honestly say I don't."

"Allow me to break it down for you then." Camilla spun on her heel and stalked the length of Vlad's office, ticking things off on her fingers as she spoke. "First of all, addressing Petrik in any manner will present itself as a challenge to him. The man is a predator, and his prey just made itself ten times more intriguing by giving in to his provocations."

"Oh, for crying out loud, are you actually suggesting I should ignore him so he'll go away?"

"There's truth to that idiom. Second of all, you threatened his life, which now gives him further reason to want you dead."

"So what? He *killed* me, reason enough for *me* to want to see *him* dead."

"*Third* of all"—Camilla scowled at me—"you mentioned your human friends *and* threatened him with *them*. Which now gives him cause to hunt down and massacre pretty much everyone close to you."

This one caught my breath. "What?"

"In other words, you're a fucking idiot," Eli snapped.

I rolled my eyes when he rose from his seat. He was the very last person I needed to hear from right now.

"Vlad could have handled it," Eli scolded.

"I'm not saying he couldn't or wasn't. I just didn't like hiding behind him like some coward."

"As you pointed out," Camilla interrupted. "You're freshly turned. What can you possibly bring to the table to inspire fear in Petrik? Your little threats did absolutely nothing except make you a much more interesting target. So, congratulations. You just made this ten times harder for us all."

My gaze leapt between the five of them. Vlad still cradled his head, like I'd done the worst thing imaginable. Eli glowered at me like I was little more than a stain on his life. Rebecca pitied me, but that didn't endear her to me at all. And Breccan appeared amused more than anything. He even chuckled under his breath and whipped his hand through his tousled brown hair.

"You guys don't understand," I whispered. "He *terrifies* me. I can't just stand there and let someone else fight this battle for me."

"Why not?" Vlad questioned.

"Because how would I live with myself? Knowing that I was such a coward that I put someone I care about at risk? Petrik is twice your age. He's as dangerous to you as he is to me. I can't just let you take my place."

"That wasn't my intention either." Vlad rose from his seat and approached me. When he took my hands, my nerves settled. "I was attempting to diffuse the situation."

"It wasn't working," I whispered.

"It might have, if you hadn't jumped in with your threats and taunts."

I blinked and shook my head. They didn't understand. And how could they? They hadn't been powerless like this for ages.

"I suggest we bring her friend here to stay with us," Rebecca finally chimed in. "One less target for Petrik to go after."

"Lucy?" I shook my head. "No, I don't want her anywhere near this."

"Too bad," Eli said. "You brought her into this when you made your threats. If you want her safe, she needs to be here where we can keep an eye on her."

I caught Vlad's gaze, who nodded. "Call her."

Sighing, I reached for my phone and sent Lucy a text, then faced the rag-tag group of vampires surrounding me.

"I'm sorry if I made things more difficult. But I refuse to hide."

"Good, because that's not an option anymore," Camilla said, storming back over to me. "Vlad brought me here to teach you to fight. So, guess what, sweetheart? We start tomorrow. And I will not go easy on you. You just brought down a whole world of trouble on all of us, so now you need to learn how to fight for yourself."

"Perfect." I lifted my chin and met her stare. "I don't want you to go easy on me."

Camilla's mouth twisted. "Believe me, you're going to wish Petrik killed you."

I squared my shoulders. I refused to let Camilla cow me. I didn't care if I was a walking bruise for the next month. I would show them all that I could handle this.

Or die trying.

CHAPTER
EIGHTEEN

"Come on, Anna! Put some damn effort into it!" Camilla shouted. "Show me you've learned *something*."

I doubled over and drew a deep breath. Maybe I didn't need air to function—except to speak and smell—but it was a habit. Comforting. Reminded me that once upon a time, I'd been something other than this walking zombie.

Two weeks had passed since the "night of the pathetic taunts," as I'd come to call it. The night Vlad and I had run into Petrik at the Vampire Lounge. Camilla hadn't been kidding when she'd said she was going to make me regret surviving, and damn, had she delivered on that promise. Since I was technically dead, I didn't bruise. But I sure as hell *felt* them. Every inch of me ached in some form or another. She'd broken my limbs, snapped my neck, paralyzed me, unleashed every physical torment she could think of, all in the name of defense. Every night, I woke healed, only for her to put me through the wringer once again.

Needless to say, my last two weeks had *sucked*.

Camilla pushed me, trained me, broke me. Every few nights, she tagged in Eli. Those nights were my least favorite. Whereas Camilla sometimes pulled her punches, Eli refused. In fact, I was pretty sure he got off on abusing me.

What few glimpses I caught of Vlad, he seemed equally tormented by my training. More than once, he'd pulled Camilla off to the side. I'd caught snippets, thanks to my improved senses, him imploring her to ease up, but Camilla had just laughed off his concerns. "What doesn't kill her makes her stronger," she'd said. And since I was a vampire, that pretty much left everything except stakes, fire, and beheading.

This was what my life had become.

Worse, Lucy barely spoke to me. She was angry with me. Her first night here, I'd explained the situation, and the moment I'd told her Petrik wanted me dead—again—she'd lost her shit on me. Accused me of throwing away my life and reminded me that I'd promised I wouldn't seek him out. She'd refused to listen when I'd tried to explain how he'd found us. We hadn't really spoken since.

What fleeting moments of peace Camilla offered, I spent them with Vlad, though nothing fun ever came of them. He often appraised my broken body, then shook his head and fetched me blood.

On the upside, I was far too exhausted to care that the house teemed with humans again. Harold and the rest of the staff had returned along with a new harem for Vlad's guests and me. I'd become a pro at feeding, or so a few of the walking Happy Meals told me. I hadn't had the chance to learn their names yet. Their blood was the only thing that kept me going, but I was too focused on feeding and healing to learn anything else.

"Are you listening to me?" Camilla demanded. "Get your arms up. Defend yourself."

My arms? The ones she'd practically snapped in half a few minutes ago? I could barely lift them, let alone use them to block her attacks.

Gritting my teeth, I ignored the agonizing pain and lifted my broken limbs.

Camilla rushed forward and unleashed another series of attacks I could barely follow. I managed a few blocks before her leg swept out and took me down. I crashed to the mats, a torturous jolt zipping up my arms and ringing in my head. My vision dimmed, and I gasped. How the hell was I supposed to defend myself when I couldn't move?

"Get up!" she shrieked. "For crying out loud, it's like you haven't learned anything! What the hell are we here for if you're not even going to try?"

Rage simmered in the pit of my stomach. I *hated* this—hated *her*. I was so sick of the insults, sick of the complaints, sick of *everything*. I was especially sick of training. She was right. I hadn't learned anything. And why? Because two weeks wasn't enough time to master a skill like fighting. People trained for years to learn how to do this shit. What did they expect from me?

"Get up!" Camilla shouted again.

"Shut the fuck up," I rasped.

"Excuse me?"

"I said shut up!" I shrieked.

The simmering rage exploded within me like an erupting volcano. Heat spilled through my limbs, and with a deafening battle cry, I launched off the ground and retaliated. My movements were liquid fast, so much so that I couldn't even follow them. I simply let my instincts take over and attacked. Everything Camilla had beaten into me for the last two weeks came rushing out of me.

"Yes!" Camilla cried out, fending off my blows.

I growled and launched a fresh attack. I didn't want her blocking me. I wanted her broken and bleeding on the floor. I wanted her unconscious. I just wanted this to *stop*.

My fist grazed the side of Camilla's shoulder and set her off balance. While she fought to correct herself, I darted around her and pounced on her back. Then, without thought, I struck like a snake, my mouth zeroing in on her pale throat.

The instant my fangs pierced her golden flesh, she shrieked.

Her sweet blood filled my mouth, and my eyes fluttered shut, even as she whipped us around. Her hands clawed at my shoulders and neck, but I held on for dear life, draining her of blood. It was the only way I knew how to win the fight.

"Anna!" a deep, commanding voice boomed through the room.

My eyes snapped open to find Vlad standing across the room, his face twisted with horror.

"Get off me!" Camilla screamed.

Her blood helped me regain a sense of myself, and I scrambled off with a sharp gasp. "I—I'm sorry. I don't know what happened."

I backed away from Camilla, my trembling hand touching the blood droplets clinging to my bottom lip. I fought not to lick it off, knowing it might insult her.

Camilla glared at me with all the anger she could muster.

"I'm so sorry," I mumbled around my fingers. "I wasn't thinking. I just reacted."

She heaved a sigh, then touched her neck. The holes had already sealed over. "It's not the most orthodox method, but I suppose it works. I don't recommend trying that again though. Petrik is older than all of us combined. Who knows the effect his blood would have on you."

I gave a frantic nod. Even Camilla's blood, rich with age, had me craving more. She wasn't as old as Vlad, but she was close enough. I needed to be careful. Drinking from older vampires was addicting, Vlad had warned me of that. And I'd likely ingested more ancient blood than any other newborn out there.

"A break might be prudent," Vlad suggested.

Camilla nodded. "I'll find a quick meal to top me back up, then we'll get back at it. Before you bit me, Anna, you were onto something. You were attacking instead of defending. Your hits were solid and strong. Definite improvement. I don't want to lose the momentum. Meet me back here in twenty minutes."

I finally licked my lips, then nodded. Thanks to Camilla's blood, I didn't need to seek out a harem member for once. I glanced at my arms to find them already healed. Amazing, the things blood could do for a vampire. In fact, I felt better than I had in two weeks. Her blood was just the pick me up I'd needed.

"You must be cautious, Anna," Vlad said as he approached. "Consuming our blood—"

"I know," I whispered. "I honestly don't know what came over me. I was just so angry and in pain, and I wanted it to stop."

Vlad sighed, then slipped his arms around my back and drew me into his chest. "I hate seeing you like this, but Camilla will do right by you. She'll make you strong, and should there come a day when I can't protect you—"

"Hey." I lifted my head and gazed up at him. "It's not your job to protect me."

"It is. I'm your sire. It's in the job description."

My smile wavered. Was that the only reason he cared?

As though sensing my concerns, Vlad leaned down and kissed me. It was the first one we'd shared in weeks, and my body reacted instantly. Flushed with fresh blood, the feel of his mouth against mine shattered all my defenses. I stretched up on my tiptoes and ravaged his mouth, devouring him until we both came apart, breathless and, for lack of a better word, randy.

"I miss you," he murmured, his hands sliding up my back and into my hair. "And Lucy doesn't care for my presence." He gave a haughty laugh. "I think she's the first person to reject me. Most fawn over me."

I winced. "You know that's not why I like you, right? The fact that you're Dracula means nothing to me."

"I'm well aware," Vlad teased, brushing his lips across the tip of my nose. "I believe Lucy is lonely, though. I feel it's important the two of you spend some time together tonight before we retire. I'll have Camilla end your training a few hours early."

I brightened inside. "Really?"

Vlad nodded. "It's my understanding that 'girl time' is equally as important as training."

"Lucy said that, didn't she?" I started laughing.

"Among other things. She's not afraid to express her opinion."

"She really isn't." I cupped the back of his head and brought our mouths together, showing him with my tongue how appreciative I was of this small schedule change.

Lucy and I desperately needed some bonding time. She was still mad at me, but I knew she was going stir crazy. Much like I had during my first week. It was worse for her, though. No one to talk to or hang out with other than the stuffy humans Vlad had hired to feed us. I highly doubted Lucy had connected with any of them.

"I also feel a little 'us time' is imperative too," Vlad murmured against my mouth. "I want to take you out tomorrow evening, before you resume your training. Would you like that?"

"What do you think?"

Vlad offered me a small smile, then with a final kiss, left me to continue sparring. Camilla wouldn't return for another ten minutes or so, but in the meantime, I could pound the salt out of the Petrik-shaped dummy she'd designed for me. If there was anything that would help me blow off steam, it was that rubber atrocity.

🦇

THE SMELL of wafting popcorn led me to my bedroom. I'd told Lucy to make use of the space however she liked, since I was too busy to enjoy it myself, and from the smells of it, she'd done exactly that. During the last two weeks, my senses had grown exponentially, and my nose was no exception. With this many humans in the house, I would have preferred that one remained dull, but alas, it was something all vampires had to endure. I was slowly learning how to tune certain things out, such as the sound and scent of someone relieving themselves, and focus on other things, aka: popcorn.

I slipped into the bedroom and chuckled at the sight of Lucy sprawled on the bed, a giant bucket of popped kernels next to her, and the movie *Vamps* playing on her laptop in the background. Because of course it was. Lucy and I had watched this flick years ago. At the time, we'd found it downright hilarious. I wasn't sure what I'd think of it now, seeing as it hit a little closer to home.

Lucy rose from the bed with a tentative smile. "Hey."

"Hi." I closed the door behind me and leaned against it. "Um, thanks for getting me out of training for a few hours."

"Oh, of course!" Lucy scooted over and brushed any lingering crumbs off the bedspread. "I figured you could use a small break."

I nodded, a little unsure of what to say. Things had been strained between us since Vlad had turned me. I understood her apprehension. It had to be hard having a vampire for a best friend. The lifestyle was so unlike anything we were used to. I'd gone from being a cherub-faced vlogger to a predator in the span of a single night. That wasn't something one just adjusted to.

"Come sit," Lucy patted the space next to her.

I couldn't help but smile. Her eagerness made me think nothing would ever truly separate us. Except death. And boy, did that thought kill the mood.

"What part are you at?" I asked as I perched on the edge of the bed.

Thankfully, I wasn't driven by the scent of blood anymore. And after gorging on Camilla, I was feeling pretty sated. But I didn't want to make Lucy nervous by sitting too close.

"The part where Stacy draws Goody so she can see what she looks like."

I slowly nodded. Man, that part made me nostalgic. We'd laughed the first time, and "aww'd" at their friendship. Now, I was wondering who would do that for me in two hundred years.

"So, how have things been going?" I asked.

"Eh." Lucy shrugged, then hit pause on the movie so we could chat. "It's boring here. Like *insanely* boring. I told Count Fangerton that he needs to update his place. I'd like to stream some shows without being confined to my room."

I chuckled. Yeah, Vlad's place was certainly outdated. The most modern thing he owned were the fireplaces. Not a single TV or radio in the house. No computers or laptops. Not even a single tablet. I'd even spotted an old accounting ledger on his desk that he used to keep track of his finances. Modern, Vlad was not. But what did we expect from a guy that old?

"What did he say to that?"

"He agreed. I think he had your needs more in mind than mine, though."

I shrugged. "I don't know. I haven't been feeling the need for modern technology lately. Staying *off* the Web is more my style these days."

Lucy pushed her laptop aside. "Have you been online at all in the last couple of weeks?"

I shook my head. It was best for my own sanity to stay incognito. I didn't want to read any more comments about how I'd brought my death on myself, how as a twenty-something-year-old woman, I should have known better than to endanger myself that way, that I was lucky Vlad had been there to save me. I'd seen it all, then shut it down. And honestly, my own self-worth had improved dramatically since. Odd how strangers' opinions could affect us.

"They... uh, they're calling you The Countess of Blood."

I winced. Of course they were. Ms. Rainn from The Vampire Lounge had been incredibly quick to tell everyone online her story about how she'd served the Count and the new Countess that night. She'd graciously left out the part about us necking in the booth, but people had latched onto my new nickname and run with it.

"Have you spoken to your mother recently?" Lucy asked.

Ugh, now there was a line of questioning I didn't want to answer. "Not since that first call. She's ignoring me."

Lucy's hand covered mine. "Give her time. Once she sees you're the same person, she'll reach out to you."

"She can't see that if she doesn't *let me* reach out to her," I said.

"What about your dad?"

"Radio silence," I admitted. "Guess she hasn't told him yet. I don't know. And I don't have time to think about this. I have other more important concerns right now."

"Right. Like Petrik."

Yet another discussion I didn't want to have.

"Have you or Vlad heard from the reeve yet?"

"No. He's been eerily quiet about all this. I'm starting to wonder..."

"What?"

I met Lucy's gaze, then scraped my fangs across my bottom lip. I'd perfected the art of *not* biting myself, but that was one human tell I'd held onto. "I'm wondering if something happened to him. Vlad assures me not. That we'd know if the local reeve had gone missing. But two weeks is a long time not to hear anything, right?"

"Dunno. Guess it depends on how long it takes their queen to see him?"

"You'd think she'd make this a priority," I groused.

"Yeah. Her sire is going all bananas. That definitely seems like something a queen would wanna stamp out ASAP."

"From what Camilla's said, I'm not the first sign that he's been losing his marbles."

"Oh, even better. Let's just let a crazed, powerful vampire on the loose, hey? Wonder if our president knows about any of this. I can't imagine she would sign the treaty if she did."

"Let's forget about politics tonight," I said. "I'm sick to death of worrying about all this stuff. Tonight is supposed to be 'girls' night,' so what do you have planned?"

"Okay, okay." Lucy clapped her hands together and giggled. My eyes widened at the sound. I think the last time I'd heard her giggle was high school. "So I've been thinking."

"Oh, Lordt," I muttered. "What diabolical plans have you been concocting in that head of yours?"

"Hear me out first, 'kay?"

My eyes narrowed. "That depends."

"First, a pedicure." She scrambled off the bed and fished a foot spa out of the closet. "Since it's not safe for you to go out yet, this will have to do. I was thinking we could paint our nails, and if you're willing, I could give you some fresh highlights in your hair?"

"You know I hate pedicures," I growled.

"Yes, but you'll be doing all the work yourself! No one touching your grody feet but you."

I mulled over that and finally consented. So long as no one else touched my feet, I could work with that.

Lucy brought her hands up to her mouth and bounced on her toes. "Then I was thinking... we record a vlog!"

Every bit of me shut right down. "No."

"Anna, hear me out—"

"No, Lucy."

Lucy sighed and threw her hands down. "Would you just listen? You're popular right now. Like, incredibly popular. All of your previous vlogs have millions of views now! You've made it big, baby. Just like you always wanted."

"Yeah, because of this!" I tapped my fangs.

"I know. So, let's use that to our advantage."

"Vlad said the queen has every vampire under a hush order right now."

Lucy waved a dismissive hand. "Who cares? The people want to hear from *you*. They're clamoring to get your take on everything."

"Lucy." I shook my head. This was a bad idea just waiting to happen.

"Look, I know you don't have a reflection anymore. But they'll still be able to see your clothes, right? So let's slap some massive sunglasses over those bloodshot eyes of yours, a hat to cover up that dire situation called your hair, wrap a scarf around your scarred neck, and boom, the Invisible Woman on camera."

I couldn't help but chuckle at the image she painted. "You've got to be kidding me."

"It could work! I think people would love it. And you'd be the first vampire on camera, the first to give an interview, the first to do *anything* modern. You could welcome vampires into the twenty-first century."

Her idea was engaging, but I knew it couldn't happen. At least, not right now. And I told her exactly that. "Petrik is literally chomping at the bit to kill me right now. I really don't need to give the queen *another* reason to hate me. I love your enthusiasm and the idea, but we can't, okay? Not right now, anyway. Let's wait until the dust has settled."

Lucy clucked her tongue, then slumped onto the bed next to me. "Yeah, I guess it wouldn't be smart to broadcast you to the world when there's some psycho out there gunning for you." She cast me an anxious glance. "What are you going to do about him?"

I glanced at the closed door, then leaned over and started the movie before cranking the volume. The house was too full of sensitive ears to have this discussion without any sort of precaution.

Once the movie was blaring at full blast, I leaned into Lucy and whispered, "Easy. Kill him first."

"Anna—"

"No. I know what I promised you, but everything's different now. I'm not going to sit around like some daft heroine and wait for him to attack me. You know who does that?"

"Smart people?" she hissed.

"Cowards. I won't live my unlife in fear of this vampire. He wants to break me, kill me, whatever. Well, I say let's kill him first."

"And how do you plan to accomplish that?"

"Find his daytime resting place and light it on fire."

"What? How the hell do you think you can manage that?"

I eyed her with raised brows. Funny how quickly she clued in.

"Anna, no! Are you trying to get me killed?"

"You won't be in any danger," I assured her. "We're dead to the world during the day. You sneak in, set him on fire, and get out. Simple as that."

"There's nothing simple about your plan!" Lucy expelled a heavy breath. "What does Vlad think about that?"

I folded my hands in my lap to keep from twisting my fingers. "Vlad doesn't know yet. But I plan on talking to him about it. I think we'll need his help. I don't intend to rush into anything or do something that puts you at risk. If he doesn't agree, we won't do it. Simple as that. But the question is, what do you think?"

Lucy eyed me, her mouth a grim slash. "A lot of this hinges on me."

"We'd help you as much as we could. We'll send in a team of humans—I don't know. I wouldn't ask if I didn't think you could handle it."

"And fire kills them? You?"

"Him, and yes. I'd prefer it if you kept the flames away from me, as an FYI."

Lucy gave a weak chuckle. "Okay, fine. I'll do it. But only cuz it's you, and I love you. And only if Count Fangerton agrees to help. We can't do this alone."

"Definitely." I slung an arm around Lucy's shoulders and grinned triumphantly when she didn't cringe away from me. We were getting there. One night at a time. Soon, it'd be me and my best friend against the world once more.

CHAPTER

NINETEEN

New Orleans was beautiful at night. The city skyline combined with the twinkling stars lent the world a magical ambience. I hadn't been able to experience much of NOLA since my dramatic foray into the vampire world, but Vlad seemed determined to fix that tonight. Which was why we now stood on the City Park docks, ready to board a cute gondola.

"Are you sure this is okay?" I took Vlad's extended hand and let him help me into the boat.

"It's a short ride, less than an hour. Hardly enough time for you to cause trouble."

"I dunno about that."

I took a seat in the passenger cabin and noted the fancy bucket with two miniature wine-shaped bottles of blood in it. My gaze flew to the gondolier, but he seemed entirely nonplussed about the whole thing. I guess when you lived in New Orleans, *real* vampires weren't exactly a startling revelation. It'd almost been a month since vampires had made their stunning debut. Plenty of time for people to adjust, I suppose.

"What if Petrik makes another appearance?" I asked.

Vlad settled into his own plush seat, then nodded to the gondolier, who started rowing. "I highly doubt Petrik will know to look for us on a boat in the middle of a lake."

"Trouble seems to follow me everywhere lately," I surmised, thinking back to Lucy's and my discussion. Before retiring to my coffin this morning, I'd dared to read the posts Lucy had mentioned. And sure enough, Rainn had taken it upon herself to announce to the *entire* online vampire community that I'd risen as a vampire and visited her place of work. Rainn had outed Vlad as my sire and had innocuously dubbed me The Countess of Blood. Welp, that name had stuck. I'd finally turned my phone off when my brother's text message came rolling in at a bright and early six a.m., accusing me of destroying the family name.

Best family ever. A mother who wouldn't take my calls—angry that I'd hung up on her—a father who hadn't even called to check up on me, and a brother who blamed me for everything. Made a girl realize who her true family was. And the Perishes weren't it.

"Yes, but you're worth the trouble." Vlad took my hand and lifted it to his mouth, brushing a light kiss across my knuckles. I'll admit that I had to clench my thighs. There was something about Vlad's gentlemanly, aristocratic demeanor that set my hormones aflame. But we were in public. And even though we were safe from photographers, I really didn't need our home boy gondolier here selling his experience with us to the tabloids. Especially a naughty experience. My reputation had taken enough of a hit as it was without adding "vampy slut" to the mix.

"Your life can't be wholly comprised of training," Vlad continued. "Everyone needs a break now and then to stop and smell the roses."

The roses, really? I nudged his shoulder. "Is this your way of telling me that *you* needed a break?"

Vlad cracked a rueful grin. "If I have to listen to any more of Eli's obnoxious complaints, I may tear his throat out myself just to shut him up."

I burst out laughing. "I think that's the most impolite thing I've ever heard you say."

"I do have my moments, I'm afraid," he said with a small, panty-melting wink. "We both desperately needed a respite. So I thought this might be a nice chance for us to spend a few minutes alone while enjoying some wonderful scenery, fresh air, and fresh blood."

"Fresh?"

He reached for the two bottles and handed one to me. "Businesses have been popping up all over the city, including those who wish to provide blood for us fangers, as they've started calling us."

Sigh. Yeah, I used to be one of them. Funny how I really didn't like the word now.

I cracked open the bottle, took a whiff, then moaned at the delicious scent. "Has anyone checked to make sure they aren't poisoned or something?"

Vlad shrugged. "Poison wouldn't harm us to begin with, so I don't believe anyone cares."

Fair point. "How are they getting the blood? I mean, I know The Vampire Lounge has humans employed to serve us on the spot, but how does this bottled stuff work?"

"Similarly to The Vampire Lounge, except these are ordered to go. I had one of my employees pick them up tonight and deliver it here for us to enjoy."

"No illegal stuff? Like people stealing humans and draining them into bottles for profit?"

Vlad gave a slow blink. "Your mind goes to some truly dark places."

"That's my job."

"Is it? I was led to believe you've had some doubts as to whether you should continue your vlog."

I lifted an eyebrow. "Eavesdropping on me and Lucy, are we? Hasn't anyone ever told you how rude that is?"

"If you didn't wish to be overheard, you shouldn't have had the conversation in the house."

I chuckled and nodded. That was why I'd cranked the volume up last night before discussing my *burning Petrik alive* idea. I hadn't wanted anyone else to overhear that particular part of the conversation.

"I honestly don't know what I want yet," I confessed. "My vlog was a part of my life—my human life. But I'm not human anymore."

"Perhaps not, but it's still a part of who you are."

This time, I was the one blinking. "Wait, you *want* me to continue my vlog?"

"While I don't approve of it right this moment, I do believe you should continue with the things you love. Once this entire Petrik matter is handled and the queen has lifted the hush order, perhaps you can revisit the idea. I know you had a few ideas you wanted to explore, such as a channel for newborn vampires. I think that might be helpful—if I'm understanding this vlog concept."

"You're such an old fart," I teased.

Vlad grinned and leaned in. "Young enough to still teach you a thing or two."

I rolled my eyes playfully. "So, where are we going on this thing?"

"Absolutely nowhere." Vlad slid his arm around my waist and drew me flush against his side.

I couldn't help but rest my head against the swell of his chest and just listen to the sound of the local wildlife and the boat cutting through the water. I could hear the hustle and bustle of New Orleans, but I was learning to tune out the less important things and focus on what mattered. Like right now, I wanted to focus on the boat ride and Vlad. Nothing else.

"Hard for Petrik to find us if we're literally nowhere," I jested.

Vlad's arm tightened around me. "I just wanted a few minutes alone with you."

"Well, we're hardly alone." I pointed at the gondolier.

"He knows what he's doing. I paid him extra for the illusion of privacy."

I chuckled under my breath. Of course Vlad had gone that extra mile. He didn't seem the sort to half-ass anything. As a boyfriend, he was quite attentive.

Boyfriend? Huh. Was that what he was to me? We'd shared a few heated kisses with a definite desire for more, but did that mean we were "together?" Could someone even date Dracula? The concept seemed a tad laughable. The man had more years under his belt than most people did spare money. But what else could I call him? Boyfriend was legitimately the only applicable word I could think of. And it made me laugh aloud.

"What's so funny?"

"Nothing." I snickered. "Just a random thought I had."

"Oh?"

"I thought of you as my boyfriend. Funny, right?"

Vlad huffed. "I fail to see the humor in that."

"Because it's *you*. Dracula. I highly doubt anyone would describe you as a boyfriend."

"Hmm."

For a moment, I wondered if I'd offended him. I glanced up and found his gaze locked in the distance and could practically hear the gears spinning.

"I suppose there isn't a better word," he mused. "We aren't lovers. Yet."

My whole body warmed at the thought. If we weren't in public right now, I'd rectify that issue. Immediately.

"But you mean far more to me than simply a 'girlfriend.'"

Ah, damn this man. He knew how to make a girl melt.

"We aren't married, so I can't address you as my wife."

Ignoring the terrified implosion in my head at the sound of the word "wife," I meandered a wee bit off topic. "You were married once though, weren't you?"

"A very long time ago. Before I even knew vampires existed, let alone became one."

"Mina?" I whispered. "Right? That was her name?"

"I see Camilla has been running her mouth."

I shrugged. "She wanted to test me, I think."

"Yes, she would. That woman is infamous for sticking her nose where it's unwelcome. Such as my private life."

"If it bothers you to speak of Mina, we don't—"

"Why would it bother me?" Vlad repositioned himself so I could straighten and meet his gaze.

"She was your wife, and she died—"

"A long, long time ago. Believe me, I'm not still pining for her. This is not a fresh injury. Nor do I miss her. Not anymore. I did once, of course. She was my wife, and I loved her dearly. But her memory hardly stands in the way of me finding love with someone new."

I was *so* not ready to be dropping the L-word. So I rushed onward, completely ignoring that particular line of discussion. Returning to the original discussion seemed safer. "I suppose we could simply say we're dating."

"Dating." Vlad's fangs peeked out when he laughed. "How modern."

"I can only imagine the tabloids now. Who's Dating Dracula Now?" I snorted with laughter. "Then they can call us The Count and Countess of Blood."

"The what?"

"Oh." I waved a dismissive hand. "That's what they've dubbed me online, thanks to Rainn. The Countess of Blood."

Vlad groaned. "That does not paint an inviting image."

"Yeah, I'm not a fan of it either."

He slid his arm around my back once more and tucked me close before laying a gentle kiss against the top of my head. "Perhaps we don't need to assign a word to us."

"Is there not some fancy vampiric term?"

"We were once human, so we tend to use the same words. But for those in our situation, most would call themselves mates."

My brain jumped back to the information I'd read from the council. How vampire mates were rare and the bond unbreakable. That was some pretty heavy stuff.

"The term runs deeper than partners and spouses," Vlad continued. "A mate is someone you are destined to meet and fall in love with. You spend your eternal lives together."

Ah, stupid destiny again. Okay, this conversation was taking a path that scared the bejesus outta me. A lot of four-letter words were being thrown around. And if I couldn't handle the ones that started with L and W, what the heck made him think I could handle this new M-one?

"You dreamed about me." My voice trembled as I recalled how he'd mentioned we were destined to meet. I cleared my throat. "Does that mean we are, uh, mated? Mates? However that word is used."

Vlad chuckled. "Don't have an embolism on me now."

Nervous laughter rose from my throat. "Can vampires even have those?"

"Of course not." He sighed and shifted his weight, throwing the boat a little off-kilter. "Are you sure you want to have this discussion?"

"Nope. Not in the least. But I mean, don't I *need* to have it? To be aware of what's going on? Instead of blindly trudging through the swamps?"

"It's merely a word, Anna. It means two who are destined to be together. Nothing except death will part them."

Well, when he put it like that, I definitely got some warm, tingly feelings. But then I remembered that was the exact same thing people said in their marriage vows—'til death do us part and all that nonsense.

"Who decides all this? Who's pulling the strings on the other end?"

Vlad raised a brow. "Destiny. Fate. Choose whichever word you prefer."

"But *who* is that?"

He laughed. "I don't have an answer for that. I imagine few would."

"You understand how mind-boggling this is for me, right? For cripes' sake, I'm twenty-four. And you're sitting here telling me that

I'm your mate and destined to be with you for the rest of our undying lives."

"I never said that. You inferred."

"Oh, don't get cute," I groused.

"Does knowing you're my mate frighten you?" he asked.

"Hell yes." I canted my head to the side. "And also, no. It's a terrifying concept but also reassuring. My head is a very confusing place to be."

Vlad chuckled, then leaned in and kissed me. I wanted to pull back and tell him how unfair that was, using his wicked mouth to distract and disarm me. But that would mean I had to stop kissing him, and that seemed like a crime. The man was a pro with his tongue, and it would be shameful to ignore his talents.

With a soft moan, I practically climbed into his lap and melted against him. There was something about Vlad that called to me like a moth to a flame. His heat and passion stoked the embers of my own inner fire, whipping it into an inferno that only he could extinguish— with his dick, if that wasn't clear.

"Anna," Vlad murmured. "Not here."

"I know." I sighed and leaned back, ignoring the gondolier's bemused expression. "Sorry. Just getting a tad impatient."

"As am I." Vlad touched his forehead to mine and breathed me in. "Soon, it'll just be the two of us, and we can enjoy each other's body without anyone listening in."

I shuddered. Yeah, the thought of his four vampire buddies listening to us during our first time did not inspire romantical thoughts. At least Lucy's hearing was as dull as a human's, but we wouldn't be so lucky with the others.

"It's getting a bit hard," I admitted.

"Mm." Vlad nipped my earlobe, then whispered, "It is."

It took a few seconds for me to realize his joke, and when I did, I burst out laughing and slid off his lap.

"Feel better?" he asked.

"Yeah, that mouth of yours has magical powers. Makes me forget everything else that's going on around us."

"I did notice that."

"Oh, shut up." I laughed. "Don't make me destroy that ego of yours."

Vlad clasped my hand and tucked it against his chest. He then gestured toward the gondolier, who started rowing us back toward the docks.

"We should return," Vlad said. "I imagine Camilla is eager to resume your training. She's quite pleased with your progress, by the way."

I scoffed. "Thank goodness all it takes to heal me is a little blood. Otherwise, I'd be dead right now."

Darkness shuttered his face. "Yes, there are certain upsides to vampirism."

We fell into a comfortable silence, with me resting against Vlad's side and his fingers idly playing with mine. When we arrived at the docks, he slipped the gondolier a tip, then helped me disembark.

"As important as I know your training is, I wish we didn't have to return tonight. There are so many other things I long to be doing with you right now."

"You and me both, big guy," I told him. "But really, just the *one* thing." When he raised his brows, I wiggled mine, and said, "Like the horizontal tango, doing the nasty, shag like the devil, hump our brains out."

I swear he blushed. And I'd never seen anything more endearing than Dracula blushing in the streetlights.

"The things you say." He sounded almost impressed by my urban lingo.

I stretched up and brushed my mouth against his. "You love it."

"Mm. Indeed."

I refrained from teasing him about his stilted *indeed* and, instead, led the way back to his town car. I still had a long night of being brutalized to look forward to, after all.

CHAPTER

TWENTY

THERE WAS no warm welcome awaiting us when we returned to Vlad's home. No happy greetings, no friendly nods. Instead, it was like a grim funeral. Everyone stood gathered in his entryway, their faces as bleak as a dark winter night.

"Oh, this is encouraging," I muttered as I slowly stepped inside.

Camilla and Rebecca stood in the front with Eli and Breccan in the back. And in the center stood Reeve John Johnson. Even Lucy hovered on the stairs, her anxious expression telling enough. Something bad had happened.

You know, I was getting a little tired of this. Becoming a vampire had done nothing but introduce a hell of a lot of melodrama into my life. There always seemed to be one catastrophe after another. Couldn't we have one night of peace? One night that didn't end with me broken and bleeding on the floor or worrying about my incredibly long future?

"Alright." I kicked off my shoes and nudged them up alongside the wall. I was the only one who did this. Everyone else wore their shoes inside, but there was something about socked feet on linoleum, or marble in this case, that I just loved. "Let's have it. What happened?"

"John." Vlad stepped forward and greeted the reeve with a polite nod. "I've been waiting to hear from you. It's been a while."

"Let's talk in your office," John said by way of greeting. "I brought some files to share with you."

Joy of joys.

Vlad's eyes narrowed on the reeve, but eventually he nodded and gestured everyone onward. Seemed this was to be a group affair then.

I hung back and waited for Lucy. Once the vampires had left the room, she skittered down the stairs and clutched my hand.

"What's going on?" I whispered.

"I don't know. He arrived about half an hour ago. And since then, everyone's been incredibly tense. Especially Camilla. Did you have fun with Vlad at least?"

I nodded. "It was nice to get out of the house for a bit. I did learn one interesting thing."

"Oh yeah? What's that?"

"Apparently, I'm Vlad's mate." I didn't go into further detail.

Lucy stared at me like I'd lost my mind, before finally hissing, "What does that mean?"

"I have no idea," I said, laughing. "Something about how we're destined to be together. Soulmates type thing."

She reared back from me, eyes wide with shock. "Seriously?"

"I'm still figuring this stuff out myself. Shall we join the others? See what has John Johnson's panties all in a twist?"

Lucy bit her lip. "I mean, we won't learn anything out here."

"You are correct, madam," I teased, then led her into Vlad's den.

All six vampires had spread out, giving us a false sense of security as we entered. I felt for Lucy. It had to be hard being surrounded by a group of blood drinkers. Thankfully, everyone here had mastered their appetites, and I was even more grateful that I could now be included in that list. I no longer lost my mind when I caught the scent of a nearby human.

"You have the floor, John," Vlad said. He sat in his office chair with the air of a noble, his gaze intent on the sheriff.

A sheriff who looked quite perturbed.

"Let me start from two weeks ago." He rubbed his face, as though attempting to wake himself. Come to think of it, he looked downright exhausted. Harried, even. A word I'd learned from Vlad. "First, I approached Queen Genevieve with Anna's grievance. I detailed how Petrik abducted her from Fallen and attempted to murder her in the alley. I explained how Drac saved her, thereby saving the queen the hassle of explaining to the human president why one of his Americans had been murdered by a vampire no less than one week after the signing of the peace treaty."

We all nodded. We knew the story. Intimately.

John eyed each of us, then carded a hand through his hair. "The queen didn't care."

"Excuse me?" Vlad's voice had deepened with unmitigated anger. He rose from his seat, his body practically vibrating with rage. "The queen didn't care?"

I released Lucy's hand and slowly made my way to Vlad's side, quickly taking his hand. His fingers clenched mine almost painfully, but I didn't ask him to let up.

John sighed, and his body practically deflated, as though he himself had given up. "I don't know what to tell you, Drac. She was entirely unfazed by the situation. Said Petrik was within his rights to feed on whoever he wanted."

"But that's against the law!" Lucy suddenly shouted from the back of the room.

Every vampire turned toward her, and she cringed backward, clearly regretting her outburst.

"She's right." I drew their attention back to me. Except, my voice was oddly calm. Almost frighteningly so. "It *is* against the law."

"How can Genevieve not care?" Rebecca demanded. She took a spin around the room, her face knotted with concern. "We are her people. Anna is now one of hers. She signed a peace treaty with the president and agreed to outlaw all vampires who feed on nonconsenting humans. She is literally breaking her own treaty."

"Petrik has always held a special place in the queen's heart," Eli grumbled. "It's why I didn't care for this plan to begin with."

"Yeah, yeah, shut up," Camilla snapped. "Like you're so smart."

When Eli opened his mouth to retort, Vlad straightened and glared at them both. Without uttering a single word, the two fell into an uncomfortable silence. I definitely needed to learn that trick. But right now, I was more focused on the developing situation.

"So, Genevieve essentially pardoned him," I mused aloud. "He's been given free rein to do as he pleases."

"This is where it gets worse." John stalked over to Vlad's desk and tapped a pile of folders. "These are files I found on other victims."

"Other victims?" I released Vlad's hand and approached the precariously teetering stack. "What other victims?"

John swallowed, then met my gaze. "Petrik's victims. It took a bit to track them all down, which is what took me so long to report back here. I had to check with the different morgues and request photos so I could measure the bite radius and confirm they were his kills."

"How many?" I whispered.

John sighed. "Thirty-four that I've found so far."

The room fell deathly silent, and I felt the world start closing in on me. My vision tunneled on the folder, and I reached out to flip the first one open.

"I wouldn't recommend that," John said.

But I ignored him. Because of course I did. Who wouldn't?

I lifted the file with trembling hands and leafed through the papers. "Blonde, dark eyes, average build, twenty-three years old." I dropped that file and moved on to the next. "Blonde, dark eyes, average build, twenty-five years old." Then the next. And the next. And the next. Until I'd gone through the entire pile. Tears burned my eyes, but I *still* refused to let them fall. Instead, I glanced at Vlad. "They all match my description."

"Or rather, you match theirs," John said. "You didn't start this. You ended it."

"What do you mean?" I whispered.

"You were his last, or rather, his latest victim."

I blinked away the tears. Now wasn't the time. "He hasn't killed anyone else since me?"

"Not yet."

"Why? What's he waiting for?"

"You," Lucy murmured from her spot against the bookcase.

I turned to face her. I must have looked as confused as I felt, because she continued without anyone asking her to.

"You survived, in a manner of speaking. All the other women are dead?"

John nodded.

Lucy's face broke, but she swallowed and pressed on. "It sounds like this Petrik is a bit of a serial killer. But you're the one victim who got away. You survived. What did he say to you when you ran into him at The Vampire Lounge?"

"That he would have fun breaking me," I whispered.

Lucy quickly closed the distance between us and took my hands. "He hasn't killed anyone else yet, because he hasn't *finished* with you. By surviving, you upped the ante. Made the game more exciting for him."

"And the queen doesn't care that this monster is roaming the streets?" I asked.

"Genevieve and Petrik have a long history." Vlad rested a hand on my shoulder. "We haven't had time to get into Genevieve's history yet. But you should know, she was born with a different name. One I'm sure you'll recognize."

Lucy and I shared a concerned frown.

"Genevieve's birth name was Maria Antonia, better known as Marie—"

"Antoinette," I whispered. "What? How? But she...."

"Petrik saved her from execution. The night before her scheduled death, he replaced her with a prostitute named Nicole who looked eerily similar to Marie. The world believed Marie was beheaded, when in truth..."

"Nicole died in her stead, and Marie was turned into a vampire," I surmised, utterly stunned by this revelation.

"The queen is intimately fond of Petrik. Even though she's found herself a vampire husband, she and Petrik have been known to indulge in each other over the centuries."

"Holy shit... Marie Antoinette is the vampire queen?" I just couldn't wrap my head around that. Talk about history coming to life.

"You mustn't ever mention that name in her presence," Vlad urged. "That name is dead to her. She had to choose a new one, because her former name is as infamous as mine."

I nodded, completely understanding. It wasn't like she could rule the vampires while using a name renowned for inciting the French Revolution.

"Back to the problem at hand," John said. "The queen has denied Anna's grievance and refused to punish Petrik. Nor will she publicly admit to his crimes."

"Once a bad queen, always a bad queen," I mumbled.

"Talk like that will get you killed," Eli warned.

I waved off his complaints yet again. I didn't have time for his whining. "Maybe Petrik has lost interest? It's been two weeks without any word from him, and I haven't seen him."

"You haven't seen him, because you've been locked up here training with Camilla," Lucy commented.

"She's right," Rebecca chimed in. "I've had a few of my own allies keeping an eye out for him in town, and Petrik's been spotted every single night."

"He lives here. Of course he's been spotted."

Camilla gave me a reproaching look. "My sweet summer child, Petrik doesn't live in New Orleans."

"Then why is he even in town?" Then it clicked. "The blood orgy. He was partaking in it that night, wasn't he?"

"Vampires come from all over for those events. They travel clear across the world for them, since they're only permitted in certain locations," Camilla said.

"Just my luck to stumble across a serial killer with a penchant for blondes."

Vlad's hand came to rest at the small of my back, and I took comfort in his touch. "I told you, this was all preordained."

"Meaning I was destined to run into Petrik that night."

"Fate will always find a way. It isn't always pleasant, but nothing will keep it from happening."

I pressed the heels of my hands against my eyes and groaned. I hated this. All of it. It felt like I had zero control over my life. For fifty years, Vlad had known we would find each other. And then fate, like a bitch, threw me into Petrik's path and ensured Vlad was nearby to save me. Had I no choices in life? Was it all dictated by some higher being who may or may not even exist? It was too much to wrap my brain around and made me feel small and inconsequential.

"Do the human authorities know about the other victims? That they're vampire kills?"

John shook his head. "We know how to cover something like this up. And it's incredibly important that it remains that way right now. We can't do anything that might disrupt Genevieve's negotiations with the president."

"So, what do we do?" I asked, needing to focus on something other than the unraveling of my life. "I refuse to stand around and wait for Petrik to make his move."

"Then we don't," Lucy said, gripping my hands tighter. "Tell them."

"Tell us what?" Vlad immediately demanded.

When I didn't speak up, Lucy repositioned her grip and squeezed, offering me silent encouragement. She was right. I needed to tell Vlad my plan. But it needed to be in private. I hadn't intended on discussing Petrik's *murder* in front of five other vamps, one of which was the local reeve.

I turned to Vlad and attempted to convey the need for privacy through some form of mental communication neither of us possessed. I guess I was just hoping he would read my discomfort and understand what I needed. Silly, right?

Well, color me surprised when Vlad cleared his throat and asked his vampire companions to leave.

Huh. Maybe there was something to this mate craziness. We couldn't speak telepathically, but he certainly knew how to read my facial nuances and mood.

Vlad crossed the room and flicked on a record player, which, if the mood weren't so grim, would have had me laughing. Of course he had a record player. The man didn't own anything modern.

Jazz music filled the room, loud enough to hopefully keep anyone from listening into my murderous scheme. Ugh. This wasn't going to be easy.

I grimaced, then took his seat and hung my head in my hands. How the hell was I going to approach this topic with him? *Oh hey, I thought maybe we'd commit a little murder? Kill him before he kills me?* That would go over about as well as a fart in church.

"I know what you're thinking," Vlad said.

"Doubtful."

"I was there, remember? I heard the threats you cast at Petrik. Only one made sense."

"And let me guess—you think it's a stupid idea."

"I think it's a reckless, dangerous idea."

"That's me," I mumbled. "The reckless one. The one who doesn't think things through. Who stumbles into a vamp club, only to find herself on the business end of a serial killer's fangs. What are the chances? And don't talk to me about fate and destiny. I've had about as much of that as I can take."

"I can't pretend any of this is easy," Vlad said, his voice softening as he crouched in front of me.

I lifted my head and found myself caught by his somber gaze. "So, what do we do then? If burning him alive isn't an option?"

"I never said it wasn't an option."

My eyes widened. "What?"

"I said you had one idea that made sense. Setting him aflame while he is trapped in his coffin is likely the only idea that would work. He's far too old for either of us to attack directly. Perhaps even too old for all of us to handle together."

I clutched Vlad's hands. "You agree to this? You want to help me burn Petrik? Kill him before he can get his hands on me?"

"If I must choose between you and Petrik, I choose you. Always. Forever."

My undead heart shivered with affection. "Even if that means angering the queen?"

Vlad's steadfast gaze never wavered. With a smile, he leaned in and kissed me. "What is it you Americans say? Duh?"

This time, I lost the battle, and the tears spilled over. But at least they were happy ones, and I couldn't stop them even if I tried.

CHAPTER

TWENTY-ONE

VLAD REACHED BEHIND HIM, snatched a tissue off his desk, then returned to quickly wipe my cheeks. I gave a watery laugh and sniffled. I must have looked quite the sight. One of those sad clowns with red makeup running down their cheeks.

Once the waterworks finished, I clutched Vlad's hand in mine and squeezed. I couldn't believe my luck to have found someone like him. He was nothing like the fictional Dracula I'd grown up reading about. The man didn't possess a single cruel bone in his body. I realized in that moment I didn't care that fate had forced us together—I wanted him in my life.

I also wanted him in a dirtier, schmexier way, but alas, we had evil plans to machinate and a villainous vampire to kill.

"So, how do we do this?" Lucy asked, drawing my attention back to the matter at hand. "Does anyone even know where Petrik lives?"

"Camilla has a contact who's been keeping an eye on him. I believe she knows his resting location."

Hmm. I wasn't sure how I felt about bringing the others into my plan. When plotting and scheming nefarious acts, less was certainly best. Spread the word too far, and wham-o! No longer a sneak attack.

"What about the vampire registry?" I asked. "Could we learn his location that way?"

Vlad shook his head. "When John checked, Petrik still had his European address listed."

"Great. And I don't suppose there's any other way of finding his local address?"

Lucy gave a haughty laugh. "Not unless he uses the internet so we can track his IP address."

"You've seen too many movies, my friend," I teased.

"Well, sorrry, Little Miss Smarty-Pants. It's not like I go around planning murders in my spare time."

I brought a finger to my lip but still chuckled. "All right. Then we ask Camilla. Maybe make it sound more like we're hoping to talk to him to resolve things peacefully."

"Because that's believable," Lucy grumbled.

"Girl!" I threw Lucy some shade. "Can I go two minutes without comments from the peanut gallery?"

"I'd like to say yes, but...."

"Yeah, chances are slim."

When I glanced at Vlad, I found him chuckling softly into his hand. "You two are quite the interesting pair. Have you ever...?" He flicked his finger back and forth between us.

"Ever...?" I let the word hang like he did.

"Had naked sleepovers?" Lucy chimed in.

"Lucy!" I scolded.

"What? We both know that's what he's asking!"

"You're incorrigible, seriously."

"I learned from the best, sweetie. The best meaning you, in case you didn't piece that together."

"Yeah, I did," I snapped.

"Ah, good. Because we all know you're not the smartest tool in the shed."

"Sharpest!" I bit out, my cheeks flaming. Lucy knew how much I hated when she mixed up her idioms.

"I know, but I wanted to really make sure you got it." She tapped her head.

I unleashed a playful growl. "Keep it up, Juicy Lucy, and I'll literally bite you."

"Oh, you did *not* just go there, Anna Banana."

"If we could return to the topic at hand?" Vlad interjected.

I threw Lucy a final glare before exhaling. "Right. What were we talking about again?"

Vlad pushed to his feet and clasped his hands behind his back. He strode toward his desk, then opened the top drawer and pulled out what looked like a cellphone.

"Ohmigosh." I practically tripped over my words, then my feet, when I darted to his side. "You *do* have a phone! I didn't think that was possible."

"I'm not completely out of touch with modern technology."

"Says the guy using a record player."

"I prefer the sound. It's deeper. Less synthesized."

And also a tad grating on the ears, but who was I to judge his musical preferences? I watched his fingers fly across the keyboard as he—le gasp—texted Camilla, asking her to join us in his war room, I mean office. Color me surprised. The man knew how to text. Why the hell did I find that so hot? Ugh. I definitely had some problems.

It only took a few moments for Camilla to push open the door and stride in. She cast a disparaging glance at the record player, then closed the door behind her. "You summoned?"

I snickered. I couldn't imagine anyone summoning Camilla or ordering her to do anything. She certainly was her own... vampiress? Ooh, I liked that. Maybe that was the word I'd use from now on.

"If you wouldn't mind, could you find Petrik's address for me, please."

Camilla didn't even bat an eye. She simply pulled out her phone, typed out yet another message, then glanced up at Vlad. "Planning to go a-murdering, are we?"

"What?" I choked. "No! That would be illegal, wouldn't it? We're just going to talk to him."

"Sweetie, please." Camilla's laughter rang through the room. "No one goes to *talk* to Petrik. And technically, we vampires don't abide by a set of laws. The queen's rule is absolute. If she determines you've done something reprehensible, she calls for your death. It's as simple as that. Since most don't wish to be hunted down by every single vampire known to her, they behave themselves."

"That's insane," Lucy said. "Your society is fucked up."

"A conversation for another time," Vlad commented. "The address?"

Camilla stole a peek at her phone, then read out his location. If my memory and knowledge of New Orleans and the surrounding area served me right, Petrik lived about an hour away from us.

"So, what's the plan, boys and girls?" Camilla demanded. She crossed her arms over her chest and stared each of us down. "Attack en force?"

"I appreciate the offer and your loyalty, Camilla, but no. Your part in this is done."

"The hell it is." She closed the distance between us and slung an arm around my shoulders. I was tall. Camilla was taller. Unnerving to say the least. I was used to being the most vertically blessed woman in the room, but she towered over me. "Our girl is in danger. I'm here to help."

"Our?" Vlad rumbled. "There is no 'our' here, Camilla. I will not share Anna, not even with you."

"Share? Whoa." I held my hands up. "Nobody is sharing anything."

"Precisely." Vlad returned his phone to his desk drawer, then faced us, his gaze locked on Camilla.

"Can't blame me for trying." She snickered, then released me and practically danced over to Lucy. "What about you, sweetie. You digging this?"

Lucy's eyes grew comically wide. "Um, I prefer to drive stick."

Camilla threw her head back and laughed. "You and me both, sister. But sometimes it's nice to enjoy the fairer sex."

For one brief second, I thought I caught a whiff of intrigue from Lucy, but she shook her head and took a step back from Camilla.

"No fun." Camilla sighed. "I'm still here to help, though. I won't abandon you or yours in a time of need, Vlad."

"You know what this means, right? If Queen Genevieve ever learns that you were involved...."

"I know. She'll hunt us all down like the dogs we are."

Fear tweaked my nerves. "No, we should think of a different plan then. Something that doesn't paint a target on your backs."

Vlad took my hand and pulled me up against him. "Petrik won't stop until you're dead. You saw the files as well as I. His victims are numerous. And if the queen refuses to see the truth, then we must deal with it. Her treaty with the president depends on *all* vampires obeying the word of this new law."

"But you guys just said vampires don't have laws."

"Times are changing. We do as our queen orders. Most of us, anyway. She has ordered a peace treaty with the humans, and Petrik has already disobeyed. Our queen is blinded by her affections for him. So, we must step up and rid the world of him."

"Gee, Drac, you almost sound altruistic," Camilla teased. "And here I thought you were just doing this for a hot piece of ass."

"Camilla," Vlad growled, his chest vibrating against me.

She waved a dismissive hand, then sat in the only free chair in the room. "If you guys are serious about this, then we need to establish a plan. One that's well thought out. I assume, since little miss human is here, that your plan is for her to set Petrik's house on fire?"

Vlad nodded.

My stomach twisted. This was my idea, but I hated the thought of putting Lucy's life at risk.

"Then we need a solid plan," Camilla continued. "Taking Petrik's age in consideration, he likely rises before dusk. How early, I can't say. But I think it's best to assume he'll be awake by late afternoon."

"Then whatever we do, it has to be before that."

"Midday is best," Vlad offered. "Based on my own sleep habits, it seems safe to assume that he can also remain conscious longer after sunrise too. The sun currently rises around six-thirty in the morning. To keep Lucy as safe as possible, I would suggest between eleven and one, when the sun is at its zenith."

"Oh, sure. Just go set a house on fire in the middle of the freaking day," Lucy grumbled. "It's not like I'll have other humans or police to worry about."

"You can't set his house on fire from the outside," Camilla said. "We must be smarter than that. Simply setting his place ablaze risks him surviving. Fire is a definitive way to kill us, but what if the fire doesn't reach his coffin before the authorities arrive and put out the flames? You will need to enter his house and start with the coffin."

"You're freaking kidding me, right?" Lucy shot the three of us a terrified stare. "You want me to enter Petrik's house, alone, and set his coffin on fire, then escape before I, myself, burn to death?"

"And what about servants?" I asked. "This place, as an example, is never quiet. Vlad has a human harem."

"Petrik doesn't," Camilla informed us. "I've been inquiring about his living arrangements since we put him under surveillance. It seems our boy prefers hunting for his meal."

"Evidenced by my neck," I groused.

Camilla inclined her head. "If my information is accurate, he lives alone, and much like us, his coffin is kept in the boarded-up attic. He leaves upon waking to track down a meal, then spends the rest of the night at The Vampire Lounge or getting his jollies off at Fallen."

I shuddered. That was one night club I'd never go back to.

"So, if Lucy can sneak into his place, she could, in theory, be able to open his coffin, set him on fire, and escape before the flames spread."

"That would be the ideal plan." Camilla rose and stretched out her shoulders. "Things rarely go as planned, though."

"Then what do you suggest?" Vlad asked.

"I don't believe Lucy should go alone."

"Agreed." Vlad's arms tightened around my waist. "Who do you have in mind?"

"Now, hear me out before saying no."

"Oh, I look forward to this."

"I think it'd be wise to send her in with Samuel."

I felt Vlad tense even before the stern "No" left his lips.

Camilla spun in the chair and glared at Vlad, her arms once again crossed over her chest. A power pose, if ever I saw one. She clucked her tongue and rolled her eyes. "You and I both know that Lucy will need some muscle in there. But more than that, Samuel will help her find Petrik's coffin faster. And he'll be able to help steer her clear of any human authorities."

"I'm sorry." I lifted my hand. "Who's Samuel?"

Vlad cursed under his breath, and I startled. It was the first time I'd heard him swear.

"Samuel is the brother to one of *my* harem members," Camilla told me. "Dear ole Drac here doesn't like him, because he's a—"

"His nature has nothing to do with why I dislike him," Vlad snapped.

I stepped out of Vlad's embrace and tiptoed toward Lucy. If a fight was about to break out, I really wanted nothing to do with it. Nor did I want to be near either of them when the shit hit the fan.

"Vlad, you need to get over this—"

"He *urinated* on my coffin, Camilla!"

I bit back a sudden laugh. "I'm sorry, he what?"

Camilla sighed. "What do you expect? He's a—"

"I expect your guests to be better trained than that."

"Better trained? He's not a damn house dog!"

Vlad held up his hands as though to say *well*? "It wasn't just my coffin, Camilla. He also relieved himself in Harold's quarters. Not to mention his hair. It took the cleaners months to get it all up. He sheds more than any mutt I've ever met."

"He was younger then, Vlad. Come on. You can't hold those transgressions against him."

"Can't I?"

I shot Lucy a startled glance. "Do you think we're talking about an actual dog here?"

"I have *absolutely* no idea, but I'm freaking riveted right now. Want to take bets?"

"Pomeranian," I said. "Twenty bucks."

"No way. Not if he's shedding that much. My money's on Bernese Mountain Dog."

Vlad unleashed a glare on us, and I pantomimed zipping my lips. No need to anger my sweet Count any more than necessary.

"Look, you won't even know he's here. He'll meet Lucy during the day, and they'll leave together for Petrik's."

"He's coming to me?" Lucy whispered. "Must be well-trained. Wonder if I'll need a leash."

"Dunno. Maybe a muzzle, just to be safe?"

"For crying out loud, he's not a dog!" Camilla barked. "Samuel is a werewolf. And Drac here is a little... prejudiced against the shifter-kind."

"Not even close," Vlad muttered. "Just him."

I couldn't say I blamed him. I couldn't imagine befriending someone who'd peed on my coffin. I burst out laughing the second a new thought crossed my mind. "He was marking his territory."

"What?" Lucy asked.

"He's a werewolf. In a vampire house. He was marking his territory."

Vlad's stony expression darkened. Apparently, he didn't see the humor like I did.

I cleared my throat and wiped the smile from my face. Guess this was all a sensitive topic for Vlad. "Honestly, I would prefer someone go with Lucy. And who better than a werewolf? I assume he's preternaturally strong like us? And quick? He does more than pee and shed hair, right?"

Lucy pressed her lips together to keep from laughing.

"Yes," Camilla said, clearly exasperated with our antics. "He'll keep your darling best friend safe and help her handle the job."

"Then I'm all for it." I commented, unleashing upon Vlad what my mother had always called "those darn puppy eyes."

It seemed he wasn't immune to them either. He worked out his jaw, then grumbled a harsh, "Fine. Take the damn werewolf with you. But don't blame me if he starts humping Lucy's leg."

I lost the battle and started laughing. "Could you imagine? Lucy trying to beat him off with a rolled-up newspaper!"

"Hey! Different expression, please." Though, even Lucy was laughing. "I'm not beating anybody off with anything. Especially not some wolfman."

"Werewolf," Camilla corrected.

"What's the difference?" Lucy asked.

"Absolutely nothing." Vlad shook his head. "When should we do this?"

I flicked a glance between Camilla and Lucy. Really, the plan hinged on the two of them. One had to fetch this Samuel—and yes, I giggled at the word fetch—and the other had to start the fire.

"Immediately," Camilla said. "The sooner, the better. The last thing we need is for Petrik to catch wind of our plan somehow."

"Agreed. This afternoon." Vlad' s jaw tightened. "Is that enough time to send for Samuel?"

"Plenty."

"Wait, so soon?" Lucy whispered. "I mean... that's *soon*, guys. I've never murdered someone before, you know? Can't I have a few days?"

Camilla, Vlad, and I all shared a glance. This entire plan hinged on Lucy. I suppose we could just send in Samuel, but I didn't like the idea of resting my future on a stranger's shoulders. Especially one known for peeing on vampire coffins. Still, I wouldn't force Lucy to do anything she wasn't comfortable with.

"We can wait a few days," Camilla hedged. "But the risk factor increases."

"No one here is going to go blabbing about our plan, right?"

"Right. But he could leave town. He could murder another woman. He could somehow learn about our plan. There are many uncontrollable factors at play."

Lucy took a deep breath, then bent in half and rested her head against her knees. I could hear her pulse thrumming away like a hummingbird's. I'd seen this once before, when she'd tried to ask her crush to prom. Poor thing nearly had a panic attack right in the middle of the hallway. Only my quick thinking had saved her from reliving that embarrassing moment for the rest of her life.

I crossed the room and took her hands, softly telling her to count to three. Lucy wasn't the impulsive one in our relationship, so this had to be difficult for her. Everything had to be planned with the utmost care before she willingly jumped into anything.

"We can take some time—"

"No," she rasped. "Camilla is right. The longer we wait, the greater the risk that Petrik finds out. She's right. We need to strike while the iron is hot. We know where he's staying in the city."

"Luce, you don't need to do this—"

"Who else will?" She gripped my hands so hard. "The wolfman? Do you trust him?"

I didn't answer. Her question was rhetorical anyway.

"I can do this." She sucked in a shuddering breath and rose to her full height. "I won't be alone, right?"

"Right."

"And this will save your life?"

"You are correct, my lady."

A tiny grin cracked through her panicked exterior, exactly as I'd hoped. "Then let's do this."

"You're sure?"

She blew out a trembling breath. "Not even remotely. Think I can handle a thousand-year-old vampire?"

"Girl, you can handle anything."

"Okay. Summon the wolfman."

"Samuel," Camilla said, sighing.

"Him too."

"Thank you, Lucy," Vlad said. "I wish there was more I could do, but alas, we vampires are all slaves to the sun."

"I get it. I'd do anything for my sista here, and she knows it. But don't think I'm not gonna be calling in a million favors once this is finished."

I chuckled. "A million and one, just cuz I love you."

Camilla and Vlad excused themselves to finalize the plan and call the wolfman. Vlad brushed a light kiss against my cheek, patted Lucy's shoulder, then left.

Once alone, Lucy and I dissolved into nervous giggles.

"The wolfman? Seriously?" Lucy stage-whispered.

"You're not even a dog person at the best of times."

"I like dogs," she said with a shrug. "Just not enough to own one. Or care for one. They're so much work. Plus, I'm allergic, so that sorta puts a damper on the whole cute, loveable part. It's hard to like something when you're practically dying whenever you get near one."

I bit my lip to keep from laughing. I'd seen Lucy's allergic reactions to dogs, and it wasn't pretty. Gasping, coughing, sneezing, hives... the whole kit and caboodle. Hopefully, this Samuel didn't set her off. I couldn't imagine how difficult it would be to set Petrik on fire while snotting and weeping all over herself. But what a sight.

I choked down a laugh, the sound coming out more like a snort. "This is a disaster waiting to happen."

"Tell me about it." She groaned and palmed her face. "It's a million and *two* favors now."

Slinging my arm over her shoulder, I pulled her into my chest and ruffled her hair. "Girl, you do this for me, and you can have as many favors as you want."

"I'm gonna hold you to that."

TWENTY-TWO

WITH TWO HOURS UNTIL BEDTIME, my energy was waning. I hadn't noticed it when I first woke as a vampire, but I was keenly aware of it now. An awareness I possessed that told me the sun was on the rise. It was like I possessed this internal clock tasked with reminding me every few minutes that my daily death approached.

Such a strange feeling.

Thankfully, the rest of the night had gone by peacefully enough. Lucy had gone to bed around two a.m., determined to get a good night's sleep before she went a-murdering in the morning. Camilla had gone to fetch Samuel. Eli was off sulking in his room or something—honestly, I didn't care what he was doing. Vlad had retreated to his office. Rebecca was reading in the sitting room. And Breccan... well, he was off engaging in a little hanky-panky with one of the harem members.

And boy, was I glad Vlad insisted we wait to consummate our relationship. I'd overheard people having sex before. It's inevitable these days. But *nothing* compared to the sounds my vampire ears now picked up. The squishing, the moaning and grunting, the skin slapping... ugh. I'd snuck into Lucy's room and stolen her headphones just to block out the sounds of Breccan feasting on his human companion. One, because it was embarrassing to listen to. And two, because it was turning me on just a little. No way in hell could I have sex with Vlad though, knowing *everyone* was listening. Sure, I sometimes watched porn, but this was a whole new level of voyeurism I wasn't interested in. I wanted Vlad's and my first time to stay between us. It seemed Breccan didn't share the same opinion.

I rose from the couch I'd been relaxing on for the last couple of hours and stretched. The book I'd been trying to read lay discarded on the cushion. Knowing what we had planned for the day had made it hard to unwind. I kept imagining all the many ways things could go wrong. What if Lucy somehow got caught in the flames? What if Samuel failed to protect her? What if Petrik somehow woke during the day—an impossible feat, I know. But it didn't stop the fears from pestering me all night long. Lucy meant the world to me. I couldn't lose her. More than once, I'd had to stop myself from storming off to Vlad's office and insisting we put a stop to this plan.

Instead, I reminded myself of a few facts. One: Petrik would be dead to the world in his coffin. Two: Lucy wouldn't be alone. Three: She could accomplish anything she put her mind to.

In a few hours, I would go to sleep. And when I woke, it would be to a new world. One where Petrik was dead, I was free, and Lucy and I could return home.

Home.

Another thought that made me anxious. At this rate, I'd need to invent some sort of antacid for vampires. The idea of returning to Perish and seeing my family nearly gave me hives. The rest of Perish, I could handle. Hell, I'd just bite them if they pissed me off. But my family? That was a whole other hornet's nest.

I still hadn't spoken to my father, and my mother continued to refuse my calls. For all I knew, they straight up considered me dead. Maybe going home would help them see nothing had changed—other than my strictly liquid diet and new nighttime schedule. Or maybe my return would inspire a mob armed with pitchforks and fire.

The sound of Vlad's front door opening broke that train of thought.

"Please behave yourself," I heard Camilla whisper. "Vlad is stressed enough as it is without adding any of your werewolf antics into the mix."

Someone grunted a nonverbal response.

Could this be him? The infamous Samuel of the coffin-urination? I chuckled and strode toward them. But the second I turned the corner and spotted them, I froze.

"Holy shit," I murmured under my breath.

I wasn't sure what I'd expected.

Half man, half hairy beast? The way Vlad and Camilla had spoken about Samuel, I'd pictured some monstrous caricature of the Wolfman. Something more akin to the old movies. A beast lumbering around on awkwardly bent hindquarters with a face the shape of a wolf.

But this....

I whistled appreciatively.

Samuel was all man. And I mean *all* man. My gaze started at his feet and tracked up his six-foot five-ish height. The dude was massive, and his stacked muscles seemed to take up the entire entryway. He was like a giant lumberjack, especially considering he wore a plaid shirt—which, I shit you not, *strained* against his biceps—and dark, crisp jeans. When I finally made it to his face, I sucked in a sharp breath. The guy was beauty defined. And that was strange to think, considering he was male. But everything about him screamed *perfection*, right down to his piercing amber eyes.

If I wasn't taken, and happily so, I might have wondered if I could get a piece of that action.

"Who's this?" Samuel demanded, his voice deep like a wolf's growl.

"Anna," Camilla said. "Vlad's new paramour."

No one could blame me for being mildly gobsmacked. I hadn't seen a man this attractive since... well, ever. Don't get me wrong—I had zero interest in Wolf Boy here. And Vlad was downright luscious. But a girl could appreciate good art, right?

Samuel arched a dark eyebrow and raked me over with a scathing glare. "Really. Someone actually warmed up to Count Deadula?"

I tried not to laugh, but my lips twitched in response. Samuel's glare eased when he caught me stifling a chuckle, as though he realized I might not be the stuffed-up vamp he'd imagined.

"It's nice to meet you, Samuel." I offered my hand.

He slowly reached out, his giant, meaty hand engulfing mine entirely. "Sam."

"Sam."

I made sure to immediately release his hand. "Thank you for coming and for helping us with this."

His mouth cracked into a smile, and I damn near fainted. "Any time. Since you're a fanger, I assume you're not the one I'm escorting into the demon's den?"

"No. You'll be escorting Lucy. My best friend."

His head bobbed, and he took to studying his surroundings as though recommitting the place to memory. "Human?"

"Yup. And... uh..." I didn't know how to approach this. "She's..." I flicked Camilla a glance, then decided, *fuck it, just say it*. "Look, she's allergic to dogs. I don't mean any insult by this. I just want to make sure that you're not gonna set her off or something. We need this to all go down without a hitch."

Sam's brows shot up into his hairline. "Did you just call me a dog?"

"What? No!" I sputtered. Shit, this was awkward. "I just mean"— I cleared my throat—"ah, fuck. Look, Vlad mentioned that last time you were shedding all over the house, and Lucy is allergic to dogs. Well, fur. *Their* fur."

Camilla rubbed her brow and exhaled.

Sam crossed his arms over his chest. His massively manly chest. And holy crickets, I think those biceps were literally winking at me.

"The last time I was here, I was in wolf form," Sam commented. "I assure you, I don't shed while in human form."

"Right. Right. Sorry. I'll just...."

Footsteps approached. I glanced back and spotted Vlad approaching. He cocked his head and studied me, clearly confused by the sight of my flushed cheeks. I cleared my throat and stepped back. Thankfully, my fluster was from the things I'd said and not a reaction to his looks.

Vlad came to a stop next to me and eyed Sam. "Good to see you again."

Sam's mouth slipped to the side, but he didn't respond. Definitely no love lost between these two.

"Lucy's asleep," I informed the group, even though no one asked. Anything to cut through the awkward tension. "I could wake her if you want."

"Let her rest," Vlad said. "Camilla and I can go through the plan with Samuel. It won't take long."

No, it wouldn't. It was a rather simple plan when it came down to it. Break in, find Petrik's coffin, set him on fire, escape. All without dying or leaving any evidence behind that might harm Lucy in the future.

Cripes, I really did hate this. I hated that I had to rely on Lucy for this. She was just a human, for crying out loud. If the queen caught wind of this, she'd kill us *all*. Including Lucy. I needed to make sure that never happened. Lucy was the most important person to me.

My gaze shot to Vlad. Make that second most important. Tied for first? I couldn't decide. I just knew that if anyone ever tried to harm Vlad or Lucy, my face would be the last thing they saw—including the precious queen.

I turned back to Sam, my face wiped clean of all humor. "She set her alarm for eight a.m. She needs a good night's sleep before this, since she's been working on our schedule. Once she's awake, meet her in the kitchen, and I'll leave a note telling her where she can find you."

Sam nodded. He lifted his head and sniffed the air, his nostrils flaring. "I have her scent. I'll be able to find her wherever she is now."

Did that sound ominous to anyone else? And how the hell did he know which scent was hers? The house was full of stinky people. Believe me, I knew. "In the house, you mean?"

"Sure."

Before I could dig a little deeper, Vlad and Camilla led Sam into the office. Seconds later, the music cranked on, and I knew they'd entered secretive planning mode part *deux*. At least I didn't need to attend this one. Thanks to my extreme aversion to sunlight, I couldn't even be involved in the process. My idea, but I couldn't execute it, and I really hated that.

Sighing, I climbed the stairs to the second floor and started toward my bathroom. Maybe a warm shower would help soothe my nerves before settling in my coffin for the day.

After all this, Vlad and I really needed to investigate alternatives. I hated sleeping in the attic. Made me feel like some monster from a creature feature. Over the past two weeks, I'd researched UV Protection windows. So far, they claimed only to block ninety-nine percent. But maybe with the new interest in vampires, someone could look into inventing full protection windows. I hadn't had a chance to discuss it with Vlad, but that didn't keep it from percolating in the back of my mind.

"Anna."

I paused at the sound of my name and turned to find Eli in one of the guest rooms. He stood out on the room's balcony, a cigarette dangling from his lips. I'd never seen a vampire smoke before. Not that I'd met many yet.

I gave him a small nod, about to keep moving, when he waved me over. "I'd like to speak with you for a moment, if that's all right?"

I didn't hold back my sigh. Eli was exhausting at the best of times. I honestly had no idea what Vlad saw in him. The man constantly complained about his circumstances and made idle threats. Yet, he'd stuck around for the past two weeks to help protect me. The dude was a walking enigma.

"It won't take long. I just wanted to apologize."

Oh? Interesting.

I stepped into his room and spared a quick glance. His room was neater than mine, but then again, Lucy was bunking in mine. She'd done a lot of shopping over the past few weeks to supply us with everything we needed. Needless to say, my room was bursting at the seams with a new wardrobe for each of us.

Eli turned and gave me his back, leaning his elbows against the balcony railing. Mine didn't have a balcony. But it also didn't have this view. Vlad's land was spectacular. Even from here, I could see the surrounding swampland and wildlife. The world seemed so quiet right now, on the cusp of dawn, but that didn't stop me from taking it all in.

I came to a stop next to Eli and cocked my hip against the railing.

"Did Vlad ever tell you how we came to meet?"

"No."

Eli tapped his cigarette, knocking the ashes to the balcony floor. I couldn't imagine Vlad would like that, but I managed to keep my mouth shut for once.

"I fought for the Union Army, way back in the day. It seemed the thing to do back then." Eli shot me another glance as though to gauge my reaction.

I kept a blank face, even though inside, I grew excited. The one upside to being a vampire was having access to all these real-life historical figures.

"Unfortunately, I never saw the end of the war. At least, not as a human. I'll never forget that night. We thought the enemy was advancing, launching an attack on us. We heard the screams. But before we could retaliate, this *thing* swept in and massacred my unit." Eli dropped his cigarette butt to the ground and scuffed it out with his boot. "It wasn't until I lay bleeding to death that I realized it wasn't the Confederates, but a monster. Vampires back then took advantage of a good war to gorge themselves. The deaths were simply blamed on an enemy attack. I think he meant to leave us there, but just as he was leaving, I must have made a sound. He came back and stared down at me. I'll never forget the look in his eyes. At the time, I thought he was the devil coming to drag me to hell. He was leaning over me when another vampire appeared and, right before my eyes, tore off the first vampire's head. I doubt you've ever seen a decapitation, but it's messy. Quite a bit of his blood found its way into my mouth."

"And the other vampire was Vlad?" I asked, horrified.

"Good ole Drac. Never could resist a little decapitation. Nicest guy in the world, salt of the earth. But if you piss him off, he sheds that gentlemanly façade of his and unleashes the monster within. He's not Vlad Tepes, but our Vlad is hardly innocent. The longer you live as a vampire, the more you'll start to become one of us.

"Drac didn't realize what'd happened to me. He was simply disposing of a problem. The vampire who'd tried to kill me had been raiding up and down the front lines, massacring any human he could sink his teeth into. Vlad took him out and left."

A dark avenging angel.

"So, I became a vampire. Sired by a murderous monster. The first few months were the worst. I couldn't control myself. Without someone to teach me how to properly feed, I turned into the same monster as the one whose blood made me. I eventually gained control and learned how to hunt discreetly."

"I'm glad to hear it," I said.

"I ran into Vlad a few times over the next century or so. I eventually confessed to him how I knew him. Told him about that night. Vlad was horrified. It wasn't Vlad's blood that sired me, but his actions caused it. He told me all that he knew about my so-called sire, then invited me to live with him. I turned down his offer. I'd already learned how to be a vampire and had my own life. But from that moment on, we stayed in touch, coming to each other's aid whenever needed."

"Including now," I whispered.

Eli canted his head and stared at me in the darkness. "Vlad's never shown any romantic interest in anyone, vampire or human."

"Were you in love with him?" I asked, wondering if his dislike of me came from jealousy.

Eli chuckled. "Not even remotely. Our relationship is platonic. But I was curious about you when he came to ask me for help. Who was this woman who'd stolen Vlad's heart? And what do I find but an annoying newborn vampire hellbent on getting us all killed."

I sucked in a sharp breath. "What?"

"I've known Vlad longer than you ever will. I'm his friend and ally. Which means sometimes doing things your friend can't stomach. When it comes to you, he's like any other man in love. He's blind, made weak by you. He's made choices that could end his life. And I won't let that happen."

This was not the direction I expected this conversation to go. "I thought you wanted to apologize?"

"Oh, I do. But not for anything I've said."

"Then what the hell do you want to apologize for?"

Eli stepped back, kicked the extinguished cigarette butt off the balcony, then stared blankly at me. "This."

A loud thump resounded behind me. I whirled around and gasped at the sight of Petrik looming over me, his back blocking the moonlight behind him. I opened my mouth to scream, but Eli's arms came around me, his hand clapping over my mouth and smothering the sound.

Oh hell no!

This wasn't happening!

After all the training, all the preparing, I couldn't let *this* be how Petrik won.

I squirmed against Eli in a mad struggle to free myself, but the man's arms were like steel vices. I couldn't so much as budge. Camilla's training was proving useless! How could I defend myself if I couldn't even move? Eli was like some ridiculously strong boa constrictor, choking the damn life out of me.

"I will not let Vlad take the fall for your stupidity," Eli hissed in my ear. "Vlad never should have saved you that night. So, I'm going to fix this problem for him. Once Petrik's finished with you, you'll be nothing more than a stain on Vlad's memory."

My muffled scream barely carried across the balcony. I fought against Eli's hold, stomped his feet, kicked his shins, anything and everything I could think to break his hold. Nothing worked. Eli's cold grip held me hostage.

Petrik closed the distance between us, his icy gaze staring down at me. He lifted a hand and brought a lock of my hair to his nose. "I've been looking forward to this, little one."

Well, he could just keep waiting, because no way in hell would I let this happen.

I stilled my body, even held my breath. Eli probably didn't realize it, but his body instinctively responded by slightly relaxing.

It was now or never.

I wrenched my head to the side, freeing my mouth from Eli's palm. The second his fingers slid across my lips, I *bit*. My fangs tore into his fingers, and like a crazed dog, I shook my head, ripping through his flesh and muscle while his blood gushed into my mouth.

Eli sucked in a sharp breath, but not once did he cry out. Instead, he shoved me toward Petrik. I dug my heels into the balcony, then used what little momentum I'd gained to snap my head back. Pain bloomed across the back of my skull the instant I connected with Eli's chin, but it was enough to daze him.

With a sneer, I whirled around and implemented Camilla's first lesson of defense.

I grabbed Eli's face and shoved my thumbs into his eye sockets.

This time, he *screamed*. I grinned triumphantly. That scream was all I needed. Vlad would hear it and know something had gone terribly wrong. Unfortunately, I wasn't the only one who realized that.

The second Eli screamed, something hard smashed into the base of my skull, and I tumbled headlong into darkness.

TWENTY-THREE

Consciousness slammed into me with the force of a bus. My eyes snapped open, and I scrambled to my feet, absolutely terrified of what I might find. Last I remembered, Eli had betrayed me. Us. Everyone. And Petrik—oh, holy guacamole, Petrik.

Eli must have planned it all. He couldn't give Petrik permission to enter the house, so he'd stood on the balcony and waited for the perfect opportunity. Once he'd found me alone and lured me outside, kaboom, perfect opportunity.

For fuck's sake, I was going to kill him if Vlad hadn't already.

With a deep, unnecessary breath, I took in my surroundings.

Four concrete walls surrounded me, and two of those walls had windows. Windows that were starting to let in daylight.

"Oh, fuck," I whimpered and darted to the farthest corner, hiding in the weakening shadows.

I had no way of knowing how long I'd been unconscious, but considering I could see the darkness fading to the light, I could guess it'd been long enough.

Where the hell had Petrik taken me? What was this room? Where was Vlad and everyone else? Did Petrik kill them after knocking me out?

Panic spread through my limbs until they tingled.

"Okay, okay, calm down," I whispered to myself. Petrik wouldn't have been able to kill everyone in the house, right? Vlad and the others were younger, but surely four vampires could hold against one ancient one. I hoped. I *prayed*.

I couldn't lose Vlad, couldn't face an eternity of darkness without him.

No. I needed to focus on something else. Think rationally. Like how the hell I was going to get out of here before the sun turned me into fried vampire wings.

Petrik wanted me. Not Vlad. I had to believe they were safe—it was the only thing that would keep me sane through this.

And even worse. I *had* to stay awake.

I wasn't even sure if that could be done. Vlad had once mentioned that vampires could remain awake when under duress, but could I do that? I was a month old, barely out of my training fangs. The only thing I knew was that once that sun rose, I was out like a light. If I allowed that to happen today, I'd never again wake up.

"Thought you might like it here."

My head snapped up with a gasp to find Petrik standing across the room, cloaked in shadows. Had he been there this whole time, watching me? My flesh pebbled into goose bumps. "What are you doing? Why am I here?"

"To enjoy one last sunrise," he said, pointing to the windows. "It'll be your last, of course, but I thought you might appreciate it."

"Why the hell would you think that?"

Petrik stepped out of the shadows with a nasty grin. "You were never meant to be one of us, Anna. Everyone knows that. It was sheer dumb luck that led Vlad to you."

"It was fate," I argued, shocked by my own words.

"Fate." Petrik tipped his head back and laughed. "Yes, I suppose the boy would believe that. He's always been a romantic, that one."

Vlad *did* have a romantic side to him, but right now, I needed his strength. I needed *him*.

"Did you kill him?" I demanded, forcing my voice out strong and steady.

"Does it matter? You won't be leaving this little place of mine. You'll remain here as a pile of ash for all eternity. I like it. The one who escaped my clutches, trapped with me forever."

Holy shit. He was downright insane.

"The queen has hair like yours, you know," Petrik mused as he stepped toward me. "Beautiful blonde hair. But her eyes are blue. Like ice. Like mine. Perhaps that's the reason I chose to take her as one of my children instead of ending her."

I shuddered and pressed my back against the wall.

The room brightened another degree. Dawn was approaching, and my eyes grew leaden with sleep. It was becoming difficult to keep them open. To stay focused. But I couldn't give in. If I slept, the sun's rays would sweep over me and reduce me to nothing.

"You, my little bird, are nothing like the queen, though. Where she is cordial and intelligent, you're brazen and ignorant. But you amuse me. Who would have thought you'd attract the attention of the famous Dracula?"

"If you're going to kill me, just do it," I snapped. "I'm tired of your voice."

"A shame," Petrik said, laughing. "For I dearly love the sound of it."

"Not surprising."

Petrik closed the distance between us in four strides. He grabbed my shoulders and slammed me up against the wall, rattling my brain. "Would you prefer to make this a little more exciting? I suppose I don't need you alive to watch you burn. Your corpse will do just fine."

I stared into his monstrous face and squared my jaw. The only thing that mattered was proving he *didn't* scare me. Not anymore. Funny how facing your worst fears helps purge you of them.

I lifted my chin and sneered. "Get *out* of my face."

Petrik's eyes widened a fraction, as though surprised by my confidence. Gone was the woman who'd cowered before him, who'd hidden behind Vlad rather than face him. I refused to give him the satisfaction.

As much as I wanted to lash out and strike him, I didn't. I remembered John's warnings, that I was nothing more than a nuisance to one as powerful as Petrik. Striking him would accomplish nothing except getting my ass handed to me. Surely he'd soon leave, and then I'd find a way to escape. Even if it meant running out into the sun myself. I could smell trees in the near distance. Maybe they could provide cover before I burned away. Or maybe I could bury myself in the earth. So long as the sun didn't touch me, I'd be fine.

"This chamber of mine won't kill you," Petrik finally said. "There's space enough to move around and avoid the sun. Provided you can stay awake, of course."

So, he meant to torture me, then.

"Vampires *can* stay awake, you know," he continued. "I've never known a newborn capable of such a feat, but it can be done. We give ourselves to the darkness every morning. But that's because it's expected of us. I haven't been a slave to the sun for centuries now. As long as I keep out of direct sunlight, I can remain awake during the day."

"That's impossible," I whispered.

"Why? Because your precious Dracula told you so? He may be famous, but he doesn't know everything. With power comes great opportunity."

"And what about your queen?" I asked, grasping at straws. "What are you going to do when she decides your behavior has become a hindrance to her?"

"My sweet Genevieve would never harm me. She knows who I am better than anyone else. As long as she rules, I have my freedom." He released me and eased back into the shadows. "I think I'll stay. To see if you survive the sun."

It wasn't the worst thing he could do to me, so I took some relief in that. But the thought of being enclosed with him in this tight space for the next few hours didn't appeal to me. I couldn't think with him nearby. Couldn't plan an escape. Not that I even had a lick of an idea. The only way out was the door, and to reach the door, I had to get through Petrik.

"In case you haven't realized, no one will be coming for you," Petrik unceremoniously announced. "Your vampire friends are all crawling into bed right about now. Poor Vlad. I can only imagine how devastated he must be, staring at your empty coffin."

Relief washed through me. Vlad was alive, then. Knowing that bolstered my resilience.

My vision had grayed around the edges, but I had to keep fighting. This was the time of day when I tucked myself in and slept. If I succumbed to that need, I had a feeling Petrik would leave me exactly where I fell and let the sun take me.

I pressed my back against the wall and slid to the ground, tucking my knees into my chest. The first ray of sunlight eased into the room. I whimpered at the sight. Minute by minute, it crept across the floor, heading toward my feet. I had no way of knowing how long it would take to reach me. Not long enough, though.

What felt like an eternity later, my head started to droop.

No. Stay awake. Don't fall asleep. You'll die.

The sun touched the tip of my toes, and pain instantly shot through my body. My head snapped back up, and I screamed myself awake, tucking myself farther into the corner. Light bled through the entire cement room. Everywhere I looked, it spread. Petrik stood in the only remaining darkened corner.

What was his plan here? He couldn't leave the room and walk out into the light—it'd kill him. But there was nowhere in the room for him to hide. Did he intend to remain here all day, awake and watching?

Fire blazed across my feet, and I cried out in pain. The sunlight was like a cancerous cell, spreading, reaching. And it burned everywhere it touched. The scent of charred skin assaulted my nose, and I watched in horror as I started to burn. I couldn't move, though. Exhaustion had me trapped in the corner, pinned like a butterfly. I wanted to duck the sun's beams, run to the darkest corner of the room and sob, but I couldn't muster the strength.

"Ah," Petrik spoke. "Finally."

"Fuck you," I rasped, then screamed when the rays reached my ankles. It wouldn't be much longer now.

Petrik stepped out of the shadows and watched me with such intensity. It wasn't until that moment that I realized he was *enjoying* watching the sun torture me.

The sunbeam rose to my shins, and I moaned. The pain was damn near unbearable. I'd never felt anything like it. I had to move. *So move! Don't give in!* I turned and clawed at the wall, using it for leverage as I dragged my battered body across the floor. Every inch was pure agony, but I couldn't give up. Not yet.

I'd barely escaped the sun's rays when something massive slammed into the chamber door.

My head slowly rose, my energy depleted, but I managed to catch sight of the door bursting open, practically exploding at the seams. Fresh sunlight poured into the room, and I screamed when it washed over my hands.

Lucy and Samuel came barging into the room. Sam didn't even bat an eye before he lifted his arm and pointed something black and shiny at Petrik. I heard a soft puff of air and marveled at the sound of Petrik's immediate anguished scream.

He dropped to his knees, clutching at what looked like a massive chunk of wood protruding from his chest.

"What about stakes?" I heard my voice echo in my head, closely followed by Vlad's. *"Regretfully, quite effective at killing us."*

There was nothing regretful about this. I only hoped a single stake would be enough to take Petrik down. He was a thousand years old, after all.

Sam rushed forward, punched Petrik in the face, then slammed him to the ground and straddled his chest. Petrik barely twitched, his hands gripping the stake as though afraid to move it. Without hesitation, Sam unsheathed what looked like a machete from his side and pressed it against Petrik's throat.

"Wait!" I rasped.

Both Sam and Lucy both turned, and Lucy cried out the second she spotted me. She bolted to my side and ripped off her jacket before laying it across my back. It wouldn't guard against the sun, but I appreciated her efforts.

"Blood," I panted. "I need blood."

Sam shook his head. "Too risky."

My mouth felt drier than the Sahara Desert, and my throat had practically shriveled from thirst. I needed blood *now* if I was to survive this.

"Lucy," I moaned.

Her hands hovering above me as though afraid to touch me. I must have looked quite the sight.

"Ohmigod, ohmigod, Anna, what do I do? Take my blood!"

I shook my head, then gestured weakly to Petrik. I didn't trust myself to feed on her. Thirst blazed down my throat, and I knew I'd kill her if I so much as laid a fang on her.

"Okay, this might hurt. Just bear with me."

Her hands slipped under my arms, and she heaved my weight across the room. I bit down to keep from screaming. Once back in the shadows, my body relaxed, which brought about a new torment. My charred flesh didn't appreciate my slackening muscles. But I locked it all inside and kept quiet.

Lucy brought me to Petrik and eased me down on my back next to him. I could barely move, but I caught sight of his pale face. His eyes were closed, his mouth slack. By all appearances, he looked as dead as any other dead man. All from a stake?

I coughed, blowing up a puff of dust from the floor. "Is he gone?"

"Almost." Sam gripped the stake tighter. "The stake is made of hawthorn and was treated in holy water and monksblood—werewolf secret, so don't tell anyone. It will keep him restrained until I take his head. Just as a precaution."

I didn't nod for fear of my brain imploding. "Blood."

"Anna, he's ancient," Lucy warned me.

Right now, I didn't care. Someone needed to open a vein for me. Human, werewolf, or vampire, take a pick. I had no way of knowing what werewolf blood would do to me, and I couldn't risk draining Lucy. I didn't want to be gentle right now. I couldn't submit her to that.

So, with claw-shaped fingers, I grabbed Petrik's wrist and brought it to my mouth. I chomped into him with absolutely no manners, my teeth ripping through flesh and sinew. His blood poured into my mouth, and it took every last drop of strength remaining to swallow. I could hear the excess spilling out of my mouth and splashing on the floor, but it didn't matter.

Cool relief spread through my body, and my skin began knitting itself back together. Of all the blood in the room, Petrik's by far was the most powerful, and it healed me with every gulp.

But what else would it do to me?

Vlad had mentioned the repercussions of drinking ancient blood. The madness, the exponential power growth. Right now, I couldn't stop to consider the ramifications. I just knew I needed blood to heal.

"Enough," Sam barked.

I didn't let go.

"Anna," Lucy whispered. "Stop. You need to stop!"

Her panicked voice seemed to wake something in me, and I managed to release Petrik's mangled wrist.

Though still utterly exhausted, I managed to glance down at my legs to find my skin flush and pink. No injuries remained. Hallelujah. Now if we could get me somewhere safe, I could sleep.

"Look away," Sam ordered.

At first, I thought he meant me, then I realized he was speaking to Lucy. My head lolled against the cement floor, and I watched as Sam beheaded the bastard who'd tried to kill me. His head detached from his body with ease, *thwomp, thwomp, thwomping* as it rolled across the floor.

"Good riddance," I mumbled, barely able to get my lips to work.

"Anna, are you okay?" Lucy asked, leaning over me.

I stared up into her face but couldn't answer. Instead, I closed my eyes and let the darkness take me.

CHAPTER
TWENTY-FOUR

By some miracle, I woke.

Darkness surrounded me, so I gave a relieved sigh and took inventory of my body. For someone who had been left out in the sun, I felt... well, good. Better than good. Hell, I felt amazing. Powerful. I probably shouldn't have munched on Petrik, but in all fairness, the asshat deserved it. I knew the Bible was all *forgive and forget*, but that would never happen.

I knew from the comfort beneath me that I was in my coffin. Lucy and Sam must have somehow managed to bring me home. I'd need to ask about that, considering the whole sun dilemma. Either way, though, I was home and alive. Ish.

Placing my palms against my coffin lid, I pushed it back, then climbed out. No lingering pain, no weakness, no debilitation whatsoever. Huh. Maybe I needed to drink more ancient blood. It certainly seemed to do the trick. Like a spinach smoothie—chock full of all those nutrients and vitamins a growing vampire needed.

I stretched out my neck and shoulders, then headed for the attic door. Had I been looking, I might have noticed some oddities. Oddity number one: the attic's ambience was far brighter than normal.

Oddity number two: Vlad's coffin was still sealed. But I didn't notice either of these things until I climbed down from the attic and landed soundlessly on the floor.

Sunlight streamed in from *everywhere*.

I cried out and clutched at the attic ladder, about to dart back upstairs, when I noticed oddity number three: I wasn't screaming in pain.

A shuddering breath slipped past my lips, and I lifted my hand, studying it. Every window in the house was open, allowing fresh air to breathe through the house. Sunbeams scattered across the floor, creeping in from the windows themselves, though none had touched me yet.

What had Petrik said? That he hadn't needed to sleep during the day in centuries?

Was this because of his blood?

I crept forward, then dipped a trembling hand toward a pure sunbeam resting on the floor. The instant my digits dipped into the warmth, my flesh sizzled. I gasped and wrenched my hand back. Okay, so direct sunlight was still a no. But I was *awake*, in the middle of the day.

I brought my injured hand to my mouth and touched my lips.

Holy guacamole.

"Anna?"

I turned at the sound of Lucy's voice. Tears immediately welled in my eyes, and I rushed toward her, scooping her into a tight hug.

"Oof, woman. You're... really... strong," she wheezed.

"Sorry, sorry." I loosened my grip and rested my head on her shoulder. "Thank you so much for saving me. I don't know what I would have done without you."

It wasn't until I felt her body trembling that I realized she was crying. I pulled back and wiped her tears, then gave her a steady nod. "We're both okay and alive."

"Ish," she mumbled, uttering my favorite joke. "How are you awake?"

"Petrik's blood, I think. Vlad's told me multiple times that drinking ancient blood can bolster a newborn's power."

"He also said those vampires went insane, Anna!"

I cocked my head and pursed my lips. "I don't feel insane."

"That's what they all say. Betcha Petrik didn't think he was insane either."

We shared an awkward chuckle.

"Come on. Let's get you some blood," Lucy said.

I looped my arm through hers and followed her down the hallway, careful to avoid all direct sunlight.

"I'll see if we can get someone to close the windows."

"No, leave them open. Please."

She shot me a concerned look but eventually nodded.

The smell of the fresh air, heated by the sun, was a beautiful thing. I wanted to enjoy it for as long as possible.

Lucy sighed. "Vlad isn't going to like this."

"Yeah, but there isn't much I can do about it."

"How about you just stop drinking ancient blood for a while, 'kay?"

"So long as they stop trying to kill me, we're good."

Lucy chuckled.

"Care to fill me in on what happened after you and Sam saved me?"

She expelled a heavy breath, one that smelled of toothpaste. She must have just woken from a nap herself. Probably in preparation of spending the night awake with me. With my newfound resistance to the sun, maybe our schedule could return to normal. I might not be able to go outside, but at least I wouldn't be confined to my coffin all day now. And maybe sleep in a bed! So long as we blocked out all the rays.

"Once you passed out, Sam and I sat in that stupid crypt until nightfall. We couldn't risk moving you. I was worried that even the smallest amount of sunlight would set you on fire."

"You sat there all day?"

She raked her teeth over her bottom lip and nodded. "Then when the sun set and you didn't wake, Vlad immediately came to get you."

"Wait, I didn't wake up? How long have I been asleep?"

"A few days," she admitted. "It's been stressful on all of us. Especially Vlad. He hasn't moved from your side, waiting for you to wake up. He never admitted it, but I could see he was terrified. He mentioned once that you were taking too long to wake."

Holy shit. "I had no idea."

"Of course you didn't."

"Eli!" I suddenly shouted.

Lucy jumped at the sound of my voice and clutched a hand over her chest. "Shit, Anna. Scared the hell out of me."

"He betrayed us. He lured me out onto the balcony so Petrik could abduct me."

"Yeah, Vlad figured that out pretty damn fast. Eli tried claiming his injuries were from Petrik, but Vlad and I had been watching your training closely. Camilla taught you that... that disgusting attack in the beginning. Did you have to shove your thumbs in his eyes?"

"It worked, didn't it?"

"Only too well. Vlad said his eyes would heal—had Vlad let him live, that is."

"Eli's dead?"

"Ohhh yeah," Lucy muttered. "Vlad's... terrifying."

I frowned so hard my head started aching. "What do you mean?"

"Well, he may not be Vlad Tepes, but he took a page out of Tepes's book."

Oh, that didn't sound good at all. "What did he do?"

Lucy cupped her face and rubbed her temple. "He staked and decapitated the traitorous bastard, then stuck Eli's head on a pike out front for everyone to see what happens to those who betray him."

I whistled under my breath. Maybe a tad excessive, but considering Eli betrayed me, I really couldn't find it in me to care about his demise. I just hoped I didn't stumble across the head.

"He's been scary, Anna. Like, vampire scary. Angry. Violent.

Losing you almost broke him, I think. He absolutely lost it at the crypt once we told him what happened. Utterly destroyed the entire thing. He demolished the building with his bare hands."

I sucked in a sharp breath. That building had been made of cement.

"Are you sure he's the right guy for you?" Lucy asked. "He's dangerous, Anna."

"No more than any other guy. And yes, I know without a doubt that he's mine."

Her lips pressed into a grim slash, and she eyed me. I sensed a question hovering on the tip of her tongue.

"Spit it out."

"How do you know he's yours?" Her words rushed together. "How do you know you're meant to be together?"

I pondered her question as we strode into the kitchen. One of the harem members stood next to the fridge, a popsicle hanging between her lips. Her eyes widened the instant she spotted me. She blinked her surprise away, then darted over to me with her arm extended.

"Thirsty?"

"Thank you... Malinda, is it?"

"Yes, Countess."

"Oh, please don't call me that."

She squished her lips together and lifted her arm higher. I cradled her wrist gently, then slowly eased my fangs into her skin. Warm blood filled my mouth, but that was all it was. Warm fluids. Frowning, I extracted my teeth and stared at the two tiny puncture marks. Her blood was fine, but it just wasn't hitting the spot for me.

"What's wrong?" Lucy asked.

I shook my head, then returned to my meal. Her blood would suffice. Maybe it was because I'd just fed off Petrik. Perhaps I wasn't quite as thirsty as I'd thought.

After I'd had my fill, I drew back from Malinda and thanked her. She scurried away with a polite nod, the popsicle still dangling in her mouth.

"I know it deep down," I told Lucy, returning to her previous question about me and Vlad. "When I'm near him, I feel this connection. It's so strong."

"Could the connection exist because he's your sire?"

"No, it's far more intimate than that. I honestly can't explain it. It's just this knowledge I have. He's the *one* for me."

Lucy grimaced, then turned away.

"What's wrong? Do you not like him?"

"No, it's nothing like that." She waved a dismissive hand. "I was just hoping for a more useful answer."

"Useful? What do you mean?"

Lucy dug into the drawers and pulled out a bag of Cheetos. Then she hopped up onto the counter and ripped it open. The smell of plastic and cheese invaded my nose, and I grimaced. Even the blood in my belly soured. For a moment, I thought I might throw up, but the nausea quickly passed.

"So, obviously I met that Sam guy."

Seeing as how they murdered Petrik together, yes, I think I'd figured that out already. I frowned, wondering if she was trying to change the conversation. But from the reddening of her cheeks, it seemed safe to assume that this was all related.

And then it clicked.

"You like him?" I asked with a teasing grin.

She sighed and dropped the bag of Cheetos, then cupped her face. "He says I'm his mate!"

I blinked, convinced I'd misheard her. "I'm sorry. He said *what*?"

"That I'm his mate! He says he knew it the second he stepped in the house and caught my scent."

After a few seconds, I burst out laughing. "So, *that* was what he meant!"

"What who meant?" Lucy demanded, lifting her head to give me the stink eye.

"Sam!" I snickered into my hand. "He told me in a very deep and manly voice that he had your scent and could now find you anywhere."

"He said the same thing to me! Ugh. I'm really starting to dislike this whole paranormal nonsense."

I snorted. "Okay. Because what woman *wouldn't* want the Lumberjack Wolfman as her mate? And does mate mean the same thing to werewolves as it does vampires?"

"I think so," Lucy admitted. "I didn't ask him to elaborate. But I definitely got that feeling. Together... forever."

"Ohhh. Damn, girl!"

"He's just so... so... big!" Her cheeks flamed when she caught sight of my smirk. "That's not what I meant, and you know it!"

"I can think of a few more adjectives too. Sexy. Gruff. Manly. Stacked. Take your pick."

"Careful. Don't let Vlad hear you say things like that."

This time, I waved a hand. "He's snoozing away in his coffin. Besides, I can look. Especially because the only one I'm interested in has fangs."

"Oh, Samuel has fangs all right."

"Really," I hedged. "Do tell."

"Gah. You're such a lech!"

"In the flesh, baby girl. But let me guess—you plan on rejecting that manly hunk of muscle?"

"Reject him? Right now, I'm just trying to keep my damn hands off him!"

I burst out laughing. Now this was the type of gossip I was here for. Lucy never let her emotions get away from her before. I found it immensely enjoyable to see her step outside her comfort zone for once. And Sam seemed like the right guy for the job.

"Is he here right now?" I gasped, then gave Lucy a salacious wink. "Is he in your bed—*our* bed—upstairs right this second?"

"Cripes, Anna! You make it sound so bad."

I snickered. "That's my job."

"No, he isn't here right now. He doesn't particularly like Vlad.

And with the mood Vlad's been in, Sam thought some distance would be best."

Insightful.

I glanced at the microwave clock and noted the time. Four-thirty in the afternoon. Another hour or so and Vlad would wake. Excitement zinged through my body. I couldn't wait to see him, especially after everything Lucy had told me. I just wanted to hold him, show him that I was perfectly fine, then maybe jump his bones.

"Where's everyone else?" I finally asked, shelving the wolfman conversation.

"Camilla, Rebecca, and Breccan left last night. They also felt it best to give Vlad some space. They were concerned with his mental health, but he refused their help. The only thing he wanted to do was sit and watch you sleep. They told me to call them when you woke up."

"Let's wait until tomorrow to make that call," I said. "It couldn't hurt to give the three of us one night of peace, right?"

Lucy nodded. "That sounds good to me. I really wasn't looking forward to another night of creepy vampires all standing motionlessly around the house, waiting for you to so much as twitch a finger."

Yeah, that didn't sound like fun to me either.

"Do you want to go see Sam?" I asked.

Lucy shot me a sharp glance, as though she understood exactly what I was doing. "You just want me out of the house."

"Maybe. But don't feel you have to. If you'd rather avoid him for a bit, that's fine too. But I definitely want to spend some time alone with Vlad tonight. I just don't want you to feel like I'm abandoning you."

"Oh, please. Go do what you need to do. I'm just glad you're okay and back with us again. These last few days weren't exactly my favorite."

I wrapped Lucy in a hug and breathed in her scent. "Yeah, same."

"I can't imagine what you went through in there...."

"Then don't." My voice came out harsher than intended. "It's best *not* to imagine it." Unfortunately for me, I knew the nightmares would hound me for the rest of my life. "We all just need to move forward and leave the past where it belongs."

Lucy nodded.

I released her from the hug and stepped back. "I'm going to go shower. I need to get all the grime from that disgusting place off me."

"And any residual Petrik stank."

"That too."

Lucy grabbed my hands, then with a naughty wink said, "Get some, girl."

I left the kitchen laughing, all the while wondering if she intended to do the same.

CHAPTER

TWENTY-FIVE

I'D BARELY finished towel-drying my hair when my bathroom door burst open. Vlad hovered in the doorway, wearing a cautiously optimistic expression. I drank in the sight of him, my heart practically bursting at the seams.

Neither of us said a word.

Instead, I dashed across the bathroom floor and threw myself into his arms. Vlad caught me, his hands bracing my ass as he stormed into the bathroom and slammed the door shut behind him. I angled my head and slanted my mouth over his, eagerly plunging my tongue into his mouth. My hands were everywhere, in his hair, cupping his neck, his face. I couldn't keep them still. I wanted to touch every inch of him—wanted *him* to touch every inch of me.

No more excuses. No more waiting.

If Petrik had won, we never would have had the chance to explore this passion for each other. And I refused to let that happen again. Time to seize this vampire by the fangs and impale myself on him. *Get it? Impale myself? Cuz he's Vlad?* I giggled against his mouth.

"Is this a joke you should be sharing?" Vlad murmured, his lips straying across mine.

253

"Later," I breathed.

Vlad didn't argue. Clearly, this wasn't the time to talk—and I couldn't have agreed more. His tongue had a far more important task to accomplish. And it was doing quite the thorough job at the moment. I loved the way he kissed. Desperate, with a sense of urgency that I found incredibly hot. Like he couldn't wait another second to take me.

He pressed my back against the wall, then tore his mouth from mine and moved to my throat. I sucked in a sharp breath when his teeth scored my flesh. He still needed to feed—I could *feel* the hunger within him. And I was more than happy to provide that for him, to once again experience his fangs buried in my neck. God, I wanted him to bite me. But not quite yet. Anticipation would only make it that much better. The teasing thought of his fangs *and* dick buried in me at the same time made me shiver. Oh yes, please. A girl's got needs, and right now, that one was foremost on my mind.

As much as I loved the feel of him between my thighs, I couldn't strip in this position. And I needed to be naked, to feel his skin against mine. I squirmed down his torso until my feet were flat on the ground, then grabbed the edges of my towel and threw it off. Vlad sucked in a breath when he caught his first sight of me, but I didn't wait to let him look his fill. There'd be time for that later. Right now, I needed a good dicking. I needed to feel close to him, to feel him under me.

I grabbed his shirt and ripped it open, distantly aware of the scattering buttons. Whatever. He had people to clean that up afterward. The belt was next, then went his pants and everything else, until he stood stark naked before me.

My fingers instantly found their mark, encircling his hardened length. The feel of him pulsing in my hand seemed to soothe my inner horndog just a smidgen. Enough that I could tip my head back and meet his gaze while slowly stroking him.

"Anna," he groaned, leaning his forehead against mine.

I had the sense neither one of us wanted to take our time. A couple's first time together was usually slow and explorative with the intent of learning each other's body. But after everything Vlad and I had been through, time seemed like the enemy.

"I need—"

"I know what you need," he grunted.

He gripped my thighs and shot me back up into the air, balancing my legs on his shoulders. Before I could so much as move, he buried his face between my thighs. I cried out, my back arching away from the wall. Only his steel grip kept me upright, while his tongue unleashed the naughtiest and most pleasurable sensations within me. It was like he could read my body, knew how to lick and suck just the right way to send me into a euphoric tailspin. I shuddered against the wall and tightened my thighs around Vlad's head, not that he cared. The instant I orgasmed, he bit, sinking his fangs deep into my inner thigh. I almost screamed with pleasure, only managing at the last second to choke it back. The house was devoid of other vampires, but I didn't need to let every human know what we were up to in here.

Piece by piece, the world slowly returned to normal. But before I could catch my breath, Vlad unwound my thighs from his head and sat me on the counter, legs spread. He met my gaze, holding it for what felt like eternity, then drove his cock into me.

I cried out and let my head fall back, resting it against the mirror. Utter bliss. I couldn't believe we'd waited this long. We'd been insane to torture ourselves like this. Hopefully, we'd never need to go without each other again, because now that I'd felt him inside me, I never wanted to let go.

It was like my whole world made sense again. Like he was that last missing puzzle piece that I hadn't *known* was missing until the puzzle all came together. That elusive center piece. Now, my puzzle was complete. Time to frame it for all time.

Vlad gripped my hips and pulled me closer, softly grunting in time to his thrusts. I locked my ankles around his backside and matched his movements, riding him just the right way to spark that warmth within me once more. One orgasm certainly wasn't enough.

And I was glad to see that Vlad seemed just as eager to push me over the edge again.

His hand came between us, and his thumb found that perfect spot. Every stroke brought me that much closer, until finally, colors exploded behind my eyes. I'd never had a multicolored orgasm before. It was like little fairy lights twinkling in the sky, stealing my vision.

I clamped around him, milking him for every inch he could give. His breath wavered for a beat before he shuddered and lost himself to his own release. His movements slowed, and his touch grew gentle, but he didn't pull out of me. Instead, he rested his forehead against mine and sighed contentedly. I joined him, my eyes slipping shut as I breathed in this moment.

Whatever I'd felt for him before this had just grown exponentially. Our connection was strengthened by this physical bond. And I loved it.

"I thought I lost you," Vlad said, breaking the silence after our mind-blowing sex. "I can't fathom living in a world without you. Don't scare me like that again."

I hummed and cupped his face. When he opened his eyes and met my gaze, I kissed him, allowing my lips to linger a second longer. "I found my way back to you. I'm not going anywhere."

Darkness shuttered across his face. "Do you want to talk about it?"

Did I? Hell no. But I could tell *he* needed to. "There's not much to say. Eli betrayed us. Lured me out onto the balcony. Let Petrik take me."

I felt Vlad shudder. "And he paid for his crimes."

"So I heard."

"Samuel told me what happened in the crypt. The sunlight, your burns, drinking Petrik's blood."

I shivered—and not from pleasure. I never wanted to hear that name again, especially when there were far more pleasurable things we could be doing right now.

"How do you feel?" he asked, brushing my damp hair back from my face.

I took a moment to consider his question. Petrik's blood was potent and aged to perfection, but I understood Vlad's concerns. Since becoming a vampire, I'd had a myriad of ancient blood. Vlad's, Camilla's, and Petrik's.

"I feel fine," I told him. "Honestly. No madness or homicidal urges. Just the small surprise of waking earlier than you."

"Good." Vlad rested his forehead against mine and released a small breath. I felt the tension melt away from his shoulders and hated that I'd worried him.

Hoping to reassure him that all was well, I kissed him and reveled in his tongue's slow and seductive dance against mine. When he pulled back, I gave a small, displeased whimper.

"We'll need to discuss all this in further detail and decide how to proceed. The queen will eventually find out—"

I chased after that mouth of his and silenced him with yet another hungry kiss, one that made his dick twitch with eagerness. Only when we'd had our fill of each other did I pull back and smile at him. "Those are tomorrow's problems. Tonight, let's focus on each other. No thinking about the queen or any other vampire. Just you and me."

"If only it were that simple."

"We can make it that simple," I said. "We deserve this. We've waited so long for this moment. I don't want to spoil it with evil schemes."

"I thought we were the good guys?" he teased.

"Good is boring," I joked. "Now, what can I do to distract you from all this?"

With a salacious wink, I separated us, then slipped off the counter and strode to the shower in all my naked glory, swishing my hips just a little extra. From the sound of his chuckle, he'd noticed.

The shower would distract him from further questions—especially if I was in it and all lathered up. Once I had the temperature set to my liking, I extended a hand toward him and waited for him to take it. Then I pulled him into the shower and closed the curtain, sealing us away from the rest of the world.

Here, we could enjoy the heat and each other's body without any worries about what might await us out there.

And that was exactly what we did.

Tomorrow, everything would change. The queen would learn of Petrik's death and call for our beheadings. I mean, she was Marie Antoinette after all. I would be very disappointed if she didn't once try to sentence us to the guillotine.

But until then, I planned to spend every moment in Vlad's arms, because that was my happy place. And I deserved happiness.

EPILOGUE

Well, the shit definitely hit the fan this past month.

I met a serial killer, became a vampire, fell in love with Dracula—shh, don't tell him that. I haven't admitted it out loud yet—killed said serial killer, although that was more Sam and less me, and likely pissed off a queen. Not too bad. All in a day's work, right?

People continue to stalk me and Vlad. It's hilarious. They snap pictures of us when we're out and about. Pictures that literally only show our clothing. And the headlines are ridiculous. *The Count and Countess Out for a Midnight Stroll. The Count and Countess Looking for a Midnight Snack.* Just last week, someone did an entire article on a bathing suit I wore to the beach. Next thing I knew, the entire town sold out.

I asked Vlad how vampires had managed not to expose themselves prior to all this if we vanish in photos. He'd given me a long-winded explanation about how it was the vampire's duty to keep the secret, even if it meant silencing a photographer. That answer hit uncomfortably close to home, so I stopped digging. Thank goodness such extreme measures aren't necessary anymore.

The Vampire Lounge has become the newest hot spot for all vampires, especially ones hoping to glimpse what they've dubbed "The Royal Couple." We aren't part of the monarchy, but that hasn't stopped anyone from calling us that. Bet Queen Genevieve is super pleased about that one.

And speaking of the queen... she's extended an invitation to us. I burned it, but unfortunately another arrived, and Vlad spotted it before I could destroy the evidence. Meeting the queen is literally the last thing on my to-do list, behind getting staked and resurrecting Petrik. Like, I would fight a zombie apocalypse before meeting her.

She chose her precious sire over me, so for all I care, she can rot in hell.

What about Lucy? Well, she's avoiding her wolfman for now. She's a little overwhelmed and terrified by the concept of being someone's forever mate. Eh. I rather like it. But every time I bring it up, she plugs her ears and starts singing "The Itsy-Bitsy Spider." I love the girl, but I'm starting to wonder about her mental state.

Vlad spends most of his nights making me scream his name, all while monitoring me for any negative effects from Petrik's blood. He finds it quite amusing. It's all right. I got him back. A few times. *Wink.*

Camilla returned a few nights after I woke. She doesn't trust us to survive without her protection. Since she's a kick-ass fighter, I don't mind. She's continuing to train me, convinced I'm going to need it. She could be right—only time will tell.

Breccan left for home a few nights ago. Told us to call him if ever we needed help again. I like him, so I hope we do see him again in the future.

Rebecca never resurfaced after I woke. Whether or not she was part of Eli's dastardly plan, we aren't sure. Maybe Vlad's dismemberment scared her off. Hell, I refused to step foot out of his house until he took down that terrifying pike and burned Eli's head. *Shudder.*

Then there's my family. My mother finally reached out again and begged to see me. I told her I'd think about it. Perish isn't my home anymore. New Orleans is. And Lucy, while avoiding her Lumberjack Wolfman, has no desire to leave either. If I do return home, it won't be without Vlad. He's a part of my life, and I wouldn't have it any other way. Rumor has it my brother finally told my dad. But I haven't heard a peep from him. Lucky me.

For a story with such a grim beginning, I must say it turned out rather well.

Of course, that could change. The queen still wants to meet us, after all. If I have any say in this, the answer is hell no, because meeting the queen will be the shittiest shit-show ever. But we all know how it goes when a monarch demands your presence. You aren't given a choice. So, I guess we'll see you then.

Hopefully.

***

BONUS STORY!

Thank you so much for reading! I have a small treat for you. I've received multiple requests from readers who wanted to see Drac's perspective of this book. Particularly, the scenes after Anna is abducted by Petrik. Well, I decided to whip something up for you guys! **When Vlad Met Anna***, is now available for download when you join my newsletter. Go forth, join and download! Hope you enjoy the Count's story.*

Click here to join and download! *(Make sure to use this link, as it's the only one that sends you the book!)*

***

And don't forget to join my newsletter so you never miss out on a Drac and Anna release! Join here!

Keep reading for Loving Dracula...

LOVING DRACULA

DATING MONSTERS BOOK TWO

PROLOGUE

Once upon a time, in a far-off land called New Orleans, a beautiful princess met the love of her life. Nothing bad ever happened, and they lived happily ever after....

Kidding!

If only it were that simple, right?

The true story—much like *real* fairy tales—is far grimmer. Death, deceit, decapitation, all our favorite D-words. Not to mention non-marital sex. Gasp! I know.

For those who missed everything, allow me to fill in those pesky little details. First, I'm the aforementioned princess. Second, I'm not an *actual* princess. And third, I really did meet the love of my life. Not that he knows how I truly feel about him. Yet.

As for the finer minutia....

The death was mine—I'm now a vampire.

The deceit was personal—a so-called ally handed me over to a nasty enemy who tried to burn me alive.

The decapitations were well-deserved—the love of my life (aka Dracula, aka Vlad) punished our betraitor, and a local werewolf cut off my enemy's head to save me.

As for the non-marital sex? Well, that's pretty damn self-explanatory. Dracula and I did the nasty, and it was *awesome*. We're already doomed, considering we're vampires, so what's a little sinful lurvemaking on top of that? Completely worth eternal damnation, believe me. Vlad is over five-hundred years old. Meaning his sexual prowess is off the charts.

Unfortunately, even after all the decapitations, there's still no happily ever after in sight. And that's because of our Vampire Queen Genevieve, Miss Formerly-Known-As-Marie-Antoinette. Apparently, she hates me. Why, you ask? Well, that enemy I mentioned? He was her sire—*was* being the operative word. Even vampires can't live without heads.

I doubt word of his death has reached the queen yet, but she's sent us a summons regardless. One I promptly burned before anyone else spotted it. But she sent another, and another, and *another*, until finally Vlad noticed. I told him there's no way we're responding. A trip to Europe sounds romantic and all, but the reality of this situation isn't as pretty. And why should I be the one to pay out of pocket to die? If the queen wants me dead, then it seems only fair she cough up the airfare.

The optimistic side of me hopes this will deter her. Maybe she hates America or maybe she'll tire of waiting for me and move on.

Or *maybe* I'm just daft.

I mean, vampires are eternal, and from my understanding, they hold grudges for an effin' long time. So, something tells me she won't wait much longer.

Lucky me.

Maybe I should get my affairs in order? Because, damn, my life sure has become dangerous since I died.

CHAPTER
ONE

"Shh!" I clapped a hand over my best friend's mouth and giggled. "He'll hear you!"

Lucy—the aforementioned bestie—sniggered against my palm. An evil glint shone in her eyes seconds before she slopped her tongue across my hand like a frigging dog.

"Ew!" I snorted a laugh, then smeared my palm—and her drool—across her face.

Seriously disgusting! Everyone knew the human mouth was a dirty, nasty place. Okay, yes, I was a vampire and therefore impervious to all forms of diseases, viruses, and bacteria. But that didn't mean I appreciated being bathed in her gross cooties. And yes, I understood the irony, considering I rather enjoyed playing tonsil hockey with my vampire beau. Then again, Vlad preferred to lick *other*, more pleasurable parts of me.

"I swear, you're as bad as Sam," I grumbled.

Sam was our local Wolfman—aka werewolf—*and* Lucy's mate. We couldn't leave out that little tidbit of info, even though she desperately wished I would. My dear sweet Lucy was trapped in the denial phase of their relationship. It'd only been three months since vampires had announced their existence to the entire world. I think learning werewolves also existed was the overwhelming icing on the mind-boggling cake for her.

Lucy wasn't the sort who rolled with the punches. That was my role in this relationship. I was the go-with-the-flow sort who made impulsive decisions, which usually landed me in trouble. Hence why I was now a walking, talking creature of the night. Freaky, right? Not.

Lucy was the steadfast one and my austere counterpart. Always there to remind me to smarten up—not that I ever did. Where would the fun be in that?

I suspected my life had become a little too much for her. The same day we'd learned werewolves existed, she'd also learned one of them was her mate.

I absolutely shipped their relationship. Not only because Sam had saved my life by beheading an evil vampire hellbent on burning me alive, but also because I believed he'd be good for her. Force her to loosen up a little. You couldn't have two serious people in a relationship. And I didn't see Sam loosening his reins at all.

From what I'd managed to drag out of Lucy, she and Sam had only spoken a few times over the past couple months. Instead, most of their conversations were through text. It wasn't ideal, but at least she hadn't written him off entirely. Now, if only I could get her to take the next step with him. She'd admitted to me more than once, in confidence of course, that she was absolutely hot for his bod. I didn't blame her. Much like Vlad, Sam scored a solid twelve out of ten. They were two different men, but both were abso-fucking-lutely mouthwatering. Except her man's body was going to waste, which was an absolute travesty.

Lucy swatted my arm, then pointed at the television and howled with laughter. "I love this part!"

I glanced up in time to watch as Dracula—a fictional one—leaned over a woman—also named Lucy—and bit her. When he started drinking her blood, it sounded like he was slurping it through a straw. I had to admit, there was a definite comedic value to that. One *my*

Lucy found downright hilarious. The way she clutched her sides and rolled across the bed had me snickering alongside her. *Dracula Dead and Loving It* was old as balls but so very worth the hour and a half run-time.

"You should include this one in your next vlog," she said between laughter. "Use this scene to show the differences between the movies and reality when it comes to feeding."

Oh, definitely.

Ever since I'd become a vampire, Lucy and I had made it our mission to watch every single vampire flick out there, genre be damned. Then we tallied up all the fiction versus fact points and scored each movie accordingly. Sort of like a report card. Once we finished that, we recorded a video for my vlog and up it went, released into the webosphere. It was a far cry from my previous "the truth is out there" channel, but people were eating this new one up. My online popularity had skyrocketed since I was one of the few vampires pandering to the public. And because of that, not only was I raking in the dough, but I was also considered the first "vampire influencer."

My connection to Vlad certainly increased my popularity, but I couldn't help that. Even now, I had interview requests rolling in. Podcasts, radio shows, guest starring on other vlogs, you name it. Everyone wanted to meet a real-life vampire, wanted me front and center on their channels, even though I had no reflection. But hey, my bank account was loving it. I was twenty-four years old and made more money than all my friends combined. Mind blowing when I compared even half a year ago to now. A real rags-to-riches story.

When vampires first came out, the queen had issued a gag order to keep any eager vamps out there silent. But she'd lifted the order two and a half months ago. Lucy had insisted I jump on the opportunity ASAP, and I'd taken her advice, knowing she'd never steer me wrong. She was now my social media and content manager and made a beautiful chunk of change herself.

Unfortunately, I hadn't told Vlad yet. Part of me feared he'd disapprove, the other part of me feared this would all blow up in my face. Fame was a fickle beast. One moment, you're walking on air, buying the newest Louis Vuitton pumps, the next buying secondhand shoes from Goodwill. I didn't want him to see any of this until I knew for sure it was more than a passing trend. He adored me, and I wanted to keep it that way.

"Oh, this is just perfect!"

Lucy's voice cut into my thoughts, and I glanced up in time to watch the scene where Van Helsing stuffed their Lucy's room full of garlic in an attempt to repel the villainous Dracula. My Lucy, on the other hand, was laughing so hard, tears spilled from her eyes.

I couldn't help but join her. Garlic truly was a treat for us vamps. And I didn't mean that in a pleasurable way. Even now, I couldn't handle the memory of that scent, and Vlad had only shown me one clove to give me an idea.

The thought of filling someone's room to repel one of us would *absolutely* work. And the image of it was so downright ridiculous, even my stomach had begun to cramp from the hilarity.

"Ohmigosh, Lucy." I dashed blood tears from my eyes. "Keep it down, Vlad's gonna hear you!"

"So?" She threw a handful of popcorn at the screen. "If ole Battikins pisses me off, I'll just chuck some garlic at him and run away."

I burst out laughing at the image, then clapped a hand over my mouth to muffle the sound. Lucy *loved* the new nickname she'd come up with for him. It'd quickly become her favorite after she'd somehow managed to sneak up on Vlad—a feat I still had no idea *how* she'd accomplished. But she'd startled him so badly, he'd spontaneously shifted into bat form. She'd just about laughed herself into an early grave that night.

Vlad didn't approve of our movie selection. Considering he was *the* Dracula, these movies possessed a completely different tone for him. I respected that. I'd gotten my own taste of that when I stumbled across a fanfiction website featuring thousands of stories written about me. I'd tried reading a few but stopped once I'd stumbled across the Anna x Lucy ones. I loved Lucy, of course, but not that way. And it weirded me out to read love stories about us. I had to imagine that was how Vlad felt about the movies based on him, especially considering his deceased wife's name had actually been Mina. Bet that felt like a donkey kick to the nuts.

Halfway through this ridiculously awesome movie, I noticed Lucy's phone lighting up across the room. From the faint flicker in her eyes, she'd noticed it as well, but refused to acknowledge it. Which could only mean one thing.

"Sam?" I asked.

Her jaw tightened, but she didn't answer. Like I said, denial, denial, denial. But I bet she had a journal at home. A diary—because even grown-ass women sometimes needed an inanimate object to bitch at—and I bet it went something like this:

Dear Diary,

Sam is, like, soooo hot. Like fry an egg on his pecs hot. He also has this lumberjack beard that's to die for, and abs worthy of a Norse god. Like Chris Hemsworth. I know he wasn't actually Thor, but he did portray him, and his body is absolutely lickable. The things I would do to him, if I wasn't a little scaredy cat afraid of my own shadow.

I stayed in New Orleans so I could eye hump him every time we saw each other, but I never let it go any further than that. Because I'm a celibate nun at heart, even though I think I love him.

THEN SHE'D PROBABLY DRAW Sam's name with hearts all over the page, and doodle Mrs. Wolfman in the corner. Yeah, that sounded about right. Girl had damn googly eyes for him, like I did for Vlad. But at least I had the ovaries to jump Vlad's rickety old bones. Frequently. Happily.

Lucy's phone lit up again, distracting me from my immature

thoughts. I couldn't help but chuckle at the image of Emo Lucy, scribbling in her journal, her hair draped in front of her eyes.

Hmm. If she didn't want to speak to Sam, maybe I would. He and Vlad didn't get along at all. But Sam liked me. He thought I was a breath of fresh air in Vlad's otherwise stuffy life. I didn't find Vlad stuffy at all, but he held grudges. And he disliked Sam because of some... uncouth behavior. Let's just say, while in wolf form, Sam behaved in an unbefitting way. If I remembered correctly—and I did because it was funny as shit—Sam had urinated on Vlad's coffin as a giant *fuck you*. The two definitely didn't get along.

When her screen lit up a third time, I smirked, then dashed across the room and snatched up Lucy's phone.

"Anna Perish!" Lucy shrieked, her face a mask of pure horror.

I grinned, held my fingers to my lips, then answered the call. "Sam! Hi!"

"Anna?"

"Yup!"

Silence crept across the line. Sam wasn't loquacious at the best of times. One-word answers were his repertoire. I often wondered what the hell he and Lucy talked about, or if they just sat there in awkward silence, panting and lusting over each other's bodies.

"I take it you're looking for Lucy?" I dragged out my words, hoping to get him talking.

He grunted.

I almost busted up laughing. *Of course* he grunted. I was really starting to wonder about the man's vocabulary. Did he just prefer not to speak? Or maybe he didn't know many words? So many questions!

Lucy, on the other hand, was shooting daggers my way. Ah well, she'd get over it once she got *under* him. Their relationship needed a little nudge anyway. The guy definitely had to be worth it considering he kept trying even while being strung along. Don't get me wrong, Lucy was incredibly hot for him, but the second the word "mate" or "werewolf" came up, she slammed on the brakes so fast, we all had whiplash.

Maybe I could help. Or interfere, whatever way she wanted to look at it. I needed to get these two somewhere they couldn't avoid each other anymore. Somewhere small and cozy. Somewhere Lucy would be forced to sit and speak to the poor wolf.

A nefarious plot bloomed in my head like a Venus Flytrap.

If Lucy wouldn't go to him, then I needed to bring Sam to us. And I knew exactly what to do. Lucy would *hate* me, but I could handle a little best friend hate for this.

"So, Samuel..." I rarely used his full name. Even Lucy's eyebrows rose. "Lucy's and my parents have been begging us to come home. They're getting pretty insistent, actually, and I don't see how we can avoid them any longer."

The blood visibly drained from Lucy's face. Look how quickly she caught on. Oh, I was going to be paying for this for the rest of her life.

"Whatd'ya say? Wanna come with? Meet our families? I'm gonna drag Vlad along too, so we can make it a sort of double date type sitch. You in?"

"Where's home?" Sam asked.

"Perish. About an hour and a half from here. We can have you back by the end of the weekend. So you can... do whatever it is you do with your time." I literally knew nothing about him other than he turned into a wolf. "Just think, four days with Lucy. Maybe you two can resolve some matters."

Lucy chucked a pillow at my head. Too bad I saw it coming a million miles away. And too bad my vampire reflexes were far more advanced than her human ones. I snatched it out of the air and whipped it back at her. I choked on a laugh at the sight of a pillow knocking her flat on her back. Maybe I'd used a little too much force.

"Sure," Sam said, drawing my focus back to our conversation.

I grinned mischievously. Lucy didn't possess supernatural hearing like me, but my smile told her everything. She swatted the pillow off the bed, then sat up and mouthed very slowly, "I hate you." I mouthed back, "Love you too."

"Welp! Guess it's settled then. We'll leave on Wednesday night if that works for you." It was currently Sunday. Which left him a couple of days to get his stuff in order for a small road trip. "Be here around nine p.m.?"

"Fine."

When he didn't hang up, I winced. He was waiting for me to hand Lucy the phone. "She isn't available to talk right now."

"I can hear her in the background."

Right. Werewolf. Forgot they could hear as well as us.

"Ah, well. Truth be told, she's too busy having a panic attack to speak. But don't worry! I'll calm her down and make sure she packs something super sexy for you."

"Anna!" she shouted, knowing her cover was blown.

"Okay, see you Wednesday night. Byeeee!" I ended the call before Lucy could snatch her phone back and slid it into my back pocket.

"Give me my phone right this second, Anna!"

"Nah." I backed away from her, then darted for the door, once again using my unmatchable vamp speed. Poor Luce. She really didn't stand a chance.

"That's cheating!" she shouted at me.

I paused at the door and threw a sassy glance back over my shoulder. "Oh, sweetie, it's only cheating if you're caught. And you can't catch me."

"I won't forget this!" Lucy cried out as I vanished through the door and raced down the steps.

Laughter bubbled in my throat.

Sometimes it was good to be a vampire.

CHAPTER
TWO

I WAS STILL CHUCKLING to myself as I snuck into Vlad's office. He sat at his desk with his back to me, his rigid posture the absolute definition of him. He drummed his fingers against the veneer top while his other hand held a phone to his ear.

Before I could utter a word, he canted his head in my direction, showing me he'd heard my approach. Because of course he had. So how the hell had Lucy startled him? Every time I insisted she tell me, she just laughed harder and harder. She loved lording this over me. Somehow, she'd snuck up on Count Dracula, the Big Bad himself. What wasn't there to love about that?

"That's right, yes," Vlad murmured into the phone.

I paused and perked an ear. It was rude to listen in on private conversations, but honestly, nothing was private in this house, thanks to our heightened senses. Privacy was a thing of the past, especially considering Camilla, one of Vlad's friends, now lived with us. She seemed utterly convinced Vlad and I would die without her annoyingly persistent presence. I'd never imagined myself living in a communal household, but it'd happened. Vlad's mansion was practically bursting at the seams with its many residents. His staff alone inhabited the lower floor guest suites, while the second floor contained the main bedrooms for me, Vlad, Camilla, and Lucy. Then, of course, there was the attic where we vamps kept our coffins for sleeping.

Usually, this sort of arrangement wouldn't bother me. Except, Camilla had taken it upon herself to tease me whenever she overheard Vlad and I being intimate together. It was like living in a college dorm, for crying out loud. I'd walk downstairs and she'd make kissy faces at me, or she'd provocatively flash her fangs and tongue the instant Vlad turned his back. I was hardly shy, but it did squick me out knowing she could hear everything that went on between me and Vlad in the bedroom.

At least Lucy had human ears. The most she overheard was a loud giggle now and then. But Camilla overheard the sweet words Vlad whispered to me—among other things. Trust me, it wasn't fun sitting across a room from someone who suddenly started dramatically acting out the sounds you made during sex.

We needed to kick Camilla out, as simple as that. She had her own house and harem, which was on a permanent hiatus while she hunkered down here. But that didn't mean she couldn't leave. In the past few months, she'd grown distressingly obsessed with me. If she wasn't bashing in my skull while teaching me how to fight, or teasing me like some high school bully, then she was updating my wardrobe, introducing me to other random vampires, and texting me stupid historical vampire facts.

I appreciated her efforts, but holy hell, there was only so much a girl could take.

"And your company guarantees complete UV protection?" Vlad asked, drawing my focus back to him.

Ooo, now *this* sounded promising! Back when Vlad first changed me into a vampire, he'd promised to look into new and improved sleeping arrangements for me. I absolutely loathed waking in a stupid coffin with a stupid lid and stupid small walls. It made me feel like a real monster from all the creature features Lucy made me watch. There had to be other options, especially now that vampires were no longer a secret. Everyone and their dog were starting up new business ventures catering to us fangers.

The problem wasn't with the products, it was with my crusty old boyfriend who was set in his traditional ways. Having lived this way for five-hundred years, he didn't see any other possibilities. Because sleeping in a coffin was safer than sleeping out in the open where any human could stumble across him and ram a stake through his chest. I tried telling him the same thing could happen in a coffin, but he'd completely ignored my comment.

So, instead, I'd suggested blackout curtains. His response? *They're not foolproof.* Of course. Anyone could fling them open, thereby frying us in our sleep. Fine. How about blacking out the windows with paint? But that "isn't aesthetically pleasing and will lower the house's resale value."

After that, I'd gone a wee bit overboard and suggested full military security, complete with trained werewolves to guard our rooms so no one could assassinate us in our sleep. I believe his exact answer had been, "Very amusing, Anna."

Ugh. Fine. If he wanted *serious* suggestions... I went and did some research and found there was a new company launching a product called SunGuard. Fancy-dancy windows that would protect us from those dastardly UV rays. In the words of their company, "SunGuard defends and protects you from the sun, allowing you the best sleep money can buy." I would be the judge of that, thank you very much.

From what I'd read on some forums, there were a few vamps around the country who'd experimented with basement suites now that we no longer had to hide. But thanks to our location, Vlad's estate didn't have a basement. And when I asked why we couldn't turn the attic into a suite, his answer had chilled me to the bone. *Because a hurricane could rip through and tear off the roof, leaving us unprotected.* Yikes.

Thanks to Petrik's blood, the sunlight wasn't *as* big a concern for me anymore. I still couldn't withstand direct sunlight—*boo*—but I woke earlier than Vlad, and so long as the sun's beams didn't touch me directly, I was safe. That didn't mean we didn't need to take the right precautions though. And I would do anything to sleep in a bed again. Coffins were morbid and downright ghastly. I would empty my bank account for these SunGuard windows, so long as it meant never crawling into the dank darkness again.

"Has this product received approval from all required channels?"

Vlad's head bobbed as he listened to the other side of the conversation—as did mine. Queen Genevieve and her council had recently approved their windows, as had the new Vampiric Health and Safety Division created by the humans.

My excitement grew.

According to the man on the phone, they'd recently installed a set of windows in a local vampire's house, who hadn't reported any problems. So, either the product worked, or the vamp had been fried crispy in the middle of a bed somewhere and no one had noticed yet.

I couldn't wait to try out these new windows. I wanted nothing more than to go to sleep cuddled up next to Vlad on a California king, surrounded by mountains of pillows and blankets. I'm talking quilted and down-filled duvets on top of a plush pillow top mattress. One upside to vampirism was we didn't overheat, even in southern temperatures. Tell me that didn't sound like heaven.

"Very well. When can we book an installation?"

I nodded eagerly. Yes, yes, when? Tonight? Tomorrow at the latest?

"August sixth will suffice."

My heart dropped. That was two damn weeks from now! *Whhyyy?* I mean, part of me understood. They likely needed to order in parts, then fit us into their installation schedule. But damn it, how many jobs were they doing that we had to wait so long?

I guess it didn't matter. We would be leaving for Perish in a few days anyway. After we returned, it'd be another week of waiting, which sounded agonizing. Impatience was a weakness of mine. When I wanted something, I wanted it now. Waiting was the absolute definition of torture.

Vlad thanked the customer rep, hung up, then finally turned in his chair, giving me the chance to really look at him. I never tired of admiring his beauty. There was something about his darkly hypnotic eyes that always seemed to entrance me. I knew he didn't possess the power of compulsion, so it was definitely just an effect he had on me. His dark, wavy hair fell to his ears in a purposely tousled look that made me want to comb my fingers through it. And then came his chiseled jaw and strong chin. All in all, the man rated "sexy AF" in my book. Certainly sexier than me, but I didn't mind that one bit, since I was the one doing all the looking.

Clearly enjoying my attention, Vlad's mouth curled into a slow smile. He wasn't big on showing affection, but for me, he always made the effort. We may be vampires, but that didn't mean we couldn't enjoy life. If I was going to spend an eternity with someone, then our romance needed to be epic and all-consuming. None of this simply putting up with each other for the sake of the relationship.

I gestured to the phone on his desk and chuckled. "You remembered."

Just when I thought I couldn't love this man more. Of course, Vlad didn't know I was in love with him yet. That was one part of our relationship I'd been holding back on. The thought of uttering those three little words terrified me. Part of me worried I only *thought* I loved him. I mean, we'd only met three months ago. Was it possible to fall in love with someone that quickly?

Vlad, on the other hand, had always known we were destined to meet, so he saw things differently than me. Thanks to his gift of foresight, he'd dreamed of me for fifty years, knowing that one night, we'd meet. His gift wasn't infallible, and it often withheld more information than it provided—for instance, the fact that I would die the night we met—but he'd never doubted that we were meant to be.

That pretty much told me how he felt about me. But I hadn't been given the same advantage. I hadn't dreamed of him for fifty years, longing and waiting for this mystery man. For me, this was all so new and fresh and exciting. I wasn't ready to say those three little words yet. I wanted to make sure this was real and not some trick being played on us by some unknown deity with powers beyond my comprehension.

I mean, who even controlled our fates anyway? What if the rush of emotion I felt for him was nothing more than me lusting after a sexy, famous vampire who made me all mushy in the knees? What if it was all purely physical? So many people confused good sex with love. Add in Vlad's drop-dead gorgeous looks, and a girl was bound to be a little confused.

Thankfully, Vlad hadn't told me he loved me yet either. Which helped a lot. Took the pressure off. Except I kept fighting the urge to just blurt them out. Especially during sex, thanks to Vlad's mad skills in the art of pleasuring the female body. When he touched me, I melted into a pitiful puddle of goo. Then there was the way he looked at me—like I was the only thing that mattered in his eternal life.

But that definitely didn't mean love. At least, I didn't think it did.

Gah! I was a mess of emotions and confusion. Lord, someone send help. Seemed my hormones were screwing me up six ways from Sunday.

"Of course I remembered. You might wake earlier than me now, but I'm still aware of your dislike for the coffin."

"It's just so cramped," I complained. "And dark. And stifling. Now picture us snuggling together in a bed full of pillows and soft blankets, holding each other, touching each other...."

"That doesn't sound like sleeping to me," Vlad mused.

"That's the joy of sharing a bed. We can sleep *after*."

Vlad chuckled.

"Trust me. You'll love it. You haven't experienced luxury until you've slept on a pillow top mattress, snuggled in a bunch of soft blankets."

Vlad lifted a brow and gestured to the room surrounding us. I couldn't help but snicker. His entire house was the definition of grand luxury. Chandeliers, marble tubs, velvet couches—which I despised—and top of the line technology, thanks to me and Lucy. Pre-Anna, as I liked to call it, the Count had lived like it was the nineteenth century. No televisions, stereo systems, computers, tablets, nada. Lucy and I had changed all that. We'd taken his house under our wing and modernized it. Now, we had a computerized fridge that informed us when supplies were low, and two family rooms complete with big screen TVs and gaming consoles—one for Vlad's employees and one for us vampires. I'd recently convinced Camilla to play a zombie apocalyptic game called *Last of Us*, and I regretted it. That woman loved murdering her some zombies. So much so that Lucy and I never got to play anymore.

I closed the distance between us, then eased onto Vlad's lap. I looped my arms around his neck and slid my fingers into his thick, wavy hair. "You're gonna love it. After five centuries of sleeping in a coffin, even a twin-sized bed would be an improvement."

"If it makes you happy," he told me, his nose brushing against the hollow of my throat.

It was one of Vlad's favorite places on my body, among a few others farther south. I never complained—I'd quickly learned my throat was incredibly sensitive, and his touch often sent little pleasurable shivers coursing through me.

"This house could be a hovel, and I'd still be happy," I whispered as I leaned my head to the side to grant him more access. When his lips brushed my throat, I shuddered. "All I need is you."

Vlad chuckled, his breath brushing my flesh. "Well, in that case, allow me to call SunGuard back and cancel the installation."

I playfully slapped his hand away from the phone, then lowered my head and eyed him. "Don't even think about it. Or I will feed garlic cloves to your harem for a month."

"Vicious," Vlad mumbled, laughter rumbling deep in his throat. In our time together, I'd noticed he didn't laugh with anyone but me.

So, I took a moment to revel in the sound. I loved that he let down his walls and opened himself up to me.

"What were you and Lucy doing up there? Sounded like the two of you were having fun."

I bit my lip to smother a laugh. "Uh, watching a movie."

Vlad's eyes narrowed teasingly. "What *kind* of movie?"

He knew of our recent fascination with vampire movies. Again, no privacy in the house. But he didn't understand *why* we were watching them. I still wasn't ready to tell him about my new vlog, and we'd somehow managed to keep it a secret.

"Lucy wanted to watch another vamp flick. A satirical one."

Vlad grimaced. "Do I want to know more?"

"Well, an aging white-haired man with a penchant for the ucipital mapilary played you," I said, referencing a specific part of the movie.

Vlad's eyes widened. "Penchant for what?"

I pointed to the hollow notch at the base of my throat. "This right here."

"Mm. Well, it is lovely," Vlad said.

"You also had a man-servant who enjoyed eating bugs."

Vlad's mouth thinned. "I think I've heard enough."

"Probably." I leaned over and gently nipped at his bottom lip, hoping to perk it back up. "It's just a silly movie we used to watch while we were in school." I smiled at the memory. "We weren't really popular, so when no one invited us to the cool kids' parties, we spent the night at my place, binging on B-rated movies."

"I don't know what either of those things mean."

I chuckled. "Means indulging in low-budget films. Thing is, though, most B-rated movies have a warped charm about them that makes them better than the mainstream releases."

"As long as you're enjoying yourself."

"I know another way I could enjoy myself," I suggested, hoping to lure him away from this topic. The last thing I needed was for him to question my purpose behind watching these movies.

He lifted a brow. "Oh?"

I wiggled mine in response.

Vlad's smile grew until his fangs winked at me. And damn, did that make me shiver. His dick wasn't the only thing I liked inside me. I couldn't drink his blood anymore—a decision we'd made after I'd feasted on Petrik like it was no big deal. But that didn't mean Vlad couldn't bite me. Luckily, my blood seemed to have no effect on him, considering he was ancient in his own right. Our sexcapades usually ended with both his fangs and his dick buried so deeply within me that I had no idea where I ended, and he began. I was A-OK with that, and I was quite sure you could guess why.

Mind. Blowing. Orgasms.

Who knew that was all it took to make me happy?

Well, not all. But enough to distract me from the other issues in my life. And there were so, so many. Queen Genevieve for one with her annoying, holier-than-thou summons. My vlog, which demanded a lot of attention. Then my family, who I really didn't want to think about right now. Not while seated in Vlad's happy little lap with his fingers gripping my happy little ass.

"Is Camilla here tonight?" I whispered, while running my teeth down his throat.

I couldn't bite, but that never stopped me from teasing. It teased me too. Just the thought of sinking my fangs into his throat nearly brought me to the edge of climax. I *loved* biting Vlad. But it was too dangerous. Younger vamps who consumed older vamp blood tended to go a little bit insane. The older the blood, the more powerful, and we youngins weren't able to process it well enough. I'd tasted Vlad before, but after I'd fed off Petrik—a thousand-year-old ancient— Vlad had insisted we cool it on his blood. Much to my dismay.

When my teeth scraped his flesh, Vlad's breath hitched, and his fingers squeezed my butt. I could feel the tension building within him and the hardening of his body in every delicious way possible.

"I sent her on a few errands," he murmured, his fingers almost bruising my ass cheeks.

"Thank Jeebus." I seemed immune to most godly curses, but

other vampires weren't, so I took care not to mention the G-word in front of them.

With no time to waste, I ripped off Vlad's shirt, then unzipped his pants and freed him through the open fly. I'd barely glanced at the Count's gloriousness before he pushed me back onto his desk, popped open my pants, and wrenched them around my thighs.

Vlad leaned over me and devoured my mouth seconds before he slid his fingers into me. Usually we took our time, teased one another, lavished in every form of foreplay known to man. But neither of us knew how much time we had before Camilla returned or someone else came knocking at his door. We were literally racing the clock. Vlad knew *exactly* how to work me up, which he proved right now with his talented fingers.

It didn't take long to send me spiraling toward a climax. The second my inner walls clamped around his fingers, he withdrew and filled the emptiness with a different, albeit deliciously harder organ. He wrapped my thighs around his waist, then clutched my hips and began moving within me.

I nearly screamed with delight but managed to bite it back into a moan.

His desk shuddered against the floor, the force of his movements sending his papers and stationary scattering to the floor. Neither of us so much as paused to look at the mess we'd made. Instead, I slid my fingers into his hair and fisted them, tugging gently on his roots. Vlad's eyes shuddered closed, and he groaned. He loved when I did this. He seemed to enjoy a bit of an edge to his lovemaking, which didn't surprise me. He was a vampire, after all. He liked to bite, pull, and push, but he especially loved to withhold orgasms as a form of beautiful torture. Lead me to the edge until I was ready to scream with frustration before finally letting me fall over it.

Tonight was different though. Tonight was rushed and merciless. And yet still so wonderful, I could have died—again. He drove into me with a divine force that had my head thumping against the wall. But I didn't care.

When I finally cried out my release, Vlad wasn't far behind me. His head dropped forward as he groaned, his hands convulsing against my sides.

Quick, dirty, and amazing.

Just the way I liked it.

CHAPTER

THREE

A door slammed open seconds before Camilla's not-so-dulcet voice rang through the room. "Oh, good. You're done."

I *screamed* and flew off Vlad's desk. My hands scrambled to fasten my pants, but I couldn't seem to get them to stay done up. The damn button kept popping back out! I nearly tore the stupid thing off in my panicked attempt to redress myself.

Once I finally got my pants buttoned, I whirled around and swept my mussed hair off my face. "For fuck's sake, Camilla! What the hell is your problem?"

"No problem." She stood in the doorframe, inspecting her nails as though she hadn't a care in the world.

I eyed her tall stature, from her golden heels to her wavy black hair, and snarled. She looked the picture of beauty and grace, while I probably looked like... well, freshly fucked.

"Would it have killed you to knock?"

I shot Vlad a glance to find him standing deathly still, his hands gripping his office chair as though his deceptively calm temperament relied on it.

"No, but where's the fun in that?" She sighed and pushed off the

288

door.

I listened to the sound of her clacking heels as she approached, my eye twitching with every step. I liked Camilla. I truly did. She'd been a key factor in my survival a few months ago. Since my little adventure with Petrik, she'd taken her role as my trainer quite seriously. But this was pushing it too far. We had zero privacy with her around! If she kept goading me, she was going to find herself dumped in a pit right before sunrise.

And from the look on Vlad's face, it seemed our thoughts aligned.

"This is entirely inappropriate, Camilla," Vlad snapped.

His deep voice sent a shiver down my arms.

"I'd apologize, but maybe you two shouldn't engage in freaky sex in the middle of your office."

"This is my house," Vlad stated, his upper lip curling back to reveal his fangs. "If you're unhappy with the circumstances, you do have your own home. Perhaps you should consider leaving."

"Can't. Too busy," she said. Her gaze darted to me seconds before her hand clamped down on my wrist and she wrenched me toward the door. "Come on. We have places to go and people to see."

I backpedaled. We so did not. The only plan I had consisted of a shower. Right this second. Vampire or not, sex was delightfully messy. Fuck, I hadn't even had a chance to bask in the afterglow. Okay, scrap my earlier comment. I no longer liked Camilla. Rob a girl of her post-orgasm bliss and you rob her of life.

"Quit squirming," Camilla shot back at me. "We have a date."

"Excuse me?" I tugged on my arm.

With a dramatic sigh, Camilla whirled around to face me. "Look, while you've been content just existing, the rest of us have been busy trying to keep your ass alive. In case you've forgotten, the queen sort of has this personal little vendetta against you."

Man, the sarcasm was thick tonight. Sometimes I wondered if my presence was having an effect on her.

"So, let's go. You have an appointment with VA."

"With... what?" I glanced back at Vlad. I could only imagine the unpleasant thoughts running through his head.

"VA. Vampires Anonymous. Hurry up. Go shower and put on something a tad more appropriate."

What was wrong with my current outfit? I glanced down at my clothes. Jeans and a long-sleeved designer shirt. I mean, wasn't this a pretty standard look for most women my age?

Camilla growled. "Let me spell it out for you, sweetie. The queen doesn't like you. Which means other vampires don't like you. Your first week of life consisted of you slaughtering Petrik. And while no one *knows* you're responsible, they *know* you're responsible. Get me?"

Talk about stating the obvious. "So?"

"*So*, we're trying to fix your reputation. One of the requirements for new vampires is that they attend Vampires Anonymous."

"That sounds like something for humans who are addicted to vampire bites."

Camilla rolled her eyes and stared at the ceiling, as though begging it for patience. "I texted you about this earlier tonight."

"You so did not!" Okay, even I winced at that one. I sounded like a whiny teenager.

"I *so* did," Camilla mocked. "Check your damn phone."

Cursing under my breath, I stuck a hand in my back pocket and came up empty. Right. My phone had probably fallen out during— well, just *during*. I eyed Vlad's desk, heat rising to my cheeks at the sight of the mussed papers. I'd never be able to look at his desk the same way again. Sure enough, laying amidst his scattered documents were both mine and Lucy's cells.

I snatched mine up and flicked it on, only to find Camilla's missed text. Along with half a dozen more explaining the vampire hierarchy to me. Well? How the hell was I supposed to know she'd actually texted me something useful among the countless boring texts about the monarchy?

"Alright, *fine*. What the hell is Vampires Anonymous?"

"A nonprofit, self-help program for all newly turned vampires."

"Um, I think I'm a little beyond that now, don't you?"

She shook her head, her waterfall of inky black hair glimmering beneath the office lights. Once upon a time, I'd been jealous of her beauty, but that envy had dimmed once I'd gotten to know her annoying personality. Looks only went so far.

"The queen has been looking into you. We need her to believe you're like all the rest of us."

"But I *am* like all the rest."

"You aren't," Vlad commented. "No newborn vampire can wake before sunset or walk around during the day like you. Such a feat will attract the attention of the queen, considering she would know Petrik possessed the same talent. I understand Camilla's concerns, and while I absolutely do not approve of her methods, I think you might benefit from this program. If anything, it'll show your commitment to the vampire community and allow you the opportunity to network."

To network with whom? And why?

"Hurry up!" Camilla hissed. "It starts in an hour, and you need to make yourself presentable. If the queen is watching, you can't go looking like...this."

Again, I stole a glance at myself. Maybe I was biased, but I thought I looked fine. What'd they expect? For me to show up in a dazzling ballroom gown complete with heels and tiara? It's not like I had a crown or anything.

"Just go shower." Camilla shoved me toward Vlad's office door. Apparently, I wasn't even allowed a kiss goodbye. "I'll have an outfit waiting for you on your bed by the time you're done."

"Lucy is in my room," I warned Camilla. Not that I needed to. The two didn't like each other—a little best friend animosity, I suspect. But I still felt the need to warn Camilla.

"Fine. She can help, I suppose."

Oh, Lucy would love that.

Not.

CRIPES, this was ridiculous. What the hell was Camilla thinking bringing me here? I suppose on some scale, I was still considered a newborn vampire, regardless of the three months I had under my belt. But I was a happily adjusted fanger, right? I had a werewolf buddy, a human sidekick, a deliciously sexy boyfriend, and well, Camilla. I didn't need *therapy*.

Camilla had practically dragged me kicking and screaming into the room—albeit without the dramatics and just a whole lot of glaring—then forced me into a chair before she beat a hasty retreat. Couldn't be bothered to stick around, I guess.

Now I sat in a large half-circle, surrounded by at least eight other vampires. And boy, did the majority look green, both in experience and appearance.

Hell was a four-letter word, and I was in it.

What did Camilla and Vlad expect from me? To make friends—or network, as Vlad put it? To open up to these *strangers* about my experiences as a vampire? I couldn't do that. If I revealed anything too personal, that information could somehow get back to the queen.

So, here I sat, dressed in a flowy skirt, strappy sandals, and silk blouse. All because Camilla had insisted. The entire ride here, she'd lectured me on the importance of maintaining mystery. *This isn't high school*, she'd said. I wasn't here to make a new bestie or join the undead chess club. I was here to make an impression. To show the queen I was a good little vampire, brushing my little vamp fangs, and making vamp friends.

Ugh. Just stuff me in a box and mail me to Transylvania. I did *not* want to do this.

"Hi," someone murmured at my side.

I glanced over to find two people seated next to me, one a young woman, the other a bedraggled looking man. Both stared at me like I was the most interesting person to have walked through the door. Damn. They were in for a shocking surprise. I was just as boring as the rest of them. Of course, the little voice in my head chose that moment to laugh at me. Since it was my voice, I was essentially laughing at myself. There really wasn't anything normal about me at all. And I wasn't sure how I felt about that.

I focused first on the woman, biting my inner cheek to keep from sighing. Her outfit absolutely *screamed* college student, and I secretly hated her for it. Jeans, a light sweater, and scuffed sneakers. Was that so much to ask? Well, not the scuffed sneakers bit. Wouldn't catch me *dead* in beat-up, no-name shoes. But skirts? Dresses? Both were emphatic hell no's from me. Why would anyone want to wear anything that limited their movement? If I wanted to run, I sure as shit didn't want to be worried about flashing someone my lady bits. Camilla didn't give two craps about my feelings, though, and had dressed me in exactly that. A stupid skirt that showed far too much thigh for my liking.

"I'm Violet," the woman said.

I bobbed my head. "Nice to meet you."

The disheveled man next to her leaned forward and flashed me a gap-toothed grin. "And I'm Graves."

Holy guacamole. I mean, I'd seen people with missing teeth before, but never quite like this. Dude had zero teeth *except* for his fangs. What a mildly disturbing sight. And by mildly, I meant immensely. He was all... gums and fangs. Fangs and gums.

"Um, sorry, did you say Grays?" I reached out to take his extended hand.

"Graves," Violet repeated for me, rolling her eyes. "Don't pay any attention to him. He has fake teeth he could wear, but he refuses to."

"Ain't comfortable with these now, are they?" Graves gestured at his sharp fangs. "And we ain't need fake teeth for nuthin' now."

He wasn't wrong. And I couldn't imagine fake teeth felt too comfy with his fangs pressing against them. I wasn't even sure if dentures would work with fangs. I wasn't a dentist. But I did know implants wouldn't. His body would reject anything surgical like that while he slept during the day. We were the undead, which meant unchanging. We would forever look the same as we did the night we transitioned. So, instead, I merely nodded and forced my gaze away from those gaping, pink gummy holes.

"What's your name?" Violet asked.

Right. Introductions. Strange how something as completely simple as missing teeth had befuddled my brain. "Oh, sorry. Anna?"

"You askin' or tellin'?" Graves questioned.

"Um, telling."

"It's nice to meet you." Violet tucked a strand of pastel rainbow-colored hair behind her ear. I had to wonder if she'd dyed it that way before transitioning or if she woke up every single night and colored it. I also wasn't sure which sucked more. I would hate to be stuck with permanently dyed Easter egg hair, but coloring my hair every single night sounded worse. Far too much effort.

It made me stop and think though. My mother used to always tell me to make sure I had clean panties on in case I—wait for it—got hit by a car and died. There were so many things to unpack in that sentence, like one, *of course* I changed my underwear daily, but also, did doctors really care about a dead person's underwear? Seemed to me they had more important things to waste their time on.

I didn't extend Violet the same compliment, because honestly, it wasn't nice to meet her. Or anyone else for that matter. I was here under protest, and I wanted to make sure everyone knew it. Screw the queen and her "spies." I honestly didn't give a fuck about any of that anymore.

"So, haven't seen ya here before, darlin'," Graves mumbled.

Great, another southern boy with a penchant for calling me darling. Had to be something in the water. I was as southern as they came, but I didn't walk around calling people sugar or sweetheart.

"First timer," I said.

"Oh!" Violet clasped my hand and threw me a sickeningly sweet smile. "Welcome to the group!"

I grimaced and slowly extracted my hand from hers. An image of Emperor Kuzco flashed through my mind because I was definitely feeling a *no touchy* moment coming on. Instead, I asked, "You?"

"Two months."

I blinked. I'd been hoping for a one-and-done sorta deal. Definitely wasn't looking to come here the next eight Sundays—or longer! I was all for mental health and healing yourself, but this wasn't for me. I didn't need therapy, and I certainly didn't need to make a good impression for the queen. She'd already formed an opinion of me, and I doubted it was a good one.

"It's Graves's third time here. He's fairly new too," Violet continued.

I shot dear old Graves a passing glance. He ran his hands through his greasy hair, then rammed a finger right up his nose and started picking. Oh wow. Charming.

Violet scoffed and leaned in close to Graves. "You know, just because we don't have reflections doesn't mean other people can't see you."

I almost burst out laughing when he shrugged and dug a little deeper. Someone was mining for green gold, that was for sure. I looked away before he did something disgusting, like wipe a goober the size of his knuckle on his leg.

Violet sighed and straightened in her chair. "I'm so sorry. I'm his sponsor, but I haven't been able to instill any manners in him. The man is like a cockroach."

"Sponsor?"

"Sure. You know, helping those who don't have sires."

My eyes widened. Wait. There were vampires out there without sires? I thought sires were required? I'd read through all the information the queen's people had sent me after transitioning. After transitioning, the newborn vampire had to remain with their sire for three months. Afterward, they were free to go.

But the more I thought about it, the more it made sense. Much like how mothers abandoned their newborn babies, surely vampires did the same thing. I just couldn't believe it'd taken me this long to clue into that. Man, I really didn't know shit.

On the upside, Violet had been attending these meetings for the past two months, so she likely knew everyone here. Meaning I could now begin networking. Maybe I could needle her for information, find out who else was new here. I still believed Vlad and Camilla were overreacting a wee bit to this whole situation, but it couldn't hurt to investigate a little, right? Make a new friend? Then grill her for all the information I could?

Famous last words and all that.

"So, how do these things usually go down?" I waved a hand toward the other six vampires.

Graves gave a wheezy chuckle that made me wonder if he'd smoked in his previous life, then flashed his gums at me once more. I had to admit, they fascinated me. And I truly didn't understand why.

"The speaker"—which sounded like *theaker*—"will welcome us, chat 'bout himself, then open the floor to us plebs to share anything we might wanna yak about."

"Like?"

"Anythin', darlin'. Becomin' a vamp is hard. Some people ain't got a support network to help, ya'know? So, they come here, spillin' their secrets and spinnin' their yarns for y'all to listen to and offer sympathy."

Made sense. Especially if they didn't have a sire to help them through these trying times. I mean, just because the council dictated that a newborn had to remain with their sire for the first few months didn't mean everyone followed the rules. The council had also made it illegal to change nonconsenting humans into vamps, and see how well that one turned out for me? I was a prime example of how much people loved to break the rules.

Violet shot me a haunted look, as though she understood my thoughts. Hell, maybe she did. Damn vampire tricks. "The point of this group," she said, "is to know that we're all going through the same thing."

"Aw, sweetheart"—which sounded a whole lot like *thweetheart*—"the real point of this group is to meet other fangers and get lucky. Amiright, Miss Anna?"

I shot Graves a startled look. "What?"

"Come on, now. Don't play all shy and innocent with me. I know the look. Seen it in your eyes the second you sat down there. Scopin' us out with a hunger I only seen on them prowlin' ladies."

"Prowling?"

"Ya know, them cougar ladies. Yer a bit young, but you got that look aboutcha."

I snorted on a cough, then started laughing. "I'm most definitely *not* here looking to get lucky."

"Sure ya ain't." Graves winked, then grinned at me. "But don't you worry, I won't tell. A lady's gotta keep her secrets, amiright?"

I gave another chuckle, one I had to swallow when someone at the front of the room cleared their throat.

My head snapped up and I spotted the presumed so-called *theaker*. He stood before a small podium, his fingers rifling through a stack of papers. When he lifted his head, his sharp blue eyes snagged mine before moving through the rest of the room.

"Alright. Welcome everyone." He gathered his papers and knocked them against the podium, straightening them into a flat pile. "Welcome to Vampires Anonymous. My name is Noah Bradshaw, and I'll be leading this meeting. Before we begin, I'd like to remind everyone that this is a safe place for all newly turned vampires. However, no humans are allowed. So, if you haven't been turned yet, please excuse yourself."

"Yeah, no bleeders allowed," Graves teased.

I squished my lips together to keep from chuckling. Graves was a character, for sure.

Movement caught my attention, and I turned in time to watch as two humans slipped out of the room. With them went the subtle sound of their heartbeats. It wasn't until they left that I realized how silent the room had become. Humans moved, squirmed, twitched, breathed, blinked, and fiddled. Vampires... didn't. We sat still as the grave. Unnerving to say the least.

"Okay." Noah tapped his papers once more. "As most of you

know, and as I just said, my name is Noah. I've been a vampire for going on ten years and have mentored my share of newborns throughout that time. When Queen Genevieve announced our presence to the world, I saw the opportunity to expand this service and help others on their journey."

Next to me, Violet nodded. When I spared her a glance, I noted the reverence with which she watched him. Graves, on the other hand, looked entirely too bored for his own good. He kept tapping his tongue against his fangs, a sight I definitely hadn't prepared myself for. Who'd ever heard of a toothless vampire before? He must have lost them all before he'd died. Either that or—and it twisted my stomach to think of this—he pulled them out every night after rising.

Oh, I was gonna throw up just thinking about that.

"Usually, this is the part where I allow everyone to introduce themselves. Let's begin, shall we? How about you?"

It took me a few moments to realize Noah meant me. For cripes' sake, why did I have to sit *right next* to the podium.

"Me?"

Noah nodded.

Great. Me.

Graves chuckled, then leaned in and whispered, "*Theaker's* pet."

I nudged him back over into his own chair, then lifted my head and faced the group. Wow. There were... a lot of vampires. And all eyes appeared to be on me. You'd think I'd be used to this now, thanks to my vlog's recent success, but here was the thing. The viewers couldn't actually see me on the channel. All they saw were the heaps of clothing Lucy piled onto me to make me visible on camera. Sweaters, scarves, massive sunglasses, wide-brimmed hats. Everything she could think of to give me some semblance of shape on camera. Knowing my audience could see me without actually seeing me lent me a freedom I adored.

This? This wasn't freedom. And I most certainly did *not* adore the many eyes tracking me, waiting to hear my woeful tale.

"Um. Hi, everyone." I gave a pitiful wave. "My name is Anna Perish—"

A quiet murmur spread through the room. Even Violet appeared shocked by this information. Insulted, even. As though she didn't appreciate me withholding that information earlier.

Graves, however, chuckled and leaned back in his chair with a knowing smirk. "So, you really ain't looking for some vamp-on-vamp action then, huh? Pity. Mighta been interested, ya'know?"

"Graves," Noah warned.

I laughed, hoping it would silence the whispers. "Right. So, like I said, Anna Perish. I've been a vampire for three months thereabouts, and this is my first VA meeting."

I had every intention of leaving it at that, but apparently Noah had other plans for me.

"Care to share a little more?" He leaned his elbows against the podium. "How were you changed?"

If my heart could still beat, it would have sputtered to a dead stop right this second. I didn't want to discuss this. Even now, months later, I still felt Petrik's breath on my throat, and the heat of the sun on my skin. The bastard had tried to murder me. Twice. Once in a dark alley, the other in a cement crypt. I didn't enjoy thinking about him—he wasn't worth the brain power. And it seemed a safe bet to assume the people here had already seen plenty of images online. Just my luck, a reporter had stumbled across me and Vlad in the middle of him turning me. Since I'd still been human—albeit pretty much dead —I was entirely visible in the images. Too visible. Those photos haunted me to this day, and there wasn't anything I could do about them. On the upside, they were a direct line to my bank account, so that had to count for something.

"Right. I was... uh..." My gaze shot to Noah, who nodded in open understanding.

"This is a safe place, Anna. We don't share other people's secrets or stories."

Well, my story was far from secret. The whole world had seen the pictures. So, I highly doubted Noah's assurances. In my experience, whatever I said here would soon be posted online. Therefore, anonymity really wasn't a thing for me. I couldn't let fear stop me, but I also had to be careful with my secrets. Guard them in case the queen truly was watching.

"Well," I hedged, wondering how much to say. "I'm sure most of you already know my story. It's no secret. A friend and I were partying at Fallen when I was attacked." I lifted my hands, palms up, as though to say *what can you do*. "I got more than I bargained for. I thought we'd be safe, thanks to the treaty, but I was naïve. One thing led to another and a vampire—who shall remain nameless—dragged me outside and drained me before tossing me into the trash."

I think that was the part that stung the most. He'd discarded me like I was nothing more than garbage. A wasted meal he hadn't had room to finish.

Soft whispers swept through the room. I did my best to ignore them *and* the memories sweeping through me. Petrik didn't deserve the real estate in my head.

"Lucky for me," I continued, raising my voice above their murmurs, "another vampire found me and saved me."

"Dracula," someone whispered reverently, confirming my suspicions that I was no stranger here.

I rolled my eyes, a small smile tugging on the corner of my lips. "Yes, *Vlad*. He sired me and has been teaching me the ropes for the past few months."

Noah's nod drew my attention. When our gazes met, I noted the emotion flashing within his eyes. Pity, definitely. But perhaps a hint of something else? Something I couldn't quite put my finger on. Admiration, perhaps?

"And what happens now that your sponsorship is coming to an end?"

My mouth parted. I'd asked Vlad months ago what would happen to us when our time finished. He hadn't explicitly said we'd remain together. But Vlad loved me. And I—*ahem*—loved him. Surely, he wouldn't kick me out, right?

"I, uh..." Truth be told, I didn't know the exact answer to this. Hell, he didn't even know we were visiting my family this week.

Noah's head bobbed before he addressed the rest of the group. "These are questions you all need to ask. Regardless of your relationship with your sire"—he pinned me with a quick but piercing glance—"you need to know specifically what happens to you at the end of your term. Will your sire leave you? Will he or she expect you to branch out on your own? These are all important questions. As new vampires, it's in your best interest to prepare yourselves. To ensure you know how to survive on your own when that day arrives. Know what your future holds, otherwise..." His gaze lingered on me for a few seconds longer before he studied the group. "Who would like to go next?"

Violet raised her hand and started regaling the group with her story. Honestly, I didn't catch most of what she said. My mind was too busy running in circles. I had no reason to doubt Vlad. He meant far more to me than a sire, and vice versa. He'd waited for me for fifty years, promised to protect me from Petrik. We'd slept together, expressed emotions for one another.

But Noah's words kept circling my head, along with the knowledge that Vlad had never explicitly explained what would happen to us at the three-month mark. I didn't want to be set free from him. New Orleans and Vlad's mansion had become my home. The thought of leaving literally made me ache.

No, I couldn't let a stranger's words upset me. Vlad and I were soulmates. I had to trust in that.

CHAPTER

FOUR

SOMEHOW, I found myself wandering City Park after VA wrapped up. Camilla had left me strict instructions to wait for her in the parking lot, but the meeting left me with a great deal of restless energy. I found myself longing to be alone, even if only for a few minutes. I hadn't noticed it until Noah pointed it out to another vampire, but I hadn't had any time alone since I'd been turned. The other vampire had confessed that he was too scared to even go for a walk by himself, afraid he'd lose control and kill someone. Memories of me attacking Harold had flashed through my head, and I'd sympathized. But things were different now. I wasn't fresh out of my grave. And damn it, I wanted a few minutes to myself so I could think.

For three long months, everywhere I went, Vlad or Camilla followed. My only time away from them was when Lucy and I vegged out watching a movie or gave ourselves pedicures. But even then, Lucy was there.

So, after the meeting, I'd bailed. Slipped out the back door and just... started walking. It wasn't until I reached City Park and found myself staring at a gondola that I realized where my feet had led me. This place was special to me. Vlad had brought me here on a quick date to get us out of the house and away from the madness. He'd wanted a few moments for us to enjoy each other's company without someone breathing down our necks. And I'd loved every moment.

I stood on the dock and stared out at the lake. It was incredibly quiet tonight. Hardly any tourists on the water, and the wildlife was calm and subdued. Almost as though the world matched my mood.

I'd always loved New Orleans. Even as a child, before my parent's divorce, my family and I had come here frequently. The city was always so vibrant and full of life. It stank to high heaven, but that was part of the charm.

As a vampire, I still appreciated the beauty, especially when the city lit up the night sky. But I also understood the darkness a bit better now, like the monsters that lurked in the shadows and the businesses that catered to them. The Vampire Lounge, for instance. Located in the French Quarter, it was a vampire blood brothel. As a human, I'd thought it nothing more than a tourist trap. A Gothic "bar" catering to a certain crowd. Their true crowd, however, had sharp fangs and no reflections.

Like every other human out there, I'd lived my life in this safe little bubble, believing us to be the most dangerous creatures in the world. Then we'd learned about vampires and had been forced to adjust our worldly perspective.

Such a change had forced me to grow up and to open my eyes to the truth. It'd taught me to ask the hard questions. And right now, there was one *very* hard question I needed answered. It shouldn't frighten me to ask Vlad about his future intentions, but damn it, the reality had me quaking in my newly purchased Valentino shoes.

What if I didn't like Vlad's answer? What if *his* truth was different from mine? What if this all came crashing to an end? Was I ready for that? Ready to branch out into the world on my own, knowing that eternity literally meant *forever*?

One day, Lucy would die. And my family would be gone. Without Vlad, I'd be left with nothing but memories that would eventually fade.

I'd thought of these things in passing, but never really *considered* them. Passing thoughts in the night that meant nothing because I still had Vlad and Lucy. But what if I didn't?

Sighing, I took a seat on the nearby grass and stared up at the stars.

Now, *this* was something I loved about being a vampire. The stars were virtually impossible to see here with human eyes, thanks to the light pollution, but my eyes were sharper now.

"Beautiful, right?" a soft voice murmured next to me.

I glanced over, a small frown furrowing my brows at the sight of Noah. Had he followed me here? And what was beautiful? Me? The backdrop? Or the stars? Better not be me... just saying.

"Anna, right?" he asked.

I refrained from rolling my eyes. Like I believed he wasn't sure about my name.

When I didn't immediately respond, he seated himself next to me, then pulled his knees up to his chest and stared up at the sky. He let out a long, albeit unnecessary breath. "It really is beautiful here."

"Did I forget something at the meeting?"

"No, of course not. I just wanted a chance to speak to you privately."

I caught the inside of my cheek with my teeth, my senses now on high alert. I'd already told him and all the others my story. There was literally nothing more to know about me.

Again, when I didn't respond, he lowered his head and caught my gaze. His eyes were a warm honey brown color, his hair sandy blond. No distinguishable features that I could see, but when he smiled, I noticed one of his teeth had a small chip.

"You can tell a lot about people from the things they say," Noah commented. He paused briefly, then finished with, "And the things they don't say."

"Okay..."

"For instance, you never mentioned who attacked you in the alley."

All my inner alarms blared in warning. "Because it's not important."

"Not important to mention the vampire who attacked you?"

"Why do you care?" I retorted.

"That's my job, Anna. I'm here to listen and help new vampires adjust to this world."

"And that involves pestering me about the details?"

"Pester." He chuckled, then picked at a blade of grass next to his knee. "I suppose some would see it that way. You know, before I became a vampire, I was a therapist."

Oh god, a shrink. Yup, he was evil. All that remained was establishing *how* evil.

"As a human, I was pretty tuned in to people's emotions. As a vampire..." He let his sentence hang.

I sighed, taking my time to exhale. "Let me guess, you developed an interesting ability to actually read people's emotions."

Because why wouldn't he? Vampires developed supernatural gifts over time. Vlad had visions of the future. I actually had no idea what Camilla's special ability was. Being annoying? Kicking my ass? Either of those two would fit.

Noah cracked a smile. "An uncanny ability, some might say."

I rolled my eyes. "Great. An empath."

"It's a trait I've come to rely on."

"I'm sure. What does all this have to do with me?"

Noah eased back onto his elbows and stretched out his legs. He looked the picture of ease, as though he hadn't a care in the world. All for show though. I was intimately familiar with vampires and the mind games they played.

"Everything," Noah finally said. "I can feel the disquiet in you."

"Hooray for you. What, you want a cookie or something?"

"I wouldn't turn one down."

He delivered the line so smoothly, I couldn't help but laugh. "You know we can't eat them, right?"

"I'm not here to discuss our peculiar diet." He laid back on the grass and tucked his hands under his head. "You never dealt with what happened to you."

I shot him an unimpressed glare. "Says you."

"Yes, says me. I can feel your emotions, remember? That would make me an unequivocal expert in the field."

"Yeah, well, no one asked you to go rummaging around in my feelings. Especially considering we don't even know each other."

I dusted off my hands, about to push to my feet, when Noah's fingers grazed my knee.

"Just listen, please. What harm can it do?"

I rolled my eyes, then turned to stare at the lake. The fact that I hadn't left yet was permission enough for him to continue. Doubtful I was going to like what he had to say, but once he *said* it, I could move on.

"I know you believe you've adjusted. But I can feel your fear. It's hidden deep within you, buried beneath layers of sarcasm and snippy thoughts. Those feelings need to be addressed and dealt with, otherwise they'll fester like an infected wound."

"Then don't pick at it," I grumbled.

Noah's deep chuckle made my mouth twitch. "Clever, Anna. But cleverness will only get you so far. Until you tackle your unresolved emotions, that wound *will* fester. These things don't heal naturally. If you had a broken limb, you'd see a doctor for it, right?"

I couldn't help but laugh. We were vampires. We didn't need doctors. A fact I'd become intimately familiar with over the last few months. When Camilla trained someone to fight, she didn't hold back.

"Your analogy is dated," I commented. "We're vampires, remember?"

"True. But my point still remains. Have you ever considered speaking with a therapist?"

Hell no. That was the last thing I needed. "No. And thanks for this little chat, but I—"

"Vlad can't protect you from everything," Noah suddenly said.

I froze. "What?"

"You feel safe in his little world. But his world is what killed you in the first place, or don't you remember?"

"No. I remember *me* getting *myself* killed by sticking my nose where it didn't belong."

"Into *his* world," Noah argued. "And what about the queen? Do you think she's just going to let this all go?"

I sucked in a sharp breath and leapt to my feet. "Who are you? What do you know?"

Noah held his hands out peaceably, but there was a fire to his gaze now that wasn't there before. "I mean you no harm."

"Like hell you don't."

"Anna, any vampire with his ear to the ground knows the queen is gunning for you."

Gunning for me? No. She'd summoned me, but there was no evidence she wanted me dead. My frown must have given me away because Noah slowly climbed to his feet. He held my gaze as he plunged his hands into his pockets, as though trying to appear like the friendliest little vampire ever.

"What's the point of all this?" I whispered. "Why are you here? Why are you digging into my life? What do you want from me?"

"That's the thing. Nothing. I don't want anything from you."

Impossible. Everybody always wanted something. "Try again."

"No, Anna. I'm serious. I just want to help."

"Well, you have a funny way of showing it. Do you work for the queen? Are you spying on me for her?"

Noah chuckled, his fangs flashing in the moonlight. I instinctively took a step back, one he noted with an arched brow. "See, that's what I mean. You don't trust vampires. And why should you? We didn't exactly welcome you into our community with open arms."

"So?"

"So... I think you need to deal with that. Before you can deal with anything else. Before you can happily move on."

"You never answered my questions," I accused.

"True. But then, you really didn't answer any of mine."

I ground my teeth and glared at him. Just like that, I knew I didn't like this guy. Noah was far too pushy for his own good. I may not be an ancient vampire, but I'd survived the last one who'd come after me. I wasn't weak or helpless.

Sighing, Noah shifted his weight, then pulled his hands out of his pockets. Clutched in his right hand was a crisp envelope, somehow in pristine condition. "Here. Take this."

I didn't take it from him. Nope. No way. A sealed letter from an unknown vampire. Nuh-uh. Didn't matter that my curiosity *burned* to see what was inside. I'd grown up *a lot* in the past three months, grown wiser and more worldly—or so I hoped—and accepting this letter smacked of stupidity.

"No thanks." I turned to leave.

"Anna." Noah's voice made me pause. It wasn't rude or mean, but his voice possessed a strength it'd lacked moments ago.

When I glanced over my shoulder, he strode toward me and slipped the envelope into my back pocket, careful not to touch me. Then he threw me a two-fingered salute and vanished.

What the hell had all this been about? Empath or not, this was about more than my unresolved issues. Had he sought me out after class specifically to give me some note? And who was it from?

I slowly pulled the envelope out of my back pocket and studied it. Absolutely nothing stood out to me. No stamp, no name, nothing but a blank slate. There was certainly something inside though. I could feel the edges of a card.

Nibbling on my lip, I turned it over and let my fingers rest against the sealed flap. I could wait to open it until I was home. Until I stood next to Vlad. I could. Or I could open it now. The nosey side of me won out. Maybe I *hadn't* grown up much then.

Cursing under my breath, I caved to my curiosity, ripped open the envelope, then pulled out what looked like a business card. *Noah Bradshaw, Therapist to the Undead.*

I couldn't help but laugh. Undead therapist? Seriously? Did he actually think I'd call him?

Shaking my head, I slipped his card back into my pocket and headed toward the VA building. It would take a hell of a lot more than this to get me to talk to a shrink—but I had a feeling he already knew that.

CHAPTER

FIVE

I groaned at the sound of Camilla's voice. Busted. I knew she would ride my ass for wandering off, but damn, couldn't a girl get a moment to herself?

Apparently not, considering the way she marched toward me, armed with a fierce glare.

"Whoa," a voice rose next to me.

I glanced over just in time to see a mess of pastel hair bob into sight. Guess Violet had also hung around for a bit after the meeting.

"Is she a friend of yours?" Violet asked, staring at the shitstorm heading my way.

With her nose crinkled and fangs bared like a pissed off kitten, if I didn't know her, the sight might have concerned me. But I was so used to her kicking my ass now that a little temper tantrum really didn't bother me.

"Well, she thinks she is."

Violet chuckled and tucked her hair behind her ears before turning to face me. "I just wanted to tell you how brave I think you

310

are. I know your transition hasn't been an easy one. Oh, and I love your vlog."

I inwardly winced and silently prayed that she didn't start fawning over me. I'd had enough of that recently.

"I don't know why I didn't recognize you when you sat down at the meeting, but—"

"Ixnay on the og-vlay," I said, absolutely mutilating the Pig Latin, then gestured subtly to Camilla.

Violet's eyes widened. "She doesn't...?"

"Camilla," I bellowed. "I've been looking for you."

"Oh, have you now? I've been sitting out there for thirty minutes, waiting for you to show your little ass. Did I not tell you to meet me in the parking lot?"

I mean, close enough, right? We were only about a block away. I didn't argue with her though. I knew better. The woman was a she-bat from the inner realms of hell when pissed.

"Who is this?" she demanded, jabbing a finger toward Violet. "You know what? I don't care. Let's go."

"Sorry," I muttered to Violet. "See you next week?"

"Oh, um. Yeah. See ya!"

Once she strolled off, I prepared myself for the brunt of Camilla's tantrum. Instead, she huffed and started toward her car. "Let's go. We have a training session tonight."

No, we didn't. She was just pissed that I'd made her look for me, and now she was making shit up as she went. First it was the VA and now training. What was next?

I planted my hands on my hips and faced her. "Camilla, are you ever gonna climb outta my ass?"

She jerked to a stop and unleashed a stare worthy of Medusa. "What did you just say to me?"

Okay, so a wiser person might have retracted their statement, then dropped to their knees and begged for this goddess's forgiveness. But because she wasn't actually a goddess, just a trumped-up vampire with an ego the size of Vlad's dick, I felt no need to prostrate myself before her. Instead, I waved goodbye to Violet, then marched to Camilla's ride.

"Well?" I grabbed the passenger side door handle. "You coming or what?"

"One of these days..." Camilla growled as she circled the front of her car and slipped behind the wheel. "One of these days, Vlad and I won't be around to save your sorry little ass, and that's the day you'll find yourself in deep shit."

"Ooo, I'm shaking in my heels. Just admit it. You don't have a life anymore, and that's why you won't leave us alone."

"Are you kidding me right now?" Her fingers gripped the steering wheel so tightly, I wondered if the leather stitches would pop. "Do you have any idea how much trouble you're in?"

"Oh my god—"

Camilla jerked, her slitted eyes flashing at me.

"—I am so sick and tired of hearing about how much trouble I'm apparently in. You sound like a broken record. I'm starting to wonder if it's all in your head. The queen is pissed, I get that. But where is she, huh? You're all jumping at shadows."

"And I suppose it's all in Vlad's head too?"

I shrugged, then braced my hands against the dashboard the instant Camilla slammed the car into drive and tore out onto the street. I'd learned very early on that she wasn't exactly a safe driver. Some nights I even wondered if she had a license.

"I swear by all things bloody, there is nothing more exasperating than a newborn vampire."

"And yet, you continue to punish yourself by hanging out with me."

I was definitely pushing her buttons tonight. Her flushed cheeks and narrowed eyes told me everything I needed to know. But guess what? The woman had literally burst into Vlad's office postcoital, so if I was needling her, it was because she deserved it. She'd been annoying me for months. A little payback wouldn't hurt.

"I hang out with you to train you. To make sure that when the queen calls for your head, you can defend yourself! And to make sure someone is there to pick up the pieces when she murders your ass."

"She isn't going to murder my ass. Geez. Are all vampires this melodramatic?"

Camilla growled and gripped the steering wheel even tighter. I watched the leather strain beneath her fingers and wondered if the poor thing could handle her strength.

"I want you to listen very closely, Anna. You are in over your head right now. You have absolutely no fucking idea what the queen is capable of. So, when Vlad and I tell you that you're in danger, you need to listen."

"Vlad doesn't seem as concerned as you."

"Vlad is hiding it from you, idiot! He doesn't want to scare you. I've told him he needs to be upfront with you about all this stuff, but he refuses. So you know what, I'll do it for him."

I rolled my eyes and settled back against the seat. This wasn't the first time I'd borne witness to Camilla's theatrics. She had a dramatic flair that rivaled my mother's.

She took a hard right-hand turn, the wheels screeching against the pavement. Distantly, I heard someone shriek, "asshole!" I glanced back but couldn't see anyone. I did spot a stop sign though. One she'd blown right through.

"There was a stop sign back there," I told her, not that she listened.

"Haven't you wondered why no one complains about the queen? Why no one ever fights back against her rules? Why there's never been a revolution against her?"

"Considering Genevieve is actually Marie Antoinette, I always figured it had something to do with her past. Maybe everyone loves her for letting them eat cake?"

Camilla spared me a stunned glance, running through a red light. "You truly are an imbecile."

I shot her a beaming grin. "But you love me."

"I... don't even know what to say to that. Vlad could have chosen anyone, but he chose you."

That didn't sound like a compliment.

"The reason no one argues about the queen's rules is because every time she catches the slightest whisper of rebellion, she slaughters everyone involved."

Well, that got my attention.

"I can think of three times in my lifespan alone where the queen rounded up her inquisitors and unleashed them on the entire vampiric community. Everyone was questioned, and if the inquisitors weren't unequivocally convinced that you were the utmost loyal citizen, they burned you, your house, and everyone you knew to the ground."

"That's murder."

She pinned me with a look that clearly said "duh." "Vampires aren't governed by the same laws as humans. This peace treaty with your president is all for show. The queen doesn't care about peace with humans. She only cares about what humans can do for us. The economy has quadrupled since the treaty. New businesses, new products, new jobs. Where do you think that money goes?"

Was this a trick question?

Camilla sped through a yellow light. "By the blood, you really are stupid. The money goes back to Genevieve and her people. As the principal investor in all these new companies, she's lining her royal coffers while playing nice with the humans. And then you came along and threw a lynch pin into all her plans. Not only that, but you did it publicly. Your photos from the night Vlad changed you are still everywhere. You caused a scene. You gave humans a reason to distrust the treaty, to distrust her. And on top of all that, you killed her sire."

"I didn't kill—"

"He's dead because of you. You're responsible. Sam went tearing in and decapitated the queen's sire to save your life." She shot me another glare. "The queen isn't just summoning you for a quick interview. She wants to make an example of you. To kill you and prove to the rest of us that you're nothing more than a minor nuisance."

My silence seemed to settle Camilla's nerves. Her fingers loosened from the steering wheel, and she stretched them out, all while running yet another stop sign.

"Do you get it now?" she asked.

Oh, I got it, all right.

I was well and truly fucked.

And not in a good way.

"ANNA MARIE PERISH!"

I whirled around at the sound of my name. The first thought that slammed into my head was "Mom?" But that voice definitely didn't belong to my mother. Oh no. It belonged to Lucy. My bestest best friend who was storming down the hallway toward me, anger crackling in her eyes. Damn. Was she seriously still mad at me? So I invited Sam to Perish. So what? It wasn't like she had to sleep with him or anything.

"Where's my cell phone?" she demanded, her long, dark-brown hair swishing behind her back. Ooh baby, she was definitely pissed. "You give me my phone. Right this second!"

I pressed my lips together to keep from laughing. Lucy was hardly a scary person. More like a little mouse. Sure, she had teeth, but they weren't as sharp as mine. She was all bark, no bite. I loved that about her.

"Well?" She came to a stop in front of me, her toe tapping the tiled floor.

"Sorry, girl. I don't know where it is." Which wasn't true. I knew exactly where it was. It'd fallen out of my jeans' pocket when I was getting my groove on with Vlad. It was probably still sitting on his desk, dinging nonstop. Bet it was driving Vlad insane. He wasn't a fan of technology at the best of times.

"Anna!" she shrieked. "You give me my damn phone—"

"Why?" I asked, interrupting what I was sure would be a fabulous tirade of threats that never frightened me.

"It's my phone! I don't need to tell you why I need it—"

"Nope, but you could tell me why you're so mad about it."

"You took it!"

"And?"

"And I want it back."

"Why?"

Anger tinged her cheeks a wondrous shade of red. Poor Lucy. She'd never been able to hide her emotions. With her fair skin, the slightest thing often set it off.

"Anna..."

"Tell me why you're so desperate for your phone."

"I hate you," she growled.

"You love me. Now tell me what's going on, otherwise you'll never see your precious phone again."

"You wouldn't."

"Please. You know I would. I'm officially holding your phone hostage until you tell me what has your panties in a twist."

Lucy cursed under her breath, then raked her hands through her hair, her nails scraping against her scalp. "I just... want it back, alright?"

"Why?"

"Oh my god, you're a pain in my ass today!"

"Watch it," I warned. The G-word didn't affect me, but I wasn't the only vampire living on these premises.

Lucy sighed, then dropped her arms to her side. "Fine, I'll tell you. But don't laugh at me."

I held up my hand. "Scout's honor."

"Oh, don't you scout's honor me. You were never a scout."

I chuckled, enjoying the exasperation in her voice. Man, I was in a mood today, and it was all thanks to Camilla. It should be against the law to ruin a girl's post-orgasm bliss.

Lucy averted her gaze, then muttered, "I need to text him."

It didn't take a genius to know exactly who she was referring to. And I promised I wouldn't laugh. But that didn't mean I couldn't still tease her. I never promised that.

But the second I saw her face, I bit back my words and instead nodded. She'd masked it with her anger, but I could see now that she was miserable. And I completely understood. Lucy was holding herself back from her mate, denying their relationship. I couldn't even imagine how that felt. Being with Vlad made my world feel complete. If I applied that to Lucy, it seemed pretty safe to assume that her world felt a little broken right now. And since texting was all she allowed herself, it was no wonder she was going a little crazy.

"Come on," I told her.

"Where are we going?"

"Vlad's office."

"Anna, please, I just want my phone."

I offered her a tiny smile, then took her hand and slowly led her toward his office. "I know. It's in there. We'll get it, then you can text Sam."

I sensed the relief in her. Her fingers loosened against mine and her shoulders relaxed. This whole "mate" stuff was serious business. She'd be happier if she stopped fighting it, but Lucy didn't know how to do that. She tended to make everything just a little bit more complicated. But that was part of her personality. Type A individuals didn't know how to easily adapt.

Voices rose to my ears as we neared Vlad's office. At the sound of my name, I gripped Lucy's hand tightly and pulled her to a stop. She glanced up at me, intending to question me, but I held a finger to my lips, then listened. If I could hear them, they could hear us, and I didn't want to give our presence away, not when I wanted to know what they were talking about. Rude, yes, but hey, so was talking about people behind their backs.

"She's being purposely obtuse," Camilla whined. "Either she's deliberately ignoring this or she's so naïve that she literally doesn't understand how much danger she's in."

"She understands," Vlad's voice rumbled. "We must be patient with her. A few months is hardly enough time for someone to adjust to all this. Her entire world has changed."

"That's exactly what I mean!" Camilla's heels clacked against the floor in a sharp pattern. Pacing, I realized. "Yes, her world is completely different, but I really don't think she understands. She's acting as though she's the same girl who stormed into Fallen."

"I disagree."

"Oh, you disagree?" Camilla's heels fell silent. "Is that why you're sheltering her from the truth? Acting as though everything is perfectly fine?"

"I don't see a reason to cause her undue stress."

"You have to be kidding me." Camilla sighed, then I heard the sound of a creaking chair. She must have sat down. "I swear, you two are utterly perfect for each other. She doesn't want to face reality and you don't want to force her to."

Vlad groaned, and I could picture him pinching the bridge of his nose. "Camilla—"

"You *have* to tell her, Vlad! You can't keep hiding something like this from her. She has every right to know, and maybe it'll smarten her up a little."

My mouth pursed. Tell me what? What exactly was Vlad hiding from me?

"It isn't the right time."

"The right time?" Camilla belted out a frustrated groan. "Listen to me, because I'm going to make this very clear. If you don't tell her about your latest vision, I will."

A chill rippled down my spine. Another vision?

"You've heard the whispers as well as I, Vlad," Camilla continued. "The queen wants her head. And if Anna refuses this latest summons, which I expect her to, there's talk of the queen unleashing a few of her inquisitors to track Anna down and drag her before Genevieve. I've heard this from very reliable sources."

"As have I."

"And you haven't told her?" Camilla demanded.

"What would that accomplish? She's terrified, Camilla. I don't think it's that she refuses to believe the truth, but rather that she's too frightened to face it."

Ouch. I definitely didn't like hearing that. Especially from Vlad. Was Camilla right? Was I being purposely obtuse? Closing my eyes to the truth and just hoping for the best?

"Then we have to make her."

I gripped Lucy's hand, squeezing perhaps a little too tight if her sharp intake of breath was evidence of anything. Thankfully, Camilla and Vlad were too busy arguing with each other to hear her.

"Vlad, you have to talk to her about this. She thinks I'm exaggerating because you're downplaying the danger. She trusts you more than me."

"Understandably."

"Yes, because you're her mate! It's your job to—"

"Protect her?" Vlad suddenly snapped. "I know this. What do you think I've been doing? It's my job to help her. Defend her. But it's also my job to love her, Camilla."

Tears sprang to my eyes.

"I will do whatever it takes to keep her safe."

"Including keeping her in the dark?"

Vlad didn't answer.

"You're both fools" was Camilla's parting retort before I heard the door click shut.

Unfortunately, I was starting to agree.

CHAPTER
SIX

Lucy dragged me into the kitchen, then wrenched open the refrigerator door and grabbed a bottle of water. I watched longingly as she leaned against the counter, popped the lid, and took a massive swallow. The sight of those wet little water beads gliding down the side of the bottle parched my throat.

Interestingly, it wasn't sweets or even steak I missed the most. It was water. The first cool, refreshing sip. A few months back, I'd attempted to steal a sip, just to see if I could tolerate it. The water had tasted like heaven in my mouth, but it'd scalded like fire on the way down. Lucy suggested just swishing and spitting, but I refused. Why torture myself like that?

Lucy wiped a hand across her mouth, and I blinked, forcing my thoughts back to the present. She recapped the bottle, then glared at me. "You're being ridiculous. You know that, right?"

Hmm. Much like lipstick, there were varying shades of ridiculousness, from Puckering Asshole Pink to 50 Shades of Perverted Grandma Red. Currently, I ranked somewhere in the middle. Maybe somewhere around the Peachy Orgasm shade.

In all fairness, I didn't feel ridiculous. I actually felt quite justified in my decision to ignore Vlad and Camilla's conversation. Why bring it up? Why even mention what I'd overheard? What would it accomplish?

"Anna, listen. I know you."

Oh here we go. Bring it on. The best friend speech.

"And I know you'll continue to avoid this conversation until it grows into a massive elephant-sized secret. Just *talk* to him. Is it really that hard to do?"

Sarcastic laughter slipped past my lips. "Talk about the pot calling the kettle black."

"Huh?"

I rolled my eyes, then imitated her voice. *"Just talk to him, Anna."* I shook my head. "Pretty sure I've been telling you to do the exact same thing with Sam for months now."

Her mouth pursed. "That's different."

"Oh, hun. It's so very not."

Lucy grumbled under her breath and slammed back another mouthful of water. Pretty sure she was doing it on purpose just to annoy me. And I seemed incapable of ignoring it. My damn tongue shot out and licked my lips of its own accord.

So I gave her my back and started fiddling with the few dishes left in the sink. "If Vlad doesn't want to talk to me about any of this, why should I force it?"

"I don't know, maybe because it's your *life*? Don't you even want to know what he saw in his vision?"

My fingers paused on a bread knife, and I sighed. "Lucy, stop pushing."

"For crying out loud," she snapped. "You two are like toddlers, I swear. You wax poetic about all this soulmate shit, how you're destined to be together, how nothing will tear you apart when really, the two of you are literally terrified of each other."

I burst out laughing. "I'm *not* scared of Vlad. Please. At least I can be around him without turning into a frightened little schoolgirl."

"Hey!" The scent of blood rose, so I knew she was blushing. "We're not talking about me and Sam."

I glanced over my shoulder and lifted a brow. "How'd you know I was talking about you and Sam? Unless you *know* you're being a little chicken shit."

"I'm sorry, *who's* being the chicken shit here? All you have to do is tell Vlad you overheard his conversation with Camilla and ask him to be honest with you. Tell him you want to know exactly what's going on. Clearly, he's been hiding stuff from you. Doesn't that piss you off?"

On some level, it did. On *all* levels, really. I didn't like being treated like a simpering damsel in distress. And I certainly didn't appreciate that he didn't trust me with the truth. But secretly—or maybe not so secretly—I was terrified. Lucy wasn't the only chicken shit here. This whole queen nonsense was getting way out of hand. If Camilla could be trusted—and I knew she could—the queen hated me. Which was just my luck. But it also raised some questions. Camilla made it sound like those who were disliked by the queen were "handled." As in, killed. So how come no one had attempted to kill me yet? After all, I was a newborn vampire who lacked any real power.

Okay, so I could wake up before the sunset, but that literally meant nothing in the grand scheme. And yes, maybe I was the first human changed into a vampire after Genevieve established the peace treaty, but on a scale of one to ten, that little blip ranked a solid negative five. It didn't matter in the slightest bit.

So why hadn't anyone tried to kill me yet?

I could only think of one answer.

Vlad.

He was well thought of in the vampire community. Famous, rich, powerful, and ancient. The man could shapeshift into two different animals and had visions of the future. He was probably the only thing standing between me and countless vampires hunting for my head.

Of course, I also had Camilla on my side—a three-hundred-year-old vamp with an innate ability to kick anyone's ass. A talent that rivaled what's-his-face in that *Rocky* movie from the '70s or whatever.

Then there was the whole "I murdered Petrik" thing. Not that I actually had. But from my understanding, very few vampires knew about Sam. Werewolves weren't a secret, but the actual werewolves themselves guarded their identities like spies. No one knew *he* killed Petrik. Instead, word spread that I had done it. Lil ole me. That took some *major* skills. Ones I definitely didn't possess, but they didn't know that. I suppose that little tidbit could be giving them pause. If I could kill a millennium-old vampire, imagine what I could do to someone half that age.

Truthfully, the answer was absolutely nothing. But hey, maybe this little white lie could work on my behalf.

"Anna."

I briefly closed my eyes and centered my thoughts. Lucy wouldn't quit pushing this because she *never* quit pushing things. The only way she'd shut up was if I agreed. "Okay, fine. I'll talk to him about all this. Alright?"

"Thank you—"

"But only if you talk to Sam."

Her mouth clicked shut while mine spread into a victorious grin. I had her now. For some reason that she didn't feel obliged to share, the thought of talking to Sam downright terrified her. But both of them were utterly miserable. Someone had to crack.

I hadn't tried it, but I couldn't imagine it was easy to avoid and ignore your soulmate. Even now, I felt the pull to seek out Vlad. He made me happy. He completed me. Why would I want to deprive myself of that?

Lucy lifted her chin and met my stare. I spotted the tightening of her jaw and the steel glint in her eyes. She wouldn't ignore my challenge, which was why I'd issued it. If she could push me into doing something I didn't want, then I could return the favor. She wanted me safe, I wanted her happy. So, I refused to feel guilty about my methods. Sometimes a girl had to fight dirty.

"Fine," Lucy bit out through gritted teeth.

I knew better though. "And I don't just mean a hello and goodbye. I'm talking a full conversation about what the two of you expect from each other. Have you even heard his side yet? Has he told you that he wants you as his mate? That he wants to be with you?"

"Well, no..."

"Have the discussion, Lucy. The full blown 'where's this relationship going' discussion. Learn each other's hopes and desires, wants and needs, likes and dislikes. Everything. Sort out what both of you want from this relationship, whether that means jumping each other's bones or walking away forever. But stop dragging him through your emotional mess and stop leading him on. The man has a right to know."

"You know, I like it better when I'm the one counseling you."

"Sucks when the tables are turned, huh?"

"Oh, shut up."

I grinned, then hopped up onto the kitchen counter, my feet dangling next to the lower row of cupboards. Of all the rooms in a house, the kitchen was the one I missed most. Especially the smell of baking. Not that I could bake. Lucy often quipped that my cooking could kill, and I believed her. Now, my mom... she could cook. Damn woman won the Miss Louisiana Best Pie baking contest every single year, which was totally a point of contention between us. When I was a human, she'd loved to hound me about it, ask me how I planned to provide for a husband if I couldn't create the simplest dishes.

Well, I showed her, didn't I?

Now all I had to do was open a vein—and my legs—to keep Vlad happy. There was more than that to our relationship of course. Depth and substance, and all that razzmatazz. But my mom didn't need to know all the finer details. Just the ones that would piss her off.

Yes, I knew that made me a little bit immature. But I didn't care.

"So, you're gonna talk to Vlad then?" Lucy pressed.

I cocked my head and stared at her. What the hell had I done in a past life to be gifted with not one but two naggy mothers? Well-meaning or not.

"Guess that depends. Are you going to talk to Sam?"

"I already said I would, didn't I?" she snapped.

"Then yes, I'll talk to Vlad."

"Good. When?"

Oh, sweet merciful baby Zeus. "Lucy."

"No, I'm serious. When? Because I know you. Procrastination is your middle name. You'll keep pushing it off until hell freezes over."

"Hmm. Hell freezing over does sound like fun. I could go ice skating with the devil. My parents would *love* that."

"Anna!" Lucy bit out.

I rolled my eyes. She was sucking the fun right out of this room. "Tonight, alright? Is that soon enough for you?"

"Then I'll speak with Sam this week once we're in Perish, whenever we can find a moment alone."

"Cuz that doesn't sound awkward."

"Well, I can't have that kind of conversation over the phone, now can I?"

Wasn't that the truth. "Guess we both have our assignments then."

She nodded, then stole another sip of water. You know, I'd never noticed how sensual the throat was. As a human, it hadn't once entered my thoughts. But now? I often found myself staring at the smooth column, watching it bob and dip, staring at the curve, studying the veins—

"Hey!"

Cold water splashed me in the face. I sputtered and mopped at my eyes. "What the hell was that for?"

Lucy stood next to me, her hands wrapped around the bottle she'd just squeezed. "You were doing it again! Gazing all longingly at my throat. It's creepy! Go suck on someone's wrist if you're hungry, but stop staring at my jugular."

"I wasn't gonna bite you!" I yelled.

"I don't care! You don't realize how disturbing it is. Your eyes get hazy, and you flash your fangs. It's just..." She shuddered. "Do it elsewhere."

"Spoilsport," I groused.

Grumbling under my breath, I jumped down from the counter and headed toward the nearby guest rooms where Vlad's harem lived.

Humph, guess I was a little hungry after all.

⚜

I PACED the length of the hallway in front of Vlad's bedroom.

After Lucy's and my little chat, I'd snuck a quick nip of blood, then wandered the house and considered my options. Really, there were only two. I could continue to play naïve and pretend like I didn't understand the gravity of the situation, or I could be upfront about it all and tell Vlad I'd overheard his conversation. The first option avoided an unpleasant discussion, the second welcomed a whole lotta trouble into my life. Naivety was starting to look mighty fine right now, but I knew Lucy would kick my ass all the way to the moon if I played that card.

Besides, I didn't run away from things. I'd always been the sort to face them head-on. Fearless and adventurous, 'twas I.

Of course, my last impetuous stint had landed me in a cement room filled with sunlight. But hey, I highly doubted that sort of luck struck twice in a lifetime.

Which left door number two. Being upfront.

Damn. I really wasn't looking forward to this conversation. Yes, we were soulmates. But we'd also only been together for three months. That wasn't a lot of time to build a relationship. And I was already about to test it.

But I'd promised Lucy. And I wasn't a coward.

So I squared my shoulders, pushed my hair off my face, then opened Vlad's bedroom door. This time of day, I often found him in here, undressing and unwinding from the night's events. Tonight, he stood on the attached balcony just outside his window with his back to me.

My eyes widened at the sight of him shirtless, his black slacks hung low on his hips. He gripped the balcony railing and stared out over his land, as though inspecting every last inch of it.

If ever there was a prize for hottest vampire, Vlad would win it hands down. The man was drop dead gorgeous with the hips of an Adonis. I couldn't see that fancy little V-thing right now since his back was to me, but it was always there, directing my gaze *downward* like a bright and shiny arrow. I wasn't a sex-crazed teenager, I swear. It was just my body's reaction to Vlad. He commanded attention, and I seemed completely willing to give it.

"I was beginning to wonder if I would see you again before sunrise," Vlad commented.

My attention dropped to his fingers, and I watched as they tightened around the railing. It surprised me to find him out here. Ever since the fiasco with Petrik, Vlad and I had avoided the balconies. A sort of unspoken rule. We hadn't known it at the time, but according to vamp logic, they didn't consider balconies part of the house, meaning they didn't require an invitation. Petrik had taken advantage of that little loophole and used it to abduct me. Needless to say, I didn't like balconies as much anymore.

I strode into the room. "Missed me, did ya?"

Vlad turned to face me, a soft smile curving his lips. "Always."

Ah, the things he said. Made a girl weak in the knees.

"How did the VA meeting go?"

I shrugged. "As well as expected, I suppose. I met a few vampires, heard a few sob stories that rivaled my own. The speaker was an odd man. An empath apparently, which wasn't fun. He told me I need therapy and handed me his business card."

"I've heard of him," Vlad said, nodding. "He's been around for a while."

"So, not one of the queen's spies then?"

"Unlikely."

Damn. That meant I really had no reason not to take his advice. Oh wait, yes I did. Because I didn't want to. Reason enough in my books.

"So, speaking of the queen..." I hedged, wincing at the horrible segue.

Vlad lifted a brow.

Ugh. I hated these types of conversations. They always set off my nerves and made my body tremble. Deep down, I knew I didn't have anything to fear—I hadn't done anything wrong, after all. But emotions didn't always follow logic. My traitorous hands were already shaking as I considered my words.

Vlad clasped my hands, then slid his upward, caressing my arms. "Whatever's bothering you—"

"I overheard you and Camilla tonight," I blurted. Best to just get it out there.

His fingers paused and his gaze lifted to mine. "Aren't you the one always telling me it's rude to eavesdrop?"

A weak chuckle slipped past my lips. "Yeah. That's me. But it's hard not to listen when you hear your name."

"I imagine so."

I snuck another covert glance, then turned away and braced my elbows against the balcony railing. We were surrounded by lowlands infested with gators, turtles, and a plethora of birds, and I absolutely loved it. Before moving here, I had cared little about Louisiana's wildlife, but living for the night had changed my perspective somehow. I appreciated nature's beauty more now that I was excluded from it.

"Well? Are we going to talk about it?"

"If we must."

"We must," I parroted. "We can't hide things like this from each other. If you had a vision about me, I need to know about it."

He nodded, then turned and pressed his side against mine. Warmth flushed my entire body, but I couldn't let that distract me.

"Am I in danger?" I asked.

He shot me a sorrowful look, then nodded. "Yes, I believe you are."

My nerves kicked into overdrive. I had to fist my hands together to keep them from visibly shaking. "How... How much danger?"

Vlad curled an arm around my waist and pulled me against him. "A great deal, I suspect."

"Tell me."

"It's all flickers right now. Which is how it always begins. It started this way when I first saw you in my dreams. Eventually, the dream becomes clearer. But until then, I'm at as much of a loss as you."

"But you know I'm in danger?"

"Of that, I have no doubt. I saw..."

"What?"

Vlad sighed, and gripped me tighter. "Your death. In my dream, I held you in my arms, and you were gone."

A shiver screamed down my spine. "Anything else?"

"Not as of yet."

"What can we do?"

After a moment's hesitation, he leaned in and kissed the top of my head. "Convince the queen you aren't a threat. We have proof of your innocence. The video you took at Fallen before Petrik attacked you. Allies who bore witness to your abduction from my house. Testimonials detailing what Petrik put you through. Her sire is dead, but it was a welcome, justified death. It may take an audience with her and the vampire council to prove your innocence, but I believe it can be done."

"Then you think the queen is the one responsible for my death?"

"Yes."

"Okay."

Vlad shifted his weight and peered down at me. "Okay? That's all?"

"What else is there to say?"

"I swear, Anna. I will never let anything happen to you. I'd sooner die."

"How about neither of us die? I like that scenario best."

"Me too," Vlad said, hugging me close. "I... apologize for keeping the vision from you. I didn't wish to frighten you. Perhaps we need to work on being open and communicative with each other."

"I haven't had much luck with relationships," I admitted with a nod.

"What's the word you use for that? Twinsies?"

I burst out laughing. "Ditto. It's ditto."

"Ah. Ditto. I like that word."

I snickered quietly. "Speaking of being open and communicative..."

"Mm."

"I told my mother that we'd come home this week."

"You did?"

"And I, uh, may have invited Sam along."

Vlad tensed. "You didn't."

I choked back a third laugh. Vlad and Sam were not the bestest of friends. Not even on the best of days.

"I would love it if you came with us," I said. "I want to introduce you to my mother."

"Anna..." He groaned and dropped his head forward until his brow rested against the railing. "Your mother? Seriously?"

I bit my bottom lip to keep my laughter in check. Our time together had certainly had an effect on Vlad's vocabulary. I wasn't sure he'd noticed the change, but I had. Far more sarcasm now than when we'd first met. And I absolutely loved it.

"We should probably reach out to my father too. Since we'll be in the neighborhood."

Vlad scowled playfully at me, his eyes catching the earliest morning light. We didn't have much time left. "What day did you say we'd leave?"

"Wednesday. Back on Sunday. It won't be a long trip."

"Long enough," he groused.

I stretched up and brushed a light kiss across his cheek. "Don't worry, I'll protect you from my big bad parents."

"You better," he growled.

This time, he lifted his head and captured my mouth in a hungry kiss. One we didn't have time to act upon.

Instead, I pulled back with a pout and glanced back at his bed. "Just think, in a few weeks, we'll hopefully be able to fall asleep together here, instead of locking ourselves in coffins."

With a bemused chuckle, Vlad swept me off my feet and bolted into his bedroom. I squealed and wrapped my arms around his neck. But before I could even blink, he tossed me on his bed and climbed on top.

"Vlad! We don't have enough time," I protested, laughing breathlessly.

"Want to bet?"

His head lowered and my laughter died on a soft gasp.

Best way to end the night.

CHAPTER

SEVEN

"Underwear?"

"Check."

"Socks?"

"Check."

"Ass-kicking Weitzman boots?"

"Double check."

"Garter and bustier?"

"Che—wait, what?" My head snapped up, and I blinked at Lucy. "I don't own a garter and bustier."

Lucy snorted and rose from the bed, notepad in hand. Since it was Tuesday night, and tomorrow we were leaving for Perish, she'd taken it upon herself to help me pack. Organization was next to godliness, or so she claimed. *Snooze alert.* But hey, she always made sure I didn't forget anything, so there was that.

"Girl, just who do you think you're talking to?" she asked, laughing under her breath. "I helped you buy them, remember?"

Ah, yes. That embarrassing moment when she forced me to strut my half-naked self around a lingerie shop, preaching that the right underwear would land me the right man. Cuz apparently, every man must see my underwear to help me decide if he's the right one for me or not. Whatever. She had some strange ideas in that head of hers.

What that underwear had actually landed me was a one-night stand with a man who had more attachment issues than a newborn baby. The experience had scarred me for life, so much so that I'd never worn it in front of Vlad—and never would. In fact, *that* particular underwear was locked in my apartment back in Perish. And when I finally moved out, it would go in the garbage.

"What about you?" I suddenly asked, turning the tables. After all, *she* was the one hopefully getting laid this weekend. I could only imagine what her travel bag looked like. Ziplocked bags full of perfectly folded clothing, separated with flimsy dividers meant to keep her things perfectly organized. Whereas mine, I just shoved everything in, then sat on top, attacked the zipper, and hoped for the best. "Did you pack condoms? Lots and lots of condoms?"

"No, I did not." She stuck her tongue out at me. "The agreement was I'd speak with Sam, not bone him."

"Ha. Bone him." I chuckled before returning to my packing.

"Oh for crying out loud, knock off the dog jokes, will ya?"

"Never," I vowed.

I mean, Sam was a werewolf. That pretty much ensured an eternity of jokes. Unless werewolves weren't immortal. Another question I needed answered. I actually didn't know much about the furrier kind, other than the fact that they knew how to hunt and kill ancient vampires. Sam had taken care of Petrik like it was no big deal. Impaled him with some special kind of stake made of hawthorn and treated in holy water and monksblood. A trade secret, Sam had said. And one I'd gratefully kept to myself. My issues with older vampires seemed to be a reoccurring theme, so that was information I knew to keep to myself. And if I could create such a stake, or maybe convince Sam to hand one over to me, I'd feel a lot better. The queen wasn't as old as Petrik, but she still had a couple hundred more years on me.

I reached for my toiletry kit, about to unceremoniously stuff it into the corner of my bag, when I caught the sound of a sharp, high-pitched sigh, followed by almost indecipherable grumbling. Frowning, I crooked my head and focused all my attention on the sound. It wasn't coming from Lucy. Or even from my bedroom. I strained a little harder, then nodded. The kitchen. Someone was in the kitchen.

"Nasty little vampires. And they call me filthy. Me! I'm a clean girl. Clean. Not them. Not clean. Not clean."

The fuck? Did we piss off one of Vlad's harem members or something?

The grumbling continued. A little quieter now. Yet higher pitched. It didn't match any of the voices I knew. I knew Beauregard's voice like the back of my hand. Dude was always in the way somewhere, tending to *Master Vlad's* needs. And the needs of the harem. Then there was Malinda, the youngest of the harem, and definitely the squirreliest. I still hadn't heard her full story, but for some reason, I imagined it involved a lot—and I mean *a lot*—of candy. The woman was *addicted*. Like, to the point where I never saw her without. It made *my* teeth hurt to drink from her sometimes.

"Filthy vampires!" the shrill voice squeaked again.

Geez, this person reminded me of that Gollum character from *Lord of the Rings*. Hated the movie but loved that little devil. Just the right amount of schizophrenic behavior to keep me invested. Lucy had shaken her head when I told her I was rooting for him. And when he bit off that other hobbit's finger, I was the only one who'd cheered.

Okay, maybe I liked a good underdog, so what?

"No food. No eats. Why? Filthy vampires."

I chuckled under my breath. Someone was definitely having a bad day. We kept the house stocked with plenty of food. Maybe Malinda had run out of candy and was crashing.

"What's so funny?" Lucy asked.

I blinked, the sound of her voice cutting me off from my eavesdropping. "Sorry. Someone's having some trouble finding a snack in the kitchen."

"And that's funny?" Lucy asked.

"You'd understand if you could hear them. They must be hangry.

They're bitching about how we don't keep enough food in the house."

Lucy lifted a brow. "Eavesdropping isn't polite, you know."

"Thanks, Mom."

"Hey." She held her hands up peaceably. "You're the one that's always telling Vlad to turn off his vamp ears. You should do the same."

"Do as I say, not as I do?" I retorted with a slight chuckle.

"Sure," she said, shaking her head. "So, have you told Vlad about the vlog yet?"

My smile instantly slipped from my face.

"I take it that's a no," she pressed when I didn't respond.

I eyed Lucy from across my suitcase. She stood next to a window, bathing in the late afternoon light that I couldn't touch, reading off a list she'd put together of everything we needed to bring.

"What's the hold up?" she demanded. "He knows you're a vlogger. I'm not sure he understands it, but he knows that was your profession before turning. Why are you hiding it from him?"

"Lucy..." I sighed. She didn't understand my apprehensions. Hell, I didn't even understand them. "I just haven't found a good time yet."

"Seriously?" She lowered her list and pinned me with an exasperated expression. "The two of you are together pretty much every minute of the night. The only time you aren't with him are the golden hours before he wakes or when you and Camilla are training. You actually expect me to believe that you haven't found a moment to tell him about it?"

I pinched the bridge of my nose and centered my thoughts. Lucy didn't realize this was a sore subject for me. Especially considering Vlad's and my chat last night about how we needed to be more open and honest with each other. That would have been the perfect moment to come clean about it, but no, I'd brought up my family instead. That one had a timeline, or so I'd told myself.

"Look, just tell him. The longer you take, the more upset he'll get. Your vlog is a success, has been for a while now! Have you seen the response to your most recent episode?" She tossed her phone across the gap, and I caught it single-handedly. She'd opened her email for me to look at, and it was riddled with notifications.

"The last episode already has over half a million views, more than a hundred thousand likes, and over five thousand comments. You've made it, baby. That's your tenth successful episode in a row."

"I know," I murmured. "I just..."

"What other proof do you need to see you're a success? Tell him."

"Lucy."

"What's the big deal?" she pressed. "Just walk up to him, show him the vlog, then tell him you're raking in the dough. He'll be happy for you!"

"Lucy," I growled.

"Stop being such a coward, Anna. The longer you wait to tell him—"

"Lucy! For crying out loud, back off!"

She startled and stared at me with wide eyes, as though shocked I'd raised my voice. Granted, I rarely yelled at her, but for cripes' sake, she was pushing my buttons tonight. Usually, I just ignored her bullheadedness and pushed past it, but tonight seemed to be one of *those* nights. The sort where her scolding and nagging shoved me over the edge.

I wasn't ready to tell Vlad about the vlog yet, and I honestly couldn't explain why. Imposter syndrome maybe? I'd never been this successful as a human. Which made me wonder if my success stemmed from me being a vampire. And if that was the case, how long till the fame faded? Nothing lasted forever.

"What's going on?" Lucy demanded. "I don't understand what the big deal is. You literally just need to shove your phone in his face and show him your channel. Problem solved. You're making this into a bigger deal than it needs to be."

I bit back a curse. Lucy was incapable of leaving anything alone, and I knew that. Just like I knew she'd keep picking at this until I finally caved and told Vlad. But I didn't want to be rushed into it. Nor did I want to listen to her berate me for not being open with Vlad. I *knew* all this already. I didn't need it from her as well.

But this was Lucy. *Peck, peck, peck.*

"You know, I'm getting really tired of you always butting your nose into my business every night," I complained, my words sour. "Don't you have your own life to live? Your own shit to pack? Your own relationship to meddle with?"

The instant the words left my mouth, I froze. I hadn't meant for it to come out so... combative and mean. I loved Lucy. I loved that she loved me enough to involve herself in everything in an attempt to protect me. I certainly didn't want to push her away.

I quietly cursed, but before I could apologize, she propped a hand on her hip and glared at me. "I do have my own life, thank you very much. A very normal, human life. But I can't live that life anymore because *you* went and got yourself killed, dragging me into this mess" —she waved her hands around the room—"you call *your* life. But you know what? Maybe it *is* time I returned to my life. And dealt with my own problems. Have fun packing by yourself." She stomped across the room and snatched her phone back from me.

"Lucy—"

She lifted a hand, effectively silencing me. "Have a nice night, Anna."

On that note, she turned and marched out of my room, slamming my door shut behind her.

Great. I sighed and plunked myself down on the bed. *Just fucking great.*

~➤~

I SAT in the kitchen with a steaming mug of blood sitting in front of me, but I couldn't bring myself to take a sip. The rancid smell turned my stomach, and I knew it would taste even worse. But tonight, I had no energy to track down one of the harem members, and even less inclination to sink my teeth into them. Fighting with Lucy always depressed me.

Seeing how our friendship spanned more than a decade, this was hardly our first row. Nor would it be our last. I'd always imagined us as little old ladies with blue and purple hair, sitting on the front porch, clutching glasses of sweet tea, yelling at them there youngsters to get the hell off our lawns. Neither of us had seen ourselves as loving little grandmas who knitted blankets for their kids and grandkids. That wasn't us.

But now that I was immortal, the image of us rocking together on the porch while spraying water at the neighborhood hoodlums and shouting at them to get off our lawns had vanished.

Lucy would grow old and gray, and I would remain exactly the same. It was actually a devastating thought. She was my partner in crime. My sister from another mister. We fought, we argued, we bickered, but we always came back to each other.

For the first time, though, I wondered if maybe I shouldn't apologize. If I should sever the friendship here and now, for her sake.

She'd said it herself: I'd dragged her into my mess of a life. Brought a human into the paranormal world. A world where she could very easily be eaten alive. It'd already happened to me, after all.

When I was first turned, Lucy had made me promise I wouldn't let the same thing happen to her. She believed there was nothing worse than becoming a vampire.

Keeping her in my life made me a selfish friend.

Maybe it was time to let her go. To break all ties and call it a day. Lucy hadn't promised Sam anything yet. She could turn around and walk away. Return home. Get a job at the local grocery store, go to school, find a husband, have a *life*. A human life.

She deserved that, and so much more.

"Well, don't you look like a barrel of sunshine tonight," a voice said, intruding on my thoughts.

I sighed and unleashed a miserable glare on Camilla. She stood in the kitchen doorframe, looking drop dead gorgeous, arms crossed above her chest. I knew that stance. That was her battle stance. The "time to kick your ass" stance.

"Not tonight," I mumbled.

I reached for the mug sitting in front of me and lifted it to my mouth. Heat touched my lips, but it didn't comfort me. My thoughts had taken a dark turn tonight.

"Yes, tonight," Camilla countered. She shoved away from the doorframe and stalked toward me. She hitched her hip against the counter, then leaned down and sniffed at the blood, her upper lip curling in distaste. "I can't believe you drink that shit."

I shrugged. I could count on one hand the number of times I had, and I'd hated it each time. But sometimes, a girl needed to hold a soothing warm mug between her hands. Coffee had been my go-to in my pre-vampire days, but the smell made me retch now.

"Alright." Camilla hooked the nearest chair with her foot and dragged it closer. "What's wrong?"

My lips flattened into a grim line. I so didn't want to talk about this with Camilla. I knew she considered me a friend, and I appreciated her efforts. Over the past three months, she'd molded me into a fighter. Something I hadn't believed possible. I wasn't the best, and I certainly wouldn't be winning any martial arts competitions. But she'd taught me how to attack and defend myself, shaped me into a strong, confident vampire. None of that meant I wanted to open up to her though. At least, not yet. Maybe one day.

When I didn't respond, she sat and braced her elbows against the counter. Then she grabbed my mug and dumped the contents into the sink. I watched as the thick liquid poured down the drain. Ugh. I couldn't blame Lucy for not wanting this. I literally fed off blood. And nothing else. Yes, I'd live forever, but as what? A shell of my human form? This monster that needed the lives of others to survive. We didn't need to kill, but that really didn't change anything.

We were vampires. Nosferatu. Creatures of the night, if we wanted to go more dramatic. Yes, I woke before sunrise, but I couldn't let the sunbeams touch me. If they did, I burned. I knew the stench of my own seared flesh, thanks to Petrik. And I'd survived with no visible scarring, thanks to my immortality. I woke every night looking exactly the same as the day before. If I cut my hair, it grew back. If I changed my nail polish, it reverted. We literally never changed. There was some sort of magic involved, something that hit the reset button for us every single night. The only thing that had an effect was permanent death. And even that wasn't easy. Decapitation, fire, or magically enchanted werewolf stakes. We never changed.

But Lucy would.

The day would come when she wanted a real life. When she wanted to settle down and have babies. I couldn't keep that from her. That'd make me every bit the monster I already believed I was. I had to be better than that.

Camilla sighed, then pivoted on the chair to face me. "I had a husband before I was turned, did I ever tell you that?"

Surprise widened my eyes. I shook my head, still not ready to speak, but I could listen.

She nodded, her eyes growing sad as she lost herself to her memories. "James was..." She hummed quietly to herself. "Amazing. James was everything I could have asked for in a husband. Nostalgia has probably made me forget his little annoyances because I only remember the good. He was kind, giving, loving, features that weren't common in husbands back then. Men were raised to be strong, dependable, and women were raised to listen to their husbands. James never expected that of me. He'd always treated me as his equal. And I him."

I wanted to ask what her point was, but for once, I just listened.

She gave a somber chuckle. "The night I became a vampire wasn't anything out of the ordinary. My carriage had broken a wheel. That was it. And while my driver was fixing it, darkness set, and..."

"A vampire found you," I murmured.

She nodded. "Back then, vampires were more akin to monsters than they are now. My maker—and I say maker because he was *never* my sire—slaughtered my driver first. Took his head clean off in his blood frenzy. Horrified, I watched as the creature slurped up the blood, his face bathed in it. Shock had frozen me through and through. Unlike most, I didn't scream, I didn't so much as take a breath. I couldn't move for fear he would see me next."

I forced myself to swallow. I knew the feeling she described oh so well. Petrik had savaged my throat when he'd attacked me.

"It wasn't until he looked up, face smeared in blood, that his teeth caught the moonlight and I screamed. I screamed so loud I thought everyone in the world must have heard me. He was on me before I could even take my next breath. I think he was a freshly made vampire himself, he seemed to have no control whatsoever."

Camilla drew a deep breath and caught my gaze. "He tore out my throat. I remember choking on my own blood. A fear like nothing I'd ever experienced came over me, and while I bled out, I attacked him. I actually managed to tear off his ear and claw up his face."

"He bled into your mouth," I surmised.

"He didn't know that. There was so much blood everywhere, he wouldn't have had any way of knowing whose blood was whose. He left just before I died. Then three nights later, I woke buried in the ground."

I shuddered. I'd woken in a coffin. It wasn't a pleasant experience.

"I did the only thing I could think of. I tunneled out and returned home. At that time, I had no idea what had happened to me. I simply thought there had to have been some mistake. James would never bury me unless he thought I was dead. But maybe there'd been a mistake."

Oh, I didn't like the sound of this.

"I returned home and nearly scared my husband half to death. He'd been drinking, likely for three days straight. He didn't believe his eyes. He thought I was a vision, an angel. The things he'd said to me."

Blood tears shimmered in Camilla's eyes, and she swiped them away before they could fall. "He told me how sorry he was. That he hadn't been there to protect me, that he loved me, that he'd miss me for the rest of his life, that I was perfect. When he finally sobered up, he realized I wasn't dead, he was so relieved, he nearly collapsed at my feet."

"Tell me you didn't hurt him," I pleaded. I couldn't handle that.

A faint smile crossed her face. "No. I was one of the lucky ones who managed to keep from slaughtering their loved ones. I told James what happened, about the monster. He didn't believe me. Thought I'd hallucinated from my injuries. It wasn't until we realized that I *needed* to feed off blood that he fully believed my story. But you know what?" She turned to look at me, her smile a bit fainter now. "He *chose* to stay with me. He told me we would endure. That he'd seen what his life looked like without me, and he never wanted to return to that dark place."

Oh my god. Could my heart melt any faster?

"He helped me find ways to feed. We tried animal blood, to no avail. So, he offered me his. Eventually, we realized we needed more people, so I learned to hunt discriminately. I learned how to sneak a sip here and there without anyone knowing. Lure men into back alleys for a small taste. And James helped. Because he loved me. He wanted me to survive."

"That's an oddly morbid but beautiful story."

"My point is, give Lucy the chance to make her own decision."

I went rigid. "What?"

"Oh, come on. I can see it all over your face. I heard the end of your argument as I woke."

"Did Vlad hear it?" I demanded, shock rippling through my nerves.

She frowned. "Not that I know of. Why?"

"No reason."

Camilla blinked, then shrugged. "I saw you sitting here, moping over your mug, and I figured you were probably considering cutting her loose. Every vampire goes through this thought process at some point. But Lucy is a grown ass woman. And your best friend. Don't make decisions for her. Don't force her to make choices she doesn't want to make. The day will come when she might move on from you, but in the meantime, enjoy your time together. And don't do something you'll regret in a few years. Because living with regret is different for us vamps. It's eternal."

I winced at the thought.

After a moment's pause, Camilla pushed to her feet. "Now, let's go. Time to train since we didn't get to last night."

I groaned and rested my head on the counter.

"No whining. No excuses. Let's go."

With a final sigh, I lifted my head, stared at the empty mug, then dragged my ass after Camilla. At the very least, maybe the training would give me something else to think about—for a few hours anyway.

CHAPTER

EIGHT

I woke the next night to an unusually quiet household. Generally, I could hear Lucy and the harem members moving around, playing games, talking, laughing, but today was an eerie silence. I laid still and took everything in, but the only sound came from outside the house, considering it would be about three or four hours or so until Vlad woke.

I slowly eased back my coffin lid and sat upright. White noise assaulted my ears, making them ring. The harem members had been given the rest of the week off—thanks to our upcoming trip to Perish —but I hadn't expected them to leave until we did. Seeing as how Vlad's house was quiet as the grave, guess I was wrong.

After a few moments, I climbed out of my coffin and gazed at Vlad's, right next to mine. Camilla's coffin usually sat near the back of the room. But after our training session last night, she'd moved it back to her house, knowing we were leaving for Perish tonight. I hadn't invited her to meet my mother, and Camilla hadn't insinuated a desire to come. So, for the first time in months, we were without her. It felt almost freeing.

Smiling, I touched Vlad's coffin lid. I couldn't wait until the new windows were installed. No more sleeping alone in a pine box. Soon, my life would return to normal—or as normal as I could get it—and I'd be able to cuddle with Vlad till we fell asleep, and wake in his arms. That sounded pretty heavenly to me, even for damned creatures such as us.

Sound rose to my ears, and I listened. Seemed Lucy was shuffling around downstairs, likely checking her bags for the umpteenth time before we left tonight. She hated forgetting things. And when she did, it would bug her until she remembered exactly what it was she'd left behind.

The thought made me chuckle. Until I remembered last night's fight.

We didn't speak again after it. In fact, I hadn't seen her since. Camilla had kept me absurdly busy with training. For once, I hadn't ended up battered and broken on the floor. Cause for celebration. Even Camilla had commented that I was starting to hold my own. I still hadn't successfully beaten her, but hey, I'd kept her from severely injuring me. A win in my book.

Lucy's and my fight, however... that one I didn't consider a win.

I recalled Camilla's story, and her advice to let Lucy choose for herself. I truly wanted to, but I wasn't convinced that was the right way to go. Camilla had put James's life in great danger. What if they'd been discovered? The authorities would have strung James up and burned Camilla at the stake. Yes, things were different now, seeing as how humans knew all about us, but that didn't make the danger any less real. Especially considering my recent issues with the queen. One day, Genevieve would come a-calling, and I didn't want Lucy caught in the crosshairs when that day came. If I let her choose, and she chose to stay with me, what kind of friend did that make me? I couldn't unlive with myself if something bad happened to Lucy because of me.

Regardless of that, though, I did need to apologize to her. I shouldn't have snapped at her like I did. My business was her business —always had been. And I wanted to bury the hatchet before we began the trip home. I couldn't imagine anything more painful than an hour and a half drive with two feuding friends.

I reached for the attic ladder, about to descend to the main levels, when I heard a strange sound. Soft at first, then a bit louder. Footsteps, maybe? Not Lucy's. She was still in her bedroom, and I could hear her counting something under her breath. No, this came from the front of the house, near the main door.

A visitor, maybe?

If so, that was unusual. First, we never received visitors, because who would willingly visit a house full of vampires? Everyone we knew practically lived with us. And second, it was still daylight out. I didn't have my phone on me, but I tended to wake around four p.m. these days. Which meant no vampires would be awake yet, except me, but we'd kept that little tidbit a secret from everyone. Yes, I woke early, but I'd never announced that to the world, and I was careful to stay off social media until sundown. No need to suggest any further connection to Petrik's death.

I paused with one foot balancing on the first ladder rung and strained my senses. While I could certainly hear someone moving around on the porch, I couldn't smell them. The nearby swamps were a bit overwhelming today in the late afternoon heat, and that was all I could pick up on.

Gripping the sides of the ladder, I quickly descended. I landed soundlessly on the floor, then folded up the ladder. No need to advertise Vlad's resting spot.

"Anna?" Lucy's voice came from her room.

"I'm here," I murmured, hoping not too loud to scare off whoever was mucking around on our porch. I wouldn't be able to answer the door, but that was what Lucy was for.

For as long as we'd lived here, no one had ever just dropped by uninvited. It was an unwritten rule among vampires that you waited for an invitation first.

Lucy padded out into the hallway, arms wrapped around her

middle. She looked oddly innocent and vulnerable, and I hated it. It reminded me of her human weaknesses.

But that was a problem for a different time.

First, I needed to focus on this.

Logically, our visitor couldn't be a vamp. Even though some of us could wake early—exhibit A—we still couldn't step out into the sun. Its rays roasted us like a crispy marshmallow. Believe me, I spoke from experience, and that was an incident I hoped never to repeat. So logically, I shouldn't be concerned about our visitor. Maybe it was a delivery person, or someone with the wrong address, or maybe someone's car had broken down and they needed help.

Except, I knew better than to believe that.

"Someone's at the door," I said.

Lucy's mouth pursed, but she didn't say anything.

"I can hear them moving around out there. Can you open the door and see who it is?" I asked as we descended the stairs together. "Peek through the hole first. Let's make sure it's not anything serious."

She gave a single slow nod.

Okay, her silence was disquieting. I shot her a second glance and noted her pale complexion. "You okay?"

She shot me a narrowed glance. "Fine."

Ah. Just great. Nope, she wasn't sick. She was throwing a classic Lucy-esque temper tantrum. Hers never resulted in yelling and screaming, just the effing silent treatment. I knew this Lucy well—and I hated her. Digging any information out of her would be like pulling teeth. Guess I really had stepped in it last night, and now I had some apologies to make.

But again, now wasn't the time. So, instead, I scrubbed my hands down my face in an attempt to wake myself up a bit more, then gestured toward the door. My apology could wait until after we figured this out.

"Are you expecting anyone?" I asked.

She shook her head.

"What time is Sam supposed to be here?"

"Nine."

It took every ounce of willpower not to growl at her. I hated these moods of hers. It always reminded me of my parents prior to their divorce. First came the bickering, then the silence. I never could decide which was worse.

I glanced at the hallway clock. "That's five hours from now."

"I'm aware."

"Lucy." This time I did growl. My upper lip even curled up over my vamp fangs.

She startled at my tone, but immediately gathered herself together. Instead of apologizing for *her* childish behavior, she lifted her chin and held my gaze, almost as though silently challenging me to say something. Oh, I was about to say something all right. The short and terse answers were immature, and she *knew* I hated them. Which, of course, was why she did it.

The sound of scuffling feet on our porch reminded me we had other issues to contend with.

"Just... go look through the peephole." I waved her forward, then pinched the bridge of my nose. Lord love the girl, because some days, I couldn't. "Tell me what you see."

She leaned forward and peered through the glass lens, then shook her head and whispered, "Nothing."

"Can you see the full range of the porch?" I whispered back.

"No. The field of view starts at the stairs. There's no one out there, Anna. Are you sure you aren't mishearing things?"

Well, at least she was talking to me now. An improvement, at least.

I padded closer and snuck a peek. Lucy was right. We couldn't see anything, but I sure could hear something. I closed my eyes and listened. Footsteps padding back and forth on the front porch deck. I followed their movement. They swept from one side to the other, pausing every now and then. Peering through the windows, possibly? Whoever it was, they wouldn't see much. The house was carefully designed so that the common areas were at the back of the house. Not quite so easy to get back there with the brush.

"Someone's definitely out there," I muttered.

"I don't hear anything."

I turned and stared at her, my expression quite droll.

"Oh, right. Vampire."

Glad *she* could forget.

"I can't go out there. The sun is still up."

"Well, I'm not going out there," she whisper-hissed.

"Oh, calm down. It can't be anything too bad. All vampires are a-snoozing right now."

This time, she pinned me with a droll look.

"Okay, fine. But they won't be playing outside in the sun. Just open the door and see who it is. See what they need and send them on their way."

Lucy scoffed under her breath. "Fine." Her hand closed around the doorknob, and she slowly began to turn it. The anticipation was eating me alive here. I almost barked at her to move a little faster, but what would that accomplish?

When she finally pulled open the door, we were greeted with a bright burst of sunlight that sent me skittering back into the shadows.

"Sorry," Lucy mumbled.

I lifted a hand to shield against the rays, then whispered. "Well? Who's out there?"

Lucy shrugged, leaned forward, and peered around the corner. The second her head popped out of the house, she gasped and clutched at her chest. "Jesus, you scared the hell out of me! Who are you and what do you want?"

So someone *was* out there. I knew it! I practically danced a little jig in the foyer.

"Oh, I'm so sorry! I didn't think anyone would be awake," came an unfamiliar voice.

Gah! I was dying to see who it was. But that would require me peeking outside, and hell with that. I'd felt the sun's wrath on my flesh once before. Really didn't need to experience the sequel.

"Then what are you doing here?" Lucy demanded, crossing her arms over her chest.

I could imagine the stare she'd unleashed upon our unwelcome visitor, considering I'd just borne the brunt of it a few minutes ago.

"Oh, um, I was hoping for a few pictures."

I rolled my eyes. A freaking vampire junkie. Awesome.

"Pictures of what? You do know vampires live here, right?" Lucy shook her head. "They can't be photographed."

"Uh, right. Um." Our unseen visitor sighed. "Look, I'm just going to level with you. Five hundred bucks, and you escort me inside and show me their coffins."

Oh. Sweet. Lord. Was this really happening? Was someone actually attempting to bribe their way into our house?

"A thousand, and you leave, and I don't call the police for trespassing."

I almost burst out laughing, but I was trying my hardest to keep quiet. If this person was some sort of vampire wannabe or whatever, I really didn't feel like exposing myself would help matters.

"I know Anna Perish lives here with Dracula. I'm a reporter for *Fang and Fur Lifestyle*—"

"Great, a gossip columnist," Lucy commented dryly.

Was that the sound of grinding teeth I heard? The woman cleared her throat and tried again. "We're one of the top ten popular magazines—"

"Save it. I don't need to hear your speech. Leave."

"Two thousand," the reporter countered.

"Two thousand bucks. To see a coffin? Are you serious? All for some stupid article showing how vampires sleep in coffins, which everyone already knows?" Lucy unfolded her arms and leaned against the doorframe. She didn't shoot me a glance, which told me she also didn't want the reporter to know about my presence.

Footsteps echoed on the porch as the reporter neared Lucy. "Two thousand, you take me inside, and show me their coffins. I'll snap a few pictures, then I'm out of your hair. Ten minutes tops. Ever made a cool two G's in ten minutes?"

"Yes," Lucy deadpanned.

This time I did snort. Loudly. In retrospect, that was the moment things went downhill fast. Before Lucy could slam the door in the reporter's face, which honestly should have been the first thing she did, the reporter stepped into sight.

"You," she breathed, her face melting into a look of pure astonishment. "You're Anna!"

Well... shit.

"Close the door, Lucy," I snapped.

"No! Wait! How are you awake right now? Anna! Let me interview you. We can pitch your vlog, get you more followers—"

"Lucy!" I barked, inadvertently flashing fang.

A flash of light blinded us. I cried out and stumbled backward, my hands lifted to shield my vision. Was she seriously snapping my photo right now? In my own house? And what the hell would that even accomplish?

"Oh my god, you really don't show up in pictures. So, you *are* a vampire. And awake during the day!"

"Lucy! Shut the fucking door!"

"I'm trying!"

I shook my head and blinked back the damn white bulbs glowing in my vision to find the reporter forcing her way inside. She'd braced her shoulder against the door, then lodged her hip against the frame, preventing Lucy from shutting her out. Lucy stood on the other side of the door, her weight pressed against it and getting absolutely nowhere. This damn reporter knew exactly how to keep someone from slamming a door in her face, meaning she pulled this shit far too frequently for my liking.

When she lifted her camera and snapped another photo, I snarled under my breath. I couldn't let her get inside. This was our sanctuary. Not a damn museum.

I stormed forward, violence clouding my mind. Without a second thought, I snatched her camera out of her hand, snapped it in two, then gripped her shoulders. I nearly caved to my hunger right then and there. Seemed the dam had burst, and all my vampire feelings and instincts were rushing to the surface. Enough so that I was incredibly tempted to wrench her to my mouth and bite.

It was the sudden searing pain of heat splashing over my arms and the scent of burning flesh that broke the spell. The sun scalded my hands and arms, and it took every ounce of willpower I possessed not to scream in pain. Instead, I locked eyes with the reporter and wordlessly flashed her my fangs. The woman before me paled, then screamed when I gave her a good hard shove out the door.

Dark memories flashed to the front of my mind, of me trapped in Petrik's cement crypt, the sun burning a path up my legs and blistering my flesh. The familiar scent pervaded my nose, and I had to hold my breath to keep from retching.

"Anna!" Lucy shouted, her voice centering me in the here and now.

Her fingers gripped the back of my shirt and hauled me back inside. I fell back against a wall and slid to the ground, staring at the charred mess that'd once been my arms.

"Holy shit," Lucy sputtered, collapsing to her knees at my side. "What the hell were you thinking?"

"They'll heal," I grunted. Granted, they'd heal faster with blood. But guess what? We were fresh out of harem members tonight, and Lucy would never open a vein for me—I knew better than to ask.

Maybe I should have taken a bite out of the reporter. But I couldn't allow myself to become that sort of monster.

Which meant I would be dining on bagged blood tonight.

My favorite.

At least the situation was handled. Pieces of her camera were scattered throughout our foyer. But there wasn't anything more I could do, other than possibly sue her for an invasion of privacy and trespassing. Reporters like her, though, lived for that sort of drama.

They believed that celebrities gave up their rights to secrecy by becoming famous. More than likely, her company would foot the legal fees, knowing all press was good press.

Maybe I should just go back to bed. Forget the whole trip to Perish nonsense. My arms hurt like hell, I was hungry, cranky, and fighting with Lucy. The last thing I needed was to add my mother into the mix.

But we had plans and we'd told Sam to meet us here at nine. My mother was expecting us around eleven. And while most of my mother's lessons never really stuck with me, this one had. You didn't break plans unless you were sick or dying. I was neither. In pain, yes, but blood cured all ails.

"Who the fuck pulls that sort of shit?" I demanded. "Storms into someone's house to take their photo?"

"It's what happens when you're famous. What, in all your years of longing for this, you never gave it much thought?"

"No, I did, but I thought I'd enjoy it more."

Lucy chuckled. "Sorry."

"I mean, we live out in the middle of freaking nowhere. And it's a house full of vampires, for crying out loud. Talk about lack of self-preservation. If we were any other vampires, we would have just dined on her and called it a night."

Lucy shivered. "I really hate when you talk like that. Makes you sound..."

"Inhuman?" I offered.

She had the good grace to look away. "Should we call someone? The police or something?"

"Nah." I waved off her concern. "Her camera is broken, that alone is going to cost a pretty penny to replace. And I saw her eyes at the end. She knows she screwed up. Hopefully, she learned her lesson."

"You sure?"

I nodded. "Help me up, gently."

I extended a crispy arm and caught the flash of panic in Lucy's sharp green eyes. Yeah, I wouldn't want to touch them either. I looked like a deep-fried mummy. Eventually, she cupped my elbows and guided me to my feet.

"Now what?"

"Well, unless you're willing to crack a vein for me—and I'm not saying you should, but just remember I got burned because you couldn't get the reporter out, so a little gratitude wouldn't hurt—I need to get some bagged blood."

"C—Crack a vein?"

"I'm kidding, Lucy." Sort of. Fresh blood definitely would have helped right now. But alas.

"Kitchen?" she asked.

"Kitchen."

If I had to, I'd plug my nose and swallow it in one gulp.

By the time we reached the kitchen, my jaw ached. I had to grit my teeth to keep from crying out in pain. My arms were an ugly rainbow of reds, pinks, and oranges, complete with blisters and scales worthy of a dragon. I must have looked like a hot mess.

Lucy hurried over to the fridge and grabbed a bag of blood. She poured it in the mug, then popped it in the microwave. The scent of quickly warmed blood filled the room and turned my stomach. I definitely wasn't looking forward to this.

"Here," Lucy mumbled as she carried the warmed mug toward me.

"Mm. Yummy."

"Shut up and drink it."

I stared at my crispy palms and winced. This was going to hurt like a mother.

"Let me," Lucy offered before lifting it to my lips.

Our gazes met over the rim, then I held my breath and nodded. I truly did hate this stuff. But right now, there was no other choice. So, I opened my mouth, placed my lips on the ceramic edge, and waited for Lucy to upend the liquid.

She hadn't warmed it enough. Dear god, it was tepid and horrifyingly disgusting. My throat closed off in rebellion, but I squeezed my eyes shut and chugged as fast as the sludgy liquid would allow. Best to just get it over with, but someone definitely needed to give Lucy lessons in preparing blood, because sweet lord, this was like drinking copper flavored mud.

"Better?" Lucy asked once I drained it dry.

My stomach convulsed, and I turned away, pressing a partially healed hand to my gut. No. Not better. Not even remotely. Not only were my arms on fire, but now I had to worry about vomiting up nasty ass blood.

"Anna?" Lucy's hand touched my back.

"Might... wanna... move back," I rasped. Because she was totally standing in the splash zone.

I forced myself to draw a few deep breaths. For some reason, it seemed to help soothe my stomach. Might have been a placebo effect, but I honestly didn't care. It worked.

After a few gut-wrenching moments, the nausea passed. I glanced at my arms and grimaced. I wasn't sure what was worse. Drinking more of that shit hoping it sped up my recovery, or just waiting for them to heal naturally. At the moment, I was leaning toward the latter.

"More?" Lucy asked.

The second she wafted the cup near my face, my stomach lurched. "No."

Maybe my arms didn't hurt that bad after all. In fact, I could barely feel them now. Whatever lie I needed to tell myself so I didn't have to drink that nasty shit again. Imagine swigging absinthe and this was similar. They tasted completely different, but both were abhorrent swill that made you retch.

Except, my arms didn't feel better *at all*. And with about three hours more to go till sundown, I really didn't feel like wallowing in misery for that long.

So, with a brave face, I pointed at the microwave. "Warm it some more."

Lucy did so without a word. Once she returned with a steaming mug, I blew on it to cool off the fetid liquid, then plugged my nose, closed my eyes, and chugged back every last drop. Once finished, I lowered the mug and pressed a hand to my cheeks. Thanks to the blood, they were warm to the touch.

"I think I'm just going to lie down," I mumbled.

"Really? Did the blood not help?"

"It did. But I just... I'm going to lie down." Maybe I'd feel better after a nap.

"Okay." Lucy reached out and touched my shoulder. "Feel better."

I threw her a grim smile, then dragged myself back up to the attic and into my coffin. I laid my arms on my stomach and winced. Hopefully, after a small nap, they'd be healed, and I could get a fresh start on the night.

CHAPTER
NINE

For crying out loud, what would it take for a dead girl to get some honest rest around here?

It felt like I'd only just closed my eyes when a heated argument woke me. I released a heavy breath, then forced open my eyes and stared at the attic ceiling. Wooden rafters hung over me, and for the first time, I wondered about my safety. Vlad had once told me we slept in coffins, even in the attic, because if a hurricane rolled through, we needed as much protection as possible. At first, I'd thought he meant from the sun, but staring up at those rickety old rafters, I now had another fear impregnating my poor, innocent brain. Nothing like sleeping beneath wooden beams to understand the fragility of life.

"You expect me to believe you could not handle one single human? That you are so frail and so utterly incompetent that you failed to push someone outside and lock the door?" Vlad's heated voice penetrated my morose thoughts.

Oh, yikes.

Someone was pissed.

"Of course not—"

"Then explain to me why *she* is burned."

Still, huh? I glanced at my arms. In all fairness, they were much improved, but apparently not enough to appease my boy toy. I didn't blame him for being mad, they actually looked pretty damn gross. Blistered in some places, crusty in others, charred in most. I honestly looked like I'd held my arms over an open flame. Felt like it too. Stiffness had settled in nicely, and I knew if I so much as moved, I would be in utter agony.

A great start to my Wednesday night.

"Vlad," I muttered. The last thing I needed was him developing a hate-on for Lucy. Or vice versa.

Darkness settled over me as Vlad suddenly appeared at the side of my coffin.

I caught his gaze and smiled. "I'm fine. It wasn't Lucy's fault."

"In your immortal words, the hell it isn't."

The absolute sassiness in his voice made my grin grow. His sarcasm was coming along just fine.

"Honestly. It wasn't. It was mine. Lucy said something funny, I laughed, and the reporter heard me. I should have just kept quiet."

"I don't see how that has any relevance to this."

"She was determined to get in once she spotted me. Lucy tried to shut the door, but the damn reporter fought back. She was pretty damn good actually. But I got mad when she started forcing her way in. The last thing we need is someone writing an article about how I'm awake during the day."

Vlad's expression darkened.

"Yeah," I said, nodding. "Figured that'd be a bad thing. That reporter thought we'd be asleep. She was trying to break in to photograph our coffins."

"Bold and utterly stupid." He sighed and pinched the bridge of his nose. "I suppose we'll need to take proper precautions to ensure this doesn't happen again. Security, perhaps."

"Yay, more people in the house."

His lips twitched with amusement. "Yes, well, we can't ignore this."

I agreed. But under protest.

"I'll look into this after we return from Perish. Perhaps others are experiencing similar annoyances."

I grimaced. There were probably some, but I had to imagine my vlog was contributing. Vlad and I were one of the most popular vampire couples right now. Every night, Lucy showed me a new article regarding us. Even the tabloids loved to feature us. They always seemed to claim one of us was having an affair, or we were splitting up, or my personal favorite, I was pregnant with baby bats. Considering we both had a lot of fame surrounding us—him with his Dracula persona, and me and my vlog—I had to imagine things would only get worse from here. The last time we'd ventured out into public, a woman had practically swooned at the sight of him. I didn't blame her —I swooned every night. But at least I had the grace to do it in private.

I opened my mouth to mention the vlog, confess about everything right here and now, when Lucy swept into my peripheral.

"How are you feeling?" she asked.

Vlad curled a lip in response, clearly still angry with her.

"I'm fine," I answered.

But the judgy arch of Vlad's brow told me he didn't believe me. He shot Lucy an accusatory glare. I could practically read his mind and hear the many questions he still had whipping around in that brain of his. Why hadn't she been able to force the reporter outside? Why not stop me from stepping into the sunlight? Why let me get hurt?

I didn't answer his unspoken questions—I didn't want to admit aloud that I'd lost my temper.

When Vlad's lips parted—I assumed to ask the questions I suspected—I subtly shook my head. No point beating her over the head with it when the damage was already done.

Vlad's mouth thinned, but he finally nodded. "Fine." Then he eased one of his hands beneath mine and held them to the dim light. "You need blood."

"I had some bagged before napping. Honestly, they feel much better than they did." *Liar.*

Vlad's sharp stare told me he saw right through me.

He helped me out of the coffin, then studied my full arm. After a moment's consideration, he lifted his wrist and pressed it to my mouth. "Drink."

"What?" The scent of his arm beneath my nose did funny things to my body. Funny, sexy things. I *liked* biting Vlad. If I started now, I wasn't sure I would be able to stop. Which was why he never let me bite him anymore. Too dangerous. Too addicting.

"You need fresh blood. I assume you still wish to go to Perish tonight?"

I nodded.

"Then drink. Your mother would be distraught at the sight of you."

He wasn't wrong. And not the good kind of motherly distraught. More like horrified and disgusted. "Are you sure about this?"

His only response was to brush his wrist against my lips. I stopped thinking and let my instincts take control. My mouth parted and I bit.

The second Vlad's blood washed through my mouth, I moaned and sank into him. My arms began to slowly knit themselves back together and the pain abated.

Vlad's other hand swept my hair back from my neck, and his fingers began caressing. Oh boy, if he kept this up, Lucy would need to leave ASAP. I grabbed his wrist with freshly pink fingers, all healed and blister free. Relief coursed through my body, then sparked into something a tad more dangerous. Desire. Heat. Need.

Vlad's arm slid around my waist and pulled me flush against him, his stuttered sigh telling me everything I needed to know. Warmth bloomed within me, and I leaned against the swell of his chest, struggling to tamp back the emotions rising within. I had to remember Lucy was present.

When we parted, I gazed into his eyes and slowly licked my lips.

Lust flashed in his dark depths, promising me a wickedly sinful time. Just not right now.

Instead, his fingers trailed down my healed arms, and he lifted them to the light. "Much better." He brought my fingertips to his lips and pressed a soft kiss against each one.

My dusty ovaries nearly burst right then and there. Some nights, I wondered how the media could see him in one light when I saw him in an entirely different one. To the movie and literature industries, Dracula was an evil, maniacal creature who murdered without conscience. Vlad was the stark opposite of that. He was kind, caring, sweet, and attentive. Moments like these made me fall all the more in love with him. And I wasn't even sure that was possible.

After kissing all ten fingers, he leaned in and pressed a firmer, final kiss to my lips. "Do you still wish to visit Perish? I can cancel our plans and handle the fallout with your mother if you wish us to stay here."

That he even thought to offer... I swear, I probably had a little bubble heart emoji flying around my head right now.

"I'll be fine," I assured him. "They're healing up nicely, and my mother would probably set me on fire if we didn't show up."

"She sounds like a lovely woman."

I chuckled. My mother wasn't *really* the harbinger of evil, but it was my responsibility to prepare Vlad for the worst, because guaranteed, she was going to bring her A-game tonight. And not in a good way.

"Everyone is all packed and ready to go," I continued. "I don't want to disrupt our plans. The sooner we get there, the sooner we can come home, which means the sooner we get our new windows and can sleep together during the day."

Vlad frowned. "Time will pass at the same speed regardless of when we leave."

I chuckled. The man was so literal. My sarcasm appeared to be rubbing off on him, but I was far from a perfect teacher.

"Anna, I-I'm sorry," Lucy suddenly spoke up.

So swept up with Vlad, I'd almost forgotten she was still here.

When I glanced her way, I found her standing next to my coffin, arms wrapped around her waist, and her gaze locked on my pink arms.

"I should have been able to handle that reporter," she muttered. "I could have—"

"Pointless to focus on the what ifs," I told her. "It's done. I'll heal. Don't worry about it."

She nodded, then swiped at her unfallen tears and left, quickly descending the attic ladder.

"I was perhaps a little hard on her," Vlad observed.

"You think?" I teased.

"I'll apologize. I admit I lost my head a little when I woke up and saw you laying here in an open coffin, half-burned." Darkness tinged his eyes, and I knew why.

I reached up and cupped his face. "Are you still having visions about my death?"

He nodded, then turned his face into my palm and kissed me. "I had another tonight. Unfortunately, I've yet to see anything new. Right now, it's little more than me holding you after you've died. And I can't, I *won't*, go through that, Anna. I refuse to lose you."

"Hey..." I rose on my tiptoes and pressed my forehead against his. When his eyes fluttered shut, I allowed mine to do the same. "I promise you, I'm not going anywhere. We'll figure it out and stop whatever it is from happening."

"I failed last time," he whispered so low I almost didn't hear him.

"What do you mean?"

"The night I turned you. I was almost too late. Another minute and I would have been."

"I remember," I said. It was a moment forever burned into my memory. "But let's not focus on what could have happened. We'll use your visions to figure this out. I promised you an eternity, and I plan to deliver on it."

He kissed the tip of my nose, then straightened. "In the meantime, I'll apologize to Lucy for yelling at her. Did you by chance know this reporter? Perhaps I will speak with her boss. Put the fear of Vlad in them.”

“No. But she did mention her magazine. *Fang and Fur Lifestyle.* She had shoulder length brown hair and green eyes, a splattering of freckles across her nose. I’m sure that description will help them figure out who she was.”

“Very well. Why don’t you go gather your things for the weekend, and I’ll give this magazine a call they won’t soon forget.”

I kissed his cheek, then descended to the lower levels. Sam would arrive soon, so I only had an hour to handle all the final arrangements. We couldn’t waste any more time playing out this melodrama.

🦇

AT NINE O’CLOCK on the dot, the sound of the house’s dignified doorbell brought a grin to my face. I legit dropped everything I was holding—makeup (because even a dead girl needed to look like a hot girl), hair products, and my fang brush—and bolted down the stairs. From the corner of my eye, I spotted Vlad strolling casually toward the door, so I put on a little more speed and beat him there.

“I see you’re feeling much better,” Vlad commented wryly.

Ignoring him, I threw open the door and squealed, “Sam!”

All six-foot-five of him ducked into the house. “Anna.” His nose wrinkled. “Your house reeks of burned flesh.”

“Thanks for the reminder,” I said, laughing. A typical Sam greeting. Right to the point and with little warmth.

I chuckled, then reached up for a hug, one I quickly modified into an awkward shoulder pat the second I heard Vlad growl. Regardless of my attempts, the two men still loathed each other, and would till the end of time, I suspected. Vlad wasn’t jealous of me hugging another man, but he certainly didn’t want me getting all snuggly with his self-pronounced archnemesis. Their animosity toward each other cracked me up. The whole vampire versus werewolf nonsense. I was proof that

363

it was exactly that. Nonsense. We both had fangs. Sam just happened to be half-furry. I, however, had always loved the canine kind.

"I'm so glad you're here." I stepped back and took Vlad's hand, as though to reassure him that I hadn't switched teams on him.

Sam's gaze flicked to mine. I caught a hint of warmth in those amber eyes of his, one that turned cold the second his attention latched onto Vlad. "Why does your house stink?"

"We had an incident today."

A dark eyebrow arched high on Sam's forehead. His focus leapt to the staircase, as though he expected Lucy to suddenly appear. I knew better though. She would avoid him until the absolute last moment. Or until I shoved her face-first into the car.

"What kind of incident?" Sam demanded, his already growly voice deepening.

Vlad tensed, his fingers tightening around mine. "It's been handled and there's nothing for you to worry about."

Sam unleashed a fierce glare on Vlad. "Lucy is my mate. And she lives here. I'll decide what warrants my concern."

Phew. Even I could smell the rising testosterone in this entryway. These two rarely spoke to each other, but when they did, tempers tended to spike. Sometimes it made for good drama, but more often than that, their arguments sent me and Lucy for the hills.

"It's fine," I assured Sam, giving Vlad my own reassuring squeeze. "Some reporter tried to bust in on us today. No one was hurt"— except me, and Vlad's sharp glare reminded me of that—"and we're all perfectly fine."

Sam's grunt had me biting my lip to keep from laughing. "Where is she?"

"Upstairs. She's moping."

This time Vlad grunted. "As she should be."

Even I tensed when Sam shot Vlad a scathing scowl.

"Okay. Alright." I pulled my hand from Vlad's and held them up peaceably for all to see. "I'd like to take this moment to remind certain people that we have a long drive tonight as well as an entire weekend together. My family is batshit crazy, so how about we take a breath and remind ourselves who the true enemy is?"

Vlad lifted a questioning brow.

"My parents," I said. "We're vampires about to descend into the seventh circle of hell."

"An interesting concept," Vlad mused.

With a small, encouraging smile, I leaned in and brushed my lips against his cheek. His arm instantly snaked around my waist and pulled me into him seconds before he stole a heated kiss.

I scoffed and playfully slapped his chest. Dead or alive, men were men. And my man apparently felt the need to mark his territory.

"My bags are upstairs," I commented. "I'll go get them and drag Lucy down. Are we taking one car?"

"Absolutely not," Vlad barked at the same moment Sam uttered a resounding, "No."

My gaze flicked between the two men. "We're not?"

"If this weekend will be the epitome of hell, then I want to spend some time alone with you beforehand. Sam and Lucy can take his vehicle." Vlad shot him a droll look. "Assuming the mutt knows how to drive?"

"Vlad!" I hissed.

Sam rolled his eyes. "The mutt can drive better than a corpse."

"Sam!" I shouted. "What is the matter with you two?"

The two stewed in competitive silence, one that had me shaking my head. And people thought *women* were catty.

I started up the stairs. "I'm going to get my bags and Lucy. Try not to kill each other."

"No guarantees," Sam muttered.

"I heard that."

"Meant to."

Still shaking my head, I took the stairs two at a time, afraid to leave them alone together. I'd learned of their little feud when Sam and I had first met, but I'd hoped they'd outgrow it. Especially considering Lucy and I were best friends. Guess my hopes were aiming a little too high. I just hoped I didn't find them at each other's throats when I came back downstairs.

I hurried into Lucy's room and saw her seated on the edge of her bed, staring morosely at the wall. I didn't want to startle her, so I rapped my knuckles against the doorframe and murmured, "Sam's here."

Her head rose, almost of its own volition, but her gaze was distant when it landed on me. "Hmm?"

"Sam? He's here. We're ready to leave if you are."

"Oh. Right." She didn't move.

Frowning, I slipped into her room. "Want to tell me what's going on?"

She blinked and her vision seemed to clear a little, sharpen with clarity. She seemed a bit shocked to find me here, as though she hadn't really realized who I was at first.

"Lucy? What's wrong?"

"Would you say I'm a good person?" she asked, her voice barely a whisper.

"What? Of course. I don't befriend assholes."

That gained me a tiny smile. One that faded as quickly as it came on. She dropped her gaze and picked at the bedspread, her movements almost aimless.

"I knew the sun would hurt you," she finally said. "I knew. And yet, when you dove forward and grabbed her, I did nothing. I could have pulled you back right then and there. Except, I didn't. Vlad's right—I let you get hurt." She lifted sorrowful eyes. "What kind of person does that make me?"

"You didn't know that woman would be so brazen. It doesn't mean anything, Lucy."

"Please." She scoffed under her breath. "I've seen a hell of a lot worse than a reporter trying to break into the house. I'm friends with you, remember?"

"Um. Sorry?"

She waved a hand. "I was mad at you because of last night. And then when that woman rushed inside, it caught me unaware, sure. But I just stood there and let you handle it... and you... burned."

I wasn't quite sure what the point of this conversation was. "Somehow, I highly doubt you did any of that purposely. Were you standing there thinking 'Muahaha, I'm going to let Anna get hurt? That'll teach her!'"

"What? No, of course not."

"Did you stand back with a grin and watch with a sickening sense of perversion and self-satisfaction?"

"For crying out loud—no, Anna, I didn't."

"Then why make this out to be anything other than a mistake? Okay, so you probably could have done something other than stand there. But you pulled me back in the end."

"Yeah, after you handled the situation."

Sighing, I plopped down on the bed next to Lucy. "Look, I'm all healed." I held out my arms so she could see. Not even a tiny bit of redness remained, thanks to Vlad's blood. The best medicine. "Why are you dwelling on this? We have places to go and people to see, so let's get moving."

"I'm sorry," she blurted. "I just... wanted you to know that. That I'm sorry."

When she turned to face me, I spotted the tears in her eyes, and my heart dropped. "Lucy. You're not a bad person. You're not even remotely mean. There isn't a cruel bone in your body. I know you better than anyone, and I absolutely do not believe you purposely let me hurt myself. You weren't maniacally laughing or plotting some nefarious scheme to hurt me. Because that's not you. So, let's drop this, okay? There's nothing to forgive you for."

Her bottom lip trembled, but she eventually nodded. "Okay."

"Good. Are we done?"

Another weak nod.

"Great. Because you need to stop beating yourself up. Tonight's gonna be hard enough for you as is."

Fear flashed across her face. "What? Why?"

"Because you and Sam are driving to Perish together, alone, in his car. Vlad and I are taking his car."

The color utterly drained from Lucy's face. Her hands clutched mine, and she squeezed so tightly, I thought for a moment it might hurt.

"No. No. You can't do that to me. Anna—"

Her panic almost made me laugh, but I didn't want to ruin the moment. "It'll be fine, Lucy. Sam can't make you talk about anything you're not ready to talk about. Just remember that."

"That's not what I'm worried about!"

"Then what—" Understanding dawned, and this time I did burst out laughing. "Ohmigosh, you're worried you might jump his bones!"

"Anna!" she hissed under her breath, her wide eyes darting to the door.

"Oh, please. They've both been listening to this entire conversation, and you know it. Here, I'll make it simple for you." I drew in a deep breath and shouted, "Sam! No hanky panky in the car tonight, no matter how horny Lucy gets!"

"Oh my fucking hell! I hate you, you know that?" Lucy spat out, her face red as a beet. "I can't believe you just did that! Maybe I *should* have pushed you into the sunlight today!"

So glad we could laugh about it already. I snickered, then leaned in and brushed a light kiss across her temple. "Maybe you should have. Now, get your things. We have to leave. You know my mother, she will be pissed if we're even ten minutes late, and we're pushing it already."

"Nope. I'm not going." Lucy sat firmly on the bed, arms crossed over her chest.

"That's okay. I'm sure Sam wouldn't mind staying here with you all weekend, alone in this big ole mansion, with no one here at all to stop things from getting too heated. Just think... four days alone with him."

Her anger bled away. "You're just the worst, you know that?"

"You love me."

"I *hate* you."

"I love you too."

Lucy muttered a string of curses at me, but she finally rose from the bed and started gathering her belongings. Which only meant one thing. It was finally time to go home. To introduce Vlad to my parents. To see my family for the first time since dying.

Hell was starting to look more like a vacation now.

CHAPTER
TEN

"Woooo!" I lifted my arms above my head and cheered, all while reveling in the feel of the wind against my face. I'd always had a thing for convertibles, a love affair I shared with Vlad, apparently. The second he'd unveiled his baby—a black 1962 Ferrari Cabriolet—I squealed, screamed "shotgun" even though there was no one else to claim it, and dove into the passenger seat.

"Enjoying yourself?" Vlad asked from the driver's seat, his hands lovingly wrapped around the leather steering wheel.

I leaned back against the seat and sighed contentedly. There was something so freeing about the open road. For a brief window of time, I could leave behind all my worries and concerns and just *exist*. Which was exactly what I planned to do. I refused to think about this weekend's impending disaster or Lucy or the queen or anything.

Instead, I lowered my arms and rested my hand on Vlad's thigh. The hard muscle packed beneath his slacks brought a smile to my lips. One advantage to road trips at night was fewer people to witness any naughtiness. Naughtiness such as, say... stroking his inner thigh.

Vlad's mouth quirked and his gaze briefly flicked to mine before returning to the road.

With an impish grin, I unbuckled myself and scooched closer.

"What are you—"

Vlad's question cut off the instant my mouth found his earlobe. We hadn't had time alone in ages, as Vlad had pointed out earlier, so I wanted to take full advantage. I tongued the edge of his ear while continuing to rub his inner thigh, my fingers achingly close to the mark I knew we both wanted me to land on. The thought of unzipping his pants and having my way with him out here on the open road had me squeezing my own thighs together.

"You're aware of how dangerous this is?" Vlad rasped.

"We're vampires," I murmured, my fingers climbing just that little bit higher.

Vlad twitched in his seat, and I caught the sound of the steering wheel leather straining beneath his grip. I would have laughed if it wasn't so damn hot seeing him this close to losing control. Careful not to prick his flesh with my fangs, I moved south, my lips landing on his throat. Every inch of me fired up the second my mouth found that perfect little bite spot. I wouldn't, of course, but the temptation always turned us on.

"Anna..." Vlad rumbled.

"Yes?"

"You're going to cause an accident."

"Focus on the road then," I told him, grinning.

I marched my fingers up his thigh, then paused at the junction between his legs. For one moment, I hesitated. I could do what I longed to and free him from his pants, or I could sit back and enjoy the ride.

Vlad seemed to hover on that precipice as well, his body rigid in all the right ways.

Nuzzling his neck, I glanced behind us and noted the dark open road. Not a single headlight in sight. I wasn't sure what route Lucy and Sam had taken, but apparently it wasn't the same as ours. And right now, I was A-OK with that.

A smile claimed my lips when I remembered her deer in the

headlights look as she climbed into Sam's car. It was a memory I quickly banished. Tonight was about me and Vlad. And just like that, my decision was made. I gave into the temptation.

The second my hand cupped Vlad through his pants, he shot to the side of the road and slammed on the brakes. My laughter carried on the wind as he parked the car, rolled up the windows and roof, then shut off the engine. I barely had a chance to utter a word before he shoved his seat back. Next thing I knew, he had me by the hips and swung me up onto his lap. He buried his fingers in my hair and pulled me down for a searing kiss that no amount of thigh squeezing would cool.

He broke from the kiss and pushed my hair back from my face. "Is this all right?"

My dead heart swooned. Because of course Vlad would think to check before taking action. Nodding, I returned to my favorite pastime. His mouth definitely qualified as the eighth wonder of the world, one I fully intended to take advantage of from now until forever.

"Take off your pants," he mumbled against my lips.

Hot. So fucking hot.

I did as he commanded and stripped bare from the waist down, not even asking if he wanted my panties gone or not. Then I made quick work of his. I couldn't remove them entirely in this position, trapped as we were in the front seat of this ridiculously sexy car, but I was able to shuffle them down past his hips, granting me full access to the gearshift I wanted most of all. The car was nothing compared to him. He had more horsepower than any vehicle ever, with one hell of a piston that I definitely wanted to ride until the end of time. Whatever, I didn't know enough sexual euphemisms for cars. Nor did I care about that right now.

Vlad's fingers got to work, preparing me for the main attraction. If I were an amusement park, he'd be slicking up the slides right about now. I shuddered above him, reveling in the feel of his expert touch. Warmth pooled in my stomach and spread through my limbs, all in anticipation of that perfect moment. So attuned to my body, Vlad knew I was about to climax. But instead of granting me that bliss, he grabbed my hips and seated me on top of him, thrusting upward in one smooth motion.

Ah. So that was what heaven felt like. I'd always wondered.

Bracing my hands on his chest, I closed my eyes and slowly began to move, riding him like the stallion I believed him to be. Sweet, sweet torture. If I moved even the slightest bit faster, I would be *right there*, about to tumble over the edge into ecstasy. But I wanted to drag this out, make him moan a little. So, what if we were a few hours late. Totally worth it, right?

Tap, tap, tap.

Vlad and I both froze, my eyes now wide open and locked with his. We couldn't have both misheard that, right?

Tap, tap.

A shadow moved outside the vehicle. Thanks to the steamed windows, I couldn't see what it was, but I could *definitely* see the flashing red and blue lights behind our car.

"Oh my god," I whispered, the words slipping past my lips without thought.

Vlad flinched at my quiet curse, but didn't scold me. Likely because he'd realized the same thing as me.

We'd been caught. Having sex. In the middle of nowhere. By the cops.

"Sir?" a voice carried through the closed windows. "Ma'am? Please step out of the vehicle."

"Holy shit!" I cussed, biting back the startled laughter threatening to rush past my lips.

I'd never been caught canoodling in a car before! And from the astonished look on Vlad's face, neither had he. I clapped a hand over my mouth to silence my nervous giggles, then dipped my head forward, my hair brushing Vlad's throat.

"I swear, I never heard him," I whispered.

"Nor I," Vlad admitted.

Which said *a lot*, considering we were vampires. Had we gotten so wrapped up in each other that we hadn't even heard the vehicle approach? That seemed impossible, right? But one glance at Vlad, and I knew it wasn't. He absolutely befuddled my senses on a daily basis.

Even more unfortunate, Vlad didn't possess the stereotypical Dracula hypnotic qualities, meaning we'd have to talk our way out of this.

I lifted my head from Vlad's chest and finally put my ears to use. The officer was pacing the vehicle, likely jotting down the license plate number. Just behind him, I caught wind of a wheezy half-chuckle, half-bark of laughter. His partner, most likely, sitting in the car as he typed in what information they'd gleaned so far.

"Bet they're humping it up in there," a rough voice commented. "Classic."

I groaned. "Yeah, they know what we're doing in here."

"That much is obvious. Would you mind...?" Vlad gestured to the passenger seat.

"Oh, right."

As much as I enjoyed riding Vlad, now *really* wasn't the time. With as much grace as I could muster, I climbed off Vlad and started scrambling back into my pants, which wasn't as easy as it sounded. It was one thing to rip them off in the heat of the moment, and another when you were frantically rushing, without knowing which way was the front or back, or where your underwear had run off too. Worst. Sexual. Experience. Ever.

"This has never happened to me before," I mumbled, unable to bite back a bewildered giggle. "I can't believe this. Who gets caught screwing in the middle of the highway?"

Vlad shot me a strange glance, then fixed his pants and climbed out of the car. He certainly seemed more confident than me. I was practically sweating blood, freaking out about what the hell we were going to say to the officer. The thought of joining him out there horrified me. It was different for men—they congratulated one another on their embarrassing sexcapades. Not women. We took the slack and bore the insults. I had to be a slut if I was willing to screw in a car, right?

Still, I couldn't let Vlad face this alone, and the officer had requested we both step outside. So, I did what any woman would. I straightened my clothes, fluffed my hair, wiped my face, then stepped out of the car.

"I understand, Officer."

"I do remember what it's like to be young and in love," the cop continued.

I nearly choked on my saliva. Vlad was *far* from young. Then again, I'd been the one to initiate the sexy times, not him. Guess his comment still applied then. Just to the wrong person.

"But it's illegal, you know. Indecent exposure, even though there isn't anyone around this time of night. Next time, keep it in the bedroom, 'kay?"

"Of course." Vlad gave a respectful nod.

The officer shot me an appraising glance. I had to wonder about the questions running through his head. Like what sort of girl would willingly hop on a man's joystick out in the middle of the boonies. Thankfully, he didn't ask. Instead, his mouth curled into a sly grin, then he retreated to his car.

My focus shot to the passenger seat, but I didn't see anyone.

Huh. Odd. I'd definitely heard someone earlier. I lifted my chin and scented the air, but could only pick up the scent of the single officer. When the cop's hand grasped the door handle, I finally caught movement in the back seat of the car.

A criminal then?

But finally, two giant pointed ears popped up. And even though it was pitch dark out, I could easily see the furred face and lolling tongue. A German Shepherd.

"You dawg!" came the same growly voice, quite rough around the edges.

A voice that had distinctly come from the dog.

I gasped, then shoved my finger into my ear and wiggled it around.

Surely, I'd misheard or had imagined hearing it? I stared at the mutt, waiting for him to speak again, except he did nothing but pant, his eyes latched onto his handler.

"Alright, you two," the officer drawled in a classic southern accent. "Drive safe."

"Thank you," I mumbled, half-assing a wave.

The cop slipped into the car and started pushing buttons on his computer system. The K-9 in the back seat simply rose on all fours and repositioned himself so he could look over his handler's shoulder, absolutely silent. Because *of course* he was silent! He was a freaking dog. And dogs couldn't talk.

I'd officially lost my mind.

"Anna?"

I turned at the sound of a voice and found Vlad standing next to the driver's side door, his hand extended toward me. Right. We had places to be, but at least we'd be on time now.

Hurray?

CHAPTER

ELEVEN

WELP, we'd finally arrived.

After what felt like an eon of waiting, we were here in Perish. And absolutely nothing had changed. It was still the same small town I knew and hated. Compared to New Orleans, Perish was more like a blip on a map, a place most people didn't even know existed. I wish I didn't know it existed. That would make my life much happier. Alas, this was my hometown, born and raised, and my entire family still lived here. No escaping that.

Sam and Lucy had beat us here, unsurprisingly. For some reason, I didn't really feel the need to indulge her with the tale of Vlad and Anna versus the police right now. We'd just pretend that we drove a little slower.

After parking, Vlad circled the car and opened my door, offering me his extended hand. I took it happily and climbed out, all while running my thumb across his knuckles. Unfortunately, our little rompus interruptus hadn't quelled my lusty desires. So even just touching his hand sparked that fire within me. From the tiny smirk curving Vlad's lips, he knew it too. One downfall to vampirism, a girl couldn't maintain mystery anymore. Half the time, he knew what I was feeling before I did. Ah well, didn't mean I couldn't play it up and tease him. A concept I very much implemented when I squeezed his ass with my other hand.

Vlad's eyes shot wide, and his gaze dropped, as though startled I would dare do such a thing. Glad I could still keep him on his toes.

Chuckling, I headed toward Lucy and Sam. Now, *their* scent was that of frustration. Guess the car ride hadn't gone as well for them as it had for us. I'd hoped they would talk out their differences, but Lucy was a stubborn ole girl. It would take more than trapping her in an enclosed space with Sam to get her to open up.

I shot Sam an apologetic glance, then glared at Lucy.

"What?" she snapped in an extremely bitchy tone.

Alrighty then. Someone wasn't in the mood to share. I didn't bother responding. I refused to let her foul mood sully mine. Regardless of the cop, our ride had been quite pleasant, once I banished the cop's K-9 partner from my mind. No reason to worry about something I had no clue about.

"Y'all ready for this?" I asked.

My gaze scanned the neighborhood. Everything looked exactly the same here too. Mrs. Bitterly still lived next door, according to her pompous little mailbox, and the family just down the road was still here, if the mountain of toys piling up in the front yard meant anything. Behind us was the local school with the dilapidated monkey bars I'd hung from every day at recess. Everything was the same. Sure, it'd only been three months since we'd left, but my entire world had changed, so for some reason, I thought Perish would have changed too.

"Um, Anna?" Lucy murmured.

I glanced over, only to find her staring at my mom's front yard. I did the same.

And my jaw dropped.

"Holy. Hell."

Honestly, I didn't know what else to say. What *could* I say? My mother and I had spoken on the phone a few times since I'd agreed to come home. She *knew* we'd be arriving tonight. I'd explained how we would leave New Orleans the instant the sun set and would arrive in Perish no later than eleven p.m. A quick glance at my phone showed it was quarter to. So, I'd held true to my estimate.

How could she not prepare for my arrival?

Or, holy shit, was *this* her way of welcoming us? I knew my mother inside and out. Knew her habits, her beliefs, her mannerisms. I *knew* she was a narcissistic drama queen with a penchant for gossip. I also knew she was a former Miss Louisiana runner up. Lastly, I knew she'd married my father out of necessity, since she'd been baking a cute little bun in her supposedly virgin oven—aka my brother.

So, when I said I knew my mother, I meant it.

But this? This was beyond the pale. And I had absolutely no fucking idea how to respond.

"Is that...?"

I nodded when Lucy's voice trailed off. Oh, it was indeed.

My vainglorious mother had put the nativity scene on full display. Yup. In the middle of her yard. At the end of July. Complete with baby Jesus and angels. And we couldn't forget the three wise men who weren't particularly wise, oh no.

Was I blaspheming?

Probably.

Did I care?

Not particularly.

And why? Because I was a vampire. And my mother had chosen to welcome me home with baby Jesus. Now, this didn't affect me. Thanks to my atheistic ways, religious artifacts, items, and words didn't bother me. Vlad, on the other hand, very much believed in the Big-G up high.

I swallowed and shot him a wary glance.

I wasn't sure what to expect. Anger? Annoyance? Neither

apparently. Instead, he wore a bemused expression I found a little off-putting. As though he found this little display to be the cutest thing he'd ever seen.

Not for the first time, I wish I could take a selfie right now. Because my *mother* had chosen to greet me and my vampire mate with a bunch of religious crap.

My mouth parted, but no words came out. So I closed my trap, swallowed, and tried again. This time I managed to squeak out, "I'm so sorry. My mother... she's..."

"Insane." Lucy's gaze leapt from the scene to my face. "She's freaking insane! You know that, right?"

"Considering I was raised by the woman, yes, I would say I'm well aware of her mental status."

My mother had never been diagnosed as clinically insane, but there were days I wondered about her mental health. Her ability to blatantly ignore the truth while only focusing on the things that mattered to her was impressive. A few years back, I'd found out that she'd known about my father's affair the entire time. Politician he may be, he was still a shitty liar. The only reason she hadn't said anything was because she'd liked being the mayor's wife. It wasn't until Caleb and I found out that she did anything, and even then, it was so she could play the victim. Then came the fake tears and temper tantrums and drama. She'd stomped around town calling my father's mistress a floozy, a grave robber, a bimbo, a desperate doxy, you name it. But prior to it becoming public knowledge, she hadn't cared. That was my mother.

And now this.

"I mean... I knew she was a lot of things, but this..." Lucy released a slow breath. "This takes the cake."

"The very religious cake," I quipped.

"And Caleb allowed her to do this?"

"You and I both know Caleb can't control her, no matter how much they both pretend otherwise. Hell, my father couldn't even control her when they were married, and he's the freaking mayor."

Lucy ran a hand through her hair. "I'm torn. On the one hand, I'm dying to know what else she has in store for you. On the other hand, I have my own family to see. I also need to get Sam settled in the hotel."

I shot her a look. "He's not staying with you?"

Crickets. That was all I could hear. Sam and I shared a glance, but he resorted to his signature half-shrug. Oof, I felt bad for the poor bugger. Perish hotels weren't known for their quality. But I couldn't offer him a room here. Between me and Vlad, my brother, and my mother, there weren't any rooms left. I only hoped Lucy was footing the hotel bill, since she was making him stay at one.

There really wasn't any point in arguing with her either. I could hear Lucy's reasoning in my head without even asking. She and Sam hadn't slept together, but if she asked her parents to put him up, they'd automatically assume they were a couple, and she still wasn't ready to take that leap.

"Go," I told them. Whatever else was waiting for us beyond those doors, Lucy and Sam couldn't help. "Your parents have been dying to see you. At least your mother is sane."

"I don't know about that," Lucy grumbled.

"Please. The worst thing she did was send you to school with little 'I love you' notes. My mother slept with the football coach, then egged his house when she realized he was married. She knew his wife, for crying out loud! Who does that?"

Lucy choked on a laugh. "I forgot about that!"

"I see where you get your impulsiveness from then," Vlad commented.

"Do not start with me," I growled. "Allow me to impart one life lesson to you. Never compare me to my mother."

A smile teased Vlad's lips.

"Oh, seriously, don't." Lucy shook her head. "Not unless you want to suffer an eternity of itching powder in your pants."

"Hmm. Not good enough. An eternity of garlic shavings in your underwear, holy water in your shampoo, wooden stake shavings mixed in your blood."

Vlad's eyes widened. "Diabolical. And they call Vlad Tepes the most notorious torturer of all time."

"And don't you forget it," I harrumphed.

Still chuckling, Vlad leaned in and pressed a kiss to the top of my head. "And your father? Should I concern myself with him? What sort of antics await me?"

"A shotgun to the chest?" Lucy shrugged. "I swear, when they were handing out responsible, well-meaning parents, you got shafted."

Didn't I know it. "I doubt my father will even notice you. We speak to one another once or twice a year, and all the conversations revolve around him, his life, and his wife, who is only a few years older than me. Did I ever mention that?"

"You didn't."

This time, I sighed. It was like the Fates had conspired to bring together the worst couple ever, just for shits and giggles. When we were younger, Caleb and I begged our parents to get a divorce. Thankfully, they'd listened, but not until after my father's affair, and after their incredibly public separation that to this day was considered the worst town scandal.

Made me wonder if my undead status rivaled it now? We Perishes sure did bring a good name to the town named after us. Guess scandals ran in the family.

"Alright, get lost, you two," I said. "And tell your mother hi for me."

Lucy rolled her eyes, but after a quick wave, she and Sam ducked out of the front yard and climbed back into his car.

"Dare we go inside?" Vlad asked once we were alone.

That was the million-dollar question, wasn't it? A part of me wanted to run back home to New Orleans. I honestly wasn't sure what we'd be facing here. This was my mother, after all. The woman who'd stuffed a hive full of pissed off bees into my father's car, then blamed someone else.

With a wish and a prayer—which was just so ironic at this point that I couldn't help but laugh—we braved the front porch. I studied every nook and cranny, searching for anything out of place. A bucket of holy water teetering atop the door? A cross nailed to the frame? An army of Jesus statues scattered across the entryway?

Who the hell knew?

I squared my shoulders, then opened the screen door and knocked. Technically, I'd lived here my whole life, but thanks to the whole "invitation" rule, I couldn't enter my family home without one. Talk about awkward. At least I wouldn't need another after this. Once a vampire was invited in, the invitation was good for life or until a change of ownership.

The door flew open, and the putrid stench of garlic smacked us in the face. Both Vlad and I choked back a cough and stumbled down the front step. Sweet baby Zeus, the place reeked of it. Had she diluted it in water and cleaned the entire house with it?

I waved a hand in front of my face and blinked back stinging tears. The damn stench assaulted my eyes and nose. What the hell was she even cooking in there?

I intended to ask, but froze when I spotted my mother. She stood before me, hovering on the threshold, clad in—I shit you not—a *Catch Up With Jesus* apron. And draped around her neck were two massive cross necklaces that had to weigh an effin' ton.

"Oh!" My mother's jaw dropped at the sight of me and Vlad cringing on her stoop. "Anna, I didn't realize you were bringing home a guest."

I choked on the poisoned air. "Wh—what the hell are you... cooking?"

"Dinner?" Her perfectly drawn brows rose as though she had absolutely no idea what I could possibly be talking about. "It's just pizza. You like pizza."

"That isn't pizza," I rasped.

"It's chicken and herb."

"And what herbs did you use?"

"Oh, a little bit of everything. You know how I cook. Some paprika, rosemary, basil, and—"

"Garlic?" This time I coughed.

My mother's cheeks pinked. Not a hint of confusion lingered in her eyes. She knew exactly what she'd done. The only thing I didn't understand was why. Was this all some sort of test? Or an insult? Or maybe she found it hilarious?

"Well, are you coming inside or what?" She waved a spatula in the air.

"Or what," I parroted. "First, you need to open some damn windows."

"Anna Marie," she hissed. "I raised you better than that. No cussing in front of guests."

I threw Vlad a look of exasperation. He hardly qualified as a guest, but who was I to argue with my mother?

"Windows, Mother."

Her mouth pursed.

When she didn't move, I drew my lips back and exposed my fangs. "Now!"

I wasn't sure what I expected, but a scowl wasn't it. "Anna Marie!"

"It's just Anna, Mother. Has been my entire life, and that's not about to change now."

"I'm your mother. I think I know your name."

"Do you?" I eyed her sternly. "And are you going to handle this situation or not?"

After a moment's hesitation, she sighed and stomped back inside. From the porch, I could hear her slamming open windows and muttering under her breath about her ungrateful wretch of a child. Lucky for me and Vlad, we could hear every word.

An eternity later, she returned, minus the spatula but still donning that ridiculous apron.

"Well?" She waved at the kitchen. "Is that better?"

Considering we were no longer under assault, yes. Though I still had so many questions about the apparel. I'd lived with this woman for eighteen years before moving out, and never had I laid eyes on this stupid thing. Or the necklaces.

"Hurry up then. Dinner is getting cold."

Dinner. With vampires. I blinked and stared at my mother as though she'd grown two heads. Was she going senile? Surely, she knew vampires didn't eat food, right? I mean, *everyone* knew that. And I highly doubted she was inviting us to snack on her, so...?

I decided to start with the more obvious problem. "You need to invite us in first."

"What? But you lived here."

"Lived, as in past tense. I don't live here anymore, and didn't when I was turned, so we can't enter until you invite us in."

A flicker of emotion flashed in her eyes before vanishing just as quickly. Almost as though she feared the idea of welcoming us inside. Was that what this was all about? Her way of pushing me out the door without having to say the words? She'd been the one nagging me to come home. But maybe now that I'd agreed, the idea of having a vampire under her roof terrified her. As much as it pained me, I didn't blame her for it.

"Mom."

"Fine, fine. C-Come in. Please."

Vlad and I shared a glance, then together stepped over the threshold. To this day, it baffled me how one moment there could be a barrier holding us out, and the next, presto, nothing but air. Magic, obviously.

Once inside, I kicked off my shoes and gently placed them aside.

My mother chuckled when she saw my fancy Weitzman boots. "Some things never change."

I glared at her offensive rubber croc shoes. I'd never understood her fascination with them considering her upbringing. Thankfully, she never wore the atrocities in public. Small favors. "No. They certainly don't."

"Well, introduce me already," my mother commanded.

I grimaced at the sight of her standing in the kitchen doorway, hands planted on her hips, with her Jesus apron just... staring at us.

"Can you take that off, please?" I sounded as exasperated as I felt.

Her brow furrowed. "But Mrs. Bitterly gave me this. It was a gift."

"And let me guess, she gave it to you after she learned I'd been turned into a vampire?"

"Oh, darling, don't be so absurd. Not everything is about you."

I arched a brow. Right. Because it was absurd to believe that our extremely Catholic neighbor hadn't done such a thing. Mrs. Bitterly was the sort of woman who taught abstinence at the local high school. And not as a means of preventing pregnancy. More like as a means of keeping girls and boys apart. Especially "colored" boys and white girls. She was *that* sort of woman—one who wrapped her bigotry in a blanket of religious piety. Needless to say, she absolutely would give my mother such an inappropriate gift after learning I'd fallen from grace.

"Take it off."

"Anna. There's no need. It doesn't bother me." Vlad's hand brushed mine. I nearly clung to his fingers, using him to steady me. Five minutes in my mother's presence, and I was ready to murder her.

"Well, it bothers me. It's rude." I leveled my mother with a heavy glare.

Her colored eyebrows winged up. If there was one way to get her attention, it was by insulting her manners.

With a dramatic sigh, she removed the apron and tossed it aside.

"What's with the display outside? And the necklaces? What's your goal here?"

"My goodness, Anna. It's like you aren't happy with anything I do."

"Because I'm not. You knew I was coming home tonight, and this is how you chose to welcome me? What could you have possibly hoped to accomplish?"

She shrugged, then turned and vanished into the kitchen without another word.

Ah, avoidance. Another of my mother's fine traits. So maybe I was ragging on her. But believe me, she deserved it. If I didn't ride her, who knew the other stunts she'd pull. Even now, the thought of entering her house terrified me. I could only imagine what the rest of the place had in store for us.

"Maybe we should go," I offered. "She's in a mood. Sometimes it's best to just ignore this sort of behavior. We can go find a hotel or something, come back tomorrow."

"A hotel is hardly required." Vlad braved a quick glance into the kitchen, but he seemed unconcerned with what he found. "I've arranged proper accommodations for us."

"Proper? What's that mean?"

"Well, your apartment would hardly house us and our coffins."

I nodded. I'd considered that. They built my apartment with bachelors in mind. And the windows were westward facing. Which tended to make things a bit toasty in the afternoon.

"When you first mentioned this trip, I purchased a house for us."

It took a few moments for my brain to comprehend that. "Wait. What?"

"I found us a place to live. Perish is your hometown, so I felt it best to own something we could call our own. We certainly can't depend on your family to shelter us. That responsibility is ours alone."

Well, he wasn't wrong there. But still! He bought us a house? And why hadn't he discussed this with me? What if I'd wanted a say in the location or the person we were buying from? He didn't know the town or the people like I did. I could have helped. I could have—

"I can practically hear your thoughts," Vlad mused.

"Yeah, well, I'm a loud thinker when surprised... or mad."

"Why would you be mad?"

I couldn't get into that right now. I wasn't like hopping with fury type mad, but definitely annoyed he'd taken this step without me.

Still, we had more than enough to focus on right now. So much so that I needed to put a pin in this whole house thing and come back to it later. Especially considering my mother was returning from the kitchen with her hands full of garlic pizza.

Oh yeah, *way* more than enough to focus on.

Someone remind me why I came home again?

TWELVE

"Well?" My mother stood in the kitchen, framed between two wooden crosses I knew hadn't been there when I'd left, and tapped her toe. "Are you going to tell me who your friend is?"

"Mom, this is Vlad. I told you about him, remember? The man who saved me?"

She harrumphed. "You mean the man who killed you?"

I bit back a groan. I knew this game, knew her goal. To create drama. If I fed into it, we'd be here all night listening to her tantrums and antics. Instead, I hit her with a few truth bombs. "No, that would be Petrik. Vlad turned me so you wouldn't have to bury your daughter. Say thank you, Mom."

"Thank you, Mom," she parroted in a saccharine voice. And people wondered where I got my sarcasm from.

"Vlad, allow me to formally introduce you to my mother, Penelope Perish. Mother, this is Vlad Vasek." I left off the Dracula bit. I honestly didn't see a point in bringing that up. As evident by the Christian artifacts tacked to her walls, my mother was a God-fearing woman. Somehow, I just knew mentioning Dracula in any facet would result in an epic meltdown. Best to keep the information as PG as possible with her.

Her gaze swept over Vlad, but from the downturn of her lips and the slight narrowing of her eyes, I knew she didn't approve. The classic "mom look." The one she broke out every time I brought a boy home. Manners dictated that she behave politely, but the second they left, she'd break out into one of the many lectures she loved to spout at me. Not that they ever worked. I pretty much did what I wanted when I wanted, and I never stopped to think about my mother's preferences, much to her dismay. More than once, she'd told me I should try to be more like her. All proper and polished. Then I'd remind her it wasn't the 1980s anymore, a comment she never appreciated, which of course was why I'd bring it up. Anything to shut her up.

"He's dark," she finally said.

I... honestly didn't know what to make of that comment. Vlad's skin was quite pale, thanks to his ethnicity and the fact that he was the undead. Maybe she meant his clothing? The man didn't own a single piece of colored clothing. Everything was black, right down to his socks. He did have an image to uphold, after all. Or maybe she meant his features? His raven black hair and midnight eyes definitely stood out against his stark pale face.

"And he's tall," she continued, as though his height offended her somehow.

I simply laughed and shook my head. She was looking for something to complain about, and there wasn't anything I could do about that.

"Don't you need to eat?" I asked her. "Before your food goes cold?"

She blinked as though waking herself from some little reverie, then nodded and marched into the kitchen. "Yes. Let's eat."

Vlad and I shared a startled look. I didn't think I'd have to explain this to my mother, but apparently, I'd been wrong.

"Um, Mom?"

She glanced over her shoulder with a raised brow.

"Vampires... don't... I mean, we don't..."

Her other brow rose. "Don't what?"

I sighed. Best to just jump in feet first. "Eat. We don't eat."

"You don't eat," she repeated, her brows furrowing as though this concept baffled her. "Then how do you—" She gasped, her hand leaping to her throat. "Oh dear. Oh my. No, I can't... You... drink... *that*?"

Shame colored my cheeks. I didn't think I'd have to explain this to her. Everyone knew vampires drink blood. It was the one myth that never changed.

"Oh God," she panted, collapsing into the nearest kitchen seat. "Oh dear God."

Vlad stepped back, as though the sound of her curses would be easier to bear with distance. Maybe they would. Pity swelled within me, and I swept into her kitchen and crouched in front of her. I took her hands and held them tightly. Maybe I didn't like my mother, but she was still my mother, and even I could see she was on the brink of an absolute meltdown. I needed to curb it before it devolved into a panic attack.

"It's okay," I told her. "Deep breath."

Her gaze met mine, and she shook her head.

"Yes. You can do this. Deep breath. Come on."

After a moment's hesitation, she finally caved and sucked in a shivering breath that shook her entire body.

"Good," I told her. "Exhale through your nose." Then nodded when she did. "Good. Keep doing that. It's okay. It doesn't matter what we eat. All that matters is I'm alive, and I'm here. Right?"

She gave a jerky nod, her normally perfectly coiffed blond hair slipping free of her bun. When she didn't immediately move to fix it, I realized this was a true panic attack.

I imitated her deep breaths and listened to the slowing of her heartbeat.

"I can't do this, Anna," she warbled, her voice weak. "I hate this. I hate knowing someone hurt you and that you died."

My shoulders rounded and I nodded. "I know. Just focus on the present, okay? Forget the past."

"I can't! Your past is literally staring me in the face. I knew when you left that you were going to get hurt. But I never said anything because you are just like me. Impulsive and careless. If I told you not to go, you'd refuse to listen and would leave just because I told you not to. I thought maybe you'd see the club, see a vampire, and come home. I didn't think *this* would happen."

"No one did, Mom."

"Chris did," she muttered. "Do you know I ran into him at the grocery store the day you left? He told me what happened. How you broke up with him because he forbade you from leaving. He told me you were going to get yourself killed."

Anger erupted within me. Who did that? Who told someone's mother that their daughter was going to get herself killed? If I ever saw that little shit again....

"Chris is an asshole, Mom," I told her, hoping to make her smile.

When her mouth curled upward, I grinned, pleased with the result.

"Someone should run him over with a car," I said.

She burst into a giggle, then clapped her hand over her mouth. "What a horrible thing to say."

"But oh so true. He never should have said that to you. He was probably still angry with me."

"Yes, you do tend to break little boys' hearts." Her gaze rose to Vlad.

"Don't worry, he's not a boy," I said, winking.

I glanced back and shot Vlad a soft smile. He stood in the living room, simply watching with a keen eye. I appreciated his silence right now, as though he knew it was best to just keep out of the way.

"Believe me, next time I see Chris, I'll slap him for you," I said.

"Probably not a good idea, sweetheart. You are a v-vampire after all."

Ah, she said it out loud. My grin widened. "Look at you, using the v-word and everything."

"Yes, well, I guess I better start owning it. There's no chance of you turning back?"

I shook my head. That she'd asked that question told me how desperate she was for it to happen. "That's not possible, Mom. Vampirism is permanent."

"You just had to go to New Orleans, didn't you?" she scolded gently. "But that's who you are. Always at the front of the line when something new and exciting happens. Nose deep in everyone else's business. I always thought you'd make a good reporter."

Well, those dreams had died alongside me. But that was okay, I had new dreams now. Ones I'd never known existed.

"I guess if you can't eat, then this whole pizza thing was pointless."

"But we appreciate the effort," I said, lying through my fangs. The house still reeked of garlic, and even if I'd been human, I never would have touched a slice. My poor gut would have rebelled just on principle.

"Do you have plans to see your father while you're in town?"

I sighed. My saint of a father hadn't once called me since I'd transitioned. Guess my father had skipped *How to Be a Good Father 101*, cuz the dude sucked. Miserably. "I texted him a few nights ago and told him when we would be in town. He didn't respond. I was considering dropping by tomorrow night, but I haven't decided yet."

"As much as I would love to say screw the bastard, I really do think you should make the effort. He is your father, after all."

A father who had proven time and time again that he didn't give a shit about us. Why should I make the effort when he so clearly refused to do the same for us? This was the man who'd cheated on my mother, then left her with absolutely nothing before settling with his mistress. Classy, right? I could count on one hand the number of times he and I had spoken in the last five years.

"Anna, listen to me."

I locked eyes with my mom.

"Talk to your father and fix your relationship with him. If this whole lesson has taught me anything, it's that family matters. If you'd died without burying the hatchet, your father would have had to live with that the rest of his life."

"And? How's that my problem?"

She sighed and gripped my hands tightly. "Your father isn't the sort to admit he's wrong. You have to be the one to take that first step."

"Well, that won't be happening."

"Anna..."

"Leave it alone, Mom. I came home so you could see me and meet Vlad. I'll make an effort to see Dad, but I never said I'd forgive him."

She released my hands and cupped my cheeks. "So much of me in you."

Oh, ouch. I definitely didn't like hearing that.

"Now, let me meet this handsome young man of yours."

I snorted a laugh. "Mom, Vlad is five hundred years old."

Her eyes shot comically wide. "Oh my."

I snickered and waved Vlad over. Hopefully, I'd diffused the situation enough that she'd be polite to him.

Sure. And pigs could fly.

🦇

THE INSTANT we left my mother's house, I drew in a deep breath in an attempt to clear the garlic from my nasal passages. Man, that shit really stung. And lingered. It felt like it pervaded every single one of my pores and orifices. I couldn't even imagine trying to ingest any. It'd probably rip my stomach to shreds.

"Well. That was... interesting," Vlad commented.

I nodded but kept my gaze locked on his car—our escape vehicle. My mother had calmed down a bit after our little chat, but she'd been incredibly curious about Vlad. More like intrusive, honestly. She'd asked questions I never would have thought to ask. Like what'd it been like living in the Middle Ages. I reminded her that he'd been born slightly afterward, but that hadn't swayed her. She'd also asked him about his parents and his life as a human. Vlad had responded graciously, but holy crap, I couldn't take another minute in there.

"Oh, Anna!" my mother called from the kitchen window.

I grimaced. "Yes?"

"Caleb is coming over Friday night. Do drop by."

Oh yay, another round of *this*. Except this time with my egotistical yet oddly stupid brother. "Sounds fun."

My mother waved at us through the window, then pulled the curtains shut, likely to keep her nosy neighbors from peeking in on her. Neighbors who had their faces plastered against their windows, openly gawking at me and Vlad.

"Lovely," I muttered with a curl of my lip.

Vlad tracked my gaze and nodded. Every single house surrounding us had people crowding their doorways and porches. I knew we were the most exciting thing to happen to Perish this year, but I honestly hadn't expected this level of prying. They even had their phones out, the distinctive camera flashes giving them away. I clicked my tongue against my teeth and started toward the car. Guess they didn't realize that 1) we couldn't be photographed, and 2) it was the dead of night. What the hell kind of results did they expect? They'd be lucky if the photos showed the trees in their yards.

"Sorry about all this," I said. "Guess you're not used to this level of attention."

Vlad clasped my hand and lifted my palm to his mouth, pressing a light kiss on my wrist. Shivers lifted the little hairs on my arms, and it took every ounce of sanity I had left to remind myself that I couldn't jump him right here and now.

"You have no need to apologize to me," he said. "While I'm not accustomed to meeting someone's parents, I'll survive."

I chuckled. Of that, I had no doubt.

"Come." He gestured to the passenger seat, then opened the door.

I slipped inside and belted myself in, even though I really didn't need to. Still, we didn't need to tempt fate a second time and land ourselves a ticket for not obeying traffic laws. We'd seen enough of the police tonight.

Once Vlad climbed in next to me, I turned down the radio and faced him. "You bought a house."

His gaze briefly flicked to me, then back to the road. He turned the ignition and the car roared to life. "No, we bought a house."

See, that irritated me. "*We* didn't do anything. *You* did it all. You chose the place, you paid for it. All you."

A slight frown marred his perfect features. "Yes. For us."

Yeah, he definitely didn't understand my point here. The old Anna would have jumped down his throat and insisted he treat me fairly and equally. But the new and improved Anna knew she needed to look at this from both sides. Vlad wasn't a modern man. To him, buying a place for *us* was exactly that. It didn't mean he didn't value me, more like he felt it was his responsibility to provide housing for us.

Keeping that in mind, I centered my thoughts. What could I say to help him understand my concerns? "While I appreciate that you handled this problem for us, I would have liked to have been included. Not only because Perish is my hometown but also because if we buy a place, I want to have a say in it. I want to choose a home with you, as partners."

Vlad fell silent and considered my words, his expression pinched. What I would have given to hear his thoughts right now. After a few moments, he nodded. "Next time I'll consult with you before making such a decision."

I almost laughed. What a typical Vlad response. But I appreciated it. He could have been a typical man from the middle ages and assured me that he could handle it all himself and didn't need the "little woman's" opinion, but he was so much better than that. It was one of the things I loved about him.

Huh.

Just like that, I realized how clear things were. I *did* love him. It wasn't physical or all lustiness. I loved *him*. I loved the way he listened to me, and the way he adapted and grew. I loved his generosity and compassion. The way he only shared that side of himself with me. The way he let his guard down to show me the real man behind the Dracula façade.

I loved him.

And he deserved to know. Especially with all that was going on in our lives. I would regret it if I never told him, then died tomorrow.

With a smile, I reached up and gently stroked his cheek. "Did you know that I love you?"

Vlad froze.

I burst out laughing at the sight of him startled into complete stillness as he stared out the window. But my laughter soon died as doubt set in. Oh shit, should I not have said it? Did he not feel the same way? Fear twisted my insides, and when he didn't immediately respond, I drew away from him.

I hadn't made it far before his hand snatched mine back.

Tears pricked at my eyes as dread nested deep in my chest. What if I'd just ruined everything? Could I handle that? Could I walk away?

Noah's words came back to me from the VA meeting, how every young vampire needed to know where they stood with their sire. If Vlad didn't echo my sentiment, at least then I would know. It'd hurt like a motherfucker and would probably take decades to heal my broken heart, but it *would* heal.

Vlad's fingers tightened around mine, and he lifted my hand to his mouth. When he pressed a tiny kiss against my palm, I metaphorically flatlined.

"I love you too," he replied, his voice gruff with emotion.

Relief loosened my muscles, and my whole body seemed to deflate like a popped balloon. "You do?"

He pressed my palm against his cheek and held it there. I reveled in the feel of his light stubble. He must not have shaved before his transition, but I didn't mind. I loved a man with stubble.

"I loved you the second I saw you. You were everything I'd been missing. You're my sun, my light, my heart. All things stolen from me. When I say I love you, know that I mean it, that I've never spoken those words to another."

Shock rendered me silent. Not even to Mina?

"You are everything I've lost and everything I've gained. Know that I'll never let anything happen to you. You're mine, in every sense of the word. And I very much intend to love you until the end of time."

Phew. That gave me all the feels.

I needed a moment to collect myself. The man certainly knew how to give a speech. One that had me tearing up. Startled by the tears pricking my eyes, I half-sobbed, half-chuckled, then wiped them away. Vampire tears weren't a pretty sight, and I really didn't feel like walking around with blood-streaked cheeks.

"Um." I released a shaky breath. "Ditto?"

A knowing smile curved Vlad's lips. "Ah."

My mouth moved soundlessly as I contemplated what to say. I wasn't as loquacious as Vlad. I didn't speak fancy words and make undying proclamations that could spin a guy's head. But I definitely needed to give him more than a *ditto*.

Determined to try, I climbed over the car's console and slowly slid into Vlad's lap. My head was pushing against the roof, but I didn't care. This sort of moment demanded closeness.

"I've never told someone I loved them either. I mean, other than Lucy," I admitted. "I can't even remember the last time I said it to my parents. Before you, I didn't really believe in it. I believed in lust and friendship, but not love. You changed my mind. I've never had that *one* person I thought about more than any other. The one person I wanted to spend every day with. But here you are. You're always on my mind, always invading my thoughts and emotions. We're going to live forever, and I couldn't imagine spending eternity with anyone else."

A small smile spread across his face, one that transformed him into a prince of darkness.

I cupped his cheeks, leaned down, and kissed him, reveling in the feel of his lips against mine. Once I had my fill, I sat back and stroked my fingers through his hair. "So, now that we have that out of the way, how about you take me to our new home? I would very much like to strip you naked right now."

Vlad's grin turned naughty. "That can be accommodated."

I fell back into my seat, but Vlad kept hold of my hand, our digits intertwined. He lowered them to the gear shift and put the car in drive. I wasn't one for symbolism, but I liked to think it represented our willingness to navigate our lives together.

With luck, we'd get our happily ever after, even if we had to fight tooth and nail for it.

CHAPTER

THIRTEEN

OHMIGOD. He bought the Barker house.

The *Barker* house.

Because *of course* he had. He couldn't have bought a normal house. No. He had to go for the *one* house in Perish that was unequivocally haunted. There wasn't a person in Perish who didn't believe this place was haunted. Usually, parents tried to convince their children that there was no such thing as ghosts, but not with this house. Growing up, our parents had actively told us to stay away from it. They never admitted it was haunted but venturing near this place often landed a child with a blistered backside and chores for months. That's how terrified people were of this place.

I didn't realize I'd taken a step back until Vlad's hand found mine and he tugged me closer. "Shall we go inside?"

Oh hell no. *Hell. To. The. No.* I wasn't stepping foot anywhere near this place.

Memories of my childhood came flashing back. Some kids like to dare others to go inside and spend the night, but no one *ever* did. And oddly, no one ever held it against them either. Because we *knew*. We knew there was something wrong with this place. The closest I'd ever come was the sidewalk leading up to the house. The second I'd touched the grass, goosebumps had pebbled my flesh and my stomach twisted. You can bet your ass I tucked tail and ran. Who wouldn't?

"Anna?" Vlad's hand touched my waist. "Is something wrong?"

I gave a jerky nod. "That's the Barker house."

"Yes. I bought it from the lawyer managing the estate. The house has been sitting on the market for decades without any interested buyers."

"Because it's the *Barker* house!" I hissed.

"Yes. It is."

"It's haunted, Vlad. Like, deathly haunted." I startled at the sound of his chuckle and whirled around to face him. "This isn't funny! The reason this place has never been purchased is that it's haunted."

"Anna, I assure you, it's not haunted."

"Oh, like you would know!"

"I do know, in fact."

I tried not to sulk, but I had a feeling I was failing at it. "*How* could you possibly know?"

"Come. Let me show you."

I slammed on the brakes and dug my heels into the pavement. Nuh-uh. No way. No how.

"Anna." Vlad bit back a full laugh. "You're being silly."

"*I'm* being silly? You're the one who bought a haunted house. Ohmigosh, we have to sell it. ASAP."

Vlad's hand fell away from my side, and he sighed. "Do you trust me?"

I waved his question off. Of course I trusted him. But he didn't know the area like I did. And clearly, he didn't understand the housing here. One did not just *buy* the Barker house. One kept a hundred feet *away* from the house and never looked at it, lest they upset the spirits trapped within.

The thing even looked creepy. While the foundation seemed to be in decent condition, the roof certainly needed some love. And the yard. Definitely the yard. It was overrun with weeds and dead dandelions that dared grow that close to the house.

Vlad thought I'd want to live *here*? Was he insane?

"It's a fixer-upper," he admitted. "But the price was decent, and the bones are good. I rather liked the thought of renovating it into a place we could call home."

I shuddered at the word bones. I bet the place was littered with them. Like an ancient burial ground or something.

"Okay. No." I faced Vlad and summoned my best *don't mess with me* look. "The Barker house hasn't been occupied since before I was born! And you want to know why?"

"Because it's believed to be haunted?"

"Yes!" I threw my hands up into the air. "Because Beaty Barker's ghost has been haunting this place since before any of us can remember. Supposedly, she lost her mind one night and took a chainsaw to her family, Vlad. A chainsaw! Then she did herself in after."

"Is any of that true?" he asked.

"What? Of course it's true. Why wouldn't it be?"

"Because myths and legends have a way of flourishing. Take me for example."

My mouth twisted. "You're different."

"How so? People believe I am the same person as Vlad Tepes. They believe that I beheaded and piked thousands of men."

"No, just one," I said wryly, reminding us of Eli.

Vlad cleared his throat. "My point is, has anyone actually looked into the story of Beaty Barker?"

"I honestly don't know."

Vlad nodded, his hand finding its way to the small of my back once more. "Well, I did."

"You did?"

"Yes. You think I would buy a home without knowing its history?"

Maybe? I mean, he'd turned me into a vampire without knowing my history. Though I suppose the two things weren't quite the same.

"Beaty Barker lived here until she was eighty-three," Vlad said. "Her husband, Robert Barker, died of natural causes three years prior. Their children, who all grew up in this house, eventually moved on, as children do. All have passed. Only the grandchildren remain, one of which sold us the house. He assured me the legends were simply that. Stories concocted by the townspeople because his grandmother never left the house. She didn't enjoy socializing and in her old age, she'd preferred to remain indoors knitting, until the day she passed. She died with her knitting needles in hand."

Skepticism had me crossing my arms over my chest. "How do you know that story is true?"

"Because, my sweet Anna"—Vlad leaned down and brushed a kiss against my heated cheeks—"vampires can see ghosts. If this was a true haunting, I would know. As would you."

"Wait. What? We can see ghosts?"

"Of course. We're the undead. As are ghosts. They're just a bit more dead than we are."

Okay, that was a bit too mindboggling for me. Because first, "You're saying ghosts actually exist?" And second, "You're also saying we can speak to them?"

Vlad chuckled. "I don't see why that would surprise you. Vampires are real, after all. As are werewolves. Why not ghosts?"

Why not indeed.

"And you're saying the Barker house isn't haunted?"

"Not that I saw. Unless the ghost is a quiet one, which in my experience, they never are."

Well, okay then. I would need some time to wrap my head around this one. I'd been told this house was haunted my entire life. And while I actually hadn't believed in ghosts, I had believed in the haunting. Odd, how people's brains worked. And now Vlad was telling me the opposite. That ghosts truly *did* exist, but the house wasn't haunted.

My life had really become topsy-turvy in the past few months. Almost as though the Fates were trying to teach me that I well and truly knew nothing. Life was a dichotomy, that was for sure.

"Are you ready to go inside now?"

I honestly had no idea. But the one thing I did know was Vlad would never purposely endanger me. So, with a forced smile, I took his hand and let him lead me into the house. From the outside, the place gave off an *Amityville Horror* vibe, but the interior of the Creole cottage told a whole different story. Surprisingly, the interior seemed to be in good shape. Vlad led me through the gallery and into the parlor, stopping to point out the well-kept pine floors and pristinely painted walls. Someone had clearly been handling the upkeep. Or they'd tackled some renovations hoping to sell the place.

Pleased by the house's condition, I dropped Vlad's hand and strolled through the entire place, taking in the different bedrooms and bathrooms. Everything seemed pretty standard. Honestly, with a little love, the exterior could easily match the interior's quality. A new roof, some new shutters for the windows, and voilà.

"Who's there!" a squeaky voice chirped above me.

I jumped in my skin, clapped a hand to my chest, then spun in a tight circle, studying my surroundings. I stood alone in the master bedroom, not a soul in sight.

Before I could call for Vlad, the voice came again. Followed by another.

"Who... Who's there?"

"Someone's here?"

"You don't smell it? It smells off. Like old blood."

"Can you see it?"

"I can't see anything, ya dolt, I'm blind, remember? You go see!"

"I'm not going out there!"

"Chicken!"

"Don't you call me a chicken, ya old bat!"

Holy shit. Holy shit. *Holy shit!* Vlad had promised this house wasn't haunted, but I was very clearly hearing voices, almost as though they were in the next room! And from the smell of it, there wasn't anyone here but me and Vlad and some animals. I'd caught the musty scent of opossum when we'd stepped inside, but that'd seemed normal, considering this house was virtually abandoned.

"Is... someone there?" I asked, my voice pitiful and weak.

"Shh! Did you hear that? I know I heard something. There's someone here!"

"Oh, calm down. They won't find us. We're safe up here. We blend in, like monsters in the night."

My eyes rose to the ceiling. Up here? As in... the attic? Oh god, we had ghosts in the attic! Nope, that was enough. I didn't need to know anything else. I *refused* to stay here if there were ghosts. "Vlad!"

The panic must have carried through my voice.

Vlad appeared at my side seconds later, his hands grasping mine. "What's wrong?"

"Ghosts," I hissed, pointing up to the ceiling. "I can hear them up there, chattering away."

His concerned expression slowly morphed into one of amusement. "Anna, there's no one up there. I would know if someone was in the house."

"They're up there, Vlad! Bickering like an old married couple."

"Shh. There's another one now," the squeaky voice added.

"See!" I jabbed a finger in the air, practically jumping into Vlad's arms. "I told you! I told you! There's a ghost up there."

"Anna..." Vlad stepped close to me and peered into my face, his brows deepening as he studied me. "There aren't any voices."

I dropped my arm and sighed. "This isn't funny. I'm serious! I can't share a home with a ghost."

"All right." He took my hand and tugged me toward the door. "Let's go upstairs. I'll show you there's nothing to fear."

"Nope." I dug my heels into the floor. "I am *not* going up there."

A hint of frustration chased across Vlad's face. "Fine. Then I'll go look. Will that suffice? I assure you, there aren't any ghosts here."

"Sure, go look. But when you find a pair of ghosts up there, I'll be down here, waiting for an apology."

Vlad threw me a wry glance, then started climbing up the steep staircase.

Fear had me wringing my hands together and straining my ears to listen for any movement or commotion.

"Quiet, quiet!" one of the voices hissed. "He's coming."

"Who is?"

"The person, you nitwit!"

"Don't nitwit me, you wanker!"

I trailed between the rooms, listening to the sound of Vlad's footsteps. "Do you hear them?" I shouted up at the ceiling.

"Anna, there's no one here."

"That's not funny, Vlad!" I shouted.

"Ah, there he is! Go, go, go!" the one with the squeaky voice complained.

"Go where?" the second voice demanded.

"Just go!" Squeaky yelled.

"Vlad..." I bolted to the staircase, ready to climb like his life depended on it. "They saw you. Can you hear them yet?"

No response.

"Vlad!" I shouted.

Oh shit, had something happened to him? Had the ghosts attacked him or something? I couldn't hear any sort of commotion up there, and even the voices had stopped. Everything was blissfully silent again.

"Vlad, answer me!"

His head popped into sight at the top of the stairs. "Everything is fine. There's nothing up here. Would you like to come see for yourself?"

"Are you insane?"

"Generally, yes," he said with a playful wink. "Come, Anna. The attic will house our coffins for now, so you may as well look."

I cursed and tightened my hands around the railings. I *really* didn't want to go up there.

"Anna."

My gaze leapt to Vlad's. I could see the reassurance in his eyes. Regardless of my fears, he wouldn't let anything hurt me. And for all I knew, ghosts could be benign. Just because I'd watched every poltergeist movie out there didn't mean ghosts were evil. Maybe they were like us, just trying to get by and survive their new existence as some earthly ephemeral being.

"Okay, okay, I'm coming," I said. It helped that I hadn't heard the ghosts speak since they'd supposedly left the room. Maybe Vlad had scared them off? Could ghosts even be scared off? Wasn't it their job to scare us off as the new owners?

I slowly climbed the staircase, then took Vlad's hand as I entered the attic. Dusty, yes, but haunted, no. In fact, the place looked pretty standard. Dusty and unused, but standard. A typical belfry.

"You're sure this is the house you want?" I asked.

"If you don't like it, I can put it up for sale and find another that meets your liking. I would never force you to live somewhere you were truly uncomfortable with."

"What about New Orleans?"

We joined hands and Vlad led me through the attic, taking the time to test the flooring. Once he declared it to be safe—since we *really* didn't want to be falling through wooden floors—he faced me. "New Orleans will always be our home. I merely wanted a place we could use when visiting Perish. Clearly, we can't entrust your mother with our safety. And I haven't high hopes for your father either. Our safety is paramount during the day."

I nodded.

"But I don't intend for us to be here often. I know you prefer New Orleans. As do I."

Relief eased my muscles. "Good. I love New Orleans. Not only because my family isn't there, but it's easy for us to grab a meal. It wouldn't be quite so simple here."

"A few of the harem members have agreed to accompany us whenever we come here."

"Well, isn't that gracious of them," I teased.

"Gracious of *me* to up their salary as recompense."

I chuckled. Now *that* sounded more like it.

"Do you hear any more voices?" Vlad inquired.

Shaking my head, I released his hand and strode across the attic. It was nice, as far as attics went. Nothing spectacular. Just a closed-off room lacking any and all light and fresh air. I understood the need for such a room, but this just made me realize how eager I was for the new SunGuard windows. This place didn't feel like home to me, not like the house in New Orleans. But he was right. We would need a sanctuary here.

"I did hear them though," I told Vlad. "They were bickering, calling each other names, and then ran away when you entered the attic."

Vlad's expression darkened. "I heard no such thing."

I threw my hands up in frustration. "I don't know what else to say. I very clearly heard their voices. I didn't imagine them." My thoughts suddenly screamed to a stop, and I lifted my hand to my mouth, touching my fingertips to my lips. "Wait, I heard another voice."

"What? Just now?"

"No. Earlier tonight. In the cop car."

Vlad crossed the room and grasped my forearms. His hands slid down until they cupped mine. "What do you mean?"

"When you and the cop were speaking, I heard a third voice. It sounded like it'd come from the patrol car. I'd immediately assumed the cop had a partner in there, but when I peered closer, I saw a German Shepherd." I craned my head and gazed up at Vlad. "He called you a dawg."

"A dog called me a dog?"

"No, he called you a *dawg*, like a player, because of how they caught us... canoodling."

Vlad shook his head. "I often find myself frustrated when you speak. I never understand anything you say."

I would have chuckled if his comment hadn't hit so close to home. My thoughts continued racing back to the strange Gollum voice I'd heard in our house back in New Orleans. It'd been squeaky too, similar to the ones heard here tonight. It called us "filthy vampires," so I'd assumed it was one of the harem members. But now that I was thinking about it, I hadn't recognized the voice. And I knew all the harem members.

I lifted my head and sniffed the air. Smell wasn't my strongest sense, but it wasn't weak either. The air was stale and musty, but beneath that came a note of something subtle. A strange odor I'd never sampled before.

With the scent lingering in my nose, I tracked it. It didn't take long until I found something in the corner of the belfry, a small pile of dark pellets.

"Hmm. I'll need to hire cleaners. I'll want them here tonight before we settle in for the day," Vlad commented. "I don't recall there being any mention of animal feces when I spoke with the inspector, and this looks fairly fresh. Within the last few days. Bat, I'd assume."

My head snapped up. "What did you just say?"

"I said I needed to hire a cleaner—"

"No. After that. What sort of feces?"

"Bat. That's guano," Vlad said.

What had one of the voices said? Something about being an old bat? "Holy shit," I whispered.

"What? What's wrong?"

No, this couldn't be possible. I mean, if my suspicions were true, then obviously it *was* possible, but it still didn't seem possible, ya'know? But what other explanation could there be? Everything lined up. All the recent strange occurrences, the odd voices... I thought they were in my head, and maybe they were, but not in an imaginary way.

"Anna, talk to me."

"Vampire powers, tell me about them again."

Vlad lifted a brow. "What?"

"Just... I'll explain after. Tell me about vampire powers."

"You already know everything there is to know. As vampires age, we gain power. And as our powers grow, we develop gifts."

"But at what age do they normally present themselves?"

"Often around the hundred-year mark."

"What about for a vampire who's been known to drink ancient blood quite frequently?"

Understanding dawned on Vlad's face. "Are you suggesting what I think you are?"

"I don't know," I whispered. "Maybe?"

I honestly couldn't think of any other explanation, other than maybe I was losing my mind. Could it be true? Could I possibly have the ability to speak to animals?

Because all vampires wanted *that* power, right?

CHAPTER

FOURTEEN

I RETREATED into the unfurnished living room, my thoughts spinning in senseless circles. This couldn't be possible. I was far too young to have gained my first superpower. And even if it was possible, why animals? Why their thoughts? That had to be the least helpful power ever. Vlad gained foresight and the ability to shift. Me? I got to hear Lassie's thoughts.

Just my luck, huh?

"Anna, you haven't been undead for half a year. You couldn't have developed your first gift yet."

"Then you try explaining it," I said, tossing my hands in the air. "I've been hearing odd voices over the past few nights, but I kept finding a way to explain them away. A begrudged harem member, for instance. But tonight, that dog. I swear that dog spoke. Not out loud, but in my head."

A shadow flickered across Vlad's face. "Anna."

"Yes, yes, I know. It's not possible. I'm not old enough. Blah, blah, blah. Vlad, I drank the blood of a thousand-year-old vampire. And I've had yours more than once. You're not exactly a young whippersnapper yourself. I've also had Camilla's. She's not as old as

411

you, but compared to me, she's ancient. You told me ancient blood was dangerous to younger vampires because they couldn't handle the power boost. Power boost, Vlad! As in, developing my first vamp gift at a younger age."

He held a hand up to end my tirade. "Be that as it may, I've never heard of anyone being able to hear animal thoughts."

I scoffed under my breath and spun toward the window. I peered out into the night, then squinted at the sight of a moving truck pulling up in our driveway.

"Ah," Vlad said. "Our coffins and such have arrived."

Right. Because we needed those tonight. The red taillights shone in the darkness, signaling their approach. I didn't want to discuss this in front of human movers, but I certainly wasn't ready to move on from the conversation either. This explanation was the only one that made sense to me. My thoughts kept centering on the K-9 dog in the patrol car. I knew without a doubt I'd heard that silly beast's thoughts. I'd heard it so clearly that I'd wondered if it was the cop's partner.

I was right about this. I knew it. It all lined up, regardless of my age.

Turning away from the window, I stared at Vlad. I needed to prove it to both of us. The way I saw it, we had a few options. Either we could randomly stalk the sidewalks in search of someone's pet Fluffy to see if I heard anything, or....

"Shift," I said.

Vlad's brows winged upward. "Excuse me?"

"I need to confirm this. Need to know without a doubt that I'm hearing animal thoughts. I've never been able to converse with you when in your animal form. But I'll bet dollars to donuts I can now."

"Anna, I may be able to shift, but I'm not a true animal."

"Maybe that won't matter. We won't know until we test this theory."

Vlad sighed, but eventually nodded. "If this will make you happy."

"So happy," I groused.

"You know, I may be old, but I'm not ignorant to sarcasm."

I rose on my tiptoes and kissed him. "I know. Now shift."

"When did you become so bossy?"

I chuckled, then dipped my fingers under his shirt and pushed it up. "I can be sweeter if you'd like. Oh so sweeter."

"Well, you did promise to rip my clothes off tonight."

"Once the movers are gone. Can't scandalize the poor humans, now can we?"

Vlad leaned down and brushed the tip of his nose against mine. "I could take care of them right now, if you wish."

"Hmm, tempting. But right now, I want you to shift. As soon as we confirm this, we can do whatever you like for the rest of the night."

Vlad's brows waggled at me. "The rest of the night?"

"Mm-hmm. Hours and hours of mindless pleasure." So long as the movers had a couch or bed in their truck.

"That sounds..."

"Heavenly," I teased. "Now, strip and shift, baby."

Vlad chuckled, then grabbed the bottom of his shirt and tugged it over his head. I took a moment to admire his beauty before I slipped my fingers into the waist of his slacks. Just because he had a task didn't mean I couldn't assist.

"What happened to me shifting," he murmured, nuzzling his nose against my throat.

"You're still gonna shift. I'm just admiring the view."

He hummed under his breath, then hooked his pants on his thumbs and shoved them down. The movers hadn't yet left their truck, but I bent an ear in their direction, determined not to let yet another person surprise us tonight.

Once nekkid, Vlad called upon whatever magic let him shift. The air popped a second before his glorious male form vanished and a cute little bat hovered before me.

I chuckled and *booped* his teeny black nose. I'd always loved bats as a child. I had memories of chasing them around the attic in my parent's house, and Lucy and I watching them from our treehouse at night. We'd always left a single light on to watch as they streaked through the air. They looked like winged puppies, and who didn't love puppies?

"Anna?"

Vlad's voice resounded through my head.

I gasped and cupped my mouth. Holy shit. I was right! "I—I can hear you..."

Vlad's beady eyes blinked at me. *"You can hear my thoughts?"*

I nodded. "Cripes, Vlad. I was right! I was fucking right!"

Vlad's wings beat against the air, pushing my hair back from my face. He stared at me, wonder filling those dark eyes. Seconds later, the air popped once more, and a wolf stood before me, his silvery coat catching what little moonlight streamed through the windows.

"And now?"

I laughed and nodded again. "Oh, wow. This is insane. Vlad, I can hear animal thoughts!" This was astounding, in a boring kind of way. I mean, if I'd had a choice, I would want the ability to fly or move things telekinetically. What good could come of hearing animal thoughts? Honestly, it just sounded like a perpetual headache. But at the same time, I had my first gift! At less than half a year old.

"We need to keep this a secret," Vlad ordered, his grim tone popping my small bubble.

"Why?"

"If the queen learns that you've already developed your first gift, it'll just give her another reason to hate you. You're threatening enough without suggesting you might be more powerful than most other vampires."

"Pfft. Power has nothing to do with it. It's just because of Petrik. I'm guessing the mixed cocktail of his blood and yours probably did it. Accelerated the process."

He crooked his silky soft head and studied me with ice-blue eyes. Vlad's wolf form was my absolute favorite of the two. Beautiful didn't begin to describe him like this.

"Exactly. It makes you a threat. How do you feel otherwise?" He pressed his nose against my stomach and snuffled. It made me giggle. *"No yearnings for ancient blood?"*

"Only yours," I teased, brushing his nose away from my navel. My desire for Vlad went far deeper than a simple feeding.

"That's a relief," he said, his voice resounding in my head. *"But we must keep this between ourselves. Word would spread and I can only imagine the fallout."*

"What about Lucy?"

His lips curled up over his long fangs, but he nodded his assent. *"Fine."*

"And Sam?"

Vlad snarled, his lips curling up over fangs longer than my fingers. *"Absolutely not. The man is a werewolf, our natural enemy, and you want to hand him this information? That you might be able to hear his thoughts, and the thoughts of his brethren, when they're in wolf form? Think what they might do when they learn that information. Their secrets won't be secret anymore."*

Only when they were in animal form. But I understood his point. "Geez, okay. No Sam, then."

Vlad huffed. *"Thank you."*

Movement pricked at my ears, and I glanced out the window to see the movers unloading the back of the truck. They unloaded my coffin first and set it down on the grass. I swear, every kitchen light in the neighborhood suddenly flicked on at the same time. Nosy busybodies watching as the new local vampires had their coffins delivered. I knew this had to be unusual for them, but my god, they had their noses practically flush against their windows in an attempt to catch sight of us.

Shaking my head, I placed my hand on the top of Vlad's head and stroked his fur. I was the only person he let do this. Lucy had tried once a few months ago, and she'd nearly lost a hand to his massive teeth. *All the better to eat you with, my dear.*

"Might wanna shift back and get dressed. The movers are about to start carrying stuff inside."

Vlad side-eyed the door, then with a quiet huff, he trotted over to the front door and sat. I bit back my laughter and watched as he waited for them to enter. The instant they approached the porch, Vlad stood and yawned, showing off his big ole teeth.

The instant the movers opened the door, they shrieked and fell back on their asses, scrambling to escape the porch. I doubled over with laughter, my hand cupping my stomach. Vlad might be ancient, but his sense of humor seemed more attuned to my age. Or maybe I was just rubbing off on him. Yeah, that seemed more likely.

Vlad vanished before the movers could pick themselves up.

I strolled into the foyer and stared down at them. "The coffins need to go in the attic. Everything else you can put wherever you'd like."

"But... the wolf?" one asked.

My lips twitched with amusement. "What wolf?"

"That... wolf." They fell into a stunned silence. "I... I could have sworn there was a wolf right there."

"Last I heard, there weren't any wolves left in Louisiana."

"But..." The closest of the two movers leaned around the corner of the foyer and peered into the kitchen. Vlad was nowhere to be seen. Apparently, I'd turned the stuffy old bat into a prankster.

"Um. I... We'll get right to work then."

"Thank you."

The movers shuffled out of the house, both rubbing the back of their necks. "I could have sworn I saw a wolf."

"You and me both, brother."

"I told you this place was cursed!"

I snickered under my breath, then gathered Vlad's clothing and retreated upstairs, where I could hear him moving. With luck, he wouldn't have a need for the clothes any time soon. And yes, I paired that statement with a sly wink.

"ANIMALS? LIKE... ANIMALS?" Lucy asked.

It was the next night, and we'd agreed to meet at the coffee shop once the sun set. Lucy sat across from me, her arms crossed, and her coffee forgotten as we caught each other up. I could smell the heavenly beans and the sweet vanilla creamer, and my mouth watered. I used to love a steaming hot cup of coffee. Stupid blood diet. It robbed food of all excitement. All I could do was sit here slavering over Lucy's coffee, wishing I could steal a sip. It didn't help that I hadn't had a sip of blood since Vlad's last night, and my belly was *hungry*, nearly reaching the hangry stages. If I didn't feed soon, god help the first person to cross my path.

"Yup, animals. Threw me for a loop, let me tell you. Damn dog was sitting in the cop car, cheering Vlad on, and I couldn't figure out what the hell was happening."

Lucy snorted back a laugh, then cupped her hand over her mouth to silence the offensive sound. "I still can't believe you got caught snorking in Vlad's car."

"Oh god, call it something else, would you?"

"Like what? Making lurrrve?"

"Egads, Lucy. Even humping sounds better than that."

She snorted again, then finally took a sip of her coffee. I watched longingly, watching the motion of her throat, then quickly averted my gaze, remembering how she felt the last time I stared at her throat.

"It was nighttime," I said, shrugging. "I doubt the cop even saw anything."

Lucy choked on her coffee. "This truly would only happen to you, Anna."

"Please. Like you've never been caught by the police?"

"Having sex? Never! I would die of mortification."

She probably would too. "You're telling me nothing fantastic happened between you and Sam on your way here? The sexual tension is so thick, I'd need a sword to cut it."

"Ugh, crass." She grimaced, then sucked back at least half of her coffee, procrastinating her answer.

I merely sat back and crossed my own arms, watching her with wide open eyes. I knew this game. Lucy would keep avoiding my question until she was blue in the face. You have to make severe eye contact with her and hold that damn gaze until she cracked. Almost like a police interrogation.

"Nothing happened! I swear. We just sat there in awkward silence."

"Bullshit."

Heat colored her cheeks, proving me right. Girl was lying through her damn teeth.

"You really are the worst. Okay, fine. It wasn't entirely silent. Mostly he talked and I sat there like a nervous wreck, too frightened to say anything. And it's your fault!"

Taken aback, I frowned. "My fault?"

"I was expecting you to be there as a buffer, to crack jokes and break the awkwardness."

I sighed. "Lucy, I can't always be there to help you overcome uncomfortable situations. And it really isn't my place to be that buffer between you and Sam. If you don't want to be with him, then you need to be open and honest with him."

"That's the thing," she said, gripping her coffee cup so tightly, I thought it might collapse inward. "I want to be with him so badly, Anna. Desperately. Like, my thighs vibrate when I'm around him."

A grin spread across my face. *Now* we were getting somewhere. And hallelujah too. I wasn't sure how much more of Saint Lucy I could take.

"Did you tell him that?"

"Oh, he knows." She scowled at the table. "Apparently, he can smell emotions just like you guys can."

I gritted my teeth to keep from laughing aloud. Lucy wouldn't appreciate that. I'd already known that, considering the man had tracked me clear across the city after Petrik had abducted me. Based on that, I think it was easy to assume they had pretty sensitive noses.

"So I can't lie to him," she groused. "He knows I'm hot for him. He knows I'm interested. How do I tell him to back off then?"

"Exactly like that," I said. "You tell him you need some space to think and come to grips with your emotions."

Something flickered behind Lucy's eyes, an emotion I couldn't quite put my finger on. Her lashes fluttered as she glanced down at her hands, a clear sign she was hiding something.

I sat straight in my chair and braced my elbows against the table. "What is it?"

"What?" she asked, playing the part of the sweet little doe.

"You're hiding something."

"Am not!"

The sudden rise of octave told me otherwise, and I didn't need to point that out to her. She'd clearly heard it.

Exasperated, she draped her torso over the table and dropped her forehead down. "Okay, so I need to tell you something. I just learned this last night."

"Okay."

She peered up at me from under her lashes. "You can't freak out."

I held my left hand up. "Scout's honor."

"Wrong hand, doofus."

"Ah, you get the point anyway."

"I ended up bringing Sam home to meet my parents."

Excitement burst in my chest. "You did not!"

"I don't know what I was thinking! I just felt so bad. I didn't wanna force him to stay in the hotel last night. I mean, you know Perish hotels, they're all roaches and mildew!"

She wasn't wrong.

"So I told him he could come with, have a home-cooked meal. I swore he'd love my mother and my mother would love him. I mean my mother loves *everyone*."

"Even me, and that's saying something," I teased.

My joke earned me a slight huff. "Well, he walked in and my mother *lost it*, Anna. She sputtered, turned red in the face, and kicked him out."

I blinked at Lucy, not sure I heard her correctly. "Your mother kicked Sam out? *Your* mother? Sweet little Elly? Your mother wouldn't know how to kick someone out if her life depended on it. She takes in strays of all kinds."

"Yes, I know my mother, thank you."

When Lucy didn't immediately continue, I rocked forward in my chair. "And? What happened?"

"Well, I asked Sam to go check into his hotel and told him I'd call him later. Then I demanded to know what was wrong. Why my mother was so upset about Sam."

"Okay. What'd she say?" Damn, the anticipation was killing me here.

"Um." Lucy's bottom lip trembled.

Oh, this was bad. This had to be really, really bad if she was about to cry. "Hey, whatever it is, it'll be alright. I can talk to your mom, or we can force her to get to know Sam. She'll come to love him like she does everyone else, I swear."

"That's the problem. My mom loves everyone," Lucy whispered. "And apparently, she loved someone else before my dad."

I frowned. I mean, that wasn't surprising, everyone had a past. But I was more confused about how this related to Sam.

"I guess the man she loved before my father was..." Lucy leaned forward and uttered in a conspiratorial whisper, "the werewolf alpha of the Mississippi pack."

Shock rendered me still. Surely, I'd misheard Lucy. Maybe the coffeehouse chatter had affected my nearly perfect hearing? Or maybe I'd picked up on someone else's conversation? It was hard to tune everyone out sometimes. "I'm sorry, but I thought I heard you say—"

"A werewolf, Anna. *And* he's my real father."

A metaphorical bomb exploded in my head. *Kaboom.* "Wait. Your father isn't your father?"

"Not biologically, but he's definitely my father. I don't care who donated the sperm."

Well, that was a very healthy way of looking at this. Kudos to her for that. "But biologically, you're..."

"Half-werewolf," she hissed. "The human half anyway, I guess. My mother says that when a human and werewolf have a baby, the child can swing either way. And I swung human. So this alpha guy discarded us like we were nothing."

Shit. That was harsh. What kind of egotistical, misogynistic asshole did something like that? Oh wait, my father did the same thing. Poor Elly. And poor Lucy.

"And she just knew Sam was a werewolf? Like that?"

Lucy nodded. "I guess it's just an instinct you develop."

"This is a lot to take in," I whispered, understanding her need for a bit of privacy right now. "So, you're the daughter of an alpha werewolf. Oh my god, please don't tell me Sam is his son or something."

"What, ew! No! Two different packs, ya goof."

"Thank goodness."

"Yeah." This time Lucy chuckled. "That would be gross. But my mom thinks Sam is playing me because he knows who my biological father is."

Wow. This was *a lot* to take in. Like a minefield worth of information to navigate. One wrong step and kablooey. "Do you believe that?"

"No. I don't know. Maybe? He swept into my life with all these claims that we were mates and destined to be together and blah, blah, blah. What kind of fool falls for that?"

"Um, me?" I said.

Lucy's eyes widened. "Oh, Anna, I didn't mean..."

"It's fine." I waved a dismissive hand. Her mind was running at a hundred miles a minute right now. I could forgive her for this small slight.

"The thing is, I don't even think Sam knows that my dad isn't my real dad. He just knows me as Lucy Williams. I don't even know my biological father's name, so how could he? Unless the werewolves keep, like, family records or something? A history?"

"They may. We'd have to ask to know for sure."

"I don't like having these thoughts, Anna. I don't like thinking that Sam might be playing me."

My mouth twisted to the side as I contemplated her situation. First, I couldn't believe her dad wasn't her biological father. That blew my mind. And to know that her mother *knew* about the paranormal and never told us. The secrets she must have kept! The things she must know. I needed to hit her up for some learning.

"Can I offer my opinion?" I asked.

Lucy nodded eagerly.

"I don't think Sam is that kind of guy. I don't think he's the sort to use another. And I certainly don't think he'd care that you're the abandoned daughter of some Mississippi alpha. I mean, what would that knowledge even gain him? It isn't like you're a favored daughter or something. You aren't even a werewolf."

Lucy considered my words, her head slowly bobbing. "I think you're right."

"Look. The only way you're ever gonna know is if you talk to him. And if you want, Vlad and I can be there when you do. I think Vlad can tell when someone is lying. Something about the heartbeat and pulse."

"You would do that for me?"

"Girl, please. What wouldn't I do for you?"

She beamed a smile at me, one that made me feel all heroic inside.

Sadly, it was a feeling that quickly joined me in the grave when a familiar—and *very* unwelcome—voice said, "Ladies. Heard you were back in Perish."

CHAPTER
FIFTEEN

THE SIGHT of Chris's leering face made me want to vomit. Not that I could, but I *wanted* to. I knew returning to Perish meant I might run into him, but I'd hoped with every last fiber of my being that I didn't. We'd hardly had the worst break up, but apparently, he'd seen things differently than me. We'd broken up right before Lucy and I left for New Orleans because he had the audacity to forbid me from going. That'd been the nail in the coffin for me. Didn't matter that he was my boyfriend, he had zero rights to forbid me from anything. So I'd shown him the door. A result he hadn't taken kindly to, according to social media.

After I became a vampire, some reporter came sniffing around Perish, trying to dig up dirt on me, and Chris had practically handed it to them all wrapped in a shiny bow. His version of revenge, I suppose.

So when I said he was the last person in the world I wanted to see, I meant it. The bastard was lucky I had a "no biting unless given consent" rule, otherwise I might have taken a big ole chomp out of him right this second in front of all these prying eyes.

"Christopher," I drawled, purposely using his full name. "To what do we owe the honor?"

"Dragged your ass home, I see." His smarmy gaze appraised me. "Like a dog with its tail tucked between its legs."

I let loose a sarcastic laugh. "Is that the best you could come up with? And how long did it take you to muster the courage to come over here? You've been here as long as we have."

"Noticed me, did'ya?"

"Don't let it go to your head." I tapped my nose. "I could smell your foul odor the second I stepped through the door." Which wasn't true, of course. The bitter coffee bean stench had sorta fried my sense of smell at the moment.

"I heard you were back. Heard you and your new vamp beau moved in last night. Everyone's talking about your coffin... Is that what you really sleep in?"

I rolled my eyes. "Man, you really need to work on your insults. If that's seriously the best you got—"

He leaned close, his hands braced on the top of the table. The man knew how to invade someone's personal space, that was for sure. Sadly, he didn't realize that he'd woken the beast within. The one hungry for blood.

"No, an insult would be to call you necrophiliac coffin bait. You're literally nothing more than the walking dead now. A piece of trash that doesn't know how to stay dead. I said you were going to get yourself killed by going to New Orleans, and you laughed in my face. Lo and behold, hey? How the mighty have fallen. So, who's laughing now, Anna? You're nothing more than a filthy leech, sucking the life out of everyone around you."

Anger uncoiled within me, burning my synapses until nothing remained but an irate vampire staring into the eyes of an ex she now hated. I felt the monster within come to life, felt it stretch its limbs out as though waking from a deep slumber. The snack in front of me had dangled himself too close for comfort.

"You might want to back the fuck up," I snarled.

Chris's mouth spread into a victorious grin, then froze the instant his flight or fight instincts kicked in. I saw it in his eyes, the moment he realized he'd become prey. His throat was in pure striking distance, and I was hungry. Oh, I wanted nothing more than to strike like a viper and bury my fangs jugular deep.

With Vlad giving his harem the weekend off, I had no one to feed from tonight. Which meant my stomach was rumbling and my inner vampire was displeased. Then here came this prince, offering the juiciest vein I'd ever seen.

"Chris," Lucy said, her voice soft and low so as not to set me off. "I highly suggest you back down. Slowly. No sudden movements. I don't think she's fed yet tonight."

The idiot made the mistake of glancing away. And the second he averted his gaze, I lunged. My hand gripped his throat, and before I could even consider my actions, I whirled him around and slammed his back down onto the table. Chris whimpered and struggled against me, his fingernails clawing at my arms. But I barely felt it, a touch lost to my blood lust. He was weak, defenseless, and had pissed off a hungry vampire. Why shouldn't I take a bite?

"Anna," Lucy whispered. "People are watching."

"Let them," I growled.

My eyes zeroed in on that blue throbbing vein, my parched mouth suddenly salivating at the sight of it like one of Pavlov's dogs. One taste was all I needed. It wouldn't take long at all.

"Anna!" Lucy gripped my wrist. "You only drink from the consenting, remember?"

"He hasn't said no yet."

Chris's wide, terrified eyes bounced between the two of us. His lips parted as he panted for breath. He tried to speak, but my hand squeezed his throat just a little harder. He couldn't say no if he couldn't talk.

"Maybe he wants this," I murmured, caressing his pale cheek with my fingernails. "Maybe he intended to anger me. Maybe he wants my teeth buried in him. *Maybe* I'm not the only coffin bait here."

I loosened my grip, and Chris immediately sputtered for air. "I—I didn't mean it." He choked on a cough. "I'm sorry, I—Ohhhh..."

An acrid stench perfumed the air. It rose above all the coffee beans and slapped me in the face. I blinked, then stared down at the junction of his legs, where a stain began to slowly spread through his khakis.

"Jesus," Lucy laughed, then clapped a hand over her mouth. "You literally made the guy piss his pants from fear. Can you let him go now, please? People are recording this."

"I can't be seen on videos," I said, shrugging, wondering how much further to take this.

"Well, I can! And I really don't want to be the focus on all the stupid vamp sites now."

I didn't tell her it was too late. Guaranteed the videos would be online within ten minutes. The internet loved anything vampire related right now. Instant fame.

With a slow sigh, I released Chris's throat and straightened. Sure enough, everyone around had whipped their phones out and recorded everything. Not a single soul had thought to assist Chris. No, instead they'd opted for their five minutes of fame by recording this little transgression.

Typical humans.

"Let's go." Lucy tugged on my arm. "We definitely need to find you a willing meal before you do something to Chris that you'll regret."

With what I hoped was an evil grin, I braced my hands on either side of Chris's head and leaned in, hoping I'd successfully mirrored his power pose from earlier. "Next time you want to run your mouth, think about who you're talking to. Running your mouth about me will just get you dead, get it?"

His eyes widened before he started nodding frantically.

On that note, I followed Lucy out of the coffee shop. The second the door closed behind us, we both burst into nervous laughter. I had a feeling the coffee shop would permanently ban us, but it was completely worth it just to see Chris's face.

"He totally pissed himself!" Lucy said, her shoulders shaking uncontrollably. "Like, that's on video. He peed his pants!"

"What can I say?" I brushed imaginary lint off my shoulders. "I'm terrifying."

"Oh, undeniably. I actually thought you were going to bite him at first. Your eyes got this unnatural glint, like you suddenly saw him as prey. Freaky!"

I didn't admit aloud that I'd considered feeding off Chris, even if it'd only been a fleeting thought. Lucy didn't need to know that my control had slipped, all because he'd angered me. I wanted to think I had better control of my temper, but truth be told, even as a human, I'd been a bit hotheaded. I couldn't imagine that changing just because I had fangs now.

"Speaking of, where are you and Vlad intending on eating while here?"

My mouth pursed. "I'm not sure. There's nothing quite like The Vampire Lounge here. I wish he hadn't given the harem the weekend off. Even one of them would have been a big help. The movers were unloading furniture all day today. Thankfully, they didn't disturb our sleep, but it would have been nice to have someone there to direct them."

Lucy nodded. "I still can't believe he bought the Barker house."

"Me too," I chuckled. "But he was right. It absolutely isn't haunted. Unless you consider the bats."

"Did they come back?"

I shook my head and started walking down the street. "The place was empty when we woke. I don't know if they sensed us and decided not to return or what."

"Next time you see an animal, you should try talking to it, see if they understand you as well."

"Because that's what I need, people catching me having an imaginary conversation with a random stray cat in the middle of the street."

Lucy laughed. "I'd definitely pay to see that. What are your plans for the rest of the night?"

"We have to meet with my dad," I said, wincing. "Wanna come? You can be our buffer. You know how my dad and his little tramp are."

"You couldn't pay me enough to tag along. I know exactly how you and your dad are, and I know it isn't going to be a pretty visit. Besides, I have my own daddy issues to sort out."

Fair enough. I slowed and placed a hand on her arm. "You know that this alpha werewolf isn't your father, right? Doesn't matter that you came from his sperm, he's nothing to you. Your father raised you, loved you, kissed your skinned knees, held you when you cried—"

"I know, Anna," Lucy said, laughing. "Surprisingly, I don't even care that he isn't my biological father. He's still my daddy. This information changes nothing for me."

"Good," I said.

"Don't get me wrong. I'm pissed my mom and dad lied, but I'm not going to let this information ruin our relationship."

"Are you gonna go looking for this werewolf?"

Her face knotted. "I haven't decided yet."

"Well, let's start with asking Sam if he knew anything about this and then we can go from there."

Lucy nodded. "Tomorrow. You have enough on your plate tonight. Tonight, I just want to talk to my mom again and get all the information I can."

I was just about to agree when I remembered my mother had asked me to come back again tomorrow night. "Has to be late tomorrow night. I have to go see Caleb. Ugh."

Lucy grimaced. "That's fine. Caleb, really?"

I nodded. "Mom didn't give me much of a choice."

"Joy. What are you going to do for blood tonight?"

I considered her question. I didn't relish the idea of walking down the street, hollering at anyone who passed to feed me, but next to that, I had no idea how to go about finding a meal. It was so much easier in New Orleans, thanks to the inherent mystical atmosphere.

"I'll figure something out," I told her. "Maybe Vlad has a plan already. But I definitely need to be fed before arriving at my dad's, otherwise, I can't promise I won't bite his wife."

Lucy looped an arm around my waist and rested her head on my shoulder. "You know I'd offer, but…"

"I know, and don't feel guilty about not wanting to feed me. That's definitely not a path I want us to go down."

She sighed and straightened. "All right. Well, text me once you leave your dad's. I want to know all about it. I'll swing by your place tomorrow before sunset with Sam."

I gave her a half-hug, then turned toward the Barker house—er, Vlad's and my place. That was going to take some time to get used to. "Night, Luce."

"Night!"

Now… time to find a quick nip of blood. Otherwise, I couldn't be held responsible for what happened tonight.

THE INSTANT I neared our house, I knew something was wrong. I couldn't explain it. Just this shiver that ran down my spine and the feeling that someone was watching me. I stopped on the porch, then bent down to fiddle with my shoes. They hardly needed the adjustment, but it gave me a chance to inspect my surroundings.

Sound wise, I only heard the wind and aimless chatter in our many neighbor's houses. Talk of bedtime and tomorrow's plans. All normal considering the time—half past ten. Next, I gave the air a sniff, drawing the myriad of scents deep into my nose, yet nothing stood out to me. Moss, leaves, swamp, nothing out of the ordinary.

Fingers still pretending to adjust my straps, I pivoted slightly on the porch. Doing so gave me a clearer view of the street. But even from this angle, everything looked right. A few neighbors stood on their porches, their silhouettes illuminated by dim cigarette light. Others sat on their porch swings, swirling their brandy and wineglasses. A third sat on a rickety bench, reading a book beneath the light.

All living their normal lives.

Yet, still, something felt off. Somehow, I *knew* without a doubt someone was watching me. My brows furrowed as an uncomfortable thought wriggled through my head. Maybe *everyone* was watching me. Which wouldn't surprise me, given the current climate. The last vlog Lucy and I posted had now reached two million viewers. And I would have bet any money there were a ton of videos going up right this second of me and Chris at the coffee house. The neighbors currently peering at their smartphones were probably watching it right now, then me, waiting to see what I did next. All this had to be super exciting for the sleepy town of Perish.

So, maybe that was all this was. The unnerving realization that all eyes were on me. Fame comes at a price, right? I'd learned that lesson at the beginning of all this. And seeing how Perish didn't receive many "VIP" visitors, I needed to expect this.

I dusted off the tips of my shoes and rose with a sigh. When nothing out of the ordinary happened, I opened the door and slipped inside. The second I closed the door, that slimy feeling of being watched vanished, and I stretched out a kink in my neck.

At least it was quiet in here. Safe.

"Anna?" Vlad called out.

I toed off my shoes, then followed the sound of his voice into the kitchen, my bare feet silent on the tiled floor. I found him seated at our spiffy new dining room table with a glass of red in front of him— and no, I didn't mean wine.

When I'd woken this afternoon, I'd found the entire house all furnished, thanks to the moving guys. Vlad must have tipped them well to set it all up for us. That or he'd hired an interior decorator. Huh. Never thought to ask. I'd merely been grateful to have a furnished house complete with books to read to pass the time while waiting for sunset. I'd given Vlad a grateful kiss as he brushed his fangs and hair before I'd taken off to go meet Lucy.

"Mmm," I hummed as I lifted his glass to my nose. "Where'd you get this from?"

"Bottled," he said. "They sell some in town. I had it delivered an hour or so ago."

My gaze drifted to the half-emptied bottle on the table, and I nodded, now understanding how we'd feed while in Perish. Vlad had purchased these bottles before. They belonged to a new company that had sprouted up almost immediately after vampires joined society. Much like donating blood to hospitals, the company farmed fresh blood from volunteers, then bottled it up for the night and sold it to us vamp-folk. Far better than bagged, and only slightly less delicious than fresh from the tap.

Throughout history, humans had always excelled at innovation, and it seemed they'd taken the concept and run with it these past few months. Every time I turned around, there seemed to be a new company idea catering to my kind.

"O positive," I murmured before resting my lips against the cool glass and draining it dry. The feel of fresh blood coating my throat soothed the inner beast within, *and* my murderous intentions. Interestingly, I felt a bit ashamed now for lashing out at Chris. Not that he hadn't deserved it. But the poor guy had literally pissed his pants on video, which guaranteed it was already online. His friends would never let it down.

"By all means," Vlad teased with a wry smile. "Help yourself."

I grabbed the bottle, topped up his glass, then held it to his mouth. His lips twitched, but he played along, allowing me to offer him a sip.

Once finished, he looped an arm around my waist and guided me into his lap, my favorite place ever. "How did your visit with Lucy go?"

I snuggled into his chest and gave him a quick rundown of everything Lucy had told me. Vlad made noises where appropriate, appeared shocked when I mentioned her bloodline, then stiffened when I started to talk about Chris.

When we reached the part about necrophiliac coffin bait and how he called me a leech, Vlad grew deathly still. For a moment, I wondered if I'd just signed Chris's death sentence.

Eventually, Vlad's tension bled away, and his body relaxed. "Be glad I wasn't there."

His statement brought a rousing smile to my lips as I pictured that scenario. Vlad wouldn't have publicly lashed out at Chris like I had, but that didn't mean he wouldn't have handled the situation. I just suspected he would have handled it privately. Somewhere Chris would never again see the light of day. Not that Vlad would murder him... I didn't think. Sometimes, I couldn't tell. The man had beheaded one of his oldest friend's for harming me, after all.

"And how are you tonight?" I asked. "Any more visions last night?"

His expression shuttered. "Unfortunately."

I splayed a hand against his chest and offered him a few soothing caresses. "Any new information?"

"Yes, but nothing helpful. Two shadows, working in tandem. They attack you, kill you, and walk away. And I'm not there. I don't understand. I'm *not* there."

"Maybe it's just a dream."

"It's a vision," he said sharply. "I know the difference."

I nodded. Of that, I had no doubt. I'd only hoped to comfort him. So, I decided to change the topic. "You haven't noticed anything strange tonight, have you?"

"Strange how?"

I tucked into his chest and rested my head in the crook of his shoulder. "I'm not quite sure. But before I came inside, I swear, I could feel someone watching me."

Vlad leaned to the side and studied me. After discussing his vision, I had to imagine this conversation was going to put him on edge. "Where?"

"I couldn't place it. I didn't smell or hear anything odd, but I definitely had this feeling. Like eyes on the back of my neck. You know that feeling? Like you've been marked as prey?"

All emotion vanished from Vlad's face. "No."

I almost laughed. Of course he hadn't experienced that before. He was never prey.

"Did you feel like you were in danger?"

"Hmm. No, I don't think so." I sighed and snuggled back into him. "It's probably just all in my head. Everyone is watching us right now. That's probably all I'm feeling."

He pulled me tight against him. "Let me know if you feel it again."

I agreed with a small smile. I loved that he took me at my word and didn't suggest it was all in my imagination. Vlad was the sort who knew not to discount things simply because they didn't make sense. He trusted my instincts. As I did his.

A quick glance at the clock told me we had places to go and people to see. "Think we can blow off my father?" I asked. Our night had just begun, and honestly, the last thing I wanted to do was spend it with my estranged father and his two-bit whore—oh, excuse me, wife. "Just think. We could stay here, wrapped up in each other, touching, kissing—"

"Careful what you wish for," Vlad jested. "Keep heading in that direction, and we might not make it out of the house tonight."

"What a shame." I chuckled.

"While I would love nothing more than for us to be alone tonight, I do think we should make an appearance, even if only for a few minutes. Your father would be insulted if we didn't show, don't you think?"

"Relieved is probably more accurate," I muttered. "All he cares about are his wife's new boobs and how much he can play with them."

"I sincerely hope your father isn't that immature." Vlad tilted his head. "Or that crass."

"He's both. The man cheated on my mother for three years before she confronted him. When she did, he simply shrugged and said he was relieved she finally knew, so he could stop hiding. No remorse for breaking his wife's heart or destroying his family. Just relief. Then he kicked us out of our family home and took all his money with him. Caleb and I were already adults, so there was no need for child support, and thanks to my mother's inheritance from her parents, she was denied alimony. So off my father went, spending all his money on his mistress-turned-wife's new boobs, face, teeth, you name it."

"Charming."

"Next came a pool installation in his backyard. After that, a fancy new sports car. The man destroyed our lives and got off scot-free."

"It's a wonder you turned out so perfect," Vlad murmured.

Inwardly, I melted. But outwardly, I chuckled and kissed his cheek. "Now who's the charmer?"

"I aim to please." After a gentle kiss atop my head, he scooted me off his lap and rose. "Shall we get this over with?"

"If we must," I said with a sigh.

"We must. But if it improves your mood, just imagine all the depraved things I intend to do to you once we return home. Such thoughts should help get me through the night."

I sputtered out a laugh and swatted at Vlad's arm. "You're incorrigible!"

"I learned from the best." He offered me another kiss, then gestured to my shoes.

As I slipped my feet in, I watched Vlad step out onto the porch and scan our surroundings, likely searching for some unknown threat. His devotion continuously stirred up emotions within me. And I couldn't help but compare him to my father. Of the three of us, Vlad and I were vampires, but my father was the true monster. At least with Vlad at my side, I felt like I could handle anything.

Ah, the silly lies we tell ourselves.

SIXTEEN

WE'D MADE it a whole whopping ten minutes into the supposed "get-together" before I wanted to rip out some throats. Excuse me, no. I misspoke. Not *some* throats. Just one very particular throat smeared in some fancy Hermès perfume and wrapped like a Christmas tree in the gaudiest diamond choker I'd ever seen.

Christina had certainly dressed for the occasion, even a vamp baby like me could see that. She'd dolled her neck up in every way she could think of. The only thing lacking was a literal "come bite me" sign pinned to her throat.

And all that attractive window dressing seemed intended for one person in particular.

Vlad.

Now, I was hardly a possessive or jealous woman—I prided myself on that—but Christina seemed incapable of keeping her mitts to herself. As though her blatant scent and jewelry hadn't been invitation enough, she'd found a reason to touch Vlad not once, not twice, but eight times. And every single time, she'd waited until my father's attention was diverted.

Not mine though. Oh no. I was blessed enough to witness every arm stroke and finger brush, along with the subtle lean-ins and smiles. If she wasn't flashing her throat, she was brandishing her breasts or displaying those pearly whites. Both of which my father had paid for.

Classy, right?

If she kept this up, I was gonna have to show her *my* teeth. The ones I tended to sink into people's jugulars. Just sayin'.

Fortunately, Vlad was all too aware of Christina's attentions. My father seemed the only blind one in the room. When the ninth touch came, I gave her a slow, dangerous blink, and flashed my fangs in a wide smile.

"Christina," I purred. "How long have you and my father been together now?"

"Oh..." Heat flushed her cheeks as she shot Vlad a surreptitious glance. "How long has it been, sweetheart? About ten years now?"

"Nine, darling," he mumbled.

Nine. Confirming that they'd definitely begun their whirlwind affair when I was the tender age of fifteen. Explained why he'd missed all my extracurricular activities.

I shot my father a glare, but his back was still to me as he washed their dinner dishes in the sink. He'd barely paid me any attention tonight. And I'd yet to figure out the exact reason why. Either he wasn't comfortable with my new vampire existence, or he honestly didn't give enough shit about me to even look at me. Considering my father and I barely ever spoke—even before my transition—I would bet all my money on the latter.

Such a sweet, caring man. *Cue snorting laugh.*

"Oh, right. Nine," she said with a smile so sweet, it gave me a toothache. "But you don't want to hear about us!" She stroked the back of Vlad's hand with the tip of her index finger.

I ground my teeth, about to say something, when Vlad simply sighed and brushed her advances away like she was an annoying gnat. The sight of her wide, unblinking eyes almost made me laugh. She shot him a stunned look, as though confused someone would dare reject her. My father might have turned her into his little doll, but her intolerable personality rotted through her exterior.

Vlad, on the other hand, barely spared her glance. Instead, he looped his arm around the back of my chair and idly stroked my shoulder.

Now, I was the one smiling oh so sweetly.

Of course, his dismissal didn't sway her. Nerp. What Christina wanted, Christina got. That'd always been her way. When I'd first learned of their affair, I'd asked her how she could sleep with a married man. Her answer had been, "He's cheating on your mother, not me." Such a charmer.

And she wondered why we absolutely loathed her.

"So, tell us about yourself, Vlad." She reached toward him once more, almost as though she couldn't help herself.

That was the last straw.

"Woman, do you want to lose that hand?" I snapped.

She startled, her heavily lined eyes snapping to mine. "Excuse me?"

My father finally turned away from the sink and shot us a quick, but hazy glance. One that told me he was already half-in-the-bag. The man seemed completely oblivious to his wife's actions right now. Which had me wondering how often this happened. Had the tables turned on him? Was his former mistress sleeping around? Le gasp, right?

This woman had destroyed my family. She'd ripped through it like Hurricane Katrina and left nothing in her wake. I absolutely despised her. Tonight was about playing nice and seeing my father, but I didn't give a shit about his wife. Not that he understood or cared about our feelings though. So, her flirtatious advances were risking her life, and I had absolutely zero qualms about telling her that.

"Ever heard the saying 'eyes bigger than the stomach'?" I asked.

"Anna..." Vlad murmured.

Christina glanced between us, but nodded.

"Take that concept and apply it here," I warned her. My lips curled into what I hoped was a psychotic smile. One that said "fuck with me and I'll eat your face off."

Seemed my warning worked because she wrenched her hand back from Vlad and tucked it under her rear.

"Um." She straightened her posture and cleared her throat. "So, Vlad, you were telling us about yourself?"

"I wasn't actually." His fingers continued to doodle on my bare shoulder. "Perhaps you'd rather hear about Anna."

Christina scowled at us both. Guaranteed, the last thing she wanted was to hear about me. I was the fly in her ointment, and the one who made her relationship with my father just that bit harder. I took pride in that small accomplishment. They'd made our lives difficult. Why couldn't I return the favor? Maybe it was petty, but sometimes, being petty felt really damn good.

"Personally, I'd rather hear about you, Dad," I said. The bastard hadn't even bothered calling me after I'd turned into a vampire. Such love. "We've only spoken like once this year. I assume you've been busy?"

"No more so than normal," he mumbled, his back still facing me as he continued to wash their dishes.

"Okay. What have you been up to, then?"

He half-shrugged, then pushed his cuffed sleeves further up past his elbows. "Same as always. Work and whatnot."

I shot Vlad an exasperated glance, one he acknowledged with an encouraging nod.

"Dad, I'm only here for the weekend. Could you maybe... try? I know that's asking a lot—"

He sighed and dropped the plate back into the water. "Don't start, Anna. I'm not in the mood tonight."

"To what, exactly? Converse with me? Or even just look at me?"

"I can't," he confessed, his voice barely above a whisper.

"Can't what?"

He blew out a heavy breath, one that perfumed the air with alcohol. Yup, he'd definitely had a few before our arrival tonight.

Calming himself after a busy workday? Or preparing himself for this visit? I had a feeling I wouldn't like the answer if I asked.

"Can't *what*, Dad?" I demanded.

"Can't look at you!" he shouted, slamming his palms down on the counter. He dropped his head, and his shoulders rounded inward while he panted for breath.

Yeah, I knew I wouldn't like the answer. But shame on me for asking, right?

Vlad's hand gripped my arm to keep me from rising to my feet. Instead, I nodded and blew out a completely unnecessary breath. It was no secret that my father and I weren't particularly close. Even as a child, I hadn't wanted much to do with him. His busy work schedule had created the divide between us, but his cavalier attitude had widened it. But if I had to guess, I'd say me becoming a vampire didn't jibe with him.

All that remained was deciding whether we left. One half of me wanted to stay. And no, not to repair our relationship, but rather just as punishment. To annoy him. To force him to spend time with the daughter he'd ignored her whole life, the one he couldn't bear to look at right now. The other half of me wanted to bail. Why put myself through this? Why bother?

The man hadn't even bothered to call to check up on me after Vlad turned me. Even before that, he'd chosen his new life and family, and hadn't been shy about his choice. Some families survive divorce. The parents make the effort to separate amicably, and everyone maintains a polite demeanor. I didn't know of any personally, but I'd heard of them. On the news or some shit.

My family had gone full kamikaze. Imagine World War II. And thanks to my father's position in the political arena, the rest of the town had been dragged along for the ride. Sides were chosen and bonds were broken. Such as mine and my father's.

He and Caleb had tried for a bit. But after a while, they'd called it. DOA. Neither had enough interest in the other to keep on trying. So why continue torturing ourselves, right? Just shout out the time of death and abandon ship. Save everyone the hassle.

Well, this was the result of that.

A tumultuous relationship where a father couldn't even bear to look at his daughter. Not exactly the loving daddy-daughter relationship most people hope for.

"We couldn't even give you a funeral," he whispered.

Anger erupted within me. I took Vlad's hand and pushed to my feet. "Bye, Dad."

"What?" He whirled around and finally made eye contact with me. "You're leaving?"

"Yes. I'm not going to stand around here and listen to you while you mourn me or some morbid shit like that."

"Language!" Christina snapped.

"Bite. Me."

Her face paled. I guess the sight of my fangs had stuck with her because she simply swallowed and pouted in her chair like a petulant child.

"I refuse to stand here and cry with you, not when I'm not actually dead. I'm standing right fucking here"—I shot Christina a warning glance before she could utter a word—"and even if I weren't, you don't give two shits about me. So, I'm not going to listen to you bemoan and complain about how you lost your daughter. You lost me a hell of a long time ago, you're just too fucking stupid to see it."

My hand shot to my mouth as the room fell into stark silence.

"Perhaps we should leave," Vlad suggested.

I slowly nodded, my eyes clashing with my father's. He seemed too stunned to speak, a sentiment I definitely shared. I'd never spoken to him like that before, and I wasn't quite sure how I felt about it. At least it was honest. And that had to count for something, right?

My mouth opened, but nothing came out. And since my father seemed less inclined to speak, I took Vlad's hand and let him lead me out the front door.

And this time, I didn't look back.

I SANK into our new luxurious Chesterfield sofa and just sighed. We'd been gone two hours, tops. Honestly, we should have stayed home, could have enjoyed two hours of mindlessly pleasuring each other. Didn't that sound better than arguing with my dad and watching his wife try to feel up Vlad? Sounds a hell of a lot better to me.

"I must say..." Vlad kneeled before me and eased off my shoes. Knowing their worth and how much my shoe wear meant to me, he gently placed them aside before he started kneading my calves. The instant his fingers dug in, I moaned and practically melted into a puddle of goo on our ridiculously expensive couch. "Your father's quite the—"

"Asshole," I mumbled. "Don't say I didn't warn you."

"You very much did."

"He's always been like that. Everything is always about him, all the time. If he was worth even a grain of salt, he would have at least texted an apology or called or something after we left."

"And did he?"

I plundered my phone from my purse and held it up so Vlad could see the missed notifications screen. A few texts from Lucy, a missed email, and a phone call from my mother. Nada from dear old dad. As always.

"You know what? Let's just forget about him," I said, pushing up from the couch. "The man literally means nothing to me. So why let him ruin our night, right? Let's have a dance party, instead. A naked dance party, of course."

Vlad blinked. "I have absolutely no idea what that is."

"It's exactly what it sounds like. I slap on some music—from my generation—and we strip and dance."

"No."

Vlad's resounding response made me laugh. I could tell from his stern expression there would be no negotiating this either. If negotiation wouldn't get me what I wanted—which was Vlad in his birthday suit—then maybe I needed to lead by example.

With a wink, I turned to our new sound system and quickly found the song I wanted. The dulcet tones of Harry Style's "Watermelon Sugar" swept through the house, and I spun back to Vlad, grinning. It wasn't my favorite song, but even I had to admit, it had a great beat. Something you could wiggle your hips and ass too. Vlad immediately noticed the instant I started grooving. I danced my way up to him, then hooked my thumbs in my pants and slowly started pushing them down.

"Anna, what in the world are you doing?"

I grinned, then stepped out of my pants and spun around, grinding my bottom against him.

"Anna..."

I cast a sly glance over my shoulder. "Yes, Vlad?"

His faint growl was music to my ears. My shirt went next, casually tossed aside. I danced before him in nothing but a bra and panties, shimmying and shaking to the energetic beat.

"Well?" I asked, scootching my booty up against his groin. "You gonna join me or what?"

I needed this. Needed to blow off some pent-up steam. I didn't realize how much my relationship with my father upset me. But being upset about it wouldn't accomplish anything. Honestly, neither one of us had any interest in repairing what was broken. So fretting about it wouldn't help either. What I needed was to dance. To burn off all that excess energy. To have fun. To smile. To laugh.

"This isn't dancing," Vlad said.

But before I could argue, his hands shot out and snatched me by the waist. He pulled me flush against him, then kissed me. The passion was intense, burning through us like a wildfire. Everywhere he touched, heat followed, sparking a familiar desire. It didn't matter that we'd sated ourselves last night for hours on end. Our hunger for one another seemed endless. And I was completely okay with that. I didn't want a relationship that went stale. That became a chore. We were only three months in, so I couldn't speak for the future, but something within me told me this was forever.

Vlad grabbed my thighs and lifted, then locked my legs around his waist. He walked us back toward the couch, then slowly sat, his fingers gripping my flesh so hard, I had a feeling there'd be marks afterward. But I didn't care.

Instead, I succumbed to the kiss and the inevitable pleasure heading my way. We hadn't had a chance to break in the couch last night, but it seemed he had every intention of remedying that right now.

I moaned against his mouth as my fingers found his pants zipper. I'd just opened it when a sudden knock echoed through the door.

Gasping, I pulled back from Vlad and glanced backward.

"Are you kidding me?" I hissed. "Who the hell is knocking on our door at half-past midnight?"

Another firm knock, almost insistent. As though this person had every right to be here.

"The scent isn't familiar," Vlad said, his brows deepening.

Which meant no one from my family. I had friends here, or at least I had before New Orleans. I honestly didn't consider any of them friends anymore. Not after they'd handed over every facet of my life to the reporters. But even I could tell from a quick sniff that it wasn't anyone I knew.

"I don't know them either," I said.

A worrisome concept. Who would come knocking on our door in Perish?

"Get dressed," Vlad said, helping me to my feet.

I threw on my clothes, then followed him to the door. Vlad shot me a quick glance, then yanked it open.

There, on the other side, stood an unfamiliar man. I studied him with a frown, wondering if I should know him. Maybe he was a neighbor? He wasn't as tall as Vlad, and he was thinner. Almost anemic looking. Except he was a vampire. And one thing we vampires weren't was anemic.

"Ah, you must be Anna," the man said, his beady dark gaze appraising me as I had him.

I didn't respond. No point confirming something he apparently already knew.

"And you are?" Vlad asked.

The man barely glanced Vlad's way. Instead, his dark eyes held mine and his thin lips pressed into a thin line, as though he wasn't impressed with what he saw. Likewise, little man. Likewise.

"Well?" he demanded. "Are you going to invite me in?"

"Oh, that would be a no," I said. "Sorry, let me rephrase. That would be a hell no. My mommy taught me not to invite strangers into my house."

His upper lip curled in annoyance. "Cute."

"I try."

"I must insist."

"Insist all you want." I crossed my arms over my chest, hoping I looked every bit as intimidating as Vlad. "Until we know who you are—"

"My name is Michel," he said. "Michel Aubert."

I had every intention of commenting on his very French name when I caught the stiffening of Vlad's shoulders. Before I could ask, his arm shot out and he pushed me behind him, shielding me from sight with his body.

The last time he'd done that, we'd found ourselves squaring off against Petrik in the middle of The Vampire Lounge.

My blood ran cold.

Something was wrong then. This Michel must not be a nice guy if Vlad was that frightened.

"Michel Aubert," Vlad repeated. "How nice to finally meet you."

"And you, I suppose," he responded, his thick French accent creeping into his words. "The queen sends her warmest regards."

Holy shit. Did he just say the queen?

"Now. Will you invite me in?" Michel asked. "Or do I need to return to England with a report of your reluctance to acquiesce?"

Oh, this sounded bad. So very, *very* bad.

I felt Vlad's muscles coiling, but instead of attacking, which he clearly wanted, he stepped back and gripped my hand, almost painfully.

"Please, come in," he said, his tone cold and unwelcome. "Inquisitor."

CHAPTER

SEVENTEEN

THIS MUST BE what a panic attack felt like for a vampire. My body couldn't react physically thanks to my lack of pulse and heartbeat, but my stomach was tighter than a puckered asshole and my vision had gone all fuzzy.

Inquisitor? Had Vlad said inquisitor? As in one of the queen's most trusted warriors?

Hell. This was bad. Extremely bad. Apocalyptic bad.

I struggled to remember everything Camilla had taught me about the vampire hierarchy. I'd only skimmed the messages, thinking I could always come back to them when I needed them. Except I highly doubted this Michel would appreciate me whipping out my phone right now to see where he sat on the vampire hierarchy.

If I remembered correctly, the order consisted of the queen, her consort, their heirs, the council, then the inquisitors. She and the consort were mates, and their heirs had been hand-chosen before being turned into vampires. The council consisted of her most trusted allies, those she could rely on when she needed advice. Then came the inquisitors. Men and women she depended on to eliminate heresy and other issues contrary to her

446

laws. They meted out justice as deemed necessary with the power of the queen backing them. Her own little Gestapo, apparently.

Suddenly, Vlad's vision came to mind. We didn't have much to go off, but he'd mentioned two shadows. Could Michel be one of them? And the queen the other?

I honestly couldn't think of a single soul in this world who wanted me dead—well, maybe Christina—except for the queen. Had she sent her inquisitor here to finish me off? To take care of her little problem? Wasn't that an inquisitor's job, after all?

Michel stepped into the house with a cocky little smile while my entire body kicked into flight mode. Vlad's hands were the only thing keeping me still when every bone in my body urged me to run. No good could come of this. I highly doubted the queen sent an inquisitor to simply investigate. This made me think of the Church in the medieval days. Their inquisitors hadn't been friendly people then either.

"Thank you for that generous welcome," Michel stated, his wry voice grating on my nerves. "I see you two have settled in rather nicely."

"How did you know where to find us?" Vlad demanded.

"We've been keeping an eye on you two for a while now."

I shook my head and scolded myself for not trusting my instincts last night. I'd felt the bastard's eyes on me, and we'd both brushed it aside like it was nothing.

"Must be nice to have such services available to you now, yes?" Michel pointed at our furniture. "Before Queen Genevieve brought us into the twenty-first century, such things like buying and furnishing a house were far more difficult to organize. We'd needed proxies to negotiate on our behalf. Men and women we employed but who remained unaware of our secret—"

"What do you want, Inquisitor?" Vlad demanded, interrupting the man's annoying tirade. I really didn't care about the days of old.

"I assumed that would be obvious." Michel strode into our living room and studied the furnishings with what appeared to be an approving eye.

I kept my comments to myself. I might be impulsive, but I wasn't suicidal, and I had a feeling anything I said would be used against me in the vampiric court of law, if such a thing existed. Camilla had mentioned something to me earlier, about how the queen was organizing a tribunal of sorts for naughty vampires. A means of showing humans we were more than murderous bastards. But I hadn't heard much else on that front.

"Queen Genevieve insisted I come meet the elusive Miss Anna Perish on her behalf, since all the queen's invitations have gone unanswered."

"What invitations?" Vlad asked, his hand squeezing mine to keep me from speaking.

We both knew exactly which invitations Michel spoke of. The first had arrived shortly after Petrik's death, and it'd soon met a fiery ending. I hadn't let anyone else see it. Then came the second and the third. Eventually, Vlad caught on, but that didn't mean we needed to admit anything to Michel.

"Come now, Vlad. Let's not play that game." Michel turned and tsked quietly at him. "You know as well as I that the queen's council has issued multiple invitations. We're all quite curious about the result of certain recent matters. Such as the condition of one Petrik Kamen. He hasn't been seen or heard from in some months now, which is rather unusual for him considering his close relationship with the queen. Last we heard, your local reeve had issued paperwork requesting Petrik be punished for attacking a human. One Anna Perish. The same woman now standing before me. This raised many questions, ones the queen herself would like answered, had either of you responded to her summons."

"Summons or invitation?" Vlad asked. "Invitation suggests we have the right to decline."

"So, you admit you received the summons then?" Michel asked.

Vlad didn't utter another word.

But my stomach sure leaped into my throat. The queen had sent someone to investigate this whole situation. Did that mean Vlad was in danger of being punished as well? Not only for ignoring her summons, but for getting involved in this entire matter? He'd only ignored the invitation because I'd begged him to. I'd been too afraid to deal with the queen myself, so I'd opted to just ignore it all. And in doing so, I'd dragged him, and possibly Camilla, into this mess.

I couldn't let either of them pay for my stupidity. I refused to. Vlad was my sire, but we loved each other. I refused to let him take the fall for any of this. And knowing him, that was exactly what he planned to do. The man was the "throw yourself on the sword" type. No. No way would I let that happen. I loved him too much to let him sacrifice himself like that for me.

"I did it," I murmured, dragging my hand out from Vlad's. Our fingertips briefly touched before I tucked my hands into my back pockets and walked out from behind him. "I saw the invitations but got rid of them before anyone else did. Vlad had no idea."

"Anna—"

"In fact, I burned them all," I admitted, cutting Vlad off before he said or did something stupid.

Throughout all this, there was one thing I knew without a doubt: Petrik had tried to kill me. Surely, I couldn't be punished for defending myself. No court in the world would prosecute someone for that. Twice he'd tried to murder me. Was it my fault that he'd been killed in the process? That hardly made me guilty of murder. Especially considering I hadn't dealt the death blow.

"You burned the invitations?" Michel repeated.

I nodded, then met his gaze. Maybe it was time for a little honesty. Maybe they would appreciate my candor and return to England. I could hope, right?

"I'm a new vampire. Not even four months old. I had no idea the queen's invitation was a requirement instead of a request. So I burned them. That might seem stupid to you, but I was frightened. I honestly didn't know how else to respond."

"You could have written a letter, an email, made a phone call—all of which were made accessible to you when you were first turned."

Like the queen would have listened to my "no thanks" response card. This wasn't like some wedding where I could decline to show, apparently.

"Let's be real. If you're here now, that means the queen never would have accepted an email or phone call from me. So how about we stop beating around the bush and you tell us exactly what you want."

"Anna," Vlad growled.

"No. Please." Michel held up a hand, his lips curling upward. "I appreciate a little candor. Sometimes picking and choosing my words is exhausting. If Anna wishes to speak openly, I very much would like that."

My eyes narrowed for a fraction of a second. I didn't trust this new direction of Michel's. Camilla hadn't been able to teach me much about the hierarchy, but I could lean on my own education regarding the current English monarchy. It seemed safe to assume that every single thing I said would be used against me. I also suspected the queen would hear all about our little meeting right down to every last detail.

I needed to approach this carefully. Wisely. I only hoped I had it in me.

"Please," I said, gesturing to the kitchen table.

Michel marched past us to take his seat, shrugging his jacket off as he went.

I locked eyes with Vlad and gave him a small nod. We couldn't read each other's minds—at least not while in human form—but I could reassure him the only way I knew how by offering him a small kiss. It was quick and passionless, unlike anything we'd shared earlier tonight, but I felt his hand relax in mine in response. Seemed he'd needed it as much as me.

I followed Michel into the kitchen and took the seat across from him. No way in hell he'd catch me sitting next to him.

Vlad took the seat next to me and tucked his hands under the table, where he rested one against my thigh. I reveled in the small touch, taking comfort from him. Regardless of what happened here tonight, I knew without a doubt that Vlad wouldn't let Michel hurt me. But I also needed to remember to control my temper. This wasn't just my life on the line anymore.

"Very well then." Michel folded his hands on the table. "Anna asked what I want. The answer is quite simple. I want to find out what happened to Petrik."

Cold fear struck my nerves.

Neither Vlad nor I spoke.

"I shall be perfectly frank with you, Anna. My instructions are quite clear. I'm not to leave until I learn what happened to Petrik and establish whether disciplinary action is required."

"Disciplinary action," Vlad repeated. "Such as?"

"You've been a vampire for over five hundred years," Michel said. "I believe you already know what's meant by that."

"Yes, but Anna doesn't. If you truly mean to be frank, then do so."

Michel bowed his head in concession. "If I deem Anna's actions to be malicious in any way, it will be within my rights to arrest her."

"Arrest me?" I whispered. "And what? Send me to prison?"

"Vampires have no need for prison," Vlad commented. "Do they, Michel?"

"The queen is trying very hard to prove to the humans that we are more than soulless monsters. I admit, ever since our reveal, she's struggled in this aspect. Humans have centuries of folklore and myths, none of which paint us in a very appealing light. Quite a few politicians have expressed concern regarding our judicial system. They've stated that our process is rather brutal. Humans never understood that we need such extreme measures to maintain control of the population."

"I don't understand—"

"Vampires who are found to be too dangerous are eliminated,"

Vlad said, filling me in. "It's a quick, merciful death. We don't imprison criminals like humans do because there are too many risky elements at play. Our aversion to the sun, to start. Not to mention how we grow more powerful as we age. How can you lock away creatures who cannot be contained?"

"So someone who is found guilty of a crime is punished with death," I said, stating it as clearly as possible in the hopes that they'd stop dancing around their words.

"Correct." Michel rapped his knuckles against the table, as though congratulating me. "However, the humans see our methods as barbaric. She wishes to prove them wrong. So she's attempting to implement our first court system. Vampires with legal experience have been brought into the process. Should I deem your situation requires legal action, I'm to detain you until such a hearing can be arranged."

On the one hand, at least it wasn't immediate death. That was something, right?

"Furthermore, I've also been tasked with assessing *you*, Anna."

My gaze bounced between Vlad and Michel. Vlad's hand tightened on my thigh, so I knew this couldn't be a good thing.

"How?" I asked after my hand came down on Vlad's.

"The queen asked that I determine whether you're a danger to yourself or other vampires."

I blinked. A danger? Like psychotic? I could easily prove I wasn't. "Um. Okay?"

"She has placed you in my charge for the time being. To test your abilities as a vampire, to question you about your intentions, and to investigate your little... what's the word, vlog?"

Vlad's head cocked. "Her vlog?"

Ah. Shit. Holding back on telling Vlad was about to bite me in the ass.

"Yes. That little online channel of hers where she explores fact versus fiction and hands over all our secrets to the humans."

A forced breath rushed past my lips. "What? No, I don't—"

"Don't what?" Michel pressed. "Don't betray our kind to the

humans? The last episode I watched, you very clearly explained how to kill a vampire, in great detail might I add. You compared it to the movies, explained how they were wrong, and described the correct method."

I stammered out an illogical response. He made it sound so much worse than it actually was! "It's just a vlog," I whispered. "I just talk about what it's like to be a vampire."

"And our weaknesses and strengths," Michel continued. "To…" He dug his phone out of his pocket and stared at the screen. "Three point seven million followers. Does that sound correct?"

"What? No." I turned to stare at Vlad. "He's making it sound so much worse than it is."

"You've been working on your vlog?" he asked, his brows furrowed.

"Well, yes, but—"

"And you didn't think to mention that to me?"

"Vlad. I meant to tell you. But with everything that's been going on, I just… I didn't… Lucy suggested—"

"So Lucy is involved then," Vlad stated, his eyes turning cold.

I squeezed my eyes shut and took a moment to think about my next words. I could actually smell Vlad's anger. It perfumed the air like a sharp spice, and I didn't like the way it pricked at my nose.

"Lucy suggested I strike while the iron was hot. After everything we went through three months ago, it would have been stupid not to capitalize on our fame—"

Vlad laughed under his breath. "Three months ago."

Oh my god, I was making this so much worse than it needed to be.

"During the last three months, you expect me to believe you couldn't find a single moment to tell me you'd been working on your vlog again. And successfully, might I add."

"It's not that successful," I murmured.

"You recently had a deposit for one hundred and sixty-two thousand dollars into your bank account," Michel said.

"Christ," I cursed, not caring when both flinched. "Would you shut up for a moment? I'm trying to explain something. And what the hell right do you have to access my bank account? That's illegal!"

Vlad shook his head, then with a tight jaw, stared at Michel. "What does her job have to do with anything?"

"If I deem her vlog to be too dangerous, the queen has permitted me to issue punishment, whether monetary or otherwise."

"Otherwise? What's otherwise mean?" I asked, panic rising in my voice.

Vlad turned and finally met my gaze. I cringed at the sight of his expression. I'd never seen Vlad angry with me before, and I hoped after tonight I'd never see it again. He watched me with such disappointment in his eyes, but even worse was the hint of betrayal hiding beneath. That one stung the most.

"Meaning Michel may decide to arrest you based on your vlog alone," he finally said. "Or worse."

Or worse.

Considering our previous conversation, I immediately understood Vlad's implication. Worse could really only mean one other thing.

Guess my vlog really would be the death of me.

CHAPTER

EIGHTEEN

Ugh. This night well and truly sucked. I guess visiting my father hadn't been torturous enough. Now Vlad was angry at me, and I had a French inquisitor hovering over us like an annoying little gnat I wanted to swat across the room. At least Vlad had rejected Michel's request to sleep here. We truly didn't need him seeing how early I woke. But in the meantime, I was hiding, slipping in and out of rooms whenever I heard Michel approach. He kept demanding to talk about Petrik, and I wasn't ready to have that discussion. Not after the whole vlog fiasco downstairs.

Thankfully, after the third failed attempt to corner me, he'd left to sort out his sleeping arrangements with a promise to return tomorrow night. It seriously felt like a giant sword was hanging over my head, threatening to make the cut any second now.

Once Michel left, Vlad vanished soon after, claiming he needed some space to think. About what, I had no idea, but I didn't like the sound of it.

My phone rang, distracting me from those dark thoughts. I glanced at the screen and almost smiled at the sight of Camilla's name.

"Pissed off your old man, hmm?" she said the instant I took the call.

"What? How do you know about that?"

"Vlad phoned me an hour ago," she admitted. "Updated me on the night's events. Asked me to check into your vlog to see what I could find. The man wouldn't know how to google something if his life depended on it. And oh, look, it does."

I sighed. "He could have just asked me."

"Yes, well, that's what happens when you keep secrets. You anger those you care about. How about you tell me about it instead."

My eyes fluttered shut. I was starting to wish I'd never revamped it. I'd even gone so far as to blame Lucy for forcing me into it. Almost texted her that same accusation, but thankfully smartened up before pissing off my best friend the same night I pissed off my boyfriend.

The only person to blame here was me. So, I needed to suck it up, own my mistake, and apologize. I just needed to get Vlad to speak to me. But he was too busy avoiding me, like I was Michel.

"This whole thing is a mess," I mumbled.

"Planning on cleaning it up?" she asked.

My fingers tightened around my phone. When all this began, I'd hated Camilla. She was so beautiful, like an Egyptian goddess come to life. Her sun-kissed skin and long, dark hair had probably been the envy of most women when she was alive. But her attitude sucked. She was sarcastic and sometimes purposely malicious. But I'd come to expect that from her now, and almost idolized her viciousness. I never thought she'd become a friend, but here we were, gabbing on the phone together in the middle of the night, like some slumber party.

"He won't talk to me," I said, resting one hand under my head.

"Oh, sweetie. He doesn't need to talk. He needs to listen."

I chuckled and shook my head. "Tell him that."

"Not in my job description. So, rumor has it you've been giving away vampire secrets?"

"No!" I grunted loudly and shook my head. "I swear, I didn't! *Everyone* knows how to kill a vampire, Camilla! Seriously. Everyone knows about stakes and decapitation and fire. So why is it so bad that

I simply confirmed it? How is it any different from someone walking down the street, thinking to themselves, I bet a stake could kill a vampire?"

"I don't think it's the information so much as you not telling him," she said. "He feels betrayed."

"Yeah, I get that. But it's not like I gave up any state secrets or something. I don't tell my viewers where they can find us, or mention anything that might endanger us. All I do is take a specific movie and discuss its accuracy. I mean, come on, how is that dangerous?"

"My sweet summer child," Camilla said, which told me I was in for a verbal smackdown. "It's dangerous because of *who* you are. The humans consider you some sort of ambassador because you were the first one to be changed after we became public knowledge. They relate to you. They follow you in every way they can. Which means every single thing that leaves your mouth is taken as gospel. Maybe the information isn't dangerous, but what they can do with it is. And that's how the queen and every other vampire is going to look at it. Right now, they're wondering if you're more loyal to the humans than your own kind."

"My own kind," I repeated harshly. "What the hell is that supposed to even mean? I was a human for twenty-four years, Camilla. I've been a vampire for three months. And I'm supposed to what? Forget I was ever human?"

"Yes. That's exactly what it means. Especially to the queen. By revealing our secrets, or whatever you want to call it, she sees you as a traitor."

"Oh for crying out loud. Has anyone ever told you that vampires are dramatic?"

Camilla burst out laughing. "Many, many times, my dear. As for Vlad, I think he's just angry that you didn't share this part of your life with him. I don't believe he thinks the vlog is dangerous. More that you kept something from him, withheld a part of yourself. Is it true you earned nearly a couple hundred thousand dollars this week?"

"Okay, yes—"

"How much have you made in total since you started your vlog up again?"

"I... actually don't know the full value," I admitted. "Lucy has been handling it for me."

"So, more than enough, since you don't know how much."

"I suppose that's one way to look at it."

"Do you see why Vlad is upset then? This is a massive change for you. From rags to riches, and you didn't share it with him, didn't tell him about your success. He loves you, Anna—"

"I know."

"You do?"

I nodded, then scrubbed my hands down my face. "And I love him, Camilla."

"Have you told him that?"

"Yeah, last night. After we visited with my mother."

Camilla gave another laugh. "It must have been a horrible visit if it got you to confess your love to him."

I snickered and nodded. "Yeah, it was pretty damn terrible. Did Vlad tell you about it?"

"No, he didn't."

I placed my phone on speakerphone, then sat cross-legged on the bed and started idly braiding my hair, all while regaling Camilla with "The Tale of My Mother." Camilla's responses went from amused to horrified pretty damn fast.

"She wants us to go back tomorrow night to meet with Caleb, but no way in hell that's happening now. I may not like my family, but I refuse to put them in any danger. And Michel is like a freaking viper. He's coiled to strike. I won't put my family in harm's way."

"I agree. What's your game plan then?" Camilla asked after I finished telling her about the wretched visit with my father.

"I can't say I have one at the moment. I just need to prove to Michel that I'm not a danger to anyone or anything and hope for the best."

I could practically hear the wheels turning in her head through the phone. "Maybe you should go to England."

My jaw dropped. "Are you kidding me?"

Camilla sighed. "The queen clearly wants to meet you, Anna. So much so that she's sent an inquisitor. Now, I know you didn't pay much attention to my texts, but inquisitors are about as bad as it gets. Do you remember what I told you back in New Orleans about them?"

I racked my brain in search of her words. "Something about how the queen used them to squash any and all uprisings."

"Correct. But it's more than that. Inquisitors are steadfast in their beliefs. In the case of vampires, their beliefs always align with the queen's. Because she doesn't accept anything else. It isn't the inquisitor you need to convince, it's the queen. Only she can fix this."

I rubbed my temples and considered Camilla's advice, but I couldn't see the logic here. Yes, changing the queen's mind was important. But I didn't see any wisdom in placing myself directly in the line of fire. The queen might be interested in me, but maybe that interest would wane the less fascinating I became. If that meant shutting down my vlog and playing the role of a docile little vampire, so be it. Yes, fame was my dream. But not at the expense of my life. I'd already experienced death once, I really wasn't keen to experience it again.

"No," I finally said. "England is out of the question. There has to be another way."

"Sometimes, it's best to face a problem head on."

"Yeah, when that problem doesn't want you dead."

Camilla chuckled. "Okay, true."

"I need to convince Michel that I'm not a threat. Then he can report back to the queen that I'm just a naïve young vampire who means absolutely nothing in the grand scheme."

"I think you're forgetting one important part."

Except I wasn't. I knew exactly what Camilla was going to say. "Petrik."

"Petrik," she repeated. "The moment the queen learns that he's dead, she's going to come looking for blood again."

I sighed and closed my eyes. When had my life become this? And why? It always came back to Petrik, didn't it? The bastard had attacked *me*. Not the other way around. He'd killed thirty-four women before me. In my eyes, Sam was a hero for killing the bastard. Seemed the queen didn't agree. All because Petrik had sired her. Well, la-di-fucking-da. If Vlad had killed thirty-four girls, I would never forgive him, because it was vile, reprehensible, *evil*. Sam had done us a favor by putting the mad vamp down. The world was a better place without him. But apparently, we were the only ones who saw it that way.

"Michel isn't going to leave until he learns what happened to Petrik. He's likely under orders to remain until he has any information he can bring back. From there, the queen will render her verdict."

I shook my head. "No, apparently he can arrest me. I guess the queen is trying to create a court system for us vamps, to prove to humans we're more than bloodthirsty monsters."

"Oh." Camilla quietly tsked. "Because that's going to go over so well."

I nodded. It sounded like a clusterfuck to me as well.

"So, she's trying to make an example of you then," Camilla murmured.

"What?"

"She's trying to show the world, both humans and vampires, that we can obey, and if we don't, here's how the situation's handled. But she needs a scapegoat. Someone she can show off as the first criminalized vampire."

Oh, just freaking fantastic. "I absolutely hate this."

"Me too."

"What are our options then?"

"We don't really have any," she said. "Either we let this play out or we take action. It always boils down to those two choices, doesn't it?"

Seemed that way. Seemed like these were the same options I'd been given with Petrik as well. And he'd opted to take action on our behalf, which had nearly left me deep-fried and crispy in that creepy crypt of his. I really didn't relish the idea of going through that again.

"So, Vlad mentioned you can talk to animals," Camilla said, changing the subject. I could have kissed her.

"It seems that way. I had Vlad shift into his bat and wolf form, and I could hear him in both. There were also a couple bats in the attic when we moved in, but I guess we scared them off because they haven't come back yet."

Camilla chuckled. "Trust *you* to develop some weird inane power like that. I've never heard of a single vampire who could speak to animals. How is that even helpful?"

"Oh, thanks," I half-teased. "Talk about kicking a girl when she's down. I'm supposed to be celebrating my first gift, not listening to you tease me about it."

"Sweetie, I developed my first power at a hundred and twenty years old."

"What?" I demanded. "I didn't know you even had one!"

"Well, it's nothing flashy like Vlad's, but it's useful. Far more useful than communing with animals."

"Yeah, yeah, yeah," I muttered. "What is it?"

"They call it 'battle-sense.' It's the ability to read my opponents in a fight. I'm able to see how they're going to attack and see the fight play out in my head."

"What?" I screeched, practically falling off the bed. "Are you kidding me? Is that why Vlad put you in charge of teaching me how to fight? And why you *always* kick my ass?"

Camilla started laughing. "Yes to both. It's not the same as reading minds. It's more like this innate ability to be able to read the fight and my opponent's movements. Sometimes I get it wrong, like that night you jumped on my back and bit me. But it's almost impossible to defeat me in a fight."

"Well, isn't that just handy to have around," I sniped.

"Why do you think Vlad keeps me so close? I'm like the perfect strategist."

"So you can see when someone is about to attack you? See all the moves they're going to take?"

She hummed an agreement. "It's like a movie in my head. Once that adrenaline kicks in, I can see the entire fight play out. Then it's just a matter of taking them down."

"Okay, see, now *that's* a gift! How the hell is talking to animals ever going to help me?"

She snickered. "I honestly couldn't tell you."

"This sucks." I sat back with a pout. "Drink the blood of a thousand-year-old vampire who was probably bursting at the seams with power, and this is my reward."

"Hey, just be grateful that you didn't lose your mind or grow addicted to ancient blood."

Yeah, I was definitely thankful for that. The stories Vlad had told me were alarming. Scenario wise, this certainly wasn't the worst case. But it wasn't great either.

"Do you have your second gift yet?" I asked.

"That usually presents around the five-hundred-year mark, which is why Vlad's still developing his foresight."

I nodded. Another incredibly useful gift. One that would become invaluable the stronger it got.

"He told you about his vision?" I asked, even though I already knew the answer, seeing as I'd overheard their conversation.

Camilla grew quiet but eventually said, "He told me he dreamed of your death."

What a mood killer.

Camilla sighed. "Don't let his vision derail you. Right now, there are so many things up in the air. Vlad won't let anything happen to you."

"Yeah," I whispered.

The problem was that something bad had already happened. Michel had found us, and the queen was waiting for an update. We'd come to Perish hoping everything would blow over. Except, instead, it'd exploded. Right in our freaking faces.

CHAPTER
NINETEEN

My fingers drummed against the kitchen table as I sat—more like hovered—near the window, staring out into the night. Vlad might have gone out to buy more blood, but something had certainly delayed his return. I knew better than to fret. He was a big boy, after all. I honestly doubted there was anything in this world that could truly harm him. But thanks to Michel's arrival, I was on edge, my every nerve shot.

In the back of my mind, this clock kept tick, tick, ticking away, counting down to the inevitable. Too bad I had no idea *what* the inevitable was. Right now, I just felt this overwhelming sense of dread. As though tomorrow night would determine the rest of my life. Crazy, right? Surely Michel didn't hold that much power over me, and yet every inch of me screamed that he did. That tomorrow night was it. The final curtain call.

Much like Camilla said, we had two choices here—or rather, *I* had two choices here. Either we let this play out or we take action. But which was the right one? Neither path ended well, as far as I could tell. If we let this play out and answered all Michel's questions honestly, chances were I'd end up dead. If we took action—"eliminated" the threat—the queen would find out, respond, and lo and behold, I'd end up dead. What fun, a lose-lose scenario.

Of course, there was a third option, one Camilla hadn't mentioned, but one I was leaning heavily toward as the night progressed. I could run. Stay one step ahead of the queen and her inquisitors. Except that way lay dragons. One, I'd never get to live my own life. I'd lose my vlog, Vlad, my friends, everything that mattered to me. Two, the queen would eventually find me, which would *once again* lead to my death.

With a deep groan, I leaned forward and rested my forehead against the cool tabletop. "When all paths lead to your demise, how do you choose?" I forced out a breath and watched as it fogged up the table. The answer came to me quickly because it was the only one that made sense. "You choose the one that harms the fewest number of people."

At the end of the day, it didn't matter what happened to me. But I refused to see Vlad, Camilla, or even Lucy hurt *because* of me.

Knowing that, I broke my three options down even farther, and even came up with a fourth.

Number one: We lied and told Michel absolutely nothing. That as far as we knew, Petrik was alive and well, and murdering more women somewhere across the country. But, eventually, the queen would learn the truth, and hunt us down. Secrets like that never stayed hidden for long.

Number two: We took action and eliminated Michel, thereby placing Vlad in danger as well. The queen certainly wouldn't look the other way if he helped me kill an inquisitor. Plus, was I really a murderer? It was one thing to defend yourself, but another to actively plot someone's death. Not to mention, the queen would obliterate us. Killing an inquisitor was pretty much a declaration of war, and I had a feeling she would win.

Number three: I ran. And spent the rest of eternity running because running meant guilty. This path only delayed my death, as far as I could see, even with my lack of foresight. Yes, it delayed the inevitable, but what kind of life would I live without Vlad anyway? And if he ran with me, the queen would surely blacklist him as well. No, I couldn't ruin his life as well as mine.

Number four: I told the truth about everything and threw myself at Michel's and the queen's mercy. This path only affected me. Vlad literally had nothing to do with Petrik's death. He hadn't even been there. I'd have to adapt my story, though, because if I told the queen that a werewolf killed her sire, I could only imagine the horrific fallout. They'd likely want to know how I'd killed an ancient vampire, but I was confident I could make something up.

Honestly, scenario number four was looking like the only good one. There was an infinitesimal chance that the queen would see innocence and send me packing.

Luckily for me, my phone rang *again* before I could make my final choice. I dug it out of my back pocket and stared at Lucy's name. We had plans to meet tomorrow, but with Michel here, that changed everything. I refused to even introduce her to the inquisitor. Refused to let him tell the queen about my relationship with a human. If I could keep her safe, I would. Which meant this might also be the last time we spoke. What with my impending doom and all that.

So, I took the call.

"Anna?" Lucy's voice carried across the line. "You there?"

I didn't immediately respond. I wasn't often hit with depression but when I was, it tended to hit hard.

"Anna? Hello?"

"Hey."

"There you are. I just wanted to check in, see how your visit with your dad went and make sure we're still on for tomorrow night."

Right. She wanted us to be there when she told Sam about her bloodline so we could analyze his reaction. Well, that certainly didn't work for me anymore.

"Um, listen, tomorrow isn't good for me. You mind if we reschedule?"

"Reschedule? Why? What's going on?"

I honestly didn't know how much to reveal. If I told Lucy about Michel, she'd march here and firmly implant herself into the situation. Her loyalty had always astounded me. But now wasn't the time for that. Now was the time to look after herself. No matter what happened tomorrow, I didn't see a happy ending for me. I couldn't outright tell Lucy that. I'd have to redirect her somehow.

"Some stuff came up. Nothing serious, so don't worry." *Liar, liar, pants on fire.* "But we don't have time for visits tomorrow, and Sam shouldn't come over anyway. You know how vampires are about werewolves."

Silence stretched through the phone.

"Anna, what's going on?"

"It's nothing, honestly. Just some vampire political nonsense. But hey, I've been thinking about your situation, and I wonder if it might be a good idea to go meet this alpha father of yours."

"What?" she screeched.

A sad smile played at my mouth. I should have known that would distract her from *my* problems.

"You've got to be kidding me, right? You can't possibly think I want to meet that asshole!"

Whoa, asshole. Strong language from her. "Did you learn more about him?"

"Yeah, I spoke with my parents tonight and got the whole story out of my mom. It's not a pretty one. Apparently, werewolves are known for seeking out people they believe have strong genes in order to create the strongest offspring."

"How the heck do they know who has strong genes?"

"It's some sort of sense they have. You know, like how in the wild, animals can tell who's strong and who's weak?"

Okay, that actually creeped me out a little bit. "So, he 'sensed' your mother's strong genes and impregnated her, hoping for a strong werewolf baby?"

Lucy grunted under her breath. "That's pretty much the gist of it. Then I was born, and he gave it six months to see if I showed any signs of lycanthropy—that's what they call it by the way. When I didn't, he packed his bags and off he went, I assume to find some other woman to knock up."

"A real charmer then."

Lucy hummed her agreement. "He means nothing to me. But now I'm worried that Sam is doing the same thing."

My stomach turned. What if he was? What if it was like some natural predisposition of werewolves? "Did your father ever tell your mother that she was his mate?"

"Yeah, so here's the thing. Mates among werewolves doesn't actually mean the same thing as vampires. I dug into that one a little too. My mom said, for vampires, mate is just another word for soulmate. But among werewolves, it's exactly like in the wild, when animals mate. Sam isn't telling me I'm his soulmate. He's telling me that he wants to fuck me."

Oh, shit. No, I didn't believe that. I'd seen the way Sam acted around Lucy. He was cuckoo for cocoa puffs over her. He didn't say much, but I could see it in his eyes *and* smell it in his pheromones. Of course, pheromones were usually just a physical response to attraction.

Damn it, what if I had it wrong this whole time?

"What are you going to do?" I asked.

"Well, I'm not going to sleep with him, that's for sure! Not if he's just looking for a broodmare."

I winced. "I really don't think Sam is like that."

"Why not? My sperm donor was."

"But maybe it's not a universal rule. Maybe your sperm donor is like every other deadbeat dad out there. Maybe Sam is looking for a relationship and a wife and..." I exhaled. "Lucy, you aren't going to learn any of these answers until you ask him. I think you need to stop drilling other people and just rip off the Band-Aid. Ask him directly—and explicitly—what he wants from you."

"I was kind of hoping you and Vlad could help me with that."

That wasn't a direction I wanted this conversation to take, so I steered her away. "Ask him, okay? Talk to him. Vlad and I can have this conversation with him any time. Don't you want to give him the chance to tell you the truth first? Don't start a relationship with someone assuming they're going to lie. And don't let your mother's situation color your opinion of Sam. He's good people. I truly don't think he'd lie to you just so he can knock you up."

Lucy released a shaky breath. "Anna, I'm... scared."

My chest swelled with emotion, and I rubbed it, hoping to loosen the pressure. "I know, sweetie. Love is a scary thing. I was frightened when I realized I was falling for Vlad. Listen to me," I said, still rubbing my chest. "Love is the scariest thing out there. Because you're giving your all to someone else and hoping they won't destroy you. That kind of vulnerability is absolutely terrifying. It's also beautiful. It's hard to take that first step but think of all the steps you get to take together afterward. If Sam is *the one* for you, you'll never regret taking that risk. But being too afraid to try, that'll haunt you. Do what you need to get all the information beforehand, but never base your decision off fear. Promise me you'll take the leap if he gives you the right answers. Okay?"

Lucy hesitated. "Anna, what's wrong?"

"Nothing's wrong." I knuckled away a tear before it could fall. I had this no crying rule because vampires cried blood tears, and I thought they were hideous. But mostly, I just didn't want her to hear me sobbing over the phone. If I gave in to them, Lucy would come running. I needed to stay strong.

"Hey, go to Mississippi," I told her. "I really think you should find your sperm donor and ask him why. Ask him how he could abandon you and your mom. Find out what he's really like."

"Why? He's not my father."

"No, and he never will be. But it might help resolve these issues with Sam. Maybe you'll see they're nothing alike." And it might get her out of Louisiana when the shit hit the fan. "Ask Sam to go with you."

"I still haven't told him about any of this," she admitted.

"Well, no time like the present. If you expect him to be honest and upfront with you, then he deserves the same. He should know there's werewolf blood running through your veins."

"Except, I'm human."

"Well, maybe it'll still change things for him. Best to be open about it, right? Then no one can call you a liar later on down the road."

And the award for the biggest hypocrite goes to... Here I was telling Lucy not to be a coward and to be honest with those she loves, and I was hiding a massive secret from her. I only hoped that one day she understood.

"I can't believe you want me to go to Mississippi," she said, laughing. "I think my mom would freak out if I told her that. Oh, speaking of, how'd the visit go with your dad?"

Grateful for the change in topic, I gave a light laugh. "About as great as you'd expect. He ignored me the entire night while Christina kept trying to make a move on Vlad."

"What a cow!" Lucy scoffed under her breath. "She steals your dad, practically bleeds him dry of all his money, then goes after Vlad? She's lucky you didn't rip out her throat."

"Oh, girl, I was tempted. The night finally ended on an explosive note when I told my dad off for being a shithead. You know, after all these years of imagining what I would say to him, it didn't feel as good as I'd hoped. I just felt crappy after."

"Yeah, that's generally how I understand these things go down. How'd he react?"

"He didn't. The man is the worst. But I knew that going in, you know. At least you got a great dad out of this whole mess with your mom and sperm donor."

"Yeah, I'm definitely lucky there. My dad's awesome."

I nodded.

"Are you still going to see Caleb tomorrow?"

"No. I'll have to text my mom with a cancellation. She'll scold me, I'm sure, but honestly, anything is better than seeing my brother. I know exactly how that would go down anyway. He'll call me a stain on the family name, I'll probably punch him in the nose, and that'll be that. Might as well save us the tears and frustration."

Lucy chuckled. "Your brother's an idiot."

"Yep."

"But I heard he's got himself a new girlfriend."

I blinked. "Where'd you hear that?"

"I've been chatting with a few girls from high school."

People I absolutely refused to talk to now. The second Vlad turned me, and the photos hit the internet, a reporter had come sniffing around town here about me, they'd all given up the goods. Most had claimed to be my "best friend," and told the reporter we were like "sisters." When really, they were people I scarcely remembered.

"You have fun with that?" I asked.

Lucy exploded with laughter. "It's just hilarious, hearing about their lives and how simple they are compared to ours. It's actually kind of a relief to hear about their work or boyfriend troubles."

"Simple lives for simple people."

"Pfft. That might have been us if we hadn't gone to New Orleans."

I chose not to comment on that. Seemed like that direction lay a fight and seeing as how this might be the last time she and I spoke, I didn't want to taint this conversation with bad memories.

"Okay, well, if we aren't seeing each other tomorrow, then I assume we'll see you Saturday?"

"Probably. I'll let you know more after tomorrow night." After Michel lay down his verdict and decided my fate. "Worst-case scenario, we'll see you back in New Orleans."

"Okay..." Lucy hedged. "Are you sure everything's alright?"

"You bet."

Before I could say anything more, the front door opened, and Vlad stepped inside.

"Hey, Luce, I gotta go, 'kay?"

"Oh, okay. Text me tomorrow."

"Will do. Good luck with Sam. And Luce?"

"Yeah?"

"Remember what I said. Promise me you'll take the leap, okay?"

"Okay," she whispered. "You're scaring me."

"Nothing to be scared of. Just doing my job as the best friend to make sure you live your best life."

"Anna…"

"Night, Luce."

"Night," she murmured.

I ended the call, then set my phone down on the table and turned to Vlad. His gaze caught mine before he crouched to remove his shoes. When he straightened, I rose from my seat and came to stand before him, my hands tucked behind my back. I needed to make this right with him. But more importantly, I needed to tell him I'd made my decision and help him come to grips with it.

Unfortunately, we didn't have enough time left tonight to get into it all. Which meant deciding which conversation was more important, the vlog or my decision regarding Michel. I knew the answer without a doubt. Vlad meant more to me than anything else. He had to know how sorry I was for lying to him. I would do anything to prove it to him.

So, with a shy smile, I stepped forward and took his hands. "Can we talk?"

Vlad nodded without hesitation, his fingers squeezing mine. Relief rounded my shoulders. I would fix this problem. And then… then I'd tell him I'd decided how to proceed with Michel.

I only hoped he let me do it.

TWENTY

I LED Vlad into the living room, then glanced at the clock. Three in the morning. Ugh. Damn witching hour. As a connoisseur of nighttime, I could honestly say that nothing good happened around three a.m., almost like it was cursed. If something bad was going to happen, it would be now.

"Listen..." I sat on the couch and pulled Vlad down next to me. "I'm so sorry I didn't tell you about the vlog. I don't have a good explanation for you. I was just... scared. Nervous, I guess. I just..." I drew a deep breath. "I didn't tell you when Lucy and I first started working on it because I was afraid it would tank. And I didn't want you to see me fail. Then it started gaining popularity, and I started worrying about whether it would last. That happens sometimes. People hit it big for one video, and then there's no follow through. When there was follow through, I freaked out over *how* to tell you since by then, I'd waited so long." I sighed and raked my fingers through my hair. "There was this little voice in my head, telling me I didn't deserve any of this, that I was going to screw everything up, so by keeping it quiet, I felt safer in that little bubble. I'm not explaining this right. I know I should have just told you right away. And—"

"Anna."

I choked back the rest of my rambly tirade and met Vlad's gaze. As far as apologies went, this one pretty much sucked camel face. I could see the disappointment in his expression, in the grim set of his lips and narrowed eyes.

"I just... I'm sorry," I muttered.

Vlad sighed, then wrapped his arms around my waist and pulled me against him, tucking my head beneath his chin. "Stop talking."

Relief loosened my poor, tense muscles. I hated when people were mad at me, but with Vlad, that feeling quadrupled. There was a weight on my shoulders I couldn't shake off, and a heaviness in my chest that refused to abate. I never wanted to fight with him again—an impossible dream, I know, considering couples fight. But if we could go the next hundred years without another spat, I'd be a happy vampy.

"I realized while I was out that you have nothing to apologize for. We've both kept secrets from one another recently. Relationships require work. And while I would have appreciated a bit more honesty regarding your employment status, that wasn't the reason for my anger. I'm upset because the revitalization of your vlog has only further endangered your life. The queen will use this against you. Had you told me about it, I could have pointed that out."

I snuggled deeper into Vlad's chest and closed my eyes. The feel of his arms tightening around me was one I knew I would remember for the rest of my life. "I never thought they would use my vlog against me. To me, I saw it as a mark of freedom, a return to what makes me, *me*. And I think I was worried you wouldn't let me do it."

"Anna. I'm not your father. I have no say over what you may or may not do. You are an adult and your own person. But as *my* person, I only ask that you be open and honest with me. Never fear opening up to me. I have no desire to make your life more difficult. I only wish to share it with you."

Gah. Why was this man so good with speeches?

"If we're going to survive eternity together, we mustn't hide things from one another. We need to trust each other. I love you, Anna. I want to spend my life with you, for however long that might be. I only hope you want the same."

"Of course," I whispered. "You know I love you."

Vlad pressed a gentle kiss against the top of my head, then shifted his weight, unwrapping me from the warmth he'd cocooned me in. "Good. Because while I was contemplating all this, I realized I have a question I'd like to ask you."

Oh boy. If he was moving on from this topic, then that meant I needed to tell him about my decision. I really didn't want to. I knew it would ruin the moment. But with the sun approaching, and Michel's impending return tomorrow night, I couldn't delay the conversation any longer. Especially considering everything Vlad and I had just discussed.

He slipped a hand into his pants pocket and began rooting around for something. I rose off Vlad and scooted over to the next cushion to give him—and myself—some space. He seemed to be holding something shiny, but just as he began pulling it out, the words I'd been mulling over for the last few hours came spewing out.

"I want to tell Michel the truth."

Vlad froze, his hand still resting in his pocket. His expression tightened and his lips flattened, all signs that I'd pissed him off. He withdrew his hand—now empty—and stared at me. "I must have misheard."

I sucked my bottom lip into my mouth and shook my head. "Just hear me out, okay? I've gone through all our choices over and over. And I think our best-case scenario is me telling Michel that Petrik's dead and telling him I'm responsible for it all."

His eyes hardened. "I would love to hear your reasoning."

Yup. He was pissed.

I cleared my throat, then folded my hands together and placed them in my lap. I needed to explain this correctly. "The way I see it, we have four options." I held up a single digit. "We lie. We tell Michel we have absolutely no idea what happened to Petrik." I flicked up a second finger. "We kill Michel." My third finger rose. "We run." And a fourth. "Or we tell the truth and hope he and the queen show me mercy."

Vlad's expression darkened.

"The first option isn't ideal. Michel is a trained inquisitor and a vampire. It seems safe to assume he'll know the instant we start lying. A change in our pupils, a change in our scent. Or he'll just look at me and know, because honestly, I'm a terrible liar. Or, one day the truth will be discovered, and we'll pay the price then. Either way, a price is paid. Likely resulting in our deaths."

Vlad's lips thinned.

I forced myself to swallow and keep talking. "The second option is likely our worst. If we so much as touch a hair on the inquisitor's head, the queen will eat us for breakfast. From what I understand, killing Michel would be a declaration of war. And she has a hell of a lot more vampires on her side.

"Running is doable, but not ideal. Running suggests we're guilty of something and gives the queen every right to hunt us down and kill us. If we choose this path, we forfeit our lives, our reputations, our friends, everything. I can't imagine we'd enjoy that lifestyle.

"Which leaves telling the truth. I tell Michel that Petrik attacked me, and I was forced to protect myself. Hopefully, he'll understand, and he and the queen will move on with their lives."

A tic throbbed near Vlad's temple. Oh shit, he was incredibly pissed. We might not have known one another for a long time, but I knew a great deal about him, including that he grew quiet when angry. Downright silent meant he was livid.

"Vlad." I scootched closer and took his hands, rubbing my thumb over his knuckles. "Coming clean is the best solution for everyone. It clears you and everyone else of any suspicion. Hell, you weren't even there. But it might also wipe the slate clean for me. Meaning no more hiding. No more worrying about the queen. No more living with a sword over my head. I have to believe the queen isn't the sort to kill someone for defending herself, regardless of her relationship with

Petrik. We even have the files that show he murdered thirty-four women before me. Her relationship with the president is tenuous at best. That's something she wouldn't want getting out."

"Blackmail?" Harsh laughter burst past Vlad's lips. He shook his hands free of mine and carded them through his hair. "That's your plan? To blackmail the queen?"

"No, of course not. I just mean... there's hope."

He descended back into silence, his cold eyes locked on me as though they could unlock the secrets to my brain. Hell, I wished they could. I was trying to sound confident and determined, but inside, I was shaking like a terrified little pup. This plan involved putting my life in the hands of people I didn't trust.

When he didn't speak, I blew out a forced breath and cupped the back of my neck. I didn't know what else to do. The other three options sucked. I didn't see Vlad enjoying a life on the run. Hell, neither did I for that matter. What else could we do?

"Vlad—"

Before I could utter another word, he grabbed me by the shoulders, pulled me close, then crushed my mouth beneath his. Surprise widened my eyes for a fraction of a second before they fluttered closed, and I sank into the kiss. Now this, I understood. He didn't know how to respond without showing his true fears, so instead, he reacted. Showing me physically what he couldn't say with words.

He pushed me down on the couch, then rose above me, his hands bracing his weight on either side of my head. His kiss was devastatingly tender and heartbreakingly emotional. Almost as though he knew this would be the last time we could be together. I refused to accept that. Michel would return tomorrow night, and I would tell him exactly what happened, but I hoped they wouldn't kill me for it. Self-defense was a real thing, and it absolutely applied in this situation. But vampires functioned differently from humans, and we lived by the queen's rule. There wouldn't be an appeal process if I didn't like her judgement. There would just be a swift death. But I had to trust, for both Vlad's and my sake, that they would believe me.

Vlad's fingers slipped beneath my shirt and guided it over my head. He lowered his head to my lace-covered breasts and took my left nipple into his mouth, his tongue teasing through the rough material. I gasped and arched my back against him, reveling in the warmth of his mouth against the chill of the air and wet material.

He moved to my other nipple, his hands cupping and grasping as he went. I lifted my hips and eased down my own pants before reaching for his shirt. I slowly popped each button open, then slid his shirt off and let it fall to the ground. His pants were next and added to the growing pile of discarded clothing next to the couch.

Vlad's mouth skimmed my stomach as he headed south, his lips caressing my flesh. His fingers grazed my sides, then gripped my thighs. I didn't make a sound as he spread my legs, but I sure as hell quivered when his lips brushed my clit. The anticipation was almost more than I could bear. I was well-versed in his wicked talents and knew all the damage that sinful mouth of his could cause. I wasn't prepared when he unleashed himself on me, his mouth and tongue working in tandem to whip me into a lusty blaze. The man was a damn artist when it came to pleasing me. He knew exactly how and where to lick and stroke. I felt the orgasm building like a wildfire, every touch stoking those flames higher and higher until finally I erupted. Only then did he add his fingers to the equation, preparing me for the main event. When my second orgasm struck, he climbed between my legs and thrust within me.

I cried out, my head digging into the cushions as I rode the pleasure train.

"Vlad," I whispered.

"I swear, you'll be the death of me," he murmured, his movements barely pausing as he gazed down at me. "I can't bear to lose you."

"You won't," I said, realizing we were continuing our previous conversation. "I'm not going anywhere. I'm not going to let them kill me." I gasped and arched my back as a wave of pleasure crashed into me.

Vlad repositioned himself, gripping the armrest of the couch as he quickened his pace.

My eyes slammed shut as I succumbed to this beautiful torture.

"Anna..." My name came out sounding more like a whispered prayer.

"Vlad." I cupped his cheeks. "Look at me."

His eyes flashed open and caught mine. For a brief moment, I could see the pain and fear within. It broke my heart to see it, knowing I'd caused it.

"I won't let them kill me," I vowed. "If they try, we'll run. We'll fight. We'll do whatever it takes."

He nodded an instant before his eyes squeezed shut and his head dipped, his tips of his hair brushing my throat. "Bite me."

"What?" I rasped, convinced I'd misheard him.

With his next thrust, he lifted his head and stared at me. "Bite. Me."

"Are you sure?"

"Yes," he said on the edge of a groan. "I want your teeth buried in my throat right now."

I nodded, my mouth practically quivering with anticipation. I understood his need. Even though I had faith we'd survive tomorrow, that fear lingered. And what was a little ancient blood between lovers when the threat of death lingered over us?

Vlad slowed his movements, giving me a chance to thread my fingers through his hair and angle his head. The sight of his bare throat nearly undid me and sent me spiraling over the edge, knowing I'd soon be burying my fangs in it.

The moment they pierced his flesh, a massive rush of pleasure spread through me. Vlad grunted and resumed his bruising pace, driving into me with more force than normal. But I didn't complain. I loved the feel of him between my legs and the sound of us coming together. I bit a little harder, then gasped when Vlad found the perfect spot and brought me to climax. The feel of me tightening around him seemed to be all it took to send him spiraling out of control. He shuddered above me, groaning as he finished. He rode out his own orgasm, his body convulsing alongside mine, before he finally collapsed on top of me.

I slowly extracted my fangs and ran my tongue over them, reveling in his delectable taste. Then I wrapped my arms around him and held him against me. I never wanted to forget this moment, or what we meant to each other. No matter what, tomorrow would come and a verdict would be decided, but deep down, I believed we'd win our happily ever after.

Because we damn well deserved it.

CHAPTER
TWENTY-ONE

I WOKE with a sense of impending doom, which really didn't help matters. I needed to be fun and upbeat, confident that I would walk away from tonight with nary a scratch. It was a necessary façade, not only for my sake, but Vlad's as well. I sent Camilla a text early this morning before succumbing to the sun with my plan laid out, and I could only imagine her response. Camilla believed me to be stupid pretty much all the time, so I didn't see the point in trying to convince her otherwise. All that mattered was convincing Michel that I was no threat to the queen. And that meant playing a part.

So, with a deep breath, I palmed my coffin lid back and sat up. I had a few hours to kill before Vlad woke, and I intended on using that time to go over my story until I had it memorized. Not that I needed reminding. My time with Petrik was essentially branded into my brain, but I wanted to make sure I could recall every last detail without a hint of hesitation.

I took my time showering, reveling in the hot water and steam, then stood in my closet and meticulously picked out an appropriate outfit. I needed something casual, but clean. Something that suggested innocent and peaceful. But I also needed something I could possibly fight or run in. Strange, the life I led now. This wasn't something I would ever have had to think about when human. I'd always chosen my outfits based on my daily mood, not whether or not I would have to fight for my life.

I ended up opting for a pair of relaxed fit jeans—because who the hell could run in skinnies?—and a loose, flowy blouse. No heels today, for sure. I didn't own sneakers, but I did own one pair of knee-high flat boots. They weren't cushioned for running, but at least they weren't six inches tall. For a final touch, I added a pastel-colored cardigan. Because nothing said calm and peaceful like pastels.

Then I stood in front of the tall, thin mirror and studied my outfit. It'd taken a while, but I'd acclimated to the sight of my clothes hovering midair, with no body to ground the reflection. I sure did miss my reflection, though. A hundred years ago or so, Vlad had sat for a portrait because he'd forgotten what he looked like. I definitely understood that. Thankfully, I had tons of photos from before I became a vamp to remind me. But staring in the blank mirror at nothing more than clothing hit me right in the feels. Moments like these were the ones that reminded me of exactly what I'd become.

Those memories were what I needed right now.

I closed my eyes and sent myself back three months to the night I met Vlad. But more specifically, to the night Petrik brutally attacked me. I hated remembering this night. The visceral fear and the sense of helplessness weren't my idea of a good time. But I needed that tonight. I needed to tremble when Michel questioned me about Petrik, I needed to cry while recalling that moment when I knew without doubt, I was going to die. I needed to detail everything so Michel felt what I did. The terror when the sun touched me in his crypt, the scent of my burning flesh, right down to the moment I drank his blood to save my own life.

The only thing I couldn't confess was Sam's involvement. I refused to include the werewolves in this. Sam had saved my life, and he'd imparted upon me a secret even vampires didn't know—a weapon that could take down a thousand-year-old vamp. Had I known of Michel's arrival, I might have asked Sam to make me one, but I swore to myself now, if I survived this, I would whittle as many hawthorn stakes as possible and soak them in holy water and monksblood.

"You look beautiful."

My head snapped up at the sound of Vlad's voice. So lost in my memories and thoughts, I hadn't noticed the sun's descent or heard him wake. Not a great start to the night. I needed to be on top of my game here. Needed my senses primed. Because if Michel tried anything, I couldn't be caught unaware.

I turned to face Vlad with a soft smile and said, "Thank you."

Then I laughed at the sight of him. While I'd chosen every piece of clothing with painstakingly deep thought, Vlad had thrown on the same outfit as normal. Black shirt, black shoes, even black socks. I swear, the man didn't realize there were other colors out there. Or maybe he wanted to make a different statement than me. Maybe he wanted to silently threaten and intimidate Michel. A show of force in case Michel took the direction I desperately hoped he didn't.

"What?" Vlad asked.

I shook my head. No point teasing him about his outfit. Especially considering nothing could be done about it now. If Vlad was awake, then Michel soon would be too. He hadn't given me an arrival time, but I assumed we'd be hearing from him soon.

"Camilla is on her way to Perish," Vlad said, when I didn't answer his question. "Have you checked your phone?"

"No. Why?" I hadn't wanted to waste any time on social media, so it'd seemed best to avoid my phone altogether. I was an expert procrastinator when it came to social media.

"It would seem she doesn't agree with your plan and wants to be here. Unfortunately, I doubt she'll make it before Michel arrives."

"Ah." Might have been nice to have Little Miss Battle Strategy on our side, but the timing just didn't work.

"Are you sure this is the path you want to take?" Vlad closed the distance between us and enveloped me in his arms. I took the comfort he offered before I pulled myself together and stepped back.

"I really believe this is the only way to put an end to this. I'm tired of living with this fear hanging over me."

"I understand."

I lifted a brow. "You do?"

"Well, no." A soft chuckle slipped past his lips. "I respect your decision. But I want you to know, I will stand by you no matter what. Should you change your mind and decide to run tonight, I will be there with you as well."

"Can't get enough of me, huh?"

"Never." He leaned in and stole an ardent kiss. "You are mine, and I am yours. Whether that means living on the run for the next five hundred years or dying together in a glorious battle."

"You would think battle is glorious," I teased.

"There's a beauty to it."

"Well, let's avoid all bloodshed, shall we?"

"Of course." He dipped his head and brushed his lips along my throat. "Have we time...?"

I shivered with anticipation, then reached around and grabbed his ass. Because it was a fine ass, and it deserved to be cupped all night long. But someone chose that moment to ring our doorbell.

Despair tightened my chest, and my hands moved to grab Vlad's arms. Fear spiked the air, the scent triggering every instinct I had to run.

"Shh," Vlad whispered, tucking my hair behind my ears. "It's a delivery. I ordered us some blood. We need to be at full strength tonight."

I almost burst into relieved tears right then and there. Maybe I wasn't as ready for this as I'd thought. But that didn't change anything.

We descended the stairs together, and Vlad opened the door. He took the delivery, paid, then closed the door and handed me a bottle.

"Drink. This and the blood I gave you last night, should be enough to help you tonight."

My eyes widened. "Is *that* why you asked me to drink from you last night? To give me a power boost?"

He had the audacity to look unabashed. Even went so far as to *wink* at me. I nearly fainted on the spot. Vlad winks were deadly. "And other reasons, I assure you."

I upended the bottle and drained it in a series of quick swallows. Sadly, I couldn't take the time to enjoy it because we had a bit of a deadline. And from the sounds of it, that deadline was fast approaching, seeing as how a car had just pulled up in our driveway.

After swallowing the last bit, I slipped into the kitchen and discarded the bottle in the recycling bin. "He's here."

Vlad's hand found mine, and he pulled me close. "Remember, whatever you decide, I'm with you. If you tell the truth, then answer his questions thoroughly and honestly. Don't allow him to sway the conversation in any way that might imply guilt on your behalf. And do not allow him to confuse you. You've truly done nothing wrong." He swept my hair back, then lowered and pressed a kiss at the crook of my throat.

We embraced for a brief moment, then I squared my shoulders and faced the door. After three months, the time had finally come to handle this situation. Perhaps I should have done so sooner, but fear had a funny way of controlling someone.

"You ready for this?" I asked Vlad, while listening to the sound of Michel's approach.

Vlad hooked a finger beneath my chin and lifted my head, staring deeply into my eyes as though committing me to memory. Then he leaned in and brushed the sweetest, gentlest kiss against my mouth.

Only when we parted did he step back and nod. "Now, I am."

CHAPTER
TWENTY-TWO

"Please, have a seat." Vlad gestured to the couch.

I eyed Michel as he passed, scanning him for any lumps or bumps that might suggest he was armed. Truthfully, I couldn't see anything. And his outfit could have hidden any number of weapons. Guns concealed within his jacket, or knives strapped to his legs. Not that either would do any good. He could shoot us full of lead and stab us as much as he wanted, we wouldn't die. No, I needed to be on the lookout for stakes or swords. He carried a messenger bag, but I highly doubted he'd be pulling either of those out of there.

Then again, I really didn't want to put anything past him.

Michel seated himself on the couch and pulled an iPad out of his bag. He unlocked the screen, then opened a digital notepad. Next came a portable keyboard, which he quickly connected to the tablet. Guess some vampires kept up to date with modern technology.

I glanced at Vlad and lifted a brow, but he only rolled his eyes. Vlad hardly ever used his cell phone and saw no need for computers and tablets, an opinion he'd maintained even after Lucy and I outfitted his house in modern technology. Stubborn old man, Vlad.

"The queen and I have a few questions for you tonight, Anna, if that's all right. Hopefully, we'll be able to clear up this matter rather quickly and allow the rest of us to return to our night."

Even I could hear the false sincerity in his voice. I hoped I lied better than that, at least. And it seemed I wasn't the only one who noticed, seeing how Vlad had curled a lip up over his fangs.

Michel lifted his head and eyed me, as though waiting for my response. His fingers hovered over the keyboard, apparently keen to take notes. Twenty bucks said he was even recording my voice on his iPad.

This was it then. The moment of truth. Time to put up or shut up. I squared my shoulders and met his stare head-on, proving to myself and everyone in the room that he didn't frighten me. Michel was merely the queen's lackey. Yes, he might have a scary inquisitor title, but of the three of us, I put the odds in Vlad's and my favor against his.

"No," I finally said.

Michel's brow rose. "Pardon?"

"No more questions, no more demands, no more veiled accusations."

"Miss Perish—"

I held up a hand. "You're going to sit there and listen, and I'm going to talk."

"Oh?" He leaned back against the couch with the keyboard tucked into his lap. "I'm eager to hear what you have to say."

"Are you? Really?"

His smarmy expression faltered for a moment. "I'm not sure I understand your question."

"Never mind."

I glanced at Vlad, and once he gave me a reassuring nod, I grabbed the nearest chair and dragged it across the living room floor. I sat and rested my elbows against my knees, contemplating where to begin. I'd told this story countless times, but never for the queen's ears.

"The most important thing you need to know is that Petrik attacked me," I said, starting at the beginning. "I didn't even see his face until seconds before he struck. There was no connection between us, no relationship. I'd never seen him before that night. He grabbed me, dragged me out of the club, threw me up against a fence, and drained me."

I stared brazenly at Michel, hoping for a hint of emotion, something to suggest he might be on my side. But the man sat as still as stone, and just as cold.

"He left me in the alley to die. I have no doubts about that. Had Vlad not found me, I wouldn't be here right now. Petrik meant to kill me."

"You can't know that for sure—"

"He murdered thirty-four other women," I stated, my voice rising above Michel's. I wasn't in the mood to hear someone defend the bastard. "Thirty-four. And maybe that means nothing to you guys, seeing as you're vampires, but that means something to me. Yes, I'm also a vampire, but that doesn't make me a monster. Thirty-four women dead, because of him. So don't come at me with your excuses. Why would he intend for me to live when he killed every other victim? He was a serial killer, plain and simple, and you guys did nothing to stop it."

"Anna," Vlad warned, his hand falling on my shoulder.

I sucked in a shuddering breath and calmed my mind. He was right. I needed to remain composed. I couldn't give them any reason to believe that I was a danger. Once my temper cooled, I lifted a hand and placed it atop Vlad's, giving it a gentle squeeze.

"Vlad found me and turned me. He felt it might be considered bad PR if the human authorities found a woman murdered by a vampire while the queen was in the middle of arranging a peace treaty. Bad press and all that."

Something flashed in Michel's eyes then. Approval, perhaps? That shouldn't surprise me. These people didn't give a lick about me. Everything was about their damn public image.

"After I turned, we thought the matter was closed. But Petrik began harassing me. He trespassed on Vlad's land to taunt me, and a few nights later, he showed up at The Vampire Lounge and threatened both me and Vlad."

"Yes, we have a report here." Michel scrolled through something on his iPad. "A testimony from one Rainn Tremblay, a human employed with The Vampire Lounge. She claims that Petrik and Vlad were speaking when things grew heated. You joined the conversation and threatened Petrik. You were quoted as saying you have human friends who would be willing to set Petrik on fire during the day."

My chest constricted. Rainn seriously heard that? And ratted me out for it? "I wasn't threatening him, I was reminding him that I might not be as helpless as he believed."

Michel hummed a nonverbal response and continued typing. "Please continue."

"Look, I don't know what you guys think happened, but whatever it is, that isn't what went down. I might have threatened Petrik, but that was as far as it went for me." Not quite true. Vlad and I concocted a plan to kill the bastard before he could kill me, but they really didn't need to know that. "That morning, he had one of Vlad's allies lure me onto a balcony so he could abduct me. When I woke up, I found myself locked in a fucking cement crypt full of windows. And the rising sun was shining through them. Tell me how that's okay. How I'm to blame for that. The bastard tried to burn me alive, but it's my fault, right? I egged him on?"

Vlad's fingers tightened on my shoulder, silently reminding me to calm myself. I sucked in another forced breath and centered my thoughts. I didn't realize how badly this still triggered me.

"Is there anyone who can confirm these events?"

Silence crashed through the room. Vlad's hand continued gripping my shoulder. But I think it was to help steady himself. They were literally asking me to provide proof that Petrik had abducted me.

I ground my teeth together and staved off a sudden rush of fury.

This was the moment where it all came to me in perfect clarity.

Michel and the queen had absolutely no intentions of clearing me for this "crime." They wanted me as their scapegoat. They wanted to chain me up and drag me in front of the masses for everyone to see. Again, all as a PR stunt. To show the humans we had a justice system and means of punishing misbehaving vampires.

"You have got to be kidding me," I hissed. "You want a witness? To my attempted murder?"

"If you can provide one, it would greatly help your cause."

My hands curled into tight fists and only the press of my nails against my palms kept me from lashing out at this asshole. "Sorry," I bit out through my teeth. "The only witness was Eli, because he betrayed me, and he's dead now."

Michel's mouth thinned. "Yes, we received reports of his grisly death as well."

"But his death doesn't concern you, right?" I asked sarcastically. "Just the one that means something to the queen."

"Careful, Anna," Michel warned.

Careful, my ass. They were literally setting me up to take the fall here. To go down as the first vampire charged with murder. Prior to the queen's treaty with the humans, disputes between vampires often ended bloody, such as Vlad's and Eli's. The queen hardly ever involved herself. But because Petrik was dead, and he mattered to the queen, special actions were being taken.

"Well, I'm sorry, but I don't have a witness to confirm my statement. You'll have to take my word that Petrik abducted me."

Another annoying little hum fell past Michel's lips. I was beginning to hate that sound.

"So, you claim he locked you in a crypt with the rising sun. How did you survive that? You wouldn't have been a month old at this time, correct? Newborn vampires can't withstand the sun."

"Believe me, I couldn't. I was burning alive, about to become a roasted marshmallow when I managed to defend myself." Okay, so that was a lie. The truth consisted more of Sam and Lucy rushing in to save the day, but I refused to drag them into this. "Petrik grew cocky, and I took advantage of that. I attacked him and was able to save myself."

"And how did you manage that?"

This was where things grew dicey. I had to outright lie here, in order to keep Sam's involvement secret.

"Petrik had a blade on him. Once he got close enough to me, I managed to steal it from him. It surprised him, and before he could react, I cut off his head."

Michel's head snapped up, his mouth a perfect O-shape. I saw it in his eyes, the triumph he was about to lord over me. "Are you confessing to murdering Petrik?"

"Anna..." Vlad whispered.

I swallowed and considered my next words. I needed to tread carefully. "No, I didn't murder Petrik. Murder suggests premeditation. What part of he abducted me and tried to burn me alive don't you understand? If I hadn't defended myself, I would have burned to death. I did what I had to in order to save myself. And it haunts me to this day." Also not true. I was glad the asshole was dead.

"Walk me through this again—"

I sighed and shook my head. "Have you ever been burned by the sun, Michel?"

His brows creased. "Well, no, but—"

"Then there's no place for buts here. Tell me what you would have done. If someone locked you in a room with every intention of watching you burn to death. What would you have done?"

"That's irrelevant."

"It's perfectly relevant!" I shouted. "You're acting as though I shouldn't have defended myself. Are you seriously suggesting I should have just rolled over and let the sun kill me? Is that what you would have done? Are you that cowardly?"

"Anna," Vlad snapped.

"No. This is ridiculous." I shot up from my chair and waved my arm at Michel. "They're setting me up to fail this little inquisition of theirs. They want to find me guilty so they can use me as an example for all other vampires."

"I assure you—"

"You can't assure me of shit," I snarled at Michel. "Answer me. Right now. What would you have done?"

"Petrik was a thousand years old," Michel argued.

"And? Does his age mean I should have sacrificed my life for his? Did you forget the part where he was a serial killer? Where he'd murdered thirty-four other women—"

"Human women," Michel stated.

Boom. And that was the truth right there. They didn't give a shit about Petrik's victims because they weren't vampires.

"Human, vampire, who the hell cares?" I demanded. "Or are you suggesting that human lives don't matter compared to vampires? Bet the president would love to hear that. A serial killer is a serial killer. But all you care about is that he was the queen's sire. So the fuck what? Maybe she should have kept a better eye on him then."

"Are you suggesting the queen should have babysat her sire?"

I rolled my eyes. "Don't put words in my mouth."

"She is the monarch of our people and is tasked with so much more—"

"Yeah, yeah." I waved a dismissive hand, my anger still bubbling in my veins.

Michel grunted and tapped his iPad screen. "You said the sun burned you and that you were locked in the cement cellar with the rising sun. After you killed Petrik, how did you escape? How did you avoid the sun and survive?"

"Once I was out of danger, I drank Petrik's blood to heal myself and then avoided the sun's rays until nightfall—"

"Wait, what?" Michel's head snapped up, his face purely aghast. "You did what?"

Oh shit. See, this was the problem with lying! It always got you in trouble in one way or another. I was so focused on keeping Lucy and Sam out of it that I'd forgotten not to mention the whole blood drinking thing.

"Say that again?" Michel pushed. "You said you drank Petrik's blood?"

I swallowed but didn't utter a sound. Somehow, I knew speaking would make this worse.

"Miss Perish," Michel pressed. "Did you or did you not drink Petrik's blood?"

Fear zipped through my veins and lifted the hairs on my arms. I snuck Vlad a glance to find him withdrawn and paler than normal. He stared at me with such a sorrowful expression that I knew I'd screwed up. Bad.

I wrung my hands and turned back to Michel. "I-I had to. The sun had fried my legs, I needed to heal so I could move and keep out of the rays."

"You're confirming then that you drank his blood?"

It was almost like he needed me to say the words. "I—yes, I drank his blood."

I didn't even see Michel move. One moment, he was seated on my couch, his keyboard in hand, the next, he had me thrust up against the wall with a machete pressed against my throat.

Holy shit. A fucking machete! Where the hell had that come from? And how had he moved so fast? He had to be old to move like liquid silver. But how old? Older than Vlad? Were we actually at the disadvantage here?

"Thank you for your candor," Michel hissed in my face.

"Get your hands off her!" Vlad shouted.

My gaze rose over Michel's shoulder, and I spotted Vlad hovering behind him, about to attack.

Michel seemed aware of it too. He tightened his grip on me and pressed the cold blade harder into my flesh, drawing blood. "Don't. Move."

Vlad froze, fury alight in his eyes. I could read the desperation in his face, knew he wanted to rip Michel to shreds, but couldn't. Not without beheading me. So, this was it then. The vision Vlad had been having. The shadows haunting him.

"Anna Perish, I find you guilty of the murder of Petrik Kamen," Michel announced in a cold voice. "The queen authorized me to deal with you in any manner I saw fit. You are a danger to my queen and our people. I hereby declare your death as recompense for Petrik."

"What?" I sputtered, my fingers opening and closing into fists to keep me from lashing out. If I so much as twitched, that blade would cut clean through to the wall behind me.

"What the fuck are you doing?" Vlad snarled, his voice thick with restrained violence. "If you kill her, I assure you, I will rip you apart with my fucking bare hands."

My bottom lip trembled. I'd never heard Vlad curse before. Somehow, that frightened me more than the machete at my throat.

"Silence," Michel barked. "I suggest you remove yourself from this situation right now, Vlad. You don't want to see this."

A deep and threatening growl rose from Vlad's lips. He sounded animalistic, almost feral.

"I will not ask you again," Michel said, his head slightly turning toward Vlad.

I whimpered when the blade pushed deeper. The feel of cold steel lodged in my flesh wasn't something I ever wanted to feel again. It took every ounce of willpower I possessed not to claw at Michel. *Don't move,* I told myself over and over. *Don't fucking move.*

"We appear to be a stalemate here," Vlad uttered in a deeply aggressive voice. "Believe me when I tell you I will make you regret it if you kill her."

"She is a danger to the queen and to our people!" Michel shouted. "How can you not see that?"

"She did nothing wrong!" Vlad yelled.

"She drank the blood of an ancient vampire! You know our laws. That cannot be forgiven."

Terror infused my body and held me frozen against the wall. Vlad and I had never discussed this outcome. And with how fast everything had taken this turn, I'd never given thought to Michel's age or strength. Maybe he was older than Vlad. Maybe Vlad would lose a fight between them.

"Vlad..." I whispered. "J-Just go."

His livid gaze shot to mine. "Like hell."

Okay, okay. Maybe I could diffuse this situation somehow. Maybe I could change Michel's mind. Maybe I could save everyone's life here.

"How?" I whispered. "How am I dangerous? I drank his blood two months ago with no negative effects. There's no threat here."

"*You* are the threat," Michel snapped, his one hand pressing harder in my chest, trapping me against the wall like a pinned butterfly. "I see through your lies. You pretend to be innocent, but you're an insolent child who cares nothing for the rules."

"I-I'm a nobody," I stammered.

"A nobody with millions of human acolytes."

Acolytes was a terrifying word. "You make me sound like some cult leader."

"Are you not?" he retaliated. "Your followers fawn over you. They believe every word that falls out of that bewitching mouth of yours."

Bewitching?

"One word from you, and the humans might rise up against us. We are woefully outnumbered. So I can't allow that. I can't allow your manipulative words to bring harm to our queen. She's been our sovereign for nearly three hundred years. And she will reign for three hundred more. Long after you are gone."

Holy shit. There was so much to unpack here, I didn't even know where to begin. "So, this is all about Genevieve then?" *Keep talking. Keep distracting him.*

Michel's eyes flashed with rage. "You will address her properly."

Actually, I wouldn't. She wasn't *my* queen, but it really didn't feel wise to point that out right now. Not while one of her inquisitors was literally trying to murder me.

"What's this really about?" I rasped. "Me drinking Petrik's blood, my vlog, or your natural dislike of me?"

"All of it!" Michel shouted in my face.

He pressed the blade a little deeper. I gasped and pressed myself deeper into the wall, trying to gain an inch of freedom. Pain burned through my throat, but I couldn't focus on that right now. I needed to turn this conversation in a more pleasant direction. Needed to calm everyone down before someone did something stupid—like behead me.

Vlad stepped closer, and Michel responded with another press that had me crying out.

"I truly recommend you leave," Michel said to him. "And before you get any ideas, know that I have a dozen inquisitors stationed throughout this neighborhood. You may kill me after I dispose of Miss Perish, but my inquisitors will kill you before you can escape. Think this through, Vlad. Are you ready to die for her?"

"Unequivocally," Vlad snarled.

No, no, no. I couldn't let that happen. No one was dying here tonight. Least of all, Vlad. "You're seriously going to go through all this trouble for your queen?" I babbled.

"I would do anything for my queen," Michel crowed, lifting his chin as though offended I'd dare doubt his commitment.

I'd heard Marie Antoinette had cast a similar spell on her people when human. She'd somehow commanded a loyalty from her most dedicated people, enough so that one of them had been willing to die in her stead. Maybe that power had carried over into her undeath, given her the power to command such loyalty from her people. If that was the case, doubtful I'd be able to break Mikey's fealty. To him, Genevieve was the sun and the moon.

"Let's think this through. You kill me, then what?"

"Stop stalling," he snapped. "And I will only ask you once more, Vlad, out of respect for you. Leave."

Every nerve in my body came alive, and I panted for unneeded breath to center my thoughts and focus on anything but the pain. Funny, the things panic did to you. The way it warped your thoughts, and made you feel almost human again. Alive. Vulnerable. Emotions I didn't appreciate right now. I couldn't lose myself to mindless terror —no, I needed to remain focused.

"You planned this," Vlad suddenly growled.

Michel's body twitched in response. He didn't deny the accusation.

"I did no such thing. Miss Perish herself confessed to murdering Petrik and drinking his blood. Even if we ignored her so-called vlog, in which she told millions of humans how to kill us, there remains the fact that she's sampled ancient blood."

"But that was months ago!" I shouted again, desperate to drive the point home. "If something was going to happen, it would have already."

"You expect me to believe you aren't also drinking Vlad's blood? You two are lovers, are you not?"

His question startled me into silence.

"I thought so," Michel said. "You are far too dangerous to let live."

I felt it then, the moment his unwavering conviction won this battle. Michel's body shifted against mine, his weight leaning into the blade. I cried out and lifted my eyes to Vlad's. If this was to be my last moment on this earth, I wanted to only see him. Not the crazed lunatic at my throat. I wanted to go surrounded by sweet memories and loving moments.

I opened my mouth to tell Vlad I loved him, but before I could so much as utter a sound, Vlad lunged.

CHAPTER

TWENTY-THREE

HOLY SHIT. My life flashed before my eyes.

And all I saw was Vlad. He *was* my life.

Fuck, I hope I didn't die here tonight.

A gust of air whipped by my face, and I squeezed my eyes shut so tightly my face screwed into a horrible knot. But there was no fresh pain at my throat, no agony as my head detached from my body, nothing but literally sweet *nothing*.

I slitted a single eye and found myself standing alone against the wall. The machete was gone from my throat, and Michel missing. For a moment, I had to wonder if I truly *had* died, when the disturbing sound of two animals fighting drew my attention.

My head snapped to the side, and I barely caught sight of Vlad before he charged Michel like a freaking bull. I'd never seen him like this before. So livid and violent. He was always so composed in my presence, calm and gentlemanly. But this situation didn't call for any of those behaviors. I knew of his darker side—I'd seen it stuck on a stick in our front yard back in New Orleans. Lucy had told me the whole story. How he'd ripped Eli's head clean off, then walked away like it meant nothing to him.

497

But it was different this time. Michel was armed, and I knew from experience that blade was wicked sharp.

Chaos descended the instant the two crashed together. I felt my eternity with Vlad growing shorter and shorter every time he deftly dodged Michel's swings.

I felt so useless just standing there, watching. But what else could I do? Their movements were so fast, *too* fast. Camilla had trained me to fight, but she hadn't shown me anything like this. It made me realize how much further she and I had to go before I could hold my own. The two were literally clawing at each other's throats and faces in a brutal brawl.

In a series of movements I could scarcely follow, Vlad shoved Michel's arm aside, knocking the machete out of the way, then dealt a series of blows that sent Michel staggering backward into the wall. Vlad struck again, but Michel dodged, and Vlad's fist caved through the wall. While distracted, Michel retaliated, swinging out with his machete.

I almost screamed at the sight of that damn blade closing in on Vlad. I rushed forward, determined to help, but Vlad wrenched free of the wall, grabbed Michel's arm, then bent and twisted until it snapped in half.

Michel hardly grunted.

I skidded to a stop and stared at him. What the fuck? How could he *not* feel a broken arm? Or did he just not care?

Vlad latched onto Michel's damaged arm and forced it backward, then grabbed his fingers and snapped them one by one until the blade slipped free. It clattered to the floor, but neither made a move for it. Doing so would break focus and allow the other to sweep in for the kill. Fighting a vampire wasn't the same as fighting a human. Humans had weaknesses that could be exploited, whereas vampires only had to worry about decapitation. Everything else would heal.

I needed to be the one to retrieve the blade. Neither had so much as glanced at me. It would give me the chance to gain control of the situation and help Vlad. With the machete in hand, I only needed one single second and a clean line of sight.

I bounced on the balls of my feet, waiting for the perfect moment to dive in. This certainly wasn't how I'd seen tonight ending, but there wasn't any other option now. Michel had thrust us down this path, and I didn't see this fight finishing without a death. I just needed to make sure it was Michel's and not Vlad's, or mine.

I tore my gaze from the machete in time to catch Michel taking control of the fight. He had Vlad's arms pinned to his sides, his fangs bared as he aimed for Vlad's throat. But before I could so much as cry out a warning, Vlad snapped his head back and smashed it into Michel's face. Blood erupted from his newly busted nose and gushed down his face.

This was getting bad. So very bad.

I needed that machete.

I needed to end this fight.

Then Vlad and I needed to get the hell out of here before the other inquisitors came a-knocking. That was our only option now. This had gone way too far for any other solution.

Michel staggered back from Vlad, his hands instinctively cupping his nose. He hadn't cared about his broken arm, but it was hard to ignore a smashed face. I jumped at the opportunity, tucked low, and dove between the two men. The instant my fingers instinctively curled around the hilt, I snatched the blade out from between them.

I scrambled back to my feet, about to see how else I could help, when the sudden sound of shattering glass rent the night. My head whipped up just in time to catch Vlad sailing through the living room window.

"Oh shit," I whispered.

This was the very last thing we needed, and outside was the absolute last place we wanted to be. Michel's warning about the inquisitors came rushing back to me, and I peered into the darkness, watching as shadows suddenly descended like locusts. We had to move quickly now. Once they got their hands on Vlad, we were done for. I couldn't allow that to happen.

Having completely forgotten about me, Michel climbed through the broken window and stalked toward Vlad. His hands were fisted at his sides, even though his arm hung awkwardly. I had to give him credit for playing through the pain. Unfortunately, I could read the intentions in his body. Camilla had taught me how to analyze an attacker's body language, and I could see it now, clear as day. He was like a walking viper, coiled to strike, and the scent of his fury riding the air only confirmed my assumptions. Without a doubt, Vlad wouldn't survive this fight. Not with a dozen inquisitors barreling our way, not with Michel leading the charge.

I knew exactly what I needed to do to level our playing field. I needed to turn the attention away from Vlad. Keep him safe. Because at the end of the day, that was all that mattered. I could live with myself dying—in a manner of speaking—but I knew I wouldn't survive Vlad's death. And I couldn't let him take the fall for me. No way in hell.

So I repositioned my grip on the machete, then launched myself through the window after Michel.

I could practically hear Camilla's voice in my head, shouting at me to survey my surroundings, map out an exit strategy, *then* attack. But I didn't have time for any of that. Not tonight. Not with Michel bearing down on Vlad.

Michel's position gave me the upper hand. He wasn't facing me and couldn't see my approach. I needed to be quick and quiet. If I so much as tipped him off, he could block my attack and turn the blade on me. Camilla had shown me that move once. Except, this wasn't like my training sessions, and we weren't in a controlled environment. This was terrifyingly real, especially the part where Vlad's life depended on me.

Tightening my grip, I made my decision. The inquisitors were only seconds away. And Vlad's life hung in the balance. With a determined breath, I rushed forward and tackled Michel from behind.

"Anna!" Vlad shouted, struggling to his feet.

I didn't let his voice distract me, nor did I hesitate. Camilla would have been proud. I lifted the machete, placed it against the back of Michel's neck, and *pressed*.

I heard the cut. Felt the blade slice through bone and sinew. Watched his head detach from his body and roll across the yard. Smelled the blood as it poured onto the grass.

My stomach turned.

Before I could climb off Michel, someone grabbed my shoulders and wrenched me back. Unfortunately, they weren't familiar hands.

"Get off of her!" Vlad shouted.

It was good advice because I could feel the heat rising in my throat. I'd never killed someone before. Petrik had died because of me, but I hadn't actually been the one to do it.

I couldn't say that anymore.

This would haunt me forever.

Knowing I'd stolen someone's life.

Deep down, I knew it'd been an untenable situation. Him or us. He hadn't given us a choice, but that didn't make this pill any easier to swallow. For all I knew, he had little vamp babies and a vamp wife out there somewhere waiting for him to come home.

But he never would.

Someone forced me onto my knees in the grass and wrenched my arms behind my back. I was too shocked to focus on them. Too stunned to do anything other than stare at the beheaded corpse sprawled in my front yard. His blood looked black in the darkness, seeping through the soil, creeping toward my knees.

"Whoa!" came an unfamiliar, high-pitched voice. *"Did you see that?! She cut that guy's head clear off! Did you see it, did you?"*

"Duh! I'm standing right here! Of course I saw it!"

The odd voices cleared the fog, and I lifted my head. My surroundings came roaring back to me. There was so much yelling, screaming, crying. My neighbors, I realized. Except the voices hadn't come from them.

Because of course not.

"When that other dude came through the window, I thought damn, he's done for!"

"I know!" the second voice commented. *"Me too!"*

I followed the sound, then groaned at the sight of two squirrels standing in a nearby tree, clinging to the branches, their tails and whiskers twitching with excitement as they recounted the fight to each other.

"And that blade. Wicked, right?"

"So wicked. Don't go near it."

"Why would I go near it? I'm not stupid!" A slight pause. *"Think she's okay? The girl who cut off that dude's head? She doesn't look okay. Does she look okay?"*

"I'm fine," came my own thought before I could stop it.

"Whoa! Did you hear that? Was that her?"

"Yeah, that was her! She can talk to us! Hey, hey lady! Can you hear us? If you can hear us, just know you kicked ass! That dude had it comin', you know?"

I groaned and closed my eyes. I *really* didn't need to be talking to squirrels right now. Not when my life was falling apart around me. But at least now we knew for sure that I could communicate with animals, for as much good as that did me.

"Anna Perish!" someone shouted, clicking their fingers in my face. Yeah, maybe I'd let the squirrels distract me a little.

I jerked and glanced back at the unfolding mess. Vlad knelt in the grass across from me. Glass particles shimmered in his hair, but he looked otherwise unharmed. Thank goodness.

An awkward silence fell over us as the other inquisitors inspected the gruesome scene. There was blood everywhere. The machete, the grass, me... everywhere. Decapitation was a messy business.

God, I was going to throw up.

I caught Vlad's gaze again and held it, all while forcing myself to swallow. He lifted a questioning brow, and I nodded, reassuring him wordlessly that I was fine. My neck had already healed thanks to the infusion of Vlad's blood early this morning and the bottled blood this evening.

But just like Michel had said, there were a dozen inquisitors surrounding us. Damn. This situation had gone from bad to worse in the blink of an eye.

"Anna Perish." Someone clicked their fingers in my face yet again. Made me wanna bite it off. "You are hereby under arrest for the murder of Michel Aubert and Petrik Kamen."

Great. Why not just add Eli into the mix then? Go for a hat trick while we were at it.

"Ohhhh, damn. That sucks. They arresting her?" the stupid squirrel asked.

"Yeah, definitely arresting her. She did kill a dude!"

"Thought you said he deserved it?"

"Well, he did... I think."

"Shut up," I snapped in my head.

The inquisitor remained completely oblivious to the noise in my head. "You will be detained and transported to England, where you will stand trial. Do you understand?"

Wait, *what*? Transported to England? What the *fuck* was going on? Michel hadn't mentioned *any* of that.

"Do you understand?" the new inquisitor demanded.

I didn't understand anything right now. I simply stared at him and blinked. Unfortunately, with Michel, I really didn't think I could claim innocence. Twelve inquisitors had witnessed me kill him.

"What about Vlad?" I asked.

The inquisitor gave my cheeks a sharp slap. "You are under arrest for murder. Tell me you understand."

All I could do was nod, even though my brain was little more than a jumbled mess of thoughts.

"He was going to kill me," I mumbled.

"He totally was going to kill her," one of the squirrels confirmed. *"I saw everything."*

Somehow, I doubted a court would allow a squirrel's testimony.

"You seem fine." The inquisitor sneered as he slapped a pair of reinforced cuffs around my wrists. "Load Ms. Perish and Mr. Vasek for transport. The queen will want to see to them personally."

The queen. England. Trial. Murder.

Oh fuck.

THEY LOADED us none too gently into a massive van. Except this vehicle had been rigged specifically with vampires in mind. One of the inquisitors shoved me down, chained me to a bench, then pressed a button that activated floor to ceiling stakes. I gasped and squeezed my eyes shut, praying that nothing nudged me into one, like the driver purposely speeding over any bumps or potholes.

Vlad climbed into the van next, and my body relaxed at the sight of him. For a moment, I'd worried they would load him in a different van. He sat on the bench across from me, his gaze locked on the inquisitor handling him. Even I could see the rage within. Vlad was definitely plotting their deaths. Surprisingly, I was perfectly fine with that.

Once he'd chained Vlad, the inquisitor sneered, then slapped the button next to Vlad's head, activating his own personal wall of stakes. "Enjoy your ride."

Vlad didn't respond, and the inquisitor retreated, slamming the door shut behind him.

Finally, we were alone.

I shivered and glanced at Vlad. "So, this is romantic."

His mouth quirked. Glad to see he hadn't lost his sense of humor throughout all this.

"Um, you don't by chance know how to pick handcuffs, do you?" I asked.

"No."

Yeah, I kinda figured that'd be the case. It wasn't a skill in my repertoire either.

The sound of voices faded as the driver fired up the van and pulled away from our house. "I gotta say, this is not my idea of a fun time."

"Nor mine," Vlad said. "Are you okay?"

"I'm fine, I promise. What about you? Are you okay?"

"Not in the least," he growled.

"Are you hurt?"

"No. He was going to kill you."

That was for damn sure. I still felt the cold steel of the blade cutting into my throat, and I suspected that wasn't something that was going to go away soon.

"I'm so sorry that I dragged you into this," I whispered.

"You haven't dragged me into anything, Anna. What don't you understand? I would die for you."

"Right. About that." I shot him a tentative smile. "I'd really like if you could stick around to actually spend eternity with me."

Vlad met my gaze, then smiled grimly. "I'll tell you what. When people stop trying to kill you, I'll stop risking my life to save you."

"Aww, such a romantic," I teased, hoping to lighten the situation a little. I didn't want to think about our coming days. They seemed like they were going to be pretty bleak.

The van hit a pothole, and I gasped, squeezing my eyes shut. This entire vehicle was a death trap. Twenty bucks said they wanted to stake us before reaching the airport. Would probably make this trip a little easier for them.

"Do you see any way out of here?" I asked.

"Not unless we can free our hands."

Hands that were currently chained behind our backs and to the benches. Not to mention, the obscene number of stakes pointed at us. I had a feeling that if we so much as twitched, the driver could likely hit a button that would release every single one of them, effectively turning us into stake cushions.

"Well, this sucks," I announced.

"Indeed."

Vlad stretched out one of his legs and touched my foot with his. I melted inwardly. Would he never stop charming me? I hoped not.

"I think I can improve matters a little bit though," he said.

"Really? Can you get out of your chains? Shift into your bat form?"

"Not in the least. These cuffs are enchanted to keep vampires from being able to shift. I'm not going anywhere anytime soon. And neither are you." He chuckled quietly. "So since we're both stuck here, there's something I've been meaning to ask you, and now seems as good a time as any." He glanced around the van. "What's more romantic than a van full of stakes and chains?"

"A lot of things," I joked.

"Yes, well, our lives don't seem conducive to flowers and picnics."

"Couldn't hurt to try," I said, laughing. "But hey, I'm flexible."

Vlad caught my eye and winked. "Yes, you are."

"Tease."

"I can't reach into my pocket at the moment," he said. "But that doesn't mean I can't ask my question. Anna, you know I love you. More than I ever thought capable. You breathed life back into me and made me remember what it means to feel."

Holy shit. Was this... was he...? Here? Now?

"I've lived an incredibly long time. And no one has inspired me the way you do. No one has stirred within me the things that you do." He laughed quietly. "No one has brought out the worst in me like you do."

"Vlad—"

"Hush. Let me finish."

"Here?"

"Yes, here," he huffed. "Who knows what awaits us in England, and I refuse to miss this opportunity."

Holy guacamole, he was really doing this, right here, right now, when our lives were an absolute shit show.

"Anna Marie Perish"—I was going to kill my mother for revealing my middle name—"you already know I intend to spend all of eternity with you, so this is more of a formality, but one I eagerly await to hear your answer to. Marry me. Be with me through the good and the bad, the ups and the downs. Love me like I love you."

Oh, I hated him right now. Because the jerk had gone and made me cry, and I couldn't wipe my tears away, not with my stupid hands chained behind my back.

"I—I can't believe you chose this moment to propose," I laughed weakly.

"I enjoy keeping you on your toes," he retorted. "I highly doubt you anticipated this."

"Of course I didn't! No one proposes after they've been arrested and chained up."

"I'm a unique soul."

I burst out laughing. "You can say that again."

"I await your reply," he commented, as though this was just any other day for him.

Meanwhile, my damn chest had grown so tight, I had to wonder if it was about to explode. "I fucking love you, you know that?"

"I had an inkling."

"Are you sure you want to marry me? I seem to attract a lot of trouble."

He stared me in the eye and said, "Unequivocally," reminding me of the answer he'd given Michel before the fight. How the hell did I get so lucky as to find this man?

I laughed quietly, astounded by this turn of events. "Of course I'll marry you, you fool."

An easy smile chased across his face, as though nothing about this fazed him. Not me. My head was spinning. Engaged to Vlad. Dracula. The Count. The legend.

Somehow, he'd managed to turn the worst night of my life into the best. And that was saying something, considering I'd been arrested for murder.

Here was hoping we survived this somehow.

Because I desperately wanted to marry this man.

EPILOGUE

Oh boy, where do I even begin?

I know you probably hate me right now, ending my story here, but honestly, this seems like the best spot for now. Things are certainly grim. Grimmer than grim. They're downright dismal. When I was a little girl and imagined my life, this was *not* the direction I saw it taking.

I don't know what the coming days have in store for us, but I can't imagine they'll be good.

So, here I am again, caught in this mess because someone else tried to kill me. Why does this keep happening? And how the hell are we going to get out of it?

Ever feel like you're the butt of some huge cosmic joke? Like everyone else in the world is in on it, and you're the last one, running to catch up? That's how I feel right now. This *has* to be a joke. They can't actually intend to ship us to England to stand trial for murder.

Yeah, I'm definitely the butt of the joke.

I suppose there's some sort of irony here. That everything I've been avoiding is coming to pass. Makes a girl wonder just what sort of control she has over her life.

Vlad believes we were fated to meet—his dreams told him so. Does that mean this was all preordained? I became a vampire only to meet the love of my life, then be executed less than a year later? There's gotta be some irony there, because half a year ago, humans didn't even know vampires existed.

Now look at me, chained to a vehicle stuffed with stakes. Like, there's literally one resting six inches from my chest. It'll be a miracle if Vlad and I even make it to England alive.

I pray Camilla and Lucy are safe. Knowing they're out there somewhere gives me a sense of calm. I have hope they'll find us. They wouldn't abandon us to these jerkoffs.

But there's also this little voice in my head telling me they don't know where we are. Vlad and I will likely be in another country before they even learn about all this.

I can't think like that.

Happy thoughts, Anna. Happy thoughts. That's the only way we're getting out of this. Because if I let the darkness in for even a second, I might lose myself. And I can't let that happen. I have to stay strong.

Because there has to be something of me left to marry Vlad.

BONUS STORY!

Thank you so much for reading! I have a small treat for you. I've received multiple requests from readers who wanted to see Drac's perspective of this book. Particularly, the scenes after Anna is abducted by Petrik. Well, I decided to whip something up for you guys! **When Vlad Met Anna**, *is now available for download when you join my newsletter. Go forth, join and download! Hope you enjoy the Count's story.*

Click here to join and download! *(Make sure to use this link, as it's the only one that sends you the book!)*

And don't forget to join my newsletter so you never miss out on a Drac and Anna release! Join here!

Keep reading for Marrying Dracula...

MARRYING DRACULA

DATING MONSTERS BOOKS THREE

PROLOGUE

PREVIOUSLY ON *My Life's a Shit Show...*

You know that voice people have in their heads? The one screaming *bish, this ain't right! You in trouble, girl!* That voice? Mine comes out when I'm watching horror flicks. It screams at the heroine to run *anywhere* but upstairs, to get her ass outta that house, to watch out because the killer is right around the corner!

Well, I've been living with it for a while now. And it won't shut up.

How long, you ask?

Six. Fucking. Months.

That's right.

Six months of imprisonment.

Six months without Vlad.

Six months of complete isolation from the real world.

Meaning, no Lucy, no Sam, no Camilla, no *social media*, nothing.

Just me and this dark, dank cell full of what I'm sure is old blood (from the stench), decomposition (did I mention the stench?), and rotted human defecation ('cuz the stench, remember?). I've been here since the queen's inquisitors arrested us back in the States. All I know is we're somewhere in England, being held in the dungeon of some massive tower. Would you believe I haven't even met the queen yet? Apparently, she hasn't found the time to greet her prisoners. Rude, right? I mean, common courtesy is to introduce yourself at least. And here I thought the British were supposed to be well-mannered individuals.

To that, I say, *ha!* And *ha* again! If the inquisitors are evidence of anything, these British vamps are the surliest, meanest, and, dare I say *ugliest*, vamps I've ever met. Not that I've met many. But that's okay. At least they're fun to play with. And by play, I mean manipulate and insult. Anything to piss these fuckers off.

Don't mind me.

I might have gone *a wee bit* insane these last few months.

Minimal blood supply, no fresh air, no hygienic opportunities, and no socialization other than the nearby rodents.

I mean, who wouldn't go insane from all that?

Welp, at least I have the voices in my head to keep me company.

CHAPTER

ONE

I hum-a-lum-lummed a silly song. For the unlife of me, I couldn't remember the words, only the melody. I knew it was a song from Disney's *Snow White*, something about wishing for the one I love to come find me, but that was all I remembered. Oh well, the lyrics didn't really matter. I preferred to make them up anyway, if only to piss off my captive audience.

"I'm wishing... I'm wishing...," I sang, horrendously off-key. My mother had always said my voice could peel the skin off an onion—whatever the hell that meant. "For these guards of mine..." My fingers tapped to my imaginary beat. "To fuck off... to fuck off... today... today."

A long, drawn-out sigh came from outside my prison cell.

"I'm hoping... I'm hoping...," I continued, raising my voice an octave. "And I'm dreaming of... the ways that... the ways that... they'll die... they'll die."

I continued humming, all while purposely dropping some idle threats and chipper F-bombs along the way. When I grew bored with that annoying song, I quickly dug through my mental library for something I *knew* would piss off Tweedle Dee and Tweedle Dum out there.

"This is the song that never ends," I belted out, tapping my toes against the cement wall. "Yes, it goes on and on, *my friends!*" I shouted the last two words so loud, my voice went hoarse, and the sound echoed through the prison. "Some people started singing it, not knowing what it was—"

"Shut the bloody 'ell up!" one of my guards barked. He whirled to face me and slapped his sword against the metal bars. "Fucking nutter. Can we kill 'er yet?"

A small smile pulled on my lips.

"Just ignore her," the other guard commented, his tone practically limp with boredom.

Considering I'd been abusing them with nonsense like this for six months, I had to give the guy credit. He was steadfast and calm. In all our time together, I couldn't remember a single time he'd raised his voice or cursed at me. That didn't make him a friend, though. I'd overheard his private conversations detailing how he'd love to drain me, just to shut me up. Between the two of them, he concerned me the most. He didn't lose himself to anger like the other one. That made him far more frightening and unpredictable.

"What'll it be next, boys?" I asked, running my hands through my slick, greasy hair. Gross, right? Well, not my fault. The queen was the one who refused to let me leave my cell. Considering vampires didn't require potty breaks, she seemed to feel showers were equally unnecessary. "Beyoncé? Or maybe a little Britney Spears? How about I serenade you with a little 'Toxic'? Or maybe 'Criminal'? I feel like I could pull that one off."

"If you open yer trap one more time—"

"Oh, come on!" I retorted. Tweedle Dee's threats didn't frighten me. I'd learned early on that neither of the Tweedles had permission to enter my cell. And I'd been listening to them for nearly two hundred days now—yes, I kept count. "Who doesn't like music? Or do you prefer the Disney songs?" I twirled a lock of grimy hair around my finger. "I mean, I *am* a Disney princess, after all. Locked away in a tower, singing songs, guarded by two brutes. Did you know Rapunzel lived in a tower? I'm blonde, so I guess I could be her. What do you think? Of course, we could just dye my hair black, and then I'd be Snow White. She talked to animals, you know. Hmm, maybe I have more in common with her, what with the whole evil queen thing—"

"For the love of everything unholy, shut yer fuckin' trap!" Tweedle Dee shouted. "I swear, if you utter another word, I'm gonna—"

I sat up and spun to face him with what I called my "innocent eyes." Mostly, it just involved me batting my eyelashes. "You're gonna what? Talk me to death? You and I both know the queen forbade you from touching me."

Fury blazed in his dark eyes, and a promise lurked in those depths. One that involved my death. I admit, it amused me. I enjoyed pushing Tweedle Dee's buttons. Wonder if there was a trophy for pissing someone off so badly that they actually wanted to kill you?

"Accidents are known to happen, ya get me?"

"Ooo." I mock-shivered. "You've got me shaking in my boots."

He bared his teeth. "Keep this up, and…"

Laughter slipped past my lips. I rose to my socked feet and skipped playfully across my cell, all the while singing aloud.

Tweedle Dee's face mottled, and his knuckles bleached when his grip tightened around his sword's hilt. I pretended not to notice and instead began a one-woman-performance of the *Phantom of the Opera* musical. I'd never seen the actual Broadway show, but I'd watched the movie starring Gerard Butler—because who hadn't?—so I had something to work with. It wasn't until I reached the second chorus of "Think of Me" when I heard a familiar squeak. I continued singing, slowly moving into "Angel of Music," but my gaze swung to the side of the room where a small, albeit familiar, beast crouched in the shadows.

"Ignore her already," Tweedle Dum commented, his words hanging on the edge of a heavy sigh. "She'll lose interest if you stop reacting."

I quirked an ear and listened to their conversation, all while belting out the Phantom's part in a bass register I sorely lacked.

Tweedle Dee mumbled some crass curse and turned his back to me. He sheathed his sword, then fisted and unfisted his hands at his sides. I'd definitely pricked someone's nerves and wasn't ashamed to admit it. In fact, I felt a small swell of pride. My antics were childish, but hey, they kept me sane. Not that my guards understood that. They thought me well and truly mad, which was exactly what I wanted.

I slowly crept back toward my bed, now belting out the main theme song, and sat on the steel edge. I lowered my hand and rubbed my fingers together, silently summoning the small animal.

Weasley scurried over to me, careful to keep hidden in the shadows, and bumped her soft head against my palm. The Tweedles seemed determined to ignore me, so they didn't notice the arrival of my little friend. Weasley was a common weasel. Nothing fancy about her other than her cutie patootie face that I desperately wanted to smoosh between my palms. I couldn't, though. It was crucial that her presence remain a secret, considering she was my spy.

Six months ago, before the inquisitors had stuffed me and Vlad into a plane and shipped us across the Atlantic, I'd discovered I could communicate with animals. Luckily for me, I'd also learned I didn't need to speak out loud for them to hear me. It wasn't a particularly powerful gift, like shifting or telekinesis, but it was the only thing I had working for me right now.

Rats infested the tower dungeon, so I'd spent my first month here practicing communicating with animals. Those disgusting critters were *not* my favorite. Too twitchy and demanding and, well, gross. Just thinking about them gave me the shivers.

But Weasley? She'd sought me out during my second month of incarceration. How the heck she'd found her way into the dungeon, I had absolutely no idea. But I'd welcomed her comforting, furry face. I had absolutely nothing to offer her, but she didn't seem to mind. A gentle soul, this one. She genuinely enjoyed helping me, and I appreciated that quality like no other.

I drew my hand back to perform an air piano solo, one that had Tweedle Dee cringing.

"Are you okay?" I asked Weasley.

"Weasley good!" she chirped in my head. *"Weasley happy to see Anna!"*

"And Anna is happy to see Weasley. Alright, fill me in on everything, Snicker Doodle."

The sound of her humorous snuffling filled my mind and I grinned, even as I continued serenading my guards. She loved the nickname I'd given her during a low point in my incarceration. Something to cheer me up.

Learning to mind-speak with animals while talking—or in this case, singing—aloud had taken *so much* effort. To this day, I still couldn't believe what I'd accomplished in my time here.

"Queenie has summoned you! Her men come now. I bite one?"

I had to choke back a laugh, one I disguised as a cough. *"No, no biting. They can't find out about you."*

"Boo. Queenie mean. Don't like."

"You and me both, girlfriend. What does the queen want?"

"Don't know. Only heard her men coming, so came to see you."

I scritched her little head and listened to the sound of her contended purr. *"Guess we'll just wait and see what she wants then. How's Vlad?"*

"Sir Battikins?"

Another laugh rose in my throat. I almost regretted telling her about Lucy and Vlad and the nickname Lucy had given him. Keyword, *almost.* There was something entirely too adorable—and comical—about listening to my weasel friend call Vlad *Sir Battikins.*

"He not okay."

Her words sparked fear in my chest. I rubbed the aching spot and stopped singing.

Tweedle Dum shot me a quick glance over his shoulder, but he clearly saw nothing out of the ordinary because he faced forward again immediately after.

My throat thanked me for finally shutting the hell up. Sometimes these games of mine exhausted me, but they were important. I had to do whatever it took to keep the guards focused on *anything* other than me and my animal friends. If they even so much as suspected us, I'd lose everything, including my one way of checking on Vlad.

"Tell me," I whispered in my head.

"He miss you. Every time I visit, he darker. Angrier. A black aura around him."

Well, that certainly didn't sound good. I wished I had a way of communicating with him, but since he couldn't speak with animals, there wasn't much I could do. This was the extent of my one and only power. I could hold conversations with them, but Vlad couldn't. And my animal friends couldn't make a spectacle of themselves, otherwise Vlad's guards would immediately notice.

"Any news regarding him?"

Weasley trilled in my head, and her whiskers tickled my palm. *"Queenie only interested in you. Battikins safe for now."*

I considered our situation. There had to be something I could do to show him I was fine and hopefully perk him up. These past six months had been harrowing to say the least, and lonely as all fuck, but we were in this together. I just needed him to hold on.

The inquisitors had taken everything but the clothes on our backs when they loaded us into the van. I stared down at my filthy shirt and inspected the cuffs that'd once had buttons back before imprisonment. Now, all that remained was one tiny brown button hanging on by a loose thread. Grinning, I plucked it off and held it in my hand. It was only a button, yet the thought of communicating with Vlad in *some* fashion bolstered my mood.

I *missed* Vlad. The agony of being separated from him was unlike anything I'd ever experienced before—including death. Right now, I would do anything to see or speak to him, both of which I knew were impossible. For now, this would suffice.

"Okay, Weasley. Can you take this to Vlad? Don't let the guards see you. Stick to the shadows. Just sneak up to him and give him this button."

Weasley's nose touched my fingers, and her little grabby paws snatched the prize from my hands. *"For Anna, I do anything."*

Her loyalty brought tears to my eyes, but I quickly blinked them back. Sadly, we vampires cried blood tears, and if the guards so much as caught a whiff of that, they'd know something was up. Thankfully, they remained completely unaware of Weasley's scent, but considering the stench of my cell, that didn't surprise me. Blood was different though. Much like sharks, vampires were excited by the scent—no need to incite the Tweedles more than I already had.

"What about queenie?" Weasley asked. *"Her men come soon. They take you."*

Fear tightened my throat, but I tried not to show it. *"I'll be fine. You wouldn't be able to come with me anyway. Stay with Vlad if you can. But remember—"*

"Stay hidden, yes. Weasley know."

I smiled and stroked her side, reveling in the feel of her clean fur. Strange, the state I'd been reduced to. Filthier than an animal. I tried not to think about it. Tried not to think about the condition of my hair and clothes. At least the filth clinging to me was nothing more than dirt and grime, and I no longer had any biological urges. I couldn't imagine the condition I'd be in if I still had to obey a bladder.

"Weasley?"

She stilled against my hand, her head cocked to the side.

"If you can find some way to touch him, even if all you can do is brush your nose against him, please do it. I think he'll understand it's coming from me."

Weasley chittered in my head, then she touched her nose to my palm and backed away.

I rolled my head and stared out the cell bars. The Tweedles stood with their backs to me, their ears primed, but their eyes were facing forward.

"Go," I told her.

"I come when you're back. We see each other again."

A faint smile curved my lips. I had to admire Weasley's optimism. If the queen was finally sending for me, I knew it wasn't for anything good. She hadn't once summoned me or stepped foot inside the dungeon since our arrest. Not that I expected her to sully herself here. But I *had* expected an audience. As the weeks passed without, I began to wonder if she intended to leave us here forever. The day that realization dawned, I began working on my new ability. Who knew when I'd require animal assistance? I needed to be ready. At the very least, there were fifty or so rats housed within the dungeon that I could unleash on the Tweedles. I'd been tempted a few times in moments when they particularly pissed me off. But doing so would reveal my one power, and I needed to keep the queen in the dark for as long as possible.

Weasley vanished without a sound. I listened to her thoughts until I couldn't hear them anymore. Clearly, Vlad's cell was far removed from mine—purposely done, if I had to guess.

I started humming to myself again, this time for my own pleasure. Silence had never bothered me before, but now, it made me itchy. I truly didn't enjoy isolation. And seeing as how the Tweedles were my only form of entertainment and communication, I took great pleasure in pissing them off.

Tweedle Dee sighed and shifted his weight, obviously unamused by my decision to start humming again.

It didn't last long. A few seconds into the new song, I picked up on the sound of approaching footsteps. If Weasley was right—and she was never wrong—these newcomers belonged to the queen.

The Tweedles snapped to attention when three new guards appeared.

I didn't rise from my bed and instead, watched them from the corner of my eye. All five were dressed identically, right down to the silver swords strapped to their belts. Silver didn't harm vampires, but it *did* poison other paranormal creatures, such as werewolves. That didn't make the blade any less lethal, though, considering it could still lop off my head.

"Queen Genevieve has requested the prisoner."

Tweedle Dee mumbled something like "About damn time," then turned with a malicious grin. Whoever this man had been in his human life, he'd had a thing for pain. Or maybe I just inspired such sadistic tendencies.

He rooted around in his pocket and produced a long, shining key, one that had been polished recently. He unlocked my cell and yanked open the door.

I rose to my feet. For a moment, I debated fleeing. But where would I go? And how far would I get before my five guards caught me? I was unarmed, outnumbered, and greatly undernourished. A bag of blood a day was all I received. Hardly enough for a growing girl.

"Don't even think about attempting to escape," one of the new guards uttered. "We have permission to cut you down if you resist."

My eyes widened. After six months of forbidding anyone to touch me, *now* the queen gave them permission to harm me? Why?

Two of the guards drew their swords and held them at their sides as though convinced I needed to witness their show of strength. I had no intentions of running now, for reasons previously stated. But also, Vlad. Even if I could escape, I wouldn't leave without him. No way in hell.

Nodding, I stepped toward the cell door. My eyes flashed to the Tweedles, and I threw them my own little grin. I might not be armed, but I did have a few weapons of my own. My gaze bounced between them, and with a ruthless smirk, I said, "My *god*, you two stink to high *heaven*."

The two shrank away from me, their lips drawn back to reveal long, whetted fangs. My lack of faith meant the G-word had little to no effect on me. That wasn't the case for other vampires. So far, every single one I'd met had issues with God. And I loved to take advantage of that weakness. It didn't do much other than make them uncomfortable. But right now, it was the only weapon I had.

Laughing, I pranced out of my cell, knowing it would aggravate them to no end.

The other three vampires surrounded me, clearly confused by the current dynamics. I shrugged, then started toward the next door, one that would lead into a corridor. It swung open to reveal yet another guard out in the hall. Snickering, I glanced back, then pushed my luck a little further. Wiggling my ass in front of all of them, I danced my way out into the corridor, all the while singing, "Oh my *god*, look at her butt." I made sure to repeat the god sentiment every chance I got.

Because I was just pure evil like that.

CHAPTER

TWO

I'D BARELY MADE it through the door when a meaty hand found my back and shoved my face into a cold stone wall. Pain erupted in my head, and my eyes immediately welled. I choked back a groan and blinked rapidly. Guess these guards didn't appreciate my show.

Rubbing my head, I pushed off the wall and glared at the bastard behind me. He towered over me, his behemoth size both impressive and intimidating AF. My eyes tracked upward until our gazes clashed, his a stormy steel gray that promised me a whole world of pain if I caused a ruckus. Damn. Ruckus was my middle name. I had a feeling he and I weren't going to become besties.

"Walk," he commanded.

I blinked at him. "And here I thought I was already doing that."

His expression turned thunderous, and he landed a well-aimed kick against my side, one that sent me staggering down the hall.

"What the hell!" I shouted.

"Shut up. Keep moving."

"*Et tu, Brute?* How about you keep your damn hands to yourself," I muttered.

The air spiked with tension, and I cringed inwardly, expecting

527

another blow. Thankfully, Brutus here ignored my comment.

I marched down the hallway while rubbing my side. Clearly, someone had pissed in his blood bag this evening. What the hell had roused the queen's attention? Why did she no longer care about my treatment and well-being?

Maybe it was me? Maybe I'd pushed the guards beyond their breaking points. That *did* seem possible. Plausible, even. I had a way of getting under people's skin—a talent I often took pride in.

Another door opened, leading us into a different section of the dungeon, where three more guards joined us. I hadn't visited this part of the tower yet, seeing as how I'd been confined to my cell, but it did amuse me that a whole contingent now surrounded me. Geez, someone thought highly of me.

I mean, I *had* killed Michel, inquisitor to the queen, but that'd been a stroke of good luck. Dude had been so focused on killing Vlad that he'd turned his back to me, giving me the opportunity to attack.

Even so, I was hardly dangerous and certainly didn't warrant this much supervision. But it seemed best to hold my tongue, considering Brutus's presence behind me. I had a feeling mouthing off at these guys would land me a shit-kicking from hell. And considering the lack of blood they provided, I really didn't feel like healing the old-fashioned way.

We trudged through the dungeon. I studied every single cell we passed in search of Vlad, but they all sat empty. Disappointment knotted in my gut until, finally, Weasley's thoughts brushed my mind.

"Anna? Why you here?"

A cocktail of emotions burst within me. If Weasley was nearby, then Vlad must have been too. Relief rushed through me, and I quickened my pace, eager to see him. Brutus grunted something behind me, but I didn't catch his words, too engrossed with finding Vlad. It wasn't until we reached the final cell that I caught sight of a tall shadow hovering near the back wall.

"Vlad!" I cried out.

Fingers snatched at the back of my tattered shirt, attempting to restrain me, but I threw off Brutus's hold and dashed toward Vlad's cell. My fingers wrapped around the thick metal bars, and I choked on a pained cry before wrenching them back. I'd learned early on that the bars were saturated with magic. Touching them was like being hit by a hundred different tasers at once. Quite unpleasant.

"Anna," Vlad rasped.

He stepped out of the shadows and approached the bars. He eyed the vamps at my back, his face as hard as stone. His jaw's sharp angle told me he was gritting his teeth, but it was the sight of his fisted hands that told me exactly what he thought of our unwanted audience.

"You're okay," I whispered, the muscles in my body briefly relaxing. Weasley had kept me apprised of his condition, but it helped to see him myself.

His gaze darted to me, and I watched as he took inventory, his mouth flattening at the sight of my disheveled self. I couldn't even imagine how I looked right now, but my money was on disgusting and filthy. Not that he looked much better. Six months in captivity would dull even the shiniest gem.

"Are you okay?" he asked, his voice doing wonders to my state of mind.

My eyes fluttered shut, and I reveled in the sound. Of course I'd missed him—because, duh—but I hadn't realized just how badly. His voice suffused every inch of me and lent me strength.

"I'm fine, I swear," I said, wishing we could touch.

"Keep moving," Brutus growled. His colossal hand gripped the back of my neck and wrenched me back from Vlad's cell.

I heard the snarl seconds before Vlad lunged forward. He gripped the bars, his face a mask of rage and hatred. "Get your fucking hands off her!" He slammed his body into the cell bars, trying to break free.

"Vlad!" I hissed. "Stop! You'll hurt yourself."

The cell sizzled with power. Golden electrical sparks crackled in the air every time he connected with it, singeing his clothing and skin. Not that he cared.

Brutus's grip tightened on my throat, and he casually threw me toward the next door. "Say goodbye to your lover boy."

I glanced over my shoulder, but I couldn't see him through the wall of vampires surrounding me. "Vlad?"

"Anna!" he hollered. But it was the sound of his body slamming into the bars over and over that chased me into the next hallway.

I staggered forward, my foot catching on an uneven stone. "What the hell was that all about?" I demanded, tossing a glare over my shoulder. "Why even let us see each other?"

Brutus shrugged. "Why not? It was funny."

Seriously? It took every ounce of restraint I possessed not to haul off and deck the asshole across the face right here and now. But the giant sword at his side convinced me otherwise. Unlike the other guards, this one seemed willing and able to smack me around, and that sorta put a damper on my whole annoying them quest.

I ground my teeth and faced forward. "Now where?"

He gave me another hard shove to the right and pushed me toward a flight of stone stairs. "Up."

"Up," I muttered, mimicking his voice. Petty, yet enjoyable.

He cuffed the back of my head.

I was really starting to hate this guy. Not that I'd liked him before he'd paraded me past Vlad. The bastards thought they were funny, dangling us in front of each other with no purpose other than to torment us. When we got out of this—and note, I said *when*, not *if*—I intended to drive a hawthorn stake through each and every one of their asses. If I couldn't find one, well, Brutus's sword would do. Suddenly, I was in the mood for a little decapitation. Usually, that was Vlad's area of expertise. But hey, a girl could learn.

"Move," Brutus grunted.

"I *am*."

"Then move faster," he barked behind me, yet again shoving me.

Okay, hands first, then his head. If this jackass so much as touched me again—

He cupped the back of my neck and frog-marched me up the

stairs. "Hurry your ass up."

Oh, that was it. I spun on my heel mid-step and faced him. Even now, two steps up from him, our eyes were level. The other five guards slowed, their hands falling to their sword hilts.

"Stop. Manhandling. Me."

Brutus lifted a thick brow. Something sparked in his eyes, but he quickly blinked it away. I couldn't tell if I'd impressed him or pissed him off, but I was betting on the latter. "Pick up the pace, and I won't have to."

A deep growl rumbled in my throat—a sound I'd never made before.

Sadly, it only made Brutus grin, as though he found my antics adorable. He lifted a hand and circled a single finger, indicating for me to turn around. Then, you guessed it, he jabbed me in the back to get me moving again.

Holy hell. Rage inflamed my nerves, and thoughts of murder took up residence in my head.

At the top of the flight, he slapped open a door and gestured me through. "Third door on the right."

I hesitated. What exactly was in the room behind the third door on the right?

"Don't make me force you," he grumbled.

"I *really* don't like you," I sniped.

"Believe me, the feeling's mutual."

"Good. Then when this is all over—"

"Don't worry. I already know how this will end."

I sneered. "Yeah, with me standing over your decapitated body."

Brutus's eyes flew wide, as though he hadn't expected such a response. Maybe no one ever dared to speak to him that way, but I was beyond pissed. And this asshole knew how to push my buttons.

"Get—"

"Moving, yeah, I know," I griped. "Broken record much?"

"You know that mouth of yours—"

"Save it," I snapped. "I've heard it all before, thanks. Try being original for once."

Brutus gnashed his teeth and closed his eyes. Probably searching for a semblance of calm. Rolling my eyes, I stomped into the room he'd indicated, then froze. I wasn't sure what I'd expected, but it hadn't been this.

The room itself contained little more than a bed and a chair. But it was the long maxi dress draped over the mattress that caught my attention. I didn't wear dresses. Ever. My style ran a bit more toward skinny jeans, heels, and leather jackets. To me, dresses were abominations.

"What am I supposed to do with that?" I jabbed a finger at the offensive garment.

"There's the bathroom." Brutus pointed at the small opening attached to the room. I couldn't help but notice there wasn't a door. "Get washed up and changed."

Under normal circumstances, I might have dashed into the bathroom and drowned myself in water. Anything to clean myself up. But why? Why now, after six months, were they giving me an opportunity to clean myself? And why the outfit?

"Don't make me tell you again," Brutus snapped. "Do it. Now."

I ground my teeth, then plucked the hideous peach-colored dress off the bed and hauled it into the bathroom, laying it across the sink. There really wasn't a door, so apparently, they expected me to strip in front them. I spun and stared at my guards. All six pairs of eyes were trained on me, as though they expected me to attempt some sort of escape.

"A little privacy?" I demanded.

Brutus shook his head. "Get cleaned up. The queen is waiting for you."

If I still had a heartbeat, it would have stopped dead in my chest. "The queen?"

"What do you think is going on here?" He stomped across the room and crowded the bathroom. Then he wrenched on the shower taps and sent me sprawling under the icy spray.

Frozen water drenched my clothes and spilled down my body, filling my socks and shoes. I gasped, my body rebelling against the chill by tensing up.

Brutus gripped the back of my head and dunked me beneath the water, effectively blinding me. In uncultured places, I was pretty sure this was a form of waterboarding.

"Get it now?" he shouted at me. "Get out of these rags, clean yourself up, and get dressed. You have ten minutes."

Then he was gone.

I sputtered, even though I didn't need to breathe, and quickly manipulated the taps. Warmth quickly creeped in, and my body relaxed. I wiped the water from my face, then glanced back. Six guards stood in the joined room, watching me.

Cursing, I kept my back to them and stripped bare. This was utterly humiliating. To maintain control of my emotions, I let my mind wander. I thought about Lucy, Sam, and Camilla, and wondered where they were right now. At Vlad's place, most likely, back in New Orleans. They probably had no idea where we were.

I scrubbed my skin and hair, all while thinking about Lucy. Six months was a long time. I had to wonder if she and Sam were a couple now. Or if she'd kicked him to the curb entirely. I thought about my vlog and wondered if she'd been able to maintain it for me in my absence. Doubtful. Without me there, she'd have no content. Most likely, my channel had dried up, and I'd gone bankrupt. That seemed more like my life.

"Six minutes left," Brutus announced.

Muttering quietly to myself, I shut off the shower and reached for a nearby towel. Even with all them peeping Toms out there, I would have given anything to spend another hour in the shower. Strange the things we take for granted. Prior to this, I barely gave showers a second thought. Now, I knew I never wanted to go without again.

I patted myself dry, then wrapped the towel around my hair and reached for the dress. No way would I put my undergarments back on, so I left them discarded in the corner of the room, ready to see them burned to ash, then slipped the dress over my head. Luckily, my chesticles were fairly small, and could brave the world without a bra.

Once dressed, I released my hair and let it fall down my back in a wet, blond curtain. Apparently no one had seen fit to provide me with a brush—or any toiletries really—so I finger-combed my hair until it lay flat against my shoulders.

I cast a final glance at my soaked socks and shoes and decided against them. No torture was worse than wearing that. I could handle a little barefoot living in a dungy castle, though the thought did make me cringe.

"Good. Let's go," Brutus said.

He reached into the bathroom, grabbed my freshly cleaned arm, and hauled me out. His bruising grip tightened as he dragged me out into the corridor, then he shoved me forward. Man, this douche canoe was *rough*. I had a feeling he'd never been gentle a single day in his unlife.

"Last door on the left," he grumbled.

The second my gaze landed on the ornate doorknob, my throat tightened. Twenty bucks said the queen was waiting behind these doors. After being imprisoned for so long, I'd convinced myself we'd never meet.

Well, we all know what they said about assuming...

I didn't want to do this. Maybe there was some way I could, like, go back in time and *not* infiltrate Fallen that night. Then the queen's sire wouldn't have attacked me. Which meant he would still be alive. It was all one massive domino effect. But then, not going to Fallen meant never meeting Vlad. And I refused to live in a world without him.

Six of one, half a dozen of the other.

Vlad was the path I'd chosen.

A path that could only have led me here.

So, with my head held high and my shoulders squared, I pushed open the door and strode inside. Guess it was finally time to meet the queen.

CHAPTER

THREE

THE SCENT of fresh blood smacked me in the face the instant I stepped inside. The fragrance overwhelmed me, and my stomach twisted. Six months of limited sustenance sparked a hunger I'd never experienced before, not even in my first days as a vampire. It took every ounce of willpower I possessed not to lunge forward like a starved animal.

I followed the scent and found myself staring at an immortal woman seated upon a gilded chair in the center of the room. Plush red velvet cushioned her ass, and her arms sat on two upholstered rests. In one hand, she held a crystal glass, while the other rested atop a man's head, her long-tipped fingernails combing through his hair as one would a pet.

The queen had yet to meet my gaze. Her attention seemed locked on the male perched at her feet. My eyes dropped, and I choked at the sight of his ravaged throat. Three long slits cut his flesh, and his blood flowed freely. His gaze briefly flickered to mine, and I saw a flash of pain within. But I knew in that moment, this man wasn't human. A wound like that would have killed a mere mortal. No, he was a vampire, forced to sit at the feet of his queen while she drank his blood.

Horror welled within me.

Was *this* how she treated her subjects? Or was he being punished for something? Would this be my fate? To kneel submissively at Queen Genevieve's feet while she drained me dry? The worst part was knowing it wouldn't kill me—much like how it hadn't killed this vampire.

The queen lifted the glass to her ruby red lips and took a long, slow sip.

I knew a power pose when I saw one. She was trying to intimidate me. Rather successfully, I might add. But if there was one thing I'd learned from Camilla back when she was teaching me how to fight, it was never to *show* weakness. It didn't matter if I was quaking inside—which I so very much was—I had to put on a good show.

I pictured Camilla and wondered what *she* would do in this situation. I needed to be strong and show the queen that her little antics meant nothing to me. So, channeling my friend, I crossed my arms over my chest, lifted my chin, and wiped my face clean of all emotion.

"Miss Anna Perish," Genevieve finally said, her lilting voice heavy with a French accent. I knew from my research that she'd been born in Austria but had lived in France after marrying Louis XVI. I hadn't expected an accent since she now lived in England—and had for the past few centuries—but perhaps she still preferred to speak French.

Vlad had once warned me never to address her as Marie Antoinette since that name had died the night she'd supposedly been beheaded. Afterward, she'd taken the name Genevieve Bisset.

"It is good we finally meet," she commented, swirling the blood in her glass.

"Queen Genevieve." I refused to curtsey or bow or whatever it was she expected in these moments. As far as I was concerned, Genevieve was *not* my queen. Vampire or not.

Brutus's foot slammed into the back of my knees, and down I

went. Hard. Baring my teeth, I glared back at him. If I ever had a chance, I was going to murder his ass. And I would take great pleasure in it.

Okay, maybe I was channeling Camilla a little too much.

"Ah." Genevieve took another sip of her glass, then held it out to the side.

A human swept forward, a girl about my age. She carefully took the glass from the queen, cradling it between her hands as though terrified to drop it. She shot me a glance before stepping back, removing herself from sight.

Genevieve gathered her long skirt and rose from her seat. I sat back on my haunches and peered up at her. She offered me her hand, and at first I wasn't sure what she meant for me to do with it, until the realization dawned, and I nearly burst out laughing. She wanted me to kiss her hand. Like I was some humble peasant.

If Brutus wasn't hovering behind me, I might have let the laughter out. Instead, I climbed back to my feet, then took her hand and gave it a strong pump. A good ole handshake. "Nice to finally meet you." And yes, that was sarcasm.

I felt Brutus move behind me, but Genevieve held up her other hand, stilling him. She stared at me, our eyes level with one another, and her mouth twitched with humor. "Ah. An American custom."

I highly doubted it was only an *American* custom, but maybe she just didn't socialize with *plebs* enough to be familiar with handshakes. Either way, she seemed entirely ignorant to my giant *fuck you*.

Genevieve released my hand and stepped back, her skirt swaying around her ankles. Interestingly, she wasn't dressed as I would expect. When one heard the name Marie Antoinette, they imagined massive gowns, crowns, and high poufy hair—her trademark style, supposedly. But the vampire before me wore a floral skirt with a white blouse. The high collar brushed the bottoms of her ears as she moved.

"Tell me, how have you enjoyed your stay?"

"My stay?" I barked a laugh. "My imprisonment, you mean?"

She turned and cocked a regal brow. "You object to your quarters?

Did you not murder Inquisitor Michel? And my sire, Petrik? Should I reward such behavior with a guest suite and king-sized bed?"

Christ, I was getting *really* tired of having this same argument over and over again. What was it with these vampires? Why was *I* the one to blame for other people's stupidity?

"Need I remind you that your so-called sire murdered thirty-four women before he attacked me? That I would have been number thirty-five if not for Vlad? Not to mention that Petrik came after me *again* and locked me in a crypt to face the rising sun?"

Anger flashed in the queen's eyes. Guess she hadn't expected me to defend myself. Queenie—as Weasley called her—truly was crazy if she thought I would placidly fall to my knees and beg for forgiveness.

"And Michel?" she pressed. "I presume you have an explanation for his death as well?"

That one was a bit harder. "He also tried to kill me." Even I winced at the sound of that. It was true, though. He'd deemed me *too dangerous* to let live. Vlad was the only reason I was still standing.

"It would appear many of my followers wish you dead," Queen Genevieve commented. She reached out and stroked the arm of the girl who stood next to her, the one holding the queen's glass. The sharp scent of her fear pricked my nose, but no one seemed to comment on it.

"Yeah, well, maybe your people just plain suck," I groused.

"Petulance is not an attractive quality, Miss Perish."

"Neither is ignorance," I lobbed back.

She turned, her long lashes fanning her cheeks. A simpering gesture meant to disarm, but I saw it for the truth. She was playing with me. "You believe me ignorant?"

"I believe that when presented with facts, you chose to ignore them and instead, came after me."

"Facts." She laughed, exposing her sharp fangs. "You expect me to believe the word of a vampling over that of my sire's reputation? Or Michel's loyalty?"

Oh, Michel had been loyal alright. To a fault.

"What about Vlad? Does his word mean nothing?"

She waved a dismissive hand. "Men are so easily swayed by women. We merely spread our legs, and they turn into docile puppies."

Um. Okay. That was one way of looking at things. "So, you think I've, what, turned Vlad into my own little sex slave?"

Her smooth chuckle lifted the hairs on my arms. "Have you not?"

"I'm pretty sure he has his own mind and opinions."

"Yes, and they so perfectly align with yours."

"Because he knows the truth!" My god, we were going in circles.

"The truth. Such an American belief. May the truth set you free." She spun on her heel and faced me from across the room. I caught the flash of darkness in her gaze, and I knew right then and there that she didn't give a rat's ass about the truth.

I didn't stand a chance. Somehow, that thought emboldened me. If she didn't care about facts, then why should I care about sparing her feelings?

"Do you want to know the *real* truth?" I asked, stepping closer.

"By all means..."

"You don't give a shit about any of this." I waved to the room. "You have your servants, your blood slaves"—I gestured to the poor man still kneeling in front of her throne. I started at the sight of steel cuffs locked around his wrists and ankles. I hadn't noticed those before—"and your guards. All you care about is Petrik's death. And much like Michel, you don't care that he murdered thirty-four innocent women before finally being brought down." The air spiked with tension, but I pressed onward before Brutus could strike me again. "You let your people do whatever the hell they want on threat of death if they go just that little bit too far. The truth is, you were a shit queen when you were alive, and you're a shit queen now."

Genevieve's expression turned murderous.

Yup, I'd gone and done it now. Nothing said *suicidal* quite like pissing off the queen.

She stalked toward me, the sound of her heels clicking angrily against the tiled floor. "*Non*. The truth, dear Anna, is that *you* should have died that night, strewn about the rubbish. The only reason you still live is because the treaty I signed with your precious American president decrees that *all* vampires must be given a fair hearing."

Now that we'd dispensed with the pleasantries, I scoffed and shook my head. "A fair hearing? Seriously? You expect me to believe you're actually going to honor that? I don't even have a lawyer, for crying out loud!"

She came to a stop in front of me, her breath fanning my face. It reeked of old blood, but I didn't cringe away. Instead, it rallied me. This woman was *evil*. And were it not for Brutus and his men, I might have done something rash, like kill this bitch. The queen was only two-hundred-and-twenty-ish years old. Yes, that was a fair bit older than me, but I'd been trained to fight by Camilla, who had a good three hundred years under her belt. Camilla hadn't just taught me how to fight—she'd also taught me how to win. And the adrenaline now coursing through my veins assured me I could take the queen. She probably hadn't fought a day in her unlife.

Genevieve must have seen something in my face, something that spoke my thoughts aloud because her eye twitched, and she forcibly swallowed. Did I make her nervous? I sure as hell hoped so. I might be young and a newborn compared to her, but I wasn't weak. And I absolutely refused to cow to her simply because she was a queen. Her title meant nothing to a modern woman like me.

"I will abide by the treaty," she finally said. "But know this, dear Anna. The treaty says nothing about the verdict, only that a trial must be given. And I am queen. The outcome *will* rule in my favor. I guarantee it." On that note, she strode past me and approached Brutus. "Return her to her cell. Her trial begins next week, so no obvious harm must come to her."

My jaw tightened. I understood the threat woven in her words.

"Yes, my queen," Brutus rumbled.

Genevieve's heels clacked against the floor as she circled behind me. I ground my teeth and forced myself to remain still. It was a hard-won battle. No one liked having an enemy at their back.

"My men have told me of your antics," Genevieve commented. She rounded my side and slowly lowered into her regal seat. "Trust me when I say these games of yours will no longer be tolerated. We may not be able to kill you yet, but I have ways of making you wish you were dead. And while we can't harm *you*, I implore you to consider one thing." She leaned forward in her seat and caught my gaze, hers blazing with hatred. "The same cannot be said for your precious Vlad."

A cold knot of fear slammed into my chest and my eyes widened.

Quite pleased with herself, the queen sat back and resumed stroking her blood slave's head. "*Tu comprends?*"

I jerked my head in understanding. I didn't speak French, but even I could ascertain that one.

"*Bon. Au revoir*, Anna."

Brutus's hand clamped down on my shoulder. Before he yanked me out of the room, I watched as the queen's tapered nails sliced through her blood slave's throat once more, reopening his wounds. His tortured eyes met mine, a silent plea screaming within. But there was nothing I could do for him. Hell, there was nothing I could do for myself. I knew then and there, I would do anything to ensure his fate didn't become mine. I would die first.

At least there was an upside to my trial. If found guilty, I wouldn't live long enough to become the queen's next blood slave.

CHAPTER

FOUR

Brutus dumped me in my cell, then vanished without even a backward glance. And here I thought we meant something to each other.

Guess not.

Ah, well. I still had every intention of killing him whenever the opportunity arose. Funny how the thought of killing other vampires didn't even spark the slightest hint of guilt within me. Throughout my short eternal life so far, only a handful of vampires had bothered to show me a lick of decency. Vlad, Camilla, John—I considered them family now. But this tower was infested with fangers, and not a single one had shown me an ounce of kindness. I would remember that when I razed this place to the ground. Not that I had a plan yet, but that didn't stop me from picturing myself standing on the ashes of this place.

"Thank the queen, they finally bathed her," Tweedle Dee grunted.

Since their backs were to me, I flipped them both off, my lips pulling back over my fangs.

According to the queen, I wasn't permitted to continue my "antics," as she'd called them, which meant no singing and dancing.

Part of me was relieved. It was exhausting upholding the façade. But another part dreaded the coming silence. At least my games kept my mind occupied. Now I had, what? A week of silence and isolation to look forward to? That sounded far worse than my singing and dancing. Not to the Tweedles, I suppose. But their opinions didn't matter much anyway.

"Anna?" came a soft voice.

My gaze darted to the farthest, darkest corner of the room. Weasley hovered in the shadows, her whiskers twitching as she stepped forward.

"Snicker Doodle." My voice sounded like a soft sigh in my head. She was certainly a sight for sore eyes. *"How's Vlad?"*

She twitched and twittered in my head, her jumbled thoughts raising a sense of alarm within me. *"Not well. Seeing you not help Battikins."*

Yeah, it hadn't done much for me either. While at first, I'd been ecstatic to lay eyes on him after all this time, that euphoria had quickly withered when they'd dragged me away. Our separation was eating away at me like a cancerous tumor. I didn't depend on him, but I *did* love him. I wanted to be with him. The man was my soulmate. I would have bet any amount of money that the queen had purposely done this. Just to torture us a bit more.

Meeting her had convinced me now more than ever that she was an *evil* bitch. I hadn't had high hopes for her to begin with, considering her past. But seeing her in person had proven all my suspicions. I knew without a doubt she'd intended to intimidate me into submission, but all she'd managed to do was light a fire under my ass to see her dead—as quickly as possible. Her existence was a clear threat to mine. And if it came down to her or me, I knew my pick. Sorry, but queen or not, I wasn't giving my life up for anyone.

The only question was *how* the hell did I get myself out of this mess? Escape was damn near impossible here. Not only were the cell's bars spelled, but there were also three levels of vampire guards. Certainly not an easy escape scenario. And unfortunately for us, these asshats had slapped some magical bracelet on Vlad's wrist to keep him from shifting.

Even if I did escape, how would I get him out of his cell, and how would we evade all the guards? This place was like freaking Alcatraz!

"Is Anna okay?" Weasley stuck to the shadows, but her voice echoed in my head.

"I'm okay. The queen just wanted to talk to me. Threaten me, more like."

"Weasley could bite queenie. Teeth sharp!"

I fought not to chuckle. I couldn't alert my guards to her presence. They thought I was insane, but I had a feeling unwarranted laughter would certainly gain unwanted attention.

"Or poop in queenie's shoes! They smell bad."

As much as I would have loved to see it, I couldn't risk Weasley's life like that. Down here, the stale stench of rot, decay, and rats masked her scent. But upstairs, someone would certainly notice a little weasel ripping through the queen's closet in search of some shoes to defecate in.

"No pooping in the queen's shoes. Did Vlad understand that I'd sent you?"

Weasley's little head bobbed, her whiskers twitching. *"He smart."*

Yes, he was.

"I like Battikins."

Such a benign statement, and yet, it made my eyes well. I quickly blinked back the tears, then shuffled over to the bed. My dress was clean, but it wouldn't remain that way for long. Not in this place. I almost didn't want to lie down for fear of dirtying the garment. I hated dresses, but right now, I would wear *anything* that wasn't a six-month-old outfit, caked in grease, dirt, and who knew what else.

"Anna sad?" Weasley asked.

"I'm okay, Snicker Doodle. Just... tired."

"You sleep. Weasley stay. Weasley protect you."

God, I loved her. If I ever did get out of here, I planned on taking her home to America. You couldn't put a price on love or loyalty.

I stretched out on my bed and sighed. This was going to be a long week.

❧

BELIEVE IT OR NOT, the week passed rather quickly. Probably due to how much I'd slept. Boredom truly was nature's sedative. When I wasn't awake and staring at the ceiling, I chatted with Weasley. I told her more about home, Camilla, Lucy, my family, anything I could think of to keep us entertained. She was a rapt audience and enjoyed asking me questions, particularly about the local rodent selection. According to her, squirrels were her favorite. I admit that one threw me a little. Not sure why—she was a weasel, after all. But I'd never given thought to her diet. Once I promised her there were plenty of squirrels to nom on in Louisiana, she started chattering about her other favorite foods. She lost me there, my stomach churning at the thought of dining on raw rabbit.

Tonight—officially one week after my last *tete-a-tete* with the queen—Weasley came slinking into my cell and bumped my lowered hand.

"Queenie summoned Anna," she chittered in my head.

Her words plucked my nerves. Guess that meant the court case began tonight. And holy fuck, did that terrify me. I'd known all along that the queen had planned for this spectacle, but knowing and actually attending were two very different things. Tonight began the most consequential moment of my life. It didn't help knowing the queen had it out for me. And her bias would absolutely affect the outcome of my trial. She was the *queen*, for crying out loud. And according to *everyone*, she ruled with an iron fist. No one would dare go against her to help me. To the other vamps, I was a traitor— someone who had revealed precious vamp secrets to the unknowing public in the name of fame and wealth.

"Thank you, Snicker Doodle," I responded. *"I think you should go be with Vlad. He isn't going to be happy when he sees them taking me."*

545

She brushed her side against my palm, and I stroked her fur, reveling in the feel of a living, breathing creature. I was so tired of being surrounded by cold-blooded vamps. I needed Lucy. There was something about a warm, breathing bestie to perk an undead girl up.

Footsteps echoed out in the hall.

"You should go before they see you," I told her.

She affectionately nibbled my finger, careful not to break my skin, then disappeared. I knew the moment she was finally out of reach, the chaotic jibber jabber of her thoughts vanishing entirely and leaving me in silence.

The door flung open, and in strode Brutus, along with two extra guards. They marched to my cell and gestured at the Tweedles. No one spoke a word as they opened my cell door and waited. Guess they expected me to come of my own free will.

Once more, the thought of fleeing clouded my mind. But logic immediately reared its ugly head. I didn't stand a chance against five guards, all of whom were older than me. Not without Vlad.

Brutus lifted a thick brow, an unspoken challenge forming between us.

Bet he wanted me to run. Bet he wanted a reason to lay his hands on me. I refused to give up on the idea of escaping, but I also knew I had to be smart about it. Choose the right moment. And this sure as shit wasn't it.

"Well?" Brutus demanded, his voice booming in the small enclosure.

Sighing, I strode out of my cell with my head held high. The guard next to Brutus lifted his hand, brandishing a pair of shiny, magically-enchanted cuffs. I'd seen them before on the night of my arrest, and I knew what they were capable of. Since I didn't have any physical powers, they wouldn't do much, other than restrain me.

Brutus took them from the other guard, then gestured me onward. Guess the cuffs were for later.

"You will proceed up to the third floor," Brutus commented. "You will shower, dress, and prepare yourself for court. You will make yourself presentable without any hassle, and you will do it in a timely manner."

"Or what?"

The muscles at his temple ticked. "Or I will do it for you."

"Aww. Did someone's mommy refuse to let him play dress-up as a child?"

Hate burned in his gaze. "Get. Moving."

With my hands tucked against my stomach, I strode through the door and began the trek. It took effort to keep my pace even. Part of me wanted to run so I could see Vlad sooner. But I refused to let these bastard guards see any sort of emotion.

The empty cells passed in a blur, and I sucked in a breath when I caught sight of Vlad's silhouette. I bit my lip to keep from crying out his name. Instead, I fisted my hands and just stared at him. He jerked at the sight of me, his dark eyes narrowing on my surrounding entourage.

"Are you alright?" I asked, slowing my pace. Oh, how I wished to ask more. To make sure they were treating him with kindness. But I knew better.

His head dipped once. "You?"

"Trial" was all I said.

Brutus flattened his palm against my back and shoved. "Keep moving."

Vlad's snarl echoed through the cell block. Thankfully, this time he didn't rush the bars. Guess we were both learning. Not that it made it any easier to walk away. I would have given anything to jump into his arms right now, feel his fingers in my hair or his lips on mine.

Instead, I stumbled through the doorway and listened as the door slammed shut behind me.

"Upstairs," Brutus barked.

"Yeah, yeah." I knew the drill already. Before he could cuff me yet again, I stomped up the flight, all the while imagining the many, *many* ways I could kill him. None of them were possible, but the fantasies were helping me maintain what little sanity remained. That had to count for something, right?

At the top of the stairs, I slunk into the first room—the same as last time—and stared at the open concept shower. Hanging from the door was yet another dress, this one a bleak gray. Appropriate, considering my circumstances. Would have preferred a suit, but we all knew I had no choice in any of this.

Sighing, I ducked into the bathroom and began the embarrassing process once again. At least this time, Brutus hung back. I made quick work of the cool shower, missing all the luxuries of Vlad's place, then ducked out and dragged the woolen dress over my head. With my skin still damp, the material clung to me, but since the guards had already seen me in all my naked glory, who the hell cared, right?

I dragged my fingers through my hair, laying it flat against my back, then turned to face my warden. "Decent enough?"

He rolled his eyes a second before gripping my arm and hauling me out of the bathroom. He held up the handcuffs and waited. I gritted my teeth and thrust out my arms, wincing inwardly at the sound of the metal bracelets snapping around my wrists. Nothing like being handcuffed to really make a girl feel like a criminal. I suppose in their eyes, I *was* a criminal.

"Let's go," Brutus said. "Your trial begins in an hour."

Panic churned deep in my gut. After six months, this was it. The moment of... well, just *the* moment. I might have said *of truth*, but even I knew the truth held no relevance here. If the truth mattered, this stupid trial wouldn't be happening. All the queen cared about was revenge. Which had me curious. Why bother with this circus act? If she wasn't going to follow the due process, why even concern herself about the treaty? Why not just quietly kill me off? Alas, mind reading wasn't one of my powers, so I lacked answers. And didn't that just drive my curious nature crazy.

Brutus manhandled me out of the room, then pointed at the stairwell. "Down one flight. Then take a left."

I followed his instructions, only to find myself outside.

Oh lord, I was *outside*.

And damn, was it cold. For some reason I hadn't given thought to the seasons. But even though I *knew* I'd been locked up for six months, it startled me to realize it was January.

My eyes fluttered shut and I sucked in a cold, albeit unnecessary, breath. I didn't need air, but right now I *wanted* it. After months of suffering the rank dungeon stench, even London's particular aroma of diesel fumes mixed with stale river water was refreshing.

Brutus navigated me toward a nearby van, one that looked unpleasantly familiar. When he pulled open the back doors, I grimaced at the interior. I climbed inside and sat on the bench. Brutus followed me in, then latched my handcuffs to a long chain connected to my seat, then pressed the magical button that activated a series of floor-to-ceiling stakes surrounding me. Did it make me a bad person to hope one stabbed Brutus? Probably. But I also didn't care.

Brutus climbed out of the van, then slammed the doors shut. Silence descended. Last time I'd found myself here, I'd been with Vlad, and he'd proposed. Somehow, he'd given me hope in a hopeless situation. Not this time, though.

This time, they were dragging me to my trial. And this time, I wasn't sure I would be coming back.

CHAPTER

FIVE

Ten minutes into the drive and I was already bored. One would think after six months of imprisonment, I would relish a change of scenery. But truthfully, this van was merely another form of confinement and a reminder of my dire situation. Even worse, I had no one to annoy other than myself, which was a difficult task, considering I was me.

My legs ached, and I longed to stretch them out. Except, any sort of movement would likely end with me staked. I hated these vans. Could hardly blink without fearing a wooden stake through the chest, let alone sit comfortably while riding over potholes. Thankfully, my driver seemed aware of the precariousness and was careful to avoid any rogue bumps. Guess Brutus wasn't the one driving. For some reason, I had a feeling he would have purposely gone out of his way to "accidentally" stake me.

A few more minutes passed in ghastly silence before a small window suddenly slid open, revealing the front cab. A dark-haired head popped up, and startling gray eyes appraised me. I didn't recognize this guard at all. It certainly wasn't one of Brutus's entourage, but that didn't mean anything. Twenty bucks said there were more insults and threats about to come my way. These people seemed to take absolute pleasure in tormenting me.

I lifted my chin and steeled myself, prepared for the oncoming verbal assault.

"Doing okay back there?" His deep voice echoed through the small confines.

I blinked. "Uh, peachy?"

He flashed me a quick smile, then ducked out of sight for a few moments. He seemed to be seated on the left, telling me he was the passenger, seeing as how this country did everything backward.

"Let's see... ah, got it."

A second later, the stakes surrounding me retreated with a satisfying snap. I gasped, then squeezed my eyes shut. Here it came. They were playing with me, toying with me like a cat would a mouse. Waiting for me to shift my weight so that when they reactivated the stakes, they'd pierce me. These people were the literal worst! And I wanted to kill them all.

"Hey, you okay?" came that voice again. "Did one of the stakes nick you?"

I cracked open a single eye and stared at the guard. His eyes were like liquid silver, but they held concern as they watched me.

When I didn't respond, he frowned. "You *are* okay, right?"

What kind of sick game was this guard playing?

"Shit. You're not okay. Camilla is going to *kill* me."

I snapped to attention, every muscle in my body going taut. "Camilla? Did you just say Camilla?"

The guard's concern melted into amusement. "Oh, good. She told me she'd skin me alive if you were harmed during this process, and I very much like my skin where it is, thank you."

I scooched forward on the bench, my ass practically hanging on by a single butt cheek. "You said Camilla. You know her? Where is she? What's going on?"

The guard lifted a hand, his boyishly handsome grin soothing my nerves. "Just hold on to something, okay? And don't die."

"Hold on?" I glanced around. "Hold on to *what*, exactly? In case you haven't noticed, I'm handcuffed and—*aahhhhhh!*" I hadn't meant to scream. But while I was blathering, the van took a sudden hard turn, sending me flailing across the bench.

Pain flared through my wrists, compliments of the enchanted cuffs.

"Keep holding on!" the guard shouted back to me, his voice carrying over the sound of two loud pops, followed by an almost flopping sound.

Next came the screech of brakes, but not from us. Instead, my van lurched forward, gaining speed right before it took another hard left that threw me to the ground. Cursing, I peeled myself off the bottom of the van and wrapped my arms around the bench, knees tucked into my chest.

"What's happening?" I yelled.

No one answered. Instead, I heard the gray-eyed guard shout an obscenity, then order the driver to take another sharp turn. Thankfully, this time, I was prepared. I hugged that bench so hard, I thought it might crack.

"Okay, here!" the guard called.

I felt the van jerk as the driver slammed on the brakes. Tires squealed as the whole vehicle shuddered to a stop. Doors opened up front, and I caught the sound of hurried footsteps padding against the cement outside. Before I could even begin to piece everything together, the back doors flew open, and in the pale moonlight stood Gray Eyes. He clambered into the van and quickly crouched at my side, his hands brandishing a familiar silver key. He inserted it into my handcuffs and twisted. The silver cuffs fell away from my wrists, and a small, relieved squeak slipped past my lips.

Oh my god. *Freedom.*

A large part of me wanted to clock my guard on the head, knock him the hell out, and run. But a smaller part of my brain told me to wait. He'd mentioned Camilla. He'd retracted the stakes. He'd freed me from the cuffs. Logic dictated he was on my side. And right now, I needed all the allies I could get.

"Come on," he said, oblivious to how close I'd come to giving him a concussion. "We need to go. Right now."

I gripped his arm before he could move. "Who are you?"

The guy had the audacity to wink at me. "Name's Alastair. Now, are you ready to get the eff out of here?"

Oh, baby. I was more than ready. I rose from my crouched position and darted outside. This time, when I inhaled the fresh air, it seemed even sweeter than before. Sadly, I didn't have time to relish in it.

"Where are the others? Brutus and whatnot?"

"Who?" Alastair questioned, landing next to me on the road.

"I don't know his real name. The head guard in charge of my unhappiness. Yay high, mean SOB, ugly as sin—"

"Oh, Finley." Alastair whipped a hand through his hair. "Don't know. Don't want to know. My job was to get you out. Camilla's job was to take care of the guards. Let's go."

"Wait." I dug in my heels before he could wrench me away from the van. "Where's Camilla?"

Alastair blew out an annoyed breath. "You gonna question everything?"

"Pretty much. Best to just give in, ya'know?"

"Americans," he groused.

"Ya coming or what?" an unfamiliar voice asked from the front of the van.

I whirled around and caught sight of yet another vampire, this one standing next to the driver's side door. My jaw dropped at the sight of him. I'd seen some tall people throughout my life. Vlad, alone, towered over me. But this guy was a damn giant. He stood taller than the freaking van.

"Who the hell is that?" I demanded.

"Mateo," Alastair said. "And we've both put our lives at extreme risk to save yours. So, can we dispense with the twenty questions and get your pert little ass out of here before the other guards come a-lookin'?"

I shook my head. "I'm not going anywhere without Camilla. That might make me an idiot, I know. But I refuse to let her end up in the same situation she's trying to rescue me from. So either take me to her or get the hell out of my way."

Alastair groaned and tipped his head skyward. "Just make sure you tell her I *tried* to stop you, yeah?"

"Sure, whatever."

"Let's go, Mateo." Alastair gripped my hand and pulled me through the streets, leading me back the way we'd come.

The two other transport vans came into sight, one laying on its side, the other dented nearly in half. And surrounding the vehicles was a fight unlike anything I'd ever seen. I'd watched Camilla fight before, but apparently, she'd been holding back.

Before my arrest, she'd confessed to me that the ability to read her opponents in a fight was one of her powers. She'd called it *battle-sense*. Supposedly, she could see how the fight would play out in her head, making her a formidable opponent.

Three vampires surrounded her, but she evaded them deftly, striking out at every opportunity. Another dove into the battle, and I gasped at the sight of Breccan. Even in the dark, I could make out his sandy-blond hair as he rushed around one of Camilla's opponents and knocked him clear out.

A third figure moved into view. One I never would have expected. Rebecca's long, black hair swished behind her as she darted in and out of sight. She masterfully took out another opponent, leaving Camilla to deal with the last one.

Within seconds, Camilla rendered the remaining guard unconscious. More guards lay scattered across the pavement. From the looks of it, my entourage had consisted of what appeared to be eight or so vampires. And there, in the middle, lay Brutus himself. Sorry, but I couldn't think of him as Finley. What a horrible villain name.

"There, see?" Alastair commented, the relief evident in his voice. "Told you Camilla would be fine."

Actually, he hadn't. But that seemed silly to point out. Instead, I rushed toward Camilla because damn, she was a sight for sore eyes. The thought cracked me up, seeing as how six months ago, I'd been begging for some time away from her.

"What the hell are you doing here?" Camilla demanded. "We had a plan, Alastair!"

"Yeah, well, tell your little friend that."

Camilla's dark eyes narrowed on me. "Can't you for once do as you're told?"

"Nope," I said, popping the *P*. "I needed to make sure you were alright."

"I'm clearly fine, you dolt."

My mouth cracked into a grin. "It's good to see you too."

The annoyance faded on Camilla's face, and she started smiling. "Yes, well. We couldn't let the queen kill you, now could we?"

I wasn't a huggy person, but for this, I hugged Camilla.

She chuckled, then gave me an awkward pat on the back.

"Oi, what about us?" Breccan demanded, his long arms wrapping around the both of us.

I laughed, relief easing my muscles. "Thank you, guys, seriously."

"Our pleasure," Rebecca murmured behind us. She and I had never really clicked, and I wasn't quite sure why, but I appreciated her presence here.

Truth be told, Vlad and I had wondered if she'd taken part in Eli's betrayal, the one that had landed me in Petrik's loving care. But if she was here, maybe our assumptions were wrong.

Camilla stepped out of my embrace, then eyed me with a pursed expression. "Don't take this the wrong way, but who the hell dressed you? You look like a nun."

"These guys," I said, toeing Brutus's side. He didn't so much as flinch. Good. Sadly, since no one had been staked or beheaded, I knew they weren't dead. Shame.

"Figures." Camilla reached behind her back and produced a wicked-looking dagger. "It isn't much, but it'll do the job."

I had nowhere to stash the blade, so I merely gripped it and thanked her. "What now?"

"Well, the *plan* was to meet you at our safe house and get you the hell out of this wretched country. I guess we can just travel to the safe house together now. A bit... anticlimactic, I must say."

"What? No. We can't leave. What about Vlad?"

Camilla sighed, as though she'd expected this argument from me. "We'll discuss it at the safe house."

I stepped out of reach. "Absolutely not. I'm not going anywhere without him."

"Anna," Camilla groaned. "Do you know how long it took us to plan this little intervention? We had to wait this long just for them to transport you. Why, you ask? Because we knew we couldn't infiltrate the tower. That's a suicide mission. Rescuing you during transport was the safest bet."

I sputtered for words. I honestly didn't care a lick about the logic behind their plan. There was no way I would abandon Vlad. It was hell being separated from him, and I refused to put us through it for another night.

"Now, come on." Camilla reached for my hand, but I snapped it back out of reach.

"She'll kill him, Camilla!" I snapped. "And before you ask, yes, I know that for sure. She's already threatened to kill him if I so much as stepped a toe out of line. Twenty bucks says this qualifies."

When she didn't immediately respond, I sighed and raked a hand through my hair. "The best time to free him is right now. These vamps"—I swept out my arm—"encompass most of our guards. And the queen is likely waiting for my arrival at the courthouse with her entourage. The tower is at its weakest *right now*. We have to take advantage of that." I scrambled to think of more points, anything to help convince Camilla to help me free Vlad. "If we wait even one more night, they'll double their numbers and reorganize. We can do this—we *have* to. And if you won't help me, I'll just do it myself."

"For crying out loud, shut up," Camilla hissed. "You know I love Vlad too. And I understand you want to free him—"

"Of course I want to free him! You don't know what that place was like—"

"Did they torture you?" she demanded.

"Oh, well, no. But—"

"So this is all about you getting your soulmate back."

I mean, when she put it that way... but I refused to back down. "She *will* kill him, Camilla. Can you live with that?" Time to pull out the big guns. "Vlad would do it for you."

Silence descended over our small motley group.

Camilla finally sighed and shook her head. "Get in the damn van."

"Are we—"

"Just get in the damn van, Anna!" Camilla barked.

Her frustration suggested we were indeed going after Vlad. And since that was exactly what I wanted, I didn't argue. Instead, I wrenched open the passenger-side door and jumped inside, my toe eagerly tapping the floor.

Camilla climbed in through the driver's side but scootched into the middle. Mateo slipped in behind the steering wheel while the others all hopped in the back.

Mateo navigated a hundred-and-eighty-degree turn, then started down the road—I assumed toward the tower. I had no concept of geography here.

"We were fortunate tonight," Camilla said. "We incapacitated your guards before they could radio or call for help. So, the tower should be completely oblivious to the current circumstances. And you aren't due at the courthouse for another thirty minutes. With luck, we might be able to get in, free Vlad, and get out before anyone notices."

I honestly didn't see that happening, but hey, I could try to think positively. I would do whatever it took to be back in Vlad's arms tonight. *Come on universe, I'm looking for a little help here.*

"Tell me about the layout," Camilla ordered.

So I did. I painted the best word picture I could. How they'd always kept me in the dungeon, how there was only one stairwell in and out. How Vlad was in the first cell nearest the exit—thank goodness. Camilla listened with rapt attention until Mateo came to a stop one block away from the tower. We all climbed out, but this time, I wasn't energized by the night air. Instead, it gave me a chill. Likely due to the foreboding sense of doom weighing on me. I hated this place. And I'd never imagined myself sneaking back *in* after escaping.

But for Vlad, I would do anything.

"Let's do this quickly, people. Incapacitate any vamps we come across. Do not give them the chance to raise the alarm. Aim for stealth. We do not want to be caught here tonight."

True dat.

"Um, I might be able to help," I said, raising a hand.

Camilla faced me with a stern expression. Someone wasn't happy with me. I didn't mind. I'd suffer Camilla's wrath if it saved Vlad.

"For the past six months, I've been honing my ability to speak to animals."

Vlad had mentioned it in passing to Camilla, but from the look on Breccan and Rebecca's faces, they'd had no idea.

"That tower is infested with rats," I told them.

"So?"

"So..." I shrugged. "I mean, I could ask for their help. Set them on the vamps."

"Oh, blimey, that's cruel," Alastair said, laughing. He turned to me with a wink. "I love it. What other little tricks do you have stashed in that gorgeous head of yours?"

"Cool it," Camilla muttered. "She's so *very* taken, and if the Count hears you..."

Alastair's eyes twinkled as his laughter grew. "Always loved me a challenge."

I forced myself to swallow. The last thing I needed right now was a distraction. Instead, I closed my eyes and reached out with my power. I honestly wasn't sure how far it could extend. Down in the dungeon, I'd lost track of Weasley after about fifty feet. She and I could never communicate when she was in Vlad's cell.

"I need to be closer," I finally admitted. "But that's fine. When we're inside, I'll rally the rats. Once they swarm the tower, we can take advantage of the distraction and free Vlad. If we come across anyone along the way, we take them out, nice and simple."

"Then we have a plan, as basic as it is," Camilla said. "Everyone on board?"

Breccan cracked his knuckles, Rebecca gave a regal nod, Alastair clapped a hand on my shoulder, and Mateo grunted. Guess that was as good as we were going to get, but I wasn't gonna complain. So long as they helped me kick a little vamp ass and free Vlad, I was one happy panda.

CHAPTER

SIX

THIS WAS IT. My time to shine. The last six months had been in preparation for this moment. Not that I'd known it at the time.

Camilla grasped my hand and pulled me up against the side of the building. The entry stood right around the corner, the very same one Brutus had led me through an hour or so ago. Strange, the turn of events the night had taken.

Two guards stood outside the door, their hands resting on their sword hilts. They reminded me of Queen Elizabeth's Guard, standing sentry in front of Buckingham Palace, except without the dashing red uniforms. Red on vampires was a tad overkill. Even I could admit that much.

Camilla touched my shoulder, then leaned close until her lips brushed my ear. "Is this close enough?"

I nodded. I could feel the minds of the rats inside, their scrambled thoughts as erratic as their twitchy little movements. But there was someone else I wanted to reach out to first.

"Weasley?"

I wasn't sure if she'd even be able to hear me. The dungeon was only one floor down, but maybe that was far enough to disrupt our connection.

"Anna!" Weasley trilled in my head. Her panic immediately sparked mine.

"What's wrong?"

"Queenie's men take Vlad! The guards hurt him!"

Pure, unadulterated rage erupted within me. I gripped Camilla's hand and squeezed. Hard.

She sucked in a sharp breath. "What's wrong?"

"Where is he, Weasley?"

Claws scrambled against the stone floor, and I glanced around the corner in time to watch Weasley come flying out of the tower, her sinuous body hidden in the tower's shadows.

"Anna, come!"

My body lurched forward in response. Only Camilla's grip kept me from dashing out into the open and ruining everything. She gripped my shoulder and pressed me against the stone, then caught my gaze and slowly blinked, pantomiming a deep breath.

I nodded and followed her lead, even though my insides were a churning mess.

"Weasley said the guards have Vlad, and they're hurting him."

"Weasley?" Breccan repeated behind me. "Who or what is a Weasley?"

I crouched down and scooped up my friend the instant she skittered to a stop in front of me. She purred contentedly before climbing onto my shoulder and winding around the back of my neck.

"Bad men have Vlad. Upstairs."

"Where upstairs? Second floor, third?"

Her confusion rankled my mind. Of all the animals I'd talked to, Weasley seemed the least intelligent of them all, and normally that was fine, but right now, I needed to know everything.

"Okay, when we get inside, you lead the way," I told her. We'd just have to make do. Then I turned my mind toward the rats. I couldn't reach them all—the distance was too great for some—but the more I

lured in, the more intrigued the others grew. As word spread among them, the rats ventured closer.

"Please, help me," I sent out into their thoughts. *"These people are bad. They kick you, kill you, trap you. Time to show them what happens to those who hurt you."* I put together an image in my mind of the rats swarming the tower and attacking our enemies. The instant the concept hit them, I felt their interest and determination rise. Maybe teaching rats how to defend themselves and attack vampires wasn't the best idea, but what other option did we have? We were sorely outnumbered. I only hoped vampire blood couldn't infect animals. Because I had a feeling some of these beasts would die here tonight. Guilt slammed into me, but I couldn't let it stop me.

The rats gathered themselves instantly, and without any warning other than a brief flash in my mind, they launched their attack. I listened raptly to the sound of them scurrying through the tower. They raced up the stairs, poured out of tiny hidey-holes in the walls, and dashed through the doorways. It was an infestation unlike anything I'd ever seen before except for the time a hurricane had flushed all the rodents out of downtown New Orleans.

Screams rose instantly. Vampire or not, no one liked rats. And I was sure they liked being attacked by them even less.

"Now!" I whisper-hissed.

Camilla bolted around the corner, and I followed suit, racing toward the entryway. The others pulled up the rear guard, ensuring no one snuck up on us. The two guards spun in manic circles, screaming as they attempted to knock off the rats. I almost laughed as I passed, listening to the rodents' triumphant war cries. Some swore at the vamps, while others promised to gnaw out their eyeballs and bite off their junk. It gave me the heebie jeebies just thinking about it. Suddenly, I was glad they were on our side.

"Up!" Weasley shouted in my head.

I scrambled for the staircase and climbed it two steps at a time. I kept my ears primed for any sound of Vlad, but all I could hear was endless screaming and squeaking.

"Okay, this is disturbing," someone whispered behind me. Alastair, maybe? "But also kick ass." Definitely Alastair.

"It's something alright," Rebecca whispered. "I've never heard of anyone controlling the thoughts of animals before."

That so wasn't what I was doing, but now wasn't the moment to correct her.

"Left!" Weasley yelled.

I latched onto the nearest wall and used it as leverage to turn left. Another corridor full of rooms.

"Go!" Weasley pressed, her little body tightening around the back of my neck. Her clawed paws gripped the collar of my dress, holding on for dear life.

I lunged forward and raced down the hallway, my thoughts a blur. If they so much as hurt Vlad, I would murder every single vampire in this tower. The queen had threatened to harm him if I stepped out of line, but there was no way she knew of my escape yet. By my count, we still had ten minutes remaining until she learned of it. And if the guards already had Vlad, that meant they'd taken him after loading me into the van. Which also meant the queen had planned this.

Sadistic bitch.

I was so going to take pleasure in killing her.

A pained grunt rose to my ears, and I skidded to a stop.

"Here!" Weasley said, her excitement rising. *"Guards take Battikins here."*

"Yeah, I figured that out."

"Hey!" someone shouted.

As a group, we all spun around to find a guard stalking toward us, sword drawn. He marched down the hallway, his face a mask of grim determination. His sheer size alone intimidated the hell out of me. Thank god I wasn't alone. I might have pissed myself at the sight of him.

"Go," Camilla growled. "I've got this."

We locked eyes until I finally nodded. Camilla could handle one guard, and I was needed elsewhere. Like inside this room, murdering anyone who dared touch Vlad.

Camilla dashed down the corridor and engaged the guard, clocking him in the jaw with a tight fist. He reeled back, his sword slicing through the air. I couldn't watch. And I couldn't delay any longer.

I lifted my leg and unleashed every ounce of strength and rage on the door. My foot crashed into the solid wood and sent it flying off the hinges.

With a battle cry worthy of the rats downstairs, I charged forward, Camilla's dagger clasped in my hand. I lifted it, about to start cutting, when the room finally came into focus, and I skidded to a stop.

There, standing in the center of the room, was Vlad. And dangling from his grip was one of the queen's men.

Weasley's warnings had made me imagine the worst-case scenario. I'd pictured Vlad sprawled on the ground, beaten half-to-death, broken, moaning in pain. Except, he was perfectly safe, healthy even. The guard, on the other hand, was a different story.

Vlad turned, and our gazes collided. My chest grew tight, and my breath hitched.

It'd been six months. Six. Fucking. Months. And here he was. Right in front of me. Finally.

Emotions flooded me. Relief. Adoration. Happiness. Gratitude. And I didn't know how to handle it all. I refused to let myself cry— because ew, blood tears—but a sob did catch in my throat and came out like a mangled whimper.

I lowered the dagger and slowly started toward Vlad. With every step, my speed increased until I was practically racing across the room. I didn't care that we were in the middle of escaping, nor did I care that we had an audience. Reaching Vlad was all that mattered.

And it seemed he was of the same mind.

Without hesitation, Vlad reached up and quickly snapped the guard's neck before tossing him aside like a broken rag doll. Then he turned toward me, arms opened wide, and I threw myself into his embrace. The second his arms wrapped around me, I squeezed my eyes shut and sagged against him.

"Anna," he rumbled. "Ah, my Anna."

My body trembled, but I instead focused on the feel of Vlad's fingers smoothing down my hair and the hard swell of his chest pressed against my cheek. Finally, I tipped my head back and gazed up at him, recommitting his features to memory. The sharp angles of his face, the tousled hair, the dark eyes... They seemed darker than I remembered—if that were even possible. Hunger, maybe? I felt it too. A relentless gnawing in the pit of my stomach.

I lifted a hand and ran the pad of my thumb along his lower lip. God, I missed his mouth, and the way it made me feel. Vlad seemed determined to remind me, though, because without another word, he leaned down and kissed me.

Of all our kisses, this one had to be the most tender. The soft press of his lips made my knees weak, and I damn near swooned against him. It wasn't until his hands tried to cup my cheeks that he paused and drew back. His gaze dropped, and I almost burst out laughing at his expression when he spotted Weasley.

"Ah. Your little friend," he commented before stroking her furred cheek. "We've become quite acquainted."

"I like him," Weasley purred in my head.

"Me too, girl. Me too."

"Can we get moving, please?" an exasperated voice muttered, shattering our moment. "In case you two've forgotten, we're sorta in the middle of an escape here? And the clock is ticking."

I sighed, then spun and glared at Alastair. He and Mateo stood half in the room, half in the hallway, while Rebecca and Breccan hovered just behind them. Fine, maybe I'd gotten a bit caught up in the moment.

"And you are?" Vlad demanded, his voice threatening.

"Vlad, Alastair. Alastair, Vlad. He's a friend of Camilla's. Helped me escape. The gentleman behind him is Mateo. Obviously, you know Breccan and Rebecca already."

"Yeah, yeah. Come on, girly. Time to get moving."

"Hmm." Vlad's fingers laced with mine. "Shall we?"

"Oh, yes." I tugged him toward the door, then updated him on the developing situation as quickly as possible. Camilla rejoined our ragtag group, all while wiping blood from her own blade. She and Vlad shared a quick nod before we bolted down the stairs.

The screams had faded. And from the looks of it, my rat friends hadn't won the battle. Unsurprisingly. In a fight, I couldn't imagine rodents beating the undead. But they'd served their purpose, distracting the vamps while we retrieved Vlad. Now it was up to us to escape without being captured *again*. Thankfully, the odds seemed more in our favor now. With all my friends at my side, I felt invincible. I didn't know enough about Mateo and Alastair to gauge their strengths, but I had enough faith in Camilla to know she would bring only the best.

The instant my foot hit the final step, I knew something was wrong. I felt it in the air. Almost like a shimmer of intuition. My head turned to the left just in time to catch sight of a silver blade coming right at me.

"Down!" I screamed.

Vlad's hand gripped my arm hard, and he wrenched me to the ground just as the sword sliced through the air. Right where my head would have been. Strong arms wrapped around my waist and rolled me to the other side, stuffing me up against Camilla. Then they were gone.

I lifted my head just in time to catch Vlad engaging Brutus in a fierce battle.

"Shit!" Camilla hissed. She scrambled back to her feet and snuck a quick peek around the corner. The doorway lay just beyond, and past that, the courtyard. We needed to clear both to reach the road where our van sat waiting. But Brutus's presence told me the other guards were likely here somewhere too.

"We should have killed them," I muttered.

"Oh, sure. Because *that's* what we need. More murder charges," Camilla snapped.

Yeah. There was that. And seeing as how the queen was salivating over my trial, it definitely seemed like bad PR to go around murdering more of her men.

"What do we do?" I demanded.

Camilla cursed under her breath, then shot to her feet and gripped her sword. "What do you think?" Before I could call back to her, she, Breccan, and Rebecca bolted through the door and out into the courtyard. Three guards immediately descended on her as though recognizing she was the bigger threat.

Ah, screw this.

I slapped a hand on the stone floor and launched myself back to my feet. A quick glance behind me showed Vlad and Brutus beating the literal shit out of each other. But their fight was one-on-one while Camilla fought three vampires on her own, and Breccan and Rebecca handled another three.

"Let's go!" I yelled at Alastair and Mateo.

"We go where you go," Alastair said. "Those were Camilla's orders to us. To remain by your side no matter what."

Oh, perfect. Well, I refused to watch either Vlad or Camilla die. While any day of the week, Vlad would have been able to handle his own, he and I were both undernourished and weak. Camilla, on the other hand, was severely outnumbered.

I had to choose.

Growling, I gripped my own blade and raced into the courtyard to help Camilla. Vlad might be weak right now, but his fight was one-on-one. I had to trust he could handle it.

"Get the hell out of here, Anna!" Camilla shouted.

Right. Like that was going to happen. She'd spent months training me to fight. Seemed only useful to put those skills to use now.

"Weasley will help!"

Weasley darted off my shoulder and scurried down my side. I

barely caught sight of her darting in and out of the fight, her teeth flashing as she took chunks out of their ankles.

Curious, I tilted my head back and stared upward. I'd heard stories of the Tower ravens. This wasn't the *actual* tower, which meant the legendary ravens weren't here. But that didn't mean there weren't *other* birds present.

I focused on my power and sent out a call as far as I could possibly push it. It didn't take long before I heard them. First came the *cawing*, then came a swooping black mass, dive-bombing our group from above. I'd never learned the difference between crows and ravens, but I had a feeling these were the former, considering their size and numbers.

The murder descended with a cacophony of noise and flapping wings and chaos erupted, targeting the ones I imagined. Vampires ran amok, crying out as the crows pecked at their faces and eyes. A part of me felt bad. I couldn't imagine being pecked to death felt nice. But at least my plan had worked.

"Good," Camilla rasped as she and the others returned to my side. "Now, let's get Vlad and get the hell out of here."

I gave a single nod, then dashed back into the tower. He and Brutus had utterly destroyed everything in sight. Rubble and dust spread across the floor. Chunks of walls were missing. Broken doorframes. But it was the sight of a blood trail leading into the next room that sparked a fresh wave of panic.

I bolted into the next room, leaving Camilla and the others behind.

At the sight of Brutus standing over an unconscious Vlad, sword raised above his head, I screamed and launched myself between them. Stupid. I know. But I wasn't thinking. The only thought in my head was to protect Vlad. I loved him so damn much.

Silver flashed in my periphery a mere second before I felt it. The icy grip of pain. It ricocheted through me and nearly brought me to my knees. Someone screamed. It might have been me. But honestly, the world had gone a little... fuzzy. It could have come from anyone.

My head dropped and I stared at the blade wedged into my side. Strange to see something buried in you. Something that didn't belong. My whole body rebelled against me, and I staggered backward.

"Huh." Brutus leered at me. "I'd meant to kill your lover boy there. But you'll do."

I lifted my head and eyed him. This wouldn't kill me. But it sure did hurt like a son of a bitch.

It wasn't until Brutus reached for his sword hilt that I understood his intention. He meant to rip it free of my side and finish me off.

Oh, hell no.

Before he could grasp the weapon, I lashed out with my foot and clipped him in the knee. The strike took Brutus by surprise, and with a small cry, he dropped to one knee. I grabbed the hilt, sucked in a deep breath, then ripped it out of my body.

The scream that erupted from my mouth deafened me. But I couldn't stop to acknowledge the agony. I had to finish this. If I showed an ounce of weakness, Brutus would win.

"Anna!" Camilla screamed.

I lifted my dazed head and caught sight of her trying to fight her way back to me. Seemed the other guards had chased us inside. Camilla, Breccan, Rebecca, Alastair, and Mateo were locked in another battle.

Time to end this then.

Sword in hand, I faced Brutus. I already had two murder charges against me. What was a third? I gripped the hilt and lifted my arms, my body swaying with pain.

Understanding seemed to dawn within Brutus. His eyes widened, and he attempted to scramble away. But I was quicker.

With a battle cry, I swung the blade. And it sliced through his neck like butter. A brief moment of euphoria chased away the pain, but it didn't last long. Neither did the satisfaction of watching Brutus's head thump across the floor.

"Anna?" Vlad's soothing voice rose behind me.

I stumbled back from Brutus's body and turned, bloody sword in hand.

Vlad's gaze swept over my length, and his jaw tightened at the sight of my wound. I knew it wasn't fatal. Joy of being dead already. But that didn't mean it didn't hurt like a mofo. I needed blood. And more than bagged blood. I needed a warm vein stat if I was going to heal and avoid passing out.

"Stay here," Vlad insisted, his voice vibrating with rage.

Then he vanished from sight.

I slowly turned to check on Camilla and instead, found Vlad sweeping through the room. One by one, heads flew. Guess we weren't playing around anymore. What was the saying? It was all fun and games until someone lost an eye? Except, in this case, maybe my liver? Or spleen? I really didn't understand anatomy whatsoever. Either way, Vlad seemed determined to end this skirmish once and for all.

When the last head fell, Camilla and Vlad both rushed to my side.

"Are you okay?" Camilla demanded.

"Um. No?" I mean... I was pretty sure I'd lost like half my blood. The pool at my feet kept growing. That was bad, right?

Breccan appeared on my other side, his hands hovering over my wound. "It's deep. She needs blood."

"Not now," Vlad growled. One of his arms knocked out my knees while the other cradled my back. "Camilla. Get us the hell out of here."

"Of course."

Before we could take off, Weasley scurried up Camilla's body and wound around her neck. Weasley watched me from behind a curtain of Camilla's dark hair, concern brimming in her beady little eyes. I wanted to tell her I'd be okay, but I couldn't make my lips move. Honestly, I was just relieved to be with Vlad again. Sad, right? Here I was, bleeding out, and I was *relieved*. Because Vlad and I were together again. There had to be something seriously wrong with me.

Well, other than the obvious, I mean.

CHAPTER
SEVEN

"GET HER INSIDE," Camilla ordered the instant the van came into view. She swept ahead of us and yanked open the back doors, Weasley still riding her shoulders.

Vlad's arms tightened around me, and he hopped in. I barely felt any movement, nestled up against him as I was. Thankfully, this time, there weren't any handcuffs chaining us to the benches and we were free to move about the cabin. Not that I was doing any roaming in my condition. My side burned with agony and a phantom pain lingered, almost as though I could still feel the blade wedged into my side. This was definitely a *one star, do not recommend* moment.

The doors slammed shut behind us and I glanced up to find we were alone. Alastair and Mateo had crowded into the front with Camilla, while Rebecca and Breccan hopped into the car they'd arrived in—choosing to give us some privacy, perhaps? Or maybe they were her second and third set of eyes. We'd certainly need them to successfully escape this mess.

I didn't even want to imagine what we'd left behind. The queen was going to shit kittens.

"I admit, I'm not a fan of these vehicles," Vlad commented as he carried me across the cabin.

A small smile tugged at my lips. "Me neither. But at least there aren't any stakes this time. Huge improvement. Maybe next time we can splurge for comfier seats."

Vlad chuckled, then took a seat on the bench closest to the front. He eased me off his lap and helped me sit. I bit back a gasp when the movement jostled my side, but the scowl on Vlad's face told me he saw through me.

"How do you feel?"

"Peachy," I muttered.

After a moment's pause, he brushed my tangled hair out of my face and peered into my eyes. "How did this even happen?"

"You were unconscious, and Brutus was about to take you out..." I couldn't say *cut off your head*. It broke my heart to even think about it.

Understanding darkened Vlad's face. "You jumped between us?"

I gave a half-shrug. "What else could I have done?"

Vlad dropped his head into his hands and released a slow breath. I slowly leaned down and rested my head on his curved shoulder. A pungent smell filled my nose, and I held my breath. It wasn't Vlad's fault that he'd been imprisoned for six months. Hell, if they hadn't made me wash up for the queen and tonight's court case, we *both* would have stunk.

"I suppose asking you to stop putting yourself in harm's way would fall on deaf ears?"

"Yup," I murmured.

"Very well. Then let me see what we're dealing with."

I lifted my head from his shoulder and slowly turned, careful not to aggravate the wound. Injuries like these hurt, but thankfully, they weren't lethal. Yay for immortality?

Vlad's fingers brushed my wound, and I choked back a pained moan. I hadn't dared to steal a peek yet. Hell, I didn't *want* to look. I'd been there. I'd felt the sword embedded in my side. Felt the agony of ripping it out. One didn't forget that sort of pain anytime soon. And seeing the wound would only etch it into my memory. No thank you. Sometimes ignorance truly was bliss.

"It's healing nicely," Vlad murmured, his dark head bobbing as he inspected the wound. "A little blood would help speed up the process."

I nodded, my saliva glands instantly pooling at the thought of fresh blood. "Think Camilla thought to bring us a fresh bottle or two?" Or five.

Vlad hummed his dissent. "Unlikely. Thankfully, I have a better suggestion."

"You do?" I quirked a brow.

"Don't I always?"

I snickered, then winced when my side muscles clenched. Yeah, he pretty much always had a plan. A trait I greatly appreciated and loved about him. Except, this wasn't really a plan so much as a solution. But hey, tomato-tomahto.

Vlad cupped the back of my head and gently guided me to his neck. I shivered, desperate to sink my teeth into him, but also... honestly... a touch repulsed. Hey, with a nose as sensitive as mine, the slightest smells were enough to turn my stomach.

It wasn't that I didn't appreciate his offer, because I absolutely did. Every part of me screamed *yes*. Especially considering how badly I wanted him in more carnal ways. I *loved* biting Vlad, likely more than I loved being bitten by him. There was something so primitive about sinking my fangs into him and claiming him as mine. But he was far older than me. And there were dangers associated with sharing blood with an ancient. Vlad wasn't a relic, but he was more than five hundred years old. Not that his age had stopped us in the past, even though we both knew it was taboo. Sometimes, a girl just needed to bite her boy toy. And vice versa. But maybe it could wait until after he'd showered?

"Vlad..." I changed position to rest my forehead against his.

"It's been six months," he whispered, as though I didn't already know that. "Anna, I—"

When he didn't finish his sentence, I leaned back and eyed him. "You, what?"

Emotion flickered across his face. I couldn't read his thoughts, but I could guess the direction they'd taken. We'd nearly lost one another. If not for Camilla, who knew what would have happened tonight. The guards had taken Vlad and likely not to share a cup of tea. As for me, the trial probably would have resulted in my execution. Because Genevieve just plain sucked.

"I need you," he said simply.

Usually, I bit first and asked forgiveness later, but today, I just... couldn't. Not that I didn't find Vlad sexy, because of course he was drop-dead gorgeous and would be even if covered in manure. But sinking my teeth into him was a whole other ball game.

So, regardless of the temptation rising within me, I inched back on the bench. I would heal regardless, with or without blood. With would merely speed up the process. And I absolutely understood his need to see me healed and healthy. But honestly, this could wait until we'd both showered. Preferably together.

"What's wrong?" Vlad asked.

I cleared my throat, unprepared for this conversation. How did I tell him he stunk to high heaven without insulting him? It certainly wouldn't inspire any romantic feelings.

"I love you," I said, speaking aloud the words I'd been terrified to say six months ago. Now, I felt like I needed to say them every day.

Vlad's face smoothed, and his dark eyes warmed. "And I you."

"But..."

A fresh frown creased his brow. Clearly, he hadn't been expecting that. "But what?"

"Um. Well..." I fake-coughed, then ran a hand through my hand. "You, uh..."

When I drifted off, his brows shot upward. "Anna, you know you can tell me anything."

Sure, he said that *now*. I gave an awkward chuckle, then buried my face in my palms before blurting out, "You smell really bad!"

Silence.

After a few seconds, I snuck a peek through my finger slats. Vlad stared at me with wide, unblinking eyes. Then, once our gazes met, he burst into laughter, something he rarely did. The sound was contagious, and I couldn't keep myself from laughing along with him.

Only I would choose *this* moment to care about hygiene, right? I mean, what the hell was wrong with me? We'd been separated for six months. During that time, I'd never stopped fantasizing about our reunion. And in my fantasies, I'd never *once* imagined my nose killing the mood. But I didn't want to force anything. I didn't want to hold my breath and bite him just because he'd asked.

So, instead, we laughed.

We laughed because otherwise, I was sure we'd cry. Or at least, I would. This year hadn't been kind to me. Or Vlad.

The window separating us from the front slid open, and Camilla's head popped up. "You guys okay back there?"

"Perfectly fine," Vlad said in a reassuring voice. He clasped my hands and brought them to his mouth, placing a series of gentle kisses along my knuckles.

"Good. Just checking to make sure you hadn't gone crazy or something."

"This woman will always drive me crazy," Vlad teased, a twinkle shining in his eye. "I'm quite sure it's her purpose in life."

I nodded. Absolutely. "Just remember that in fifty years when I've turned your hair gray."

"Impossible," he muttered before dragging me close. "Now, can I at least kiss you?"

I wrinkled my nose and gave a put-upon sigh. "If you must."

"Oh, I must."

"I suppose I could just hold my breath."

"You are undoubtedly a brat, do you know that?" Vlad teased.

I booped the tip of his nose and grinned. "Definitely."

"Get. Over. Here."

Mm, there was something sinfully delicious about that deep voice of his. So much so that I overlooked his rank smell and leaned forward. The instant our lips touched, the world vanished. I forgot about the queen and our imprisonment. I forgot about the dozen or so vamps we'd left dead back in the tower. I forgot about Brutus and the feel of the sword lopping off his head. I forgot about everything except me and Vlad. At that moment, he was the only thing I wanted. And lucky for me, I was the only thing he wanted. Maybe life hadn't been kind, but Fate had made up for it by bringing us together.

BY THE TIME the van finally stopped, I was exhausted. I'd dozed most of the ride, my feet resting on Vlad's lap and my head against the bench. The blood loss had really taken it out of me. And sadly, no amount of rest appeared to be helping. I certainly needed blood. And soon, hopefully.

Vlad touched my thigh to rouse me. "Anna."

I mumbled something incoherent about not wanting to go to school today. Vlad chuckled, then eased my legs off him and rose to open the doors. I sat up with a sigh and stared outside. Camilla, Weasley, Alastair, and Mateo stood just beyond, waiting for us to climb out. From the looks of it, Breccan and Rebecca hadn't returned yet. I dragged myself to my feet and staggered to the van door. My wound had thankfully finished healing, but I felt like a zombie.

Vlad grasped my waist and eased me down to the ground, his hands careful not to push hard on my side.

"You okay?" Alastair asked, sidling up next to us. Without asking permission, he grabbed Vlad's arm and unlocked the metal bracelet latched around his wrist. The one keeping him from being able to use his powers.

I eyed his movements, finally wondering just how Camilla had convinced a guard to assist with our escape. All questions for later. There were other, more important things I needed to do first.

"Yeah," I said, finally answering Alastair's question. "Just need to get cleaned up and drink some blood."

Alastair shot Vlad a perplexed look, one I didn't have the energy to decipher, then nodded and strode through a nearby wrought iron gate. A brick fence surrounded us, separating us from a cobblestone path leading up to a massive mansion. Could this be the safe house Camilla had mentioned? From the looks of it, we were the only house in the vicinity. She certainly would have aimed for privacy and seclusion.

"Have you found yourself another pet?" Vlad asked.

My gaze immediately darted to Weasley. She sat perched on Camilla's shoulders, but her eyes were all for me. Thankfully, she seemed content riding shotgun on Camilla, who didn't appear to be complaining about the circumstances. Gave me a break and a chance to be with Vlad without spectators.

A soft smile curved my lips. "Weasley's my friend, not a pet."

"Hmm." Vlad leaned down and brushed a kiss against the top of my head. "Not the pet I was referring to."

Huh? I turned with a frown to find him now staring across the manicured lawn at Alastair, who'd turned to wait for me to catch up.

Oh. That. Right.

"Just a little hero complex, I'm sure," I said.

"That's usually reserved for the damsel in distress."

I shrugged. "Shall we go inside?"

Vlad gripped my hand and led me toward the front door. Once we reached the porch, I felt the barrier.

"Come in," Camilla said.

And just like that, presto. No more barrier. Crazy how the world worked. All it took was a simple invitation.

"Anna, I should warn you, there's someone—"

A shriek echoed through the house. Every single vampire around me reacted, crouching defensively. Footsteps thundered toward me, and my head whipped around, tracking the movement. The blur came from the left, and before I could brace myself, someone crashed into me, and we fell to the ground in a tangle of limbs.

"Girl!" Lucy squealed in my ear.

I cringed away from the sound of her lush heartbeat but found my arms immediately wrapping around her. "Lucy!"

"Oh my god," Lucy said, completely oblivious to the surrounding group of vampires. "Oh. My. God. I could kill you! I love you so much, but right now, I hate you! And where the hell have you been!" A hand slapped my arm. "You were supposed to be here *hours* ago. And why are you such a mess?"

"Sorry. I couldn't leave Vlad behind."

Lucy pulled away from me, as though only now realizing we weren't alone. Her head lifted, and she stared up at Vlad. Without a word, she climbed to her feet and took his hand in hers, giving it a single pump before she punched his shoulder.

"Dude. You smell," she said before turning back to me. "What happened? One moment you were telling me to go to Mississippi, the next, the news was reporting your arrest!"

"Well, guess you already know what happened then," I deadpanned.

Lucy rolled her eyes. "You know I need more information than that."

Sigh. As did the others, most likely. "Can we fill you in later? I'm dead on my feet here, and Vlad and I need to shower."

"Of course, of course." Lucy gripped my hand and hauled me to my feet. "I just... I really missed you, and I'm so relieved to see you again."

Warmth rushed through me. It was damn good to see her again too. Lucy and I hadn't been apart longer than a day since we'd become best friends.

"Okay. Go get cleaned up." She turned to Vlad with a sour expression. "Seriously. The shower's upstairs. There's a room set up for you two, though it doesn't have much. We honestly weren't sure we'd be able to pull this off—"

"What's this 'we' shit, Batman?" Camilla demanded in a teasing tone. "I didn't see you out there risking life and limb."

"Uh, because you wouldn't let me," Lucy retorted playfully. "Remember?"

"Hey, I wasn't the one holding you back."

"Yeah, well, you didn't argue with him either!"

"Um, guys?" I asked, waving a hand in their faces. Seemed Camilla and Lucy had bonded in our time apart, and I wasn't quite sure how I felt about that. Grateful, I suppose, but also, maybe a bit jealous? "The shower?"

"Right." Lucy hopped to attention and started toward the stairs. "This way! Camilla can show the others where they'll be staying."

Vlad and I trailed after Lucy, but she seemed to climb the stairs with an energy I lacked, so I fell behind. I wasn't used to that. As a vampire, I moved with speeds she couldn't imagine. So when she reached the landing without us, she turned and frowned at me.

"Anna? Stupid question, but are you okay?"

"Tired," I wheezed out.

One of Vlad's hands touched the small of my back. He didn't push me up the stairs, but that solid weight encouraged me to keep moving.

"I could carry you if you'd like," he offered.

"So long as it involves carrying me into the shower with you."

Vlad's chuckle echoed through the stairwell. "Now *that* can be arranged."

"Oh good, glad to see nothing's changed," Lucy taunted.

I wanted to lob back a retort, but I literally didn't have the stamina. Instead, I merely waved at her. Vlad's arms came around me, and without breaking stride, he lifted and settled me against his chest.

"The bathroom?" he asked Lucy.

"You guys have the master suite. Head to the end of the hall and take a right. There's an en suite bathroom that Camilla and I thought you might appreciate."

"Thank you."

Lucy placed a hand on Vlad's arm as we passed. "Don't feel like you have to rush back to us. We know it hasn't been easy for you guys. Take your time."

Did I mention I loved this girl? Platonically, of course. But I loved her, nonetheless.

"We appreciate that," Vlad said.

I caught Lucy's eye as we moved past and smiled. We truly did have the best people in our lives. Few would have risked the queen's wrath to rescue us. But Lucy and Camilla had.

And I would never forget it.

CHAPTER

EIGHT

VLAD BEGRUDGINGLY LOWERED me to my feet once we'd ensconced ourselves in the bedroom. Honestly, I didn't care much for the décor. Hardly enough to even spare a glance, and I only cared about us. We were finally alone. And together. And... *insert blissful sigh*.

I'd dreamed of this moment for so long. We'd been alone in the back of the van, but I didn't count that. Not with three vampires riding up front, listening to every word we said. Of course, the house wasn't private either, but it at least offered the illusion.

Vlad stared down at me, his relief practically palpable.

For a moment, I did nothing but stare back. This moment felt a bit too surreal. In a single night, we'd broken out of the tower and escaped the queen's evil clutches.

"Promise me this isn't a dream," I whispered.

Vlad rested his brow against mine and closed his eyes. I counted the dark lashes resting against his pale cheeks, afraid to close my eyes in case this *did* turn out to be a dream.

"We're really here right now?" I asked. "Together?"

"Yes."

A shiver rolled down my spine. This was *real*. It had to be because I couldn't handle any other outcome.

"I hate her, Vlad," I said, my voice low and threatening. "Like more than I've ever hated anyone."

"More than your father?" he jibed.

"Oh, ha, ha. And yes. More than my father since I don't want to murder him." Then I amended with, "Most days."

Vlad cupped my cheeks, then pushed my hair back from my face. "I'm just relieved to see you're alive. Those were the darkest months of my life."

"And mine."

"If not for your rodent friend—"

"Weasley," I told him. "And she's a weasel, not a rodent."

"She was the only reason I knew you were alive. Only you would send a rodent on your behalf."

"Pfft." I rolled my eyes. "You can't make that statement. We only *just* learned about my newfound talent."

"Yes, but it fits your personality. I was merely relieved you didn't send a rat to do your bidding."

I chuckled. If it weren't for Weasley, I would have. A girl had to make do with what limited resources she had.

"What about you?" I asked. "Why did the guards take you tonight?"

"I'm sure you've already ascertained that for yourself." He brushed his nose against mine. "Thankfully, they only sent two guards."

Two guards. For Vlad? I scoffed and shook my head. They'd stuck me with eight. But for Vlad—the infamous Dracula—they'd used two guards. Idiots.

"One left to investigate the commotion you caused, and I took advantage."

Come to think of it, Vlad had snapped that guard's neck, meaning he was still alive. He'd wake up tomorrow night, healed. Sadly, the others wouldn't. Once upon a time, that might have upset me. Not anymore. After mine and the queen's little chat, I couldn't be bothered to feel guilt for her people. They'd made their beds by supporting her. Callous? Maybe. But they'd chosen to follow her orders, and I could only imagine the things Queen Genevieve asked them to do on her behalf. I.e., killing Vlad.

"Come." Vlad took my hand and led me toward what I assumed was the bathroom.

He pushed open the door and together, we stepped inside. The instant my gaze found the massive, jetted tub, I squealed. Damn, Lucy *knew* me alright. She knew my adoration of anything jetted. And since it looked like it could fit about four people, it suited me well. So much so that the sight of it chased away my exhaustion. Excitement fueled me now, and that was just fine. I could get by on that for a few more minutes.

"Oh, hell yeah!" I scrambled toward the edge and peered into the depths. This thing was like a hot tub! And I couldn't wait to try it out. We just needed to shower first.

I gripped Vlad's wrist and practically dragged him to the nearby glass shower. I yanked open the door and turned the taps. The instant the temperature went from scalding to steamy, I stripped naked, kicking the horrible gray dress to the side of the room.

Vlad's eyes widened and a grin stretched his lips. "Well then."

"Hurry up!" I urged.

When he didn't immediately start undressing, I growled and started tugging on his clothes. Hopefully Camilla or Lucy had thought to bring us supplies because these clothes were going right into the trash bin. I yanked his shirt open and practically ripped it apart, a tad eager to get him under the spray so we could then enjoy ourselves in the tub.

"Anna," Vlad chuckled, his hands slowly working on his belt.

Perplexed by his new sloth-like movements, I popped open his fly and shoved his pants to the ground. He kicked off his undergarments, then stood before me in all his naked gloriousness. My eyes lingered—because *of course* they lingered. Vlad was no average schmoe when it came to girth or length, and after six unwillingly celibate months, I wanted to pounce on him like a randy little kitten.

But there were other priorities we had to take care of first. Namely, cleanliness.

I took his hands and pulled him into the shower alongside me. The instant the spray hit us, we moaned in unison. This was heaven. Nirvana. The Promised Land. Paradise. Whatever word best described this bliss. If it weren't for the tub beckoning me just outside the shower stall, I might have stayed here forever—or until the water ran cold.

But... the tub did indeed beckoneth.

I collected the nearby body wash and shampoo and set to work. It took more willpower than I possessed to focus on my task and not Vlad's body. I had to keep telling myself that I would enjoy it in great detail once we hit the jets.

Vlad returned the favor and washed me from head to toe, lingering contentedly in certain places that had me burning hotter than the water. I kept chanting in my head: *jetted tub, jetted tub, jetted tub* as though that would cool me off. Yeah, right.

So distracted by my thoughts, I didn't realize Vlad had leaned down and pressed his mouth against my ear until his fangs grazed my lobe. Desire shot through me like a lightning bolt.

"I think we're clean enough," he suggested.

Uh-huh. Agreed. Time to get dirty.

"Stay here," Vlad murmured. Then he stepped out of the shower and strode across the tiled floor, buck-ass naked, and started the bath. He dipped a hand beneath the spray, adjusted the taps, then tested it again. Once content, he returned to the shower. The door had barely clicked closed behind him when he placed his hands against the wall on either side of my head and leaned in, claiming my mouth in what could only be described as a panty-dropping kiss. Luckily for me, my panties were already long gone, giving him full access when his hand slid up my inner thigh.

He drew back from the kiss and tilted his head, exposing his throat. "Before we do anything, you need blood."

And this time, excitement zipped through my veins.

"You sure?" I whispered. "You haven't fed properly in six months. I could find blood elsewhere."

The spark in Vlad's gaze told me everything I needed to know. One, I wasn't going anywhere. And two, he wanted my fangs buried in him. Who was I to deny him—and me—that pleasure?

"The tub will take a bit to fill," he commented.

I nodded. It was practically a pool. I was just surprised we hadn't run out of hot water yet. Someone had excellent plumbing.

"Anna." Vlad pinned me with the lustiest of lusty stares. "Bite. Me."

I slid my arms around his neck and pressed myself against him, reveling in the feel of my nipples grazing his flesh. They pebbled in response, as eager as the rest of me. When I nestled myself in the crook of Vlad's neck, one of his hands immediately rose to cradle the back of my head. I felt his breath hitch—which said a lot considering we didn't need to breathe—and his body tensed. Oh, he wanted this. And was trying his damnedest to hold still.

I laid my mouth on his neck and shuddered with anticipation. A part of me wanted to sink my teeth right this second. But my brain took this opportunity to remind me that it *had* been six months since we'd last seen each other and to take my time. To draw this out. To enjoy every second of it.

I placed a gentle kiss against his throat, right where his pulse would have been if he weren't undead.

A strange sound escaped Vlad's mouth, one I took as encouragement.

When my teeth finally found their place, his other arm came around my waist, clutching me to him. I slipped my fingers through his wet hair and simultaneously bit.

Vlad choked back a guttural groan, but I didn't. Were it not for the warm ambrosia rushing into my mouth, I might have even cried out. As it was, my fingers fisted in his hair to help me hold on for dear life.

It was overwhelming, the emotions rushing through me. So much so that I almost pulled back. Vlad's grip held me in place, though, his arm like a steel band. I couldn't move, nor did I want to. Instead, I surrendered to it.

After a few more swallows, Vlad's hold on me loosened, and I eased back, not that I'd wanted to. But I knew the rules and how much of his blood I could consume.

"Feeling better?" he asked, his voice hoarse.

I nodded. I felt great now, thanks to him.

"No more exhaustion?"

"None whatsoever," I whispered.

"Good."

His mouth came crashing down on mine, and my lips instantly parted to allow him to deepen the kiss. Oh, goodie. Time for my other favorite part!

With his mouth still on mine, Vlad shut off the shower. But before I could complain, one of his arms swept out my legs. He caught me just before I fell and carried me to the tub. All without breaking our kiss. Now *that* was talent.

He stepped over the edge and eased us into the almost scalding water. Our lips parted long enough for him to turn off the taps and activate the jets. The second those concentrated water streams hit our bodies, we both moaned. God, could this night get any better?

The gleam in Vlad's eyes promised me that yes, yes it could.

Without a word, he ducked beneath the water. I could barely see him due to the jets, but I could certainly *feel* him. His hands found my thighs and he spread them wide. I jolted when his mouth found me, his tongue laving at my most sensitive parts. Holy shit! No one had ever gone down on me in a tub before. Why would they? Air had been sorta crucial when I was human. But as a vampire, Vlad didn't need to breathe, and he seemed quite happy to make use of that talent right now.

I gripped the edge of the tub and let my head fall back.

Sweet merciful Zeus, heat and ecstasy built within me until it reached a crucial level. My orgasm slammed into me with the force of a jackhammer, and I cried out, the jets muffling the sound. I trembled in the water, my core undulating with my release.

Vlad's fingers joined the party next, eagerly preparing me for the main event, all while his mouth continued devouring me.

After a second smaller but equally pleasurable orgasm, Vlad surfaced. Water dripped from his hair and poured down his face, but he barely paused to wipe his eyes before stealing another heated kiss. I practically climbed into his lap, eager to hop on board Vlad's cock.

It seemed Vlad had other plans though.

Grasping my hips, he turned me around and bent me over the edge of the tub. He rarely fucked me from behind, I think because he liked to watch my face, but tonight seemed to be the exception. And I had a feeling I knew why.

He positioned me until the jets hit me in just the right spot. I gasped and clutched the tub just as he thrust into me. His hands cupped my hips and held me in place, ensuring the jets worked their magic while he worked his.

The force of the water brought me to an instant climax, and this time I couldn't bite back my cry. I was sure everyone had heard it downstairs, but I also didn't give a fuck. Not right now. Maybe later.

Vlad moved within me, careful to time his thrusts with the water so it didn't slosh on the floor. Slowly, he picked up speed, his fingers almost bruising my ass cheeks. Just another thing I didn't care about, not when Vlad's cock felt so good.

He drove himself into me, the force pushing me into the jet stream once more. A guttural cry ripped free of my throat and I bowed my head to keep from making too much noise. Holy cow. After tonight, I would never look at Jacuzzis the same way.

"Anna," Vlad grunted.

I glanced over my shoulder and caught sight of him. His eyes were darker than night, his jaw tight. I knew what he wanted. What he *needed*. So I nodded.

Holding my hips, he spun me around. His hands slid up my back and lifted me until my chest was pressed against his. I locked my legs around his hips and began to move, eagerly pumping against him. He wasn't far off. I could tell from the hazed look in his eyes and his gritted jaw. I cupped the back of his head and pressed it to my throat.

Once his teeth were positioned, I quickened my rhythm and tightened my inner walls around him. Vlad groaned and briefly thickened within me, then sank his teeth into my neck the instant he succumbed to his own climax. Sharing blood was magical between partners, but it also heightened an orgasm. And from the contented look on Vlad's face, it was exactly what he'd needed.

Once the ecstasy passed, Vlad slowly lifted his head. Our gazes met, and I couldn't help but smile. Some days, I couldn't believe he was my partner. The world knew him as Dracula. They thought him cruel and evil. But me? I knew the truth. Vlad was caring and giving. He put my needs before his. He *loved* me. I loved him.

I pressed a gentle kiss to his mouth, then gently rose off him. My legs nearly gave out, which made me laugh. He'd certainly shown me a good time, and my poor trembling knees were evidence of that.

Eventually, we'd need to drain the tub and shower again. But not now. I wasn't done with Vlad yet, and from the twinkle in his eye, it seemed he wasn't done either.

CHAPTER
NINE

I awoke in a cellar stuffed to the brim with coffins. After Vlad's and my reunion last night, we'd been forced to race the rising sun and tuck ourselves away. Camilla, Alastair, and Mateo had just been getting themselves settled when Vlad and I burst inside. They'd shared knowing glances, but I hadn't cared. Strange how things had changed. There'd been a time where it would have horrified me to know others had overheard us having sex. Now, I just wanted to tell them to get some headphones and give us our privacy. Lucky for me, the impending sunrise had knocked us all out before anyone could make a rude comment.

And thanks to my ability to rise earlier than the others, I didn't have to face any of them until later tonight.

After six months of captivity, I relished my freedom. But I still hated coffins. Pretty sure I'd enjoyed my prison bed more than this. Coffins were just too cramped and—well, everyone knew my complaints already. No need to rehash them all when there was literally nothing that could be done about it. Not until we returned home.

I palmed my coffin lid back and rose. There was an eerie silence to the place, which I supposed was to be expected. Especially when ninety-five percent of the inhabitants were all dead to the world. I climbed out and quickly ascended the staircase. Definitely weird waking up in a cellar instead of an attic. But England was a whole other world than Louisiana.

Lucy's fragrance tickled my nose, and when I opened the door, I found her standing in the hallway, tapping her toe impatiently.

"Finally!" She lunged forward and tackled me in a bear hug. "I've been *dying* to see you. I could barely sleep."

I chuckled and returned the embrace, sinking against her with a contented sigh. We were still in a foreign country, but hugging Lucy was like coming home. The scent of her fruity shampoo and lilac deodorant brought back all the memories.

Once she'd decided she'd had her fill of our hug, she released me and clamped down on my hand. "Come on. I've got everything set out for you."

Everything? What exactly did that mean?

But before I could even ask, Lucy dragged me down a narrow hallway and into a living room the same size as the cellar. She'd drawn all the curtains and blinds except for one window, which let a stream of light into the kitchen, which, thankfully, was nowhere near me. She pushed me down onto a plush leather sofa, then gestured to the table before me.

"First up, blood." She grabbed a bottle, popped the lid, and poured me a glass.

I blinked at her. Before my arrest, Lucy would never have been caught dead doing something like this for me. The girl was as skittish as a bunny around blood. My fangs weren't to come anywhere near her veins, and I respected that. Just because I was a vampire didn't mean I could go around biting whoever the hell I wanted. Not that I wanted to. Lucy's and my relationship worked best without that element.

I took the glass from her and sampled the product. It wasn't fresh from the tap, but it also wasn't bagged. These bottles were produced nightly, compliments of humans willing to donate a few pints for some cash. So fresh, but not "right from the tap" fresh.

"Next, a makeover." She pointed at a small foot spa sitting across the floor, already filled to the brim with hot water. "Then we're gonna talk."

That sounded ominous. "About what?"

She frowned. "No! Just talk. Catch up. Shoot the breeze."

I quickly downed the blood. Sounded like I'd need the energy. "You do realize that I don't have anything to catch you up on, right? I've sort of been in prison for half a year."

"Oh, please." Lucy swatted my arm. "You know I have questions. And... so do your subscribers."

She picked up her phone, which was attached to a tripod, and sat it on the table across from us.

I sighed, already exhausted, and I'd just woken up. She couldn't be serious about this, could she? Vlad and I were technically on the lam. It didn't seem wise to broadcast my whereabouts. Surely the queen knew about all my social media accounts. And after last night, it seemed wise to assume they were being monitored.

"Lucy, put your phone away. I'm not doing an interview."

"You *have* to!" she complained. "Anna, you have so many people out there rooting for you. They were protesting in your name, demanding your release. They need to know you're safe from the queen."

"Except, we're not safe from the queen. Not by a long shot. And doing an interview puts all of us at risk. So, no."

Lucy's bottom lip jutted out, but eventually, she slowly nodded. "Yeah. I guess that makes sense."

"If we're ever able to resolve this matter, I promise I'll do an interview then. But right now, I'd be endangering everyone in this house. Including you."

She nodded and tucked her long, dark tresses behind her ears.

"Now, how about *you* tell *me* what's been happening these past six months."

"Oh…" She blew out a heavy breath. "There really isn't much to tell you."

"Bullshit."

"I'm not really sure what to say," she said. "Most of our time was spent coming up with a plan to free you and Vlad. Camilla and I reached out to Breccan and Rebecca, and they were happy to help, thank goodness. I guess Breccan found his mate about seven months ago, so he's been a bit busy. But when we asked him to help, he dropped everything."

Aww. How cute. But speaking of mates… "What about you and Sam?"

Lucy's face pinched. "I don't want to talk about him."

Uh-oh. Trouble in paradise? When last we'd spoken, she'd learned that a werewolf's definition of a mate differed from a vampire's. For us vamps, it meant together forever, true love, and all that jazz. Apparently, for a werewolf, it literally meant *mate*. Someone to reproduce with. No emotional attachment. I'd told Lucy to ask Sam if that was the case, instead of just assuming. Sadly, Vlad and I had been arrested before they could have that conversation.

"Well, give me something, girl," I said. "I'm dying over here."

"Oh!" She bounced in her seat. "Your father and his wife divorced!"

I swear, that had my head turning so fast, I got whiplash. I slammed my glass down on the table and stared at Lucy. "What?"

"Yeah! Whatever you said to him the night before you were arrested must have resonated with him because the next thing we knew, he and Christina were separated. Last I heard, the divorce just became official. Caleb thinks she said something about you that pissed him off, and he walked out."

"Caleb?" I demanded. "You've been in contact with my brother?"

"And mother. Both have been incredibly worried about you."

Oh, that I highly doubted. My brother didn't give a shit about anyone other than himself and his failed football career. I could see my mother caring. She was my mother, after all. But I highly doubted she understood. There were a few missing screws in that head of hers. This was the woman who had introduced herself to Vlad while wearing a Jesus apron and a cross, after all.

"Did you tell them about all this?" I waved to the house.

"No. Camilla and I thought it'd be best not to share our plan with anyone else. We were worried about it getting back to the queen. Not that we thought your family would betray us. More like, the fewer the better. Security and whatnot."

Okay, so my family still thought I was in jail. I could deal with that for now. The less phone calls I had to make, the better.

"Tell me about Alastair and Mateo."

"Oh, boy. Where to begin? I guess Camilla and Alastair go way back. She knew he was a member of the queen's guard, one who wasn't particularly devoted to the queen. Not like others."

Mm-hmm. Like Brutus.

"At first, we weren't sure if she should reach out to him. What if *he* turned us in? Eventually, we decided the risk was worth it. We needed someone on the inside if we were going to pull this off. Especially considering I couldn't help much beyond merely planning. Thankfully, Alastair had been following you on social media, so he knew all about you and was willing to break a few rules. I don't know much about Mateo. Only that he and Alastair are companions. He assured Camilla that Mateo would be helpful."

"So, you assembled the team?" I asked. "Camilla, Breccan, Rebecca, Alastair, and Mateo all came together to help us escape?" Man, that was a mouthful.

Lucy nodded. It surprised me to see tears welling in her eyes. "I couldn't just not do anything, you know? It killed me to think of you locked up. Camilla wanted to go right after the queen, but I convinced her that would be suicide. Sam helped calm her down, enough so that the rational side of her brain could kick in."

"Sam was a part of all this too?"

Lucy's face darkened. "Yeah. Much to my dismay."

Oh boy. This sounded really bad. "What happened between you two?"

She sighed, then reached for a second bottle, one I quickly identified as wine the instant she popped the cork. "I don't even know. So much. And yet, nothing at the same time."

Well, that was a conundrum. "Start from where we left off."

She bit her bottom lip, then sighed and flopped back on the couch. "Do you remember what we discussed before your arrest?"

"Sure. You wanted me there while you guys discussed the whole mate fiasco thing to make sure Sam wasn't lying about anything."

Lucy stared at the ceiling, her lashes damp. Things must have gone very badly indeed if she was crying about it.

"Once you were taken, I sorta... fell apart. We didn't know if you were alive or not. No one would tell us anything. So, I turned to Sam for comfort."

"Oh, Luce."

She nodded, her cheeks flushing with blood. "I admit, it wasn't my best idea. Afterward..."

I was pretty sure I could piece this together. "Afterward, you found out that your mother was right? That a werewolf mate was literally just someone to have their babies?"

Her tears fell freely, and she dashed them away with a frustrated grunt. "Exactly. When I dug deeper, he admitted that a werewolf mate wasn't the same as a vampire's, and yes, it was more about producing strong offspring. I lost my cool. I'm not some broodmare for him to use and dump once I have his children. I won't follow in my mother's footsteps."

Understandably. No one wanted to enter a relationship knowing there was a fifty-fifty chance the sperm donor would bail if his offspring turned out to be human instead of a werewolf.

"Oh, Lucy, I'm so sorry."

She sniffled and nodded. "Camilla wouldn't let me kick him to the curb because he was helping us plan your guys' escape. I try not to talk to him, mostly because I refuse to be in the same room as him. But back home, he was always *there*, watching, waiting. He calls me every single night since we came here."

Oof. That must have been hard. "So he's not here?"

"No. His alpha utterly forbade him from tagging along on this little quest of ours. Both Camilla and I understood. He had to think about his people, and the alpha feared the vampires would retaliate if they learned of their involvement."

And a war between werewolves and vampires was absolutely the last thing this world needed.

"Well, once we're home, you just give me the word, girl, and I'll kick that dog out on his ass. No one makes my bestie cry."

Lucy gave me a watery smile. "Thanks. I... may take you up on that offer. I hate being around him. I'm, like, hyperaware of everything he does. And when we're in the same room, I can barely think straight."

"Oh shit," I whispered.

Her eyes rounded. "What?"

"You're in love with him."

"Pfft. Am not."

She so was. And she was blind to it, which made it so much worse. Not to mention, they had a rather undesirable situation. No one wanted to be seen as just a breeder. But Sam also couldn't help how he felt. It was in his DNA to produce the strongest offspring possible.

"Enough about me." Lucy waved a hand. "How are you doing? This must all be quite a lot to take in."

"Well, I hate the queen, so that's been established."

"Never doubted that," Lucy said, laughing. "What else?"

"I killed another vamp. The guy was a real asshole, though. Definitely took pleasure in tormenting me. His real name was Finley, but I knew him as Brutus. He tried to kill Vlad last night and instead, I killed him." I winced and touched my side, recalling how his blade had felt embedded in my flesh.

She winced and took another sip of her wine. "So, that's three vamps now?"

"Two," I corrected her. "Sam killed Petrik. But no one knows that. Everyone else thinks it's three for me."

"Right."

"When did I turn into this person?" I lamented. "Before I became a fanger, I lived a normal life!" Or as normal as possible for a vlogger. We were a strange breed, after all. "Now, I'm up on two charges for murder, likely three. Probably treason, too, thanks to our escape. Plus, the queen wants me dead. Like dead-dead. Remember when my biggest worry was money? Not whether or not I'd live to see next year?"

"And here our mothers thought we'd never amount to anything," Lucy deadpanned.

"Well, you still could. Me? I'm an undead criminal and a murderer to boot."

"Is it murder if they try to kill you first? Pretty sure that's called self-defense."

I appreciated her comment. Trust Lucy to help put things into perspective for me.

"And Vlad? How's he doing?"

"Better now that we're free and together again." I glanced around the room, taking my surroundings in for the first time. "Where's Weasley?"

"I'm sorry, who?"

"Weasley. My little weasel friend."

"You have a weasel friend?"

"She came in with Camilla last night."

Lucy shook her head. "I'm sorry. I don't know anything about that."

I pursed my lips and sent a quick mental call through the house. Nothing. No Weasley. I hoped she returned tonight. Maybe she was out hunting rabbits and squirrels as she claimed to be so fond of doing.

"What are you going to do?" Lucy finally asked.

Somehow, I knew she wasn't referring to Weasley. I grabbed my glass and allowed myself another sip of blood. "I don't know. The queen will come after us again. Of that, I have no doubt. When she dragged me into her room to threaten me, I saw it in her eyes. She loathes me for killing Petrik. I guarantee she won't let this go, especially considering Vlad decimated most of her guards last night."

Lucy peered into her wineglass with a scowl. "Have you..." She drifted off.

"Have I, what?"

Sighing, she tucked her legs up under her bottom and faced me, her glass resting on her thighs. "We need to think about this logically. You want to survive this, yes?"

"Duh?"

"And you don't think you will so long as the queen is around, right?"

"Yeah, that seems like an accurate assessment."

"Well, that leads to a logical conclusion."

It did? I frowned. "Which would be?"

Lucy shrugged, then reached for the wine bottle and topped up her glass. "You need to kill the queen."

I immediately burst out laughing. "I'm sorry, what?"

"It makes sense. It's one of those situations where only one of you can survive. The queen has turned herself into a villain. Your villain, to be precise."

"Except to her, I'm the villain. I'm the one going around murdering her people."

Lucy waved a hand. "The villain always sees themselves as the good guy. If they didn't, they wouldn't make a good villain."

Right. Guess that made sense, in an odd sort of way.

"At the end of every book or movie, the villain dies."

"This isn't a movie, Lucy!"

She shrugged again. "That's just details. If you and Vlad want your happily ever after, it's pretty clear what needs to happen."

I scoffed. It was official. Lucy had lost her damn mind. "You seriously want me to kill the queen?"

"Do you see another way out of this?"

"I don't know, incite a revolt?"

She laughed. "The woman is Marie Antoinette. She knows all about revolutions. And how to escape them. Plus, a good villain still comes after the heroine, even after the heroine thinks she's won."

"So, now I'm a heroine in this story of yours."

"Well, you're the main character. So that makes you the heroine."

"You're insane."

Her mouth quirked. "Yeah, but you love me anyway."

True. No denying that. "Okay. I may have killed two vampires already, but that doesn't mean I'm looking to kill more. And if I killed the queen, I'm pretty sure the entire vampire community would turn on me. Which doesn't sound like a good situation either."

"Hmm. Guess we'll need to come up with a plan B then."

"Yes, definitely a plan B. Because plan A is cray-cray."

Snickering, Lucy leaned forward and grabbed the remote off the table.

"What are you doing?" I asked.

"We have a few hours left until the other vamps wake. I thought we'd give ourselves pedicures and watch a movie."

I blinked at Lucy. Okay. "And what movie are we watching?"

She turned to me with a shit-eating grin. "*Hunger Games*. You know, a movie where the heroine faces horrendous odds, takes on the president, and wins? Maybe it'll inspire you."

I groaned and dropped my head back against the couch cushion. Yup, my best friend was going to get me killed.

CHAPTER
TEN

THE MOVIE HAD JUST ENDED, and I was feeling all the good kind of feels when Vlad woke. I heard his approach before Lucy and scootched across the couch to mute the credits scene as he strode into the living room. Camilla usually woke about thirty minutes after Vlad. As for Alastair and Mateo, I knew nothing about them, so I didn't know when to expect them. Sunset was in about an hour. Seemed safe to bet they'd wake around then.

"There's a fresh bottle of blood waiting for you in the kitchen," Lucy said by way of greeting.

"Much appreciated." Vlad leaned down and kissed the top of my head before strolling into the kitchen.

Warmth flushed my body as memories of last night surfaced. As far as reunions went, it'd been top fricken notch, especially considering it'd been six months since we had been given any relief. In fact, last night had been *so* good, I wondered if Vlad and I should take time apart more often.

I snickered at the thought. Yeah, right. We wouldn't make it more than two nights apart before succumbing to our need to ravage each other's bodies.

Lucy lifted a knowing brow, and I coughed into my hand. Guess my thoughts weren't entirely private, after all.

Vlad reached for his bottle, which sat next to three others. A bottle for each vampire in residence. Lucy really had considered everything. I just hoped no one had found it odd that she'd purchased five bottles of blood. Not that the queen knew of our numbers. Even so, we needed to fly under the radar. What if someone had noticed and followed her here? Someone who worked for the queen. We were in her territory. I honestly didn't know what to expect.

My mind was a mess of what ifs. And I hated it. I didn't normally dwell on random possibilities. I was a hard facts kind of girl. But the queen had changed all the rules. This was *her* ballgame, not mine. And if we were going to win, we had to think of every scenario. Including sabotage.

"What movie were you two enjoying tonight?" Vlad asked.

He was no stranger to our antics. Back in Louisiana, he'd often found me and Lucy tucked into my bedroom, watching some silly comedy together. My favorite was the night he'd caught us watching *The Queen of the Damned*. He'd entered my room right as Stewart Townsend stalked across the screen, clad in a fishnet top and leather pants. Whereas Lucy and I had squealed and drooled, Vlad had clucked his tongue and left.

"Don't ask." I groaned and shook my head. Tucking my legs under my butt, I turned on the couch and eyed him in the kitchen. "Lucy has it in her head that I need to kill the queen."

Had I not been watching him, I might have missed how his grip subtly tightened around the wineglass. His knuckles whitened, and the slightest fracture webbed through the glass. Vlad's eyes darted to mine, and unspoken emotions flashed within—fear, panic, then anger. He flexed his hand and released the glass before it shattered into oblivion.

"No" was all he said.

Lucy's gaze jumped between us. "No? No, what?"

"No, Anna will not kill the queen. I won't allow it."

You bet your ass, I bristled at that. Every last hair on my body stood on end. Because *allow*? Seriously? That was some word choice there, one he might come to regret pretty damn quickly. "Excuse me?"

Vlad's gaze narrowed on me. "What?"

"Don't you *what* me." I rose from the couch and stomped into the kitchen. I came to a stop on the other side of the island he stood at, then crossed my arms and cocked my hip. "Did you seriously just say you wouldn't *allow* me to kill her?"

"Anna, it is too dangerous."

I scowled. Tell me something I didn't know. Hell, just *existing* was dangerous for me right now. Yet, I was making do. "And here I thought this was all just some big game. Color me surprised."

Vlad sighed and pinched the bridge of his nose. The scent of exasperation poured off him in waves. Maybe I felt a little bad for the guy. He hadn't even taken his first sip of blood yet and we were already bickering like an old married couple. But *he'd* been the one to go all caveman on me. So, in the words of my immortal toddler self: *he started it*.

"The queen is not merely a vampire. She is a monarch," he stated, as though I didn't already know that. "What do you think will happen if you kill the Queen of Vampires?"

"Gee, I don't know. Maybe she'll die? As for the rest, who cares?"

His expression flattened. Vlad rarely appreciated my native sarcasm language.

"At the end of the day, isn't that all that matters?" I pressed. "She wants me dead, Vlad. She told me so herself. So why should I sit back and just let her kill me? I think it's only fair to return the favor."

"I never said I didn't want her dead."

"But you just said—"

"That *you* would not be the one to kill her."

"Then who—" I froze, my mouth agape. "Oh, hell no. *Hell* no."

Vlad's eyebrow winged upward. "You want her dead, do you not?"

"If *I'm* not allowed to kill her, then what the heck makes *you* think you are? If I can't, you can't, buddy."

"Buddy?" he repeated, his brows slamming down into a severe frown. "Did you really just call me buddy?"

I shrugged. Better than calling him the other names that were rolling around in my head. I couldn't imagine any of those going over well.

"Maybe you two should take a breath," Lucy suggested.

I almost laughed at her suggestion. *Yes, let's tell the undead to breathe.*

"I didn't mean to start a fight," she continued.

I held up a hand and silenced her. This little spat was between me and the Count here. We didn't need any commentary from the peanut gallery.

"Anna, I am far older than you."

"Oh, don't give me any of that ageist bullshit. Older than me. So what? Isn't this why Camilla's been training me to fight?"

He pressed his palms flat against the island counter and leaned forward. "Not so you can murder the queen!"

Maybe I was young, but that didn't mean I didn't have a few tricks up my own sleeves when it came to power poses. He thought he could intimidate me? The mere thought was laughable. I'd grown up with a certifiably insane mother, an absentee father who drank, and a dimwitted ass of a brother who only thought about himself. I could certainly take on a five-hundred-year-old vampire who barely understood sarcasm.

I mimicked Vlad's stance, flattening my palms on the island and leaning forward. Our faces were a few inches apart, his gaze blazing with anger. I could only imagine he saw the same mirrored in mine.

"How about this?" My mouth quirked up on one side. "I call dibs."

Confusion had him blinking. "What?"

"I call dibs. You know, I get to be the one to kill the queen because I called it. Think of it like calling shotgun."

He huffed quietly. "Calling shotgun?"

Sometimes I forgot Vlad wasn't a modern man, and often the things I said went right over his head. Like now. Incredibly frustrating. Made it hard to win fights when the guy you were fighting with had no idea what you were trying to say.

I sighed. "It means that since I mentioned it first, the honor goes to me."

"That's ridiculous."

"About as ridiculous as you thinking you can forbid me from doing something. Tomato-tomahto."

"Anna..." Vlad exhaled so heavily, his entire body deflated. He closed his eyes and severed the connection between us. "This whole argument is absurd."

I pressed my lips together just in time to keep from actually telling him that he'd started it. I might be immature, but I wasn't *that* immature.

"I'm not forbidding you from doing anything," he clarified. "I simply think that of the two of us, I should be the one to kill her."

"Really. I would love to hear this logic." And if he gave me any nonsense about him being stronger than me, I was going to show him exactly where he could stuff that.

"Because..." His mouth snapped shut, and his attention darted to Lucy, who stood on the precipice of the kitchen, her wide, unblinking eyes taking in the entire scene.

He frowned and glanced back at me, clearly trying to communicate something. Thankfully, it was a look I knew well. And in all fairness, if we were about to have our first real fight, I didn't want Lucy here to witness it either.

"Hey, Luce, you mind giving us a few minutes?" I called over my shoulder.

"Oh, yeah, of course." Her hands fidgeted against her thighs. "I'll just... go elsewhere. Wait for Camilla to wake up or something."

She tiptoed out of the room, clearly not eager to draw our attention again. It was awkward enough to watch a couple fight, but I had to imagine it was worse watching two vampires snarl at each other.

"Anna," Vlad murmured. He reached across the island and took my hand.

I wish I could say I pulled back, but nope. Inside, I was just a big ole softy. So when he wove our fingers together, I relaxed and ran my thumb over his knuckles. Bomb diffused. Damn it.

"I didn't mean to imply that you are incapable. You know I believe you are capable of anything. But this is not a weight I wish for you to bear."

"You want to bear it instead then?"

"Your reputation is already quite tarnished in our community. You are the vampling who killed Petrik and Michel. Word of last night will soon spread too. Many vampires died there. If you were to kill the queen, I believe the community would rise up against you. And I'll do anything to ensure that doesn't happen."

Hmm. I wasn't so sure. True, my name had been dragged through the mud a few times now, but I believed Vlad was wrong. "Have you ever *asked* anyone what they think of the queen?"

He frowned. "Of course not."

"Of course not," I repeated. "Because that wouldn't make any sense, would it? She's the queen. Therefore, all love her."

"All do love her."

"Yeah, not from where I was sitting. And believe me, I was sitting pretty damn close."

He growled under his breath. "I don't understand what you're saying."

"Sorry." I shook my head. "There's a reason we vote for our political leadership, Vlad. We removed our monarch from power a long time ago. And for good reason. You didn't meet the queen, but I did. I saw the vamp she'd kept cuffed to her chair as a blood slave. She'd cut open his throat and left him there to bleed out into her glass. I also saw how terrified her human servants were. I could smell their fear. Maybe some of her people love her, I'm not arguing that. But look at Alastair and Mateo. They willingly betrayed her to help us escape, and we were complete strangers. That doesn't smack of undying loyalty and devotion to me."

"You believe the community would celebrate her death?"

"Honestly, I don't know. But I do know this situation isn't cut and dry. There will be some who hate me—*us*. But there will be many who thank us. Hell, maybe we can even sway them to our side and convince them to join our cause. We'll certainly need more people. She's the queen. It won't be as simple as stumbling across her in a dark alley somewhere and staking her."

"Anna—"

"Then there's the werewolves," I interrupted.

Vlad startled. "The werewolves?"

"Sam's alpha wouldn't allow him to come help with our escape because he feared any involvement would result in a war between vampires and werewolves. But what if we could promise them no retaliation. Promise them immunity from whoever takes over after the queen is gone. Maybe then they'd agree to help us. Our own personal army."

If possible, Vlad blanched. "You're speaking of a revolution."

"Well, it wouldn't be the first one she'd caused."

Vlad fell eerily silent. He stared at me, his face utterly devoid of emotion and as pale as death. I wasn't sure what to make of that, honestly. Was he angry with me? Impressed? I couldn't tell.

Without another word, Vlad grasped his bottle of blood and popped the lid. But rather than pour it in a glass, he upended it right into his mouth.

My jaw fell slack. I'd never seen Vlad down blood this way before. He was usually so refined, so gentlemanly. Had I pushed him too far already? Enough so for him to guzzle an entire bottle in five swallows? My mother had once told me I could make a sober person turn to drink.

Guess she was right.

"Okay... what's going on in here?" a voice cut in.

I glanced up and watched as Camilla slowly made her way toward us, her eyes darting between us as though sensing impending violence.

Vlad held up a finger as he finished his blood. Then he lowered the bottle to the counter and stared at it as though it could give him all the answers.

"I think I gave him apoplexy," I muttered.

"Curious." Camilla stood next to me, our hips almost touching. "I don't think I've ever seen Vlad rendered speechless before. What did you do to him? Lucy mentioned you two were sniping at each other, then vanished into her room. I would think after last night's adventures, you two would be disgustingly happy with each other."

"Oh, shut up," I griped. But inside, her comments made me smile. Camilla had never been one to bite her tongue. And back in Louisiana, she'd often commented on our sex life.

I could have bantered with Camilla and cracked some joke about inciting a revolution—shit, maybe *Hunger Games had* inspired me. Instead, I took pity on Vlad and circled the island. I came to a stop in front of him, then took the bottle and tossed it into the recycling bin.

Vlad still hadn't lifted his gaze from the counter. I shot Camilla a worried glance, then laid my hand on top of his and stroked his fingers.

"She'll kill you," he whispered.

My shoulders rounded, and all the fight fled my body as understanding dawned. The last nine months hadn't been easy on either of us. I'd become a vampire because Petrik had tried to murder me. Then Michel had tried to cut off my head. Then we'd been arrested. Our romance so far had pretty much consisted of me fighting to survive. That had to give a guy a complex.

"And you think that if you're the one to kill her, I'll be safe," I murmured.

"Anna." He turned his hand over and clutched my fingers so tightly, I had to bite back a gasp. "This *shouldn't* fall on you. You're still so young. You haven't even been a vampire for a year yet. You should be enjoying your undead life, experiencing everything it has to offer. Not scheming a revolution and planning to kill a queen."

"Ah," Camilla hummed.

I ignored her and focused on Vlad. I lifted his hand to my face and nuzzled his palm. "I don't think we have much of a choice here. The queen will come after me. She loathes me for killing Petrik, and now I've publicly embarrassed her by daring to escape. But instead of us fighting over who gets to actually kill her, maybe we could work together to figure out a way to kill her that doesn't end with either of us dying."

A faint smile pulled at Vlad's lips. "I can't lose you."

"You won't. We're stronger together."

"You say that, but our past suggests otherwise."

"Okay, valid point." I honestly didn't know what more to say. I only knew I didn't want to fight about this. I much preferred doing sinfully wicked things to his body as opposed to wanting to kick his ass. "How about we look at all this positively? We've survived this far. The queen can throw whatever she wants at us, but we're going to win in the end."

His smile grew the slightest amount. I was wearing him down.

"And if she wins, hey, I'll come back as a ghost and haunt her ass until the end of time."

This got him chuckling quietly. "You would."

"Oh, I so would," I promised. Then I leaned in and kissed him, lingering a little longer than necessary to revel in the feel of his mouth against mine. I had a feeling that was something I would never grow tired of.

"Alright, alright," Camilla chirped. "Before you two descend into a repeat of last night, how about you perk your ears and listen to *my* plan."

Vlad and I both turned to her with confused expressions.

She scoffed and shook her head. "You two forget, I've had six months to plan all this out, *including* how to handle the queen. What, you think my plan was just to grab you and go?" When neither of us responded, she rolled her eyes. "Thanks for the confidence boost."

"Camilla—"

"Oh, shut up," she said, "and listen up. Because I may just have a solution that benefits everyone."

CHAPTER
ELEVEN

Camilla—being the brat she was—made us wait until Alastair and Mateo woke before she would willingly discuss the plan. In her words, "Best to have the conversation once."

Fair enough, but the impatient vlogger in me wanted *all* the answers right fricken now. While we waited, Camilla dragged a large whiteboard into the kitchen, sat it on the dining room table, and perched it against the wall. In her other hand, she held a bunch of markers.

I couldn't help but stare at her. The Camilla I knew was an ass-kicking, take no prisoners sorta vampiress. I never pictured her lugging around school supplies. It almost made me wonder just who this place belonged to since she seemed to know where everything was located.

"Camilla?"

"Hmm?" She tapped a marker against her cheek but paused and turned to me when I called her name.

"Dare I ask... where are we?"

Her mouth crooked upward. "England, genius."

I rolled my eyes. Well, she certainly hadn't changed at all in our time apart.

"I believe Anna is asking whose house this is," Vlad interjected.

I tapped my nose, then pointed at him.

"Mine." She pulled out a chair and took a seat. "I bought it a few months ago, once we figured out where you guys were being held."

"Oh wow, it took that long to find us?"

She lowered the markers onto the table and started aimlessly rolling them across the veneer top. "We knew you were taken overseas, so we figured somewhere in England since Genevieve hardly leaves this place. But while England isn't as large as America, mainland England is still a pretty big place. The queen has multiple estates throughout the country. Castles, towers, you name it. You could have been at any of those."

"How'd you finally find us?"

"Breccan," Camilla said. "At first, it was just me, Lucy, and Sam looking for you guys. Breccan put out feelers among the other vamps he knows in this area. Eventually, word began to spread about the queen's special prisoners. Vlad has a lot of allies, so people were keeping a close watch on the queen."

I lifted a brow. I knew Vlad had friends, but I'd never stopped to ask how many. Were these people we could ask to help us? If their loyalty belonged to him and not the queen, maybe we wouldn't need the werewolves at all.

"I wasn't aware I had that many allies," Vlad said in a droll voice.

Camilla's fangs peeked out at us when she laughed. "Yeah, that sounds about right. You've always been a bit unaware of your own acclaim. Need I remind you that you are *Dracula*? To many, you're a legend."

He rolled his eyes, clearly unaffected by Camilla's words. "Please. They revere the name, not the vampire behind it."

"Be that as it may, they were helpful little minions when it came to tracking you guys down. Once we had a location, Lucy and I searched for real estate within close proximity to the tower, but not too close to risk capture. I purchased this place under a new alias. One Dorothy Caron, who tracks back to some fifty-something-year-old with a penchant for travel. According to her blog, and thank you, Anna, for introducing me to *that* world"—she rolled her eyes—"she's currently exploring South America."

Okay, color me impressed.

"Further digging would reveal that Dorothy came into her money via an inheritance she received from a dead grandmother. Anyway, you get the point. The bank accounts used don't trace back to me, Vlad, or anyone else who might arouse suspicion. We purchased this place and settled in. Then came waiting for news of Anna's trial date. Mateo has a friend at the courthouse who learned of the date two days ago. It was tight, I admit. But luckily for us, we pulled it off."

Barely. I still saw the many faces of the vampires we'd killed during our daring escape. But those were concerns for another time. Now, all that mattered was keeping my head firmly attached to my body.

"Well done," Vlad mused. "What precautions did you take to throw the queen off your trail as you traveled here?"

"What precautions didn't she take," Lucy chimed in as she rejoined us at the dining room table. She shot me a quick glance, but once she saw Vlad's arm slung around the back of my chair, a relieved smile chased across her face. "I don't even think I could tell you all the steps if I tried. But essentially, she planted about five false trails, started umpteen rumors about her plans throughout Louisiana, and told others how she was happy to be rid of you two traitors. A bit overkill, if you ask me."

Camilla shrugged. "Had to cover my tracks."

I reached across the table and grasped Camilla's hand, giving it a gentle squeeze. "And we appreciate it. Truly."

"Damn straight," she said, laughing. "You think I'd pull this shit for just anyone?"

Warmth pooled in my eyes, and I had to blink back the naughty tears threatening to fall. They knew they weren't welcome here, yet they consistently pestered me.

"Oh, don't go getting all weepy-eyed on me." Camilla rose and cocked her head. "The others are waking. We'll give them a bit to enjoy some blood and get their wits about them, and then we can discuss my amazingly genius plan that is going to solve all our problems."

"Can't wait," Vlad deadpanned.

I chuckled at his dry tone of voice. So, maybe some of the things I said went over his head, but he was definitely learning his own form of sarcasm. And I loved it.

A freaking entourage of four vampires stormed the kitchen. It was like chaos. Rebecca and Breccan reached for their bottles of blood, while Alastair and Mateo started rifling through the cupboards for what looked like coffee mugs. Guess they didn't like their blood in wine glasses.

Their familiarity with their surroundings drove home the fact that they'd all been working together for a while now. It was refreshing but also a bit overwhelming. They clearly had a routine established, one that Vlad and I weren't a part of yet. Even Lucy seemed aware of it, as she ducked and wove around them to open the fridge and pull out a snack. I watched her expression and listened to the steady beat of her heart. She wasn't uncomfortable here at all, and that spoke volumes.

"Good evening." Vlad dipped his head in greeting as everyone eventually took their seats around the table.

Man, if the kitchen felt crowded before with me, Vlad, Camilla, and Lucy, it was nothing compared to now with Breccan, Rebecca, Alastair, and Mateo thrown into the mix. My gaze leapt from face to face, but no one returned my gaze. Breccan and Rebecca were too busy sipping at their glasses, and Alastair was blowing on the blood he'd warmed in the microwave—which still turned my stomach.

"Alright!" Camilla stood at the head of the table and clapped her hands together, like she was some sort of schoolteacher. I snorted back a laugh and shook my head, one that Vlad acknowledged with his own chuckle.

"First of all, great job, everyone. We successfully managed to retrieve Anna and Vlad—"

"Woo! Go team Try Hard!" Lucy called from the kitchen as she stood over a plate full of food. As though to emphasize her point, she punched a fist in the air.

My snort grew into a loud laugh. Was she the resident cheerleader or something?

Camilla tossed Lucy a playful glare, then turned back to us. "Yes, anyway. We have Anna and Vlad back, which is indeed a cause for celebration. But our problems aren't yet solved."

Breccan grunted, then leaned back in his chair. "Got ourselves a queen we need to take out."

"Right." Camilla tipped a marker at him.

I had to admit, her markers had me increasingly curious. What the heck sort of presentation was she putting together here? And would it involve PowerPoint? I didn't see a computer anywhere, shockingly, so it seemed unlikely. Not to mention, any vampire over the age of like, twenty, seemed entirely technologically inept. I suppose I should be giving Camilla points for pulling out a whiteboard instead of a chalkboard.

Vlad pulled his arm off my chair, then rested them on the table. "Before we proceed any further, I wish to express mine and Anna's gratitude. You all went to great lengths to rescue us and have placed yourself at risk if the queen ever learns of your participation."

Everyone tipped their heads in acknowledgment.

"Yes, thank you," I said, my voice thick with emotion.

"But before Camilla proceeds, I want to ask that you take a moment and consider the ramifications of taking out the queen. These are your lives. And I would never ask that you throw your life away on our behalf. If you feel this is too much for you or beyond what you expected when you offered to help, know that you can leave. No one will hold it against you."

A heavy silence carried through the room.

When no one responded, nor rose from the table to leave, Camilla clucked her tongue at Vlad. "We appreciate your concern, but we've been working on this for months. We all know the stakes."

"And you're all willing to go against Genevieve?" Vlad asked, his eyes leaping from face to face.

Every single person here nodded.

Geez. This was choking me up. I cleared my throat and dropped my focus to my hands, tangled in my lap. I wasn't used to this. My family was a *mess*. We're talking affairs, divorces, name-calling, you name it. So the fact that these people, who were strangers to me less than a year ago, were willing to risk everything for us made me want to cry. Not that I would.

"All right, then," Vlad said. He leaned back and slid his arm across the back of my chair. "Proceed, Camilla."

"Why, thank you, Vlad," she said, chuckling.

She shot me a concerned look, then uncapped her marker and approached the gleaming whiteboard. Without a word, she scribbled the name Genevieve at the top, then squiggled an line beneath.

"As we all know, Genevieve is our queen. And she just plain sucks at it."

Laughter rose around the table. Guess everyone was in agreement there.

"Now..." Camilla drew a line to the side. "Genevieve is 'married' to one Adrian Roche, but while he's her consort, they aren't mates. Which never seemed to bother either of them, considering Genevieve had been openly sleeping with Petrik for who knows how long."

I shuddered, forcing that little tidbit to the back of my mind. The thought of anyone gettin' their freak on with Petrik turned my stomach.

"Beneath Genevieve and Adrian are Elias, Gabriel, and Natalie." Camilla wrote in their names a step down from the queen's and consort's, then connected them with single lines. A family tree then?

I quirked my head and studied those names. I'd never heard of these people.

"These are their heirs," Camilla said, then turned to us with a comical expression. "Because as vampires, it's very important we have heirs."

Everyone laughed.

It did seem odd, but the basis of a monarchy was to have an heir. Maybe Genevieve had felt it necessary?

"Then beneath the heirs is the council." Camilla wrote out the word, then circled it twice. "These are the people who assist the queen with whatever matters she deems appropriate. For instance, the registration and acclimation of all new vampires."

Ah, yes. I remembered that. The email I'd received after I'd first been changed had come from them. They'd also guided me to an FAQ that they'd expected would answer all my questions. At the time, it'd been helpful. But nowhere in that forum had there been a topic discussing the appropriate steps to take when the actual queen wanted you dead.

"The council advises the queen where they can, but we all know their power is quite limited. Adrian is essentially a figurehead, and few vampires in our community actually respect him. He mostly gorges himself on blood and ignores the queen and politics."

"Then why the heck did they even marry?" Lucy asked.

Everyone's head swiveled in her direction, but thankfully, no one criticized her question. Which was good, because I had the same one. Also, who in their right mind *would* marry Genevieve?

"Most likely, the council advised them to. But who's to say. Maybe at some point, they loved each other."

"I'm pretty sure the only person she ever loved was Petrik," I quietly commented, recalling the hatred in her gaze during our lovely discussion.

"In any case..." Camilla drew a star next to the three heirs' names. "These are the names that matter to us."

Vlad leaned forward in his seat, his arm once again pulling away from my chair. He studied the board with a severe frown. That sort of focus would have given me a headache.

"Camilla..." Vlad rose to his feet and slowly circled the table, his focus locked on the board. "You mean to suggest a coup?"

She turned with a bright grin. "A coup is better than a revolution, right?"

"It's brilliant," he commented. He propped his fists on his hips and contemplated the board. "What do we know of these three? I've met Natalie a few times, Gabriel only once, and Elias never."

"Each heir has a strong connection to the queen," Camilla replied. She tapped the *eldest* name at the top. "Elias was Genevieve's first. She calls him her son. Perhaps a touch creepy, but hey, who are we to judge. They've always had a familial connection, never romantic, so if the shoe fits. Rumor has it she found him living in squalor in 1818, and decided to offer him a better life. To this day, he is supposedly the most loyal of the three.

"Gabriel is a different story. He's their youngest son. Adrian changed him when he reached the age of eighteen. Before that, he lived in their home after Genevieve removed him from an abbey, where he was being raised as a monk. His birth mother believed it was his destiny to serve"—she pointed up toward the ceiling, avoiding the big guy's name—"but Gabriel didn't agree. Genevieve supposedly saw him as a victim of religion and raised him instead. Whereas Elias is the steadfast, loyal son, Gabriel is a bit of a rogue who chooses his own path in life. Genevieve calls him her 'wild child.'"

I frowned as I listened. Camilla seemed to know a great deal about this Gabriel.

"Lastly, Natalie, who is problematic. When she was changed, there was no rule against changing the unwilling. But beyond that, the queen turned Natalie at age ten when she came across her clutching her dead father's hand. As we all know, we don't age after being changed, so she's been trapped in the body of a ten year old for about a hundred years. Genevieve dotes on Natalie, completely blind to the madness festering within. She certainly cannot help us."

"You believe Gabriel is the best option then?" Vlad asked. When

Camilla nodded, he turned toward the rest of the group. "Have any here met him?"

"Yeah." Breccan gestured with a hand. "Lad seemed intelligent enough. But the real question is his politics."

"I'm also quite familiar with Gabriel," Camilla said, though she didn't elaborate. "He avoids politics and prefers to play the role of a spoiled prince."

"Lovely," Rebecca commented. "And you want to place him on the throne."

"Well, how is that any different from a murderous queen who ignores her own laws?"

Alastair lifted his hand. "I've met the boys. They both seemed like decent chaps to me. Gabriel and I got on the best. A bit of a jokester that one. Elias was a dud, more interested in behaving proper and whatnot."

Mateo seemed to agree with this assessment, his head bobbing.

"So, let me get this straight." I called the attention to me. "You want to place Gabriel on the throne."

"Right," Camilla said.

"And what happens to Genevieve?"

Everyone averted their eyes back to Camilla.

"She would have to die."

Uh-huh. "And you want her loyal sons to help us with that? You actually think this is possible? Who's to say they won't turn around and arrest us for treason, or worse, just kill us outright?"

Camilla cleared her throat. Even Lucy appeared a bit shocked by my intelligent question.

"Well, I suppose that's a risk we're just going to have to take."

I quirked a brow. Some risk.

"I feel Gabriel is the best fit, based on my history with the two princes. It's risky, I get that, but we don't have many other options. Or any, really."

"And what about Adrian?" I asked. "He might be useless, but I highly doubt he's going to sit back and let us assassinate his wife."

"Right. There is that."

This plan sounded like it had a whole stream of holes in it. And I didn't like it one bit. What was wrong with my plan? A revolution sounded a lot easier to organize than all this subterfuge nonsense.

"There's five of them," I said. "And six of us. Hell, maybe we can even get more. I say we go in, take them all out and find ourselves a new leader."

Okay, now everyone was looking at me again, except this time, their expressions were a mix of shock and horror.

"You want to kill the entire royal family?" Camilla asked.

"How is that any worse than just killing Genevieve?"

"And who would you choose for the throne after we wiped out the monarchy?" Vlad asked.

"I wouldn't. Thrones are antiquated."

"Then what—"

"A prime minister or president, whichever term is preferred among the community."

"A democracy," Camilla said.

I nodded. "It seems to be the easier solution than *hoping* one of Genevieve's family members will willingly betray her and help us."

"But if one is, this whole process could go much more smoothly," Camilla argued. "If we slaughtered the entire royal family, we'd all be up on charges in some fashion. Or executed."

"Which will likely happen anyway. This is literally treason we're discussing here."

"I understand your concern, Anna," Vlad said. "But our kind isn't ready for a democracy. Many in our community would rebel. The monarchy has been in place for two hundred years, when Genevieve first stepped up as queen. Her heirs were established as a fallback in case she ever died. Removing the queen would be simpler and easier for the community to accept."

I sighed and shook my head. This was insane. They were basing *everything* on the belief that one of Genevieve's sons would willingly betray her. And if that were the case, how did that make him a better candidate for the throne. Did we really want someone capable of matricide leading a world of vampires?

"Anna has some good points," Lucy said.

I threw her a grateful smile, but the voice of a human wouldn't hold much weight here.

"A vote then," Vlad suggested.

I nearly burst out laughing. Did he not realize the irony of voting on whether we should attempt a coup or a revolution?

"All in favor of the coup?" Vlad said.

Of the eight people present, five lifted their hands.

"All in favor of the revolution?"

Three hands rose. One was Lucy. Alastair was the other.

Vlad nodded his thanks. "I understand your concerns, Anna. But I truly feel the coup is the safest and best option here."

Yeah, until one of Genevieve's sons betrayed *us*. I guess there was one upside. If we all died, no one would be left to hear me say, "I told you so."

CHAPTER
TWELVE

I NEEDED FRESH AIR. After being incarcerated for so long, I found I didn't much like staying cooped up indoors right now. And thankfully, Camilla's house came with a massive, fenced backyard. The kind rich people liked to seal them away from the rest of the world.

I slid open the back porch door and stepped outside, breathing in the frigid night air. Geez, it was cold! January in Louisiana still had a crispy nip to it, but England was a whole other monster. Even though it was winter, the air still felt heavy and wet, and possessed a chill that bit deeply into my bones.

Wrapping my arms around my center, I strode to the side of the house and peered around. Thankfully, Camilla had purchased a house in the middle of nowhere. No neighbors to be found. Which meant no nearby human blood to tempt me—other than Lucy's, but she was a *no touchy* zone. The bottled blood had helped ease my hunger, but I wasn't sure how long it would last. Better safe than sorry.

"Yes, I'm fine, I swear." Lucy's voice came from the back of the yard.

Curiosity had long since killed my inner cat, so I ventured toward the sound of her voice. I found her tucked behind a thick tree, clad head to toe in winter gear. She must have dressed immediately after the meeting and headed out here to talk on the phone.

Sam's deep voice carried through the speaker and rumbled in my ears.

Ah.

She'd come out here for some privacy. Well, too bad. Rather than give it to her, I tiptoed around the tree, then sank to the ground next to her, my back also pressed against the trunk. She shot me a startled glance, then relaxed when she saw it was just me. After a moment's hesitation, she leaned her head against my shoulder and continued chatting.

"No, I didn't assist with the rescue," she said, sighing. "Yes, Camilla made me stay at her place until they all returned. Sam, listen. I appreciate your concern, and I know you're worried, but this has to stop."

Oh, ouch. Was she dumping him?

I heard his questioning grunt, and it made me smile. The guy was hardly loquacious.

"I told you I didn't know what I wanted, and I still don't. So, in the meantime, I need you to stop calling and texting me, okay? Just give me some space. That's all I'm asking." She paused, and I listened for her answer the instant I heard his next question. "Yes, Anna is here now. Safe and sound. I'm going now, okay? We'll talk when I get back."

She ended the call before Sam could argue.

"That went well," I murmured.

"He doesn't understand why I'm upset." She fiddled with her phone before finally dropping it to the ground next to her butt. "And I don't understand how he *doesn't* understand. I mean, come on. No woman wants to hear that she's been chosen specifically because she's the best match for creating the strongest offspring."

Hell, even I winced at that one.

"I'm not a baby factory. I am officially *closed for business*. But I..."

She sighed and tipped her head back against the tree trunk. "Anna, tell me what to do."

I gave a gentle laugh. "What in the name of all things unholy makes you think I'm the best person to give you advice?"

"Vlad's your mate."

"Apples and oranges, my dear. He doesn't want me to pump out babies."

"Because you can't."

"Well, yes, there is that."

"Am I being too hard on Sam?"

"Well, has he ever actually told you that he's only interested in making babies with you?"

She cleared her throat and shifted anxiously against me. "Not in so many words."

I shot her a startled look. "Okay, I'm going to need you to be very specific here. What *did* Sam tell you?"

"I don't even know anymore." Lucy groaned and closed her eyes, her breath steaming in the cold air. "Everything is so muddled in my head. You were gone, he and I had just slept together, and I was hysterical. I accused him of trying to knock me up to lock me down."

I winced. Ouch. Poor Sam.

With her eyes closed, Lucy tilted her head to the left, an unconscious sign she was trying to remember the conversation. "He said something about me being ridiculous, which just further set me off. And then I called him an asshole. He told me that just because my sperm donor pulled this shit on my mother didn't mean he would. And that was when I stormed out."

Oof. That was rough. "So you never asked him how he truly feels for you?"

Her pulse thrummed louder. Apparently, this entire topic made her anxious. "I-I was scared. What if he said I was nothing more than a possible baby maker?"

"What if he said he was in love with you?"

Her eyes shot wide, and she turned her head to stare at me. "You can't actually think we're in love."

"Girl, I've never seen you so knotted up over a man before. You keep pushing him away, yet here we are. You two slept together, then you literally crossed an ocean to get away from him. I don't think it's because you hate him."

Lucy huffed. "You just think he's cute."

"The man is downright gorgeous," I corrected her. "But that's irrelevant. If babies are all he wants from you, then fine, walk away. But if he has deeper feelings for you, don't you think you both have a right to know? If he loves you, truly loves you, does he not deserve a chance?"

"I'm afraid," she finally confessed. "My mom says werewolves are incapable of love."

"That's your mother's interpretation," I said. "And while I love your mother, there's a chance she might be a bit jaded due to her own experiences."

Like Lucy's biological father jumping ship the second he realized Lucy would never shift. Children born of human and werewolf relations could go either way, and Lucy had swung human. Daddy dearest hadn't appreciated that. Luckily for them, Lucy's mother had found a wonderful man who loved them both more than anything in the world, so much so that he didn't care a lick that Lucy technically wasn't his. He'd raised her as though she was, and she loved him dearly for it.

"I say go right to the source," I continued. "Ask Sam straight out how he feels about you. Leaves no room for doubt. You'll be able to make a rational decision based on that."

"You make it sound so easy," Lucy whispered.

"It isn't. It'll be the hardest thing you've ever done."

"Other than breaking you out of prison?"

I chuckled. "If I remember correctly, you didn't participate in that. So that doesn't count."

"Jerk," she teased. Then she waved at the house. "What do you think of everything that just went down?"

I sighed and thought back to earlier tonight. "I think their plan is going to get us all killed."

"You and me both," Lucy admitted. "Camilla never told me about any of this."

"Eh. Probably hadn't seemed relevant."

"You wanna go back inside?" Lucy asked, rubbing her hands together.

"Getting cold?"

She nodded. "Not all of us are dead out here, you know. I actually need blood flow to live. And right now, my blood is freezing."

"Nawh." I chuckled. "I'm fine, and I think I'd like to stay outside."

"Really? It's so cold."

I lifted my knees to my chest and wrapped my arms around them. The temperature was uncomfortable, but knowing it wouldn't kill me made it easier to accept.

"You okay?" Lucy asked, nudging my shoulder.

"There are a lot of vampires in there," I murmured. "And that house isn't large enough for the seven of us. I was getting anxious with all of them crowding around."

Lucy eyed me curiously. "I've never known you to be claustrophobic before."

"Yeah, well, I'd never been imprisoned before."

Lucy stilled, then without a word, she reached out and clutched my hand, winding our fingers together. Her chilly skin was still warmer than mine. "Was it that bad?"

"It really could have been a lot worse. But it was lonely. Six months without any companionship, other than the guards and Weasley."

"But no one hurt you?"

"Well, not permanently," I said, recalling the queen's words. "If you're asking if they tortured me or anything, the answer is no."

"Good. That's something at least."

"Sure."

Something rustled in the frosted brushes next to us. Lucy gasped and gripped my hand tighter.

"Lucy—"

I didn't get the chance to tell her to calm down before a dark object darted toward us. I caught a whisper of Weasley's thoughts right away and knew it was her, but Lucy didn't. When she caught sight of an animal dashing toward us, Lucy squealed and jumped to her feet.

Before she did something stupid, like kick Weasley, I leaned down and opened my hands. My little furball leapt into my cupped palms and curled up, nuzzling her cheek against my fingers.

"Anna! Weasley missed you!"

"I missed you too, Snicker Doodle. Where've you been?"

"Around. So much yum-yums. Much better than tower rats."

I couldn't help but laugh. The second the sound left my mouth, Lucy's jaw dropped. "So, it's true then. You really can talk to animals."

"I told you about that back in Louisiana," I said, still scritching Weasley's cheek.

"But I never saw it. Wow. You can actually hear their thoughts? What's Weasley thinking about?"

I chuckled. "Squirrels mostly. And a few rabbits she tormented for fun, little scamp."

"For fun, right," Lucy said, her tone dry.

Weasley uncurled in my palms and stood, her head lifted as she sniffed the air. *"Who this?"*

"This is my best friend, Lucy."

A loud trill echoed in my head. *"Weasley Anna's best friend."*

I laughed louder this time.

"What's so funny?" Lucy demanded.

"Weasley's apparently replaced you in the best friend category. She just adamantly told me that *she* is my best friend, and not you."

"Hmph." Lucy dropped to her knees next to us and peered down at my weasel friend. "Too bad, little miss. I was here first."

I felt Weasley's thoughts darken as she pictured herself biting off Lucy's nose.

"Might wanna back off there," I told her.

Lucy's eyes widened. "Okay, how about I go inside and leave the two of you be?"

I nodded. I still wasn't ready to go back in. Part of me knew I should be spending time with Vlad after being apart for so long, but I hated the idea of being enclosed in there with so many vampires. Besides, I was sure he had his own affairs to handle, what with it being his first night of freedom. Not that I had any clue what those might be.

"Anna happy now?" Weasley asked.

I tucked deeper against the tree and lifted Weasley to my chest, setting her on the top of my knees. She whirled around and faced me, our noses nearly touching. When I didn't immediately respond, she licked my nose.

"Ew, Weasley!" I laughed. *"Didn't you just eat squirrel or something?"*

"Two!" she chirped with such pride.

"Glad your belly is full."

She purred, then curled up in a tight ball and immediately fell asleep. Damn, that was fast. A talent I sorely lacked. Not that it mattered anymore. The sun knocked me out cold every day.

Approaching footsteps crunched in the snow. I didn't need to look to know it was Vlad. I'd know the sound of his walk anywhere. The slow but purposeful swagger.

"There you are," he murmured as he rounded the tree. His gaze dropped to Weasley and a warm smile crossed his face. "Are you two all right out here?"

I nodded. "Just couldn't stay inside any longer. Needed some fresh air."

"Yes," Vlad said, nodding. "I understand that need vehemently. Mind if I join you? I have something for you."

I gestured to the open seat next to me. Not that it was anything grand. Just a place to cop a squat in the snow. Maybe I should talk to Camilla about getting some furniture back here.

"I hope you know that I truly did consider your thoughts in there."

My mouth crooked upward. "I know."

"Of course, we won't agree on everything—"

That made me laugh. "I know that too."

"Good." He leaned against the tree and reached out to stroke Weasley's fur. The little stinker barely twitched in her sleep. "I'm glad she found her way back to you."

"Me too. I was getting worried there."

Vlad nodded. "When she entered my cell, I thought I'd officially lost my mind. And then the strangest thing. This little beast nudged a button my way. *Your* button. And I knew right then and there that you were alive. I can't describe the relief."

Nor did he need to. I remember how I'd felt the instant I'd laid eyes on him in his cell. I quietly hummed my understanding and leaned my head against his shoulder.

"You've developed remarkable control over your gift."

"Had nothing else to do for six months," I teased in poor humor. "Seemed only wise to develop the one talent I have."

"Those rats you set loose on the tower were brilliant."

I chuckled. "The little beasts were eager for a taste of vampire. Speaking of, can vampirism transfer to animals?"

Vlad shook his head. "Not that I've ever seen. And I've seen alligators take chunks out of some. The consensus is that they're immune to whatever affects us."

"Good." It seemed like *bad news bears* to have vampiric rats. Regular ones were bad enough as it was.

"You said you had something to give me?" I asked.

"Ah, yes."

Vlad slipped a hand into his shirt pocket, grabbed something, then held his prize up to the moonlight. It glittered as though it'd been waiting for the moonlight to finally wake it up. Without a word, he took my left hand in his and stared deep into my eyes. "Anna Marie Perish, I believe you've already said yes to this question, but Lucy informs me that the statute of limitations has passed, and I must propose again. So, here I sit, in the freezing snow, with a damp rear, beneath the moonlight, asking the woman I love if she would do the honor of marrying me."

Amusement and adoration flushed through me. Of course Lucy would make a comment like that. She loved to watch Vlad doing *her* bidding. If she ever paired up with Sam, she was going to give the poor man a run for his money. I almost felt bad for him.

Vlad held the ring poised over my fingers, his brow hitched as he waited.

"Anna, say yes," Weasley's voice echoed in my head, startling me.

"Hey, you're supposed to be sleeping," I scolded.

"Battikins loud. Can't sleep."

"Well?" Vlad asked, clearly ignorant of the unfolding conversation in my head. "I wait with bated breath."

"No you don't," I said, laughing. "And yes, of course I'll still marry you. Like I would give you any other answer."

"That was my hope," he said. "Now for the part that Lucy keeps nagging me about." He lifted my hand and slid the gold band onto my finger.

I held my hand up to the moonlight. Wonderment lit through me. The gem was utterly breathtaking. So red that I wondered if it was a ruby. "What sort of stone is this?"

"A red diamond," he told me. "It seemed fitting. It's rare, much like you."

I choked on the frigid, wintry air. I didn't know much about diamonds, but I did know reds were almost unique. And incredibly expensive. Encircling the bloodstone was a series of crystal-clear diamonds twinkling in the moonlight.

"Vlad," I whispered. "It's breathtaking."

"As are you."

Feeling a touch weepy, I leaned in and kissed him, lingering so I could get a real taste of him. Pulling back, I met his gaze. "I love you."

He cupped my cheeks, then leaned in and brushed a second, albeit lighter, kiss on my mouth. "And I you. Now, shall we return to the others?"

"Sure, why not?" I asked. "I'm sure Camilla needs some help with her subterfuge, and who better to assist than me?"

Vlad chuckled. "Who, indeed."

CHAPTER
THIRTEEN

With Weasley wrapped around my neck like a warm scarf and Vlad's hand clutched in mine, we entered through the patio door and stepped into the kitchen. I wasn't sure what I'd expected to find, but it wasn't stark silence. Camilla and Alastair hovered in front of a laptop, their faces bleached of color—a neat trick for vampires. Breccan, Rebecca, and Mateo were glued to their phones. Poor Rebecca had a hand fisted in her hair while Breccan rubbed the back of his neck.

I shot Lucy a startled glance only to find her standing in the kitchen with a full wineglass perched against her lips. She gave a subtle shake of her head, then tipped her head back and drained the glass.

Something was wrong.

"What is it?" Vlad demanded. He released my hand and strode into the kitchen, his footsteps loud in the small confines.

"The queen," Alastair replied, his voice hoarse. "She's conducting raids."

Raids? What did that even mean? My gaze darted back to Camilla. Her eyes slowly closed and she stepped back from the laptop, her mouth a grim slash.

"She's searching Greater London," Camilla mumbled, almost as though she couldn't find the right words. "Her guards are going door to door, demanding entrance to all vampire dwellings. She's trying to flush out who might be helping you."

"Okay, that's not so bad," I whispered. "I wouldn't qualify that as a raid."

Six pairs of vampire gazes shot to me and I instinctively stepped back. Even Weasley sensed the amped-up tension, her chittering thoughts echoing in my head.

"She's burning down houses, flushing out any vampires who don't immediately cooperate."

The hairs on my arms rose. "What?"

"Her own people," Alastair commented. "It's madness out there. The forums are lighting up right now from those who've witnessed the events. Hopefully word spreads, but I'm not sure it'll reach everyone in time."

"She's attacking her own people?" I asked, attempting to understand.

"If they don't cooperate and invite in her guards. Obviously, we can't enter a house without permission."

I gave a jerky nod.

"So, if they refuse to give the queen's men access to their homes to search for you and Vlad, her men are burning them out. No need for an invitation if there's no home left."

"Oh my god," I uttered, a hand rising to clutch at my chest. I caught the few winces in my periphery but not enough to apologize.

This was our fault. We'd dared to defy the queen and now she was taking her wrath out on literally everyone.

"Have any humans been harmed?" I asked.

"Humans?" Mateo's head snapped up from his phone. "Who the bloody hell cares about the humans?"

I stared at him, shocked to even hear him speak. He was always so quiet.

"No," Camilla interrupted. "No humans have been harmed.

Which is a good thing. The last thing we need is for her to piss off the human government."

"She has a treaty with the British prime minister," Lucy added, her voice soft, as though not to attract the attention of any pissed off vamps. "They signed it about four or five months ago, once the British government saw how successful her relationship was with our American government."

"Attacking any humans would threaten the treaties," Rebecca commented. "She would be daft to risk that."

"Which is why she's only going after vampire homes," Alastair continued.

My gaze kept bouncing around the room, following the conversation, but I had very little to add. "The vampires whose homes she's burning... did she kill them?"

"No deaths reported yet," Breccan chimed in, his finger scrolling down his phone.

"Where are you reading all this? The news?"

A small grin tugged at Alastair's lips, and he glanced up, winking at me. "We do know how to use the internet, you know. There're a few popular forums we vampires frequent. The news is slowly spreading there."

"This is madness," Vlad finally stated. "Has she lost her mind?"

"More like her temper," Camilla countered. "You and Anna have pushed her farther than any other vampire in history. Think about it. You escaped imprisonment, attacked her guards, even killed some. I wondered how she would respond."

"By punishing her own people," I said.

"I don't think she sees it that way. To her, she's trying to reclaim control. She's probably concerned about looking weak."

I shook my head and turned away from the kitchen to stare outside. Geez, a year ago, my life had been so different. Normal, even. Or as normal as I could make it. I'd been human, living a typical American life in my typical American apartment with my typical human boyfriend. Now, nine months later, here I stood, a vampire in a relationship with Dracula himself, *and* an escaped prisoner. It didn't get much different than that.

I aimlessly scritched Weasley's head while considering the ramifications of my actions. It wasn't just about me and Vlad now. It was about *all* vampires, considering the queen was raiding their homes. While we hid. That hardly seemed right.

A hand cupped my shoulder and I glanced up to find Vlad standing behind me, the darkness to my light.

"I hate this," I whispered, even though I knew the others would still hear. Benefits of vamp hearing.

"As do I."

"She's hurting people. Destroying their homes. And what are we doing about it?"

"What can we do about it?" Vlad asked.

"Anything!" I said, my voice rising in anger. "She's taking advantage of her status to do what she wants when she wants."

"She's the queen," Mateo argued behind us.

"That doesn't give her the right to do whatever she likes."

"That's rich, coming from you," Mateo countered.

Vlad stiffened behind me. When he started to turn toward Mateo, I gripped his wrist and squeezed gently. "Don't. Just... ignore him."

"By all means, ignore me," Mateo barked, rising from his seat. "It's not like I have a valid point or anything. You complain about the queen doing whatever she wants, but you've behaved similarly since the day you were turned."

Anger vibrated through Vlad. I gave him another gentle squeeze. Fighting would get us nowhere. And I refused to defend my actions *yet again*, especially to someone who meant literally nothing to me.

Instead, I turned and lifted my chin, all while silently congratulating myself for not biting off Mateo's head. "We have to help."

"I don't see how," Alastair commented, glaring daggers at Mateo.

My gut sank as I watched the two communicate with silent expressions. Lucy had mentioned that Alastair and Camilla were friends but that she didn't know anything about Mateo. Considering my history with traitorous allies who tried to kill me, it made me a little anxious. What if Alastair had been wrong in assuming Mateo would help us? What if Mateo betrayed us to the queen?

Vlad must have sensed my rising anxiety because this time, he gave my hand a little squeeze. I clutched at him like a lifeline.

"There has to be something," I said, my voice wavering.

Camilla frowned and glanced at me, clearly sensing my inner angst. "Word is spreading on the forums, warning people of the consequences if they don't agree to the queen's demands. I'm sure people will start inviting in the queen's men to keep them from burning their homes."

"But what if it doesn't stop there?"

"Once she sees that no one is harboring you, things will return to normal."

"And that's it?" I asked. "We just leave it? Let the queen have her tantrum?"

"What else would you have us do?" Rebecca asked. "It isn't like we can march out there and fight her guards. We have seven. They have hundreds."

"I could do a vlog," I suggested.

Vlad tensed.

"I could tell people what's happening. Explain my side of things. Warn them about the queen's actions."

"And then what?" Vlad demanded.

"I-I don't know."

I peered up at him and caught sight of his gritted jaw and dark eyes. I knew from experience that this was his *I'm pissed* face. Ah, shit.

I released his hand and paced the length of the kitchen, all while running my hands through my hair. I couldn't just stand here and do nothing. Couldn't continue hiding and waiting for things to blow over. Couldn't keep running and dodging the queen. Eventually, she would find us. She had more resources, more people, more power. If we were going to win this, we needed help.

Sighing, I dropped my arms and turned to face everyone else. "We need help. We need people on our side. This will never end unless *we* end it."

No one said a word. The house had grown so quiet, you could hear a pin drop.

Then Vlad growled a response that sent a shiver screaming down my spine, "Do you have a death wish?"

I stammered out an incomprehensible response. I honestly didn't know how to respond to that, because of course I didn't have a death wish. And who asked that sort of question, anyway?

But before I could respond, Vlad shook his head and stormed out of the kitchen. I stood in the middle of the room, my jaw agape. I honestly hadn't expected such a strong reaction from him. It wasn't like I was asking to march into battle. All I wanted was to make a vlog, something I could post online and update all the vampires watching out there.

"Well," Camilla said. "Anna?"

I blinked, then shot her a startled glance. She gestured for me to follow Vlad. I shook my head. It seemed unwise to go after him right now. I mean, wasn't there a phrase about not poking the bear? That seemed a wise idiom right now.

She gestured again, miming a *shoo* motion. When I shook my head harder, she planted her fists on her hips and scowled at me. Then she mouthed the word "go."

"Are you crazy?" I mouthed back.

She rolled her eyes before silently commanding me to, "Go. Talk. To. Him."

I crossed my arms over my chest and held my ground. If Vlad wanted to be alone right now, I wasn't going to force my presence on him. Besides, one could argue that it would be best to let him calm down before we engaged in any sort of discussion. He was mad at *me*, after all. In my mind, it made more sense for Camilla to talk to him, which I acted out with the waving of arms and a few moves I'd learned from *Pictionary*.

"Oh, for crying out loud!" Camilla finally shouted, breaking the eerie silence.

I jumped.

"*Go*," she growled.

Sighing, I flipped her the bird, to which she blew me a kiss before I turned and followed the scent of Vlad's rage out onto the front porch.

He sat on the stone steps, his back to me, staring out into the night. I paused with one hand on the door, giving him a chance to tell me to leave him be, but he didn't. That had to count for something.

Releasing the door, it swooshed closed. I sat next to him on the step before collecting Weasley from around my neck and lowering her to the ground.

"Why don't you go find yourself a midnight snack?"

She turned and eyed me, her beady gaze glittering in the moonlight. Then she dipped her head and vanished into the snow.

Still, Vlad didn't speak.

After a few moments, I sighed and pulled my knees up to my chest. "I didn't mean to upset you."

"I know."

Okay, improvement. At least he wasn't giving me the silent treatment. I'd always hated when Lucy did that. Thankfully, Vlad's five hundred years made him a bit more mature, aside from him storming out.

"I just hate feeling useless," I admitted.

"I'm aware. I feel the same way."

"Alright, then why are you so upset about my vlog idea?"

His shoulders shifted when he sighed. "I understand how important your vlog is to you, truly. You take such pride in your work, and I admire that. However, it also frightens me beyond belief."

"My vlog frightens you?"

"No." He turned and pinned me with a severe stare. "Your popularity frightens me. Or perhaps I should say notoriety."

"Interesting word choice," I hedged.

"You have so many eyes watching you. How can I keep you safe if the entire world knows about you?"

Ah. That darn light bulb lit up in my head like the Fourth of July.

"Sure, I have a lot of followers, but the great part to being a vampire is none of them know what I look like." I nudged his shoulder in an attempt to lighten the mood.

And failed.

Vlad scowled. "If you think anonymity is enough to protect you, you're sorely mistaken."

Geez. Mood killer. "So, you're scared that if I do a vlog, the queen will see it?"

"I think you walk a fine precipice as it is. The queen loathes you. She's already expressed her desire to kill you. And instead of lying low, you wish to further enrage her by releasing a video accusing her of all her crimes."

I mean... when he put it that way, it did sound rather impulsive and reckless. "You don't think the community has a right to know about all of this?"

"I think you're so caught up in the belief that you *can* do it that you aren't stopping to ask if you *should*."

"Vlad—"

"Do you know what the last six months were like for me?"

I started at his question. "Of course I do. I went through the same thing you did."

"Did you?" He lifted a brow. "You had two guards with you at all times, correct?"

I nodded. But I didn't see how that changed anything.

"Did you not also have your precious Weasley?"

Another slow nod.

Vlad cupped my hands. "I had none of that. No guards, no friendly animals, and no idea whether or not the queen had killed you. All I had were endless nights. And when I slept, visions."

I gasped. "You had more visions?"

He grimaced and turned away, releasing my hands, which

instantly grew cold without his palms to warm them. Vlad had mentioned his visions before we were arrested, telling me that he kept seeing my death.

"Is it the same vision?" I asked.

"Always the same. I've seen bits and pieces of the things to come, and while I can't make any sense of them yet, I assure you, they aren't pleasant. And in it, I'm always too late to save you."

I bit the inside of my lip. The first time he'd told me about this vision, he'd said he saw himself holding me after my death, cradling me against him. That hadn't yet come to pass, and considering these visions were still bothering him, it seemed safe to assume that this vision would come to pass.

I shuddered and tucked my hands in between my thighs. "Do you think that's where all this is headed?"

"Anna, Genevieve is far more connected and resourceful than you or I will ever be. She is the *queen*, and if she wants us dead, then that's the fate that awaits us."

"But see, I think we can change our fates!" I said, leaning toward him. "I think we can sway it to our side. What if I die because I *didn't* ask other vampires for help?"

"What if you die because you make a silly video that enrages the queen further?"

A catch twenty-two. Our gazes warred with each other until I finally sighed and broke contact. "I still think it's worth the risk."

"The risk being your life?" he asked.

"Yeah, yeah, I think it's worth it. I could die either way. We'll never know, of course."

"And what about me?" He repositioned himself on the porch, his elbows resting against his knees and his shoulders slumped. I'd never seen Vlad so... defeated. "If my vision plays out, I'm the one left behind to mourn your death. You would ask that of me?"

"Vlad..." I reached for him, but the tightening of his jaw made me pause. "We can't know the future—"

He scoffed, and I bit back a silly chuckle. The moment was far too somber to laugh.

"Maybe not all of us know the future. But even your visions seem... uncertain. They take so long to develop. What if we miss something important in the meantime? All we can do is make our choices and hope they're the right ones."

Vlad shook his head. "I still think the risk is too great."

I needed to get my point across to him, but I wasn't sure how to do it without further upsetting him. "I can't be that person who sits back and does nothing. If the queen is raiding people's homes and burning their livelihoods, others *need* to know of her tyranny. What if their ignorance gets them killed when I could have done something? I have the means to spread this information and the obligation to do so. I understand your fears, and I hate that you were trapped in that darkness for six months, but I can't withhold this from the community because we're frightened of the consequences."

Vlad scoffed, then rose to his feet. "Your altruism will get you killed."

Before I could reply, he shifted into bat form and vanished into the darkness.

CHAPTER

FOURTEEN

MY MOTHER HAD ALWAYS TOLD me the secret to a successful marriage was never going to bed angry. Then she'd laugh and say maybe that was why my father had a mistress. I didn't want that sort of relationship for me and Vlad. Which was why it broke my heart when he didn't return that night. It was five minutes to sunrise, and all us vamps were accounted for, standing next to our coffins. Except him.

Camilla shot me a wary glance, her face twisted with sympathy. Thank goodness she didn't say anything. I couldn't face the comments right now. I just wanted Vlad to walk through that door so I could kiss him good morning before we all tucked ourselves into our coffins.

The minutes ticked down and he didn't show. A kernel of fear bloomed in my chest. What if something had happened to him? What if the queen's men found him? What if the queen had him again? She would kill him just to spite me. And with the sun this close to rising, I certainly couldn't go look for him! We were in a foreign country. Every friend or ally we possessed was currently in this cellar with me. Where the hell was Vlad?

I must have made a panicked noise because Camilla reached out and grasped my hand before giving it a squeeze. "I'm sure he's fine."

Anger flared like the sun within me. I didn't want to hear any silly platitudes or stupid promises.

"Anna." Camilla pushed me into my coffin. "You two will wake tonight and sort all your problems out."

Except, *I* would wake before him. Meaning, I'd have to wait hours to see if he returned home tonight. If he wasn't dead, I sure as hell was going to kill him. If this was some lesson he meant to teach me, now wasn't the time. This was completely inappropriate.

I ground my teeth and laid back in my coffin, thinking of all the ways I'd kill him tonight. The only upside to sunrise was that it would knock me out cold. No way of fretting when you were dead to the world.

Camilla's head hovered over my coffin. She tapped the wooden side, then offered me a sickly smile. I could see the concern in her eyes. Just fantastic. Her worry only amplified mine. I swear, my stomach felt like it'd been infested by the tower rats, all gnawing on my innards.

Before I could say anything, the sun flared to life, and I dropped dead.

⸙

CONSCIOUSNESS WIGGLED in the back of my brain seconds before my eyes snapped open. I peered up into the dark confines and sighed. One would think a girl could get a good night's death around here, but nope. Even in the afterlife, Vlad consumed my thoughts. Part of me wanted to lay here, maybe close my eyes and just go back to sleep. Would it be so bad? Just because we were dead all day didn't mean we couldn't nap, and honestly, the thought of dragging myself out of this coffin just to spend hours worrying about Vlad sounded utterly exhausting.

"He's fine," I murmured to myself, listening to the sound of my muted voice locked up tight in here with me. "He's *fine*. He's Vlad.

He knows how to take care of himself." Not to mention, if the queen had him, she would have sent word last night just to torture me.

Then where was he?

With tired muscles, I pushed back my lid and rose. Six other coffins surrounded me, all laid out in a cramped semi-circle. The cellar wasn't exactly large, and our coffins weren't exactly small. So the only space that remained was a walkway that led to the staircase.

I climbed out and approached Vlad's coffin. The lid still sat half-open, revealing the silk-lined insides and his plump pillow. My damn heart ached at the sight of it. We'd never not spent the day together in the same room, except for our stint in prison.

Glancing down at my hand, I spun my ring and sighed. We hadn't even made it one night into the official engagement before fighting. Hell, I hadn't even had a chance to show off the ring. Off to a great start I see.

I rubbed my cheeks, then turned away from Vlad's empty coffin and ascended the stairs. I could already hear Lucy moving about. When I entered the kitchen, I found her standing next to the island, a wineglass in one hand and a bottle of blood in the other. She handed it over without a word, the top already popped. I took it from her and silently tipped the bottle back, chugging the contents down with nary a breath. Yup, it was going to be one of those nights.

Lucy didn't comment. She simply sipped from her glass and watched. Once upon a time, watching me drink blood would have sickened her. I guess the six months she'd spent with Camilla had cured her of that little delicacy. One upside, I suppose.

After I drained the bottle, I dragged my ass into the living room, slumped onto the couch, and buried my face in my palms.

"Nothing?" Lucy asked. "I was hoping he'd appear at the last moment."

I shook my head, then combed my hair back from my face and blew out another heavy breath. "He doesn't want me to do a vlog."

Lucy sat next to me, the couch hardly shifting under her weight. "I can understand that."

"But I *need* to," I practically exclaimed. "It's my responsibility! This is happening *because* of me, and he just, what, expects me to remain silent? No. I have to speak up about this."

"I also understand that."

I shot her a scathing glare. "Is that really all you have to say?"

Lucy's mouth twisted. She tucked her feet beneath her butt and leaned on the couch arm. "You guys have valid points. I can see both sides."

"Great," I grumbled. "And here I thought you'd side with me."

"Anna..." Lucy reached over and took my hand. "This isn't about choosing sides. This isn't some schoolyard spat. The man is literally terrified he's going to lose you. Can you blame him for being upset when you purposely put yourself in danger?"

"So, what? You think I should just sit down and shut up?"

"I didn't say that."

"Then you think I should do the vlog?"

She gave a humorless chuckle. "I didn't say that either."

Frustration had me biting out a low-pitched growl that probably would have scared the pants off any other human. Instead, Lucy shot me an impatient scowl.

"There isn't a right or wrong here," she finally said. "The question is, can you live with yourself if you don't speak up? Or can you live with yourself if taking such a risk does, in fact, end in your death?"

"You're awfully calm about all this," I sniped.

Lucy's lips tugged into a smirk. "The last six months introduced me to new levels of calm and panic."

Hmm. Well, glad it'd been helpful to someone. It seemed to have given Vlad some sort of complex. And me, well, I wasn't yet sure how my stint in prison had affected me.

I turned and faced Lucy head-on. "What if I don't speak up? And some unlucky vampire somehow finds himself smack dab in the middle of the queen's raids. What if she kills said vampire? My vlog could help. It could spread the word. I have, what, like four million followers?"

"Almost five and a half now."

My jaw dropped. "Oh, uh, that's more than last time."

"Yes, you've become popular since breaking out of prison. Who'd have thunk it?"

I shook off that news. "My point is, how many of those five and a half million followers are vampires? If I can spread the word about the queen's newest antics and increase awareness, maybe these vamps will choose to stand with us."

"Maybe." Lucy took another sip of wine. "It all boils down to what you're willing to risk."

I nodded. This was almost the same conversation Vlad and I had last night. At least Lucy was more willing to hear me out.

"I want to do the vlog," I announced.

"Even if it means angering Vlad further?"

I forced myself to swallow. "I refuse to live my life by anyone's rules but mine. If I don't do something, the guilt will eat me alive. Eternity sounds miserable enough without adding regrets into that."

"You might regret hurting Vlad."

I grimaced. "I-I'll just have to make it up to him somehow. That sounds fixable. Death, however, is rather permanent."

Lucy rocked her hand slightly in a so-so movement. "You're evidence to the contrary."

Okay, I couldn't help but chuckle at that. "Fair enough. But there's no bringing a vampire back from true death. Vlad's anger won't last forever."

"True." She leaned forward and placed her wineglass on the living room table.

Scoffing, I slipped a coaster underneath.

Lucy ignored me, then rose from the couch and dipped out of the room. When she returned, she had a familiar blond wig, massive black sunglasses, and a long colorful scarf. It was the "costume" we'd adopted for my social media presence to give people something to look at. She plopped them on my head, then grabbed the ring light, tripod, and her phone.

"You ready?" she asked.

I repositioned myself on the couch and considered her question. I was ready to tell the vampire community *everything*. But was I ready for Vlad's reaction?

That would be a huge hell no.

THE SUN HAD STARTED its final descent when Lucy published the video across all platforms. She assured me that she'd done all she could to keep our location private by using a VPN and other techie-geek language I so didn't understand. I made content, but I didn't understand the first thing about computers.

The instant the vlog went live, I felt this massive weight fall off my shoulders. My video was a tell-all. I'd started with the night Petrik attacked me. How he'd ripped me out of the vampire club, Fallen, and left me battered and bleeding in the alley. How Vlad had saved my life and taken me into his home. How we'd fallen in love. How Petrik had attempted to finish the job he'd started by trying to burn me alive. How I'd been forced to kill him—I still hadn't been willing to bring Sam's name into this—and how it'd led to the queen unleashing her inquisitors on me. I'd divulged everything and anything I could, including how the queen had kept us prisoner in one of her towers. In the name of transparency, I'd also discussed the escape, how we'd been forced to kill to save our own lives.

At the end, I went into as much detail as I could about the queen's response and how she was raiding—and burning—the homes of her own vampires in search of us. I discussed how horrified I was to learn of her cruel reaction. How sorry I was to hear that some people had lost everything because the queen couldn't keep a hold on her temper. I asked the community how long they were willing to let this continue. Who knew what steps the queen would take next, and were they willing to just sit back and take it?

I wasn't sure what to expect for a response. Either my story would rouse support from the vampire community or it would condemn me. Lucy assured me I had done a good job, but a part of me felt like I could have done more, begged them to take action and stand with us. But I wasn't yet willing to go that far.

"Alright," Lucy murmured. "Comments are rolling in, mostly in your favor, so that's good. Some... not so much."

I nodded, expecting that. "I don't want to know what people are saying. Not yet."

Seconds later, I heard my voice echoing through the house. My head snapped up to find Camilla and Alastair standing in the hallway, listening to my video on one of their phones. Disappointment crushed my chest. If they were awake, that meant Vlad was too, and yet he still hadn't returned home. I didn't know what to think. Was he merely avoiding me? Or was he in danger?

Panic wrapped its cruel fingers around my heart and squeezed. Grimacing, I escaped into the master suite and hopped into the shower. I couldn't stand to hear my voice on their phones, nor could I face the others right now.

I blasted the hot water, and soon the bathroom filled with steam. I faced the wall and dunked my head beneath the scalding spray, palms flat against the tiles. Had I made the right decision here? Airing everything to the public? It wasn't just vampires who would watch, but humans too. My family.

Oh lord, my family.

I hadn't thought about them.

They didn't know I'd escaped prison. At least I was overseas. My mother couldn't reach me here. Yet. But give her time, and she'd berate me for not immediately calling. Thankfully, I didn't have a phone. Only Lucy did. However, my mother knew Lucy's parents. So, it was only a matter of time.

So consumed by my fears and concerns, I didn't realize someone had entered the shower behind me until strong arms came around my waist.

I gasped and whirled around, my hands striking a bare chest. My eyes widened as I found myself staring at Vlad. Usually, the sight of him naked would render me speechless. Instead, tonight, it enraged me.

"What the hell, Vlad!" I shouted, my hands curling into tight fists. "Where the hell have you been!"

He gazed down at me, but rather than respond, he leaned down and kissed me.

As much as I hated to admit it, I melted. His kisses did that to me. They disarmed and fired me up all at the same time. My hands flattened against his pecs and I rose on my tiptoes, eagerly meeting his kiss with a hungry one of my own.

Once I had my fill, I pulled back and gave him a gentle shove, pushing him against the shower wall. "Where. Were. You?"

"I needed space last night," he said, the deep timbre of his voice a salve to my poor frayed nerves. "I apologize. I should have returned before sunrise, but I lost track of time."

"You scared me!" Tears pricked at my eyes, surprising me. I didn't realize until now how terrified I was. "I thought the queen had found you. I thought..." My words broke off with a strangled noise.

Vlad bent his head forward and rested his brow against mine. "Forgive me."

"Of course I forgive you, you dolt."

"Ah, the things you say," he murmured.

"We can't do that to each other," I told him. "We can't scare each other like that."

He lifted his head and met my gaze with a knowing expression. I winced and stepped back. "The vlog is different." I felt his anger spark, but before he could argue, I shook my head. "Don't. It's already done and live."

"I know. I watched it."

"You did?" Surprise had my brows furrowing. "Really?"

"I understand," he said. "I might not like it, but I do understand. And since the video is already live, I suppose all we can do is mitigate the response."

"I couldn't live with myself if I didn't do anything," I said, my voice barely louder than the shower spray.

Vlad nodded. "I won't pretend to understand this need for people to air their dirty laundry, so to speak, but I admit, you told your story rather captivatingly. Hopefully, it's enough to warn people so no one else suffers because of the queen."

I stared at him, watching as the steam swirled around his head. "You're okay with this, then?"

The slight twist to his mouth told me he wasn't, but eventually his eyes fluttered shut and he nodded. "I need to remember that there is an entire world out there. As much as I wish to be selfish and hide you from the queen, that isn't a long-term solution. Her day of reckoning will come. But perhaps we can prepare everyone and lessen the number of innocent bystanders caught in her chaos." He opened his eyes and pinned me with a heated gaze. "Furthermore, I love you, and I want to support you. Your vlog matters to you. Therefore, it matters to me."

Relief loosened my muscles. I slid my arms around his neck and hugged him. "Thank you."

"But you also need to realize how important you are to me. I can't promise I'll always agree with your decisions and actions, but that will never change how I feel about you."

I smiled against his chest. "I love you too."

"Of course you do," he teased. "I'm a loveable guy."

"Well, I wouldn't go that far." I tipped my head back and grinned at him. "You're pretty prickly after all."

A deep growl rumbled in his chest. "I'll show you a pricking."

I gasped, then burst out laughing. "Did you just crack a *sex* joke?" I couldn't recall ever hearing him crack one in the past. Clearly, I was a bad influence.

"It's only a joke if I wasn't serious."

I barely had time to piece together his words before he had me pressed up against the warm shower wall, where he proceeded to indeed show me a good pricking.

CHAPTER

FIFTEEN

Unsurprisingly, the second we shut off the water, someone knocked on the bathroom door. I would have bet all my money it was Camilla. The vampiress took great pleasure in pissing me off, and back in Louisiana, one of her favorite past times had consisted of teasing me about Vlad's and my sex life.

"If the two of you are finally finished in there, we have some matters to discuss out here." She paused. "You know, with the clothed people." Another pause. "The people not grunting and moaning." A third, longer pause. "Those of us not enjoying a—what was that, Lucy, like five minutes—quickie?"

"Camilla!" I shouted, my voice reverberating in the bathroom.

Lucy's chuckle rose to my ears. She must have been standing outside the door too. Bunch of perverts in this house, seriously! Vlad shook his head and clucked under his breath, but honestly, we were both pretty used to this now. Nothing was secret when you lived in a house full of vampires, and the two of us had long since stopped caring about being overheard. If we did, we'd never be intimate together again. And that just wasn't happening.

"Well?" Camilla shouted back. "Are you coming or not?"

With a naughty smirk, I called out, "Just did. A few times actually."

Lucy groaned, and I listened to the sounds of her grumbling as she stomped away. Served her right. If they couldn't take it, perhaps they shouldn't dish it out.

"We probably should head out there," I said, reaching for one of the fluffy towels.

Vlad hummed a noncommittal response and instead reached for my bare, soaked ass. I laughed and swatted his hand away.

"Come on, guys," Camilla grumbled through the door. "I'm still here and can hear you. Hurry, okay? We have things we need to discuss, and I don't know, a city full of vampires and their queen to worry about."

Yeah, she wasn't wrong.

"Talk about killing my lady boner," I complained.

Vlad blinked and lifted a brow. "What the heck is a lady boner?"

"Exactly what it sounds like," I said, laughing. When he didn't respond, I winked and grinned. "My imaginary dick. And sometimes, not so imaginary."

"You have a non-imaginary penis?"

I almost doubled over laughing. Priceless. Just priceless. Vlad had learned some sarcasm, but there were still some things that blew over his innocent little head. Truly, there wasn't anything innocent about him, but his ignorance of pop culture and modern ways always gave me a laugh.

"Every girl has a non-imaginary penis. They're usually colored—purple, red, blue—and vibrate."

Understanding warmed his face, and he chuckled. "Ah."

"Mine was ribbed for her pleasure."

"For your pleasure," he clarified.

"Definitely for my pleasure."

"I think I should like to meet this non-imaginary friend of yours."

I waggled my brows. "Pedro is a little possessive, but sure, I think he'd like to meet you too."

"His name is Pedro?" Amusement curled Vlad's lips.

"I could name him The Impaler, instead?" At the sound of Vlad coughing into his hand, I grinned. Success. "You know what, I think he's due for a name change, and I rather like The Impaler. Very formal. Regal. And so fitting."

Vlad shook his head, then climbed out of the shower and toweled off.

Guess our moment had concluded. Boo.

Sighing, I did the same, but I took the time to dry my hair before throwing it up into a messy bun. Once I had it styled just right, I strode through the kitchen to find everyone seated at the dining room table. Okay, perhaps I had taken a little longer than necessary, but you know what, after being locked up for six months, a girl needed to take a few moments for self-care. Such as blow-outs and shower sex. Surely no one could blame me.

The look on Mateo's face said otherwise.

Camilla rose to her feet and circled to the head of the table, resting her hand on the veneer. "Now that we're all here, we can get down to business. First, Anna's video-vlog-thing, whatever, is trending." She shot Lucy a look and lifted a brow as though to ask, "Did I say that right?"

Lucy chuckled and nodded.

"Okay, trending. Good."

Lucy and I both bit back identical chuckles. Bringing these vampires into the twenty-first century had to be my favoritest thing ever.

"The responses, however—"

Lucy interrupted with a subtle cough, then shared a glance with Camilla. When Camilla nodded, Lucy rose from her seat. "There's been an influx of comments from both vampires and humans alike. Unfortunately, we're seeing more concern for human well-being than vampires. But it might just be because vampires aren't speaking up for fear of angering the queen. Those who *have* spoken up are those who were present during last night's chaos. Some claim the raids were peaceful. Others have reported what they lost. Houses, cellars, sheds. Thankfully, no casualties. The queen and her men were careful to protect all life. They are apparently warning everyone that their house will be burned down beforehand to give them time to evacuate their people."

"How... kind of her?" I asked, frowning.

"Others..." Lucy hesitated, then sighed and faced me. "Others are demanding your surrender and are insisting you turn yourself over to the queen and accept your punishment."

I bit my tongue. I'd expected it. Much like with any political issue, there were always those who believed the government was always in the right.

"Over my dead body," Vlad growled.

Lucy nodded and glanced at her phone. "There's no way for us to know whether the queen has watched the video, but I would say it seems safe to assume she has. I'm sure someone from her council has likely brought it to her attention."

Seemed a wise guess.

"The raids haven't started yet tonight. But that's not to say they won't. The queen might just be organizing the troops, or perhaps they're discussing different tactics. Either way, we won't know for a bit yet. However, people are aware, and at the very least, can take action to protect themselves. Otherwise, there's not much more we can do except continue forward with the plan," Lucy said.

"And that's where I come in," Camilla interrupted.

Everyone's focus swung to her. She cleared her throat, then gestured toward the whiteboard she'd scribbled on last night. "I've reached out to Gabriel and arranged a meeting."

"You have?" Alastair leaned forward, his elbows braced on the table. A frown twisted his features, one that had me concerned. Usually, he wore a smug grin or some sort of saccharine expression.

"What's the big deal?" I asked. "She said yesterday that she could reach out to him. And she did."

"It's not that simple," Alastair murmured, sharing quite the stern stare with Camilla. When she didn't move, he gestured at her, then us.

"Uh, guys?" I asked. Clearly, we were missing something here.

"Tell them, Camilla," Alastair said. "They need to know."

"Know what?"

A question others echoed around the table.

Camilla sighed, then ran a hand through her long hair. "Fine. So most of you are, thankfully, unaware of my past."

"I believe I know a great deal about your past," Vlad argued. "Considering how long we've been friends."

Camilla nodded. "But that doesn't mean you know everything about me."

"By all means," Vlad said, clearly amused by her assumption.

"Last night, I told you that I know Gabriel personally."

I nodded.

"Well, he and I have quite the past. One I rarely speak of."

"What sort of past?" Vlad questioned.

Camilla and Alastair shared a glance. I didn't know much about their history, but it did seem as though they were closer than Camilla and Vlad. Which I found a tad surprising. I thought Camilla was one of Vlad's closest confidants, and perhaps she was. But maybe he wasn't hers.

"Gabriel is my..." Her eyes fluttered shut, as though she had to work up the strength to utter whatever it was she held back.

"Her mate," Alastair finally said.

Camilla glared at him, but he simply shrugged.

"Your... mate," I repeated, stunned. "Gabriel, the queen's youngest son, the prince?" I shared a glance with Vlad. "Is your mate?"

Camilla's mouth compressed, but she nodded. "We met soon after he was turned by the queen's consort. And similarly to you and Vlad, we instantly knew."

"Okay... Then why aren't you two, like, together? What happened?"

"His mother," Camilla said. "The queen didn't approve of..." She gestured to her face. "Well, me."

Meaning the queen didn't approve of Camilla's skin color. I growled and leaned back in my seat.

"Gabriel and I met just after he was turned," Camilla said, as though that excused it. "It's a volatile time. A new vampire needs their sire more than anything in those first months. If the queen had ordered it, Adrian would have been forced to turn Gabriel out into the cold. So when I saw how difficult I made his life, I left."

"You left," Vlad repeated. "Just upped and left."

"Brutal," Breccan said.

I shot him a stunned glance, almost surprised to find him here. He and Rebecca had been so quiet that I'd almost forgotten about their presence.

After being parted from Vlad for so long, I could easily imagine the agony Camilla and Gabriel must have felt. But for Gabriel to have let her go so easily sorta made me not like the guy. Not that I'd ever liked him. He was the queen's son, after all. That pretty much made him evil in my books.

"I never told Gabriel why I left," Camilla commented, as though she could read my thoughts. "I just vanished one night."

"And how long ago was this?"

"About a hundred and fifty years ago," she said.

"I've known you for almost two hundred years," Vlad stated. "And you never thought to mention your connection to him?"

"It didn't feel necessary. You and I met before I met him. Then he and I weren't together long before I cut ties. He stayed here in England, and I left for the Americas."

"And now you've reached out to him?" I asked.

She nodded again.

My gaze leapt between all the surrounding faces. No one seemed concerned about this news whatsoever. But I sure as hell was. "What if Gabriel betrays us? Anyone consider that? What if he's so pissed at Camilla for leaving him that he decides, screw it, I'm going to hand them all over, and good riddance."

"Gabriel wouldn't do that," Camilla argued.

"Really? And you know that, after a hundred and fifty years of estrangement?"

She blew a piece of hair back from her face and dropped into a nearby chair. "You don't know him, but he was never the golden boy like Elias. The queen and her consort raised him from childhood, but he never blindly followed their ideals and beliefs. Not like Elias. Whenever the queen steps out of line, it's Gabriel who calms her down and helps her see reason."

"A lot can change in that amount of time, Camilla."

She frowned at me. "I think I know who he is, Anna."

"Do you? Because I would argue the opposite. I would argue that you don't know him the slightest bit. For all you know, she has him under her thumb now, just like his brother."

"I know otherwise," Camilla shot back. "I've been watching him since the queen took you. I suspected we'd need his help at some point."

I understood her implication and believed she'd done her research. But how were we supposed to know for sure that he wouldn't betray us all? Could we take the risk?

"When and where is the meeting?" Vlad finally asked.

"Two a.m. at Noir Masquerade."

Lucy and I shared a glance, but we both shrugged, so I asked, "And that would be?"

"A pub," Breccan answered. "Specifically, a fanger pub. Blokes come from all over to get nipped."

"Bet the ole codger will love that," Alastair muttered, chuckling.

"So like The Vampire Lounge back home?" I asked.

"Not at all. It's an actual bar. Dark, dingy, just the way us *creatures of the night* like it." She rolled her eyes. "No rules. Just vampires out looking for a meal and a lay, and a bunch of willing humans looking for a good time."

"Lovely," Lucy mumbled.

"Fear not," Alastair told her, winking. "I'll protect you."

"We have a couple of hours then until we need to leave. Camilla, Anna and I will accompany you to meet with Gabriel, while the rest remain here," Vlad said.

"What?" Voices rose around the table in a cacophony of noise.

Vlad held up a hand and waited until everyone quieted before he continued. "The queen is searching for us. Traveling in large numbers would draw unwanted attention. The three of us stand a better chance at successfully meeting with the prince."

"You're kidding, right?" Breccan said, his accent thickening with displeasure. "You two are on the queen's shit list. If anything, you should be the ones remaining behind."

"Out of the question," Vlad said. "Camilla needs a strong ally—" Everyone ramped up again, but when Vlad fell silent, they did the same. "I am the strongest and oldest here. I will accompany her."

"Fine, but Anna isn't going!" Alastair argued, his eyes practically sparking with anger.

Vlad frowned and considered the Brit with an unnerving silence. Even I bit my lip. Alastair had shown a tendency to flirt, but that was all I'd thought it was.

"Anna doesn't leave my side," Vlad finally said. He reached out and grasped my hand in a silent show of dominance. Regardless of how much I hated testosterone battles, I didn't shake it off. I liked the feel of his hand wrapped around mine too much to go without.

"Unbelievable," Alastair snapped. "You all see how ridiculous this is, right? Anna herself is worried about Gabriel betraying us, and you're just going to take her with you, essentially handing her to our enemy."

"Moments ago, this wasn't a problem for you," Vlad stated. "You seem to only care because you won't be there. I have to wonder why."

Alastair grumbled an incoherent response and leaned back in his chair like a sullen child. I shot Lucy a nervous glance, one she mirrored. Alastair didn't know me in the slightest, but Lucy had mentioned that he'd been following me on social media for a while. Was that what this was about? Some sort of fascination with me because of my fame? If so, I didn't like it one bit.

"Vlad," Rebecca interjected, her voice breaking the tension. "Perhaps it would be best to leave Anna here with us. We would keep her safe, you know that. We've done it before."

Vlad's face tightened. I knew his thoughts before he spoke them, and I winced inwardly in preparation of hearing them aloud.

"The last time I asked my allies to protect the woman I love, she was abducted and nearly killed."

No one mentioned that Vlad had been there that night too. That path seemed like certain death if anyone spoke those words. Instead, I tightened my fingers around Vlad's and turned to face him. For a brief moment, I'd intended to assure him I would be safe here. But the instant I spotted the look on his face, I knew it wouldn't happen. To others, his expression likely looked like sheer stubbornness, but I saw the underlying fear. Vlad had certainly developed a complex. One I wasn't willing to push right now. It wouldn't hurt for me to accompany them. A dark, dingy pub didn't sound at all like the queen's scene, considering she'd been targeting residential houses.

"Okay," I said, nodding. "I'll go with you. The others can stay here. We'll meet with this Gabriel, and then immediately return here."

"Anna." Lucy reached out and touched my arm. I could sense her concern, but it seemed pointless to argue it. After everything we'd been through, it seemed only fair that Vlad and I kept each other in our sights at all times. And after last night, even I wasn't quite ready to part with him. Co-dependency issues? You bet. Some psychiatrist would likely have a field day with the two of us. But these were unique circumstances, and I was more than willing to avoid logical advice right now.

"Fine," Lucy said. "But then I'm going too."

"No," both Vlad and I said at the same time.

Lucy's mouth parted with what I was sure was some in-depth explanation as to how she was better off with us, but I shook my head.

"Three vampires going to a vampire bar is normal," I said. "But three vampires plus a human attracts attention. And if word gets back to the queen, the last thing we need is her finding out about you."

"Like she'd care about me," Lucy grumbled.

"Oh, she'd care." I remembered the look on the human servant's face back in the queen's throne room. I would have bet my right fang that woman hadn't been there by choice. "Besides, she'd see you as our weakest link—"

"Gee, thanks."

"—and one of the easiest ways to hurt me. We can't risk that."

Lucy shook her head, but thankfully, she stopped arguing. Instead, she, too, sat back in her chair and pouted. At this rate, we were going to have a room full of toddlers.

"At least keep in contact with us. Everyone who's going takes a phone, just in case something happens, and you guys get separated," Rebecca suggested. "We can send messages to each other every ten minutes so we know everyone is safe."

"I like that." I glanced at Lucy with a raised brow.

"Not only are you leaving me behind, but now you want my phone too? Are you kidding me? What the heck am I supposed to do here all night?"

I chuckled at her theatrics. "I'm sure you can find something to occupy your time."

"You suck, you know that?"

A genuine smile chased across my face. "I do, indeed."

The entire table erupted in a series of groans.

"Bad form," Alastair jested. "Vamp jokes aren't welcome here."

Lucy nodded. "Especially horrible vamp jokes."

I laughed, then took her phone and pushed to my feet, Vlad's hand still in mine. "Shall we?"

He didn't look quite as eager, but I suppose, neither did I.

Camilla, on the other hand, practically glowed, she was so excited. It was almost hard to watch, considering we had no idea how Gabriel would respond to her appearance.

I only hoped he didn't break her heart.

Or worse.

CHAPTER

SIXTEEN

Wrapped in a long, white, quilted parka with a furred hood, I strolled through the streets with my arm hooked through Vlad's. Unsurprisingly, he'd found himself a mid-thigh length, black pea coat and had popped the collar to obscure the sides of his face. Though we didn't require the winter gear, my skin seemed much happier without the wind biting at it. And as a bonus, we blended in with the surrounding humans who practically shivered, even with their fleece mittens and scarves.

"There," Camilla murmured, pointing across the street. She'd chosen a puffy, apricot-colored jacket I thought looked utterly hideous on her. She seemed to like it though, especially with its white faux fur trim.

I glanced in the direction she pointed and noted the bar shrouded in shadows. This time in the morning, there wasn't much of a line, but I did note the bouncer standing guard at the front door. I scraped my teeth over my bottom lip as I contemplated our options. If we acted suspiciously, we'd draw attention to ourselves, and we very much needed to avoid that right now. We needed to act as though we often frequented establishments like this. Which would be hard, considering I'd never stepped foot inside a vampire bar and had no idea what to expect.

Back home, The Vampire Lounge was laid out similarly to a restaurant. You were given a booth with a privacy curtain, then offered a meal—aka a human—on which to dine for the evening. I suspected that wouldn't be the situation here. Guess we weren't in Kansas anymore.

"Ready?" Camilla asked. She practically vibrated with energy.

I could only imagine how this felt for her. Being parted from a mate for six months was painful enough. Camilla had endured it for more than a century. I couldn't even begin to imagine the thoughts running through her head. But I did find myself worrying about her. There seemed just as likely of a chance that Gabriel wouldn't appreciate her presence, not after she'd jumped ship and bailed on him. Tonight might not end in a happy reunion for them. I couldn't tell her that. It killed me to even think of destroying that little spark of hope within her.

Vlad laid his bare hand over the one I had tucked into the crook of his arm and guided me across the street. But I stopped midway when the first few snowflakes began to fall. I lifted my head and stared up at the sky. As a born and raised southern girl, I'd rarely seen snow before.

A splotch of cold touched my nose, and I touched the chilled spot with my finger. It melted so fast! With a breathy laugh, I unwound myself from Vlad and lifted my hands, watching as the small flakes fell into my palms and instantly vanished.

"It's beautiful," I whispered.

Vlad's hand found the small of my back, and he continued guiding me across the street. "Remind me to show you how to build a snowman before we leave this forsaken country."

A snowman!

My foot splashed in something squishy, and I glanced down to find a slush puddle surrounding my boots. The liquid seeped in, and I gasped when the cold water invaded my socks. Okay, *that* sensation I didn't like. Squishy feet. Not a fan.

I stepped up onto the curb and shook out my foot, as though that would dry it off. Wishful thinking, apparently.

"Gabriel's people said he'd meet us inside, at the bar."

I froze on the sidewalk and lifted my head. "Wait, what? Gabriel's people? You didn't actually speak to Gabriel?"

A cloud of air puffed past Camilla's lips when she chuckled. "Of course not. You can't just *call* the princes."

"Camilla!" I snapped. "If you didn't speak to Gabriel, how the hell can we guarantee that he even got your message?"

She waved a hand. "You worry too much. Any message from me would go through to Gabriel immediately. Don't worry, I didn't mention you or Vlad. I just said I was here to see him."

Annoyance flared within me, and I gritted my teeth to keep from lashing out at her. *This* was her plan? To hide from the queen's son that he would be meeting not only with his estranged mate, but also the two "traitors" she was currently helping? We were so screwed.

I turned, about to dart back across the street and put this whole ridiculous plan behind us, when Vlad's touch stopped me.

"We're already here," he said. "May as well see what happens."

"Are you kidding me right now? *Any* plan is better than this. Look, I know you guys have faith in this Gabriel-turd. But I don't. I don't know anything about him except that he's Genevieve's *son*. You know, the woman who wants to stake me dead? You lured him here under false pretenses. Camilla, he's going to be pissed!"

"Calm down," Camilla hissed. "Let's just go inside, okay? You and Vlad can hang out somewhere safe in the back, and I'll meet with Gabriel alone. If it makes you feel better, I'll tell him all about you guys and what we're asking of him before I introduce him to you."

"We never should have come to this meeting," I stated, scraping a hand down my face. "And you guys thought *my* plan was insane. Anything is better than surprising the effing prince and hoping he'll help us overthrow his mother."

"Hush," Vlad urged. "There are sensitive ears surrounding us. We wouldn't want word to spread to the queen about our location."

Quietly grumbling, I stomped forward a few steps. When neither Vlad nor Camilla followed me, I reined in my temper and spun on my wet heel. "Well?"

Both grimaced, then trailed after me. I gritted my teeth to keep from blurting out something waspish and instead marched toward the bouncer.

At the door, he held up a hand, indicating we should stop. I patted my pockets, and only then remembered I had *nothing*. No money, no phone, nada.

Camilla nudged me aside and handed over a small stack of euros. The bouncer dipped his head, then shoved open what looked like a metal door. The instant the door cracked open, heavy music thumped out into the street, the beat practically reverberating in my bones. A few people stopped to gawk at us vampires but moved on when the bouncer curled a lip.

Vlad grasped my hand and led me inside, the width of his back and shoulders blocking my view. When he finally stepped out of the way, I grimaced at the sight before us. Noir Masquerade was an elegant name for an inelegant location. Literally, one bar sat across the room, wrapping around its width. Behind it stood a bartender who slung drinks like his life depended on it. Other than that, the place was a hole in the wall. A few bar stools, some chipped benches, torn booths... nothing with the grace or class of The Vampire Lounge.

My gaze swept over the bar, and I caught sight of vampires brazenly sucking at the necks and wrists of humans. Humans who seemed rather intoxicated.

I sighed and shook my head. This was *exactly* the sort of institution I might have loved to find back when I was human. Something to prove vampires were far more dangerous than humans believed. Guess my story had proved that claim tenfold.

"Lovely," I muttered.

"It's a watering hole," Camilla called back to me, her voice mingling with the music. "Humans come here to get wasted and donate some blood. They get paid for their time and donation."

And that made it alright? This was the equivalent of slapping a Band-Aid on a broken foot and calling it healed. Guess it didn't matter that a few of these humans looked like they might keel over any second now from extreme blood loss. At least back home, The Vampire Lounge had rules about how often the humans could feed us. Rules I assumed were in place not only for their protection but ours as well. Noir Masquerade laughed in the face of those rules.

"Why don't you guys hang out over there." Camilla pointed to a shadowed corner, one barely visible from here. "Gabriel should be here any minute now, and I don't want him to see me with you two until I've had a chance to explain the situation to him."

Vlad and I did as she asked and seated ourselves on two unbalanced stools.

Honestly, this reminded me of a few dive bars Lucy and I had gone to back in the day. A place to stir up trouble. Not that we'd ever done anything too terrible. At least, not compared to all this.

"What do you think's gonna happen?" I asked.

I eyed our close surroundings, but Camilla was right. No one seemed to even notice us, let alone venture toward us. A few humans mingled nearby, hitting up every vampire they could find, but the darkness seemed to hide us from eyesight. And thank goodness for that. Fending off human advances was the very last thing I wanted to do right now.

"I can't say," Vlad said.

Nodding, I rifled around in my pocket and pulled out Lucy's phone. There was already a message from her from Alastair's phone asking if we'd made it safely. I responded, then tucked the phone away, making a mental note to send another message in ten minutes.

"I guess there're only two possible outcomes here." I leaned back in the chair, careful not to throw my weight around in case its legs snapped like little twigs. "Either he agrees to help, which, yay. Or he shows up with the queen's men and has us arrested."

"If the latter occurs, I want you to immediately use the exit behind us."

I followed his gaze to the bright *exit* sign hovering above yet another metal door. "Yeah, running would probably be the best bet. I guess we just need to hope we can outrun them."

"No," Vlad said. "Not us. You."

I froze, his words thrumming through my head along with the heavy beat. When he didn't correct his final sentence, I leaned forward. "Wait, what? Did I hear you right?"

Vlad reached out and took my hand. The second his fingers closed around mine, I knew I'd definitely heard him right. Anger rose within me.

"Listen to me." He ran his thumb along my knuckles. "Camilla and I can hold our own. If Gabriel betrays us, we will stay behind and fight. You will run and get back to the house where the others can protect you."

A bitter laugh scraped past my throat. "You can't be serious."

He didn't answer, proving he was indeed serious.

"This is ridiculous," I spat out. I pulled my hand free of his and fisted it. Then I rose from my seat and stole a few steps away from him. I needed a moment to gather my thoughts and settle my emotions before I did something I'd regret, like slap the damn stupid out of his stupid manly head. Why did men always resort to this? Me, big bad man, protect helpless puny mate. Guess it proved that vampire or not, all males had this caveman tendency.

"Anna—"

I lifted a hand and silenced him. Then I faced him with what I hoped was my *boy, you best shut up* scowl. "First of all, if you think I'd *ever* abandon you or Camilla in a situation like that, then you don't know me at all."

He opened his mouth yet again, but I pointed at him and canted my head. He immediately shut up.

"Second of all, need I remind you, *again*, that I've been trained to fight! I'm not some hapless little heroine who needs her knight in shining armor to dash in and save the day. If Gabriel betrays us, and I'm leaning heavily toward that happening, I will fight alongside the two of you." I closed the distance between us and cupped his face, all the while holding his gaze. "And for the sake of our relationship, how about you never suggest I abandon you again. The answer will always be the same."

Emotions streaked across Vlad's face, but after a moment's hesitation, he finally nodded before leaning in and stealing a light kiss. Damn straight, he better apologize with a kiss, suggesting something as idiotic as that.

"Forgive me. When it comes to you, I'll do anything to keep you safe."

"Same goes for me. No way in hell I'd leave you behind."

"Then I guess we're both fools in love," he teased.

My mouth quirked. "Guess so, lover boy."

I looped my arms around his neck and stepped between his thighs, brushing a light kiss against his cheek. He gripped my waist and held me tight. Thankfully, it didn't progress beyond that. I still remembered the night Lucy and I had gone to Fallen and the things we'd seen. My thoughts immediately jumped to the vampire couple we'd seen necking in the corner. Except, they'd been doing more than necking. *Much* more. Luckily for us, voyeurism wasn't our thing. So there weren't any eager beaver hands doing anything other than hugging here.

"How's Camilla doing?" I turned in Vlad's arms and found her still standing at the bar, looking a little dejected. This had to be tough for her, waiting for her mate to suddenly appear.

"I see no sign of Gabriel," Vlad said, his breath brushing the back of my neck.

An involuntary but pleasurable shiver rolled down my spine and arms. "Think he's going to stand her up?"

"Hmm. Hard to say. Speaking from experience, I would find it incredibly difficult to avoid my mate if I knew she'd asked to see me."

"Speaking from experience, your mate would never pack her bags and just leave."

Vlad chuckled, his chest vibrating against my back. "While I appreciate the sentiment, we can't judge her actions. We don't know the situation leading up to her choices."

"How magnanimous of you," I teased.

"Well, it's easy for me to say. However, were it me in their situation, I doubt I'd feel so forgiving."

I nodded, understanding exactly what he meant. Soulmates among vampires was an eternal thing. There was no breaking the bond. It'd likely caused them both a great deal of pain when Camilla jumped ship. But Vlad was right. Without knowing their circumstances, we couldn't judge. If the queen hadn't approved of Camilla, I couldn't imagine Genevieve had made their lives easy.

Vlad and I fell into a comfortable silence as we waited. But soon, the minutes began to feel like they were dragging. I kept glancing at the mangled clock dangling from a chipped wall and watching as the seconds ticked by. For someone who was going to live forever, time sure felt slow right now. Then again, I wasn't known for my patience, and waiting wasn't one of my skills.

I started to grow antsy and shifted my weight against Vlad. After my third or fourth sigh, Vlad's arms tightened around me, offering my nerves a bit of reprieve.

"This is getting tedious. He should have been here by now."

Vlad grunted in agreement. "Perhaps we should go speak to Camilla."

I shot her a glance to find her leaning on the bar, her shoulders slumped in defeat. It seemed she'd come to the same conclusion as us, and my heart broke for her.

"Maybe his people didn't pass the message on?" I suggested. "Maybe he has some sort of *do not disturb* sign on his door when it comes to her?"

"Meaning...?"

"Meaning, maybe he doesn't want to speak to her."

Vlad fell quiet, but his index fingers tapped against my sides. After a few moments, he pushed to his feet and clasped my hand. "Come.

Let's collect her and leave. There's no point in us sticking around. The longer we wait, the more we risk ourselves."

I nodded. Considering most of the patrons were too consumed in one another to really notice us, I wasn't too worried now about being recognized, but Vlad was right. It only took one person.

Together, we approached Camilla. She must have heard our footsteps, even over the music, because she turned.

"Camilla, I'm so sorry," I said. It was clear how much she'd hoped to see him again.

But, in true Camilla style, she shrugged and forced a smile. "Hey, at least we tried, right? I can't say I blame him. It's not like we ended things on a good note."

"Someday, I'd like to hear that story. But how about, for now, we head home?"

"Yeah. That's probably for the best. We can regroup and decide on plan B."

Looping my arm through Camilla's, we moved through the sparse crowd in search of the main door. We hadn't made it halfway through the room when someone suddenly dove inside, blood dripping down his face. He staggered to a stop just as the music cut off, then dropped to his knees.

It took a second for recognition to dawn, but I eventually realized it was the bouncer from outside.

He opened his mouth and blood gurgled out. But it was the words he spoke that turned the blood in my veins to ice.

"The queen's guards... are here."

CHAPTER
SEVENTEEN

"Camilla!" I whirled toward her, my body already trembling. Whether it was from nerves or adrenaline, I couldn't tell. "Did Gabriel do this?"

The guards hadn't raided businesses last night. They hadn't even been raiding tonight! So why now? Why here? Was it because of us? Did Gabriel betray us? Or Gabriel's people? Or had someone here recognized us? And why was the bouncer bleeding? All the raids had been peaceful. Why escalate matters now?

Vlad grabbed the bouncer by the arm and hauled him up from the floor. "How many?"

"I-I don't know," he rasped. "One of the guards approached me a few minutes ago, demanding information. I told him to fuck off." The bouncer winced both in pain and reflection. "Stupid, right?"

"Quite."

"While he was smashing my face into the side of the building, I heard him call to others. They'll be here—"

The main door slammed open, and a chilled breeze swirled inside. For a brief moment, I heard a faint voice in my head chanting, "They're heerreeee..." I might have laughed were the situation not so grim. If they were resorting to violence, that meant no one here was safe. Least of all us. Especially considering our history with the queen's men. Thankfully, no guards accompanied the wind.

"Vlad..." I grasped his arm, my fingers trembling. I silently berated myself. Had I not just been telling him I could handle this? To not treat me like some damsel in distress? I needed to suck it up and push the fear down.

"Out the back," he ordered me and Camilla, pointing toward that illuminated exit sign.

"The place is probably surrounded by now," the bouncer wheezed, gripping his stomach.

"Fucking great," Camilla grumbled. "I swear, if this is Gabriel's fault, I'll kill him."

I swung her a startled look. I highly doubted she'd be able to kill her mate, but damn, she sure sounded serious. Her hardened expression frightened even me, and she was one of my closest friends.

"We need a way out," Camilla commented, her body swiveling in every direction as she searched our surroundings.

I did the same, but I could only make out the two exits. "We'll have to fight."

"We can't just fight!" Camilla shouted. "We're going to be outnumbered."

I froze, my eyes falling on her. She had the gift of battle-sense, meaning she could see in advance how fights played out. Usually, Camilla was calm and collected because she already knew the end result before it happened. Tonight, she was crazed. Desperate. She kept spinning in circles in search of a solution. Which told me one thing.

We were going to lose.

"This way!" someone unfamiliar shouted.

A hand came down on my arm, but it wasn't Vlad or Camilla's. I spun around to find a middle-aged vampire staring at me. I recognized him immediately. The bartender. He whipped a dirty towel off his shoulder, then pointed behind him.

"Ever seen the movie *Shaun of the Dead*?"

I blinked at the vamp and shook my head, utterly baffled by such an odd question.

He gestured for us to follow him, then dashed behind the counter.

I didn't even hesitate. Anything was better than standing here like an idiot when the guards finally decided to swarm the place. Vlad and Camilla chased after me, but it was Camilla I heard cursing under her breath about trusting a stranger. But who else could we trust?

The bartender tucked us low behind the counter, then pointed at the floor. I had to squint to see it, but there was a thin square seam large enough for someone to slip through. A secret exit?

My jaw gaped and I lifted my head.

The bartender shrugged. "Always good to be prepared, right? It's an emergency exit. This ain't our first rodeo."

I had no idea what that meant, but hey, I wasn't going to look a gift-horse in the mouth. The bartender pushed on the floor, and I heard the telltale click of a lock unlatching. The door then popped open enough for him to slip his fingers under and open it the rest of the way.

"Go, quickly. If they find you here, they'll burn this place down."

I nodded. "Thank you. You didn't have to help us."

He gave another noncommittal shrug. "It's time someone stood up to the queen. I caught your video this evening, kid. Very brave of you."

I beamed with pride. At least someone didn't think I was stupid for speaking up.

"Now get. It won't be long—"

"Oi!" A shout came from across the room. I couldn't see, hiding beneath the counter as we were, but I could hear the guards filing into the bar. "By the order of the queen, we've been instructed to search this building. We're looking for two fugitives. And believe me when I say, you're gonna want to speak up if you know where they are."

The bartender held his finger to his lips, then pointed into the deep, dark hole. We had no idea what was down there, but honestly, anything was preferable to what awaited us in the bar. Last time we'd gone head-to-head against the guards, I'd taken a blade to the side, and Vlad had nearly lost his head. I wasn't eager to repeat those events.

I leaned in and gave the bartender a quick hug before slipping my legs over the edge and jumping. Air streamed around my head and my stomach flipped, but before I knew it, I was on my feet and standing in what appeared to be a dusty storeroom.

Without pause, I hurried out of the way to allow for Vlad and Camilla to join me. Both landed as quietly as cats, then Vlad grabbed my arm and pulled me into the nearby shadows, pressing my back flat against his chest and wrapping his arms around my waist. I felt the tension in his muscles and knew he was prepared to fight.

The bartender sealed us in without the slightest sound.

Movement came to our right and I nearly jumped when Camilla's breath brushed my ear. "There's an exit leading to the street, but I can hear guards out there. We'll need to wait them out."

Fuck. That sounded pretty damn miserable. My eyes fluttered shut as I struggled to settle my nerves. I didn't like it down here. Thanks to my vampiric senses, I could see in the dark, but that didn't mean I liked it. We were trapped like rats. Had I been a fool to trust the bartender?

No. No, I had to believe he had our best interests at heart. If he'd meant to hand us over, he could have just shouted for the guards.

Footsteps thundered above us, raining dust down around our heads.

"Hey! What are you doing back here?" the guard's deep voice boomed from above.

I squeezed my lips together to keep from gasping. The guard stood directly above us. Any sound would notify him of our presence.

The bartender rifled through his bottles, then dropped them down onto the counter with heavy thuds. "Thought you and your men might want something to drink. It's cold out there."

Silence reigned.

"Have you seen the two fugitives we're looking for?" The guard's British accent thickened dramatically.

"Sorry, mate. Haven't seen them. It's been a quiet night here, as you can see, so I'd know if I saw their faces."

Fear twisted my gut. If they found out he'd lied, they'd kill him and burn this bar to the ground. I couldn't stand that thought. He'd gone out of his way to protect us. We needed to do the same.

As though sensing my thoughts, Vlad's arms tightened around me like vices. I tilted my head up and caught the subtle shake of his head. His dark gaze held mine until I finally nodded. We had to trust that the bartender could handle this.

"Wouldn't be lying to me now, would ya?" the guard demanded.

"No, sir. Wouldn't risk my business on something like that."

"Hmm." The guard moved position, his heavy-soled boots practically reverberating above our heads.

Fuck, I hated this.

"Thing is..."

Oh shit. There was a *thing*.

"We received a report tonight claiming that the fugitives and one of their allies were planning to meet someone here."

My hand shot out to clutch Camilla's, and she squeezed my fingers.

Gabriel.

He truly had betrayed us.

"That might be," the bartender said, "but I wasn't lying. Maybe you got here too early? I can keep an eye out for them, though, letcha know if they do show."

"Awfully accommodating of you," the guard leered, his voice clearly suspicious.

The bartender fell quiet. Eventually, I heard him rinsing out a few glasses. I could picture him up there, doing his job as the guards relentlessly questioned him and his patrons. I only hoped no one else spoke up.

"Hmm." The guard turned and thumped across the floor.

I watched the dust shake free of the rafters and closed my eyes, listening to the sound of the guards moving toward the exit. I relaxed against Vlad and rested my head on his chest. Looked like we were in the clear.

"Burn it down."

I froze. Vlad stiffened. Camilla's hand tensed.

"What?" the bartender shouted. "Hey! I told you everything."

"And yet, I get the feeling you weren't being entirely honest with me." The guard's boots clomped. "Do as I say. Burn it down."

"But, sir—" a guard argued.

A strangled yelp echoed through the upper level before something heavy thumped to the floor.

"I *said* burn it the fuck down!"

"Eh, fuck you!" the bartender shouted. I heard the distinctive slap of his towel hitting the counter. Then he stomped across the bar, closing in on the guards. "You wanna know why people are rebelling against the queen? It's because of shit like this! You're tyrants, the whole lot of ya!"

"No, no, no, no," I quietly chanted under my breath. If he kept up this tirade—

I couldn't even finish the thought before I heard it.

The telltale sound of a head being severed.

I swallowed my cry and buried my face against Vlad as something heavy rolled across the floor. I knew that sound. I was quite familiar with it. Petrik's, Michel's, and Brutus's faces all flashed through my mind as the memory of their heads bouncing across the floor surfaced.

Dead silence carried through the bar. I stood on pins and needles, waiting for someone to reveal our location, but no one spoke. Seemed everyone was too frightened or pissed to betray us.

The guard's steps continued, easy and carefree, as though killing the bartender meant nothing to him. He shoved open the main door, but before stepping into the night, he called back, "Burn. It. Down."

"Vlad," I whispered, now that the guards were filing out of the bar.

His palms ran down my back and he released me. Then he and Camilla shot across the storage room to the cellar door. I didn't need to ask. From the looks on their faces, the guards hadn't left. Would they stand here and watch it burn? Waiting to see what the flames flushed out?

Fear rooted my feet to the spot, to the point where I felt like a statue. I couldn't move. Couldn't think. Couldn't rationalize. The only thought playing over and over in my head was we were going to die down here, burned to ash.

I heard the flames before I felt them. Heard the screams. The trampling of feet. The cries. The pleas.

Holy fuck.

They were burning the bar down with everyone still inside.

The queen had lost her ever-loving mind. Had I truly pushed her to this brink? Or had she always been this insane? Maybe she'd just been good at hiding it.

Camilla leaned forward and pressed her ear against the door, then shook her head once more. "They're still out there."

Thanks to the ruckus above, we could speak more freely. But I didn't take comfort in Camilla's words.

"We have two options," Vlad said. "We climb back out and take our chances with the crowd upstairs, or we fight our way out in the back alley. Camilla, which is best?"

Even in the darkness, I noticed when her gaze turned distant. But the grim press of her lips told me neither option was best.

Heat beat down on me from above and I glanced up to find embers starting to fall through the rafters.

"Vlad," I whispered.

"I know." He returned to my side and took my hand. "We *will* get out of this, I promise."

I met his gaze, then gave a shaky nod.

"Upstairs," Camilla finally answered.

"You're sure?" Vlad grasped my other hand and pulled me tight against his back, as though that would keep me safe.

"It's not ideal, but out there, we don't stand a chance."

At least we had a little foresight on our side.

"We'll have to break down one of the doors," I mumbled. Even now, I could hear the other vampires pounding their hands against the walls and doors in search of a way out. My guess, the guards had barricaded us in.

"We'll find a way out," Vlad assured me. "Let's go."

He tugged on my hand, and I stumbled after him and Camilla, my damn knees trembling so badly, I wasn't sure they'd hold me up.

Vlad positioned us beneath the trapdoor, then cupped his hands and lowered them to Camilla. Without hesitation, she stepped into his interlocked fingers, and he heaved her into the air. She grasped the nearest rafters, then unlatched the lock and shoved open the door. She gripped the sides and hauled herself up. Vlad turned to me next, and I mimicked Camilla's movements, stepping into his interlocked hands right before he boosted me up.

I felt the searing heat instantly.

Tucked squarely behind the counter, I leaned over and watched as Vlad shifted into bat form and quickly flew through the door, landing next to me. An instant later, he flashed back into his true form. I'd always wondered where his clothing went when he shifted like that, but that was a question for another time. Not when we were at risk of being burned alive.

Together, the three of us stood, and the chaotic scene surrounding us astounded me. Vampires ran amok, their panicked expressions doing little to ease my calm. Fire wasn't something vampires came back from, so I understood their reaction.

"Vlad!" Camilla pointed up high. "A window. You can get out."

"And then what?" he growled. "Leave you two here?"

"Yes. You can get out and break down one of the barricades."

He paused and glanced upward, his thoughts clearly racing. "What if the guards are watching all the doors."

Camilla nodded. "They likely are. You'll have to improvise."

"*This* is your plan?" I hissed. "Sending Vlad out to deal with the guards by himself?"

"He won't *be* by himself if he gets one of these doors open," Camilla argued. "Leaving through the cellar meant the three of us would face the twenty or so guards alone. Vlad opening one of the doors from the outside dramatically increases our chances. If we can get everyone out, we'd outnumber the guards."

I hated how easily she could rationalize. My thoughts were little more than *fire* and *ahhh*!

Vlad turned and faced the two of us, his expression fearless. "Be right back then."

"Wait." I clutched his hands, terrified that this might be the last moment we'd see each other. If he was facing *twenty* guards out there, how the hell was he going to get the door open before they killed him?

Vlad cupped my face, then leaned in and kissed me, his lips tender against mine. So not the right moment, and I knew that. But I couldn't help myself.

"I will come back," he avowed.

Then, without another word, he shifted into bat form and flew toward the window.

Meanwhile, the flames grew nearer. They climbed the beams, devoured the tables and chairs, scorched the floor, and charred the walls. Camilla and I huddled together near the back, the safest place in the room, and watched as the other vampires tore through the room screaming.

"Calm down!" Camilla screamed.

Some shot her startled glances, a few stopped to gaze at her but most completely ignored her.

"Hey!" she shouted. "Calm the fuck down. Or you're going to die. We need to be ready."

That got their attention.

"Ready for what?" someone demanded.

I shot the window a quick glance to find Vlad had already slipped through. With luck, we'd be reunited in a minute. Maybe two. I started counting the seconds in my head.

Camilla held up a hand, indicating that we should wait. The anxiety spiked in the room along with the temperature. It was uncomfortably hot in here. And the smoke was clogging my throat. I coughed into my palm, then covered my mouth with the bottom of my shirt. We didn't breathe, but we did talk, and that required inhaling the smoky air.

"Hear that?" Camilla called out.

I perked an ear.

Fighting.

Oh god, fighting.

"Vlad," I mumbled against my palm.

Fear pushed me toward the closest exit. Grunts and groans rose to my ears, and my already weak knees turned boneless. I sank to the ground and listened to the sound of a vicious fight on the other side of the door.

Then, right before my eyes, the door swung open, and the cold night air swelled inside.

Coughing, I lunged to my feet to find Vlad caught between three guards while four others lay incapacitated on the ground. Adrenaline surged within me, and I dashed outside into the wintry night, unleashing all my rage and hatred on the guards currently holding Vlad hostage.

My fist cracked into one's face, quickly followed by a sharp jab to another's middle. The two guards broke away from Vlad, but I didn't stop. Instead, I clutched the head of the one whose nose I'd broken and smashed my knee into his face. When he fell, I snapped out a sharp kick to the side of his head. Then, without pause, I pivoted on my heel and drove my foot into the other guard's gut. He staggered backward. Before he could gather his wits, I swept his legs out from beneath him, then pinned one of my knees against his throat. Were he human, this might have killed him, choking off his air supply until he eventually suffocated. As a vampire, that wouldn't work. So before he could grab my knee and dislodge me, I jabbed him in the face, then grabbed the sides of his head and twisted until I heard the telltale crack of his neck breaking.

Panting, I rose and turned, shocked to find Vlad and Camilla standing behind me. Vlad stared at me, his expression full of awe, but Camilla just beamed at me with pride. She was my teacher, after all.

"I told you," I said while brushing my hair back from my face. "Camilla taught me well."

"Damn right I did," she said, offering me a fist bump.

I couldn't help but laugh as we knocked our knuckles together.

From the looks of it, Camilla's plan worked. Most of the guards were immobilized, and the other vampires handled those who still presented a threat. We were safe. For now.

"Do we call the fire department or something?" I asked, not sure how it worked in the vamp world.

Camilla nodded, then jumped to the task. Meanwhile, I pulled out Lucy's phone and snapped a few pictures and a quick video.

"What are you doing?" Vlad asked.

"Proof of the queen's madness. It's important."

He shook his head but didn't argue.

Camilla quickly returned, sliding her phone back into her pocket. "Done. Now we need to get the hell out of here before the queen sends more guards."

I nodded in complete agreement.

"Let's go."

Vlad's hand pressed against my back, easing me out of the alleyway. I stole one last quick glance at the inflamed bar and shook my head.

All this. For nothing.

EIGHTEEN

"Wʜᴀᴛ ʜᴀᴘᴘᴇɴᴇᴅ to texting every ten minutes?" Lucy demanded the instant we stepped foot in the house.

She stood in the foyer, hands perched on her hips, and her long dark hair swept back into a messy bun. Definitely not her typical look. Lucy usually wore her hair long and straight, in a shimmering waterfall of obsidian, her face clean and polished to shine, with makeup that accentuated her features. Tonight, she looked frazzled. Which said a lot, considering we'd only seen each other a few hours ago.

Her appearance was the only thing that kept me from snapping back at her. She wasn't the only frazzled one. Camilla and I were utter messes. Soot and smoke clung to our skin, our hair frizzy and mussed from the heat and fight. Vlad was the only one with a calm and collected appearance, because of course.

Ignoring Lucy's question, I kicked off my winter boots and sank onto the shoe bench tucked up against the wall. I released a breath and leaned my head against the wall. So much had happened tonight that never should have happened.

"We never should have gone there," I muttered, more to myself than anyone else.

"If we hadn't—"

"If we *hadn't*, that bartender would still be alive and his bar still standing. As it is, we're lucky the bartender was the only casualty. We could have all died in that fucking building." I sensed Lucy shift her weight, so I peeled open my eyes and stared at her. "Is it on the news yet?"

"The fire? Oh, yeah. It's playing nonstop."

I nodded. It'd taken us a good hour to get back to the house. I imagine it hadn't taken the news stations that long to pick up on this story.

"They're pitching it as an unfortunate accident," Lucy commented. "But from the looks of you three, I'd wager it's not that simple. What happened?"

"Just give us a few minutes to relax, Luce." I shrugged out of my puffy winter jacket and stared at it. The furred hood was singed and the white material smeared with soot. It stunk of smoke and flames, and I knew I'd never be able to get it all out.

"I'm just glad you guys are okay," she commented. "When you didn't text, I started to imagine the worst."

"Bet you weren't too far off the mark." I slowly exhaled, then pushed to my feet and groaned. Vampires didn't get sore muscles, but I swear, mine were sore. Likely all in my head, but right now, it felt real.

Camilla and Vlad disrobed, and together, we all tossed our coats into the laundry room. I honestly didn't expect any of them to come clean. Not that I should even be concerned with something as silly as that.

"Blood first. Then story time."

Lucy nodded, then retreated into the kitchen, where the others waited. I could feel their anxiety pressing down on us, likely eager to know if everything had gone according to plan, regardless of the fire. I wasn't keen to tell them that no, no it definitely hadn't.

Vlad, Camilla, and I all tossed back some blood, then quickly briefed the group. When it came to the part about Gabriel betraying us, Camilla quietly growled.

"Gabriel would never betray me."

"The proof is in the pudding, girl," I said, so exhausted with this debate even though it'd just begun. I understood her loyalty to her mate, but clearly, the prince had screwed us over. The only question left was why the queen hadn't come herself. If Gabriel had gone to her and told her exactly where we'd be, then why hadn't she come to collect us herself? Fear? Security? Maybe the council hadn't let her? Or Gabriel?

"Camilla—"

"No." She cut Vlad off with a sharp slice of her hand. "I *know* Gabriel."

"It's been more than a hundred years since you two have seen each other. I know you don't want to hear this," I said, "but no, you *don't* know him. You don't know what's happened in the last century. Maybe he's sworn fealty to the queen in that time. You guys claim he's a rogue and doesn't obey like his older brother, but let me clarify one more time. That was *a hundred and fifty years ago.* A guy can do a lot of growing up in that time."

"Not Gabriel," Camilla argued.

"Then you explain this." I tossed my hands up into the air, my frustration building. "You heard that guard. He said they'd received a report that we would be there tonight. The only person who knew was Gabriel."

"No..." Camilla's wide eyes flew to mine. "I didn't leave the message with Gabriel. I gave it to his people."

I pinched the bridge of my nose. "So, what, you think his people betrayed you?"

"Well, why not? They might be more loyal to the queen than he is. And they might think they were protecting him."

"Okay, then riddle me this, Batman. How did they know Vlad

and I would be there with you? It's not like you told them that, right?"

"I-I don't know. Anyone who's researched you two would know I'm a close friend. Perhaps they put two and two together?"

"That's a large assumption," I said.

"Well, what else can I tell you? Gabriel wouldn't do this. Not ever."

I shot Vlad a defeated look. He merely shook his head, clearly not in the mood to engage with Camilla's arguments.

"We need to find him ourselves," she pressed. "No secret messages and rendezvous. We need to track him down and talk to him ourselves."

"Oh, sure, because that'll be as simple as it sounds. The dude is a prince, or have you forgotten about that? You think we're just going to stumble across him in the middle of the street tomorrow night?"

"Well, no. But I think I could find him."

Oh boy. The woman was delusional. I highly doubted the queen would let any of her so-called children out of her sight after this. She probably had them all locked up somewhere "for their protection."

"Come on, Anna. Think about it. If you and Vlad were separated, don't you think you could find him? Don't you believe a part of you would know *how* to find him?"

"I don't know," I said, exhausted, waving a hand in her direction. Couldn't we just all go take a nap somewhere. Or a shower? I stunk. And I hated that. Shower and bed. That sounded marvelous. Let this be tomorrow Anna's problem.

"Give me two nights," she pushed. "Two nights to see if I can track him down. If I can, you and Vlad can come with me to meet him."

Like hell! "You want us to do this *again*?"

Camilla crossed the kitchen and snatched my hands, holding them close to her chest. "You know me. You know you can trust me. And I'm telling you, we can trust Gabriel."

I stared into her dark eyes and felt my determination waver. "You really believe in him this strongly?"

Her head bobbed. "Gabriel would never set us up like that. Even if he's angry with me—which I assume he is, I'm not that naïve—he would never hand us over to be executed like that."

"What happens if you're wrong? What happens if we *do* find him, and we're all killed?"

Camilla gave a humorless chuckle. "Then I give you permission to haunt me for the rest of your afterlife, telling me you were right and I was wrong."

"We'll both be dead, genius. Ghosts can't haunt ghosts."

"That you know," she teased, winking. Then her face grew serious. "Trust me, please. I know I can do this."

I glanced at Vlad over her shoulder and caught an almost imperceptible nod of his head.

"Fine," I muttered. "But I swear, Camilla. If this gets us killed, I will drag you to hell with me."

She grinned at me. "Deal."

ONCE SHOWERED, I went on a hunt to find Weasley. I hadn't seen her since last night and wanted to ensure all was well. I slipped out into the backyard, my steps as quiet as the night. The fresh snowfall covered the yard and softened my steps as I crossed toward the tree.

I was just about to call Weasley's name when she suddenly appeared and scurried up my side.

"Anna, safe?"

"Yeah, Snicker Doodle, I'm good."

Her head bobbed and her little whiskers brushed my cheeks. *"Weasley scared."*

"I know, but don't worry. We're still good." I scratched her furred side, reveling in the feel of her warmth. *"Have you been having fun hunting?"*

She trilled in my head, then shot down my arm and vanished into the snow. The next time she appeared, she had a limp squirrel hanging from her mouth. My gag reflex immediately activated, but I swallowed it down. She was a wild animal, of course she hunted other animals. And who was I to shame her. I drank human blood, for crying out loud.

"Gift for Anna!" she exclaimed, dropping the squirrel at my feet, its blood staining the snow.

Oh, lovely. And I'd just showered too.

"Uh, thanks, Snicker Doodle. But I'm not hungry right now. How about you take it? It's all yours."

Her little body trembled with excitement, and she scooped the squirrel back up and disappeared deep into the snow. She must have made a den somewhere for herself.

Chuckling to myself, I turned to head back inside and find Vlad when familiar voices rose in the air. I paused and canted my head, listening. It sounded like Alastair and Mateo. And if I wasn't mistaken, they were arguing. Curious, I crept through the nearby bushes leading toward the south-facing walled garden, careful not to alert them to my presence. My mother would have scolded me for eavesdropping, but I pushed that thought aside and focused more on my curiosity. Alastair and Mateo seemed like close friends, so what in the world would they be fighting over?

Of course, I quickly learned the answer to that.

Me.

I peered into the snowy garden and caught a quick glimpse, the two of them standing side by side, heads nearly touching as they argued.

"You're going to get yourself killed," Mateo bit out. "The queen will execute anyone associated with *them*." He said "them" like it was a bad word. "Are you seriously willing to throw your entire life away for them? Or rather, *her*?"

"This has nothing to do with Anna," Alastair argued.

"Of course it does! You think I haven't seen the way you look at her. She's taken. You're literally risking your life for absolutely no reason."

"Maybe I believe in their cause," Alastair muttered.

"Do you?" Mateo crossed his arms over his chest and waited. When Alastair didn't respond, he shook his head. "This is so like you. You're thinking with your dick again instead of your brain. And it's going to get you killed. Well, I'm not going to sit back and let that happen."

"What are you talking about?" Alastair straightened, his eyes narrowed on his friend. "What are you going to do?"

"Look, man. I'm really sorry it's come to this. But I won't go down in flames with you. The queen is hell-bent on executing these two. Yes, they're causing an uprising right now, but do you truly believe they'll change anything? They lack all vision and are just leaping from idea to idea. There's no way they'll take down the queen."

"Mateo," Alastair growled. "What are you saying?"

His friend sighed and leaned back against the bricked wall. I could barely make out his profile, but I saw that his eyes were closed as though he regretted what he was about to say. I felt a sinking sense of dread stake my chest. This couldn't be good.

"I'm leaving," Mateo said.

Oh, okay. That wasn't terrible. I could handle that.

"And I'm going to alert the queen to this location. I suggest you smarten up and leave before the queen arrives. Don't go down with the ship, alright?"

Anger raced through my veins.

Was Mateo serious? He intended to betray us? Turn us into the queen?

My gaze shot to Alastair. Surely he wouldn't abide by this? Except, they were friends. Best friends for all I knew. What would I do if Lucy came to me and asked me to bail on something that was going to get me killed?

Oh, wait. She already had, and I hadn't listened. Which was why we were standing here right now.

"You've gotta be kidding me," Alastair said, snaking a hand through his hair. "You're actually going to hand them over to the queen?"

"It's for the best. I just hope you come to see that before it's too late."

"Mateo!" Alastair snapped. "If you want to leave, that's fine. No one will stop you. But you can't do this to them!"

Silence stretched between them until finally Mateo sighed and pushed off the wall. "So, that's how it's going to be then? You're going to side with them instead of me?"

"I'm not siding with anyone," he bit out. "I'm just asking you not to betray them. They haven't done anything wrong to us."

Mateo turned away from Alastair, his profile visible to me in the moonlight. "Look, man. I didn't wanna mention this, but tonight... I was the one who tipped off the guards."

"What?" Alastair sucked in a sharp breath. "*You* betrayed them tonight?"

"*They* dragged us into this whole mess!" Mateo snapped. "They're going to get us killed."

"I can't believe you did this," Alastair murmured. "I trusted you."

Mateo shook his head. "You're so far gone, you don't even see it. Don't say I didn't warn you."

Alastair shuffled his weight and lifted his head. It took a second for me to realize he was staring right at me. Had he known I was here this entire time? Or just now? He held my gaze, his expression heavy, almost defeated.

"Mateo...," he sighed.

His gaze never strayed from mine.

Fuck. He was going to rat me out.

And then what? Could I make it back to the house to warn everyone before Mateo bolted, or worse, attacked me? And what about Alastair? I pressed my hands against the wall, but whether it was in preparation to run or attack, I had no idea. My own thoughts were far too muddled to understand. I couldn't believe one of our own would betray us like this. Then again, it wasn't like Mateo had shown me much kindness since the escape.

Surprisingly, Alastair didn't bring Mateo's attention to me. Instead, he broke eye contact and swept Mateo into a brotherly hug. I was debating my options, the main one being to scream for help, when Alastair suddenly struck.

I gasped when he swept Mateo's legs out from beneath him. The man dropped to the ground with a hard *oof*, then Alastair snatched up a nearby wooden chair, broke off one of the legs, and slammed the makeshift stake into Mateo's chest.

Holy. Shit.

I stared at Mateo's crumpled form and watched as whatever magic infused us bled out of his eyes until nothing remained but a pale corpse.

"Alastair..." I slipped into the garden and approached, my hands cupping my mouth.

"I-I couldn't let him leave," Alastair warbled, his voice thin.

I lifted my head and stared at him. His entire body trembled, his muscles tensed as though preparing to flee.

"I couldn't let him do that to you," Alastair continued.

When he lifted his head, tears shone in his eyes, and I nearly wept with him. "I'm so sorry."

He gave a jerky nod, his blood tears spilling down his cheeks. My heart fractured, and without thought, I gathered him into a tight hug. I couldn't imagine what he must be feeling right now. If anything like this ever happened to Lucy, I'd die. Without question. She, Vlad, and Camilla were my family. And from my understanding, Mateo had been Alastair's. The choice he'd made, the sacrifice... I wasn't quite sure how I felt about it. That he could betray his best friend like that. I'd never. But at the same time, I was grateful. He'd saved us. He'd kept Mateo from turning us over to the queen for a second time. That spoke volumes about loyalty.

I couldn't thank him, though. Couldn't imagine uttering those words to him. Thank him for murdering his friend? Thank him for choosing us over his brother? No way he'd want to hear that.

Instead, I pulled back and took his hand, which shook against mine.

"Come on," I said. "Let's get you inside where it's warm. Someone else can tend to his body."

"No." Alastair's voice came out gruff. "I'll do it. I don't want—" He cleared his throat. "It's my responsibility."

I nodded, yet again understanding.

"I can't imagine how difficult this was for you."

He nodded, then forcibly swallowed. "He would have done it. I couldn't let him. I'm with you guys. The queen..." He shuddered. "Please, go. I'll take care of Mateo, then join you all inside."

"Are you sure? I can stay and help."

He shook his head, his tears still flowing. "Thank you, but no."

I drew him in for another hug, then stepped back. "We'll wait for you in the kitchen."

Alastair didn't answer. With a faint smile, I left him to his grief.

CHAPTER
NINETEEN

THE NEXT FEW nights were a lesson in patience—a talent I sorely lacked. Everyone felt Mateo's absence, but we'd silently agreed to keep our thoughts on the matter to ourselves. What was done was done, and no one saw any point in rehashing the events. Especially considering how it'd broken Alastair. The poor man looked nothing like himself. Every night he rose, but without his usual smile or charming wit. Sadly, I had no idea how to comfort him since I knew little to nothing about him, and Camilla—his only other friend—was too preoccupied with tracking down Gabriel.

Even London was on edge, and tensions were rising among the vampire community. Thanks to the human news stations, reports of the fire spread fast, and my vlog had gone viral. Vampires from all over the world were commenting, telling the local vamps to rise up against the queen, to show her they won't stand for this.

The queen never once responded, but she continued the raids in search of us.

Every night, we mapped their progress and watched as they breached surrounding neighborhoods. We wouldn't be able to hide here much longer. But our options were limited. Either we left and escaped back to America, abandoning our coup, or we gave Camilla more time to find Gabriel. Neither option looked good.

"Hey." Lucy's voice invaded my thoughts.

I lifted my head and blinked, surprised to find her seated next to me at the dining room table and doubly surprised to find the sun had already set. How long had I been sitting here? Last I'd looked, the sun had been hovering on the horizon, happily melting the recent snowfall.

"Oh, hey. Uh, sorry, I think I kinda spaced out there."

She laid a sympathetic hand over mine and smiled. "Yeah, it's been a bit rough here lately. I don't blame you for zoning out."

I nodded, then glanced around the kitchen. With the sunset, all the other vamps had risen. Rebecca was chatting with Camilla, trying to pinpoint exactly where Gabriel might be tonight. Breccan and Vlad were drinking their blood, and Alastair stood off to the side all by his lonesome. The sight struck a chord in my heart. Without his friend, he was truly the odd man out here.

His eyes caught mine, and I waved him over, pointing to the seat next to me.

He didn't appear too enthused as he plopped down.

"How are you?" I asked.

A shrug.

"I'm so sorry," I said. "I can't imagine how you must feel right now."

He threw me a weak smile, then reached for a bottle of blood and took a sip. Okay, so he wasn't in the mood to speak. And I didn't blame him. Maybe we just needed to focus on something else. Something that could occupy his mind and keep his thoughts *off* what'd happened.

Luckily for us—or rather, unluckily—Lucy gasped, snatching everyone's attention. She stared at her phone, dark shadows playing across her face.

Something was wrong. As per the usual lately.

"What is it?" I asked.

"The queen..." Her voice drifted off, then she covered her mouth with her hand and shook her head. Were those tears in her eyes? What the heck would make Lucy cry?

I eased her phone out of her grip and scrolled the page she'd been reading. It was the same forum that Alastair had first shown me, one specifically catered to vampires and their news. At the top of the page, in a bolded headline, were the words **The Queen Kidnapped My Mate**. I forcibly swallowed, then clicked the thread and started reading.

"Vlad..." My voice warbled.

I felt his hand come down on my shoulder.

"The queen." I scoffed and continued reading. "According to these posts, she's taking people's spouses and mates hostage to force their compliance."

"What?" Camilla hissed.

Everyone moved with liquid vampire speed to surround me, all waiting for an update.

"It started tonight." I scrolled, counting the names in my head. "So far, four people have stated that the queen's men instigated a raid, but instead of burning down their house, arrested their spouse. Apparently, they won't be released until I'm handed over to the queen." I cursed and carefully placed Lucy's phone on the table before I snapped it in half.

The room fell silent as everyone digested this news.

"She's upped the ante," Camilla said, her voice tired.

Fuck, even I was tired. Exhausted, really. I was so sick of this game we were playing and wanted out. But no way in hell I'd turn myself over to the queen, no matter how badly I might want to. I hated the thought of others suffering on my behalf but giving up meant letting the queen win. And I couldn't allow that.

"What do we do?" Rebecca whispered.

"Find Gabriel," Vlad ordered, his voice strong. At least someone had some energy left. "Camilla, this ends. Tonight. Find Gabriel, or we move onto plan B."

I perked up at that. "And what exactly does plan B entail?"

Vlad's fingers squeezed my shoulder. "We revolt."

Relief loosened my muscles. I'd been waiting for this moment. For them to realize that their coup plan was failing. I understood their desire to take care of things quietly, but the longer we searched for Gabriel, the longer we let this madness continue.

"Vlad." Camilla rounded the table and practically collapsed into a chair. Her naturally golden skin tone seemed pale. When she finally glanced up from her phone, she wore a weak smile. "I found him."

Disappointment rounded my shoulders. Of course she had. What timing. Finding him now, when Vlad was finally close to agreeing with my plan.

"We still can't guarantee Gabriel will help us, Camilla," I said. "For all we know, he's on board with his mother's plans. Do you really want to risk everything on him?"

She cupped her mouth and considered me quietly, her eyes dull with pain. It bothered her to imagine Gabriel selling us out. But after Mateo's betrayal, we had to consider every possibility.

"I truly believe he will help us, Anna," Camilla finally said. "I don't even think his people told him about the bar, and I can't imagine Gabriel would approve of his mother's recent transgressions. He'd always believed in fairness and equality among people. He hated that she'd made him a prince. He came from an abbey, and he was training to be a monk. All this"—she waved at the devices in front of us, indicating the current political climate—"would sicken him."

I considered Camilla's words. Were I in her shoes, I would want to give Vlad another chance too. I wouldn't want to write him off without even reaching out to him. But this was asking a lot. Another night wasted tracking down this prince who may or may not help us.

"I truly believe we should give this a shot," Vlad said, as though hoping to sway my doubts.

Well, at least they weren't outwardly shutting down my concerns this time. That had to count for something.

Finally, I nodded. "But I'm going on record to say I still think this is a really bad idea."

"Noted," Camilla said with a weak chuckle. "You'll like him, I think. You two are similar in a lot of ways."

"Yay?" I asked, not sure if even I could handle another me. "Fill us in then. Where is he and where do we have to go this time?"

Camilla typed out a quick message on her phone, then nodded. "According to my source, he's planning on visiting a museum tonight. His mother has asked him to stay out of the limelight."

Which didn't fill me with confidence at all.

"He always loved museums," she murmured, clearly taking a stroll down memory lane without us.

"And which museum is he going to?"

She blinked away the memories and met my gaze. "You probably haven't heard of it."

"Try me."

Snickering, Camilla slipped her phone into her back pocket and gestured to the front door. "Come, little vampling."

🦇

"Oh, you have got to be kidding me." I stared up at the building in front of me and sighed. "Really, Camilla? The Museum of Vampires?" Could they have found a more boring name? Granted, I wasn't a museum person. The thought of visiting one always made me yawn and groan. But god, that was a horrible name.

She rolled her eyes, climbed the stairs, and opened the large glass doors. I followed, then shook my head. Of course it was dark inside. I wouldn't expect anything different from a vampire museum.

In all fairness, Camilla was right. I hadn't heard of this museum. But according to her, it'd only opened recently. As in, while Vlad and I were incarcerated. Seemed the queen had really taken to capitalizing on vampire popularity. How she'd put together an exhibit so quickly,

I had no idea, but I imagined it had included a lot of posturing and threatening.

"Well?" Camilla gestured us inside.

Vlad and I entered, our heads ducked low in case someone recognized us. At least there was one upside to the dark interior. With luck, it would keep us hidden from sight. But I'd also slapped on a dark beanie to hide my golden blond hair and a scarf to obscure the lower half of my face. Winter had its advantages, but I was coming to learn I didn't like snow. Or cold. Or wet. Just any of it, really.

Vlad had taken similar precautions, though he looked more dapper in his high-popped collar and black woolen newsboy cap. I'd chuckled when he'd first pulled it on, but I had to admit, it lent him a certain look that I was definitely digging.

"Well?" I asked. "Where is he?"

The place reminded me of a morgue. Empty and full of dead stuff and things. See? Proof I hated museums.

"Come on." She took a left and led us into a room labeled "medieval times." Displays filled the room, all with different artifacts focused on that timeframe. I leaned over to peer at the first one we passed, wincing at the sight of a cross.

"Iron," Vlad said, chuckling.

"What?"

"The cross." He gestured with his chin. "It's made of iron. When I was a child, the townspeople would talk about the undead rising from the graves. Most of us believed it to be a superstition, but some saw truth in the myths. I remember they believed a vampire couldn't touch iron. Now it's silver. There's always some form of metal we're supposedly allergic to."

"Ah."

"My country used to drive spikes through the bodies to impale them to the earth. Anything to keep the dead from rising."

"And to think, we just burn our dead now."

Vlad chuckled, then took my hand and led me through the rest of the room. I caught sight of interesting things like ancient rocks, tombstones, funerary objects, even skeletal remains of those people had once believed would rise from the dead. As much as I hated museums, I found it intriguing to see the progression of the myths. I had to admit, if I'd lived back then and heard stories of people rising from their graves, I might have stocked my house with garlic and crosses too.

"He's not in this room," Camilla said, suddenly appearing at our sides.

I quirked a brow and watched as she peered down a nearby hall. The woman was determined, I had to give her that.

"There are a couple of rooms down here. We should check them out."

"Lovely. And when you realize he's not actually here, can we leave and start working on plan B?"

"Have patience," Vlad said, his hand squeezing mine. "If Camilla says he's here, then I believe her."

It wasn't that I didn't believe her. More that I believed she was riding on blind faith. She wanted so hard to believe that he would help us that she couldn't see that she was crippling us, wasting time.

But I told them I would give this plan a shot. So, on to room number two we went.

This one was a collection of art thought to be created by vampires. Paintings, statues, pottery, even photographs. This room didn't discriminate by date, it merely displayed the art and offered what little information it could provide.

I slowed in front of one specific series of paintings. I didn't recognize the artist's name, but the paintings called to me. All were dark, with hues of blues and blacks. The scenes consisted of belfries and catacombs. The subjects all vampires. But one particular painting that caught my eye, one of a dark-haired man hovering over a woman's exposed throat. For some reason, it reminded me of Vlad. Or rather, what someone might think Vlad looked like. Considering he was Dracula, I had to wonder if the artist had used him as the concept.

"He's not here either," Camilla stated, her voice starting to darken with disappointment.

I blinked and tore my gaze away from the image, then turned to face her. "Okay, so are we done now?"

She glared at me, then moved into the next room.

"One more room," I said to Vlad. "That's it."

His mouth pursed, but he finally nodded. "Agreed. We can't spend all evening here."

Especially considering we were no longer alone. A few other patrons were mingling about, discussing the art. Seeing as how our last outing had nearly resulted in the death of at least a dozen innocent vampires, I wasn't keen on that happening again.

Rolling out my shoulders, I trailed after Camilla into the next room. The second I stepped inside, I froze. It had been designed to mimic a graveyard. Real plants crowded the room, lending it a fresh scent. But mixed within the plants were dozens of tombstones, all jutting out of the ground, much like they would in a real cemetery. And placed between the tombstones were elegant stands holding scrolls and texts.

I stepped closer and caught sight of one book titled *The Necronomicon*. The next one merely had the word "demonology" written in gold script across the front. The next stand held a wooden box. Below it rested a sign that read "Vampire Hunting Kit."

"What is all this?" I whispered, almost afraid to raise my voice.

"An immersive room," Vlad responded. "It's meant to pull you into the life of a vampire. Show you what it might mean to be one. The vampire kit reminds us of a time when specific humans hunted us, almost to extinction. The texts serve as a reminder of those who believed themselves to be sorcerers, who would summon 'demons' and the tombstones symbolize exactly what it means to rise from the dead."

Well, wasn't that just an unpleasant thought.

"I don't like this room," I announced.

"Nor I. It brings back unpleasant memories."

"And clearly the prince isn't here, so can we go now?"

Camilla turned on her heel with a crestfallen expression. "Yeah, I guess I just hoped..."

I nodded and bit my tongue to keep from commenting on the obvious—that we'd wasted precious time on this hope of hers. I was a better friend than that.

"Look, we can do this without him," I told her, careful with my words. The last thing we needed was to be overheard.

Camilla nodded. "It just would have been easier, you know?"

I didn't respond. Instead, I shook off the shivers this room gave me and headed for the door. The sooner we were out of here, the better. I didn't like being so exposed. Especially considering the queen's recent decision to continue abducting people's loved ones until someone turned us in.

"Let's go," Camilla said, resigned.

I was just about to step through the door when a massive shadow fell over me. Gasping, I clutched my chest and hopped back a step.

"Geez, sorry about that," I mumbled, my nerves jumping. "I swear, I didn't see or hear you." Which was odd, considering my enhanced senses.

Before I could skirt around the shadow, Camilla's hand latched onto my arm and she wrenched me backward. Vlad appeared next, tucking me squarely behind him.

My stomach immediately twisted. The last time they'd reacted this way, bad things had happened.

I fisted my hands, about to ready myself for yet another fight, when Camilla's soft voice rose beside me.

"Hello, Gabriel."

CHAPTER

TWENTY

I BALKED the instant I caught my first hard look at Gabriel. For some reason, Camilla's description of him had given me the image of someone resembling a scholar. Thin, bespectacled—even though vampires didn't wear glasses—with mussed hair. But the prince standing before me looked nothing of the sort. In fact, everything about him screamed aristocratic vampire, from his square chin to his piercing gray eyes. He towered over Camilla—meaning he also towered over me—and even had a few inches on Vlad. But it was the way he moved, silent and predatory, that gave me pause.

"Camilla?" Her name left his lips as a whisper, as though he couldn't believe his eyes. Or perhaps because he was stunned to see the last person in the world he'd expected to cross paths with tonight. That seemed more likely. "What in the name of—what are you doing here?"

"Surprised?" she teased, a coy smile curling her lips.

"Annoyed, more like." And to prove it, he crossed his thick arms over his wide chest, his long, woolen coat straining across his muscles.

"Come on. Don't be like that."

"Like what? Pissed that you think you can just randomly appear after how long?" He shook his head, his wavy blond hair brushing the tips of his shoulders. "You know what? I'm not doing this. If you'll excuse me."

Wow. He hadn't even spared me or Vlad a single glance. Camilla had certainly thrown him off his game.

Gabriel moved to step past Camilla, but she intercepted, her hands held up, though not quite touching him. A solid move. Seemed the prince wasn't too keen on seeing her, so I couldn't imagine he wanted to be touched without permission. I also couldn't imagine his guards would appreciate it. And from the looks of the two men towering behind Gabriel, they were already considering violence.

"Hear me out," Camilla pleaded, lowering her arms back to her sides. "Give me five minutes of your time. That's all I ask."

"Really? Five minutes? After all this time. Wow."

"Gabriel..." Camilla pinched the bridge of her nose. "You know I wouldn't have come unless it was absolutely dire."

Oh, shit. Even *I* could tell that was the wrong thing to say. I shot Vlad an alarmed look. This so wasn't going well, and from the looks of it, this was about to bottom out pretty damn fast.

I stole a glance around the room, relieved to find it empty save us. Those who'd entered earlier had passed into the next exhibit, and we were all that remained. I metaphorically breathed a little easier and tiptoed closer to the bickering couple. One of the guard's gazes shot to me, and I quickly turned away before he recognized me. Last thing we needed was Gabriel's entourage causing a scene and attempting to arrest us.

"Listen," Camilla started, "I'm here because—"

"I don't care why you're here."

Camilla's eyes slipped closed and she uttered a quiet curse. "I forgot how truly irritating you can be."

"As opposed to your glowing personality."

I choked back a laugh. Forgetting for the moment that he was Genevieve's son, I liked him. He was witty and clever, and from the looks of it, able to give Camilla a run for her money. That certainly endeared him to me.

With my back to the guards and only my side profile visible to Gabriel, I sidled up next to Camilla and grasped her wrist. "I suggest we take this elsewhere. Somewhere the two of you can speak alone."

When Camilla's gaze darted to mine, I subtly gestured toward the guards behind him. They grew antsier with every barb the two passed, and I really didn't want to be arrested tonight.

Face grim, Camilla shook free of my grip and snatched Gabriel's hand.

Everyone sucked in a collective breath. Every muscle in my body tensed in preparation. Surely grabbing a prince broke some royal code or whatever. Gabriel lifted his other hand, signaling for his bodyguards to stand down. My body immediately relaxed, but I made sure to keep my face hidden from sight. Thankfully, this immersive exhibit simulated a real cemetery, meaning dim lighting. Not that vampires needed light to see, but the shadows were likely helping veil us from sight.

"Please, Gabriel," Camilla finally said, her voice cracking with emotion. "I only need a few minutes of your time. And then, if you want, I'll walk away forever."

A pregnant silence filled the room. We all stood on the precipice, waiting for the prince's answer. Finally, he rotated his hand and gently twined their fingers together.

"Fine. A few minutes."

"Thank you." She beamed up at him.

Her expression gobsmacked me. I'd never seen Camilla like this. She almost looked earnest and innocent. Maybe a reflection of her true self? The person she was when she was with her soulmate?

She gestured toward the back of the room, where a single bench sat. Gabriel followed her gaze and nodded.

"Take five outside, guys," Gabriel said.

His guards shared a look before retreating into the hall. Once they left, I hurried to the doors, then quietly closed and locked them.

Relief swamped me, and I leaned my head back against the door and sighed. I really hated this. Some people thought it'd be fun to be infamous. I didn't agree. The fear overrode everything.

"Well." Vlad leaned against the wall next to me, his hands plunged deep in his pockets. Somehow, he appeared completely relaxed, and a small part of me hated him for it—not that I'd ever *actually* hate him.

"This has been a real blast, but I'm ready to go home now," I told him in a faintly amused voice.

"Hopefully soon. I wouldn't mind returning to normalcy myself."

"Normal..." I tapped my chin thoughtfully. "Sorry, I don't know the meaning of that word."

Vlad chuckled. "I should expect not." He pushed off the wall and slid his arms around my waist, pulling me away from the door and into his chest. "I wish I could tell you we're almost free, but unfortunately—"

"You have no way of knowing."

He nodded, then rested his chin on the top of my head.

I slipped my arms around his waist and sank into the embrace. At least Vlad's hugs always made me feel better. As long as we were together, that was all that mattered. We'd figure the rest out later.

We stood like that for a few minutes, silent yet attentive to each other. I could have listened to Camilla and Gabriel's discussion, but I felt it best to give them privacy. Since they hadn't seen or spoken to each other in so long, I wanted to give them a few moments. It was the least we could do before demanding Gabriel betray his entire family.

"Are we stupid for thinking this is doable?" I asked Vlad.

"Possibly, though I feel we need to try. I just worry he won't help, and we'll be left with few other options."

I didn't answer. We might be giving them privacy, but for all we knew, Gabriel had an ear on our conversation, and I didn't want to give anything away in case the worst happened.

Time passed slowly as we waited, but it didn't bother me. This was a rare, peaceful moment for us, something we didn't often experience, so I didn't want it to end any time soon.

This was one of the few rare moments Vlad and I had found some alone time, so I didn't want it to end.

Sadly, Camilla didn't share my sentiment. "Anna."

I lifted my head to find her beckoning us closer.

"Here we go," I whispered to Vlad.

He brushed a quick kiss across my brow, then together, we crossed the room. We came to a stop in front of Gabriel, who remained seated on the bench with Camilla and wore a disquietingly blank expression.

"Anna, Vlad, meet Gabriel. Gabriel, Anna and Vlad."

I bowed my head respectfully, but that was as much as he was getting out of me. At least he hadn't held out a hand out to me, expecting a kiss, like his mother. Improvement.

"Ah." Gabriel leaned back and eyed me. "So you are the burr in my mother's side."

Fear churned in my stomach. Of all the things he could have said, that filled me with little optimism.

"Gabriel...," Camilla murmured.

He held up a hand, silencing her. Even I bristled. What was it with monarchs thinking they could treat other people like shit? But before I could share my rather unpleasant thoughts with him on the matter, Vlad stepped forward and bowed his head.

"It's good to see you again," he said.

Gabriel inclined his own head in response. "And you, Vlad. I must admit, I was surprised to learn of your involvement in these issues."

"It's an unfortunate position your mother has placed us in."

"Indeed." Gabriel rose from the bench and casually strolled toward the nearest tombstone, his head downcast as though reading the script etched onto the front. "I confess, I've had some concerns regarding my mother's behavior in recent years. But nothing quite so alarming as these recent days."

I stole a glance toward Camilla, wondering if I could pick

anything up from her expression or body language that might suggest which direction Gabriel was leaning.

"If Camilla is correct, you wish to see me on the throne instead?" Gabriel turned and locked eyes with Vlad.

"That's the plan," I said, interrupting their manly one-on-one. "Camilla seems convinced you'd make a better leader. Of course, a dog might make a better leader, but hey, what do I know?"

Gabriel's gaze narrowed on me, and Vlad squeezed my hand.

I rolled my eyes. "Look, can we all just agree to stop beating around the bush? This is a pretty serious thing we're asking of you. And honestly, I'd rather not engage in twenty minutes of prattle and political scheming and word vomit. Just tell us straight up, are you interested or not?"

The air spiked with tension. For a moment, I had envisioned Gabriel tearing off my head. Instead, his eyes warmed, and a hint of a smile played at his lips.

"Well, aren't you a breath of fresh air?"

Condescending, but whatevs. I didn't respond and instead, gestured impatiently for his answer.

Gabriel sighed and ran a hand through his hair. "Here's the thing. Me taking the throne isn't as simple as you make it sound. And killing my mother isn't the best way to accomplish this."

Of course not. "Then what is? You can't seriously think she'll willingly step down."

"No, my mother has never shown enough self-awareness to know when she's beaten. However, if we can convince the council that she's unfit to rule, they'll push for her 'retirement.' And that will pave the way for either Elias or me to take over."

"You."

Gabriel paused, then lifted a brow. "Pardon?"

"We're not asking for *one of you* to take over. We're asking *you* to take over. Not Elias."

Vlad cleared his throat. "Anna's correct. Between you and Elias, we decided you're the best fit."

"While I appreciate the vote of confidence, I'm not the actual heir."

"So? Enough of this heir nonsense. I don't know Elias, but from what I've heard, he's no better than your mother. Sounds to me like he's her little puppet. What good would that do us? We need someone to take the throne who would then pardon Vlad and me. That's you."

"And you assume I would pardon the two of you?"

"Why wouldn't you? Vlad and I are only in this mess because your mother refuses to see reason. She's blaming me for her sire's death."

"And rightfully so, or am I wrong?"

I tipped my head back and released a frustrated groan. "What is it with you people? It's like you're blind to the real fucking world or something. Yes, you're wrong. Incredibly wrong. And if you'd actually take a moment to understand the *facts*, literally *none* of this would be happening right now."

"We aren't here to discuss those matters," Vlad cut in. "Right now, we just need to know whether or not you agree to help us. And make no mistake, you are the one we will see on the throne. Not Elias."

Gabriel drummed his fingers against his thighs and stared at Camilla. "If I say no?"

"We have a plan B," I said.

"Ah. And I'm not privy to that knowledge?"

"Nope." I popped the *P* for emphasis.

"I assume plan B ends with the death of my entire family?"

That he could say that without even a hint of alarm in his voice terrified me. What kind of sociopath were we striking a deal with?

"Plan B is messier, or so I'm told," I commented. "Camilla seems insistent that you'll help us. She thinks you can lead this coup and resolve matters quickly."

"So, you want me to lead the coup, dethrone my mother and brother, take the position myself, and then pardon you and Vlad."

Hell, even I winced at that. But... "Yes, that's exactly what we want."

"Those are quite the demands."

"Regardless, we need your answer. And soon, I should think. The queen is balls-to-the-walls nutso right now. In case you haven't heard, she's ordered her guards to abduct people's loved ones and burn down their homes and businesses."

"Yes," Gabriel ground out. "I've heard."

The slight tightening of his jaw told me he didn't like his mother's current antics, which gave me hope.

"I do see another option here," Gabriel commented. "One I think could end all this violence rather quickly."

"Oh?" I asked.

He folded his hands behind his back and faced us head-on. "I kill you right now."

Panic rushed through my veins. I instinctively stepped back, my thoughts already spinning.

"Touch her and I'll crucify you," Vlad snarled.

"Gabriel!" Camilla shouted. "You swore."

He unclasped his hands and held them up as though to say *whoops*. "A joke, I assure you."

If my heart could beat, it would be racing right now. "A poor one."

"No one's ever accused me of being funny," he said, shrugging.

"That I believe. Look, we really need an answer. In case you didn't notice, time is sorta running out."

Gabriel sighed. "I agree to help you only if you agree not to kill my family. We will convince the council to force her to retire and Elias to abdicate. We'll make them see reason."

Wariness had me turning to Camilla for guidance. She and Vlad shared a look before she finally nodded and said, "Agreed."

"And no more talk of killing me?" I said.

Gabriel's mouth quirked again. "Agreed."

"Good!"

Just like that, all the tension in the room vanished. I almost laughed with relief.

"I suppose I should dismiss my guards and accompany the three of you back to wherever you're staying so we can begin planning."

That sounded great. Nodding, I looped my arm through Vlad's and started toward the door. We'd only made it a few steps when I caught wind of a strange smell. My nose wasn't my strongest sense, so I slowed my steps and glanced up at Vlad, only to find him pale—well, paler than normal.

"Do you smell—" Camilla's voice cut off the second the exhibit doors burst open, revealing the queen's lithe form.

She stood framed in the doorway, with a battalion of guards surrounding her, and a massive werewolf tucked at her side, restrained by a leash.

Her head rose, and her crystalline blue eyes ensnared mine. Her mouth curled upward, like the cat that got the cream.

"Ah, my dear Anna," she purred. Her hand patted the werewolf's head as though it were nothing more than a dog. "*Bravo*, Julien."

Fear rooted me to the spot, and I found myself unable to tear my gaze away from the sight the two made. The damn werewolf came up to Genevieve's chest, its teeth inches long. I'd never seen Sam in werewolf form before, and holy shit, it was terrifying to see this one now. Its muscles practically trembled with anticipation, its body the size of two mastiffs. If this thing got its paws on me, I was dead.

"Do you like my new friend?" Genevieve asked, her French accent rising with her excitement. Her gaze scoured the room and her smile wilted into a frown at the sight of her son. "Gabriel? *Pourquoi, mon fils?*"

"This has to stop, *Maman*," Gabriel said. "Vampires will begin rioting soon if you can't control yourself."

Rage shuttered her face. "You would betray me?"

His silence spoke volumes.

Devastation and fury battled within the queen's eyes. She gripped Julien's leash tighter as though it would help her retain her sanity. Her guards responded to her body language and gathered themselves.

Fuck, I didn't see this ending well. We were outnumbered two to one, plus a werewolf who looked like he wanted to turn us into chew toys.

"Fine," Genevieve growled. "Then you will die with the traitors. Kill them all."

The room erupted into chaos. I cried out when someone's hands gripped my arms and hauled me backward. It wasn't until I spotted Vlad shifting into wolf form that I realized it was Gabriel who had me.

"Run, Anna. Take Camilla and get out of here."

"Screw you! I'm not leaving you guys." I shrugged him off. Like hell Camilla or I would tuck tail and run. The queen wanted me? Well, here I was.

I dove into the fray, dodging every hit and weapon thrown my way. The sound of snarls pricked my ears, but I couldn't tell if they came from Vlad or the werewolf. Surely Vlad didn't stand a chance against a real werewolf. His wolf form was frightening, but nothing compared to a real were.

I bolted to the bench behind us and snapped it in two, then broke off a few shards of wood. Calling out Gabriel and Camilla's names, I tossed the makeshift stakes across the room and watched as they snatched them out of the air.

I needed to reach the queen. That was the only way this would end. We'd promised Gabriel we wouldn't kill her, but I had to imagine that promise didn't count anymore, considering she'd ordered her men to kill her son alongside us. One good hit, that was all I needed. But the queen had wisely sequestered herself in the farthest corner of the room, shielded by two guards. Julien and Vlad tumbled across the floor in front of her, snapping at each other's throats.

Refusing to let any of my people die, I ducked and weaved through the fight, avoiding everyone as I rushed toward the queen. If I had to take out her two guards, so be it. But the queen wasn't leaving this room tonight. This was our chance to end everything for good.

A sharp jab caught me in the side, and I doubled over, gasping for air. Luckily, I was able to dodge the next blow and deliver a startling hit that broke my attacker's nose before I quickly staked him.

Honestly, Camilla had trained me by repeatedly beating me to a pulp. If these guards thought one hit would lay me out, they were sorely mistaken.

I dove out of the way of another attacker, then quickly belted him in the face with my foot before rushing toward the queen. Her guards faced me, about to attack, when I heard it.

A sharp scream quickly followed by an agonized bellow.

I whirled on my heel, then froze at the sight of Camilla standing in front of Gabriel, her hands cupped around a wooden stake wedged in her chest.

The next scream pierced my ears, and it took me a second to realize the sound came from me. I'd never made such a noise before.

Camilla staggered backward and fell into Gabriel's outstretched arms. He shouted her name and cradled her against him, but she was already gone.

Gone.

Camilla was *gone*.

Dead. Staked.

Pain unlike anything I'd ever felt lit through me. I cried out her name and ran across the room. I didn't give two shits about anything else. Didn't care about the guards chasing me. Didn't care about the queen laughing in the background.

Camilla.

Hands grabbed me.

Cold, hard hands that weren't Vlad's.

Crying out, I spun around and unleashed all my rage. My hits were brutal and violent, and after I buried my stake in the first one's chest, then the second's, I unleashed my emotions in a terrifying scream.

Only then did I turn back to Camilla.

She lay in Gabriel's arms, so still, so pale. I dropped to my knees at her side, my hands hovering above her staked chest.

"Camilla," I whispered. "Camilla! No, no, no, no..."

"She jumped in front of me," Gabriel choked out. "She saved me."

When he lifted his head, he stared at his mother across the room, his eyes blazing with fury. "Are you happy now?" He shot up from the ground and stormed toward Genevieve. But I couldn't look away from Camilla.

A dark swath of hair covered her face. I gently swept it aside and tucked it back. Her eyes were closed, her mouth drawn, but not in pain. She'd never feel pain again.

"Oh, Camilla..."

Gabriel's tormented cries finally roused my attention, and I looked up to find him utterly destroying the place. He tore up tombstones, ripped down trees, shredded the books, anything that stood in his way as he stalked toward his mother. He raged and screamed and cursed her name. Everything I wanted to do but couldn't muster the energy.

Camilla was dead.

And the woman responsible stood at the back of the room, still protected by her two guards. But neither moved. Everyone seemed stunned by Camilla's sacrifice.

The queen's gaze found mine, and for once, I didn't see the insane mirth within. Instead, she appeared almost pained by her son's agony. She held my gaze for a few more seconds, then let the guards rush her out of the room before Gabriel could unleash his fury on her.

I should have chased after her and killed the queen, but Camilla's head lay in my lap, and I couldn't move. I couldn't disturb her. Not when she was resting so peacefully.

"Anna." Vlad's hoarse voice drew my focus.

I slowly blinked, then glanced up at him. Tears welled in his eyes, but he held his hand out to me.

An ache invaded my chest, one I suspected would never go away. I ignored Vlad's outstretched hand and glanced back down at Camilla.

"What happened...?" I whispered, even though I already knew the answer.

"We must go," Vlad said. "Before the queen returns with reinforcements."

Another slow blink. Camilla's face blurred. I think I was crying. I couldn't tell. I'd never lost someone I cared about before. I didn't know how to process this, didn't know what to do.

"Anna..." Vlad's gentle hands curved under Camilla's shoulders, and he removed her from my lap, lowering her to the ground. "We must leave. Collect Gabriel. Allow me to tend to Camilla."

I think I nodded.

But I didn't remember standing.

I must have, though, because seconds later, I stood in front of a grief-stricken prince.

It took me two attempts to say his name. "Gabriel."

When I finally managed to utter it, he turned and stared at me with wild eyes.

"We have to leave."

His gaze rose over my shoulder and his lip curled. He pushed past me, and I turned in time to watch as he snatched Camilla from Vlad and cradled her in his arms.

"I'll carry her," he said, his voice gruff.

Vlad nodded. "We have to leave before your mother—"

"Just lead the way," Gabriel snapped.

After a moment's pause, in which Vlad stared at Camilla, he finally nodded and gestured us onward. I didn't know what to do, so I did the only thing I could. I stumbled after them, my mind and heart utterly broken.

TWENTY-ONE

TIME SORTA... grew hazy.

I was distantly aware that we sat in a car and Vlad was driving us back to the house, but I couldn't tear my gaze off Camilla's face. Her head rested in Gabriel's lap, her legs on mine. The way he cupped her face, as though he couldn't not touch her, broke me into a thousand pieces. I didn't want to imagine what he must be feeling. To be separated from someone you love for so long, only to be reunited, then torn apart again so soon afterward. This time, permanently.

I had the distinct feeling Gabriel and I would never be best buddies, but that didn't mean I couldn't mourn with him. Camilla was his mate, but she'd also been one of my closest friends. I considered her family. So, I laid my hand on Gabriel's forearm and gave it a gentle squeeze.

His head shot up, and our gazes met, his blurred with blood tears. I imagined mine were as well.

Neither of us spoke. Honestly, what would we have even said? I could have told him how she'd thought highly of him, how she'd searched endlessly for days to find him, how if only his people hadn't betrayed us two nights ago, this never would have happened. But none of that was his fault. I didn't blame him.

I blamed Genevieve.

"We've arrived," Vlad said, his voice breaking the somber silence.

I blinked and stared out the window at Camilla's house. A place she'd bought solely with the purpose of protecting all of us. Fresh tears pricked my eyes, but I dashed them back and gently eased her feet off my lap.

My door opened before I could do it, and I glanced up to find Vlad standing just outside, his hand outstretched to me. For two hundred years, he and Camilla had been friends. This had to be killing him. But thanks to his tightly clenched jaw, I also saw how hard he was restraining himself.

Gathering my wits, I glanced back at Gabriel. He hadn't moved. And I didn't want him to yet. We needed to handle this carefully. We couldn't simply carry her inside for everyone to see. We needed to warn them first. Prepare them for the worst.

I cleared my throat. "Gabriel, would you mind waiting out here with Camilla just for a few moments. They don't know about"—my voice hitched and I forcibly swallowed—"I just don't think we should—"

He nodded.

Vlad's hand slid under mine, and he helped me out of the car. I slowly closed the door, then turned to face the house. Inside were Camilla's friends and allies. *My* friends and allies. We'd already lost one member of the group earlier this week—though his loss hardly stung considering how he betrayed us.

Hand in hand, Vlad and I approached the curb, but the second my toes hit the cobbled path, I froze.

"Do you smell that?" Fear twisted my stomach and I clutched at his hand.

"Blood," he whispered, his voice stark.

And it came from the house.

Panic set my body in motion before my brain could catch up. I bolted up the walkway and lunged onto the porch. In the dark, it was hard to make out, but I could see it now. How the door hung from the hinges, how it creaked eerily in the faint breeze as it moved back and forth. How it was pitch black and absolutely silent within the walls.

Had I been thinking, I might have waited before stepping inside, but the only thought in my head was Lucy. The lights wouldn't be off if she was home. And she wouldn't have left. Not without knowing if we were safe. She would have waited until we returned.

I stepped into the front entry and immediately took notice of the deep gouges in the floor and walls. Something with claws had done this. My head snapped up, and I sniffed the air. Beneath the blood came a horrifyingly familiar scent. Same as the one we'd noticed right before the queen had attacked.

"Werewolf," I whispered.

Vlad's hand gripped my arm. "Anna, wait."

I shook him off. No way in hell was I waiting. Lucy was here somewhere.

I shot down the corridor, then screeched to a stop the instant I entered the kitchen. The place was an absolute disaster. Broken dishes and lamps, shattered glasses, crushed tables, I almost couldn't inventory it all. The couch lay in multiple pieces scattered through the room, the TV hung from the mantel, swaying from its cord. The patio door was busted wide open, the tempered glass laying in a glittering pile. It wasn't until I saw the first foot among the sparkling mess that I gasped.

"Vlad!" I shouted as I dove through the carnage.

Breccan and Rebecca lay sprawled on the back porch, blood streaking their pale faces. But their heads were attached, and they hadn't been staked, so they just needed to heal.

I pressed onward, then gasped at the sight of Alastair crumpled against the tree, his head slumped forward over his chest. Again, no permanent injury. Looked like they were all lucky to still be alive. Which begged the question, why?

I spun in a tight circle, my heel crunching in the snow. Where the fuck was Lucy? I couldn't see her anywhere back here. And how the hell had all the vampires ended up in the backyard?

"Vlad," I whimpered, fear rising steadily within me. "Where is she? I don't see her."

"We'll find her."

"Where is she?" I screamed. Panic erupted within me. She wasn't out here in the snow. She *had* to be inside then. She *had to be*.

I leapt back inside, skittering on some glass, and searched the living room. Lucy wasn't anywhere to be found among the debris. I ran into the kitchen, but it wasn't until I slipped in a pool of blood that I froze.

My head slowly lowered. There wasn't a body, but the sight of blood had me panting for unneeded breath. A thin trail led out of the kitchen and down the corridor, in the opposite direction of the vampires. It had to be hers.

I pressed a trembling hand to my mouth and fought back my tears as I followed the trail. When it took a turn into Vlad's and my room, I lost control of my tears and started sobbing. She was in there. I knew it with every fiber of my being. Somehow, I could *feel* her on the other side of the door.

A shadow fell in place beside me, and I stared up at Vlad.

"She's in our room," I said, my chin quivering. I wiped my tears and sniffled. "Vlad, I can't... I don't hear a heartbeat." His form blurred as I fought back sobs. "I don't hear a heartbeat."

Vlad's hands curved around my shoulders, and he drew me back from the door. "We'll go in together."

"I don't hear a heartbeat," I repeated. I couldn't think of anything else to say.

When he reached for the doorknob, I covered my face and turned away. I couldn't handle this. Not after Camilla. Not ever. I couldn't lose them both.

The door scraped open. But there wasn't any other sound. No sigh of relief, no one calling my name, nothing but dead silence.

"Anna." Vlad's quiet voice drew me back around.

I lowered my hands, then completely shattered at the sight of Lucy sprawled on the floor. Oh god, I couldn't do this. I couldn't face the truth. And yet, something drew me into the room.

"Oh," I moaned as I sank to her side. "Lucy..."

I plucked a strand of hair off her cheek and tucked it behind her ear. She was so pale. So broken. Injuries covered every visible inch of her. This wasn't a vampire kill. They would never have mauled her like this.

"A werewolf," I forced out. "I smelled it when we walked inside. A werewolf did this..." I fought for breath and choked back my cries. "Lucy..."

Fresh tears spilled down my cheeks as a thought clicked in my head. I remembered this. I remembered lying in an alleyway, broken and bleeding, watching my body as though dreaming. Lucy could be here. Her spirit, her essence, whatever.

"Lucy," I called in a stronger voice. I gathered her body in my arms and held her close. "I can fix this. I can fix this." I rocked her back and forth. "Vlad, tell me how to fix this."

"Anna..." His soft voice nearly undid me.

"No. I can fix this. You fixed me. You fed me your blood." I lifted my wrist to my mouth and bit without hesitation. It immediately welled over the edges of the wound and spilled over my arm.

"Anna, no."

"I can *fix* this."

"Lucy wouldn't have wanted that," Vlad said, his voice achingly soft. "Remember? She asked you not to ever change her."

"I know, but she wouldn't have wanted *this*," I cried out, gesturing to our surroundings. Panic raised my voice. "She told me not to change her, but I know she wouldn't want to die like this. Not like this. Not now."

"Anna..." Vlad's hands cupped my cheeks, and he forced my head up until our gazes met.

I sobbed, my breath catching. "I can't do this." I rocked her back and forth. "I can't do this. I'm not strong enough. Let me fix her. I can fix her." My voice cracked until it was barely a whisper. "I can fix this."

"No." Vlad wiped my tears. "Lucy would never forgive you. You know that."

I broke down into full hysteria then and leaned over Lucy, weeping into her hair. She would hate me if I turned her. She'd made me swear. She'd said becoming a vampire was the worst thing she could ever imagine. And I'd promised.

I'd promised.

Vlad's hands smoothed down my back as he crooned softly to me. His compassion didn't slow my tears. Nothing would. First Camilla. Now Lucy. I never wanted this. I thought we were doing the right thing by trying to take out the queen. I thought we were doing what was right. But clearly, I was so wrong. And Camilla and Lucy had paid the price with their lives.

"This is all my fault," I cried. I rested my head next to Lucy's and laid down beside her, our bodies pressed together. "I'm so, so sorry."

Footsteps echoed in the hallway. I gasped and lifted my head just as Vlad shot to his feet, ready to defend me. Thankfully, it was only Breccan, Rebecca, and Alastair. The three stood in the doorway, each staring down at Lucy with sorrow in their eyes.

"We were attacked," Alastair whispered. "One moment, everything was fine, and the next, the house was under siege."

"Werewolves?" Vlad asked.

Breccan gave a somber nod. "There were a few vampires among them. They couldn't get inside, but I heard one of them mention that the queen ordered the local pack to track you and Anna down. They used your scents from the prison cell and some of Anna's clothes."

"H-How did you end up outside?" I asked.

"Not willingly," Alastair commented, rubbing his head. "The werewolves were well-trained. Their objective seemed to be to get us outside so the vampires could take us out. Thankfully, we were able to fight the vamps off. But the werewolves..."

"Anna, we are so sorry," Rebecca whispered. "The attack was unexpected, and we didn't even have a chance to protect Lucy."

I laid my head back down and closed my eyes. The others continued to speak together, and Vlad told them of our own challenges. When he finally confessed that Camilla had also died, Alastair stormed off.

"We'll burn Camilla tonight," Vlad said, his voice weak.

"And Lucy?" I asked.

"That's up to you. You know her best. What would you like to do?"

I couldn't even think about that right now. I shook my head, about to tell them that I needed time alone with her when I heard it. A faint thump beneath my ear.

I gasped and shot to my knees. "Did you hear that?"

"Hear what?" Rebecca asked.

"I-I heard something. I think it was her heart."

Sympathy softened Vlad's face. "In times like these, we often hear what we want to help us deal with the pain."

"No." I pressed my ear against her chest. "I heard her heartbeat." Except, it lay silent again. Dejected, I sighed and hung my head.

Vlad smoothed a hand down my hair. "We don't have to decide anything right now."

Another hard thump, one that I *knew* I heard. This time, excitement lifted my voice. "I just heard it again."

He and Rebecca fell silent. A few moments later, another hard thump.

"Vlad!" I shouted.

He dropped to his knees next to me and placed a hand on her chest. A few moments passed, but then another hard knock. Followed by a slight movement of her chest.

"Oh my god!" I shrieked, not caring that vampires surrounded me. "How is this possible? She was dead. Right?" I shot the others a frantic look. "Right? She was dead!"

"Yes." Vlad leaned down and pressed an ear against her mouth. "But now she's breathing."

Relief swamped me and I fell back against the wall, my entire body shaking. "She's breathing?"

"And healing."

That gave me pause. "She's healing?"

I scrambled back to my knees and slowly approached her. Sure enough, her wounds were closing. And quickly too. Her broken limbs snapped back into place, and the gashes closed, leaving no scars.

Vlad reached across Lucy and snatched my hand. He turned my wrist over and stared at the flawless skin. "Did you give her blood?"

"N-No. You stopped me." I stared at my own arm.

"But you bit your wrist?"

I nodded.

Vlad cursed under his breath, then forced open her mouth and peered inside. I didn't see any blood anywhere. If I'd accidentally spilled some in her mouth, we'd see remnants, right?

"My arm wasn't anywhere near her mouth," I told him, but even I heard my words waver.

Vlad peeled back her upper lip in search of fangs, but her teeth were as flat as ever.

"Anna. Vlad," Breccan said. "You guys might want to move away from her."

"What?" I demanded. "Why?"

"I don't think she's a vampire."

I turned and glared at Breccan. "Then what else could she be—"

"A werewolf attacked her," he stated.

Understanding dawned. I glanced at Lucy and watched as her body underwent the final changes. She looked nothing like a vampire. While her skin had always been flawless, she wasn't pale. And if she were a vampire, her heart wouldn't have been beating. Vlad and I had been so excited to see her improving that we hadn't connected the dots.

"She's turning into a werewolf?" I asked.

Vlad met my gaze and nodded. "Her scent is changing."

I sniffed the air, but it took a few more minutes for me to pick up on the change. Lucy's biological father was a werewolf. Did that have something to do with it? Or did everyone attacked by a werewolf change? I was surprised to learn that I knew absolutely nothing about their kind.

And honestly, right now, I didn't care.

Lucy was *alive*.

Her chest rose with breath and her heart now beat steadily. Color flushed her skin, and her wounds were healed. I didn't care that she was a werewolf, she was still my Lucy.

When her eyes suddenly flashed open, I burst into tears all over again. But thankfully, this time, they were happy tears. I still had my best friend, even if that meant putting up with her turning furry every once in a while.

CHAPTER
TWENTY-TWO

"Gabriel!" I shouted after the prince as he stormed out of the house. "Gabriel, wait!"

"No" was all he threw back over his shoulder.

I gave an exasperated grunt and bolted down the cobbled path. The *last* thing I wanted to deal with right now was a pissy vampire prince, but it seemed life didn't give two shits about what I wanted. Instead, it just kept throwing me obstacles.

We'd barely just gotten Lucy cleaned up when Gabriel stormed in and demanded to know what was taking so long. One look at the house, Lucy, and the other injured vampires, and he'd muttered something about *ending this* and took off, leaving me to scramble after him.

"Gabriel!" I bolted in front of him and held up my hands. "Please, would you just stop? Give us a few minutes to collect ourselves and strategize a plan before you go tearing off into the night."

He leaned in close, his gray eyes almost white in the moonlight. His face was so severe, his expression so devastating, that I fell back a step. The prince didn't frighten me per se, but his size and height definitely gave my nerves a small jolt. "Back. Off."

I gritted my jaw and lifted my chin. "No."

"Excuse me?" A thick brow rose high on his forehead.

When I didn't cow away, he lifted the other one, then pressed forward, shouldering me out of the way.

"Camilla wouldn't want this," I shouted.

The world froze. Hell, even I winced when the words left my mouth. Gabriel staggered to a stop, then turned on his heel and leveled me with a glare worthy of the devil himself.

"What the hell did you just say to me?"

Shit. I had no idea how to handle him. Nor did I have any idea what to say. I fumbled around for something, anything, that would make him see reason.

"Camilla had a plan. She wanted you to help us. She wouldn't want you to go tearing off into the night. I don't know what you're planning—"

"I'm planning to end this!" he yelled, his voice echoing through the night.

I fought not to cringe back. "Okay. Good. Then let's hear it. Because I don't know about you, but I can't handle any more death tonight. And I think Camilla would literally haunt my ass for the rest of eternity if I let you get yourself killed."

"Do. Not. Speak. Her. Name."

I sighed, my undead heart breaking for him. So, I said the only thing I could think of to get him to listen. "She left you because of your mother."

The night spiked with tension. "What?"

"Your mother didn't approve of her, and was making her life a living hell, so she left."

"She told you this?" he demanded, his voice cracking with emotion. "Why didn't she tell me this?"

"She loved you," I said. "I could see it in her eyes back at the museum. She probably didn't want to come between you and your mother."

Gabriel averted his gaze, his jaw so tight, I feared it might break.

"She was my friend," I continued, struggling with my own emotions. "I loved her too, you know. When Vlad first changed me, I had no freaking clue what I was doing. She made me into the vampire I am today. She taught me how to fight, she made me strong. I know that pales in comparison to the fact that she was your mate, but you need to know, I—*we all*—loved her. Vlad and Alastair were her oldest companions. I don't mean to belittle your pain. I just want you to know that you're not the only one grieving her right now."

Gabriel's eyes dimmed, and after a moment, he hung his head and scratched his forehead. "What do you want from me?"

"Just tell me what you're planning. Maybe we can help."

"Your hands are full enough as it is," he said, gesturing to the ruined house behind us. "I don't know any of you, but even I can see you're failing. That friend of yours?" He pointed at the front door. "She's going to need a lot of help. Humans don't just become werewolves. They're born. That she survived is a miracle. And a curse."

A shiver rolled down my spine. That was really good to know.

"Okay." I nodded. "Fair enough. But the best thing we can do for her right now is get her home. To America. And we can't leave until the queen is handled. Because your mother refuses to see reason."

"My mother has lost her fucking mind," Gabriel barked.

I gave another small nod. At least one of her children saw that. "Camilla wanted to put you on the throne. She assured us you would fix all this."

"And look where that got her," he growled.

My eyes blurred with fresh tears, but I blinked them back before they could fall. I had a feeling that I looked like a downright mess as it was. Tonight had definitely obliterated my no crying rule, and I hadn't had a chance to so much as wash my face.

"Then tell us what to do. How do we put a stop to all this?"

He canted his head and studied me. I could practically see the gears turning in his head. "My mother will never stop hunting you down. You killed Petrik, and she loved him dearly."

I fought to keep my revulsion hidden.

"Blood feuds like that never die. Believe me, I'm quite experienced in them."

"Okay," I pressed, hoping to keep him talking.

"The only way to end all of this is to get the council on your side. My mother is the queen, but the council has a great deal of power. Enough that they can order her to step down."

"And you'd be happy with that? If she just stepped down?"

Pure, unadulterated fury whipped across his face. "My mother will die by my hand, that I swear to you."

Yikes. A teeny tiny part of me felt bad for Genevieve. To have your own son turn against you was bad enough, but to die by his hand? But I understood. Camilla was dead because of Genevieve. Hell, I wanted a slice of that action. Lucy was apparently a werewolf now, yet another thing Genevieve was guilty of.

"My plan is still to approach the council," Gabriel said. "That's where I was heading."

Relief rounded my shoulders. "So you weren't tearing off on some suicidal plan?"

"No."

"Alright. I wanna help you. You're gonna need backup."

His eyes narrowed. "From you? The woman responsible for this entire mess?"

Ouch. That barb stung. Through gritted teeth, I forced out, "*Petrik* is responsible for this entire mess. I wish you all would start placing the blame where it belongs. For fucks' sake, it's like you guys all fault me for just surviving. I swear to god, if another—"

"Enough."

I winced. Yeah, maybe I shouldn't have whipped out the G-word. "Sorry."

He hesitated for a moment, then nodded. "As am I. You're correct. This *is* Petrik's fault. And my mother's for allowing him free rein like that. Even I knew Petrik had gone quite mad, but I'd allowed myself to believe that my mother could control him."

"She didn't even try. He murdered thirty-five women before he tried to kill me."

Gabriel's eyes widened. "That... I didn't know."

Huh. "Guess you don't watch my vlog then, hey?"

"Your what?"

I chuckled, then shook my head. A conversation for a different time. "Okay, so we approach the council. Then what? You command them to support your claim to the throne?"

"You don't command the council to do anything," he said. "We make them see reason. We show them that my mother is no longer fit to rule. So long as we make a solid case, they'll agree. Their primary concern is to protect us, not condemn us."

"What about Elias? Isn't he technically the heir?"

Gabriel nodded, then raked a hand through his wavy blond hair. "That one will be tougher. But I think I can sway them. Elias is my mother's puppet. Removing her from the throne and seating him upon it won't change matters. She'll just control him and through him—"

"The people."

He nodded. "I am truly the only option."

"What about your father, Adrian?"

Gabriel winced. "My father isn't the best politician. But I don't think it'll be difficult to convince him to side with us. Not that his approval is needed. I would prefer to spare him, though, if it comes down to such a choice."

"I can agree to that. But your mother—"

"She dies," Gabriel snarled. "There's no debating that matter. The council will force her to step down, but the first chance I get, I will make her pay for what she's done here tonight."

Right. And speaking of that... "What about Camilla? We brought her here to care for her body."

A tic leapt at Gabriel's jaw. He turned and stared up at the sky as though searching for answers. "If we're going to approach the council, it must be now. Before sunrise."

"I'll have Alastair stay with Camilla," I offered. "They were dear friends. We'll take care of everything else when we return."

"*If* we return," Gabriel grumbled.

"Hey." I closed the distance between us and gently touched his arm. "We can do this."

"Yeah." He shook his head, then strode to the car. "You have fifteen minutes to get everything in order. Bring whoever you need. But after that, I'm leaving, with or without you."

His words set a fire under my ass. No way in hell I'd let him leave without me. Genevieve needed to pay for her crimes. And I would be there to watch her burn in her own flames.

🦇

"ALASTAIR IS GOING to stay with Camilla," I said as I dashed around the bedroom, collecting whatever weapons I could find. So far, I'd strapped a dagger to my left thigh and tucked a stake into my belt. No way in hell would I face the council without protection. Gabriel might trust them, but I sure didn't. They could have stepped out and handled matters before they'd progressed this far and hadn't. So, in my eyes, that made them about as bad as the queen.

"Do you truly feel it best that we attend this meeting?" Vlad asked. He sat on the bed and watched as I ran around the room like a chicken with its head cut off. "What if they side with the queen?"

"Then I guess it's time for my so-called revolution."

"If we survive."

I slammed on the brakes and faced him. Vlad rarely made such morose statements. "Did you have another vision?"

He wouldn't meet my gaze. Which meant, yes, he had.

"It's still not clear," he said, raking a hand through his hair. "I'm at a loss. I keep seeing you in my arms. This last one I saw something else. It almost seemed like we were seated in a classroom, seeing as how we were surrounded by desks."

A classroom? I couldn't imagine any reason we'd find ourselves in one of those. "Well, let's steer clear of classrooms then, and all should be good."

Vlad didn't appreciate my humor.

"Look, everything is going to be okay. I believe Gabriel can convince the council to help us. I really don't think it'll be that hard. Look at everything Queen Genevieve's done. The local vampires are enraged that she's taken quite a few of their loved ones. Breccan just told me she's not even permitting them visitation rights."

Vlad snared my hand as I whipped by, pulling me onto the bed with him. "Anna, I'm concerned. After everything that's happened tonight with Camilla and Lucy, I'm not sure seeking the council's help is the right choice. Perhaps we should let Gabriel handle this, and we stay here."

I shook my head. "I won't abandon him. Camilla wouldn't have wanted that."

"And Lucy? What about her?"

I frowned down at our bedroom floor. Her blood still stained our carpet, but at least Lucy was alive. After we'd cleaned her up, she'd retreated into her bedroom, asking us to leave her alone. She'd very explicitly stated that she needed time alone. I'd suggested calling Sam, and she'd nearly bitten my head off—literally. Apparently, calling Sam wasn't an option. I respected her decision, but I certainly didn't agree with it. If Gabriel was right, Lucy needed help. But I knew her better than I knew me. She had to make that choice herself. We couldn't force anything on her.

"She'll be okay here for the rest of the night. It'll give her that time alone she said she wanted. We'll get this all cleared up, receive our pardon from Gabriel, then hop on a plane home tomorrow night."

"I fear I don't share that optimism of yours."

I waved a hand in the air. "We have to do something. Genevieve knows about this place now. Why she hasn't returned for round two, I don't know. But I doubt this reprieve will last. So we need to finish this before she gets a second wind. Personally, if we can get the council on our side, I'd prefer that."

Vlad drew me toward him, but I shook my head and pushed off the bed with my knees. "We don't have time for that. Gabriel gave me fifteen minutes. So, if you're coming, you need to get ready."

"Of course I'm coming."

"Good. Then gear up. I need to gather the troops."

I hurried out of the bedroom and gestured to Breccan. He'd agreed to accompany us, but Rebecca had decided to stay and keep Alastair company. After the arrangements were made, I instructed them to dispose of Camilla's body if for some reason we didn't return tonight.

Rebecca nodded, then ducked out of the house.

I had two more stops. First, Lucy. I rapped my knuckles on her door and waited, but she didn't respond. I knew from personal experience how she must be feeling, and also knew I didn't want to intrude. But if we were leaving, I needed to speak to her.

Wrapping my fingers around the doorknob, I twisted and slowly pushed it open. She lay on her bed, a pillow pressed against her chest.

"Go away," she mumbled.

Not that I listened. I stepped inside, then closed the door behind me. "Lucy, I have to leave for a bit. Gabriel wants to meet with the council, and he thinks this is the only way we can win. I hate leaving you so soon after... well, just after."

She waved a hand in the air. "It's fine. I'm fine. Go."

"You're not fine." I eased toward the bed and sat on the edge, resting my hand on her shoulder. She winced at the contact but didn't brush me aside. "I just wanted to see you before I left. To tell you I love you, and I'll be back." When she didn't respond, I sighed and pulled my hand back. "I know it doesn't feel like it right now, but eventually, one day, you'll be okay again. And I plan to help you get there."

"Help me?" She shot up from the bed, her face screwed in a tight knot. "Help me what? Adjust to becoming a monster? How the hell can you help me when *this is all your fault*?"

I reared back like I'd been slapped. "What?"

Rage lit Lucy's eyes. "Get. Out."

"Lucy—"

"I said *get out!*"

I shot up from her bed, my hand clutched against my chest. My fault? How the hell was this my fault? I hadn't changed her into a werewolf.

"Get. Out." A deep, threatening growl leaked past her lips. The instant the sound rose to our ears, Lucy clapped a hand over her mouth and turned away from me, huddling on the corner of her bed.

"I—"

"I said get out!" she screamed, suddenly whipping the pillow at my head.

I ducked, then scrambled for the door. Everyone's emotions were charged right now, including mine. I tried not to let her words hurt me, but they felt like little needles piercing my chest. I stepped out into the hallway, then spared a final glance back at her. Lucy lay sobbing on the bed, her arms shielding her head as though trying to block out the rest of the world.

"I'm so sorry," I whispered before closing the door behind me.

Vlad stood in the hallway, his face soft with sympathy. I shook my head, then brushed past him and made my way through the kitchen into the dining room. I stepped out the broken patio door and strode through the snow to the middle of the yard.

"Weasley?" I called out.

The second her name left my lips, I felt her thoughts slam into me. She was a bundle of fear and anxiety even as she raced toward me. A few feet away, she leapt into the air, her paws outstretched. The instant I caught her, she snuggled up to my neck and purred. If weasels could cry, I imagine I would have been wiping away her tears.

"Anna!" she trilled.

"It's okay. I'm just glad to see you're okay."

"Weasley so scared. The noises. Those beasts."

"Shh." I stroked her side until her trembling eased. *"I have to go again. But I wanted to make sure you were alright before I left."*

"Go? Go where?"

"I have to stop the queen."

"Queenie bad!" Weasley cried out. *"Queenie hurt Anna!"*

I shook my head. *"I'll have my friends with me."*

"Take Weasley."

This time, I shook my head, then I rested my brow against hers. *"It's not safe for you. But Lucy will still be here. Alastair too. And I'll come back. Don't worry. I'll find you once I return."*

"Anna..." Weasley turned up her head and unleashed her deep, dark eyes on me. *"No go."*

"I'm sorry," I whispered out loud. After another cuddle, I lowered her back down to the ground. But she didn't scamper off into the snow like normal. Instead, she stood there and watched as I walked away. Every step broke my heart. But I couldn't let that stop me. So much was riding on our success, I couldn't let something like fear hold me back. Instead, I told myself that I *would* come back. For Weasley, for Lucy, even for Camilla.

CHAPTER
TWENTY-THREE

OF ALL THE futures I'd envisioned for myself, this one had never even registered. I'd never pictured myself storming the castle, so to speak. But here we were, literally marching into the vampire equivalent of Buckingham Palace. Gabriel had assured us we would find the council here and in session, likely discussing the recent events, especially after the attack on The Museum of Vampires.

He'd also mentioned the queen lived here. And damn, did that have the little hairs on my arms standing up. If Genevieve found me here, she'd literally stake my ass. Nothing like marching into your enemy's domain to make a bold—and *stupid*—statement.

Gabriel led the way, his back straight as he paraded through the main hall. Vlad and I came next, side by side, with Breccan at our back. My left hand lingered near the blade strapped to my thigh, my fingers nervously stroking the hilt as though reassuring myself that I wasn't helpless. Even so, I had to keep reminding myself that the council had no power over me. Nor would Gabriel allow them to attack us. I had to trust that he knew what he was doing. This was his ballgame, after all. He understood vampire politics a hell of a lot more than me.

When we reached a double-wide door, Gabriel palmed them open with an angry flourish and stormed inside. We entered a large room lined with individual chairs. Near the back, I spotted a long table with five seats. Then, to the sides were five desks, three on the left and two on the right. This had to be where vampires came to petition the council.

In the middle of the room stood five vampires, all staring at us with equally surprised expressions. Seemed they hadn't expected our intrusion.

"Gabriel," one said, separating from the others. "Now isn't the time for—"

"Sit." Gabriel pointed a long finger at one of the desks.

"Excuse me? If you think—"

"Sit down!" Gabriel shouted.

Oh boy. We were not off to a good start. I reached out and touched Gabriel's arm, hoping the small touch would help him cool his jets. It didn't matter how emotional we were at this moment. Yelling at the council wouldn't help matters and certainly wouldn't sway them to our side.

The other four members shared a glance, then shrugged, and seated themselves behind their individual desks. The last member— the one who'd spoken—took his time but did eventually sit. I guess disobeying a prince wasn't an option here.

Gabriel clasped his hands behind his back and strode through the chairs to the center of the room. He was the kind of man who commanded attention, and every last gaze tracked him as he moved. Even ours. I had a feeling we were here as a show of support, but not to speak. And right now, I was totally okay with that. What would we say that Gabriel couldn't?

"I expect you're all aware of my mother's recent actions," he said as a statement, brooking no room for them to pretend otherwise. "I also expect you know why I'm here."

"We do, but Gabriel—"

He held up a hand, silencing the woman who'd spoken. I shot her a quick glance but didn't recognize her. Unsurprising, considering I knew very few vampires in the world. The name on her desk, however, read Sophia Lark.

"I am here to petition the council. My mother cannot be trusted as queen anymore. It's foolish to pretend otherwise. You will approve my mother's and brother's abdication, and you will approve my ascension to the throne."

Damn. Even I jolted at his words. He hadn't once asked for their permission. He'd simply told them how it was about to go down. And from their darkening expressions, they hadn't appreciated the power play. I, on the other hand, was giving him a silent high-five. Maybe we truly were backing the right horse here.

A third vampire rose from his seat, then stepped in front of his desk and leaned against it. Next to him sat his own nameplate, of which I was suddenly grateful, seeing as how no one seemed willing to introduce themselves. Arthur Evans.

"First, let me say we are very much aware of what's been happening." His gaze skirted past Gabriel and landed on me. I raised my chin instead of flinching away. They could imply accusations all they wanted. "Second, there is a process to this, Gabriel. As I'm sure you're aware. You can't simply storm through the doors and demand that we help you stage a coup."

"Your 'process' will take too long. In the meantime, Queen Genevieve is kidnapping innocent vampires and holding them against their will to force their spouses' cooperation. She is burning down local establishments. She's even gone so far as to force the local werewolf pack to do her bidding. Tell me this isn't an egregious abuse of power."

Two other vampires shot to their feet. One was named Amir and the other Shani.

"What?" Amir demanded, his gaze darting around the room. "Werewolves? Why haven't we heard of this?"

"I question where you heard this news," Arthur said, his face grim.

"I didn't hear it," Gabriel said.

Their faces smoothed over. "Ah, then—"

"I witnessed it firsthand."

Silence swept through the room.

Sophia cleared her throat, then braved a few steps toward us. "You witnessed your mother using the local werewolf pack?"

Gabriel stepped aside and gestured to the three of us. "And I am not the only one. May I introduce Anna Perish, Vlad Vasek, and Breccan O'Connor. I would like for you to hear them speak for themselves."

"Please," Sophia gestured toward us.

Before I could speak, Amir interrupted, "We're supposed to take the word of a traitor and murder suspect?"

"You *will* hear her speak, or I will have you removed from your seat on the council," Gabriel barked.

Damn. Even my eyes widened.

This time when I started to talk, no one silenced me. I told the council *everything*. Starting with the bar a few nights ago. When I mentioned that we'd only been there with the intention of meeting Gabriel, the man in question tightened his fists. From what I could see of his face, it seemed a wise guess to assume he'd never been given that information. Then, I relayed tonight's events. I recalled the queen's appearance with a werewolf at her side. I told them of Camilla's death, then went on to describe the scene we'd returned home to. I didn't particularly like mentioning Lucy, but the council needed to know.

"As you can see," Gabriel stated, "my mother has not only ended the life of someone I cherished, but she's also brought harm to a human. If word of this spreads to the prime minister or the president of the United States, our treaties will fail. Currently, they are allowing the queen to handle matters because they aren't aware that she's done anything to endanger humans. But that could change."

"Are you blackmailing us?" Shani demanded.

"Not at all. I'm just stating the obvious."

I took a deep breath, then stated, "I currently manage a vlog that has over five million subscribers. I've already released one video describing these events. I mentioned the raids, but I haven't had a chance to update everyone about the more recent events, such as the bar, museum, and my house."

"So then this *is* blackmail," Amir grumbled. "If we don't agree to Prince Gabriel's demands, you will unleash chaos on us."

I sighed. Yeah, I guess they would see it that way.

"No one is blackmailing anyone," Gabriel commented, leveling me with a dark stare. "We simply request that you see reason. As her council, you can force her renunciation of title and power. We have a vested interest in her abdication. She will destroy us all in her quest for vengeance."

"And you expect us to believe that this isn't about vengeance for you? Was Camilla not your mate?" Sophia questioned.

"She was," he said without hesitation. "But as we were estranged for a hundred and fifty years, you can hardly claim my emotions are involved here."

Oh, his emotions were quite involved, but I didn't mention that, considering I wanted him—*needed* him—to win.

Shani circled her desk and came to a stop in front of us. "As it is, we were already discussing matters when you so politely stormed in. The council and I feel the queen is unstable. A few of us have sought her out over the past few nights to discuss her choices, and she's been brusque, even going so far as to insist we fall in line, or she will force our obedience."

Gabriel scoffed. "That goes against the purpose of the council."

"Indeed," Arthur stated. "However, you are not the heir. Elias is."

"Elias is a puppet," Gabriel growled. "My mother would simply rule through him."

I pressed my lips together to keep from pointing out that Gabriel intended to kill the queen at first chance. Again, we were trying to win here, and those little tidbits wouldn't help our cause.

The council considered Gabriel, but no one argued his point.

Eventually, Amir nodded and shared glances with the other four members.

"We have heard your concerns, and we will now put it to vote." Amir turned his back to Gabriel and addressed the council. "All in favor of Gabriel's succession say, aye."

Arthur, Sophia, and Shani called a sharp "aye."

"All in favor of denying Gabriel's request say, nay."

"Nay," the fifth vampire said, who hadn't spoken once since we'd entered. I glimpsed his nameplate that read Morgan Laurent.

"And nay," Amir said. "Three against two. The council approves. We will seek out the queen and will inform her of the council's decision."

No one looked too excited about this. And I couldn't say I blamed them. Genevieve was practically insane.

"Now?" Gabriel asked.

The council members didn't immediately respond, which gave me the impression they meant to wait. A choice that clearly didn't sit well with Gabriel, if his expression indicated anything.

He pointed a finger at the door and repeated, "Now."

"Very well," Amir sighed.

I almost laughed. He sounded like a child who was being forced to do something by his parents. Almost like this was the very last thing he'd wanted to do tonight. And I couldn't blame him. How did you force a queen to abdicate? If she didn't agree, then what? I had so many questions.

When I moved to follow Gabriel to the door, he shook his head, then grabbed my arm and gently guided me off to the side of the room.

"You need to stay here," he said. "You can't be present for this meeting."

"What? You're kidding, right?"

"Not in the least. Not only are you a main instigator in this mess" —he held up a hand before I could argue—"but my mother will be harder to manage with you present. Besides, this conversation isn't privy to peasant's ears."

I bristled at his words. My inner nosy reporter wanted unfettered access to this entire meeting. Imagine the things said. Imagine being present for a soon-to-be historic moment. But the stern glint in Gabriel's eyes told me there would be no further discussion in this matter.

He lifted his head and stared at someone behind me. I had to assume it was Vlad. "Keep her here. It's for her safety as much as everyone else's."

"Understood."

I turned and glared at Vlad. "Traitor."

He shrugged, obviously unperturbed by my accusation.

Gabriel brushed past me and joined the council members at the door. Sophia shot me a final curious glance before they all disappeared into the hallway and sealed us in the room. Ugh. I hated this. I wanted to be there, to see the moment the queen realized she'd lost. I wanted to see her face when she learned that she'd lost everything.

Petty?

Fuck yeah.

But I figured I deserved to be. The woman was responsible for Camilla's death, for Lucy's near-death experience, and so much more. The thirty-five lives stolen by Petrik, the bartender who'd stood up for us, even Mateo. Her madness knew no bounds.

"So, this is it?" Breccan commented once they left. "Just stand here and wait for them to return?"

"Guess so. Maybe there's a window we can peek through or something."

"Anna, we promised Gabriel you'd stay put."

"I promised no such thing," I argued. "And don't tell me you aren't curious about how this conversation plays out."

"Of course I am, but I won't allow that curiosity to derail things for Gabriel. For the first time in nine months, we've been given a break. So long as everything goes well, we'll be pardoned and heading home tomorrow evening. Right now, that's more important to me than eavesdropping on conversations we aren't permitted to hear."

"Spoilsport," I grumbled. Why did his arguments have to make so much sense?

I crossed the room and took Sophia's seat behind her cluttered desk. It sucked that I had absolutely nothing to pass my time. When we returned to America, the first thing I was doing was getting a new cell phone. Being without any form of social media was killing me. I hated that I couldn't even scroll through Facebook or TikTok.

"Are you incapable of waiting patiently?" Breccan's voice interrupted my thoughts.

"Hmm?"

"Your foot is tapping rather annoyingly against the floor."

I glanced down and sure enough, my whole leg was bobbing. "Sorry. Just have some energy to burn, I guess. What time is it anyway?"

"Three," Vlad said without so much as glancing at a watch.

Five or so hours until sunrise, then. I might not like winter for the cold, but I certainly was enjoying the extended darkness.

With nothing to help me pass the time, I spun in the chair like a mindless toddler. Boredom had me resting my head against the metal frame and counting the rafters above. I never wanted to be without a cellphone again. Not if I could help it.

After what felt like an eternity, I lifted my head and sighed. "*Now* what time is it?"

Breccan muffled a laugh.

"Four," Vlad responded, shooting me an amused glance.

Ugh. An hour. With another four to go until sunrise. I seriously hoped it didn't take *that* long for the council to convince Genevieve to step down. If it did, I might just stake myself. I couldn't stand doing nothing.

Yet another hour passed, and I was ready to pull out my hair. Anything to escape this boredom. Two hours, seriously? What the hell were they even talking about in there?

I rose to my feet and crossed the room. My fingers curled around the doorknob, and I was about to turn it when Vlad's hand came down on mine.

"What are you doing?" he demanded.

"I'm going to see what's taking so long. It's been two hours. They've gotta be done by now."

"These things take time, Anna."

I grumbled under my breath.

"So impatient for an immortal," Vlad said, laughing.

"Oh, it's funny to you. Meanwhile, this is torturous for me."

"Sitting still is torture? I would hate to see what *real* torture would do to you."

"This *is* real torture," I snapped.

"Give it another hour," Vlad suggested. He slung an arm around my waist and drew me away from the door.

I sagged against his chest and blew out a heavy breath. Another hour? Gah. I wasn't sure I could handle that. The thought of sitting still made my skin crawl. I wasn't cut out for it. Sitting still was a talent I sorely lacked.

"Can't we just leave? Gabriel knows where to find us. He can update us when everything's handled."

"Do you truly wish to leave?" Vlad asked, a knowing smirk curling his lips.

Damn, he knew me well.

I brushed his question aside, then tipped my head back and groaned. "I hate this."

Instead of assuring me I could handle another hour, Vlad kissed me. The instant I felt his lips on mine, my own smile grew. I looped my arms around his neck and sank into the embrace.

"Now, this could help keep me entertained," I murmured against his lips.

"I'd like to remind you both that you aren't alone here," Breccan called from across the room. He sat in Amir's chair, his head resting against the desk and his eyes closed.

Boo to vampire hearing. Vlad certainly could have helped pass the time. But Breccan was right. We had an audience.

I pulled back from Vlad, about to return to my seat, when I heard movement out in the hallway. The sound of footsteps approached, including heels clacking against tile. Could it be the queen? I leaned over and pressed my ear to the door.

"Gabriel, *mon fils*, I refuse to believe you would do this to me!" came Genevieve's shrill voice.

"You left me no choice, *Maman*," he retorted, his bass tone echoing in the hall.

"They're coming," I hissed.

"I will not be held prisoner!" she shouted. "Not again! Not by you. Not by anyone. You are *my* council, not his!" Her French accent thickened dramatically. "Gabriel! *Non*, you cannot do this to me!"

"Held prisoner?" I repeated.

"She must not have agreed to step down," Vlad murmured. "There's a room on the top floor of the tower reserved for royal prisoners. They must be taking her there."

I gasped and grabbed the doorknob. If they were hauling Genevieve to prison, I *needed* to see this for myself. Without warning, I cracked open the door and peered out.

The entourage neared us. Genevieve stood in the middle, and she was surrounded by the council, Gabriel, and a couple guards. Behind them trailed a group of vampires, all of whom wore conflicted expressions. Her remaining guards?

"Gabriel!" Genevieve screamed.

I cranked the door open a little wider and watched as they passed by. The queen wasn't restrained, but it was clear from the numbers surrounding her that she wasn't being given a choice in the matter.

As they passed, she lifted her head and lanced me with a furious glare that lifted the hairs on the back of my neck.

"*You!*" she rasped, her eyes igniting with a fury unlike anything I'd ever seen. The air around her practically crackled. "You are to blame for all this!"

Man, I was really getting tired of hearing that. Everyone seemed determined to place all the blame on me. I scoffed and shook my head, which only seemed to incense her further.

With a terrifying shriek worthy of a banshee, the queen lunged, her clawed hands outstretched toward me. "I will kill you!" Somehow, she broke free of the surrounding group and barreled toward me with murder in her eyes.

Gasping, I backpedaled. But she was so fast.

"Anna!" Vlad shouted as chaos erupted around us.

Before he could reach me, the queen's hands wrenched the stake out of my belt. I threw up my arms in defense, but I was too slow. Then I felt it.

A hot stabbing pain.

Right in my chest.

I barely had a chance to cry out before darkness consumed me.

CHAPTER
TWENTY-FOUR

I couldn't make out the words, but their tone was clear. Panicked. Furious. Terrified. My ears practically rang with all the noise, and my head throbbed. What the hell just happened? Then I remembered. The queen. She'd staked me.

Holy shit! She'd staked me!

Clearly, I hadn't died though.

Someone's trembling arms cradled me, and I heard someone whispering in my ear, begging me to wake up, telling me this couldn't be happening. Vlad. I would know his voice anywhere.

"Vlad!" another voice shouted. "Is she…?"

No response. From the tightening of Vlad's arms, I had a feeling he wasn't in the mood to speak to anyone right now.

I needed to tell him I was alright. Which meant opening my eyes and speaking. But my damn eyelids were so heavy. It took a little concentration, but I finally managed to groan and lift my hand.

"Holy shit!" Breccan shouted, his Irish accent almost off the charts. "She's alive!"

Vlad froze, his arms gripping me so tightly. "Anna?"

I managed another groan and fumbled with the stake still lodged in my chest. "Pull... it... out," I rasped.

"What the hell!" someone else shouted. I wasn't sure who. Honestly, it was getting hard to keep track of all the voices amid the yelling.

Vlad quickly laid me on the floor, then covered my hands with his. "On the count of three."

I grumbled something incoherent. I just needed the damn thing out of me. Fuck, it hurt. A lot. More than being burned by the sun.

"One—" Vlad wrenched the stake out.

I screamed and my eyes flew open, adrenaline now coursing through my body. Gasping, I scrambled backward on the floor, then shot to my knees and cupped my chest.

The room fell into a dead silence.

Panting, I lifted my head and took in the scene. I kneeled in the middle of the room, surrounded by discarded chairs and at least twenty vampires, three-quarters of which I'd never met before in my life. Vlad crouched beside me, his hands hovering over my body as though he was fighting back the urge to grab me. Breccan hovered over him, his face paler than normal and eyes wide. Gabriel stood in front of me, a dagger slick with blood clutched in his hand. The council members hurried behind him, their faces all wearing horrified expressions.

Blinking furiously, I glanced down at my holey chest and gaped at the wound.

I'd just been *staked*. By the queen! Where the fuck was the bitch? I was going to rip her motherfucking head off!

I dragged my hands away from the wound and nearly retched. Thankfully, the injury had begun healing, and I watched, mesmerized, as it closed.

Wait.

How was this possible?

Stakings meant death. Even I knew that.

Vlad leaned forward and gently touched my chest, careful not to hit the wound. "Oh, thank the lord," he said, even though he cringed as he said it. "She missed your heart."

"What?" My gaze shot to his face. "She *missed*?"

He nodded. "It happens. You were lucky."

"She missed," I repeated.

Was that even possible? How did someone *miss* someone's heart? Weren't all vampires, like, naturally trained to stake each other? I mean, sure, it wasn't like the queen did a lot of staking. She had people to do that for her. But to miss? The odds had to be infinitesimal.

"Holy hell," I mumbled. I sank back onto my haunches and stared at the many faces surrounding me. "Where is she?"

Gabriel stepped aside and pointedly glanced down.

I followed the path of his gaze, noticing the body lying in a bloody heap behind him. Queen Genevieve. And without a head, no less. Considering Gabriel held a bloodied blade, it was easy to piece this all together. He'd killed her in my defense.

"Damn," I whispered in awe, my hands rising to my chest again. Clearly, the woman had lost her damned mind—which seemed fitting. "Guess she finally lost her head, huh?"

Not a soul laughed.

I cleared my throat. "Too soon?"

Yeah, if their expressions were evidence of anything, it was too soon for morbid jokes. But I mean, I couldn't resist. She was Marie Antoinette, a woman everyone had thought beheaded centuries ago. Looked like the Fates had a way of tying up loose threads.

"Well." Gabriel stepped back and handed his blade over to one of the councilmen. "It appears we won't be imprisoning my mother after all."

A few nodded, but no one spoke. I swallowed and met his gaze. There was pain within, likely from killing his mother, but there was something else there as well. Almost like triumph. He'd avenged Camilla's death. I wondered how that sat with him.

I took a moment to gather my bearings. I glanced around the room, then started laughing.

"What could possibly be so funny right now?" Vlad demanded.

"Look around. We're surrounded by chairs and desks. I think this was the 'classroom' you saw in your vision."

Blinking, he did as I suggested and surveyed the room. Surprise had his eyes widening, and he rubbed his jaw before saying, "I think you're right."

"We really need to work on these visions of yours," I told him. "Because this definitely isn't a classroom. And a little warning prior to coming here tonight could have saved us a lot of trouble."

"If you remember, I did suggest we not come."

"Yeah, yeah, you're the poster boy for brilliant thinking."

"And don't you forget it," he teased. His face briefly shuttered, then he wrapped his arms around me and pulled me close. "I feared I'd lost you."

"You and me both." I glanced at Genevieve's detached head and grimaced. I'd wanted her dead. Especially after everything. But staring down at her remains just lying there on the floor, I shivered. I was so done with all this. If I never saw anyone die again, it would be too soon.

"Very well. Let's get this cleaned up," Gabriel said. "Send for the appropriate people. We will hold a funeral for her and allow those who wish to attend to do so. But we also need to put together a statement of events and inform our people that her rule has ended. We have a couple long nights ahead of us."

He turned to face me and Vlad, then outstretched a hand. One I took without hesitation. Together, Vlad and I rose.

"As for you two, you may return home now," Gabriel said. "As king, I pardon you, Anna Perish, and your mate, Vlad Vasek. The crown apologizes for any inconveniences you may have suffered."

Did suffer more like, but I bit my tongue for once. I knew this was the best we were going to get. "We're free?"

"You're free," he repeated. "Although might I suggest waiting a couple hundred years before returning to England?"

I knew he was joking, but my head bobbed anyway. "Of course. However, you're always welcome to come visit us in the States. Any friend of Camilla's is a friend of mine."

Agony darkened his face. Without another word, he turned and marched deeper into the palace. Clearly, as the new king, he had things to do and places to be. Like establish his own brand-new regime. I didn't envy him one bit.

As for us, it was time for us to collect all our friends and go home.

I did still have a wedding to plan, after all.

CHAPTER
TWENTY-FIVE

One Year Later

I STARED at my non-reflection in the mirror and preened at the sight of me in what had to be the most b-e-a-utiful dress I'd ever laid eyes on. Surprising, right? Considering my abhorrent loathing of all things flowy and dressy. But since I'd designed this baby, it only made sense that I loved it to pieces. I mean, what woman didn't love her wedding dress?

Sadly, I couldn't see my hair or makeup—or face, for that matter —but I sure as hell could appreciate the smooth lines and sexy cut. Vlad's heart was going to metaphorically stop when he saw me walking down the aisle. Somehow, I'd managed to keep it from him for an entire year, and believe me, that'd been more challenging than *anything* I'd faced in the past two years.

A year had passed since our England adventures, or so I called them. And in that time, the vampire world had settled contentedly under Gabriel's rule. Businesses prospered, as did human-vampire relationships. Rumor had it there'd been some in-fighting at the start, and that Elias had tried to depose his brother, but he'd failed epically.

Last I heard, Elias had taken a "permanent vacation" somewhere in northern Asia, where he was to remain until he learned his manners. I had a feeling that wouldn't be anytime soon. Gabriel certainly knew what he was doing—much to my relief.

Vlad and I had sent him an invitation to the wedding, but he'd politely declined, stating he was needed in England more. Personally, I think he just couldn't face us. It wasn't as though we were friends. And Camilla's loss had affected him severely. Estrangement or not, the two had clearly possessed a strong bond. I couldn't even imagine someone killing Vlad. Just the thought made me break out in hives. To actually experience that, though... I shuddered.

No, it was time for happier thoughts.

This was my wedding day, after all.

Thankfully, someone chose that moment to knock on the dressing room door, rescuing me from my morose thoughts.

"Come in," I called.

The door swung open, and a blonde head popped in. The second my mother's gaze settled on me, she gasped and darted inside, closing the door behind her. Her hands rose to her mouth, and tears pooled in her eyes.

"Oh, sweetie. You look gorgeous."

"Thanks, Mom." I beamed at her.

I perched my hands on my hips and swayed. I'd worked relentlessly with a dress designer to create what I believed to be the perfect dress for me. I hadn't wanted something off the shelf. Our marriage would be eternal, so I felt like I needed something exceptionally perfect to match. Together, we'd fashioned a sheer bodice with nude tulle and floating lace, as the designer had called it, which covered my bust and waist. Though I'd wanted sleeveless, the designer shook her head and sewed long, lacy sleeves with a hint of a wide cuff—for Vlad's sake, she'd said. The skirt hugged my hips, then flared out at my thighs, leading into a long, scalloped train.

It was perfect. I only wished the photos would show me *in* the dress. Alas, there were some things I couldn't change, and that was one of them.

My mom dabbed her eyes. "Your father and brother are here. They just found us some seats in the first row."

"Dad's here?" My voice rose with shock.

Mom nodded. "He said regardless of your guys' difficulties, he wouldn't miss this day for the world. I think he's changed."

"Oh, Mom." I reached out and laid a supportive hand on her shoulder. "Don't fall for that again, okay? You and I both know only heartache lays down that road."

She gave me a weak smile. "It's hard not to get swept up in him."

"Just remember all the pain he's caused you."

Interestingly, over the last year, ever since my death and subsequent arrest, my mother had toned down her crazy. I wasn't sure which event had been the catalyst, but I also wasn't going to look a gift-horse in the mouth. So long as she didn't try to poison me and Vlad with any more of her homemade garlic pizza, we were good.

My father, on the other hand, had done a complete one-eighty. He'd divorced his former mistress and cut her off as best he could from his money. Since then, he'd been trying to fix things with me and my brother. I hadn't been as interested as Caleb. I had my own life now, one that didn't need my father, especially after years of estrangement. My brother thought I was being selfish, so I faked biting him just to scare the shit out of him and shut him up. It worked.

"Vlad told me that you never chose a maid of honor. Who's going to stand up there with you?"

My jaw tightened. I *had* chosen a maid of honor. That spot would always belong to Lucy. Unfortunately, she'd disappeared after England. We'd flown home, and the second we landed, she'd disappeared. I hadn't seen or spoken to her since. No calls, no social media, nothing. I'd tried tracking her down, but it seemed Lucy had developed a keen ability to remain off the grid. So much so that Sam hadn't even been able to find her.

I desperately missed Lucy. She was my sister. No one would ever replace her in my life. I still hoped she'd reach out to me one day. So, I'd opted to go without a maid of honor. No one else would have felt right.

"I'm going to stand alone," I told her. It didn't matter to me that Vlad had Breccan standing beside him.

"Oh, honey. I truly am sorry about Lucy."

I lifted a shoulder. As disappointed as I was, I refused to let this ruin my big day. I'd spent months organizing this wedding, and I planned to enjoy it. I would marry the love of my life and dance until the sun rose. Then, when we rose, we would officially be the Vaseks. Or Mr. and Mrs. Dracula. Vlad hated that one. Personally, I loved it and intended to sign all my checks that way from here on out.

"Have you seen the others?" I asked. "Is Sam here?"

"Up near the front," my mother confirmed. She'd finally met him a few months ago, when she'd popped by for a visit, and he'd been discussing recent rumors with me regarding Lucy's location. "And Lucy's parents are here. They didn't want to miss this either. Though, it seems Lucy's mom isn't keen on Sam."

I choked back a laugh. Yeah, that was an understatement. I'd never told my mom what'd happened to Lucy in England, too afraid she'd tell Lucy's mom. If Lucy wanted her mother to know, that responsibility laid with her.

"That Rebecca woman is here as well. I must say, she's quite the pretty thing."

I quirked a smile. Yeah, Rebecca was beautiful in a classical sense. "I'm glad she came."

A momentary pang stabbed me in the chest when Camilla came to mind. I hated that she wasn't here today, and for a brief moment, I feared I'd cry. No tears today, though. Blood so didn't match the décor, interestingly.

"Ah, sweetie." My mom swept forward and pulled me into her arms, as though she knew exactly where my thoughts had gone.

We'd held a small funeral in England before returning home to the

States. Alastair had remained behind since England was his home, but Breccan had returned to Ireland, where his mate waited. Vlad, Lucy, and I had traveled home together, but even throughout the twelve-hour flight, Lucy hadn't spoken to me.

"What about Violet?" I asked, referring to someone I'd befriended back when I'd attended Vampires Anonymous. I'd only gone to *one* meeting, thanks to all the shenanigans my life had rained down upon me, but I'd connected with a woman that night named Violet. And in Lucy's absence, Violet and I had grown closer. I enjoyed having another vampire girlfriend.

"She's sitting in the second row."

So, everyone was here then.

Everyone except Lucy and Camilla, the two most important people. One couldn't be helped, but the other... I sighed and turned back to the mirror. No point fixating on things that couldn't be changed. But damn, I missed her.

"Ten minutes till showtime," someone shouted out in the hallway.

I grinned, excitement twisting my stomach.

"You doing okay?" my mom asked. "No cold feet?"

"Oh, my feet are always cold, I'm undead," I teased.

My mother groaned and pinched her nose. "What a horrible joke."

"Definitely. But nope, no cold feet here. I am one thousand percent sure that Vlad is the one for me."

A bittersweet smile tugged at my mother's lips, and she dashed away tears before they fell. "You know, I always imagined this day for you. I will say, I didn't quite picture it like *this*—at night, attended by vampires—but I did always imagine you looking just breathtakingly gorgeous, and that part certainly has come true." She pulled me in for a hug and ran her hand up and down my back. "I know that you're going to live longer than me, and I have no issues with that. I'm lucky enough that I'll go to my grave knowing my daughter will live forever, and there's a beautiful comfort in that. I just hope Vlad takes care of you. Forever for vampires means something quite different than to us mere humans."

"We'll take care of each other," I assured her.

"I know, sweetie."

When she stepped back, she caught sight of herself in the mirror and gave a watery laugh. "Well, would you look at that. Now I need to fix my makeup."

I chuckled at the sight of her raccoon eyes. "You need waterproof mascara."

Her laughter grew. "I suppose so."

"How's mine? No issues?"

My mother gave me another once-over, then shook her head. "Not a thing out of place." She clutched her hand over her heart once more and gave a dopey sigh. "Okay, I need to go fix my makeup, then take a seat. I'll see you afterward, okay?"

"You got it."

My mom quickly disappeared. I turned and stared at myself once more. To think how far I'd come. Just shy of two years ago, I was this bumbling human trying to infiltrate a stupid nightclub to prove vampires were more dangerous than humans believed. I'd proven that lesson to myself tenfold. But now, here I stood, a vampire myself, someone who'd helped take down a tyrannical queen, about to marry the love of my life. Not a bad day's work if I did say so myself.

Another soft knock on the door jarred me from my thoughts. I couldn't see who it was in the mirror, so I turned and sniffled before calling out, "Yeah, come on in."

The door didn't immediately open. I frowned and tilted my head.

Had I imagined the knock?

But before I could investigate, the door slowly eased open.

At the sight of her long, dark hair and piercing green eyes, my hands shot to my mouth and I gasped. Fuck, now I really *was* going to cry, and I wasn't even married yet.

I braved a step forward, my knees trembling under my dress. "Lucy?"

She toed into the room, her hands pressed against her stomach as though to contain her own nerves. "Hi, Anna."

Every bone in my body wanted to run to her and pull her into a hug. But I held back, afraid and cautious, unsure of where I stood with her. Her last words to me had been accusations. Telling me that she was a werewolf because of me, that everything was my fault. In a way, she'd been right. They'd only come to England to rescue me. If she hadn't come, she wouldn't have nearly died, and she wouldn't have been mauled by a werewolf, subsequently turning her into one. To this day, we had no idea which werewolf was even responsible.

"What... are you doing here?" I asked.

She offered a small smile. "Where else would I be? It's your wedding day."

I lowered my hands to my sides and bit my bottom lip. I took a second to really study her, and thankfully, she looked good—healthy even. Part of me had feared for her. I had absolutely no idea how hard it was to become a werewolf. And sadly, Sam hadn't been able to give me answers, considering she was the first werewolf to ever be turned.

But here she stood, decked out in an elegant purple gown that accentuated her figure and heels that brought her up to my height.

"How did you know it was today?" I asked.

"My mom told me," she said. "When she received your invitation, she forwarded it to me."

"Your mom knew where you were?"

Lucy winced. "Um, yeah. She put me in touch with my biological father."

My jaw practically bounced off the floor. "You were with your sperm donor?"

"He seemed the best person to reach out to. I didn't have any clue what to expect or what was going on inside my body. I needed help—"

"But Sam—"

"Sam wasn't the help I needed."

I bit the inside of my cheek. I guess I could understand that. "But what about me? Why did you shut me out?"

Her lashes fluttered and her eyes closed. "Because I was mad. And I'm so, so sorry about that. I hate that I blamed you, but I did. I needed time. And Reggie helped me with that."

"Reggie?"

"My sperm donor," she confirmed.

Her biological father's name was Reggie? The Mississippi alpha werewolf? I almost snickered but reminded myself that now wasn't the time for laughing. Not to mention, I didn't want to insult Lucy and push her away again.

"Are you... here to stay?" I asked, almost scared of the answer.

The second her face shuttered, I knew the truth. She wasn't. And my heart fricken broke.

"You're leaving?"

"After your wedding. I told Reggie I would come back. He's still teaching me. But I didn't want to miss this. I wanted to come, not only to apologize but to maybe... fix this? Us?"

I squealed, then rushed toward Lucy—as fast as my dress would allow—and dragged her in for a real hug. One that would have broken her bones as a human, but as a werewolf, I knew she could take it. There was a relief to that, knowing I couldn't hurt her anymore. Not badly, anyway.

Lucy laughed and squeezed me back. "I take that as a yes?"

"Bish, I *missed* you so much. And I'm so glad you're here right now. It sucks that you're leaving again, but knowing that we aren't broken anymore makes me incredibly happy!" I pulled away from her and leaned back. "You're doing okay, though? Coping well enough?"

Lucy brushed my question aside with a playful shrug. "Girl, we're here to get you married. Let's focus on *that* and get you walking down the aisle. Pretty sure we're on a time limit here."

Indeed, we were. I clutched her hands tightly. "Walk me down the aisle and be my maid of honor?"

"It would be my honor," she said, winking.

"Horrible," I said while laughing. "Just horrible."

"You love me."

My smile widened. "I do, I really do."

Her eyes warmed. "Come on, let's get you down that aisle."

I gripped Lucy's hand hard and pulled her from the room, eager to drag her down the aisle with me. Today had now become perfect.

We stood behind a set of closed double doors. Violin music filtered through the cracks. Everyone sat inside, waiting for my entrance, but the only one I cared about was Vlad. We'd gone through so much to get here, and I wanted to ensure today went without a hitch.

Which meant there was something I had to tell Lucy, and quickly before the doors opened.

I squeezed her hand. "You should know Sam is here."

Lucy's breath stuttered, but she eventually nodded. "I assumed."

"And..." This would be the hardest part. "Um. He's not alone. He brought a plus one."

This time, she was the one to squeeze my hand, and phew, it hurt. Girl was stronger than she let on. My damn bones almost snapped, but thankfully, I was able to pull my hand loose and shake it out. I needed it in tip-top shape, considering Vlad was about to slap a ring on it.

"Guess I'll just have to win him back," she vowed.

Inwardly, I squealed. Sam had searched endlessly for her after she'd vanished. But after a while, even he'd given up. And their relationship hadn't been strong to start with before. I think he'd grown tired of the games and the waiting and had finally decided to move on. But if she wanted to win him back, I was game. I wanted nothing more than to see them both happy.

Before either of us could say anything more, the doors slowly opened, revealing Perish's exquisitely decorated town hall. It was the one thing my mother had asked of me, to marry in my hometown instead of New Orleans. Considering Vlad and I owned a house here, I hadn't felt inclined to turn her offer down. I found I appreciated family more. And my mother and I had grown closer because of it. Though, we'd still had a few knock-down fights over the decor. My mother might be saner these days, but she'd still tried pushing for us to marry in a church, with a crucifix and everything. Pass, thanks, considering half our guests were vamps.

The music swelled, but before Lucy or I could start down the aisle, Weasley appeared, dressed in the cutest little tux. Tied to her neck were the rings. She glanced back at me, then with an eager hop, dashed down the aisle, fulfilling her ring bearer job. I chuckled, then nudged Lucy forward. The second we stepped inside, I heard a few people whisper Lucy's name.

My eyes, however, were all for Vlad. He looked so dashing, dressed to the nines in a dapper tuxedo. He cut such a fine figure, even with his hands loosely tucked into his pockets. Our eyes met and I grinned, pleased by the awed expression on his face. From the looks of it, he hadn't even noticed Lucy's presence. That, or he simply didn't care right now.

Once Lucy and I reached the dais, Vlad stepped down with an outstretched hand. I placed mine in his, then joined him on the dais. With my hands in his, I felt like the luckiest woman in the world. Few were blessed enough to fall in love, let alone meet their soulmate, but I'd been given both. Yes, it'd started with my death, but I'd gained so much more in the end. And I never wanted to take a single day for granted.

Our officiant began his speech, which I'd pre-approved. There'd be no mention of God or any religious concepts whatsoever. No need to offend the attending vampires. But honestly, I didn't hear much of it. I was too busy staring at Vlad and committing this moment to memory to truly listen. It wasn't until the officiant asked us to recite our vows that I came back to life.

Vlad faced me, his eyes glowing with adoration. "Anna. You and I have faced our fair share of challenges. Not many relationships could survive the things we have. But rather than weaken our bond, those challenges strengthened it. I know now, without a doubt, that you are my soulmate. You bring out both the best and worst in me. I love you. More and more every day. And I hope to inspire the same within you. For I am yours. And you are mine. From this day until the end of days."

I sniffled and quickly dashed away any rogue tears before they dared to fall and ruin my makeup or dress.

"Anna," the officiant said, gesturing for me to go next.

I wasn't sure I could top that. Vlad was the pro at speeches here. I'd struggled to write mine and had finally decided to wing it at the last moment. Not because I didn't care, but because I knew without a doubt that anything I said here, in this moment, would sound better than anything I'd scrawled on paper. And now was my moment to prove it.

"Vlad. You are everything. My purpose for existing. Without you, I'd be nothing. Without you, I never would have amounted to anything. You know everything there is to know about me, yet you still love me. Two years ago, I gave you my life. But tonight, I give you our eternity. And I promise to walk beside you no matter where our path takes us. So long as it takes us together. You are my best friend, my confidant, my one true love. Nothing in this world will tear us apart, I know that now. So, yes, I am yours. And you are mine. From this day until the end of days. Because I refuse to accept anything less."

A low chuckle broke out among the audience.

I grinned and winked at Vlad, who quietly laughed.

The officiant continued the ceremony, and I giggled out loud when I slid Vlad's ring over his finger, and he slipped one on mine. This was so surreal. To think of how far we'd come. I never would have imagined this.

"By the power vested in me, I now pronounce you husband and wife. You may kiss the groom."

I laughed loudly, then clutched Vlad's vest and dragged him toward me. Okay, so maybe I'd made *one* additional change to the typical wedding verbiage. So what? I was tired of the groom always being the one to kiss the wife. Time for a little girl power.

I deepened the kiss and gently scraped my fangs against Vlad's tongue before pulling back. We'd agreed there'd be no bloodletting at the wedding—no need to upset the masses—but that didn't mean I couldn't tease the poor guy. And from the befuddled look on his face, I'd done exactly that.

"Ladies and gentlemen," the officiant called out, "may I present to you, Mr. and Mrs. Dracula!"

The crowd burst out laughing, and I soon joined in, unable to contain my happiness.

So, maybe I'd tweaked *two* things. But the look on Vlad's face made it *all* worthwhile.

Hey. He married me. He knew what he was getting himself into, so he had no one to blame but himself.

EPILOGUE

Phew. Some ride, huh?

At least it finished on a happy note. There were a few moments there where not even I knew how my story would end. Lots of darkness and black moments. But hey, I'm now a married woman—happily, might I add—and I got my best friend back. Sort of.

Vlad and I have settled into our new life, spending the majority of our time in New Orleans. In case you're wondering, we *did* eventually get those SunGuard windows installed, and they're perfect. Every morning, we fall asleep in each other's arms. It didn't take long for Vlad to admit I was right, and coffins are terrible. Maybe this means he'll heed my advice more often.

My vlog is as popular as ever. People love the idea of a "vampire influencer." They follow me for tips and tricks on dating or living with vampires, which has become a thing now. They also love my facts vs. fiction episodes. But my most popular installments are always ones that focus on my personal life. They're hungry to hear more about Vlad's and my marriage. Which is why the paparazzi still follow us everywhere, snapping our picture and writing stories about us. No rest for the famous, I suppose. But this is the life I'd wanted. So, time to deal with it.

What about our friends and family, you ask?

Well, would you believe Alastair and Rebecca have become a bit of a couple? Quite adorable, really. Breccan and his mate have visited us multiple times. They're even considering adopting a human child to change into a vampire when the time is right—with permission of course. Neither Vlad nor I have any desire to bring a child into our lives, but we certainly wish Breccan all the best.

Weasley is quite happy here. She lives in Vlad's backyard, which also houses many smaller mammals for her to hunt. At least once a week, I stumble across a dead animal left on the porch for me. We spend our afternoons together, hiding and cuddling in the house until the sun goes down.

My father and I have been working on our relationship, slowly repairing it. It's going to take time considering all the damage done over the years. Eh, I've got nothing *but* time now. My brother and I hardly speak, but that's nothing new. It's just the way we are, and I'm A-OK with that. As for my mom, we've continued the weekly dinners. Except I drink blood while she dines on something I once loved and now can no longer have. She's evil. Part of her charm, I suppose.

I know, I know. You want to know about Lucy and Sam, don'tcha?

Well, that isn't my story to tell. Lucy doesn't crave the limelight like I do, but I think she'll tell you everything if you're desperate enough.

In the meantime, thank you so much for being a part of my story! Without my devoted followers, such as yourself, I'd have no story to tell. I appreciate every single one of you.

Now, get outta here and go bug Lucy.

Until then!

.   .   .

Love ya,
Anna

WOOING THE WOLFMAN
SNEAK PEEK

Welcome to New Orleans, where werewolves and vampires roam.

The werewolf? *Moi*.

The vampire? My best friend. But this story isn't about her. She's had her moment of glory, her day in the sun—ironic, considering she's a vampire—her claim to fame. Fame being the operative word.

No, this story is about me.

The sidekick.

I never thought I'd play the heroine role in my own story, but thanks to a life-changing adventure across the pond, here I am. For those who don't know, it's been a year since some psychopathic bunghole went all Jack the Ripper on me and turned me into a werewolf. A feat once thought impossible. Werewolves are born and not made, after all.

Pfft, wrong.

I'm the first person in the history of lycanthropy to be born human and then changed. Huzzah! Life accomplishment complete. Not.

Believe me, there's nothing charming about being a werewolf.

The shedding, the drooling, the howling... none of it fun.

Some people talk about how awesome it would be to run freely under a full moon. But come on! Have you ever gone running before? It. Sucks. Whether you're on four legs or two.

Then there's the fact that I'm allergic to dogs, which absolutely includes wolves. Every time I shift, I descend into a sneezing fit worthy of the dwarf himself.

And we mustn't forget the whole "mate" thing. Humans are lucky. They find someone, fall in love, marry, pop out a few children, then get divorced. Rinse and repeat as many times as they like. But werewolves? We have mates. As romantic as that sounds, believe me, it's not. According to my mother, a *mate* is someone biologically designed to help you produce the strongest offspring. There's no love or emotion to it. Just a little switch inside us that gets flipped at the most inopportune moment.

I found my mate before I was turned. And for a year, I've been avoiding him. Until now. I wasn't ready to settle down and have pups. I may *never* be ready... But if that woman touching his bicep doesn't back the F-train off, I might have to go all prehistoric on her ass and show her why it's unwise to go sniffing around a werewolf's mate.

Things are about to get pretty darn hairy up in here...

About the Author

Kinsley Adams is a thirty-something-year-old author who stopped counting when she turned twenty-five. When she isn't writing uproariously hilarious romantic comedies, she's raising her womb-gremlin with the hopes that he might one day become the world's first Supreme Leader (and yes, *Debbie*, that's a Star Wars joke). You can find her and her books online at kinsleyadams.com.

If you enjoyed this book, please leave a review! Your support and feedback are greatly appreciated. And be sure to sign up for Kinsley's newsletter at kinsleyadams.com/newsletter for updates on new releases, sales, and more!

ALSO BY KINSLEY ADAMS

DATING MONSTER MAIN SERIES

DATING DRACULA

LOVING DRACULA

MARRYING DRACULA

WOOING THE WOLFMAN

MATING THE WOLFMAN

WEDDING THE WOLFMAN

SMITTEN WITH THE VAMPIRE KING

HOOKED ON THE VAMPIRE KING

HITCHED ON THE VAMPIRE KING

DATING MONSTERS SIDE STORIES

WHEN VLAD MET ANNA

MR. & MRS. DRACULA

MONSTERS & CHOCOLATE